ANDREW MACK

BELINEA

SEASON ONE

THE MISSION

ISBN (Print): 978-1-09832-963-1
ISBN (eBook): 978-1-09832-964-8

For Derec and Quinn,
I hope you never lose your love for Sci-Fi,
you are the hope of my world.

EPISODE ONE

THE MISSION - (PILOT)

BELINEA 1.1

"There would be no time," Malovex thought. He was frantically flying a spacecraft as fast as he could towards the planet's surface. The sky was full of smoke, debris, and shades of orange. All were the aftermath of multiple hours of ground warfare that bellowed into the air above. He regularly touched his screen, keeping his other hand on the center console's main thruster, in a futile effort to get his ship to move faster. The cargo ship was going as fast as possible, making it difficult for Malovex to see where he was going. Relying strictly on the computer navigation system, he was practically flying blind to the base below.

He closed his eyes. A vision appeared in his head. As if he was looking into a cockpit, much like his. The controls were almost the same. He could see the helmet, a reflection in the glass, and hands moving frantically, shooting. More troubling was the flight. It was moving faster than his cargo ship. Through multiple layers of ground artillery fire, explosions going off near the ship, and barrel-rolling through all of it. Malovex re-opened his eyes. The vision was gone. His cargo ship was getting closer to the base. There was no verbal communication from anyone. It was a state of chaos now. There would be no time.

He approached the base, reversing the thrusters and causing his ship to decelerate quickly. The wind's force almost knocked down the two guards with shoulder-mounted rocket launchers, pointed directly at Malovex's ship. One turret was guarded by another man, likely a Tiloian, though his weapon was much more significant. A 20-foot cannon was pointed directly at his cargo ship. Malovex hovered closer and went through the landing procedures. If they were going to kill him, they would have done so already. Either they were expecting him, or they did not consider a cargo ship any threat, clearly confused by its arrival here alone. Releasing the full thrusters to landing level power, he gently touched the cargo ship on the base landing circle.

This part of the base was high above the trees, some fifty meters above the ground. It provided an excellent view of the ground battle. Malovex walked through the ship, dressed entirely in black, with an additional knee-high black cloak, his standard garment. He was exiting the ship from its belly when a flash of light from a massive explosion in the distance caught his eye. A mammoth Battle Cruiser was suddenly on fire. Losing its stability, it slowly turned toward the ground below. The sound of the explosion followed, echoing and rumbling through the entire base. Malovex whispered to himself, "The signal..."

His mouth was slightly opened, and his eyes became heavy. Malovex took a long, deep breath and swallowed hard. This was not going to be easy. There was no time.

Two Lieutenants had shoulder-mounted rifles pointed at Malovex. They walked briskly up to Malovex, still locked and loaded. Both were dressed in Tiloian army gear, a green-grey brown camouflage to blend into the trees. Each had a small ring on the side of their hip that was about six inches in diameter. The ring was a silver mercury color, almost translucent, but with a blueish rock in the middle of its brown handle. As they got closer, one stopped pointing his rifle, after noticing who it was. The other, though, Lieutenant Orbo, kept it pointed right at Malovex. He said, "Malovex, why shouldn't I kill you right now?"

Malovex, who was still staring at the explosion, turned to look at Orbo. He was now closer to his face. Malovex grabbed his ring, which was inside his cloak on his hip as well. He said, "What makes you think you can?"

Lieutenant Orbo let go of his rifle, allowing the shoulder straps to burden the weight. He grabbed the ring on his side hip. The other Lieutenant butted in and said, "The Commander said, trust Lord Malovex, Lieutenant. And that is what we will do."

Both men continued to stare at each other for a few seconds. A large ship flew almost directly over them, with the man guarding the turret gun firing repeatedly at it. Both Malovex and Orbo looked up at the ship, then back at each other. Malovex spoke, "Lieutenant. There is no time. Do as I say, or every last one of you will die."

Lieutenant Orbo said nothing. The other Lieutenant then said, through all the noise around them, "Malovex, what do we do?"

Malovex turned to him. "Get everyone on this cargo ship, NOW."

Orbo almost laughed, "You want us to trust you? Get on a ship with you? And go where? Take us to our execution?"

Malovex looked down again. The other Lieutenant scurried off as Malovex whispered, "Do it."

Malovex turned to Lieutenant Orbo again. "Orbo, you know what that explosion was. Otherwise, I wouldn't be here. I don't care if you live or die, so tell me where your Medical Wing is?"

Lieutenant Orbo looked directly into Malovex's eyes. The men were roughly the same height, 6 feet. "Malovex, I will wait 50 years for you, anytime, anywhere, if you want to settle this. You will never order me to do anything."

Malovex was now out of his somber, angry with impatience. "Orbo, there is no time for this, the damn Medical Wing, where is it?"

A bomb from a craft was dropped next to the base. Again the base shook from the explosion. The Tiloian guard from the turret had managed to shoot down the jet, which had crashed landed and exploded a mere 100 yards from the base. It was evident the base was not going to survive more than 10 minutes. Orbo and Malovex saw the explosions, then resumed their staredown of each other. Orbo, still breathing hard, pointed to the steel stairwell and said, "There is a triage center two flights down to the left. "

Malovex began to jog to the metal stairs, shouting at Orbo, "Get everyone on that ship, NOW."

He quickly ran down them, skipping steps. He could hear the other Lieutenant's voice on the base intercom ordering an evacuation to landing circle fourteen. He assumed that must be the circle he just landed on. After two flights, Malovex made the left, now sprinting down the hall. He came up to the triage center exactly where Orbo said it would be, but it was overflowing. The pristine white room had smoke in it, likely from the explosions. Debris and fire marks were scattered everywhere. Soldiers, men, and women, were getting treated in every corner of the large room. There was a Doctor, a medic, and several Droid Doctors taking care of the wounded. After surveying the room, Malovex climbed on top of a chair, yelling at the top of his lungs, "All of you need to get out now! There is a ship two flights up to take you away."

One of the wounded got up next to Malovex and said, "We will stay here and fight till the end."

There was a small cheer in the room. Malovex looked over everyone. He then turned toward a wounded teenage girl on the bed next to him and spoke firmly, "And all of you, even those who do not fight, will die."

The room went silent. Another explosion went off, shaking the room. Malovex repeated, "There is no time. We need to leave now."

One by one, the Tiloians began to flood out of the room. Malovex grabbed the teenage girl and carried her out. Visibility was becoming increasingly difficult as the hall was full of smoke. They sprinted, no one was walking at this point. Even the wounded, some who were compromised to one leg, were hobbling and skipping. Malovex carried the girl up the flights and towards the cargo ship. Malovex handed the girl to Orbo, who was waiting with open arms at the ship's entrance. Tiloians were streaming onto the ship. Malovex turned and sprinted back to the stairs. As he ran down the hall towards the triage center, he passed the medic who helped a soldier walk. Malovex shouted, "Where is the operating room?"

The medic responded without looking "Through the red doors in the back of the triage room. But we got everyone out already."

Malovex went through the entrance of the triage room and spotted the red doors. The last of the patients were leaving the room. He saw a bag on the ground that was holding bloody uniforms that were removed from the wounded. He grabbed it and turned it over, dumping the garments onto the triage floor. He sprinted through the doors and began frantically searching the cabinets and shelves. About thirty seconds went by. The room continued to rock from the explosions outside, and smoke became more and more prevalent. Malovex finally found what he was looking for and dumped the entire contents into the bag. With bag in tow, he walked back through the red doors. The triage room was now on fire. Malovex sprinted across the flames and continued down the hall.

As he came to the entrance of the stairs, a soldier was shot from an overhead jet. His body rolled down the stairs to the bottom, directly below Malovex's feet. He helped him up, grabbing his arm and draping it around his shoulder. They both moved up the stairs, the soldier with no chance without Malovex's assistance. After a flight and a half, Malovex looked up at the last flight of stairs and saw Orbo at the top. Orbo quickly came down and assisted both men up the stairs. Through the smoke, Orbo and Malovex carried the soldier across the flight deck to the cargo ship's entrance. Malovex asked, "Is that everyone?"

Orbo responded, "We think so."

Malovex handed the wounded soldier over to another soldier as they walked up the belly of the ship. "We don't have time anyway. How many?"

Orbo looked grim and responded, "I don't know, eighty? Maybe a hundred?"

Malovex walked through the corridors towards the pilot's cockpit. "Where is the Doctor?"

The Doctor, who was working on a patient, stood up. He was a few feet away and walked up to Malovex. Malovex pulled off the shoulder strap of the bag and shoved it into the doctor's chest.

"What is this?" the Doctor asked.

Malovex just stared at him, not saying anything. The Doctor looked inside the bag then at Malovex. Malovex softly said, "Everyone...."

The Doctor's eyes grew wide. Orbo, who was standing next to them, said, "There has to be another way."

As Malovex began walking away, back towards the cockpit, he said, "There is not. Twelve hours."

Malovex then stopped at a corridor before the cockpit. He opened a door where there were four rocket assault rifles mounted to the wall. He unlocked a box and pulled out a small duffle bag. Opening another box, he took out four grenades and tossed them into the duffle bag. He looked up and pulled down a bag, tossing it into the duffle bag. He then walked into the cockpit area, holding the duffle bag in his hand before dropping it next to the co-pilot chair. He climbed in, as another Tiloian soldier was in the other chair. It was clear he was prepping the cargo ship for take-off. Malovex strapped himself into the chair next to him and stated, "I got this."

The soldier, taken aback, said, "I am the best pilot on this ship."

Malovex abruptly interrupted his speech and said, "You maybe, but you don't know where we are going."

Malovex took over the controls, adjusted the center console thruster, and slowly accelerated the ship over the trees. Narrowly missing an attack jet that dropped a bomb on the landing pad they left, the entire cargo ship trembled from the explosion. The base was now in flames, slowly crashing to the ground below. Malovex tapped a few spots on the control screen, turning the ship's entire exterior into a green-brown camouflage. Blending in perfectly with the trees above, the cargo ship was barely detectable, flying only a few meters above the treeline. The co-pilot asked, "Must we fly this close to the trees?"

Malovex said nothing. In the distance where the Battle Cruiser fell from the sky, he could see the area below an enormous ball of fire and smoke. His attention moved back to flying as he clipped the top of one of the trees. The co-pilot looked scared. Malovex looked laser-focused, saying nothing as he passed through the smoke. "Sir, do you hear me? Can we at least fly a little more above the treeline?"

Malovex said nothing. He could now see his destination, a second Tiloian base in the distance. Malovex turned to the co-pilot and said, "Tell them we are coming. Mandatory evacuation of everyone."

As the co-pilot began speaking into the communication device, Malovex began calculating his landing. He knew there would be little time, maybe a few minutes at best to get them out. How many were left? Could he get them all? The base came up quickly. In quite a stunning move that even impressed the co-pilot, he had reversed the engines and spun the spacecraft 180 degrees. The spacecraft had almost come to a complete stop, nose up, wings tipping to regain its balance. Malovex had it hovering and began to land the craft on top of the base slowly. At first, only a few soldiers came out, running to the aircraft's belly to board it. But soon more came, about forty in all. One soldier stopped, kneeled, and secured his rocket launcher towards the ship.

Maolvex had no way of killing him. There were no weapons or guns on this cargo ship; it was for transport only. The soldier shot and a rocket soared right above the cargo ship into the distance. A couple of hundred meters away, it connected with an incoming fighter jet and exploded on impact. The soldier then got up and ran towards the belly of the cargo ship.

The sky was still full of smoke, and now the bombs were landing at this base as well. Zooming overhead and exploding in the trees. One rocket finally hit the base, exploding near the cargo spacecraft. At least fifteen men were killed instantly as they were running across the platform. A few more were wounded. Orbo was at the bottom of the belly of the craft. He could hear Malovex revving up the engines to prepare for take-off. Malovex was not going to stay after that last bomb. Orbo ran out to the platform. Burning debris was everywhere. After running 40 meters, he grabbed a wounded female officer lying down, threw her around his shoulder, and dragged her back to the ship. Malovex could see this action through his window. Gritting his teeth, he said, "Orbo, there is no fucking time..."

Malovex began to take off. The ship, ever so slowly, lifted itself from the concrete platform. The belly door was still open. Horrified that Malovex was leaving him, Orbo reached down to the silvery ring on his hip. Malovex steered the ship, with its belly door open, towards Orbo and the female officer in his grasp. Another officer in the belly of the cargo ship lowered a line with a hook on it. As they flew over Orbo, he held his silvery ring up as it expanded in diameter. The hook caught the ring, and quickly the officer on the ship reeled both Orbo and the female officer into the ship.

Malovex, not having any idea what was going on in the ship's belly entrance, accelerated quickly. The cargo ship clipped trees as it flew. The smoke was overwhelming, bombs and rockets repeatedly going off. Malovex's refusal to gain altitude was perplexing to his co-pilot. "Sir, we have got to get higher!"

Malovex, not looking at the co-pilot, responded sharply, "You are relieved."

"But sir ...."

Malovex snapped back "Take your ass to the back of the ship, now!"

The soldier unbuckled his harness and proceeded to the back. Malovex was alone now in the cockpit. His focus was everywhere, thinking about what to do, the explosion, what was going on above. After a couple of minutes, he got to the spot he was looking for. He quickly tapped some controls on the screen in front of him, and the ship now rapidly began to climb, ninety degrees vertical. The ship was making strange noises. It was clear it was being pushed to its breaking point as it had suffered damage from the explosions. As the ship climbed, Malovex could see out the window. Smoke was coming out of the engines of the cargo ship. Pure destruction could be seen for several hundred kilometers in every direction. The surface, mostly trees before, was almost entirely on fire, causing smoke to bellow everywhere. Everything had changed so quickly. He closed his eyes. The vision he had of the cockpit returned. In the reflection off the glass, he could see the eyes barely through the helmet. The ship vibrated, and he opened his eyes, leaving the vision.

The ship was clearing the atmosphere. He could see the markers that lit his way to the giant space station above. A voice came over the speakers in the cockpit. "Cargo ship, please identify."

"This is Lord Malovex. I have a cargo ship with over a hundred wounded soldiers. Request a docking slip for immediate medical evacuation."

There was a pause. A tracer was scanning the ship for lifeforms. It would verify Malovex, but it was unclear what the rest of the scan would reveal. "Lord Malovex, can you please identify the wounded aboard your ship?"

"I will not at this time, But you will do as I say!" he stated.

The ship had now wholly cleared the atmosphere. Malovex could see the space station, markers lining a lighted path towards it. He continued to touch the control panels, now steering the ship directly towards the station. He unbuckled his straps from his seat and stood up. Malovex reached into the duffle bag and took out a grenade, attaching it to the door behind him. His hands scoured the duffle bag before finding the small plastic bag. As he ripped it open, the voice returned to the speakers. "Lord Malovex, proceed to slip B7. We will have a medical team waiting with security detail for safety precautions. "

Malovex did not respond. He sat back down in the pilot seat. With one hand on the item in the bag, the other began to steer the cargo ship to slip B7.

He slowed the thrusters to a point where the ship was less than 100 meters from the slip. Someone was knocking on the door behind him. "Malovex, what are you doing?!"

The item in his hand looked like a large mouthpiece. He put it in his mouth, which had external vents on the outside. He bit down hard, then began to breathe. Malovex knew it was working. He reached into the duffle bag and grabbed another grenade. Planting it on the control panel in front of him, he put this one on a timer. He then stepped firmly on the bag. His foot wedged so the bag would go nowhere. The ship was now 25 meters from the slip doors and began slowing down even more. The self-guided computer docking systems were locked in.

Malovex reached down to his hip and grabbed his silvery ring. Gripping the handle tightly (he too had a blueish stone in his), he pointed his ring towards the window. With his mouth firmly biting the breathing mouthpiece, Malovex grabbed the four remaining grenades in the duffle bag. The two larger grenades he put on a fifteen-second timer, attaching it to the door. He then took a smaller grenade, activated it, and stuck it to the cockpit window, still gripping the handle of his ring as tightly as he could. The ship was a mere 15 meters from the space station, and the slip B7 doors. Malovex turned his back, now facing the slip of the space station. The grenade went off and immediately catapulted him through the windows of the cockpit out to space.

His body burned, he could feel the flames on his back, as he floated aimlessly in space. The headless ship, with debris from the explosion going everywhere, was drifting away from him. The ship was also drifting slightly towards the space station, just missing its mark on the slip. He took a grenade and threw it directly into one of the engines on the cargo ship. It exploded, sending his body ten meters from the ship in a different direction. A couple of seconds went by. The grenades he planted on the cockpit door went off almost simultaneously.

The entire cockpit area exploded off. Due to the explosions, the now 'headless' ship was spinning on fire away from the station. The grenade that had caught the engine split a section of the ship off. Some of the debris found Malovex's legs and chest. It was small, hot, burning through his clothes and skin. He took his final grenade and threw it at the middle of the ship. The grenade sailed through space, slowly catching up with the spinning cargo ship. About ten seconds lapsed, and as it got to the ship, it exploded. The ship began breaking apart everywhere. It was mostly on fire, scattering through space in hundreds of pieces.

Malovex, in excruciating pain, turned around. He was now a good fifteen meters from the space station slip and floating further away. He aimed his silvery ring, pointing it at the slip doors. A stream of liquid silver shot from it. The stream reached the doors, and then somehow connected itself to the metal just outside the gate. It morphed into the metal, so the line somehow looked like it was an extension of the spaceport. Rapidly, Malovex, arm extended, allowed the silvery expansion to shrink back into the ring, somehow 'pulling' him back to the station. When he got to the doors, he hit a red button on the side, and the door slid open. Malovex climbed in, and the doors closed behind him. Another pair of doors opened from the other side. A medical doctor sprinted towards him, while two security guards, rifles drawn, stayed still.

An officer joined the doctor kneeling next to Malovex, treating his wounds from the debris. The officer asked, "Lord Malovex, are you alright? What happened?"

Malovex removed his mouthpiece, breathing the air of the station. He grimaced from the Doctor treating the wounds and spoke softly, "I'm fine."

The officer turned to look directly at him. "Sir...the wounded?"

Malovex took a deep breath and said, "The prisoners Lieutenant, the prisoners. I killed them."

BELINEA 1.2

Twenty years later....

Space Port Earth

Space Port Earth (SPE) is one of the largest space stations ever constructed by the Belineans. With over six years to go before completion, the station is home to a mix of eight thousand people, both civilian and military. SPE has one long narrow middle core, the main reactor that supplies the station's energy. It is almost eight kilometers long. Two hundred and twenty elevator shafts spoke off from the core to the outer ring of the station. On the outer ring are docks for ships to link up to. On dock 11 lied a small ship, with two current passengers inside.

Alexis Devanoe sat at a desk in the lavishly furnished living quarters of the ship. She continues to furiously touch the tablet in front of her, executing an endless list of tasks. Alexis is the Senior Advisor to the newest Earth Ambassador, Thomas Bird. At 22, she understands most view her as too young to hold such a prestigious & responsible position. In the background, a small, ten-year-old African American child was on the sofa, watching a video on her tablet. An image of a man giving a speech is lit up against the far wall. His audio is faint, but can undoubtedly be overheard.

> *"Yes we share the same vision as the Belieneans, we must let these terrorists know....that there is no place in this galaxy dark enough for them to hide, that we will find them, and shine the light of justice upon them...And while we work together on that mission, we shall also not forget our primary vision of a better Earth. We cannot tolerate becoming prisoners to a plan that will lead us into an economic abyss, simply to remove an evil we must extinguish together. No more will these shackles constrict us. Earth must, AND WILL, do what is best*

for EARTH. Earth will choose our direction. And most important,
Earth will fight for the right to protect its citizens...(applause)."

The little girl, not taking her eyes off her tablet, spoke softly. "Alexis, what is taking my father so long?"

Alexis did not stop what she was doing, either. She continued to look at her tablet while answering. "He is giving a significant speech, Savannah. He's almost done."

"Why is it so important?" the little girl asked.

Alexis, frustrated that babysitter was now part of her duties, answered in a slightly annoyed tone. "If you had been listening, you would know. He's talking to all the people of Earth about the need to be independent."

Savannah now put her tablet down. "Why does that matter?"

Alexis ran her hand through her long black hair. The child had managed to break her concentration. She stopped what she was doing to look at her. She spoke softly and slowly now, making sure she would understand. "Remember what I told you about the bad people? The terrorists? Your Dad, and other people on Earth, think we might be better off developing our own forces to fight the terrorists than only working with the Belineans. "

Savannah was now curious. "Why is that better?"

Alexis now stared directly at Savannah. "It may not be. The Council with the Belineans and other Ambassadors have their way. We are offering ours. They might just need more help. The problem is we disagree on how to do it."

Savannah replied, "Why can't we just try all the ways? Somebody's plan should work."

Alexis was trying to explain a very complicated answer in a straight-forward way. "Savannah, these plans the Belineans came up with cost lots of money and resources."

Savannah was confused. "So? If it's important?"

Alexis answered, "It is important. But your father believes we can accom-plish the same goals of eliminating the terrorists without having to contribute so many of Earth's resources and workers to the Belineans. That's money we can use for ourselves."

Savannah went back to the couch. "I don't think it's right. The Belineans care about us."

Alexis Devanoe smiled, charmed by the little girl's childish behavior. "So, what does it matter?"

Savannah continued. "I learned in school that almost twenty years ago when Earth had the pandemic that killed all those people, it was the Belinean who saved us. They are smart and our friends. We should help them if we can."

Alexis Devanoe was now actually proud the little girl had formed her own conclusion. "That is true. The Belineans came at a time when we didn't understand all the other people and planets in the galaxy and saved us with a cure for the virus that caused the pandemic. Without them, everyone on Earth would have died, instead of the five billion that did."

Savannah, looking sad, asked Alexis, "Do you remember the pandemic?"

For the first time, Alexis had a look of remorse on her face. She grabbed Savannah, giving her a half hug as if to help with the pain of the memory. "Barely, I was younger than you. My father caught the virus and died. It was awful. I will never forget what the Belineans did to help us."

The sound of a door opens. Savannah breaks away from Alexis, running towards the door. She said, "Father..."

She runs headlong into a man dressed all in black. He is wearing a cloak that went just below his knees, with a hood over his head. Malovex looks down on the girl. The girl is now taken aback. Savannah, looking scared, said, "You are not my father...."

The man removes his hood and reveals his facial scars along with his long jet black hair. He tilted his head, looking at the girl. Pondering at Savannah's facial expression, he softly responds in a deep voice, "No, I am not."

Savannah asked, "Who are you?"

Alexis, now seeing the weight of the situation, lunges up from her seat. She takes a few steps, grabbing Savannah's wrist and forcing her to take a step back. Alexis bows her head slightly, before speaking, "Lord Malovex. My apologies. No one told me of your arrival."

Malovex kneeled and looked directly at the girl. "I am Sansigar Malovex. Who are you?"

The girl was now a little nervous. "I am Savannah Bird. You have a funny name."

Alexis was speechless and furious. "Savannah, don't be rude! Apologies, Lord Malovex."

Malovex, still looking at the girl, responded. "We don't pick our names, the people who raise us do."

Savannah was still frightened, but slightly warming up. "I was born in Savannah, Georgia. I wasn't supposed to be, but I was. My mother gave birth early, so my father named me Savannah."

Malovex showed no emotion. He said in a very soft but serious voice, "I was named for a town that was wiped out by some evil men."

Savannah, now genuinely terrified, whispered, "Just like the terrorists?"

Malovex paused. He took a small deep breath before whispering back, "Worse than the Terrorists."

Savannah's eyes grew big. She was scared. She almost did not want to ask the question, but somehow it just came right out. "Are the bad men still out there?"

Alexis still had her head bowed. She had no idea what to do. "My Lord, I'm sorry, the girl is a child and does not know any better....."

Malovex waved his hand up in the air. He silently brushed away Alexis' remarks, mainly because he was okay with answering the question. But the girl was scared now, looking down the whole time, she finally looked up into Malovex's eyes. Malovex spoke softly but clearly, "No. I killed them all."

Savannah was terrified. Who was this guy? Her eyes were watery. Alexis did not know what to say. Finally, the sound of the door opened, and Ambassador Bird walked in. Savannah ran to her father and hugged his legs just as he entered the room.

Ambassador Bird first looked down at his daughter before surveying the room. "Savannah, are you alright? Lord Malovex, no one told me of your arrival."

Malovex stood back up. "That is because no one knows I am here."

Ambassador Bird was first looking at Alexis as if upset that no one told him Malovex would be here. He then grabbed his daughter's shoulders and kneeled to talk to her. "Savannah, what is wrong?"

With a tear in her eye and a whimpering voice, Savannah said, "Did you do something bad, father?"

The Ambassador was now as confused as ever. " I don't think so."

Savannah was unconvinced. "Then why is this man Malava here? Is he here to kill you?"

The Ambassador now smiled. "It's Lord Malovex, and I don't know why he is here. But he and many other brave soldiers are sworn to protect me, you, and Alexis. Lord Malovex is the head of the BRG."

Savannah now wiped the tears away. "What is that?"

Alexis had now walked up to the two of them. "It stands for Belinean Rosash Guraan. They protect The Council's two hundred and ninety-six Ambassadors that were elected by the planet's delegates. The Ambassadors elect a leader, currently Chairman Hassara, Lord Malovex's uncle."

Savannah, now turning to Malovex. "So, you are trying to catch the bad guys?"

Malovex was emotionless in his answer. "No, I am going to kill the bad guys."

There was an awkward silence in the room. Savannah was back to looking scared. Alexis looked solemn. Even Ambassador Bird knew the conversation had somehow taken a dark undertone. It was clear it was not appropriate for his ten-year-old daughter. "Savannah, why don't you go with Alexis to the front of the ship and let the officers show you the cockpit again."

Malovex interrupted. "Miss Devanoe stays, she will be useful in this conversation. I'm sure the child can find her way to the cockpit."

Alexis looked curious. Ambassador Bird, never taking his eyes off Malovex, shoed his daughter off. "Go along, Savannah. Lord Malovex and I need to speak."

Savannah walked away to the front of the craft. Bird waited until he heard the door close before speaking to Malovex. "Please, have a seat."

Lord Malovex was not into extending pleasantries. "I will stand. This will not take long. I heard your speech. Very interesting."

Ambassador Bird was concerned this was going to turn into an awkward conversation. "I felt I was speaking on behalf of all my constituents."

Malovex showed no emotion. "If you say. Ambassador, I am here on behalf of Chairman Hassara and my cousin, Defense Minister Tempest Hassara. Are you familiar with the Emmetts Rule?"

Ambassador Bird was not quite sure but vaguely knew. "It is a security measure passed by the Council years ago, correct?"

Malovex was annoyed. Bird knew little. Malovex said, "Miss Devanoe?"

Alexis was relieved to speak about something she did know. "The Emmetts Rule, passed in 17235 BD, states that the Belinean Rosash Guraan, the BRG, or loosely translated as Sacred Guard in old tongue Belinean, will be responsible for the primary security of all Ambassador's represented in the Council. Transportation and additional security for all Council sessions will be supported in conjunction with the Aultali Chlorifa, the peacekeeping military for all the planets in the Council. Ambassadors will be permitted to have their own private detail or Guard, as security for traveling within their planet and subsequent starbases. This does not permit any planet to secure their own military, or replace the duties of the Aultali Chlorifa."

Bird said, "Which is the AuFa for short?"

Malovex spoke plainly. "Precisely. The rule allows you to have your own Delegate & Ambassador Guard. This is to encourage each representative in the Council to have local security on the planet that falls out of the jurisdiction and resources of the AuFa and BRG."

The tone had now changed. Ambassador Bird first looked at Alexis, then back at Malovex. " I would not say that expanding our Delegate Ambassador Guard to help fight terrorists is forming a military."

Malovex asked, "You believe your Delegate Ambassador Guard can handle fighting terrorists?"

Bird continued. "I believe Director Kimakawa has done a fine job with the DAG. Going back to my days as a Delegate, I can assure you the DAG has provided a security level that is as good, if not better, than the BRG. Perhaps you could learn something from them?"

Malovex took a few steps. He then looked directly at the screen the Ambassador had been on giving his speech just prior. He said, "I doubt it. Please play Malovex file one."

The screen showed clips of horrific Terrorist attacks. With subtitles underneath, it listed the destruction. The attack on Starbase 12, the transport ship Circas, carrying 86 people, all perished. Then the transport ship Issinery with the Wisterian Ambassador Luliet and 28 crew all died after a bomb exploded approaching this base.

As the clips popped up on the screen, Malovex continued, "This has all happened over the last 24 months. Two hundred and forty-one deaths, hundreds more wounded. Our new intelligence suggests the attacks were led by a Terrorist named Taz. He may be working with an Avolian terrorist cell group called the Valmay."

Ambassador Bird saw the images. "What is your point, Lord Malovex?"

Malovex now looked directly at Bird. His voice increased in volume to make sure the message was heard. "You have confidence your DAG can handle these terrorists?"

Ambassador Bird was put on the spot. "As articulated in my speech, which will be echoed in front of The Council, I believe we can work together, the DAG with the BRG and AuFa, in a way to protect everyone better."

Malovex was not amused. "Chairman Hassara and I, want to be clear that *any* expansion of your Delegate Ambassador Guard is a direct violation of the Emmett's rule. The Council will advise accordingly. Your resources can be put to far greater use by helping the AuFa and BRG then wasting your time with your own DAG."

The tension in the room became evident. The Ambassador looked directly at Malovex, clearly not scared of him. "And I see it differently, Lord Malovex."

Malovex looked directly back. "Pity….."

Alexis now identified the tension in the room might get out of hand and decided to end the conversation prematurely. "Lord Malovex, the Ambassador, has a couple of meetings that he is now late to, so forgive us if we must cut this short."

The Ambassador said nothing, nor did Malovex. After a few seconds of staring at each other, Malovex turned to Alexis and said, "Of course, Miss Devanoe, you are correct. I also have a meeting with Director Kimakawa about your security detail for your passage to Belinea. Ambassador, I also bring you a personal message from Ambassador Yi. As you know, he is already on Belinea for the Council meeting."

Malovex reached into his cloak and took out a rolled piece of parchment inside a sealed tube. Ambassador Bird took the tube from Malovex's hand, not knowing what to say. He was curious to know if Malovex had read the note.

Malovex put the hood back over his head and began walking out. Before getting to the door, Malovex turned and looked at Bird and Alexis. "And no Ambassador, I did not read the message. Your world gets a lot better when you start figuring out who you can and cannot trust."

Once he left, Alexis turned to Bird, whispering, "Ambassador, you cannot say those things to him. He is one of the most powerful men in this galaxy."

Ambassador Bird said, "Relax Alexis, his primary job is to protect me."

Alexis Devanoe replied, "No, it isn't. His title may be the head of the BRG, but Ambassador protection is his second job."

Ambassador Bird looked almost puzzled. "What's his first?"

Alexis Devanoe softly said, "Same as mine Ambassador. Protecting his family."

The two look at each other for a moment before the Ambassador puts his thumb on the spot on the tube. Once the tube recognized that it was Ambassador Bird, it opened. Bird took the parchment out and quickly read the handwritten note. He then turned to Alexis and softly said, "Get me, Director Kimikawa."

BELINEA 1.3

Earth - Northeastern Japan

In blizzard conditions, the small transport ship navigated Earth's atmosphere towards the surface. Through very thick clouds and turbulent winds, it raced towards a small base located in a desolate mountainside between two ridges. The ship touched down on a landing pad with minimal white landing lights. Two men got off and walked towards a small building off to the side. Dressed in military jackets that were not quite good enough for the conditions, one man took his hand out and placed it on the scanner beside the door. The door opened, and both men walked inside, towards the elevator. As the men came off the elevator, they began to take their hats and goggles off.

Commander Avery Jones, a tall, African American, with a bald head and a muscular frame, and Commander Nolan Willits, a caucasian, also with a bald head but slightly shorter, piercing green eyes, and a salt-n-pepper stubble beard, walked in. Willits turned to Jones and said, "I forgot how cold it is here."

Both begin walking down a series of corridors. Jones sarcastically responds, "Thank you for the weather alert, I couldn't tell."

Each man had a look of displeasure on their face as if getting called into the principal's office for doing something terrible. Jones looked down on Willits, "You sure you don't know what this is about?"

Willits, sounding annoyed, replied, "Same answer the first two times you asked, no. I am just as curious as you."

Jones shook his head. "We're being punished for something."

Willits questioned. "For what?"

Jones continued, "Maybe for not reaching the Avolians?"

Willits answered, "He knows that takes time."

Jones countered, "Maybe he thinks he can find someone better than us?"

Willits smirked and said, "Don't be stupid."

The two men turned down a few more hallways, then left, then right again. The halls had steel metal grate floors, with dirt and rock underneath. It was as if the corridors were well-lit caves in a mountainside. They turned and pressed a hand on to a secure spot on the wall. The entrance of the elevator doors opened, and the two men walked in. The elevator took them down further into the mountain. When they got out, they walked down another corridor, placing another hand on the wall, to pass another secured entrance. This one had security men guarding the doors. Finally, they walked into an office where a robot greeted them.

The Robot said, "Commander Willits, Commander Jones, Director Kimakawa is expecting you."

The two men walked by the robot and into yet another set of massive steel doors that opened automatically. As they walked in, Director Kimakawa, a bald fifty-something Japanese man with a thin black goatee, sat behind a stainless steel desk. A flat computer monitor laid on the top of the desk, along with a few trinkets: a small model spaceship, a picture of him with Ambassador Yi, a few books. There was also a picture frame with a quote from Sun Tzu *"If you know the enemy and know yourself, you need not fear the results of a hundred battles."*

A second man, Vice Director Franklin Meyers, was off to the side in full uniform. He was standing in front of Kimakawa's library wall that also held his Edo period Samurai Sword. Jones and Willits stopped four feet in front of the desk, stood at full attention, and saluted. Director Kimakawa spoke without looking up. "At ease, gentlemen. I am sure you are wondering why I have summoned you from your assignment on Gitaris?"

Willits was in a mood. He said, "I am going to assume it's not to talk about Sun Tzu?"

Franklin Meyers, now uncrossing his arms, scowls angrily at Willits. A protocol had been broken. "Watch your tone with the Director, Commander."

Director Kimakawa, however, never seemed bothered and proceeded. A man of quiet but sure confidence, he knew who was in charge of the room and conducted this meeting accordingly. "A fan of Sun Tzu Commander Willits?"

Willits glanced down at Kimakawa and responded with a Sun Tzu quote, "All warfare is based on deception."

Director Kimakawa nodded slightly and said, "One of my favorites. I also like Strategy without tactics is the slowest route to victory…"

Willits continued for him "…Tactics without strategy is the noise before defeat."

Kimakawa now stood. "I would love to talk Sun Tzu strategy all day, but that is not why I pulled you off of Gitaris."

He walked over and poured himself a scotch while continuing to speak. "First and foremost, our DAG is a security unit. Nothing can compromise our primary objective. As you may have heard, Ambassador Bird has been giving many speeches defending our existence. He plans to provide a policy changing speech in front of the Council at the next session, and we will assist him accordingly."

Willits seemed more relaxed now. For once, they were not in trouble. "Of Course, sir. I am just confused about how Commander Jones and myself can help?"

Director Kimakawa now half-smiled, which is something he never did. "You will lead Ambassador Bird's security detail to Belinea. Ambassador Bird wanted the best and most experienced I had."

Jones was now confused as well. "Sir, with all due respect, Commander Willits and I have not led a security detail in over five years."

Franklin Meyers, still standing off to the side, was getting tired of Willits' continued lack of respect. He said, "Are you disobeying a direct order from the Director?"

Director Kimakawa waved his hand. "Meyers, enough. I understand it has been some time since your last security detail. But this is important to me, and I want someone I can trust."

Willits did not care about pissing off Meyers. They had never been friends. But the timing was not adding up. "Thank you for your confidence, Director. However, it will take my team some time to get here, which will delay the Ambassador's departure. I fear he may not get to Belinea on time."

Kimakawa gave Willits an enlightened look. He continued, "Correct Commander Willits. Which is why Vice Director Meyers and myself have recruited a first-class team in its place."

Commander Willits looked at Meyers, then at Director Kimakawa. "Permission to speak, Director?"

Director Kimakawa nodded as if to say yes silently.

It was still not adding up to Willits. "We prefer working with someone we trust. The faith you have in us is equal to that of our own team, which is just as qualified."

Meyers interrupted. "Well, Commander Willits, that is the thing. They are not qualified."

Willits was taken aback. "Excuse me?"

Vice Director Meyers began to explain. "The BRG has issued a new transport ship, the C-62T, for all Ambassador interstellar transport. It's a faster version of the C-58T, and Earth has only been commissioned two. However, it requires a BRG certification to fly it."

Willits had just been blind-sided. He said, "Sir, again, with respect, a pilot is a pilot. Lieutenant Rix or Lieutenant Mollanari, the pilots on my team, could learn to fly it in no time."

Meyers was almost gloating. There was no love lost between them. He continued, "The BRG Certification requires 25-plus hours flight time in the C-62T or certified simulator. We have already begun to certify all of our transport pilots in the last four months, including the flight school graduates at Odgins. As you know, I sent you a request three months ago to get Lieutenants Rix and Molinari certified, but you said they have been too busy on assignment to do so."

Willits was staring at Meyers. This was a bullshit technicality. But why? It almost seemed like personal retribution. Before Willits could make it worse, Commander Jones decided to break the tension. " When do we leave, sir?"

Meyers answered for him. "You are scheduled to leave tomorrow, 16:00 hours. The detail team and the Ambassador will be waiting for you at SPE gate 5. You have been given TS-5 security access for this mission, so anything further you need is available at your disposal. There is a briefing memo if your quarters regarding flight details to Belinea should take eight days."

Director Kimakawa was not about to answer any more questions. This meeting was done in his mind. He said, "Do not let me down, gentlemen. Ambassador Bird wanted the best, and that is what I am giving him. Dismissed."

Commander Jones and Willits saluted and walked out. As they began walking down the corridor, Jones whispered to Willits, "Told you, we were being punished."

They boarded the elevator going up, as Willits answered, "This is complete bullshit. Pulling us off Gitaris for this?"

As the elevator continued up, Jones added, "And, not using our team?"

Commander Willits was still hot and confused. "Meyers fucked us on that one."

Jones responded, "Thank you for not punching him and making it worse."

Willits said, "I am tempted just to fly the damn thing ourselves."

Jones responded, "Yeah, but you heard the Director. They have to be certified pilots, or the Dock Master won't even let us get off the slip."

Willits was shaking his head as they got off the elevator. They practically bumped into Lord Malovex, who was entering the elevator. They all stared at one another. Willits and Jones almost froze. They gently bowed their heads before getting out, "Lord Malovex."

Malovex said nothing. He stared at them briefly for a few seconds, before finally getting on the elevator. As the doors closed, Jones and Willits looked at each other in disbelief.

Jones first commented. "What the hell is he doing here?"

Willits was lost now. "This is getting crazier by the minute. I do know one thing."

Jones and Willits began walking away from the elevator. Jones answered, "What's that?"

Willits responded. "I don't trust anyone at this point. Just because we can't use our team, doesn't mean I am taking the team Meyers gives us."

Jones was confused and asked, "Where are you gonna find two qualified pilots?"

Willits, half sarcastic, half still fuming, said, "You heard Meyers. We're going to Odgins."

BELINEA 1.4

The Moon, Earth

Odgins Military Academy

Commanders Willits and Jones walked off a transport ship in full gear. The enclosed helmets secured the oxygen necessary to breathe on the moon. It was an extremely dark place, with only artificial lights that lit up the landing pads that allowed people to navigate walking around. Willits and Jones walked to the corner of the base. Sliding doors were encased into the side of a small rock mountain, with a faint dark sky and rays of orange behind it. Willits put his hand on the scanner next to the door, and it immediately opened. As they entered, they walked through the second set of doors before removing their helmets. A quick unzipping of the gear, they left the space uniforms on racks that harbored a couple of dozen suits in the room. They then entered another set of sliding doors to a place with about fifty people, all scurrying around with seemingly essential tasks to do. Many control panels, lights, desks, maps, and operations boards, it was clear this was the main operations room at the Academy.

Willits and Jones walked to the first long counter and looked to a Corporal behind the desk. She stood and gave a slight salute before saying, "Commander, how can I help you?"

Willits figured intimidation would be his best tactic. "Commander Willits for Master Sergeant Evans."

The Corporal, however, was an experienced gatekeeper. "Do you have an appointment, Commander Willits?"

Willits doubled down on the intimidation card "Corporal, I am a Commander. Go find the Master Sergeant for me."

The Corporal was not going to play this game. "Sir ...."

Master Sergeant Evans, a short, female African-American, immediately popped her head from behind the counter and got up. Walking up to the desk, she annoyingly said, "Are you going to talk to my Corporal like that? What if I was in a meeting? Teaching a class?"

Willits answered, "But clearly, you are not…."

Evans walked out from behind the desk. She said to the Corporal. "Forgive the Commander's, Corporal. They skipped the class on civility when they were here."

Jones said, "Nice to see you too, Master Sergeant."

Evans asked as she continued walking, "Don't add to the hostility Jones. Why are you here? Your transport breakdown?"

Willits and Jones followed her down a low lit hall, clearly cut out of rock and soil, with metal grates on the floor. Jones tried to keep up and spoke, "We are on vacation and decided to stop by."

Master Sergeant Evans continued to walk briskly. "Whoever told you there were bars and hookers here lied."

Commander Jones and Willits were still trying to keep up. Willits talked to the back of her head, "Maybe we just wanted to see you."

Evans, still walking at a brisk pace, replied, "If only the feeling were mutual."

Jones continued. "Come on, maybe hang out and teach the cadets a thing or two?"

Evans never broke stride as she turned the corner to walk down a second long hallway. "What you two could teach those cadets wouldn't fill a bubble gum wrapper."

Jones was stupid enough to speak. "Harsh, Sargent."

Evans walked behind another counter now and took a sip of her coffee. "And yet, true."

The three stopped in front of sliding doors that were behind the counter. Willits, speaking softly, said, "I need two pilots, preferably close to graduating, and they need to be C-62T certified."

Evans was confused. "All the graduates are now C-62T certified. Why do you need two?"

Willits was looking around to make sure no one heard him. Two cadets walked by, and other than their very slight salute had utterly ignored them. Willits spoke as they walked away, holding up a small stick that was an electronic file. "I am recruiting them for a DAG mission."

Evans sounded skeptical. "Flying a C-62T? That's not a mission. That's babysitting an Ambassador for the weekend."

Willits spoke a little louder now. "Convincing them it's a mission will be my problem, not yours. Are you going to help me, or am I going to have to go through other channels?"

Evans was now insulted. "Other channels? Really? This is only my second cup of coffee today Willits, don't push me."

Willits rolled his eyes as Jones casually smirked. Evans walked through the doors, and Jones and Willits followed. They walked into a vast hangar with lots of spacecraft maintained by a couple of hundred cadets and maintenance crew. The hangar was enclosed, approximately thirty meters high and two kilometers long. It had six large doors that led to the outside landing pads of the base. A lot had changed since Willits and Jones were here. They were both taking everything in while Evans continued to walk ahead of them. She spoke over the loud noises. "So just two cadets that can fly a C-62T?"

Willits lightly shouted, "Preferably, the best two pilots you got, based on overall scores and performance records. This may be slightly more complicated than just transporting."

Evans smiled as she continued to walk. "Someone as good as Rix?"

Willits was still looking at all the things in the hangar while he and Jones followed Evans. Jones then shouted, "That would be ideal."

Evans walked under a massive transport ship that was being worked on. She did not need to duck, but Willits and Jones did slightly. "How is my girl doing? You haven't pissed her off yet?"

Jones responded, "She's an excellent pilot, albeit a pain in my ass sometimes.."

Evans continued walking, "Well, you two aren't exactly Commanders Warm and Fuzzy. Why can't you just use Rix?"

Willits said, "We can't."

Evans walked up to a flight maintenance crew member, who quickly saluted. "I need these two prepped and ready by 0800 hours. And make sure the A-11's are ready for final testing tomorrow. All of them. (turning back to Willits) Why not?"

The flight crew member saluted and walked off. Jones said, "She caught a glimpse of Willits in the shower and has been temporarily blinded for two weeks."

Evans responded, "It would be longer for me. Sinkai is a great pilot and an outstanding student, highest marks in his class. But you don't want him."

Commander Jones looked puzzled. "Why?"

Evans was very candid. "Because he's a weasel, and high marks aren't everything. Look at the two of you. You need good pilots, but excellent soldiers. Two you can trust in combat, am I correct? That is why you are asking me. If you just wanted any two, you could've sent me an electronic order."

Willits looked at her suspiciously. He did not trust anyone at the moment other than Jones. "Maybe I just need two babysitters to fly an Ambassador on a C-62T."

Evans looked directly up at him, inching a little closer. "You gonna tell me what this is about?"

Willits and Jones just looked at each other. Evans tilted her head and continued. "If you had Rix or Molinari here, you wouldn't be looking for two rookie pilots."

After a pause, Willits said, "I need two pilots, are you gonna help me?"

Once Evans realized she was not going to get an answer, she began walking again. She said as they followed her, "The two you want are Tunsall and Trujillo. Trujillo is obvious. Excellent pilot, an outstanding soldier, moderately insubordinate. He jumps into the fire but hates rules. You will love him. He reminds me of you."

Jones spoke from behind, "Me or Willits?"

Evans slightly talked over her shoulder. "Is there a difference?"

Jones said, "I am only marginally a prick, not full-blown."

Willits looked at him disapprovingly. Evans walked up to another crew cadet. Evans said, "Fair point."

Willits asked, "What about the other one, Tunsall?"

Evans signed a tablet that the crew officer shoved in her face, as he scurried off after. "He is quiet, cerebral, not sociable. But he is the best pure pilot I have ever seen come out of here."

Jones shouted, "What's the problem?"

Evans stopped and turned to look at both of them. Trying to articulate her thoughts, she responded, "The rest of the cadets don't trust him. He is different. The medical staff cannot figure out what he is, but he is not human. He has some connections because I don't know how he got here. He is also smart, probably too smart. His aptitude tests are off the chart, and his classmates hate him for it. He should be first in class if not for a few minor incidents with Trujillo that prevented that."

Willits looked down at Evans. "They know each other well?"

Evans began walking again. "Like two peas in a pod. The cadets all respect Trujillo, and most like him. But Trujillo is the only person who even talks to Tunsall. We call them TnT. Complete opposites, but you won't find one without the other. And you won't convince one without the other. I sometimes think they share the same brain."

Willits spoke slightly more softly now, giving his orders to Evans. "These are my orders, where can I find them?"

Evans put the orders into her tablet and quickly read them. "A security transport mission to Belinea protecting Ambassador Bird. These orders say Meyers already provided you pilots."

Willits pointed to further spots on the orders "Per Commander Willits and Commander Jones discretion, DAG will provide any support crew needed. Signed, Director Kimakawa."

Evans now thought about something, curiosity rising in her voice. "This is a simple Ambassador transport mission. Why are you two assigned to it? And why is Meyers forcing you his crew instead of yours?"

Willits took a deep breath before speaking, "Well, now you have come to the root of the problem. I asked myself the same question."

Evans looked at Jones. "What did Kimakawa say?"

Jones replied, "We were cut off by Meyers and this C-62T certification bullshit. Kimakawa never gave us an answer after that. It was clear we were not going to get one."

Evans was trying to put two and two together. "Well, that's a bullshit technicality. It doesn't make any sense that he wouldn't allow you to use your own crew... unless....."

Willits now tilted his head. "Exactly...hence why we are here. I'm certainly not going to use his."

Another cadet walked up to Evans. "Master Sergeant Evans. Sergeant Murray has a problem with one of the A-11's. He doesn't think it will be ready for testing tomorrow."

Evans began to quickly punch things into her tablet and before handing them back to Willits. "I am going to have to deal with this. I attached the files for Tunsall and Trujillo onto those orders. The two of them are likely in the flight simulation room on deck 5, preparing for final performance flights with the other cadets. You remember how to get there, correct?"

They both nodded. Willits then reached into his other pocket, which was another stick, this one with a seal. He said, "Sabrina…"

She turned around, momentarily thrown off by being addressed by her first name. Willits tossed her the stick and said, "It's a simple transport. But if something happens, give that to Kimakawa, personally."

Evans, holding the stick, said, "Like if what happens?"

Willits said, "Like serious shit, that shouldn't happen. Like the reason, I'm picking my two pilots."

Evans nodded and walked off. After Evans was a good twenty meters away, Jones turned to Willits and whispered, "You remember how to get to flight simulation from here?"

Willits was still looking at Evans as she walked away. Evans was now barking orders at a few cadets. Willits slightly turned, trying to find the way out of the hanger. Reluctantly pointing, he then said to Jones, "It's that way. No…, wait, that way."

Jones rolled his eyes. "Forgive me for having zero confidence in your navigation."

Willits began taking a few steps "It's this way...I think?"

Jones quickly answered, "I would sooner follow the Devil to Confession."

Willits looked at him with another disapproving look. Jones whistled at a nearby crew cadet. When the cadet turned, he said, "How do we get to flight simulation on deck five?"

The cadet pointed to doors in the opposite way Willits was going. "Through the doors, down the corridor to the end. Hang a left, get on the elevator to deck five."

Jones smacked Willits on the shoulder as they began to walk that way. "See what happens when you just ask for directions?"

Willits mimicked Jones. "See what happens when you have to ask for help...."

Jones now gave him a disapproving look. Willits continued, now in his voice. "Next time I leave you with a hoard of ugly women, watch what happens."

Jones answered, "That's cruel. I would sooner leave you on the battlefield, alone to die."

Willits countered, "Careful what you ask for."

BELINEA 1.5

The Moon, Odgins Military Academy

Deck 5 Flight Simulator

"Bullseye...Sinkai down."

A long, narrow, tube-like room housed eight simulator boxes on each side, sixteen total. The simulator boxes were cockpit shaped—all black, with multiple wires and hoses popping out. Two red flashing lights spun on the ceiling as all the simulator cockpits slowly opened. Each cadet came climbing out, stepping up to the small, narrow, metal crate walkway that divided the room. One by one, they began filing down the walkway. Trujillo and Tunsall were last in line.

As they came down the stairs, they passed a control panel with multiple personnel operating the simulator. Trujillo looked of Spanish descent, with dark hair, brown eyes, and a muscular frame. Tunsall was taller, just over 6 feet, with sandy brown caramel hair, green eyes, and a wiry frame. Two pilots were waiting at the end for Trujillo and Tunsall. As Trujillo approached, one of them said, "Trujillo, you are the luckiest son of a bitch I have ever met."

Trujillo stopped and looked him straight in the eyes. "Is that right?"

Tunsall, not saying anything, kept walking by, behind Trujillo. The first pilot who barked and was now staring at Trujillo, said "That was complete bullshit. I've never seen somebody get so lucky so many times in a row."

Trujillo just tilted his head "If you think it was luck, let's do it again."

Tunsall, who was at least two steps past Trujillo and the other pilot, suddenly stopped. Not saying anything, he turned around, but on his helmet, and started walking back towards the steps. Trujillo never turned around to look at him, only still staring at the pilot who barked. Tunsall stopped at the foot of the stairs, waiting. After a few seconds, the pilot that barked shook his head and said, "You're such an asshole. Both of you."

He walked off. As he did, Tunsall turned around again, taking his helmet back off. Trujillo glanced behind himself, looking at Tunsall, and gave a small smile. Both men then walked out of the room, down towards the control panels. Standing there were Willits and Jones.

Willits, with his arms crossed, spoke. "That was some pretty nice flying there."

Trujillo and Tunsall stopped. Trujillo spoke, "Thank you, sir. Were you watching?"

Willits continued. "We were, on the monitors. Gentlemen, this is Commander Jones, I am Commander Willits of the Delegate Ambassador Guard. Can we speak to you over here in private, please?"

All four men walked over to a small room off to the side of the simulation room. Willits stared at Trujillo. "You must be Trujillo, and you (glancing at Tunsall) must be Tunsall?"

Tunsall said nothing. Trujillo looked apprehensive before speaking. "Yes, sir."

Willits took a deep breath while looking at his tablet. "According to this, you fine gentlemen are scheduled to graduate as officers next week. Second Lieutenants. What are your plans after?"

Trujillo raised an eyebrow. "Sir?"

Willits, now glancing back up to Trujillo and again looking at him eye to eye. "Plans, Trujillo, plans. Belinean-Earth forces for peacekeeping? Possible officers in the DAG, protecting the bureaucrats? Good enough pilot scores, perhaps trying to get assigned to a Belinean AuFa Carrier flying Fighters?"

Trujillo, still slightly confused by the line of questioning, responded. "Sir, we have no say. We turn in a request to our...."

Willits changed the tone, now not smiling. "Blah, blah, blah, yes, I am aware, it's a request. If it was your fucking choice, what would you want?"

Tunsall now understood and spoke out of turn. "We are pilots, sir. We both want to fly fighters."

Tunsall was staring at Willits intensely, almost as if he would stab him in the chest with a pencil. Jones, staring at Tunsall and noticing, with a touch of sarcasm, spoke. "He speaks. I was beginning to think he (nodding at Trujillo) did all the speaking for you."

Tunsall, still staring at Willits with piercing green eyes, nodded at Jones and said, "I was beginning to think you did the same for him."

Jones took a few paces forward, now standing face to face with Tunsall, looking down at him. Tunsall, looking up, never changed the expression on his face, still a glaring stare. After a few seconds, Jones cracked a small smile and walked back over to the desk. He crossed his arms, leaned on the top, and stared at both of them while Willits continued. "I got a personnel file in here, for both of you. Outstanding marks in Academics, Marksmanship, top of the class in flight school skill levels. Two instances of insubordination, one involving disobeying direct orders, the other a failure to cooperate, what should I know about this?"

Trujillo and Tunsall said nothing. Both did a small glance down, nothing more. Willits was now annoyed. "I can send Commander Jones down to talk to your classmates, find out the real story. Or you can stop wasting everyone's time and just tell us. What happened?"

Trujillo decided to speak candidly but did not ask for permission. "The direct order was bullshit, sir. It was an exercise."

Jones cut him off. "Bullshit? Did Master Sergeant Evans call it bullshit? Or is her version different than yours?"

Tunsall said, "Sir, in our opinion, the exercise was unfair. As for the other, we're not rats."

Jones was now amused. "Rats? What do you know about being rats? Were you tortured? Lost a limb? Waterboarded? Keeping quiet around here to protect your classmates is not exactly sworn secrecy. What did you get, an hour of detention? Sent to bed without dinner?"

Trujillo was agitated. "Seventy-two hours confinement, no passes for a year...sir."

Willits almost laughed. Jones smiled and said, "Whoah, a little testy for breaking out after curfew, no?"

The attitude of these two officers did not amuse Trujillo, but for whatever reason, he seemed to like them. "Permission to speak, sir?"

Willits, now done smiling, responded. "Granted. And dispense with the sir, it's either Willits or Commander."

Trujillo took a breath. "Commander, why are you here, did we do something wrong?"

Willits now got serious. "I'm here because the unit I'm in, you do get tortured, beaten, and killed for information. And then they find your family and do the same. I'm here because I'm looking for two officers for an assignment."

Tunsall was now intrigued. "What kind of assignment, Commander?"

Willits now began slowly pacing. "I need two pilots, adequately trained. It's to support a highly classified DAG mission that will require a month of travel log. It will require a second level of security clearance, which you don't currently have. Combat is likely. "

After a pause, Tunsall spoke. "What will we be flying?"

Jones answered from across the room, "What are you qualified to fly?"

Trujillo turned to Jones. "Everything...."

Willits, still holding the tablet but now below his belt with his hands crossed. "Cocky little bastard, aren't you?"

Trujillo, a matter of factly, said, "Speaking Mandarin Commander, no. But flying, we hold our own."

Tunsall added, "Or you wouldn't be here."

Jones, slightly puzzled, said, "Excuse me?"

Tunsall spoke. "No one goes looking for two mediocre pilots. Someone told you we were the best."

Jones barked, still with his arms crossed. "What makes you think we don't have another meeting after this with two better pilots?"

Trujillo was now deadly serious. "Because there are no two better pilots, Commander. Not here, at least. Or do you need to go watch us with our classmates in the simulators again?"

There was a long pause. Willits got face to face with Trujillo again and softly said, "I'm not talking about simulation. I'm talking about real shit."

Trujillo just stared back, took a deep breath, and sarcastically whispered, ".....And....."

There was another long pause. Tunsall and Trujillo continued to stare at Willits. Willits glanced at Jones. Jones just very slightly shrugged his shoulders. Willits then looked back at the two of them and quietly said, "Maybe we don't need that second interview."

Tunsall then spoke, "Commander, we did not say yes."

Willits turned his head in disbelief. "What?"

Tunsall continued. "This is not an order, correct Commander? This is a volunteer assignment. We do not have to go. We may have better options when we graduate in a couple of weeks."

Jones again lightly shouted from across the room. "Better options? You got some crazy connections that we don't know about?"

Tunsall and Trujillo glanced at each other before looking at Jones as he continued. "Because unless you do, here are your options. You can fly transport ships to ferry cargo and soldiers on peacekeeping missions on Earth. Maybe even fly local delegates on Earth if you're lucky. What you won't be doing is flying anything on an AuFa carrier. Because if you ain't Belinean, they won't let you drive so much as a transport cart from one side of the hanger to the other."

Tunsall and Trujillo glanced at each other before looking at Willits. Willits walked up to them and said, "This is an assignment that will get you combat experience before you even graduate. You get back after this mission for a month, graduate, and join the DAG as an experienced officer and write your ticket anywhere."

Tunsall spoke. "You mean fly a bunch of old Ambassadors to and from Belinea, Commander?"

Jones and Willits looked at each other before Willits said, "There is a lot more to it than that my two little naive officers. What do you say?"

There was again a long pause. Both glanced at each other again before Trujillo spoke, "When do we leave?"

Willits half-smiled "Tomorrow. 1300 hours, SPE Gate 14. I will arrange transport with Master Sergeant Evans."

Both Willits and Jones began walking out of the room before Willits stopped and turned around. "One more thing, gentlemen. To save us time that could otherwise be used for drinking in a bar and finding Commander Jones, the company of an attractive female, what else is in this file that I should know?

Trujillo spoke, slightly shaking his head. "Sir?"

Willits continued. "Things I find on a background check of your Master Security file?

Skeletons in the closet? Jail time? Blatant insubordination? Do you hit your girlfriend? Drug problem? You got a secret relative that's Belinean? "

Trujillo glanced at Tunsall. Tunsall didn't turn, keeping his eyes on Willits. "No, nothing."

Trujillo added, "Nothing Master Sergeant Evans wouldn't tell you."

Willits and Jones walked out of the room. Jones said, "That's a lot. See you tomorrow."

Willits and Jones turned down a corridor and got to an elevator shaft before Jones turned to Willits and said, "Arrogant little shits aren't they?"

They both got on the elevator, and Willits responded, "Yeah, I like em too. Let's get a drink."

BELINEA 1.6

Avola

Bosa Province, Valmay Group Base

Kaya Killian was watching her brother, Octavious Killian, walk along the landing pads. Inside the massive cave, Kaya walked down steps, towards the ships that were being prepped for the mission. As Octavious was walking up to two soldiers working on a crate, they immediately stood up and saluted. Octavious did not return the salute. He tapped one confidently on the shoulder and pointed at the crate, asking a question. The two soldiers smiled and nodded. Octavious smiled and gave them a thumbs-up before walking off. The two soldiers returned to the crate. Kaya had made it to the bottom of the steps, now finding Octavious engaged with two more soldiers: Cortes, a pilot, and Rendon, a weapons expert.

Both tried to salute. Octavious, tall with dark olive skin, casually touched Rendon's shoulder instead. Octavious asked, "Where are we on surveillance footage?"

Cortes, who was much shorter and therefore had to look up, said, "A Miner transport got six photos about an hour ago. No change."

Octavious looked at Rendon and said, "And the AuFa officer?"

Rendon calmly said, "Singing like a bird to Marrat in the holding cell. He gave us the codes, which is more than we need."

Kaya walked up the group. Tall, athletic, and toned, with the same dark olive skin as her brother, she only looked at Octavious, not saying anything. Octavious replied, "Alright, the rest of the crew is ready. We leave in fifteen minutes."

Cortes and Rendon both nodded, saluted, and walked off to let the others know. After they were gone from ear-shot, Kaya said, "If we get there too late, the Cargo Transport will leave without us."

Octavious began walking and said, "We'll get there right before they leave. A message from the miners said the last shuttle left five minutes ago. Those greedy bastards won't leave without it."

Kaya, walking next to him, asked, "And the AuFa Patrol Fighters?"

Octavious quickly responded, "Returning now, done for the day. "

He and Kaya took a few more steps before she asked, "And the crate?"

Octavious stopped and looked at her. He said, "Stocked and ready, waiting for me. If there is anything that potentially worries me about this mission, it is you."

Kaya, miffed at the lack of confidence, replied, "Me? Why?"

Octavious replied, "You have the hardest task."

Kaya answered, "Which is why I'm doing it."

Octavious said, "I offered to switch."

Kaya answered, "A move no one would allow."

It was Octavious who was now miffed. "Last time I checked, I was in charge around here."

Kaya replied, "Last time I checked, your aim still sucks, and you're old and slow."

Octavious answered, "Careful, you're almost the same age as me. When we get back, we can get in the ring and see who's old and slow."

Kaya began walking off and said, "Why would I embarrass you in front of your troops?"

Octavious stood there, hands in his pockets, watching his little sister walk off. After she got about six steps away, he yelled, "Kaya…."

She turned around and started backpedaling, still looking at him. She said, "Yeah…."

Octavious said, not too loudly. "Be careful…."

Kaya responded, "Anything else, Captain?"

Octavious gave a small, half-grin. He said, "Don't miss."

Kaya turned around and began walking away again. With her back turned away from Octavious, she said loud enough for him to hear "I never do."

BELINEA 1.7

Space Port Earth

Inside a bar, Willits and Jones were at a high top table that overlooked the planet Earth. Willits still had the tablet in his hand, as he was typing several things. An attractive female server came over and asked, "Would you officers like something to drink?"

Jones just smiled and said, "Yes, what is your name?"

The server smiled and responded, "My name is Julie."

Jones responded, "What a beautiful name. My name is Avery. My friend, Nolan, is a bitter, poor excuse for a man who lacks confidence, charisma, and humor. I, however, am delighted to meet you."

Julie smiled again and said, "Likewise. He doesn't look too bad to me."

Jones got a little dangerous, with sarcasm. "Ten minutes ago, he was wearing a fedora with a red velvet robe and nothing else, pondering where it all went wrong."

Julie squinted her eyes. "Midlife crisis?"

Jones responded. "He's eighty-one."

Julie grabbed Willits on the shoulder while he kept looking at his tablet. "Well, I like fedoras."

Jones quickly said, "It's pink with a neon green feather."

Julie shook her head and said, "Oooh, no. Perhaps a drink will help?"

Jones responded, "A lot of drinks to erase that memory."

Willits glanced at Julie and said, "Double Woodford, neat."

Julie's smile was gone. She nodded and turned to Jones and asked, "And you?"

Jones said, "Same. And forgive my friend Julie. Jackass is his default language until you get him some Bourbon or Scotch."

Julie smiled again and said, "Then I will hurry and be right back."

Julie walked off, and Jones waited a few seconds before quietly saying, "I haven't gotten laid by a human in over six months, and you might as well be a farting wild boar next to me."

Willits, not smiling and still typing on his tablet, said, "I can arrange that."

Jones shook his head and said, "I'd have a better chance, at least pigs wanna fuck."

Willits shook his head "I am busy getting this shit done for tomorrow."

Jones incredulously asked, "How long does it take to change a manifest?"

Willits, still typing, "Longer than you think. Besides, I am changing our departure time, as well."

Jones replied, "Best news I've heard all day. A later departure gives me more time to cure that getting laid problem, which will likely turn into a getting over hangover problem."

Willits was still typing and said, "We are leaving earlier."

Jones raised his eyebrows and said, "See, it sounded like you said earlier, which would greatly impact even my ability at getting horizontal."

Willits, never taking his eyes off the tablet, asked, "Have you known me to have a stuttering problem?"

Jones shook his head and asked, "Why the hell are we leaving earlier?"

Willits, still typing, replied, "You know why."

Jones continued. "We already changed the manifest. Isn't that overkill?"

Willits stopped typing and looked at Jones and said, "The sooner we get this shit done, the better."

Jones waited a few seconds before saying, "You are killing my mojo."

Willits, going back to typing and not missing a beat, said, "Really, I'm so sorry. Do you need a tissue?"

Jones scowled him. After a few seconds, Julie, the server returned and said, "Two double Woodford's, neat, ..."

As she was putting the drinks down, Jones replied, "Thank you, Julie..."

Julie smiled and said, "Anything else I can get you?"

Jones continued. "Normally, after a few hours and lots of drinks, you would be captivated by my charm, which can reach a certain level of sophistication and appeal that matches my rugged good looks. However, I simply do not have that kind of time tonight. Why don't we postpone that delightful evening date number two, and skip right to the instant attraction of going home tonight instead."

Julie just stared at Jones for a few seconds. She then glanced at Willits before looking back at Jones. She then turned around and walked away. After she was out of earshot, Willits looked at Jones and said, "I am killing your mojo?"

Jones sarcastically said, "You are not helping."

Willits continued. "I think your mojo reached a new level of dumpster fire, even without me."

Jones said, "Desperate times call for desperate measures."

Willits smiled as he resumed typing. Holding his fingers an inch apart, he said, "Sophistication and appeal? How did that not work? You were so close."

Jones took a sip of his bourbon, before putting it down and replying "You are right. Being a moody little shit, with a touch of jackass and annoyance, is so charming."

Willits raised his glass and said before taking a sip, "Being an annoying prick has yet to fail me. Consider it my mojo."

Jones took another sip and said, "Yep. The ladies are flocking to see it up close."

After a few seconds, Julie returned and got a lot closer to Jones this time. She whispered. "Order another round of drinks for you and me. I got someone to cover my shift, I'm off in an hour."

Jones raised his bourbon glass and said, "We will take another, and whatever the lady would like."

Julie nodded and walked away. Jones then looked at Willits, smiled, and took a big gulp of his scotch. Willits just shook his head and whispered, "Un-fucking-believable."

Jones asked, "Do you want me to see if she has a friend?"

Willits went back to typing and said, "I am fine on my own, thank you."

Jones nodded and said, "You are absolutely right, that being a cock that is working out great. You know what you should try?"

Willits stopped typing and looked up with his head tilted.

Jones, shaking his hand and pointing, said, "Sophistication and appeal...."

Willits, shaking his head, softly said, "Go fuck yourself..."

BELINEA 1.8

Space Port Earth

Alexis Devanoe sat alone in a tiny room. She was packing a small bag as a computer voice spoke aloud, "Alexis, 15 new messages in the last thirty minutes."

Still packing, and barely paying attention, Alexis spoke aloud. "Identify importance levels, please."

The computer continued aloud. "Two messages from Ambassador Bird. One message from a Commander Nolan Willits of the Delegate Ambassador Guard. One message from your mother. All of those messages are deemed urgent and important. Five messages from the Office of the Council Clerk on Belinea, moderate importance. The rest are low level."

Alexis continued to pack. "Messages from my mother are not urgent or important. What did she say?"

The computer had a different opinion. "That is not valid. Your mother has marked them important, and therefore they are. She says, 'Have not heard from you in three days. Are you still traveling to Belinea, please advise? I need to speak with you before you leave. Have you heard anything from your brothers?'"

Alexis, now smiling, said, "Respond, leaving for Belinea 16:00 tomorrow. Communication confidential, will advise later. Nothing from Nick or Connor. End message."

The computer voice responded calmly, "Understood."

Alexis was now finishing the last bag packed. "Read message from Ambassador Bird."

The computer voice responded quickly. "Message One, 1914 today, Alexis, please bring all material involving Ambassador Yi's joint investigation on DAG, mark it confidential. Do not transport ahead of time via electronic pulse. Hand transport via soft file."

Alexis now poured herself a cup of coffee, "Acknowledge, message two."

"Message Two, Copied you a recent report from the BRG. Terrorists have stolen a cargo ship on Avola containing Vait and other anti-matter properties. Negotiations have broken down. The Terrorist situation seems more grave than ever. Alert level for our transport mission has increased to RED/Severe. DAG has been alerted to the situation. "

Alexis was curious now. She put the cup of coffee down and walked over to her desk. Sitting down, she pulled up her tablet and downloaded the BRG Avola report. As she read, she asked for the other message, "Read message from Commander of Delegate Ambassador Guard."

"Message from Commander Nolan Willits, Delegate Ambassador Guard. 'Miss Devanoe. Be advised of an increase to security level Red for our trip. Please advise the Ambassador of a confidential departure change from 16:00 to 13:00 tomorrow and gate 14. Rearrange his schedule accordingly. Use discretion.' End message. "

Alexis began to type furiously. She looked stressed. "Damnit, why?"

After about twenty seconds, Alexis re-emerged into the BRG Avola file. She began combing over the pictures and stats. "Start message to Director Kimakawa. Please provide all intel files from BRG and AuFa regarding status for Planet Avola, Taz, and the Valmay Group of terrorists. Need all material delivered via secure electronic file 10:00 hours tomorrow for Ambassador Bird's review. Thank you. End Message."

She then whispered, "Play video summary of BRG Avola report from Ambassador Bird."

After a pause, the report popped up on her screen wall, all in 3-D imagery. "Planet Avola is the second from the star S-131. A longstanding member of the Council, it exports numerous raw materials used in building spaceships and spaceports. The most valuable being Vait, a mineral indigenous to Avola that is critical for the antimatter chamber that allows Hyper-EXtension speed space travel. In recent years, the Vait has been processed at a rate five times greater annually than before. Residents of Avola have been conflicted. Most following the Majavkee, a group fully supported by the Council for their ambitious mining practices. The minority of others remain loyal to the now-defunct Avolian Mining Guild. Supported by former Ambassador

Syren and the local religious Quill, they are protesting an incident in the Valmay Village. The Valmay Group, led by Octavious Killian, recently led a terrorist attack on an AuFa Garrison on Avola…."

Alexis paused the report when it showed a picture of Octavious and Kaya Killian. "Who are these people….?"

BELINEA 1.9

Avola

Lowell Province, Mining Center 14

Over one hundred lights lit up the Facility at dusk, the sky was backlit red and orange, with many dark grey clouds. Steam poured from three giant external steam smokestacks. The buildings were no more than thirty meters high, with thick walls to protect the elements. Ten landing pads surrounded the main building, all with orange, red, and white lights to navigate the cargo ship's arrivals. An AuFa flag flew from the top of the Control Tower. Two, forty meter high towers, flanked both sides of the facility, each with a rotating rocket cannon for security. One vast cargo ship, with AuFa markings and four times bigger than the other ones, was parked on the large landing pad in the center. The ship's bottom loading doors were open as several men in Belinean AuFa uniforms were transporting crates from the facility to the ship via forklifts.

One small cargo ship with AuFa markings touched down on an outside pad. Steam and sand dusted up as the bottom loading doors opened. A ground AuFa officer walked up to the doors with four armed AuFa security soldiers in tow. Octavious, in a dirty AuFa uniform, was walking down the ramp towards the soldiers. He was wearing tinted goggles and a mining ventilator mask covering the bottom of his face. Confused and curious, the greeting officer looked at Octavious and said, " We got your codes, but we do not have a manifest for this ship? What is this?"

Octavious turned, looked back at the officer on the forklift, and whistled. Seconds later, a beeping forklift carrying a vast crate wheeled out and down the ramp. "Huge discovery over in the mines in sector Ten. This is the first of two. The second ship is right behind us."

The greeting officer on the ground was still confused. "We have no knowledge of this. Why wasn't it called in?"

Octavious, with soot all over his face, very confidently said, "Captain Hansall notified you about an hour ago. I have orders, these two crates have to be on that 18:00 C-24 ship."

The other officer was now in a pickle. "That C-24 just got its last cargo put on. It's about to take off. We cannot add this to it. "

The soldier driving the forklift stopped and looked at Octavious. He asked, "Lieutenant, where am I taking this?"

Octavious asked the greeting officer, "Who are you?"

The greeting officer answered, "Sergeant Grant."

Taking one step closer, Octavious, still with the ventilator mask on the bottom of his face, looked directly in his eyes. He said, "Look here, Sargent Grant. It's not my problem who did or didn't communicate with you. What *is* my problem is this cargo needs to get on that ship, or Captain Hansell will be crawling up my ass asking why. Unless you want me directly pointing at you when he does, my problem is now your problem. Are we clear?"

The sergeant kept staring at him, not saying anything. After a few seconds, he noticed that both men were unarmed. He took one step back to acquiesce the decision. Octavious looked at the soldier driving the forklift and jumped on. Standing, with one foot on the base, and one hand gripping the crossbar, he pointed to the vast C-24 Cargo Transport. Octavious yelled, "Take us to that transport over there."

The forklift found another gear and darted off towards the transport ship. They were clear from the other soldiers, who were now turning back to walk inside the hangar. Octavious said to the soldier, driving the forklift "Four minutes."

Meanwhile, a small second transport ship flew very low, a mere fifteen meters off the desert sand and rock below. The transport ship had a crew of four plus a handcuffed man tied to a bench near the exit doors. The handcuffed man was naked except for a pair of underwear. The rest of the ship had two female pilots in the front of the craft, with two male soldiers in the back. Only this transport ship was converted with two open side doors and two colossal rocket guns on each side. Both the male soldiers were operating each weapon. Over the radio, a male voice came on "Transport ship this is AuFa Garrison 14, please identify."

Cortes, the female pilot, said, "Garrison 14, this is transport T-3472. Second added cargo from Captain Hansell. First cargo ship should already be there."

There was a long pause. The second female pilot, Kaya Killian, got up. She tapped Cortes on the shoulder and began walking to the back of the ship. A voice came over on the radio. "T-3472. We have no orders from Captain Hansell and no manifest for you. First cargo ship is here. Please advise to land on pad nine for a full inspection."

Cortes said, "Copy Garrison 14. Captain Hansall called it in about an hour ago. He said this cargo needs to be on that C-24, or someone's nuts are getting fed to the snakes out in the desert."

The voice continued. "Copy that T-3472. We've been advised. Verifying with Captain Hansall now."

Kaya Killian walked by both of the male soldiers operating the guns on the ship. She yelled, "Ready?"

They both nodded. Kaya put her tinted goggles on and put her hand up to her earpiece "Cortes, we are a go."

Cortes hit a switch to change the audio to internal only. "Standing by. Thirty seconds."

The forklift was now heading up the massive ramp of the C-24. Four AuFa soldiers were helping with the final load. The rest had already walked away from the ship. One of the soldiers on board the vessel said, "We got a full payload! Where are we supposed to put that?"

The forklift spun and stopped in a 90 degree turn at the top of the ship. It no longer was on the ramp but in the cargo bay as Octavious jumped off. The soldier driving the forklift began putting the cargo crate down. When it got to the floor, Octavious looked at the soldier who spoke and said, "Gentlemen, we need to find room on this ship somewhere. It's got something special inside. "

Octavious and the forklift driver began opening the crate. One of the Aufa soldiers asked, "Yeah, what's that?"

Octavious Killian removed his ventilator mask and took off his goggles. He said, "Catastrophe."

He then reached into the crate and grabbed his ring. It was a reddish silvery ring, with a black wooden handle and a glowing orange stone. He pulled it out, and it immediately transformed into a maroon, narrow, diamond-shape saber, with small flames. He then slit the heads off the two officers nearest him. The forklift driver grabbed a short rifle from the crate and shot it right into the heart of the third AuFa soldier. The fourth AuFa soldier raced over to his rifle, laying on top of a crate off to the side. Killian jumped across two containers almost seamlessly and much faster. As the AuFa soldier was about to grab the rifle, Octavious transformed his diamond-shaped saber into a longer, narrower one. He immediately lunged the tip straight into the stomach of the fourth soldier and drove it directly through his body. Taking it out, he looked at the forklift driver and said, "And Kaya says I've gotten slow."

The forklift driver smiled. Two more of Octavious Killian's soldiers came out of the crate. Each was holding their rings with a small red saber blade. Octavious said, "Get to the pilots. Sixty seconds."

The second inbound ship with Kaya and Cortes continued to fly extremely low. In her right hand, Kaya held the black handle of her reddish ring with the orange stone in the middle. Strapped around her shoulder was a rifle, with a barrel over a meter long and a scope on top. Her left hand still was clutched to a crossbar on the ship. As the ship came upon the Facility, it slowed slightly down. Cortes, the pilot, veered it straight up and got the ship almost vertical, seventy degrees, before leveling it out five meters above the forty meters high Tower Cannon. Kaya Killian jumped out the open side doors of the transport. Holding the bottom of her cloak, as she began to descend, the cloak's material expanded, turning it into a gliding parachute. Letting go near the Tower Cannon, she landed on both feet on the walkway.

Cortes flew the transport ship back down, flying it strategically slightly above the landing pads.

Everyone on the base who had just witnessed the transport ship do that maneuver was speechless. It took them a few seconds to realize what was going on. Octavious Killian and the forklift driver were back on the forklift, driving it down the big cargo ship ramp and onto the base surface. They turned the forklift and began driving it to the two fighters parked near the outside hanger.

Kaya was greeted by a soldier running towards her. Still trying to get the gun out of his holster, Kaya transformed her ring into the same diamond-shaped fire saber her brother had. Rolling forward and bouncing up, Kaya cut the leg off the soldier with one swing and then kicked him off the ledge. The Tower Cannon was 6 meters by 6 meters at the top. The other soldier that operated the Cannon came down off the chair. He got off one shot on Kaya, but it missed as she backflipped and sliced his head off with one motion. Two more soldiers had made their way up the stairs. Kaya began running towards them. One shot at Kaya, hitting her armor that covered her shoulder. As they made their way to the top of the stairs, Kaya drop-kicked the first one, causing him to go into the second, tumbling them both down the stairs. When she got up, she whipped her rifle around and shot both of them as they were trying to get up from the base of the stairs. Turning around, Kaya dropped her rifle and climbed on top of the cannon, pointing it at the other forty-meter high Cannon Tower on the other side of the Facility.

The gun on the Tower Cannon was loud and devastating. In five quick shots, she blew up the other cannon tower. Kaya pointed the cannon at the stairs the soldiers had tried to come up in. In two short blasts, she rendered them useless. She then began firing on the four other cargo ships sitting on the landing pads. Any AuFa soldiers on the facility who were confused before, now knew precisely what was going on. The second transport ship Cortes was piloting, was still flying slowly, ten meters off the ground. The two side gunners were providing a stable stream of recovery fire, lighting up the Control Tower, and shooting at soldiers on the ground.

Two AuFa soldiers in the cockpit of the vast C-24 Cargo Transport pulled the throttle back on the engines. Two of Octavious' Valmay soldiers came up behind them, slitting their throats with their fire daggers. They dragged their bodies out of the cockpit. After, they jumped back into the cockpit themselves. Hitting a button, they closed the main ramp door, and slowly took off.

Octavious Killian and the forklift driver were still on the ground, navigating toward the two F-81 Fighters. It was all chaos now on the landing pads. Everyone was looking at the second Tower Cannon on fire, or the second transport Cortes was flying, with its two side guns hammering away. Kaya jumped out of the chair of the Cannon and picked up her rifle. She positioned her body against the railing. Looking through the scope on the rifle, she followed her brother on the forklift. A couple of AuFa soldiers, now identifying Octavious, began firing at the forklift. One by one, Kaya picked them off, from some seventy to eighty meters away. The rifle was far more accurate than the Tower Cannon, albeit not quite as lethal in damage.

The second transport ship did a U-turn and began heading back toward the first Cannon Tower that Kaya was still on. The two gunners continued to shoot down below, with less accuracy because of the smoke. A few of the AuFa ground soldiers managed to hit Cortes' gunship transport, but it did minimal damage.

The forklift arrived at the two F-81 Sirator fighters. Two pilots had managed to run from the hangar and were climbing up the ladders when the forklift stopped. Octavious shot one of them, and Kaya, from eighty meters away, killed the other. Octavious and the other Valmay soldier jumped off the forklift and began climbing the ladders to get into the Fighters. Other AuFa soldiers were shooting at them from the other side of the bay, but Kaya kept picking them off. Both Octavious and the soldier jumped into the cockpits of the F-81's. The fighters roared to life and quickly ascended from the landing pads.

The fighters flew side by side, flanking the vast C-24 Cargo ship that was now airborne as well. Smoke still billowing from everywhere, as the facility was now entirely on fire. As the second transport Cortes was piloting made its way back to the first Tower Cannon, Kaya slung the rifle back over her shoulder. She waited until the transport ship was right next to the tower and jumped, landing on top of it. She sprinted to the back of the ship, and cartwheeling, grabbed some handles, and flipped all the way around. She landed in the open cargo bay ramp at the end of the ship. Walking toward the two male gunners, she grabbed her earpiece and yelled, "Cortes, let's go."

Kaya walked over to the handcuffed man only in his underwear, tied to the bench and gagged. She cut his ties with her saber and dragged him up by the arm. She proceeded to kick him out the cargo doors, "Captain Hansell, it's been a pleasure."

Captain Hansell fell fifteen meters to his death. All five ships flew away at a low altitude. The facility was entirely on fire.

BELINEA 1.10

Earth, The Moon

Odgins Military Academy

Cadets Trujillo and Tunsall were finishing packing their bags in their common room. Trujillo, not looking at Tunsall, said, "We can still back out of this if you want."

Tunsall let the question linger for a second before replying, "I think we should do it."

Trujillo said, "You think I should do it, or should we do it?"

Tunsall zipped his bag and picked it up. After a second, he said, "We…"

Trujillo nodded and zipped his bag. He said softly, "You got real options after graduating."

Tunsall just stared at him and said, "And you do not?"

Trujillo continued, "I am nobody. A kid whose family was wiped out by the pandemic, and happy to have three squares a day and a bed to sleep on. That's not why you are here."

Tunsall responded quietly. "You do not gain perspective seeing only one view."

Trujillo looked at him and said, "You know I want to do this. I just hope this perspective does not change your path."

Tunsall continued. "My path has not already been chosen. Besides, I cannot let you go by yourself. What happens when they ask you to actually fly something?"

Trujillo gave Tunsall a smirk. Both of them walked out of their room and down the corridor towards the elevator. They boarded it and took it to the top floor. When they got off, they took a left towards the cargo bay. At a desk before the bay doors, Sergeant Sabrina Evans was waiting for them. She said to them, "You are late."

Trujillo responded, "Master Sergeant, our shuttle is supposed to leave at eleven hundred hours."

Sergeant Evans replied, "Precisely. Thirty minutes early is on time from now on, gentlemen. You have to start thinking like DAG officers if you wish to become one."

Tunsall responded, "Master Sergeant, this is just an assignment. I have no intention of joining the Delegate Ambassador Guard after."

She answered, "That said, this is not homework in one of your classes, gentlemen. It is not an assignment to take lightly."

Evans reached from behind the desk and gave the cadets two sticks, one each. She said, "Here are your orders. When you get to Space Port Earth, show them to the Dock Master along with your credentials. Then report to Gate Fourteen. Any questions?"

Both said, "No, ma'am."

Evans then gave both of them a side pistol. She said, "And take these. Commander Willits wanted each of you issued an additional sidearm along with your taser."

Trujillo and Tunsall looked at each other for a brief second before Trujillo asked, "Permission to speak ma'am?"

Evans nodded. Trujillo asked, "Is this standard for this type of mission?"

Evans answered, "For a DAG officer, yes. For your role, no."

Trujillo continued, "So, you know what our assignment is, Master Sergeant?"

Sergeant Evans nodded and said, "Yes, I do, but it is up to Commanders Willts and Jones to explain your mission, not me."

Tunsall added, "You know Commanders Willits and Jones, ma'am?"

Evans answered, "I have worked with them before."

Trujillo asked, "Do you think we are doing the right thing? Volunteering for this assignment?"

Evans shook her head and said, "That is not for me to say. You have been picked for a reason. Now, get going, and do not let me down."

Trujillo saluted before being followed by Tunsall. Trujillo responded, "Yes, ma'am."

Evans saluted back and said, "Good look, gentlemen."

Trujillo and Tunsall walked out and put their outside suits on. Once their suits were on, they walked out another set of doors to the landing area. They continued over to the shuttle on the last landing pad and boarded it. Tunsall looked at Trujillo and said, "That wasn't exactly the most glowing recommendation for Willits and Jones."

Trujillo quickly added, "I thought the same thing. What the hell did we get ourselves into?"

BELINEA 1.11

Space Port Earth, Dock 14, 12:50 Hours

The C-62T transport ship was docked. Two dock workers were finishing the last bit of cargo provisions necessary for the long trip. Commanders Willits and Jones were there instructing a couple more dock workers on proper procedures. The two cadets, Trujillo and Tunsall, came walking down the extension ramp of the dock, each with a standard issued traveling bag in their hand. They stopped in front of Willits and Jones, saluting. Trujillo said, "Cadets Trujillo and Tunsall reporting for duty, sir."

Willits slightly saluted back, before yelling at a dock worker and addressing the cadets. "And make sure it all gets in there, quickly. We are not going to be late. At ease, gentlemen."

Tunsall kept looking at the transport ship. "Commander, that is a C-62T."

Willits was not exactly in the best mood. "Imagine how nervous I would be if you didn't know that, Tunsall. Glad to know Odgins is teaching you something."

Trujillo and Tunsall glanced at each other. Trujillo had an ever so slight roll of the eyes.

Ambassador Bird and Alexis Devanoe came walking down the platform soon after. They were flanked by two Delegate & Ambassador Guards, both carrying rifles. Two dock workers followed in the rear with the luggage. As they approached, one of the guards gave a quick salute to Willits and Jones before speaking.

The first DAG soldier said, "Commander Willits. Delivery confirmed of Ambassador Bird and Miss Devanoe. Although we had a delivery time of 16:00 hours, sir."

Willits looked at both of the guards. "Thank you, Sargent. I changed the time, we are good. Will you do a perimeter sweep on the loading dock and ramp extension before you leave. The Ambassador's luggage, along with Miss Devanoe's, can be left right there."

The two guards saluted and began their security sweep of the area. The two dock workers began walking back up the ramp. Willits did the introductions. "Ambassador Bird, Miss Devanoe, I am Commander Nolan Willits, this is Commander Avery Jones, of the Delegate Ambassador Guard. We will be responsible for the security detail for your transport to Belinea."

Ambassador Bird spoke. "Nice to meet you, Commander. Miss Devanoe tells me you were responsible for changing my departure time."

Willits stood with his arms crossed behind his back. "My apologies Ambassador. Just a safety precaution on my part."

Ambassador Bird responded matter-of-factly. "Honestly, most of the meetings needed to be canceled anyway, they were a waste of time. And who are these two?"

Willits pointed open-handed. "These are our pilots, cadets Trujillo and Tunsall."

Ambassador Bird was confused. "Cadets?"

Willits could see this might be a problem. "Yes, sir. Top of the class at Odgins, they graduate next week."

Alexis extended her hand first to Trujillo, still smiling, then to Tunsall. However, she never took her eyes off Trujillo. Ambassador Bird was confused and asked, "Commander Willits, pardon me. Are these cadets not Delegate Ambassador Guard? I spoke at great length with Director Kimakawa about getting the best for this mission."

Commander Willits would try humor to defuse the situation. "I appreciate the compliment, Ambassador. Commander Jones and I are not used to such flattery."

Ambassador Bird was now annoyed. "Commander, I was referring to experienced officers."

Commander Willits stood a little more upright now. "I understand, sir. This transport is the most advanced the BRG and Council have to offer. Most pilots have little to no hours of time in it. Luckily for you, no one has more flight time in it than these two cadets."

Ambassador Bird was still upset. He continued, "Commander, I am giving a speech to the Council, proposing to expand your Guard and become less dependent on the BRG. Miss Devanoe then keeps shoving me information about this terrorist group on Avola, and a terrorist named Taz being linked to them. Our trip is now at level red, and you're telling me these two cadets are the best Kimakawa has got? No offense, gentlemen."

Trujillo and Tunsall just slightly shook their heads. Willits waited for a second, before replying. "Ambassador, I understand your trepidation. But with all due respect, I have a great deal of experience in this. I can assure you that I am going to get you safely to Belinea."

The Ambassador did not sound convinced. "Perhaps if I had a word with the Director ....."

But Willits cut him off, with a little bit of anger in his voice. "The Director chose me for a reason, Ambassador. Talking with him will only be a waste of thirty minutes from our departure. Stick with the speeches, let me handle the security. Got it?"

There was a long pause. Ambassador Bird still looked unconvinced. A staredown between Willits and Ambassador Bird was lasting more than ten seconds. Willits finally said, "I understand the magnitude of the mission, even better than you. I will get you to Belinea, sir."

The Ambassador gave another long pause before finally saying, "I am unfamiliar with this vessel Commander. Where do we go from here?"

Willits still looked serious, adding, "Commander Jones will escort you inside and show you both your quarters, Ambassador. Cadets Trujillo and Tunsall will take care of your personal belongings."

Jones opened his hand towards the entrance of the ship. "Right this way Ambassador."

The Ambassador and Alexis followed Commander Jones onto the ship. After they were on board and way out of hearing distance, Trujillo looked at Willits with a disdain look. "You lied."

Willits shrugged his shoulders and said, "Simulator, real-time. The Ambassador doesn't know the difference."

Tunsall said, "That's not what we're talking about. You said it was a special, combat mission."

Willits, still confused. "And?"

Tunsall followed, "We are chauffeuring an Ambassador across the galaxy. I'm shocked we had to show credentials to the Dock Master."

Willits was now a little annoyed. "Well, mission experience before you even graduate, you're fucking welcome."

Trujillo was stunned. "Mission experience? We are babysitting an Ambassador and driving a golf cart."

Trujillo and Tunsall said nothing. Willits continued, "If you think I am playing games, you have permission to go back to your simulators. I can find two other qualified, more experienced pilots."

Tunsall, after a pause, said, "Then why us, Commander?"

Willits continued. "You can fly this thing?"

Trujillo responded. "In our sleep."

Willits softened his tone and voice. "Good, because the list of people I trust keeps getting a lot shorter. I asked Master Sergeant Evans for her two best, and she gave me you two."

Tunsall looked curious now. "What are you not telling us?"

Willits spoke. "What I know about this mission is a hundred times more than you. You two have zero hidden agendas, and neither of you knows jack-shit, which is why you are here. Nothing would bring me greater joy than a boring trip to Belinea. But my gut tells me something different."

Trujillo now had a different tune. "What are you not telling us?"

Tunsall asked, "What do you think will happen?"

Willits said, "You ain't carrying that sidearm for show."

Trujillo and Tunsall glanced at each other before turning back to Willits. Willits continued. "Now shut up, do as you are told, and let's get out of here. Tunsall, do a physical pre-flight check of the ship. Trujillo, help me with the luggage."

Trujillo was still a little pissed. "Why isn't he carrying bags?"

Willits picked up a bag. "Because the better pilot flies first."

Tunsall took his hand and slid it on the outside door of the ship, carefully inspecting the engines with his tablet. Trujillo looked pissed and kept staring at Willits.

Willits just looked at him and began walking with the luggage. "Did you really think I didn't read the file?"

BELINEA 1.12

Avola

Valmay Opposition Group Headquarters

Bosa Provence

The Valmay Group's Base was inside a massive cave on the side of a mountain. The enormous doors had already closed, and all five ships had just landed. Steam was still coming off them as the doors opened. Octavious and Kaya all got off with the other soldiers. They began walking over to the Control Tower Area. Octavious looked at Kaya as they continued to walk together. He said, "Are you alright?"

Kaya, perplexed by the question, said, "Yeah."

After a long pause, she asked, "Are you?"

Octavious said, "Yeah, why?"

Kaya said, "I've seen rocks move faster."

Octavious rolled his eyes. He said, "I offered to switch."

Kaya quickly answered. "And trust your shot? I'd be running for my life."

Octavious replied, "You hit a couple of stationary soldiers from thirty meters away..."

Kaya cut him off with "It was more like eighty meters away."

Octavious said, "It was thirty..."

Kaya stopped walking and said, "It was eighty meters. This is why your shot sucks. You can't tell the difference between thirty meters and eighty."

Octavious smiled and kept walking. Kaya trailed behind. Cortes and Rendon heard the whole conversation and were both smiling and shaking their heads. Rendon, Octavious, and Kaya walked up to a woman who was waiting for them outside. Former Ambassador Syren asked them both as they approached "Successful mission?"

Kaya nodded. Octavious shrugged his shoulders and said, "We got the Vait, and no one was killed, so …."

Syren was wearing a long white robe. With her hands in her pocket, she said, "Octavious, the last shipment of Vait you sold to the Invicto Guild is less than half of what you could have made selling it on the black market, let alone the Council or Majavkee…."

Octavious glanced at Rendon, who had just slightly bumped into him. He looked at Rendon and said, "Get that Vait back to Bisi. Download the intel off those ships' computers."

Rendon asked, "Paint the Fighters?"

Octavious looked at Rendon first, then turned to Syren and said, "Not yet, I may have a plan for those. Ambassador Syren, monetary gain is not the primary objective. I will not sell to the Council. The Belineans will simply use the Vait to construct more ships, increasing the military capacity of the AuFa. The Invicto Guild aligns with the Logistical Cargo and Trade Corporations, operating independently of the Council."

Rendon walked away. Ambassador Syren was trying to plead her case. "It is also becoming increasingly difficult to sell to the Invicto Guild because of the embargo."

Octavious understood, "We will cross that bridge when we get to it. Find me another independent contractor not aligned with the Council, and I am open to selling to them as well."

Ambassador Syren tried a different tactic. "Supplies and weapons cost money. You obtain more money by selling more Vait, Octavious."

Octavious looked at Kaya before speaking. "The small percentage we keep for weapons and ammunition provides security for the miners. We lose that security when we give our enemies the wealth to build more ships and weapons to defeat us."

The Ambassador countered, "The miners' wealth is basic needs. Food, clothing, shelter, and a Quill education. Your wealth is the power to hold this territory."

Ocativous sounded confident. "Principle is the greatest wealth we have, Syren. There must be righteousness in what we preach. Otherwise, we are ruling in fear, which cannot be sustained."

Kaya managed to change the subject as Ambassador Syren was perturbed. She said, "No word from the Belineans?"

Ambassador Syren, a woman much shorter than Kaya, humbly spoke. "Nothing, as of now. But keep stealing their Vait, and it will get their attention. At some point, they will send much more than a few Aufa regiments to support the local Majavkee security."

Kaya was befuddled. "Their Vait? It was never theirs to begin with. Do you think they will send more troops? "

Ambassador Syren was somewhat confident. "Sooner than later, yes. You just laid waste to one of their garrisons. I'm sure it's still burning. They aren't going to pretend it didn't happen."

Kaya sounded angry. "If we only harvested our own Vait, here, in the Bosa Provence, and stopped attacking their bases, then what? They leave us?"

The Ambassador thought it was a good question. "It's possible, Kaya. They are getting plenty of Vait from their resources. The eyes of the Council could see it as a diplomatic compromise."

There was a pause before Octavious spoke. "There will be no diplomatic compromise. They are also not going to leave. They are going to mine all the territories they control until there is no more Vait to mine. And then, they will come for ours. It will not be limited to a Battle Carrier Group. It will be a full invasion."

Ambassador Syren asked, "Is that what you think?"

Octavious began to walk away. He answered, "No, it's what I know."

Kaya looked at Syren before walking away with her brother. After a few steps, Syren raised her voice and said, "Octavious, you have brought great awareness to this cause. In history, you will be looked at as someone who saved Avola if you can barter a peaceful negotiation. But if you continue these vicious attacks, you will lose the sympathy of the Council. The other Avolian Ambassadors are calling you terrorists. You are only providing evidence to the narrative."

Octavious stopped. He turned around and said, "Evidence to the narrative? Do you truly believe there is a narrative where they don't invade, Syren? You believe in your heart, they desire peace?"

Ambassador Syren asked softly, "Octavious, what is the alternative to negotiation? War? Against them? You would not last one day."

Kaya, coolly but confidently, said," We just took out an entire garrison, stole two Sirator fighters and a giant cargo ship full of Vait, all with only nine soldiers. I like our chances."

Octavious gave a small grin. Kaya just squinted her eyes, still staring at Syren for doubting their capabilities. The Ambassador, now looking at both of them, calmly said," This is only the beginning. Eventually, the innocents will start dying."

The three stared at each other. After a few seconds, Octavious said, "I will not succumb to some form of Totalitarianism, Ambassador. Negotiation ends without basic freedoms, and our death will happen before we give that up. If innocents die, so be it, that will be on their soul."

The Ambassador quickly countered, "No, Octavious, that will be on your soul too."

The Ambassador turned around and walked away. Octavious and Kaya briefly looked at each other before turning around themselves and headed into the Control Tower.

BELINEA 1.13

Space Port Earth, 15:55

On the other side of Earth, a large transport ship in orbit slowly opened its back cargo doors. A small, black, single-pilot attack fighter emerged. The cockpit glass was lightly tinted, and the fighter had no running lights. The small angular engines fired up, a bluish hue on the inside. The attack-fighter gained speed as it flew further away from the large transport ship. The pilot was wearing a dark blood-red helmet that covered his entire head. A simple four-centimeter wide visor was cut into the helmet in a semi-circle around his eyes. The visor was entirely translucent silver, allowing him to see out but preventing anyone from seeing in. He dropped the accelerator throttle all the way, and the attack fighter moved even quicker. He hit a couple of controls then returned his hands to the stick. In the distance, but rapidly approaching, was Space Port Earth.

In the control tower of SPE, a DAG corporal surveys the flight map. Suddenly, he sees a large blip on his screen. It almost lights up the whole board, making it unable to decipher between the smaller ships coming and going. A few seconds went by, and the board almost returned to normal. But instantly, another blip hit the screen. It lit up the whole screen, making it incapable of reading anything. The Corporal turned around in his seat and shouted out, "Commander, there's a problem."

The DAG Commander, a female officer, came over to the Corporal's screen. "What is it, Corporal?"

The Corporal sounded nervous as he said, "The screen, Commander. It just lit up and froze. I can't see anything."

The screen began to come back to normal before another blip lit it up again and rendered it useless. The Commander, now beginning to realize what it was, hit a couple of controls on the Corporal's control panel. "We are being jammed. Did you see any ships on your screen before this happened that were not registered?"

The Corporal looked confused. He said, "Commander?"

The Commander was fully engaged now. "Any ships not registered, Corporal? Anything approaching the base at high speed or jumping out of Hyper-EXtension?"

The Corporal was simply bewildered "I... I don't know, Commander."

The blip went off again, this time lasting longer and causing more blindness. The Commander turned around and sprinted back to her station. Hitting a few buttons, she then shouted into the speaker. "DAG Control, this is the Control Tower Commander, get me the AuFa Operational Commander on Duty, stat, we are being attacked."

The small attack fighter closed in on SPE. It was still about twenty seconds away. The Pilot with the blood-red helmet kept hitting a few more controls. The jamming of the frequency was working. He began to run a scan on SPE, getting an entire readout of the Port. He then hit a few more controls, and the area for Dock 5 lit up yellow and was blinking. He then locked in on that area and directed the attack fighter to that position of the base.

The Control Tower was completely buzzing now. Everyone was looking out the windows, trying to see if they saw anything unusual. The female DAG Commander was now yelling into the speaker again, "AuFa Watch Deck, get those F-81's up, now."

A voice came over the speaker, "Commander, do you have a visual ID on the attacker?"

The Commander was talking fast. "Negative. But we are being jammed. I am sure you are too. So whatever it is, it doesn't want us to see it."

Suddenly, one of the officers pointing at the glass window, shouted, "Commander! Over there, across flight deck Alpha. Is that some sort of attack fighter?"

Everyone turned. Most did not see it, but a few did. The Commander spoke into the intercom again. "AuFa Watch Deck, visual on something approaching Alpha Deck."

The black attack fighter rapidly approached the Alpha deck. It slowed down to maneuver around the prodding dock stations so it could line up with

Deck 5. As it slowed, it then hovered, opening the covers to let it's two guns out. However, there was no ship there. Confused, the Pilot with the blood-red helmet rechecked his controls. Deck 5 was highlighted and currently blinking, but nothing was there.

Two F-81 Sirator's launched from the AuFa Watch Deck. They quickly accelerated and made their way around the Port. Weaving in and out, they made their way to Deck 5. One F-81 fighter identified the black attack fighter. Noticing the guns out, it hastily took a shot at it.

The Pilot of the black attack fighter was puzzled. It was supposed to be here. Where was it? He then glanced up and saw the two F-81's in the distance. He veered his ship to the right, just as one of the F-81's fired at him. It missed narrowly. He accelerated the fighter into attack speed. The two F-81's began to chase him.

The Control Tower Commander was still trying to process everything when she heard the shot from the F-81. "Watch Deck, we got a visual on Alpha deck. One unidentified attack fighter. AuFa F-81's have engaged. How long before we can get support fighters up?"

AuFa Watch Deck responded, "Stand by."

The two F-81's kept chasing the black attack fighter. In what can only be described as brilliant flying, the blood-red helmet Pilot used the Port as a shield, flowing in and out of it until it had maneuvered behind the F-81's chasing him. Now engaged, he took a shot and missed. The two F-81 pilots were stunned. One shouted to the other on the intercom, "Split up."

The F-81's split up. The pilot with the blood-red helmet kept flying his small black attack fighter in tight circles around the docks, narrowly missing them. He tightened up the distance of the one F-81 he was chasing. The other F-81 circled around and now saw the small black attack fighter chasing the other F-81. He closed in behind the chase and focused on the attack fighter. Just as he was shooting, the black attack fighter inverted the other way, circling 360 degrees. The F-81 pilot whispered, "What the...."

The pilot with the blood-red helmet completed a full inverted figure-8, and as it came back across from the side, it shot right at the F-81 pilot that had just shot at him. Hitting the engines, the F-81 fell into a death spiral towards the atmosphere.

At the Control Tower, the speaker barked out, "Deck Commander, two minutes on the support fighters."

The Commander shouted back, "This isn't gonna last one minute."

The other F-81 began circling as he spoke into his intercom "Tower Commander, I've lost visual, any site of the attacker?"

The people in the Command Tower kept looking. The F-81 pilot kept looking around, and he could not see him. The F-81 pilot began to fly in a very slow circle around the Commander Tower, looking out around the Port, trying to find anything, but there was nothing. The pilot whispered, "Where did he go?"

Then, out of the corner of his eye, he saw it. The small black attack fighter hovered directly above the Control Tower, turning with the F-81, preventing anyone from inside the tower to view it. The female Tower Commander spoke on the intercom " One minute on support fighters, no visual anyone?"

The F-81 pilot stopped his circling and pointed its guns towards the small black attack fighter, but he knew it was too late. He whispered, "Oh shit…"

The guns from the attack fighter opened on the F-81 and obliterated it. There was a silence in the Control Tower as everyone just watched the F-81 explode in front of their eyes. The Pilot with the blood-red helmet slowly moved his small black attack fighter down from the hover position and pointed his guns at the Control Tower so everyone could see. There was a hush in the room. A deafening silence, as the black attack fighter just hovered, guns aimed at point-blank range. It seemed like minutes but was only about ten seconds. The pilot spun the attack fighter around, and accelerated away, back towards the cargo ship.

His speed increased. It was possible those support fighters would try to chase him once they were out of the Port, but more likely, they would stay and defend. He quickly made it to the Transport ship and followed the lights inside the cargo bay door. As soon as the small black attack fighter was inside, the cargo door bays closed, and then another set of doors closed behind the cargo bay doors. The pilot landed the attack fighter, and almost immediately, the giant Transport ship accelerated away. After a moment, the ship gained enough speed to get away in Hyper-EXtension speed.

The pilot in the blood-red helmet climbed out of the attack fighter and jumped down. He walked over to a flight of stairs that led to the cockpit area of the transport ship. Once there, he went off to the side and began typing a message:

'Contact not at the location. Contact was NOT terminated. Minimal collateral damage. Await orders."

He immediately joined his crew from the Captain's chair, never taking his helmet off.

BELINEA 1.14

Earth, Northeast Japan
Delegate & Ambassador Guard Headquarters

Director Kimakawa was sitting at his desk, drinking a hot tea. Vice Director Franklin Meyers immediately came into the room, shouting as he was still walking towards the Director's desk. "There has been an attack SPE at 1600 hours."

Kimakawa put down his tea. He responded, "Shit. Casualties? What is the damage."

Meyers continued, "The Tower Commander said two F-81's were engaged and destroyed by a lone Attack Fighter. Pilots are dead. But no further damage."

Kimakawa stood up "And Ambassador's Bird transport? Did it get off?"

Meyers answered, "Nobody knows?"

Kimakawa was puzzled. He said, "What do you mean?"

Meyers quickly responded. "The C-62T was not there. We are looking into it, but we think it might have taken off three hours earlier."

Kimakawa raised an eyebrow. "By your crew? You weren't informed of the departure time change?"

Meyers now looked disheartened. "My crew, security detail, and pilots were at the Dock at 15:30. They are still waiting, the C-62T never arrived. Only when the Port was under attack did they suspect something wrong."

Kimakawa was still trying to process the events, " And the attack fighter? Any markings?"

Meyers: "None. It got away. It likely had a Transport ship waiting for it and jumped into Hyper-EXtension. We have a residue record that matches, still trying to verify the sequence of events."

Kimakawa took a few seconds before speaking, "How did Willits and Jones pilot the ship off the dock? The Dock Master allowed them to leave without credentials?"

Meyers responded, "It's possible, but not likely. Either way, we have to entertain the thought that Willits and Jones have possibly gone rogue, deliberately changing a departure time."

Kimakawa squinted his eyes at Franklin. He said, "But to a time that avoided an attack. Do we know if he changed the manifest?"

Meyers shrugged his shoulders and asked, "Would he even follow the manifest?"

Kimakawa thought about that for a second. After a moment, he responded. "So I have two rogue DAG officers escorting an Ambassador who is about to give the most important speech of his life, and we have no idea where they are going and how to communicate with them….."

Meyers shook his head. He asked, "What do we do?"

Kimakawa answered, "Hope the pigeon courier has a message telling us what's going on."

The two men just stared at each other for a brief moment before Kimakawa said, "Let's get to Space Port Earth."

Tunsall was inside the cockpit of the Ambassador's C-62T transport, looking at the entire control board panel. Trujillo was in the co-pilot chair next to him asleep. Willits walked into the cockpit and got behind Tunsall. He said to Tunsall, "I heard a vicious rumor that the BRG or the SS has figured out a way to put a C-Bar Transmitter on a ship? Know anything about that?"

Tunsall replied, "No, sir."

Willits said, "So no chance there is one on this ship?"

Tunsall shook his head. "Not in any of the simulators or ones that I have flown, sir."

Willits continued. "And you and the other DAG officers didn't find any beacon transmitters when you did your external inspection."

Tunsall shook his head again. "No."

Willits continued, "So no one has a tracker on us, or is somehow following us?"

Tunsall was a bit uneasy now. "I can't see how, sir."

Willits kept talking. "Alright, so despite how fast this thing is, this is a good old-fashioned Hyper-EXtension trip so far. No one can communicate with us, and no one knows where we are going, correct?"

Tunsall, after a pause thinking about it, said, "I believe so, sir."

Willits then said, "Alright, I want you to change our coordinates."

Tunsall said, "Excuse me?"

Willits looked at the control panel and saw what he was looking for. He typed in the coordinate numbers, then hit the button to execute. The ship tilted ever so slightly, changing course. Tunsall said, "Braccus, sir?"

Willits grinned and then whispered, "Change of plan. No one needs to know where we are going."

Willits got up and walked out of the cockpit.

Tunsall just stared at the controls for a few more seconds, before relaxing back into his chair.

BELINEA - EPISODE 2
OFFERINGS

BELINEA 2.1

Serpia - 2137 (twenty years prior...)

Sansigar Malovex woke up. He was lying in a bed, in an all-white pristine room. In a few seconds, he recognized he was in some sort of medical area. He glanced over to see two Medical Robots operating on his shoulder area. The operation on his burns did little to fix the scars still on his face. He glanced the other way and saw a Belinean Medical Doctor who spoke outside the room.

The Doctor said, "Lord Argo ...your cousin is awakening."

With black robes down to his knees, a man in all black briskly walked over to the bed. The Medical Doctor was ready with caution. "Sir, he is still being operated on...."

But Argo Hassara ignored this and rushed to the side of his cousin. He looked down at his cousin and asked, "Are you alright?"

Malovex was still slightly bewildered. Looking around before finally looking at his cousin, he responded. "Yes, where am I?"

Argo replied, "Medical Wing of the Space Station. We are evacuating. The Serpian's have officially declared victory. They have given us a grace period to leave. We are leaving within the hour. There are just a few more troops we need from the planet surface."

Malovex glanced at his shoulder, grimacing. Looking back at Argo, he said, "Understood."

Malovex then looked at the Robot Doctor and said, "Are you done?"

The Doctor finished 'fusing' the skin back together before spraying an antiseptic over the shoulder area. Malovex, feeling slightly better, then proceeded to sit-up. As he was, Argo spoke, "Sansigar, the explosion on the dock. What happened?"

Sanisgar whispered so only Argo could hear him. "The Tiloians, as many as I could get."

Argo was in disbelief. "They were all Tiloians? The scanners read there were 138 lives on your ship?"

Malovex whispered, "Sounds about right. I couldn't get an accurate count, because we were moving too fast. The ones I didn't get most certainly died on the surface. Help me up."

Argo, with his silvery ring attached to his side, assisted Malovex in getting up. Argo grabbed a black robe off to the side and helped Malovex put it on. The Doctor entered the room, put his hand on Malovex, and said, "Sir, what are you doing? You are in no condition to leave."

Malovex continued to put the rest of his robe on. "I am fine."

The Doctor, clearly concerned, put his hand a little deeper into Malovex's shoulder, further emphasizing the movement restriction. Malovex stared at the hand for a couple of seconds before returning his look directly at the Doctor. The Doctor, realizing what he had done, dropped his hand. Malovex continued to stare at him. Softly, he said, "Thank you, Doctor, the Robots have reattached enough today."

The two cousins began to walk out of the operating room. Argo assisted Malovex slightly as they continued through a doorway and down a corridor. Near the end, Argo let go and let Malovex walk on his own. He asked, "Are you good? My team is preparing for evac on Deck 17."

Malovex, slightly grimacing, whispered, "Go. Where is the Communications Tower?"

Argo replied, "Make a left here, two flights up, take another left. Follow the corridor to the end."

Malovex was still slightly bent over. Argo grabbed his elbow, assisting him slightly. Looking him directly in the eye, Argo needed the verification. He quietly asked, "Sanisgar, you got all of them?"

Malovex stopped, holding the ribs below his shoulder with his left arm crossed. Argo, still holding his elbow and waiting intently. Malovex replied, "The Tiloians?"

Argo nodded. Maolvex responded, "All of them."

Argo nodded back. He continued, "I will tell Father. Full extraction in less than an hour, get all your men Sanisgar."

Argo ran off. Malovex continued to walk, which was as fast as he could go. He followed Argo's instructions, down the hall, two flights up, to the end of the corridor. He walked into the Communications Tower. People were scurrying everywhere. It took a few seconds for someone to identify him, but a junior officer finally did. "Lord Malovex….."

The Junior officer ran over to Malovex and helped him. He then yelled at another officer, "Lieutenant…"

As the Lieutenant came over and assisted him, Malovex continued to walk toward a hologram map of the battle below gingerly. He said, "Let me see the board."

Both the Junior officers flanked Malovex, one holding his elbow in assistance. The other officer spoke. "Sir, the battle is over. (Pointing) We are retreating here and here, evacuating the last troops right now. This breach was lost; whatever got out is on it's way up now. No response from the Tiloians at this time."

Malovex scanned the map until he found what he was looking for. Pointing, he said, "Lieutenant, this area, what happened."

The Lieutenant replied, "BC 72, The Hunvallo, went down, in this Tiloian Province. Casualties on the Battle Cruiser are massive."

Malovex continued, "Lieutenant, some of my team was in that area. How can I find out their status?"

The Lieutenant had no real answer. "I don't know, sir. All ships evacuated the area over an hour ago. A few Fighters did a couple of final passes with two AT-11's, but…."

Malovex gave a look of anger. "But what Lieutenant?"

The Lieutenant continued, "Sir, the ships did not leave anyone behind. Eyewitnesses said total destruction. If they are not currently on any of the medical frigates coming up from the surface, they are likely gone, sir."

Malovex thought for a second. This might be the only way. "Lieutenant, check the Medical frigates, you are looking for Commander Spoon and Commander Bagget. You, I need to send a message. What are the coordinates of that crash site?"

One Lieutenant scurried off, back to his post. Mumbling, you could hear him trying to communicate the orders he was given. The other Lieutenant checked his board. "One moment, sir...... It looks like 42, 28.192, 15.353 by 44, 61.538, and 71.454. But sir, that entire area is no longer in our control."

Malovex was typing the coordinates into a computer in front of him. He had entered a few codes, then typed out a message, held his hand on the computer scanner, and said clearly " Malovex, Sansigar, ID 64190623, clearance."

The computer responded, "Clearance accepted, message sent."

Malovex then asked a second command. "Location of Quiilisar Farra."

The computer responded, "Quillisar Farra is in the Meditation Room on deck 14."

Malovex turned to the Lieutenants. "Let me know if you find my Commanders. If you find anyone else from my team, we leave Serpia in thirty minutes."

Malovex walked out, still laboring to breathe and walk normally. He went down the corridor to the main shaft elevator and took it. He yelled, "Deck 14."

The shaft elevator accelerated. Despite moving quickly, it gave Malovex a few seconds to think. He was still reflecting on the events that had transpired in the last few hours. He looked down at his wrist and saw the time on his monitor. He began to do the calculations in his head. The shaft elevator doors opened, and he briskly walked out. Malovex turned down a series of corridors until he got to the meditation room. He entered.

There were rows of pews, all empty, except for one person in a red cloak, kneeling in the fourth row. A silvery-white ring hung from around her neck in front of her chest, similar in shape to the ring Malovex had hanging from his hip. Her hands were folded in front of her face, praying to the diamond shape figure on the wall. She did not turn, however, despite hearing the doors open. Malovex walked into the room, down the middle aisle. He bowed to the diamond figure, then kneeled in the row behind the red-cloaked priest.

Malovex put hands in a prayer position as well. His heart was pounding. He quietly whispered, "Are we alone, my Quillisar?"

Quillisar Farra, still with the cloak around her head that made it impossible to see her face, gently whispered back. "We are Sansigar. Would you like to tell me your sins?"

Malovex ever so quietly responded, "Yes, my Quillisar."

BELINEA 2.2

Twenty Years Later......

Space Port Earth

Director Kimakawa, Vice Director Franklin Meyers, and Lord Malovex were in the control tower of SPE. On the hologram board, they were getting constant replays, from different angles, of the attack on the base. Kimakawa, pointing, spoke to the Tower Control Commander. "So this first jamming occurred here, at this moment, correct?"

The officer responded, "Yes, sir."

Kimakawa continued, "And all of your rear sensors and map sonar failed? They crippled the entire system, no reading on anything?"

The officer nodded and spoke, "That is correct, sir."

Malovex watched for a few more seconds. "This is Dretelli jamming code."

Meyers responded, "What is that?"

Malovex continued. "The Secret Service and the BRG have noticed this particular signature jam in small smuggler runs on different planets, mainly near the Avolian system. My cousin, Lord Argo, recently captured a ship with this hardware. The SS is still breaking it down to find a way to reverse the jamming effects."

Director Kimakawa then watched the replay again. "The ship bypassed the Control Tower and went straight to Slip Five. This was not a random attack. They expected Ambassador Bird's C-62T to be there."

Malovex asked again, maybe expecting a different answer, "And the C-62T *was* supposed to be there, but it left before?"

Meyers responded, "We know the ship left at 13:02, about three hours before these events."

Malovex asked, "Can we confirm who was on board?"

Meyers responded, "The Ambassador, his assistant Miss Devanoe, and the DAG detail of Commanders Willits and Jones."

Malovex shook his head. He asked, "How did they get it off the dock? The DAG officers are qualified pilots?"

Kimakawa replied, "No, and I doubt they could fly it in a pinch, honestly. According to the Dock Master, two qualified cadets, with credentials from Odgins, joined their team."

Meyers responded, "We know they were *not* the pilots I assigned."

Malovex turned to Kimakawa, "And the Dock Master let them pass anyway?"

Kimakawa looked directly at him. "The Dock Master would only question qualifications, not a direct order or procedure issue from Commander Willits. He has full authority on that."

Malovex still wanted answers. "What do we know about these two cadets?"

Meyers answered, "We are still working on it."

Malovex asked, "Is there any chance there are other people aboard this ship, or is it just the six of them?"

Meyers answered, "It is not likely, but we are not completely sure."

Malovex continued, "And the Manifest has them going to Braccus?"

Meyers then interrupted, "Commander Willits changed the Manifest to meeting Battle Cruiser 54 in the Corvalis System before leaving. We believe he sent a message to their ship Captain to confirm."

Malovex, shook his head, not understanding all of this. He then looked back at the map and continued. "The Corvalis System is slightly further, basically bypassing Braccus. Is it possible something caused them to leave early, something they had no time to report to you?"

Kimakawa said nothing. Meyers did not speak, but he wanted to. Malovex continued to look before finally reiterating, "Anyone?..."

Nobody said anything. Malovex finally finished, "What I am asking is, do you trust these two Commanders with this mission?"

Meyers looked first at Kimakawa, as if looking for permission, then back at Malovex. He replied, "I have had some concerns, Lord Malovex. The Commanders have much experience, but it was quite some time ago."

Kimakawa still said nothing. Malovex went back to looking at the hologram board before continuing, "Well, it could be nothing, but you could also have two rogue Commanders on your hand. It's your problem now until they get to that Battle Cruiser."

Nobody said anything for a few moments until Malovex saw something on the replay. "There, deck officer, freeze that, go back a few seconds."

They all looked at the security footage from one screen that showed a Tower Angle. Malovex continued, "Zoom in there......."

Malovex circled a spot where the black attack fighter had hovered above the Control Tower deck, and then the image zoomed in. He then identified the maroon blood-red helmet. "There, that is our attacker....Taz."

Kimakawa and Meyers stared at the monitor and could now see it clearly. Kimakawa repeated, "Taz? Are you sure?"

Malovex answered, "Yes. This was clearly an attack on the Ambassador's life. An assassination attempt. Taz will not go away if he has identified his target. He will attack again."

Meyers looked at Malovex. "So, what now?"

Malovex responded. "Nothing, I will take it from here. This is why the BRG should be handling these things in the first place. This is beyond your abilities. I will immediately notify the rest of the BRG along with the AuFa and the Council. I will meet the Ambassador and your DAG team, if they make it, on that battle cruiser in Corvalis."

Malovex walked out of the room.

BELINEA 2.3

Belinea

The Hassara Residence

In a room full of daybeds and ottomans connected together, Lord Argo had laid down on one. Tall narrow windows had drapes over them to keep the light out. One girl was naked, rubbing on his bare chest. Two other girls were on top of another naked man across from Argo. One of the girls, straddling the man's face, said, "Is this what my Lord wants?"

Argo was unamused. "Suffocating?"

Argo shook his head softly. The third girl got up, naked, and walked over to Argo and the girl rubbing on him. "I know what the Lord wants…."

Argo sounded tempted. "Do you….?"

She reached over and grabbed the knife used to cut the meat and cheese from the table behind Argo. She walked back over to her original spot where a vase had an assortment of toys. With her other hand, she pulled out a small whipping stick from the vase. The woman straddling the man's face moaned in pleasure, while the man firmly had both his hands on her ass. The third woman gently patted the man's chest with the whipping stick.

She whispered, "My Lord likes watching us…. "

Argo was watching, becoming slightly aroused. The girl that was rubbing on his chest put her hand down his pants.

Argo whispered back, "Do I?"

The third woman began working her other hand on the man's penis, until finally getting the desired effect. She then climbed on top, facing the other woman, and allowed his penetration. The one straddling the man's face began touching the other girl's breast, eventually trying to kiss the other girl on the lips, mildly succeeding. While moaning, she said, "Is this what my Lord likes?"

Argo tilted his head. The girl next to him was gaining traction with her hand in his pants, eventually moving faster. The third girl straddling the man in intercourse gently pushed the other girl away. She smacked the other girls' breasts with the whipping stick, ever so lightly, hitting the same spot repeatedly.

"This is what My Lord likes….."

Argo repositioned himself on the ottoman. The girl rubbing him with her hand down his pants could tell he was getting aroused.

Argo softly said, "Now we're getting somewhere…."

The girl with the whipping stick then changed direction and, again, ever so gently, began smacking the girl opposite to her across her face with the whipping stick. She stopped her moaning and slightly yelped in pain. The girl next to Argo, clearly sensing his arousal, began viciously kissing his neck while maintaining her hand down his pants. The girl with the whipping stick looked directly at Argo, noticing his eyes getting more prominent, and moaned out, "Is this what you want, my Lord, or something deeper?"

Now fully concentrating on the threesome in front of him, Argo spoke just louder than a whisper. "Deeper…."

The girl went back to hitting the other girl on her breasts, this time a little harder. After smacking her ten times, the last being hard enough to draw a look of slight pain from the girl, she put the whipping stick down, and ever so secretly, while still straddling the man in intercourse, grabbed the knife she retrieved. With her opposite hand, she began caressing the opposite girls' breasts, a sexual peace offering. She grabbed her cheek, and began kissing her while slowly moveing her hand to the back of her head. After a long kiss, the other girl grabbed her cheek. The third girl grabbed the other girl's wrist while she continuing to kiss her. She put the other girl's fingers in her mouth, and kissed the fingers one by one to get her fully aroused. As she got to the last finger, still holding it with her left hand, she took her right hand and cut the girl's finger with the knife.

Argo was now thoroughly aroused. The girl next to him violently moved her hand down his pants while the blood from the cut on the other girl began trickling down her finger. This allowed the dominant girl to lick it up with her tongue. Argo, licking his lip, loudly whispered, "More…"

The dominant girl began straddling the man more violently with her hips, as he got into it as well. One of his hands moved off the girls' ass and up the sofa, clinching the top of it in excitement. The dominant girl then took the knife and gently carved a small cut into the man's chest. He moaned in both excitement and pain. The cut drew blood. Which the dominant girl, with her free hand, wiped the blood off the man's chest and put it into the girl's mouth opposite her. "Is this what you want, My Lord?"

Argo now yells, "Yes….."

He was fully enthralled. The dominant girl, now sensing she had Argo's full attention, moaned in excitement. She licked her lips, completely staring at Lord Argo until she was about to climax. She then took the knife and stabbed the man she was riding directly in the hand he had clutched to the sofa. He immediately screamed in agony. The girl sitting on his face was thrown on to the floor.

Argo smiled and yelled out, "Yes……"

The girl next to him was still violently working her hand down his pants. The victim was now pinned to the sofa by the knife. Blood began to run down his arm. A buzzing broke the tension at the door.

Argo yelled, "Go away. I am busy."

A voice from behind the door yelled back, albeit politely. "Lord Argo, your father is expecting you."

The dominant girl got off from riding the man, half laughing, half excited by the whole situation. The other girl seemed almost traumatized by the site of the man's blood as she had been thrown to the ground and was now looking at the wound. Argo yelled again, "Go away. I am busy."

The voice behind the door was persistent. "My Lord, Your father, and everyone else is waiting on you for the afternoon military briefing. Your Father sent me to get you, and commanded me not to return without you."

Argo grabbed the girl's hand and yanked it out from his pants. He sat-up and reached over for his shirt, quickly putting it on and slipping on his boots. The dominant girl walked over to Argo, took her bloody fingers, and put one of them in Argo's mouth while he finished putting his second boot on. He looked up at her, not amused. She took the finger out and slapped him across the face, smiling while she was doing it. He got up and grabbed her arm. "Don't go anywhere. I will be right back. "

The other man, still moaning, was trying to free his hand, and was now being assisted by the other girl. Argo put on his knee-high length black robe and walked to the front door of the room.

Lord Argo opened the door to find a portly man in a green Belinean military uniform. An officer clearly, being summoned to do errand boy work. Argo was not amused as he walked out and slammed the door behind him. The portly man followed, claiming, "My Lord, the meeting was scheduled twenty minutes ago, and your Father is very annoyed at your lack…."

Argo, not looking, just muttered, "Quiet…."

But the portly man continued as they walked outside through the beautiful gardens and over to the main residence of Lord Hassara. "If it is a question on how to communicate better with you, my Lord, please let me know so that we can get you to these meetings on time…."

Argo, a very tall man at 6'3" and muscular, slightly rolled his eyes. He was walking briskly and still annoyed, and muttered without looking down at the portly man, "What is your name again?"

Looking surprised, he responded, "Walva, sir, Lieutenant Walva."

Argo continued, "Walla, when I want your opinion on punctuality, I will ask for it."

They continued to walk, coming to a door that was the entrance to the main residence. As they walked down a long corridor, the portly man continued. "It's actually wal-Va, my Lord."

Argo shook his head. "Walva, Walla, whatever, just shut up."

Walva continued, "The name is not important, sir. My point is, that when you are late for these meetings, Chairman Hassara seems to blame me, and I can only relay to him the fact that I did coordinate these times …"

They had arrived at the front of two massive doors with four guards outside. Argo stopped, turned to the portly man, pointing, looking down at him and whispered, "One more word, and I will cut your fucking tongue out so that you will never speak again."

Walva looked hurt and scared. After a few seconds, Argo began to slightly turn to go into the big doors before the portly man said, "Of Course My Lord…."

Argo immediately glanced back at Walva. The anger in his eyes translated that he was ready to cut his tongue out right here and there. The portly man, realizing one more word, really meant any word, immediately bowed his head as a measure of mercy. Argo paused a few more seconds before finally turning and entering the room.

Inside the conference room were Chairman Hassara, his daughter Defense Minister Tempest Hassara, Admiral Magloan of the Aufa, and Ambassador Yebba of Avola. Chairman Hassara was sitting behind his desk. Tempest Hassara and Ambassador Yebba were seated on sofas across from the desk. Admiral Magloan was standing, making a hologram presentation near the wall. He was speaking as Argo entered the room " these three locations in our estimate are the most crucial, and would require the most military intervention for security……"

The Chairman noticed Argo walking into the room. "Argo, your lack of punctuality is persistently exasperating."

There was a pause in the room. Argo looked his father down as he walked over to a side table. He grabbed a piece of Belinean fruit and before biting into it, responded, "Difficult indeed, but I squeezed you in…."

Chairman Hassara was now staring at his son in a disapproving manner. After a few seconds, the Chairman looked back at the Admiral and said, "Please proceed, Admiral."

The Admiral, clearly caught off guard by the father-son exchange, cleared his throat before proceeding. "As I was saying to Chairman Hassara, we are evaluating these three strategic areas that we feel have a large abundance of Vait. Ambassador Yebba has eliminated the Avolian Mining Guild, which has allowed The Council to negotiate contracts exclusively with the Majavkee Group to mine the Vait using our engineers to head the projects. As of now, the Vait supply is still fluid, for the most part."

Argo was still eating his fruit. "Outstanding. Nothing else? Or do we need to discuss the weather on Avola this time of year?"

The Chairman glared at Argo before saying, "No, the Admiral was putting it kindly when he said 'for the most part.' Admiral…"

The Admiral then pointed to the other side of the planet. "This area here, The Avolian Government nor the Majavkee Lords have control of. It is occupied by the Valmay Opposition Group. These terrorists are in favor of restoring the local Mining Guild and eliminating the Council involvement."

Argo was all about getting this meeting done as soon as possible. "But the Valmay Group is mining Vait as well, correct?"

The Ambassador responded, "We believe they are. Scanning the area shows cyclic residue and steam clouds, clear primary indicators of Vait mining. But they have not sold any of it. At least not to us."

Argo was still confused. "I thought you just said the Vait supply was fluid?"

The Admiral continued, "It is Lord Argo. The increase of mining by the Majavkee has our Vait levels at an all-time high. Currently, we have a surplus of Vait, and we are waiting on the approval of the Council to increase purchasing and production."

Lord Argo sarcastically asked, "Then I am not sure what the problem is. As long as we have a constant flow of Vait, let them deal with their petty disagreements."

Tempest Hassara half smiled and asked, "Do you read any correspondence I send you?"

Argo smiled and responded, "Only the naked pictures, certainly not the boring stuff."

The Admiral continued. "Well, unfortunately, that constant flow might be in jeopardy. I believe Defense Director Hassara was referring to the file I sent her of the Valmay Opposition Group, taking out an entire Belinean Garrison, here (pointing to the map area). They also managed to steal an entire C-24 Cargo ship full of Vait. It resulted in fourteen Aufa soldiers, all Belinean, and another four Majakee security detail killed in action. The area is still not secure."

Malovex responded. "Fine. Have Tempest send in a few battlecruisers. A whole battalion and a couple of AuFa regiments should end this quarrel quickly."

The Chairman now got up and sarcastically said, "Well, thank you, Argo for coming up with a conclusion that the four of us already made last week. "

Argo looked miffed. He took a deep breath, rolled his eyes, and said, "You already did that…."

The Avolian Ambassador Yebba now spoke. "Yes, the AuFa already did. I am afraid it is more complicated than that, my Lord. Our atmosphere, given our proximity to our star and the considerable mining that we do, has created a thick cloud of electric gases, often leaving the planet in a perpetual dusky haze throughout the day. It also makes travel from space to the surface nearly impossible. The exception being these four-atmosphere tunnels that block the electrical and gas currents. They allow ships to fly in and out through the 32 kilometer stretch of atmosphere. We are currently building a fifth one, but it is costly."

Argo sat directly up while his sister was still laid back in her chair. "I have read about the tunnels, Ambassador. There is no other way in or out?"

The Ambassador shook his head. "No, my Lord, not that we have figured out in centuries. There have been rumors of pirates being able to navigate tiny ships through. But those are just rumors. No one I know has ever seen it done. "

Lord Argo now had a plan. "And there is a Battle Cruiser or AuFA presence at the top of every tunnel?"

The Admiral added, "Yes, my Lord. Between the Battle Cruisers and Patrol ships, we have effectively put an embargo on the Valmay Opposition Group. They are getting no supplies and not selling any Vait, if they have it. Yet, somehow they are getting stronger."

Argo squinted. "Stronger?"

The Admiral switched gears. "We think Taz was responsible for the attack on Space Port Earth. Our latest intel connects Taz to this Valmay Opposition Group. We think he is a member."

The Chairman finally spoke. "Thank you, Admiral and Ambassador. I think Lord Argo has been made aware of the situation While we discuss the matter privately, continue to keep the embargo as tight as possible."

The Admiral and Ambassador walked out. The Chairman, still aggravated, said, "Your attendance to these meetings should not feel like a prison sentence. We are discussing important matters."

Argo sat back down, "That is what Tempest is for."

Tempest closed her tablet. "Don't drag me into this big brother. It's not my fault you care more about where you put your penis than where we put our military."

Argo half smiled, "Nothing personal sis. I can arrange for you to blow off some steam, you clearly need it. The girls work both sides."

The Chairman was not amused. "Enough. I don't have time for your petty little jabs. Despite the Admirals' concern, the conflict is inconsequential as long as the Vait supply is not interrupted."

Tempest spoke up. She saw the same angle. "Then why get involved at all? As long as we are patient, they will have to sell it directly to us or through a third party."

The Chairman began walking back to behind his desk as he continued. "Because we may not have time. Once our engineers took over mining in the region, we exponentially began yielding the Vait. Publicly, the increase is about five times more. Privately, the yield is much greater."

Argo looked alarmed. "How much greater? An unsafe amount?"

The Chairman sat down. "Correct. The removal of their Mining Guild allowed us unregulated access to all their abundant sites, and we took advantage. The rate is unsustainable. The Ambassador thinks he has decades of production, but a meeting last week with our engineers told us differently. "

Tempest now even sat up next to her brother. "How long?"

Hassara sat down, folded his hands together, and put his elbows on his desk. "They believe a few more years, at best."

Argo was now curious. "Until all the Vait is mined?"

Hassara answered, "Before internal implosion from the planet core, a result of this advanced mining. They say it is inevitable. It will be close, but they also believe we should have all the Vait out by that time."

Tempest asked, "If we slowed the mining down, would it save the planet?"

The Chairman said, "Possibly, but this current extraction is what we need to achieve our production goals. The engineers cannot get an accurate reading because of all the gases and electricity in the atmosphere. They estimate the richest area of Vait currently on the planet is in the Bosa region, controlled by the Valmay Group. Thus, sending someone to negotiate on our behalf has become a top priority."

Tempest asked a question. "Negotiate what?"

The Chairman continued, "Convincing them to sell the Vait to us, publicly or privately. Publicly and it looks like we are negotiating peace. Privately, and they probably save face with their people. As long as we get the Vait, the AuFa can stay out of their conflict altogether."

Tempest was not convinced. "And if the Valmay Group does not negotiate?"

The Chairman responded coldly, "Then we convince the Council it's in our best interest to remove them, which would require some media savvy and public outcry. But understanding all their options would only force a logical, peaceful solution that benefits all sides."

Argo then patted Tempest on the shoulder. "Great, when does Tempest leave?"

Tempest first looked at her brother, then at her father. Argo was smiling. Tempest was not. The Chairman broke the tension. "As Defense Minister of the AuFa, Tempest is too vital at the moment here with me. I need her for this upcoming Council session regarding the potential Earth situation and their own Delegate Ambassador Guard. I will need you to go to Avola and negotiate on our behalf."

Argo now frowned, and Tempest smiled. Argo was floored. "Me? *Negotiate*? Why? Why not send Sanisgar?"

The Chairman took a deep breath. " When he returns here, I need his help debating the financial implications of investing resources in private Ambassador Security instead of the BRG. But currently, he is on assignment with the Earth situation."

Argo was now upset. He stood up. "I told you the situation is under control. My contact has assured me all is going to plan."

The Chairman let out a crooked smile, "Is it? The attack on Space Port Earth?"

Tempest continued to smile. Argo kept staring at his father. After a few seconds, he regrouped. The angle of the conversation was going nowhere. Argo continued, "Why not send Tempest's deputy to Avola? Or the Admiral?"

The Chairman unfolded his hands. "I want the message to be impactful. Coming from my son, my top deputy, is the same as coming from me. And coming from the Director of the Secret Service, it can also be done discreetly as well if that is their preference. There is a possibility they say no, which is also why I am sending you to negotiate, understand?"

Argo was still standing. "Do I have a choice?"

The Chairman now stood up as well. "No, you do not. Now, my meetings are running late. I have people waiting outside. There is a SS ship waiting for you on the landing field to take you to Avola. If there is nothing else...."

Argo had been blindsided. "I am leaving now?"

The Chairman walked from around the desk and began to escort his children out. "Yes, I have arranged for your steward to pack your belongings so you can leave immediately."

Argo and Tempest walked out of the room into the corridor, where a few Ambassadors were waiting. Lieutenant Walva, Argo's portly steward, was waiting as well. Walva said, "My Lord, I have arranged for all of your gear to be transported to the SS ship, including a few weapons that I thought you might have......"

Argo looked at him and cut him off. "Quiet...."

Tempest took one more step before turning around and whispering, "Safe travels, brother...."

Argo stared at her before whispering back, "What a fucking dick-punch...."

Tempest then proceeded to kiss him on the cheek and gently slap his face. "Yes, it is. But it is your dick-punch problem now, not mine. Don't let me down. "

She spun around, taking four steps before turning back around and saying, "Oh brother,...."

Argo just looked at her, head tilted.

Half tilting her head, Tempest asked, "Your companionship? It would be a shame to let them go to waste without them earning their services."

Argo gave a scowl and paused before speaking. "In my common room.…... enjoy."

Tempest turned around and walked off. Taking a few more steps, she blindly waved behind and yelled, "Thanks."

Argo watched her walk off. He took a deep breath and proceeded the other way towards the landing field, the portly steward in tow. After a few steps, Walva deemed it appropriate to speak. "Sir, all your belongings are already on the ship, with a few of the weapons that I know you commonly like. I also.…..."

Argo stopped and looked down at him, cutting off his speech. "When I said I was going to cut your tongue out, did you think I was joking?"

Walva looked astonished. "My Lord, I must admit, I thought it to be just a figure of speech, and from my perspective, a poor one at.….."

Argo continued, cutting him off again. "I once interrogated a man for information. I hung him to a cross and, one by one, cut each of his toes and fingers off until he bled to death. He never gave me the information, but I rather enjoyed myself for an hour, despite ruining the floors."

The two stared at each other for a few seconds before the portly man kneeled his head. After a few seconds, Argo walked off, and Walva continued. "Your right, my Lord, but wouldn't it be much more advisable to keep me in my current state, one in which I can help you accomplish your basic needs.….."

Argo rolled his eyes. This day had not gone to plan. He whispered to himself, "Colossal fucking dick-punch."

The door opened into Argo's common room as Tempest walked in. Two of the girls (including the dominant one) were still naked on the ottoman, smiling slightly. The other girl held a towel around the man's hand, having removed the bloody on the table. They were walking out, each grabbing the bloody wrapped-up hand. Tempest looked at them as they walked by her and said, "Need a hand?"

The two walked out, leaving Tempest with the other two girls. The dominant one said, "Lady Tempest…."

Tempest proceeded to walk from the door to the ottomans and couch, carefully surveying the vase with the sex toys. Tempest, shaking her head, softly said, "Ta-ta-ta, another messy afternoon with my brother, how unfortunate."

The dominant girl just smiled and blinked her eyes, while the other one began rubbing on the dominant one. Tempest began taking off her shirt and grabbed one of the toys. "So unnecessary all these violent little games when a proper tongue will do."

Tempest proceeded to join the two girls while taking the rest of her clothes off.

BELINEA 2.4

Avola

Valmay Headquarters, Bosa Province

Octavious Killian sat at the head of a long rectangle table. Kaya, his sister, was next to him along with the other seven officers, including Rendon, Marrat, and Cortes. The seat at the end of the table was left open.

Kaya stood up and walked over to the screen on the wall. She said to the group, "I wanted to show you this."

When she pointed at a spot on the map, she said, "Here, the mining colony in sector twelve. My cousin Donovan indicated this colony has limited protection. A few AuFa ground troops and a couple of fighters to escort the cargo transport ships. That leaves the facility vulnerable to an attack. If it's true, that's a large amount of Vait going unprotected."

Octavious quickly added, "But it's very far from Bosa."

Kaya replied, "True, but if we fly low with no cover, casualties would likely be minimal considering the element of surprise."

Octavious answered, "Perhaps. But if there were casualties, quick extraction would prove difficult."

Kaya added, "Yes, but worth the risk. The amount of Vait is substantial."

Rendon questioned, "You trust the intel?"

Kaya answered, "It came directly from Donovan, so yes.

She paused briefly and then said, "There's more Octavious."

Octavious looked up. He quietly asked, "What?"

Kaya turned off the screen and softly replied, "Donovan said the conditions in the mining camp were atrocious compared to Guild standards. They're living in poverty, spending more hours in the caves than not, while the Majavkee Lords reap the benefits."

Ocativious paused. "I cannot free the mining camps all at once, Kaya."

Kaya countered, "They are not soldiers. They are not trained to fight. They are starving, barely able to feed their families. We have to help them."

Octavious looked up at her and said, "They need to protest. The Majavkee can not mine the Vait without them."

Kaya replied, "Do you not think they are punished for speaking? The loudest of voices can be silenced with one round to the head."

Octavious raised his voice slightly. "And we cannot echo the call of liberty by ourselves. Do you want freedom and justice, Kaya? So do I. We all do. But our decisions must be calculated, advancing the broader mission. Even at the expense of our brothers in the greatest need."

The other officers exchanged glances across the table. It was not often that Kaya and Octavious articulated their opposing views in front of the other officers. Kaya let Octavious's words hang in the air before sitting down. "If we are not saving the lives of the people, what are we fighting for?"

Octavious now paused. He then said, "No amount of violence will change what is happening. Controlling the supply of Vait, through a rebellion with the miners, will allow us the revolution we seek. We must establish a movement that includes the miners before we can move forward."

Kaya looked at him and nodded. The others at the table did the same. After a moment, Octavious calmly said, "Alright, recheck the scheduled times, and coordinate when the escort ships are away. You will use your team?"

Kaya looked at Cortes, Rendon, and Marrat before acknowledging with a nod. She then said, "Yes…"

Octavious half-smiled and said, "Let me see the final plans, but otherwise it is a go."

After a moment, Octavious hit the spot on the table and said out loud, "Send her in."

Former Ambassador Syren came walking into the room, wearing a long white robe. The entire table stood up, including Octavious, waiting for her to take her seat at the table's foot, opposite Octavious. When she did, the rest of the soldiers sat down as well. Syren said, "Octavious, thank you."

Octavious nodded and said, "Ambassador."

Syren quickly got to the point. "The Council has reached out to me. Publicly, they recognize Ambassador Yebba and all the delegates on Avola.

Privately, they concede the Majavkee Lords run the planet. They would like to meet with you, Octavious."

Octavious folded his hands together. He responded, "Why?"

Syren answered. "To negotiate a peaceful solution to the violence currently disrupting the Vait mining."

Kaya jumped in. "If the Majavkee peacefully leave, we will peacefully not attack them. Simple enough."

Syren responded, "I see no scenario where they force the Majavkee to leave."

Kaya quickly answered, "Then there is nothing to discuss."

There was a long pause in the room. Syren then asked, "Octavious, is this how you feel?"

Octavious waited a few seconds before answering. He said, "I believe everyone at this table feels the same way."

The officers made eye contact and nodded before looking back at Syren. Syren met their gaze, and after a few seconds, said, "I know what you are trying to accomplish. Nobody respects it more than me. But think about the people you are fighting for. The Miners. The children. What would Quillisar Ballera ask you to do?"

Nobody said anything. There was a hush in the room. Syren got up after about five seconds and said, "Didn't make a difference, did I?"

Octavious immediately replied, "I'm at Temple every week. She knows how to find me if she has something to say."

Syren began walking out of the room. As she approached the door, Octavious said, "Syren…"

The former Ambassador stopped and looked back over her shoulder at the table. Octavious said, "If the Belienans and the Council want to talk, I am willing to listen. But no promises."

Syren nodded and walked out of the door.

Kaya then stood up and said, "Anything else? Meeting adjourned."

One by one, the other soldiers got up, made the silent diamond shape with their fists, towards Octavious, and slowly left the room. Kaya addressed her brother once everyone had left. "You will talk to them? Why? You said so yourself; they will never negotiate a withdrawal of Avola."

Octavious turned toward his sister. "I know. And at some point, they will become much more aggressive in their defense. She is right. The Vait is too strategically important to them. "

Kaya was strong. "And we will destroy everything they send our way. No one is afraid."

Ocativous snorted, and a doubtful quarter smile, slightly shrugging his shoulders.

Kaya was confused and was more confident than her older brother. "You don't think we can win?"

Octavious looked at her, grabbing her shoulder. "Kaya, there is no win. They will be forced into a surface attack, yes, but we can only hold them for so long. We may have Vait, but we have no ships. And we have no resources to build ships, no factories, no workforce. We are forced to steal the weapons we have. Eventually, we will run out. And we certainly can't stop them from mining the other regions."

Kaya did not see it that way. "Octavious, we can beat them. One battle at a time. We are defending our home, and it's just another planet to them. They don't have the stomach for this fight."

Octavious "Stomach, no. Ambition, yes. The Majavkee are on their side, as are most Avolians."

Kaya paused for a second and asked, "Who would they send?"

Octavious answered, "Probably an Ambassador or a high ranking AuFa officer. Nobody too important."

Kaya continued, "Well when they do, I will be there with you."

Octavious gave a small smile and said, "You think this will help the negotiation?"

Kaya answered, "If only to remind them they could be dealing with me instead of you."

Octavious smiled and said, "That's a good point. Get me that intel when you can, please."

Kaya walked out of the room, leaving Octavious to study the map.

BELINEA 2.5

Somewhere on the way to Braccus

Cadet Tunasll sat in a pilot's chair of the C-62T transport. Cadet Trujillo walked in through the back cabin. He uttered one word: "Dinner...."

Tunsall hit a few commands on his screen and unbuckled himself from the pilot's chair. He got up and walked out the door with Trujillo. The two of them walked to the back and noticed a long table. Eating at it were Ambassador Bird, Alexis Devanoe, and Commanders Willits and Jones. There were two empty seats, but clearly with a plate of food in front of each one. Trujillo and Tunsall were confused. They inconspicuously walked to the table, grabbed their plates, and began walking back to the front of the ship.

Willits, sipping on a glass of wine, stopped, and said, "Where are you two going?"

Trujillo spoke "To the front of the ship to eat, sir."

Willits quickly responded, "Sit down. No one on my crew eats anywhere else but at the same table as the rest of us. We are all equal. Provided it is ok with the Ambassador?"

The Ambassador nodded in approval. "By all means, sit down. I would like to get to know these two cadets better. However, who is actually flying the ship right now?"

Tunsall responded. "It's on auto-pilot in Hyper-EXtension mode. In the unlikely event anything happens, we will be notified."

Tunsall and Trujillo reluctantly sat down. They began eating, and Willits poured both of them some wine. Ambassador Bird was first to say, "How much longer until the two of you graduate from the Academy?"

Jones and Willits glanced at each other. Maybe this wasn't such a good idea after all. Tunsall spoke first. "It was supposed to be next week, sir."

The Ambassador continued, "If I may ask, how much real experience do you have?"

Willits and Jones could see this was not going to go well. It was unclear even how to stop it. Trujillo spoke this time. "We get an abundance of time in the simulator, sir. It is virtually identical to flying in real space. I often can't tell the difference."

The Ambassador then asked, "And with this particular ship?"

Trujillo continued, "This is a C-62T, sir. A refurbished cargo transport ideal for civilian travel. Tunsall and I have over fifty hours each of simulation time flying with this ship, as required before we graduate."

Ambassador Bird was still chewing his food, nodding as Trujillo was talking. He swallowed and continued. "But no actual real flight time?"

Willits and Jones were about to put a stop to this, but Tunsall jumped right back. "No, sir, no real-time. But as Trujillo said, the Simulator is outstanding for creating space-like conditions. Unlike current AuFa pilots, we are also certified to fly twenty-two other ships, including F-81 Sirator's and all attack aircraft."

The Ambassador seemed to gain some knowledge. "Really, I was unaware of that."

For the moment, it looked like the situation was squashed. Ambassador Bird was searching for something to say but could come up with nothing. Willits and Jones had been saved and resumed eating. Tunsall then broke the tension "Sir, if you do not mind me asking, how long have you been an Ambassador?"

Ambassador Bird answered, "Six months. I served as a Delegate Representative for almost a decade."

Trujillo then added, "And how many times have you been to Belinea for an actual Council legislation session?"

The Ambassador kept chewing his food, pausing a while before speaking. He stared at Trujillo for quite some time, before saying, "This will be my second Council trip."

Trujillo slightly nodded his head. The room was a little quiet before Tunsall continued, "I am sure your lack of experience will have no bearing on the outstanding job you will do."

The Ambassador took a sip of his wine, swallowing hard. He now stared at Tunsall. It was an insult, but no more than the one he gave the cadets.

Tunsall and Trujillo kept eating. Willits cracked a small smile at Jones, who returned the gesture. Alexis asked, "Commander Willits, how long have you been in the Delegate Ambassador Guard?"

Willits smiled. "Commander Jones and I joined at the inception, over fourteen years ago."

Alexis asked, "Mostly Earth security duties, or have you been all over the galaxy?"

Willits took a sip of wine before responding. "Unlike you, Miss Devanoe, this is not my first or second trip to Belinea. I have done it plenty of times."

Alexis whipped her black hair back in a matter of fact kind of way and declared. "Actually, Commander, I have done it plenty of times as well. I was raised on Belinea."

Everyone looked surprise, except Ambassador Bird, who already knew. While everyone looked at Alexis, Commander Jones spoke first. "But you are not Belinean?"

Commander Jones knew she didn't have any of the usual markings of a Belinean, so he pretty much knew the answer despite it coming out as a question. Alexis put down her wine. "Mostly Scottish, Commander Jones. My mother sent me away to learn everything about the Belineans when I was eleven years old. I was schooled like a Belinean, only coming home, to Earth, a couple of weeks out of the year until I was seventeen."

Commander Willits "I'm sure that was a tough decision for your parents."

Alexis took another sip of wine. "A decision my mother made. My father died in the pandemic."

Trujillo interrupted. "So did my parents."

Alexis held up her glass and said, "My condolences…."

Trujillo held up his and said, "Likewise…."

Alexis continued, "My mother thought it was important to learn a Belinean education. My brothers were taught the same."

Ambassador Bird interrupted. "Which is why she is invaluable. She knows far more about Belinean culture, rules, and customs than I ever could. In addition to being the hardest worker I've ever seen."

Alexis was blushing. She said, "Thank you, Ambassador, you are too kind."

Willits had a puzzling look on his face. "Devanoe, correct? What is your mother's name?"

Alexis looked at Willits with a raised eyebrow. It was an odd question. "Annella Devanoe? You know her?"

Willits responded with a "no," but his face said something else.

Trujillo asked her, "So if you are so familiar with this trip, where is our first stop? "

Alexis put down her wine "I believe we stop at a planet called Braccus to stop and resupply."

Tunsall countered with "Well, Miss Devanoe, that is incorrect. You and the Ambassador, as dignitaries, will be going directly to a Battle Cruiser in the Corvalis System."

Jones interjected, "That is wrong, Tunsall."

Tunsall said, "But the manifest says…"

Willits cut Tunsall off. "The manifest says Corvalis, but we are going to Braccus."

Alexis Devanoe was genuinely perplexed. A slight look of apprehension was now on her face as she asked "Why the confusion?"

Willits continued in a solemn manner. " We don't entirely trust who has and who hasn't seen that manifest."

Tunsall got it immediately. "So, the Battle Cruiser has no idea where we are?"

Willits continued. "Or anyone else, hopefully."

The Ambassador was confused. "We left Space Port Earth early because of your lack of trust in your own DAG. You are changing the manifest now because you neither trust the AuFa or BRG. Do you trust anyone?"

Willits took a sip of his wine and stared at Bird. After a moment, he responded, "No…"

Alexis looked a little uneasy now. Bird was startled at the brutal honesty. Jones tried to dissolve the tension by saying, "As long as no one knows we're out here, then we are safe, sir."

The Ambassador waited a second before offering, "Should we at least notify Director Kimakawa of where we are?"

Willits finished chewing before saying, "Nope, and we have no way of communicating with him even if we did. We're on our own until we get to Braccus."

An uneasy feeling came over the table as Bird, Alexis, Trujillo, and Tunsall all just looked at each other. Willits and Jones said nothing for a few moments until Willits grabbed the bottle and said, "More wine, anyone?"

Nobody said anything.

BELINEA 2.6

Belinea

Director of Defense Conference Room

Six other Ambassadors were in the room, along with Ambassador Yebba from Avola and Admiral Magloan. All were looking at the 3-D hologram showing Vait production levels. Defense Minister Tempest Hassara was standing and conducting the meeting. "At 8,450 units, this last month of Vait mining on Avola was the best yet. We are finally over 500,000 units overall at our Grannis Facility. Admiral Magloan...."

The Admiral added, "Currently we have two Battle Carriers and eight more Battle Cruisers under construction. The expedited supply of Vait will be key if we are to expand the capacity of the facility as planned."

The Ambassador sitting closest to her asked, "Defense Minister, is this military buildup essential?"

Tempest answered, "As Ambassador Yebba can attest, the Valmay Group represents a serious threat to the extraction of Vait in the area. If we are to combat the terrorist efforts of Taz, our current levels of defense must be elevated to handle further aggression."

Another Ambassador questioned, "Is it possible that the BRG and AuFa are spread so thin that we should inquire about other measures?"

Just as the Ambassador finished speaking, Chairman Hassara walked into the room. Everyone immediately got up as he continued to walk toward the hologram, saying in a distinct tone, "What other measures are you referring to Ambassador Sedaris?"

The Ambassador was caught off guard. "My apologies Chairman, no one told us you would be joining us in this meeting. "

The Chairman continued, "Nor should I have to. Whatever the Defense Minister says might as well be a direct statement from me."

Ambassador Sedaris continued, "The Defense Minister was speaking of our need for more ships. I was wondering if the planets should assist in such a manner. The strain on production alone is troublesome."

Tempest then continued, "Which is why Ambassador Yi is here. The other facility on Earth should be completed ahead of schedule and easily double production provided we supply the necessary Vait. Ambassador...."

Earth Ambassador Yi stood up and said, "Yes, we are finishing construction details now. The addition to the current facility will have the same production levels as the Grannis facility, but cost almost 60% less to operate due to the decrease in labor costs and taxes."

Tempest added, "We are confident at those levels, with an additional tax the Council passes, that we can increase the military ship size by thirty percent over the next three years."

The other Ambassador countered. "Ambassador Yi, your other Earth counterpart, Ambassador Bird, has recently been making a lot of public statements regarding the need to expand Earth's Delegate Ambassador Guard. Is this not a direct contradiction to your support here of the BRG and AuFa expansion?"

Ambassador Yi responded, "I am very aware of the Ambassador's comments. I promise that Ambassador Bird and I want the same thing, what is best for Earth and the Council's security. When the Ambassador arrives here for the Council meeting, he will be aligned with our commitment to the BRG."

Tempest then added, "When the Ambassador hears of this latest attack on Earth, he will see things."

Ambassador Sedaris asked, "He does not know yet?"

The Chairman then spoke, "The Ambassador's whereabouts are unconfirmed at this time. His local DAG security seems to have mishandled the whole situation honestly. It is why I have Lord Malovex personally investigating the situation. Our primary concern is the safety of all of our Ambassadors."

Ambassador Yebba added, "This attack by the Valmay Group, and the terrorist attack on Earth is nothing short of a declaration of war on the entire Council. This increase in military size should be a bare minimum Chairman."

Tempest added, "And we thank you for that support Ambassador Yebba. Is it safe to say that we have the full support of every Ambassador in this room moving forward with this increased Military Initiative?"

There was a nodding of all the Ambassadors in the room, some slightly more enthusiastic than others. Tempest, after allowing all the Ambassador to see everyone was on board, finally continued, "Thank you all. We look forward to bringing this initiative to the entire Military Subdivision of the Council soon before a final vote on the next Council meeting floor. Now, I have a critical meeting with The Chairman and the Admiral, so if you will excuse us."

One by one, the Ambassadors all left the room, each giving a personal departing goodbye to Chairman Hassara. When they all had left, Tempest Hassara and Admiral Magloan were still sitting, waiting for Chairman Hassara to join them. The door closed as Tempest poured herself a glass of water. She said, "The meeting was going fine Father, I did not need your help."

The Chairman countered, "You're welcome Tempest. Actually, I convinced my twelve Ambassadors faster than you. I came down here for our meeting and noticed you were not done and wondered if you needed help."

Tempest, finishing drinking the water, said, "I did not."

The Admiral added, "The Defense Director did just fine Chairman."

The Chairman sat down. "Good to hear. Any news on Ambassador Bird?"

The Admiral answered, "Not at this time. If this DAG team keeps to their manifest, they should be rendezvousing with Battle Carrier 54 soon, and we can find out what happened on their end."

Tempest added, "I am sure I will hear from Malovex soon to offer clarity on the situation."

A buzz was heard. A female voice came over the speakers, "Chairman Hassara, Quillasar Prill is here to see you."

Tempest and the Chairman then stood up. "Let him in."

Quillisar Prill walked into the room. He was wearing a red cloak. Around his neck hung a silvery ring with blue stripes. He was flanked by four Secret Service officers, all in the SS red/black uniforms. Each had the same silvery ring with blue stripes hanging on their hips. The Quillisar walked to the center of the room and removed his hood from his cloak. He looked at the Admiral and said, "Leave us."

The Admiral looked at Chairman Hassara. He gave a very slight nod of approval. The Admiral then quietly said, "Excuse me, Quillisar."

The Admiral walked out of the room. The Quillisar then looked at his guards and seemed to say something to them telepathically. All four then walked out of the room, and the door closed.

The Chairman spoke first. "My Quillisar, what do we owe the pleasure?"

The Quillisar, very seriously, looked over at Tempest and said, "When was your last visit to Temple, my dear Tempest?"

Tempest had her head down before looking up and responding, "It has been some time my Quillisar, I have been very busy."

Quillisar Prill responded, "Six weeks to be exact. Do not think I am incapable of noticing these things. Even Argo has been there twice during that time."

Tempest frowned and said, "My apologies Quillisar, I will be there this week."

Quillisar Prill replied, "I hope so. It is the Sun Offering."

The Chairman spoke, "I hope you did not come all this way to scold my daughter for not coming to Temple? You could have sent me a note, and I would have been happy to do it myself."

Tempest gave her father a mean look. The Quillisar continued. "You took Argo off my detail and sent him on assignment. Nobody can tell me where he went. Why?"

Chairman answered, "I sent him on assignment to Avola. There is a potential Civil War developing there between the Majakee Lords and the desert Avolians over the production of Vait. He is there to stabilize the situation."

Quillisar took a deep breath. He responded. "I see. These Avolians, in the desert, who is their leader?"

Tempest answered. "They call themselves the Valmay Group and are led by Octavious Killian."

The Quillisar walked over to the map. After a few seconds, he responded. "Killian…..a religious group, no? Members of the old Quill called The Red Ring Rise."

The Chairman responded, "The Red Ring Rise? I do not think so. They cannot possibly still have members that are practicing or even alive?"

The Quillisar looked at the map and changed the hologram to Avola. He continued, "I had the SS remove them from the cities of Avola over a decade ago. I was told they had been vanquished, but I am sure some of them went into hiding in the caves in the desert and mountains. Do you understand who you are dealing with if that is the case?"

The Chairman and Tempest looked at each other. Tempest spoke, albeit unsure, "They are a Quill group?"

Quillisar Prill reluctantly responded, "Not in the way that you understand it to be. Your father, however, understands. Their version of the Quill is a different interpretation. It is based in Avola itself, a union of the rock and desert they call home. The red comes out in their sacrifice rings the same way the blue comes out in ours. That is how you will know. "

Tempest spoke, "They attacked one of our garrisons, but the security footage shows nothing like Quillisat SS soldiers."

Prill turned and looked at Tempest. "Look again…"

The Chairman interjected, "The tape shows a well-executed attack…."

But Prill cut him off and said, "Look again. This attack was done on an entire garrison, with how many of their men?"

Tempest answered. "We think eight to ten."

Prill then looked at the Chairman. He said, "Ten soldiers against an entire garrison? Does that sound like normal soldiers to you, Chairman?"

The Chairman just looked on. Not shaking his head, but acknowledging the curious statistics.

Prill turned to leave the room. "I will notify Argo and properly prepare him for what he is getting himself into."

The Chairman sputtered. "My Quillisar, I am sure I can handle that duty."

Prill stopped but did not turn around. He put his hood back on and said, "No. I will speak to him. This is a Quill matter. You do what you need to do from the Council."

The Quillisar walked out of the room. Tempest looked at her father. She then hit a button on the 3-D map and spoke, "Get me a copy of the garrison attack on Avola."

BELINEA 2.7

On the way to Braccus

Trujillo was alone in the cockpit of the Ambassador's C-62T Transport. He was half asleep when Alexis came walking up from the back. She poked at Trujillo's shoulder, and he turned around, still sitting in his chair. She smiled and said, "Hey, what's going on?"

Trujillo, slightly rubbing his eyes, said, "The sheer excitement of flying a Transport at Hyper-EXtension through the darkness of space."

Alexis looked through the window, noticing the stars going by. The smile was removed from her face as she looked before looking back at Trujillo. He raised his eyebrows and gave a half-smile. It caused her to provide a full smile back. He said, "It was a joke…"

Alexis felt relieved. She said, "Oh, right…"

Trujillo said, "This is as exciting as watching ants build a hill."

Alexis smiled and said, "Gotcha, I don't usually come up to the front. I'm always working, stuck in the back."

Trujillo continued, "We all have our jobs. You got the Ambassador. I'm stuck up here."

Alexis nodded. She then asked, "So where is it that we are going?"

Trujillo looked curious. "Willits told you, Miss Devanoe. We're going to Braccus."

Alexis smiled and said, "Please, just call me Alexis. How do you know for sure?"

Trujillo looked down and hit a few buttons. "This is our navigation setting and course right here. It is a direct path to Braccus."

Alexis asked, "Can it be changed?"

Trujillo answered, "Of course it can. But Commander Willits gave me specific instructions not to change the navigation in any way."

Alexis thought about that for a second before she said, "Alright, good to know. I'm only asking because the Ambassador was curious to know, he has never worked with this specific DAG team."

Trujillo just smirked and said, "That makes two of us."

Alexis smiled again and nodded. She said, "Right, cadets. Keep forgetting."

Trujillo quickly countered, "Graduating soon."

Alexis smiled and began walking back towards the common area. Underneath her breath, she whispered, "Not fast enough…"

BELINEA 2.8

Avola, Lowell Province

In the Mining Center, Donovan had gone outside to take a break. He was eating a granola bar. After a few seconds, a man came out and joined him. The two nodded at each other. After a few more seconds, the man said something to Donovan. "You are Donovan, correct?"

Donovan nodded. He replied, "Yeah, sorry. I do not know you."

The man replied, "Sterling, nice to meet you."

Donovan said, "Crew Supervisor on the Seven Line, correct?"

Sterling nodded. "Yeah, that's right."

Donovan said, "I recognize the name. You have been here a minute, for sure. I have heard people talk about you."

Sterling broke out his snack and started eating it. "Hopefully, good. I try not to piss too many people off."

They both smiled. Donovan said, "You are not Majavkee. That is half the battle right there."

Sterling took a few looks around to make sure no one heard him. "I would not say that too loud."

Donovan replied, "You have been here long enough to know they have fucked this whole situation up."

Sterling said, "Not for me to say. I got a wife and a kid on the way."

Donovan said, "Come on, you know how it is. Are you not working twice as hard for the same pay?"

Sterling paused for a second before responding. "I am a crew chief, so I have to watch what I say. It is not as good as it was with the Guild, but the Majavkee have promised bonuses. That will make it better."

Donovan shook his head. "You think they will make good on those promises?"

Sterling shrugged his shoulders. "I hope so. Like I said, I got a kid coming."

Donovan continued. "Crew Supervisor or not, I will tell you, Sterling. A change is coming. I got friends. My cousins are important. When you are ready to join the revolution, you let me know."

Sterling smiled. After a second, he said, "Thanks, friend. But right now, I am just trying to keep the peace. No offense, but my family comes first."

Donovan smiled and said, "I respect that. Good talking to you."

Sterling responded, "Good talking to you."

Donovan went back inside, leaving Sterling outside to finish his snack alone.

BELINEA 2.9

On the way to Avola

Secret Service ship 11

Argo was on a sofa, relaxing in a very comfortable, luxurious common room on the ship. He was wearing a red/black SS cloak, with his silvery ring on his hip. Sipping on a glass of wine, he was reviewing notes on his tablet. The portly officer Walva entered his common room, holding a note.

Argo looked up and immediately said, "How many times do I have to tell you, do not disturb me when I am reviewing notes?"

Walva walked over and said, "My apologies, my Lord. This transmission came over on the S-channel. It is directly from Quillisar Prill."

Argo took the note and put it into his tablet. As it was loading, he said, "I would throw you outside into space if I weren't so worried about your fat ass getting caught into the intake of one of our Battle Cruisers."

Walva did not understand but nevertheless replied, "Thank you, my Lord, I did not know you cared so much."

Argo read the message and then softly said to himself, "The Red Ring Rise....?"

After reading the whole message, he turned to Walva and asked, "Which of my weapons did you bring Walva?"

Walva, still upset about the comment, conducted himself and responded, "Your V-fleece armor, the TR rifle, your spare flog handle...."

Argo stood up and cut him off, "The Bolster pack?"

Walva thought for a second, "Yes sir, I believe I did."

Argo gently slapped him a few times on the face, "Well, fucking done Walla."

Walva replied, "It's Wal-VA, sir. I am really not sure what the confusion is, sir, as I have reminded you several times what my name is. I am aware that you are a brilliant person……"

Argo walked to the side and poured himself some more wine. "How about I just start calling you shut the fuck up?"

Walva, slightly upset, responded. "While you may find that title amusing and unforgettable, I do not think it would be appropriate for you to call me that in a public setting with other officers and Ambassadors…."

Argo responded, "Hey, shut the fuck up, can you shut the fuck up?"

Argo looked again at his tablet. He thought for a second. He looked over at Walva again. Argo continued. "Somewhere on this ship, we still have access to the Quill database, correct?"

Walva gave up temporarily with the name-calling conversation and responded, "Yes, my Lord."

Argo looked at him and said, "Give me all the data you can on the Red Ring Rise of Avola. Also, cross-reference the name Killian and see what comes up."

Walva replied, "Sir, I was planning on ….."

Argo cut him off and said, "Now, Walla."

Walva scurried out of the room. Argo downloaded the file that Quillisar Prill had attached. Soon, he was watching the attack on the Garrison on Avola. When it got to an angle he had not seen before, the image stopped. Argo suddenly heard the voice of Quillisar Prill through the speakers say, "Here Argo."

A circle showed up on the screen. At the top of the Cargo ship was a flash of red light. The Quillisar magnified the image for Argo. While a tad bit grainy, it was clear enough. Argo tilted his head, half smiled, and whispered, "A fire saber…."

Immediately after was the voice of Quillisar Prill coming through the message on his tablet. "The Fire Saber of the Ring Red Rise, no doubt you have seen it before."

Argo crossed his arms and whispered to himself, "Looks like Taz has some friends, who knew…"

BELINEA 2.10

Avola

Bosa Provence

The cargo ship was trailing smoke. The Belineans had managed to get one decent hit on it as Kaya Killian and her team were making their escape. Being flanked by two F-81 Sirator Fighters, the cargo ship was also carrying two badly wounded soldiers. Cortes, the pilot, radioed in from the cockpit area upfront. "Tower, this is Ranger Four. Two wounded on board, have med-vac ready."

"Copy Ranger Four. Medical Team is on stand-by."

In the back of the cargo ship, Kaya had a bandage pressed on the throat of the wounded soldier Marrat. The compression was helping, but not stopping, the soldier from bleeding out. Another soldier was working on the wounded soldier's arm. It had been severed below the elbow, and the soldier had it wrapped in bandages. There was a third wound on the leg that was being ignored. Blood was everywhere, including all over Kaya's uniform. She was shouting over the sounds of the engines. "Cortes, step on it. He is bleeding everywhere."

Cortes barely heard through her earpiece and screamed back over the radio, "Commander, still five minutes out."

Kaya replied, "Cortes, he doesn't have five fucking minutes."

Cortes is flying the ship as fast as she could. The second soldier planted a device on the forehead of the wounded soldier. It gave a small readout of vitals. The soldier read them off "Blood pressure and pulse are dropping. We gotta stop this fucking bleeding. Can we *Freeze* him?"

Kaya was losing hope. She took her other hand and grabbed the wounded arm. She yelled at the soldier, "No, it might fry his brain. Go get the medical kit. There should be a Pulsator in there."

The soldier ran to the front of the cargo bay and quickly grabbed the medical kit on the wall. Scouring through it for a few seconds, he found the Pulsator and ran back to the wounded soldier and Kaya. Kaya yelled, "Rendon, how are you doing over there."

Rendon, sitting next to them in a chair, had a bandage wrapped around his thigh. He was putting pressure on the wound himself, as his leg was stretched out. " I will make it."

Kaya then looked up at the soldier who had returned. "When I lift this bandage, get the Pulsator in there, and seal the wound. Got it?"

The soldier nodded. Kaya lifted the bandage and blood went everywhere. The soldier immediately began applying the Pulsator, which was a torch-like device that fused the skin back together. He was attempting to stop the bleeding, but not succeeding. Kaya said, "Hang in there, Marrat, we got you."

The blood though, was still seeping out of the throat and neck. The wound was more significant than Kaya had thought, and the amount of blood coming out made it difficult for the Pulsator to seal the skin back together. It was taking too much time. Kaya whispered to the other soldier "Come on, get in there. Keep working, you gotta seal that wound."

He responded, "I am trying….. There is too much blood. I can't see."

He kept working. Kaya shouted out, "Cortes, damn it….."

Cortes yelled back through the earpiece. "Two minutes…."

The blood then stopped coming out, yet the wound was still open. The device on his forehead no longer read vitals, no pulse, no blood pressure. Kaya and the other soldier continued to work on sealing the wound with the Pulsator. It was an awkward two minutes, knowing that the wounded soldier Marrat, was now dead.

Kaya whispered again. "Come on, Marrat, don't die on me."

Cortes yelled again. "Hang on…."

The ship came upon the base. The landscape was entirely red rock, mountains, and sand. A combination of steam and smoke came up through the rocks, which put a mist everywhere, making visibility scarce. The formation of one of the rocks then opened, causing a tunnel hole to appear. The Cargo ship flew in first, followed by the two fighters. Cortes brought the ship in fast and immediately reversed the thrusters, allowing the cargo ship to spin

180 degrees. The medical team was behind a barrier, preventing them from getting blasted with dust and debris the engines kicked up from the Cortes maneuver. Cortes then aggressively landed the cargo ship as it came to a thud on the landing pad. The back door immediately opened, and the medical team rushed in.

Kaya still was straddled next to the wounded soldier as a medic came up to her and demanded, "Let me in Commander."

Kaya let go and backed away. She got up and watched the team do their work. The medics began furiously working as they carried Marrat off on a stretcher. Kaya walked over to Rendon and helped him up. He limped, but walked, with his arm around Kaya. Cortes had finally gotten out of her pilot chair and then assisted Rendon on his other arm as the two walked him down the ramp of the ship. Eventually, another team of medics appeared and got Rendon onto a moving stretcher. Kaya looked down at Rendon, who casually said, "I am fine. Go check on Marrat."

Kaya gently slapped Rendon's face and said, "Hang tough."

Kaya and Cortes kept walking across the base. Cortes finally spoke. "I am sorry, Commander. I don't think I could have flown the ship any faster."

Kaya stopped, looking at Cortes and replied, "It's not your fault Cortes. That was a fatal wound. Get that ship assessed for damage and report back to me. And clean it up. I need it ready by tomorrow afternoon."

Cortes saluted and walked off. Kaya kept walking to the main building, first putting a hand on the security door before it let her in. She walked down a corridor, made a left, then a right before getting to another set of doors that required her palm print to open. The thought of changing never occurred to her, as she walked into the Control room still covered in blood. In the control room was her brother Octavious Killian, and two other officers.

Her brother Octavious was the first to notice her. "What happened? Are you hurt?"

Kaya shook her head no. She was surprised by the question until she glanced at herself when all three briskly walked up to her. She then noticed the blood everywhere. Her brother grabbed her shoulder and saw a small wound there. "Brembilla, go get me a medic."

The officer immediately walked off. Kaya responded, "I am fine."

Octavious kept staring at the wound, then at the rest of her blood-soaked clothes. "This blood is obviously not you."

Kaya's face grimaced, as Octavious poked at the wound. She replied. "Marrat. Nothing was defending the transport depot. Donovan and our intelligence were right. As we were taking off with the cargo, though, another ground cargo vessel was coming to the site escorted by a ground artillery vessel. We never saw it, and its cannon got off one clean shot before the Sirator's took it out. It tore through the middle of the cargo ship."

Octavious looked at her face now, cuts across her forehead and cheek. "How bad?"

Kaya replied, "Rendon got hit in the leg, but he will be fine. Marrat probably bled out."

Octavious looked at the other officer, and said, "Go check on him."

The officer walked off. Octavious clenched his fist. "I should have flanked your team with more protection."

Kaya responded, "It was more important to go in stealth with little cover. More ships increase the chance of detection."

Octavious took a deep breath, still looking at Kaya's wound. He quietly said, "We cannot afford these losses, Kaya."

Kaya bit her teeth down before replying softly. "We're going to have losses, Octavious. Sacrifices are a tragic necessity for survival."

Octavious replied, "True, but all losses are not equal. The Majavkee can afford to lose a hundred soldiers for every one of mine. The Council has their back. Marrat's loss was unnecessary and costly."

Kaya grew angry. "Unnecessary? He gave his life for our cause. A cause in which Avolians have no choice but to aggressively defend our homes, our planet. Tragic, yes. Unnecessary? Never say that."

Octavious turned to her. "I understand the brutal tyranny we are fighting, better than anyone. Make no mistake, every battle matters. But they have to be monumentally successful. Every, single, one. I cannot negotiate with the Council without significant leverage to discourage their commitment."

Kaya looked confused. "Negotiate?"

Octavious blurted out. " With the person, Ambassador Syren said is coming."

Kaya shook her head and said, "Still, don't know who it is?"

Octavious shook his head. "The negotiator left Belinea a couple of days ago. It sounds like they are sending a Senior Council Member if I had to take a guess. Perhaps someone that speaks for Hassara or the Defense Minister."

Kaya looked curious. "You sure it isn't a trap?"

Octavious continued. "I don't think so. Syren seems to trust it. It's a private meeting, and we're picking the site, their sign of good faith."

Kaya was not expecting this. "Why private? They don't want to look weak?"

Octavious scratched his stubble. "I don't know. A public meeting, strategically, would make more sense. The Council would appear to be offering a diplomatic solution as opposed to a military one."

Kaya had a thought. "Maybe they are just buying time until they try a more aggressive military strategy."

The officer returned with a medic, who immediately began working on Kaya's shoulder. Ocativous then said to Kaya, "Look at this while the medic is fixing you."

Octavious walked over to the screen and hit a couple of spots on his tablet. "Look at this attack on the planet Earth. It's their spaceport. This was two days ago."

Kaya intently watched. Octavious froze the image and magnified it. Her jaw slightly dropped when she recognized the pilot. She said, "No…Taz?"

Octavious responded with a nod.

Kaya questioned, "Guess his hiatus is over."

Octavious responded, "Hiatus and independence. The official AuFa response was 'terrorist attack on Earth from the Valmay Group.'"

Kaya responded, "No? After all this time? Why now?"

Octavious turned to look at her sister and said, "I don't know."

Kaya responded, "What are you going to do?"

Octavious spoke, "*We* are going to do nothing. Let's see how they address the issue first. A little added leverage could be beneficial. In the meantime, get fixed up. I have a meeting to prepare for."

BELINEA 2.11

Earth

Northeast Japan

DAG Director Kimakawa was sitting in the chair behind his desk. Vice Director Meyers walked into his office and said, "Director. We have confirmation of the ship Taz returned to."

Kimakawa asked, "Can we confirm where it was headed?"

Meyers shook his head. "It could be any number of places. But the ship made a course adjustment while Taz was attacking SPE."

Kimakawa looked perplexed. "A course adjustment? That means someone was on his main ship."

Meyers stated, "Perhaps even a crew?"

Kimakawa nodded. "Perhaps. We should get this information to Lord Malovex."

Kimakawa hit a couple of spots on his desk, and the robot assistant walked in. In a charming voice, the assistant said, "How may I help, Director?"

Kimakawa said, "I need to get a message to Lord Malovex. Please have Vice Director Meyers give you the file and title it 'Latest Intel'."

The Assistant said, "As you wish, Director. Please advise, Master Sergeant Sabrina Evans of the Odgins Military Academy has requested a meeting late tomorrow afternoon."

Kimakawa was slightly confused. "Master Sergeant Evans? Did she say why?"

The Assistant responded, "She did not. Only that the meeting was important and needed to be conducted in person, privately."

Meyers looked perplexed as well. He said, "Has she ever requested a meeting before?"

Kimakawa bit his lip. He said, "In all the years she has been teaching at the Academy, no."

Meyers added, "That's quite some time. It must be important."

Kimakawa nodded. The Assistant then said, "May I remind the Director that you scheduled a meeting in Scotland tomorrow."

Kimakawa paused for a second. He then said, "Reschedule that meeting and confirm the meeting with the Master Sergeant."

Meyers said under his breath, "Someone is going to be pissed."

Kimakawa rolled his eyes and said, "She will get over it. Any word from Ambassador Bird's transport?"

Meyers responded, "No, sir. But they should be arriving in the Corvalis System soon. If they keep their manifest destination."

Kimakawa very slightly rolled his eyes and said, "I am not holding my breath."

BELINEA 2.12

Lord Malovex's Ship

Lord Malovex was in his common room. Alone, he was eating a steak and having a glass of wine with his meal. His sleek, all-black ship was in an advanced form of Hyper-EXtension, traveling even faster than the Battle Cruisers and Carriers of the AuFa. After finishing his glass, he got up to pour himself another. The cork was jammed as he said out loud, "Speaker, please read the message from Tempest."

A hologram of Tempest appeared on the table. She said, "Efforts with the Avolians have deteriorated. Father has sent Argo to negotiate on our behalf with the Valmay terrorist group. He is confident in a successful outcome…"

Malovex whispered underneath his breath, talking to himself, "That is foolish enthusiasm…"

The message from Tempest continued. "…We have still heard no word from you about the Taz attack on Earth and the current status of the situation. Please advise Father and me when you can. Finally, I saw Quillisar Prill…"

Malovex rolled his eyes as he got the bottle of wine opened. The message from Tempest continued. "…He said to make sure you get to Temple this week for Offerings. Contact us when you can. Tempest out."

Argo poured himself another glass and went back to reading his tablet. As he was, a beeping sound went off on one of the sensors. Annoyed, he ignored it for a few seconds before it went off again. Putting the tablet down, he walked up to the front of the ship.

He sat down in the pilot's chair and hit a button to turn the beep off. He looked at the screen and saw a red blip. As the scope was circling around it, it seemed to be moving. Malovex, talking to himself, said, "There you are…."

He then hit a few more buttons to reveal some systems on the map. He looked at the maps and then back to the red dot that was flashing and moving. He said to himself, "But where are you going?"

BELINEA 2.13

Braccus

Both Tunsall and Trujillo were in the front pilot seats of the C-62T. Commanders Willits and Jones were directly behind them. The ship came out of Hyper-EXtension and was closing in on Braccus. Not going into orbit, Willits quickly scanned the planet. He then saw it and pointed.

Willits said, "Trujillo, take us over there, to the third moon."

Trujillo, after looking at where Willits was pointing, responded, "Copy that."

Tunsall added, "Engage Auxiliary Engines, copy course 2-7-0."

The engines came back to life, and quickly, the C-62T was moving towards the moon. After a moment, Trujillo asked, "Why the moon Commander? Why not just go straight to Braccus?"

Both Trujillo and Tunsall did not turn around, keeping their eyes forward. Willits answered, "Will you two just fly the damn ship?"

Jones half smiled and let Willits' answer linger for a second. Jones then said, "Noone knows we are coming here, we are trying to keep it that way."

The ship banked hard as it came to the entry lights of the moon. Trujillo asked, "Where to, sir?"

Willits and Jones kept peering out the front window. Finally, after a few seconds, Jones saw it. Pointing, he said, "Trujillo, there. The landing pad on the left."

Tunsall was skeptical. "Is that an AuFa Port, sir?"

Jones smiled and said, "No, my two cadets, that is Vandabri."

Trujillo asked "Vanda-what?"

Willits smiled and said, "Vandabri."

Tunsall said, "Isn't Vandabri a trader's port? With casinos, gambling, prostitution, and such?"

Jones sarcastically answered, "So you've heard of it?"

Trujillo asked, "Why are we going here?"

Jones replied, "Because Braccus is very much under Belinean Security and AuFa control. These outer moons offer a bit more scandalous affair, yes. But, more importantly, they are very loosely policed. The AuFa simply doesn't have the manpower to patrol it."

Tunsall was suspicious. He asked, "Is this really a safe place for the Ambassador?"

Jones looked at Willits. "Until we get on board that Battle Cruiser, we are on our own. This is the last place anyone would be looking for the Ambassador."

Trujillo kept flying the craft. They came upon the Port of Vandabri, a sprawling web of landing pads branching out from above-ground tunnels. The facility had lights everywhere, including giant rotating spotlights that lit up the stars above. Trujillo pulled up and softly landed on the empty pad Jones pointed at. Trujillo shut the engines down, and everyone unbuckled. All four men got up and walked out of the cockpit area. They reached the landing doors where Alexis met them. She asked, "Everything ok? Did we just land?"

Willits grabbed a mask and a bag of coins on the upper shelf. Looking at her, he said, "Everything is fine, Miss Devanoe. You can inform the Ambassador we are almost at Braccus."

Alexis did not seem convinced. "He is sleeping."

Jones responded, "Good, no need to wake him."

Jones began putting on a mask. Willits pointed at Trujillo's sidearm pistol and said, "If anyone other than us comes back, shoot them. And immediately take off and take the Ambassador to the AuFa Base on Braccus. Understand?"

Trujillo responded. "Where are you going?"

Willits smiled. Before he put on the mask, he said, "To make sure no one knows we are here."

Willits and Jones walked out the landing doors, with their ventilation masks on. Once they were outside, Alexis asked, "Do you trust those two?"

Trujillo and Tunsall just looked at each other and said nothing. They were all now a bit curious about this unorthodox protocol.

Willits and Jones walked across the landing pad towards the dock doors. Walking in, they took their masks off and hung them up. They proceeded to walk through another set of doors where they were greeted by a fascinating man with green skin and horns coming out of his head. Behind him were two armed security guards. He said, "Gentlemen, welcome to Vandabri. My name is Kovo. I am the Dock Manager."

Willits and Jones walked towards Kovo to size him up. Kovo was tall, a height that exceeded Jones. After looking at him for a moment, Willits said, "We are looking for Madam Rouselle."

Kovo gave the appearance of confusion. "I am sorry, I do not recall anyone here in the Port of Vandabri by the name. Perhaps you are mistaken?"

Jones responded, "I don't think we are."

Kovo looked at the gentlemen for a brief moment before looking out the window and seeing the ship. Kovo said, "Gentlemen, unless I am mistaken, that is an Ambassador transport ship outside. That leads me to believe that you have either stolen a rather expensive ship or that you could possibly have BRG security onboard, which would be rather unfortunate."

Willits smiled and said, "Neither my friend."

Willits held out the small sack of coins and gave them to Kovo to inspect. Willits continued. "Those are Belinean Qusar coins. Sort of the preferred payment for my client instead of Council Credit. Those are for Madam Rouselle if she can still provide some discreet, special attention my client is looking for. Subtract your fee, of course."

Kovo looked at both of them before looking back inside the bag of coins. He smiled and said, "Gentlemen, perhaps we got off on the wrong foot? Right this way."

Willits and Jones followed Kovo. They proceeded to get on a private carrier with one of the security guards now driving. As they scurried off, they noticed how busy the Port was. They rapidly navigated the street tunnels that were crawling with pedestrians and echoing with conversation, music, and a cacophony of other noises. The establishments had neon signs and dark windows, bars, and exotic merchandise in the shops. In and out, quick turns, a couple of near collisions before Kovo yelled over his shoulder. "My apologies, gentlemen, Madam Rouselle has gotten more discreet these days. AuFa security has begun stretching their tentacles where they are not wanted."

Jones yelled, "No problem, but does your driver have to go so fast?"

Kovo smiled. He yelled back, "He can go a lot faster than this."

They were on the private carrier for two more minutes before it stopped in front of a very dark alley situated between two shady buildings. The only light came from the glare of the neon signs. They all got off, and Kovo said, "Gentlemen this way."

Back on the ship, Trujillo, Tunsall, and Alexis were still standing at the doorway. Alexis spoke, "They have been gone a while, should we go after them?"

Both gave her a look of 'are you crazy.'

Trujillo responded, "We are following orders and staying right here."

Alexis than said, "Well, he didn't give me any orders."

Trujillo and Tunsall looked at each other. Alexis put a mask on and walked outside. Tunsall and Trujillo just stared at her as she walked off towards the doors. Once inside, she took her mask off and continued through the entrance of the tunnels. Walking along the dark enclosed streets, she could see aliens of all origins, as the steam helped mask the bars and shops. Alexis continued a bit before ducking into a bar, which was extremely dark and half-busy.

Walking up to the bar, she sat on a stool. The bartender came over and glanced at her before saying, "What will you have?"

Alexis responded, "Any Torsalli wine?"

The bartender just smirked. "Lady, what kind of place do you think this is? I got some Belinean Zollarian red wine."

Alexis smiled and said, "That will do."

The bartender returned and placed it in front of her. She said, "Thanks. Do you know where I can find a Communications Center?"

The bartender replied, "Make a left out of this place and go about fifty meters. On your left will be the Invicto Trading Guild Outpost. They can help you."

○——◉——○

Willits and Jones were walking behind Kovo and the security guard down a dark alley. They walked up to a door with no signage other than a hazy yellow light three meters above. A security guard stood out front. Kovo put his palm print on a box to open the door. Inside was a dark lobby area, a few chairs, and a doorway with beads. Kovo walked through the beaded doorway and said, "Wait here, gentlemen."

After a minute, Madam Rouselle walked out with the bag of coins Willits had given Kovo. Madam Rouselle looked at Willits and Jones. She said, "Avery, I don't know why you keep hanging out with this guy?"

Madam Rouselle, a large and very big breasted woman, came over and hugged Avery. He said, "I only get his money if he gets killed in action or by accident. I'm still waiting."

Madam Rouselle let go, looked up at Jones, and said, "I got a guy that can take care of that for you."

Willits gave a confused look on his face and said, "When did I become the bad guy?"

Madam Rouselle looked at Willits and said, "When you left a tranny with a drunk Vi."

Willits looked incredulous. He said, "I tipped them plenty to cover that…"

Madam Rouselle walked over to Willits and looked him in the eye. She said, "Ain't enough money in the universe to cover that shitshow."

Willits tilted his head and softly said, "It *was* funny…"

Madam Rouselle just kept staring before whispering, "For you…."

She waited a few more seconds before opening her arms and allowing Willits to hug her. She said, "Nolan, you look like shit."

Willits smiled before replying, "But you look great."

She let go of him and said, "No, I don't. I am just getting bigger everywhere."

Willits held up both of his hands to imply breasts. He quickly countered, "Boobs might be bigger…"

Madam Rouselle put both hands on her round belly and said, "And this…"

Madam Rouselle turned around and began walking back through the doorway with beads. Jones and Willits followed her. Jones said, "Ass looks great."

Madam Rouselle said, "That's getting bigger too."

Willits asked, "Who is this Kovo guy?"

Madam Rouselle just shrugged and kept walking. She said, "New Dock Commander. Old one got killed a few weeks back. What can I do for the two of you?"

Willits smiled and said, "I'm gonna make it up to you. I have a client on board that needs some entertainment. Two specifically, for a few hours."

Madam Rouselle was all business now. "Two girls? Any kinky stuff? Bondage? Roll play?"

Jones responded, "No, none of that. I just need two discreet professionals, ones that know how to keep their mouths shut."

Madam Rouselle, still holding the bag, began walking down a flight of stairs. Willits and Jones still followed. She said, "This more than covers that, you sure you don't need anything else?"

Willits smiled again before answering, "I have an Ambassador Transport ship out there that I don't want people asking questions about. How much do you trust Kovo?"

Madam Rouselle smiled back. "The coins buy his discretion. I have a lot of Ambassador clients. I will give Kovo a little extra to hide it in one of the private hangars."

Willits smiled. "Tell him to charge me double, and other than towing it into the hanger, not to touch it."

Madam Rouselle responded, "Got it."

The three then got to the bottom of the stairs, where they went through a doorway. Madam Rouselle said, "Now, let's go pick out a couple of ladies."

The three walked inside into another huge room. It was a lounge setting, very dark, with a bar in the middle and music playing. There were many cozy booths against the walls, with lots of women and men socializing. In the corners were elevated stages with women dancing with little or no clothes on. Some were performing sex acts on stage with each. Some were performing sex with their male clientele in the booths. Some women were watching men perform sex on each other. As they looked around, two beautiful female entertainers grabbed Willits and Jones by the arms. Madam Rouselle looked at both of them and said, "Two ladies right here from Braccus?"

Willits smiled. He knew he had to make it look like he was being specific, even if what he really needed was two mutes. Willits said, "Not quite…."

They began walking around, with Madam Rouselle now following them. They saw one girl on a table, her legs spread without assistance, and then pinning them behind her head. Jones said, "Now that is talent…"

As they passed a more enclosed booth, a woman was pleasuring herself with her hand down her pants while watching a transgender person, tits out, penetrate a man from behind. They had made their way across the room, Madam Rouselle still trailing behind. Through the beads of one room, on a large sofa, they could see a sex act going on.

A woman was in a swing, legs up. A man was penetrating her while standing up. A second woman, scantily dressed, was standing behind him. One hand was draped under his armpit, across the man's chest, grinding her nails across his skin. She was hitting the man from behind across the back of his calf with a small whip. She was whispering in the man's ear, "Are you gonna fuck that?"

The man screamed, "Yes."

She hit him again. Then whispered, "You gonna show her what a man you are?"

The man screamed again, "Yes."

Jones and Willits, still outside the beads that separate the room, continued to watch. Madam Rouselle softly said, "Two exotic, darker skin ladies from Avola. You like Nolan?"

Jones answered, "What is there not to like?"

The girl in the swing screamed out, "Fuck me!"

The second girl hit the man with the whip again. "Fuck her like she is your's."

Still standing outside, Madam Rouselle asked Jones, "Do I need to find a third for you?"

Willits interjected with "Nothing for us, thank you."

Madam Rouselle quickly countered, "Since when do you come here and not leave entertained."

Willits responded, "An enigma, I know, but we're working."

Jones, looking at Madam Rouselle, said, "You should've asked me a couple of days ago when I would've ignored that fact."

Madam Rouselle shrugged her shoulders and said, "Whatever you say."

Willits looked at Madam Rouselle and said, "These ladies will do fine. Do they play cards?"

Back in the bar, Alexis was now in a conversation she did not want to be in. Clearly uncomfortable, she said, "No, I am just waiting on my friend."

The guy was sitting next to her with a drink in his hand. He used his other hand to grab her on the leg as he said, "I don't see him. Looks like he forgot about you."

Alexis tried to look to get the bartender's attention, but he was on the other side of the bar talking with someone else. Alexis was trying to be polite, but that tactic was not working. She pushed his hand off her leg, "I really need to be going, so if you do not mind."

The guy put his hand right back on her leg and said, "Where are you going? You just got here. At least let me buy you another glass of wine."

Alexis was insistent. "No, but I must…"

The guy grabbed her wrist. They struggled for a few more seconds, the man getting more aggressive. He was digging into Alexis' arm when he whispered, "Look, lady, you shouldn't leave without getting what you came in here for."

Alexis looked right at him and said, "But I did."

The man said, "Really? Come on. You know what you want."

Alexis said, "Yeah, a glass of wine. Too bad it came with the dickless prick."

The man said, "Go ahead, bitch, you want to see this prick?"

The man stood up before he was immediately grabbed on the back of the shoulder. As he tried to turn around, Trujillo used his leg as leverage to trip him, throwing him to the ground. Alexis looked up at Trujillo, then stood up behind him. With a serious look, Trujillo said to the guy, "I think the lady said to leave her alone."

The guy on the ground was rolling a bit, trying to get back to his feet. He managed to get on all fours before muttering, "And who the fuck are you?"

Trujillo kept looking down at him before saying very clearly, "I'm the guy that guys like you are scared to fuck with."

The man finally got up, standing in front of Trujillo. He was a couple of inches taller than Trujillo, but clearly a little overweight and not as in good shape. The guy stared Trujillo down as a few people in the bar had now turned to see the ruckus. Trujillo had his jacket open. The man noticed his gun. He said, "Tough guy with a gun. I wonder how tough you are without one."

Trujillo paused for a moment. Then, tilting his head, cracking a tiny smile, he stared right into the guy's eyes. He then grabbed his gun, flipped it over, and caught the barrel side. He turned and handed the gun to Alexis. He then turned back and noticed the guy looked a little shocked. Trujillo then said, "Careful. She might pull the trigger. I'm just gonna break a few bones."

The guy swung at Trujillo, who ducked. Trujillo got two punches in the stomach before another man hit him with a bottle over his head from behind. He scrunched down and turned around. He swung and missed the guy that had hit him. A couple of blows were exchanged, mostly missing Trujillo, before he kicked the guy in the chest that sent him flying across a table. He then turned to Alexis and the other man, who had now come back up to Alexis and said, "Where were we?"

Alexis flipped the pistol over and struck the man directly in the middle of the forehead. He was taken aback but soon regained his senses. He then pulled out a knife and said, "You don't want to shoot me. You just came in here for a good time."

Alexis whipped the pistol around again and pointed it right at the forehead of the man. She tilted her head and said, "You wanna bet?'

The man stared at her for a few seconds. Alexis gave no indication that she was nervous. In fact, she was almost daring him. A few seconds went by before the man backed up and said, "Fucking bitch."

He turned and walked down to the other side of the bar, which went back to normal activity. Trujillo, now with blood running down from the top of his head, took a couple of steps towards Alexis. She flipped the gun over, holding the barrel, and gave it back to Trujillo. As she did, she said, "Both sides of it work."

The C-62T now was in a private hangar that Kovo had arranged. Alexis and Trujillo came walking up to the doors of the ship. Alexis was holding her arm, Trujillo was holding his head, the other hand on the gun. Standing in the common area next to the doors, Tunsall was sipping on coffee with a gun in his hand. On a small round table, Willits and Jones were playing cards with the two very attractive, professional Avolian girls. All four were drinking coffee. Jones then spoke as he laid down a card. "Three of diamonds."

The door opened, and Tunsall helped Alexis in, immediately noticing her arm. Willits and Jones turned as the doors opened, but didn't get up, noticing it was Trujillo and Alexis. Tunsall immediately grabbed a first aid kit on a shelf next to the doors. He threw a towel at Trujillo first, then began wrapping Alexis' arm. Willits glanced over again, still not getting up, and said, "Miss Devanoe, are you alright?"

One of the professional girls then laid a card down. "Seven of spades."

Alexis, letting Tunsall continue to wrap her arm, said, "I am fine, just a bruise."

Jones looked up and offered, "Did Cadet Trujillo try to make a move on you?"

Tunsall then asked Alexis, "What happened?"

Trujillo, annoyed by Jones' comment, was wiping the blood off his head. He then answered for her, "She went off somewhere she shouldn't have."

Willits, still looking at his cards, replied, "She looks alright to me."

One of the professional girls, looking at Trujillo, asked, "Who is the pretty boy, Nolan?"

Willits replied, "That's my security, ladies. He is so good, he needed assistance from Miss Devanoe."

Trujillo, holding a towel over his cut, tilted his head and said, "Really?"

Alexis answered, "I went to the bar across the bay to have a drink, that's all."

Then the other professional girl, still looking at her cards and never looking up, said, "That's Blutoo's girl, bad place. A lot of assholes in there. Jack of hearts."

She threw the Jack down. Jones, cards in one hand, was pouring himself some more coffee in the other. He looked at the girl next to him and said, "More coffee?"

She smiled and said, "Yes, please, thank you."

Willits continued, "Went into a bar and came out with a lump on my head. Don't miss those days. Did Miss Devanoe hit you, pretty boy?"

There was a collective chuckle at the table as Willits had called Trujillo pretty boy. Trujillo took his jacket off and unholstered his gun. "She was talking to some asshole, I intervened."

Tunsall was almost done wrapping Alexis' arm. She said, "I didn't need to be rescued."

Willits, still with his eyes on his cards, glanced up at Trujillo, before looking back at his cards. He then said, "Trujillo, didn't I tell you to stay on the ship? Two of hearts."

He laid the two of hearts down before glancing back up at Trujillo.

Trujillo replied, "I was following Miss Devanoe to make sure she was alright."

Willits, now with a slight scowl, said, "Next time I tell you to stay on the ship, you do it. Same goes for you, Miss Devanoe."

Alexis then looked back at Willits as Tunsall finished wrapping her arm. before saying, "You didn't tell me."

Willits kept looking before replying to Alexis, "But you know better. I cannot protect you and the Ambassador if you keep running off every chance you get."

Alexis just stared at Willits with a disapproving look. Jones then asked, "Anybody follow you? You didn't cause a scene?"

Alexis responded, "As long as you don't count the drunk guy, I bludgeoned in the forehead."

Willits turned and stared down Trujillo. "Really? Where were you?"

Trujillo looked right back at Willits rolling his eyes. "I was defending her...."

Willits looked at him and said, "With what? Bad language?"

Alexis then sat down with some coffee "I don't need defending....it was just a guy who had too much to drink. Nobody important."

Willits went back to playing cards. Jones said, "Hopefully not. We need to keep a low profile."

The other professional girl then laid down a card. "Queen of Spades. Don't worry, Avery. If drunk, unimportant guys were trees, Blutoo's would be a forest."

She took a sip of her coffee. The back door then opened, and the Ambassador, who had been sleeping this whole time, walked into the room. "What the hell is going on here?"

BELINEA 2.14

Battle Cruiser 54 - Corvalis System

Commander Nickalis Devanoe was the watch officer. He had control of the ship currently, or more importantly, he had the Conn, standing where the Captain would. The Corvalis system was a wide range of mostly inhabitable planets, sandwiched between two massive asteroid belts. Most of the planets had ten plus moons, making it an ideal spot for hiding. Devanoe had an entire patrol team looking for Taz. while waiting on Ambassador Bird's ship. According to the manifest, they were already supposed to be there.

The Commander sipped on some coffee. A communications officer came up to him and said, "Sir, this is a communication from Ambassador Bird's ship."

Commander kneeled down to see the message on his screen. He quickly read it, muttering, "They are on Braccus? What the fuck? Out here with our dick in the wind. Lieutenant, get me, Captain Kimmel."

A few moments went by as Devanoe began making some calculations. "Lieutenant Wilcox, status update on the patrol crafts we got out?"

The Lieutenant looked at the screen and replied, "Patrol craft two is twenty minutes from the fourth Planet, which makes it approximately two hours away from us. Patrol craft six just did a sweep of the moons on the second Planet. It is now returning to us and is two and a half hours away. The other four Patrol ships are all about an hour out after doing a complete sweep of the third Planet."

Devanoe sounded pissed. "Lieutenant, call them back in, all of them!"

Captain Kimmel walked onto the bridge of the Battle Cruiser. "Commander Devanoe, what is the status?"

Devanoe stood at attention while simultaneously giving up the Conn to the Captain. "Sir, contact has been made with Ambassador Bird's ship. The DAG team has him on Braccus and has asked that we pick them up there."

The Captain seemed agitated by this discovery. "And no explanation on the change of location or the manifest?"

Devanoe shook his head, "No, sir."

The Captain then asked, "All the patrol craft still out looking for Taz?"

Devanoe responded, "Yes, sir. I've already called them back, but it will take at least 2.5 hours to get them all on board."

The Captain thought for a moment, then realized he did not have that kind of time. "Where did this DAG team say they were on Braccus?"

Devanoe responded, "They did not say, sir. The transmission came from that area, but it's not the AuFa Base, they would've already notified us. They are likely hiding somewhere else."

The Captain was now really annoyed. "Well, the DAG team clearly does want us to know where they are, and telling the AuFa to go looking for them might send up the wrong signals if Taz intercepts the message. So, I guess we are forced to play their little game."

Captain Kimmel looked at the screen again. Then addressed Devanoe. "Take a T141 transport and load it with two Sirator Fighters. Take two of your pilots and a security detail team to Braccus. Once there, reconnect with that transmission, and get them on that AuFa base. Get the local BRG to help you. As soon as I get all the Patrol Craft back, I will meet you there."

Devanoe responded and saluted before leaving. "Copy that, Sir."

BELINEA 2.15

Braccus

Port Braccus

Port Braccus was a mammoth and sprawling facility. In the middle was a colossal Control Tower, one hundred and fifty meters high. Around it were eight smaller towers, fifty meters high and two kilometers away. The Control Tower and smaller towers were connected by elevated trains and bridges. Each of the eight smaller towers had eight concourses branching out from it to handle the volume of transport traffic. A separate elevated train with a Walkway Tunnel Bridge connected the entire facility to the Terminal of Port Braccus. The Terminal served as an entry point to Braccus City, a vast metropolis with several hundred tall buildings, each two hundred meters plus high.

A sizeable civilian transport had just landed. It's doors opened, allowing the eighty passengers to exit onto the concourse. Dressed all in red, with his hood over his head, a Quillisar Priest grabbed a bag and continued out to the concourse. The chain was visible, while the silvery ring and orange stone it held was not, hidden behind the red cloak. He boarded a train carrying a small bag in his folded hands. The train took him across the long elevated bridge over to the Port Braccus Terminal Building. Getting off with several other passengers, he made his way to the security guards. One inspected his bag of gifts and boxes with bows on them. He asked, "Gifts my Quillisar?"

The Quillisar Priest, still with his head down and the hood completely hiding his head, nodded slightly. He let the Port security guard scan his ID bracelet, and the guard let him through. The Quillisar Priest walked out and down to the immense pedestrian traffic of Braccus City. He turned down a few streets, first turning right, then left, then right again. A few times, he passed Belinean officers, who all nodded and respectfully said, "Quillisar…"

After walking twelve blocks, the Quillisar Priest found the massive Temple. He walked up the steps and then inside. The Temple was packed, with several people, including children, soldiers, and families, all in prayer. The Quillisar Priest went into one of the pews, looking up at the diamond-shaped object on the wall. In the middle aisle, people formed a line to get to the Head Quillisar in front of the altar. Each person gave him an offering, or gift, to lay on the altar. After, they made the shape of the diamond with both hands. The families then went off to the side of the altar, where another Quillisar would ask the children, "The sun is where my child?"

The child answered, "In the Quill my Quillisar."

The Quillisar then gave each a present, wrapped in a box. Both the child and parent nodded.

After a minute, the Red Priest stood up and joined the line down the center aisle. One by one, people laid an offering down in front of the Head Quillisar. After a minute, the Quillisar Priest finally got to the front altar. The Head Quillisar said, "Offering Quillisar?"

The Quillisar Priest pulled out a small red box from inside his sack. He put it down in front of the Head Quillisar, adding it to the other offerings. But the Quillisar Priest failed to make the diamond shape sign with his hands. His ring was unusually beneath his cloak. The Head Quillisar was slightly confused and miffed, but said nothing, as there was still a long line of people behind. The Quillisar Priest then walked to the side altar where the families were. He took five boxes out and put them on the pile of boxes. The other Quillisar acknowledged the offering and nodded. The Quillisar, still holding his bag, walked to the back of the Temple.

Passing several people, he made it to the back corner. He kneeled in front of a table with a hundred candles and took out a small blue box. Opening it, he took out the plastic wrapping contents with wires in it and stuck it underneath the tabletop. Getting up, he walked to the other side of the room to the other table with a hundred candles. He did the same, sticking the plastic wire contents underneath the tabletop. With the sack now empty, he disposed of it underneath the table. He walked over to the giant front doors and proceeded to walk out of the Temple. As he was going down the steps, a few soldiers bowed their heads out of respect and said, "Quillisar…."

The Quillisar Priest began to walk back to the Terminal Building, taking the same route. A small girl came running up to him with an offering in her hand. The girl tried to hand it to the Quillisar Priest. She said, "Offering…."

The Quillisar Priest stopped. Standing there motionless, he didn't extend his hands to accept the gift. After a moment, the girl, still holding the present out, said, "Offerings Quillisar…."

Finally, her father walked up and pulled the girl to the side. He said, "Sorry, Quillisar. My daughter is still learning the proper way to give offerings, forgive her. "

But the Quillisar Priest did nothing. The father then grabbed the offering from his daughter's hand, and after bowing his head said, "Offerings in the name of the Quill, Quillisar…."

But the Quillisar Priest still did nothing. He took a step to the side and just continued walking toward the Terminal building. The man and his daughter were left speechless. Baffled by the events that just took place, the man yelled, "Hey, Quillisar!"

Back at the Temple, the line began to diminish. The Head Quillisar looked over to the other Quillisar, gesturing for a break. Remembering, the Head Quillisar grabbed the red box the Quillisar Priest had left. He walked off towards the back of the Temple as the other Quillisar immediately replaced him on the altar. He turned a corner and made his way to a private room. There, he took off his glorious red priest cloak and picked up the red box to inspect. He tried to remove the top, but it was somehow taped. He opened a drawer from the table next to him. He scurried through various candles, matches, pens, and other objects until he found the small letter knife. He took it out and began cutting the tape on the box.

Out near the altar, off to the side, a father and son lined up to another Quillisar. The Quillisar asked the son when he approached, "The sun is where my child?"

The son answered, "In the Quill my Quillisar."

The Quillisar grabbed the blue box left behind by the Quillisar Priest and gave it to the child for correctly answering. The father and his son walked away, carrying the blue box the Quillisar Priest had left. They made their way to the back pews, where they entered to continue praying. The son, ever so impatient, opened the blue box and discovered a toy silver AuFa battle cruiser, with immense detail. It had a small button on the back. But when the boy pushed it, nothing happened. The father, now noticing what the boy had done, told him, "No, Samuel. The toy is for after. You must pray to the Quill first."

The boy, still annoyed that the toy is clearly supposed to light up but doesn't, kept pushing the button, waiting for something to happen.

The Quillisar Priest began walking away faster from the man and his daughter. He turned down another street and continued until he arrived at the steps of the Terminal Building. Navigating through the crowd, with the hood of his cloak still shielding his head, he moved his way to the front of security as most people let him pass by. When he got to the guard, he displayed his ID bracelet for the guard to scan. The guard signaled him through, and as he did, he reached into his bright red cloak pocket and took out a small box with a button.

The little girl and her father, still bewildered by the Quillisar's behavior on the street, entered the Temple. Holding hands with her father as they entered, she glanced off to the side. Turning toward her father, she asked, "A prayer for mother first?"

The father nodded, and the two walked over to the table with the hundred burning candles. They both kneeled in front of it. Grabbing a long match together, they lit a candle. The girl saw a bag underneath the table. Picking it up, she asked her father, "What is this?"

In the private back room behind the altar, the Head Quillisar was still trying to cut through the tape on the offering box left by the Quillisar Priest. Little by little, he eventually cut through it. The Head Quillisar put the knife down and slowly opened the box. His eyes got big as he inspected the contents. A rectangular wrapping with a couple of small wires plugged into it.

After the Quillisar Priest made it safely through security, he held the small box in his hand. He pushed the button on it.

Back at the Temple, in the back pews, the boy holding the toy Battle Cruiser immediately got excited when he saw it light up. It made a funny noise, almost as if the toy ship engaged itself somehow. The father saw the toy and suddenly got very confused. The boy began waving the toy Cruiser back and forth. He finally pushed the small button on the back of it.

The Head Quillisar was holding the box when the bomb exploded. It disintegrated him immediately. The bombs underneath the candle tables went next. A wall of fire consumed the father and the little girl, who was still holding up the empty sack. People just outside were thrown back thirty meters as the Temple exploded in front of them. In a matter of seconds, the Temple was obliterated with an explosion that went a hundred meters high and a wall of fire that spread out for blocks. The surrounding buildings all had damage, with windows blown out and heavy debris from the church flying everywhere. People on the street were even knocked back from the blast. Smoke, fire, and chaos were everywhere.

A BRG officer, knocked over from the blast, got up, and saw two bodies, fifteen meters in front of him. The heat was immense, but he ran up to the still flaming bodies. He grabbed the child's arm to pull him away, but only managed to pull burning skin instead. He squinted his eyes to look and saw there was no hope for them. After debating for a few seconds, he started walking back the other way to help others, realizing no one inside had survived.

The Quillisar Priest kept walking through the Terminal Building despite everyone clearly hearing the explosion. In the chaos, a BRG security team began running towards the front of the security station. The Quillisar Priest just kept walking in the other direction, along with hundreds of other people, now terrified. One BRG Officer, Lieutenant Storm, sprinted through the crowd toward the Temple, shouting, "Out of the way, let me through."

The Quillisar Priest kept navigating the crowd. Lieutenant Storm ran right into the Quillisar Priest, knocking him down. The small box popped out of his hand and onto the ground a few feet away. Storm landed awkwardly on his feet with the assistance of one hand. Realizing he had just run over a Quillisar, he stopped to help him back up. But first, he saw the box and grabbed it. He held it out to offer it back and said, "My apologies Quillisar….."

As the Quillisar Priest made it to his feet, Lieutenant Storm took another look at the box, noticing its button. The Quillisar Priest tried to walk off, ignoring what just happened. But Storm immediately grabbed his arm, to not let him get away. As he turned him around, Storm took his other hand and removed the red hood from the Quillisat Priest to reveal the blood-red mask of Taz. In a very swift move, Taz grabbed the silvery ring hanging around his neck underneath his cloak. He broke it from its chain and turned it into a saber, immediately slicing the hand Storm was using to hold him. In a reverse move the other way, Taz jabbed the red saber into Storm's shoulder. It was a glancing blow, enough to knock him backward off his feet.

People immediately started screaming. Two more guards who were ahead of the pack immediately turned around and saw the struggle. Taz began sprinting towards the Walkway Tunnel Bridge, which led to the Towers. One of the guards, struggling to see what was going on, yelled, "Everybody down!!!!!"

A few people began falling on the floor, but most people were still trying to scurry away. After a few seconds, one of the guards got impatient. He pointed his rifle towards the ceiling and fired three shots. That got everyone's attention. Almost everyone in the room was now screaming and got down on the floor. The other BRG officer saw Taz running towards the Walkway

Tunnel Bridge, jumping over people in the process. Aiming his rifle at Taz from forty meters away, he thought about taking a shot. But Taz reached onto his hip and dropped a smoke grenade, leaving a colossal cloud all around him. Unable to see Taz, the two BRG officers began running toward the smoke cloud.

Taz turned down a large corridor and then turned back the other way to the Walkway Tunnel Bridge entrance. The Bridge was enclosed in glass, allowing its pedestrians a full view of the Port. As Taz was running across the Bridge, the crowds were dispersing, trying to get out of his way. Taz had made it two thirds across when he noticed four BRG officers on the other side. Their rifles loaded and pointed, one of them yelled, "Everyone down!!"

As the four walked briskly toward Taz, he immediately turned around and sprinted back the way he came. As he made it to the halfway point across the bridge, he could see the other two BRG officers had made it through the smoke and were now joined by two more BRG officers coming from that side. These four also had rifles loaded and pointed at Taz. One of them shouted, "Everybody drop down on the floor!!!!!"

Taz did not move, he was stuck in the middle. Both sides had four BRG officers, rifles ready to shoot. Every time they passed a civilian lying down, they got up and ran the other way. Slowly, they made it to the center of the bridge, each team of four BRG officers ten meters away. One yelled directly at Taz. "Drop your weapon!! Get down on your knees now!!!"

BRG Lieutenant Storm finally got to his feet and began running toward the Walkway Tunnel Bridge.

Back at the tunnel, Taz was motionless as the teams were inching closer. Taz dropped down to his knees and sat on his locked ankles behind him. The BRG officers inched closer, now six meters away. Taz held out his red, hollow, diamond-shaped saber. The saber got bigger as Taz held it first, a hundred eighty degrees away from him, then as the hole in the saber got bigger, another ninety degrees upwards towards his body. He moved the diamond-shaped saber over his head. The BRG officers had stopped moving, now a mere five meters away. One finally yelled, "Drop your fucking weapon, NOW!!!!"

The saber then expanded and turned to flames. The entire saber shot a burst of fire from each side of the diamond shape. The wall of fire continued towards the BRG officers, who had stayed, and were now burning. It kept extending out down the Bridge, burning everyone in sight. The fire continued for ten seconds before it finally stopped. The eight BRG officers were charred beyond recognition. A few people further away, were not burned quite as bad, but nevertheless were rolling on the floor in agony.

Lieutenant Storm had just made it to the Walkway Tunnel Bridge when the wall of fire came down. He immediately turned to the side just outside the tunnel and felt the flames pass him into the large Terminal room. Once the flames subsided, He continued into the very charred Tunnel Bridge.

Taz got up from his squat position and punched the glass window next to him with the back of his saber. The glass broke quickly, charred by the fire, and losing its integrity. A rush of cool air from outside came through. Taz waited a few seconds. Lieutenant Storm, gun drawn, was running down the tunnel. Taz, using the red Quillisar cape as a glider/parachute, jumped from the window. He landed, some ten meters below, on top of a transport shuttle rolling underneath.

Taz looked up, noticing no security had followed him. BRG Lieutenant Storm ran past the window and saw Taz riding away below. He immediately began running down the other side of the Tunnel Bridge. Taz glanced up at the overhead train and saw a team of BRG officers heading towards the next stop that was ahead of him. Three were looking right at him, while a fourth was on his wrist radio. The transport shuttle Taz was riding came to a stop in front of a parked transport ship. Civilians began getting out of the shuttle to board the ship.

The BRG officers ran out of the train when it stopped and down the numerous stairs, before taking the extended walkway that went out to the ship. One stopped on the outdoor stairwell, and pointed his rifle towards Taz. He shot three times. Taz ducked after the first shot missed him badly. He then rolled off the transport shuttle to the ground, and back underneath the shuttle. The first BRG officer stopped in front of the transport ship, waving his hands at the pilot to turn off the engines. As civilians exited the shuttle to board the ship, the other two BRG officers were yelling, "Everyone alright? Get down!"

Meanwhile, Lieutenant Storm came down to the surface. He got in a transport car and immediately darted toward where Taz was with the civilian transport ship.

Taz, still underneath the shuttle, noticed an emergency door. He took his diamond-shaped saber, and pierced it through the door. It narrowly missed a civilian. A woman shocked to see the blade protrude from the floor. Taz twisted his blade before forcing the door open. He tossed a smoke grenade inside, which immediately filled the entire cabin of the transport shuttle. A BRG officer was at the other door. As he assisted the next civilian forced to get off, the blade of Taz's diamond-shaped saber came out from underneath the civilian's arm. Taz stabbed the BRG officer on his side, between his ribs where his protection shell did not cover. Taz then kicked the civilian down the steps from behind. The BRG officer tried to get a round off with his pistol, but Taz twisted his saber blade further into the ribs. The BRG officer keeled over as Taz removed his blade.

One of the other BRG officers, a mere five meters away, slowly turned around to see what was going on. Taz began running towards him, flipping into the air and somersaulting behind him before knowing what happened. He got off one shot before Taz sliced his head off.

The other BRG officer was on the other side of the Transport shuttle, still looking for Taz. He heard what was going on and ran around to the other side of the transport, rifle drawn. As he turned the corner, Taz was kneeling, waiting for him. He swiped his saber blade into the BRG officers' knees, immediately taking him out. Face first, laying down, Taz took his saber and pierced the BRG officer behind the neck.

Taz ran to the entrance of the Transport ship. The BRG officer from the stairwell got off another shot that glanced off Taz's shoulder, spinning him 180 degrees back towards the ground. He quickly got up and sprinted up the entrance. Taz, now bleeding from his shoulder, began running up towards the cockpit. He passed one of the flight officers, who asked, "Hey, what's going on out there?"

Taz immediately stabbed him in the stomach and kicked him off his blade. He then passed two flight crew members without any resistance. They two immediately ran out the door and off the ship. When Taz finally got to the cockpit, he saw the pilot look back, but it was too late. Taz slit his throat with his saber, then yanked the pilot out of his seat. Jumping into the pilot's chair, he immediately turned the engines back on. Within a few seconds, engines roaring, Taz got the transport ship off the ground.

Lieutenant Storm had pulled up, just as Taz was taking off. Glancing to the side, he noticed the dead BRG bodies on the ground. He drove the transport car to another side of the base.

Taz slowly turned out of the Port, twice almost hitting other ships landing on other pads. He heard over his radio, "Transport 3719, you do not have clearance for takeoff. All ships are now to be grounded, by order of the BRG and AuFa, do you copy?"

Taz hit a couple of buttons, and the voice was muted. Taz continued out of the city, accelerating but not rising in altitude. He flew a few more minutes before getting to the outskirts of the city.

Lieutenant Storm ran out of the transport car before it even came to a complete stop. He got out near two parked F-81 Sirator Fighters. He sprinted towards one, climbing up the ladder and jumping into the cockpit. Storm fired up the engines as another pilot raced to the other F-81 Fighter and climbed up the ladder. Storm got his fighter off the ground and quickly flew it in the direction of where Taz went.

As Taz cleared the city, he got to the mountains. About a minute later, he found a desolate area where his transport ship was parked. He eventually slowed down, preparing to land his craft near the transport. As Taz was about three meters off the ground, closing in on his landing, a shot came across his bow. Taz never saw the F-81 Sirator being flown by Lieutenant Storm. The second shot hit Taz's transport ship directly in the left engine. The engine exploded, spinning the transport out of control until it thudded to the ground in a cloud of smoke.

Lieutenant Storm circled around in the F-81 after noticing the crash landing of Taz's transport. The second F-81 slowed down behind him, now hovering directly over the crash site.

Taz stumbled out of the crash site and onto the landing surface. Still, with his mask on, he looked up at the F-81 that was hovering above, while the second F-81 flown by Storm had now circled back. Taz put his hands on top of his head. Storm wanted to shoot, but he needed more answers. He said on the com radio, "Do not shoot him, we need him alive."

As the words came out of his mouth, two black fighters flew upon the sands behind the F-81's and fired multiple rounds. One of the F-81's took a direct hit, spinning a hundred yards away before exploding on impact. The F-81 that Storm was piloting got hit in the engine and spun to the ground in a similar fashion to Taz's craft. It crash-landed twenty meters away from Taz.

The two black fighters circled back around, now hovering over the multiple crash site. Taz walked briskly over to the F-81 Lieutenant Storm had crashed. Storm, trying to get his bearings, began looking for his weapon. Taz walked more briskly towards Storm, now drawing his saber. Storm was bleeding from his head as Taz got to the craft. Taz jumped three meters into the air, landing on to the top cockpit frame. Storm found a button and locked the cockpit window frame from opening. Taz first tried to penetrate the window with his blade but to no avail. After staring at Storm for a few seconds, Taz reached into his red cloak and pulled out a small grenade. He ripped a tag off it and stuck it to the cockpit window. Taz quickly jumped off and jogged away from the downed F-81.

Lieutenant Storm was puzzled. The two black fighters were now hovering next to him, guns pointed right at him. The grenade was clearly on a timer, and he kept staring at it. Taz, meanwhile, walked over to his big transport that was waiting for him. Just as he took his first step walking up the ramp from the back, the grenade went off, instantly killing Evans and putting a large hole full of black smoke in the cockpit window of the downed F-81.

Taz entered the Transport ship, and within a few seconds, fired up its engines, and very slowly took off. Within a minute, the transport ship was flying away, the two all-black fighters flanking each side as they headed off to space.

BELINEA - EPISODE 3
BRACCUS

BELINEA 3.1

2137 - Serpia (Twenty years prior.)
Space Battle Station Two

The speaker was loud and clear. "Station evacuation in twenty minutes. Repeat. Station Evacuation in twenty minutes. All personnel must transfer to outbound ships to Belinea. Repeat, all personnel must transfer to outbound ships to Belinea."

Quillisar Farra knew there would not be much time. Time was the enemy. Soldiers, officers, and all forms of personnel were briskly jogging, some running through the corridors. She walked down two flights, and onto another deck. Another 50 meters and she turned to a dock loading wounded onto a huge medical cargo ship. Quickly, she walked through the chaos of medical teams and soldiers, about two hundred in all, helping everywhere they could. A steady stream of soldiers were being carried onto the ship. Only a couple managed to get out "Quillisar...." from under their lips, but the frantic pace everyone was at gave no time for pleasantries.

Quillisar Farra looked around, then saw Quillisar Sallor. Sallor was still a Quillisar in training, a red cloth for where his diamond should be. He was young compared to Quillisar Farra but was nearing the completion of his Quillisar training. Sallor was addressing a soldier, helping a doctor seal some wounds, and apply bandages. Quillisar Farra grabbed Sallor by the shoulder and whispered into his ear, "Sallor, a word, please."

Sallor turned his head and saw who it was. He immediately looked at the Doctor, who was finishing up. The Doctor nodded.

Sallor turned, wiping the blood off his hands with a towel from the wounded soldiers' gurney. A cacophony of people shouting orders and yelling commands was echoing through the area. Sallor responded, "Yes, Quillisar Farra?"

Farra was a little surprised. "Helping the wounded Quillisar Sallor?"

Sallor responded. "Four years of medical school, before I decided my passion for the Quill, overcame all other things in my life."

Farra nodded her head in approval. "The Energy finds us all in different times. How are the wounded?"

Sallor was still wiping blood off his hands. "Still coming, Quillisar. We have treated a few hundred, some fatalities. Hopefully, we can retreat with minimal losses."

Farra continued. "Quillisar, the time has come for you to do your part for the Quill."

The conversation had become much more serious. Farra was an older, very respected Quillisar. Sallor straightened up. "Anything for the Quill, my Quillisar."

Farra walked one more step away and took a peek around to make sure no one watched them. Which, given the chaos, was a solid bet. Farra continued. "I am going to ask you not to respond verbally, just nod."

Sallor nodded with a look of slight confusion on his face. Quillisar Farra reached into her pocket and pulled a small object out. She held it in her hand. "Do you know what this is?"

Sallor looked at it for a second, then after realizing what it was, looked directly at Farra and nodded his head.

Quillisar Farra then said, "Good. Do you know where to find them?"

Sallor paused for a moment, blinked his eyes, and then nodded 'yes.'

Farra then said, "The Quill is counting on you. I need at least one hundred and fifty. Get them, and meet me on Slip 41 in ten minutes. "

Sallor walked off. Quillisar Farra walked out of the docking bay, back to the corridors of the station. She went down a long hallway, turning a couple of times before getting to the elevator shaft. She rode the elevator down many flights. It finally stopped at Level 2. She got out to a circular bay with doors all around. The bay was full of broken ships, small cargo ones, a few F-36 Pirra's that had been damaged in combat. Farra looked around until she found her mark, Commander Kimmel. Kimmel was talking to two soldiers. "Leave those behind. They are unsalvageable anyway. The F-36's and the rest of these can be taken out with the C-16 if they will fit. Otherwise, we leave them behind also. We got less than ten minutes!"

Farra reached the Commander and said, "Commander Kimmel."

Kimmel responded, quite surprised to see Farra. "Quillisar Farra, what are you doing here?"

Farra saw the other two soldiers and immediately said, "Leave us."

The two soldiers scurried away. Quillisar Farra continued. "Orders to leave immediately?"

Commander Kimmel responded, "I am prioritizing damaged ships, what we can salvage. By now, everything should be off the planet. The AuFa has about twenty minutes or so to get everything off this station. I would hope the Serpians will give us slightly more time for medical and salvage ships, but the Cruisers and Carriers need to be gone."

Farra asked, "Salvage ships?"

Kimmel continued. "Yes, they clean up damaged ships, transports, fighters, and equipment. As long as all the troops are gone, the Serpians will give us a few more hours to take the ships away and properly retreat. They don't want us to lay behind any hidden bombs in the ships that could damage them."

Quillisar Farra continued. "Do you have any salvage ships left at your disposal?"

Kimmel did some calculations. "Yes, Quillisar. That TCX-46 over there (pointing to the largest ship in the bay). My orders are to triage equipment, damaged transports, and fighters, and salvage what I can on my way out."

Quillisar Farra looked intently at this ship Kimmel just pointed to. She then looked back at Commander Kimmel and said, "Sergao, the Quill needs you."

Kimmel reiterated his beliefs. "Anything my Quillisar."

Farra continued, almost giving an order. "Finish-up here, quickly. Don't worry about your AuFa orders. The Quill will need that ship for something else. Meet me at Slip 41 in ten minutes."

Commander Kimmel just nodded and muttered, "Yes, my Quillisar."

Quillisar Farra returned to the elevator. The loudspeaker sounded off again. Lights in the station were constantly flashing yellow and red. The corridors were a scene of chaos and uncertainty.

"Station Evacuation in Fifteen Minutes. You have Fifteen minutes to get to an outbound ship to Belinea. All personnel report to their Commanding officers for immediate evacuation."

Quillisar Fara rode the elevator a few more flights back up. When it got to level 10, she got off. She then went down a short corridor and turned down another corridor. Soldiers and personnel were still running through the corridors. An alarm was now on, going off every five seconds in conjunction with the flashing red lights. She got to a sliding door, put her hand on the wall for the hand ID reader, and calmly said, "Quillisar Farra."

The door opened, and Farra rushed inside. Still in her red cloak, she got a small bag and began putting things in it. Not clothes, but items. What looked like a couple of religious artifacts, a book, a handful of colorful stones, were all thrown in. She then stared at a Diamond-shaped artifact, hanging on her wall. After staring at it for about ten seconds, she yanked it off the wall and threw it into the bag. She then exited the room, bag in hand.

She went back down the short corridor and returned to the elevator, taking it upwards to level 14. She got off and began walking down a very long aisle, with clear marks for landing slips 31 through 42, even on the right and odd on the left. People were filling up the slips in large bunches, awaiting transports to take them to the large Carriers, or if it was a more significant slip, a large enough ship. The alarms and flashing red lights continued, along with people frantically running. She briskly walked down the corridor until she got to the end where Dock 41 was on the left, and 42 was on the right. There was a notable Diamond shape figure above the walkway to dock 41. Clearly, this was the religious dock used for members of the Quill.

Quillisar Farra could see out the window at the ships leaving. She diligently stood there, head down now, almost in prayer. After about a minute, Quillisar Sallor came jogging up with a bag in his hand. Farra looked at the bag Sallor was carrying and immediately asked, "You were successful? "

Sallor was out of breath, but nodded his head 'yes.'

The two stood there for a moment. Chaos was still all around them, as the docks were clearing out with all the personnel now finally leaving. Alarms and red lights were still flashing. Sallor eventually noticed the bag that Quillisar Farra was holding. Sallor asked, "Quillisar Farra, what is in your bag?"

Farra looked at Sallor and very calmly said, "Salvation."

Sallor did not understand. Before he could ask, he noticed a ship coming up to slip 41. Quillissar Farra saw it as well. "Our ship is here."

Sallor asked, "Where are we going?"

Farra and Sallor walked through the first set of dock doors. Commander Kimmel brought up the TCX-46 ship to gently dock with slip 41, and it's second set of doors. Farra said nothing.

The two red-cloaked priests waited a few more seconds until the yellow rotating light went off and turned green. The doors opened, and it led to the entrance of the relatively large salvage cargo ship. Turning the corner to greet them was Commander Kimmel. "As you asked, Quillisar."

Quillisar Farra then asked, "You came alone, Commander, yes?"

Commander Kimmel responded, "Yes, my Quillisar."

The three of them began walking back to the cockpit of the Cargo ship. Quillisar Farra finally said, " We need to get to slip seven. We have a duty to perform."

BELINEA 3.2

Twenty Years Later...

The Corvalis System

Battle Cruiser 54

Captain Kimmel had the conn of Battle Cruiser 54. He was still waiting for all his patrol crafts to return so he could leave this system and get his ship to Braccus. Kimmel took a sip of his coffee before asking, "Lieutenant Wilcox, status of the patrol craft?"

Wilcox turned and looked directly at Kimmel. Wilcox was using a pointer on the map that Kimmel could see from his conn chair. "Three heading back now, they inspected this area of the system, here, and here. These five are back onboard. So far, they have found nothing, sir."

As Kimmel took another sip of coffee, his sonar officer shouted out. "Sir, I have an unidentified incoming ship, coming in rapidly."

Kimmel got out of his Captain's chair and walked over to the sonar computer screen. He looked down at the map, as an officer pointed. "Here, sir. Bearing 2-8-0, speed is HX-12.5, and slowing down."

Kimmel responded, "Any other ships?"

The officer responded, "Negative Captain. The ship is by itself.."

Kimmel asked, "Size of the ship?"

The officer looked puzzled. "Not sure, sir, but not prominent. Can not verify but a small Transport ship at best. And I would say with some stealth capabilities given we did not see it until now. "

Kimmel looked concerned. "Lieutenant Wilcox, hail the incoming vessel. Ask to identify. Lieutenant Morrow, have torpedoes one and two locked in on the incoming target. Also, have those two F-81 Sirator's ready on standby."

Both Lieutenants nodded in affirmative. There was a very long ten-second pause. The sonar officer finally broke the tension. "Vessel is still decelerating rapidly, down to HX 3.2, still heading right for us."

The Communications officer interjected. "Captain, the vessel has identified himself as Lord Malovex, sir. The code is a match."

Captain Kimmel began walking off the bridge, over to the transport elevator. Speaking as he walked, he was still shouting orders. "Open bay door Two, tell Lord Malovex to proceed there. Wilcox, get those patrol ships back and give me a status of where Commander Devanoe is."

A sleek, all dark grey ship with black stripes, and no military markings, Malovex was slowing down to less than Hyper-EXtension speed. His ship proceeded straight to Bay Two of Battle Cruiser 54. With landing gear opening, it hovered as it came inside the bay. The massive cargo bay doors behind him began to close. The sleek ship gently landed on the Battle Cruiser's bay floor, just as the doors behind it sealed shut. The smaller doors in front of the elegant ship opened, just as Captain Kimmel came walking down a set of steel stairs from the flight deck, security team in tow.

A belly door opened from underneath the sleek grey ship, and Lord Malovex came walking out, greeted just in time by Captain Kimmel. "Lord Malovex, I was not aware of your planned arrival."

Malovex kept his hood on for a few steps, before finally laying it rest on his shoulders to reveal his scarred face. He walked directly up to Kimmel but gave no indication that he would stop or ask for permission to come aboard. He certainly did not need it. "That is because no one knows I am here."

Kimmel had never seen this ship before. "Lord Malovex, I am not familiar with this ship. It was not detected with our sonar until a rather uncomfortable proximity to our ship, at an outstanding speed as well."

Malovex kept walking towards the flight deck. "Good, then it works. It is experimental; the SS has been working on it. Speed capabilities are outstanding. Record time on my trip to Earth, and to here I imagine."

The two began walking together back to the Flight deck, side by side. A security team followed them, albeit a bit more relaxed now that they confirmed it was Lord Malovex on this ship and not anyone else. Kimmel continued as they walked. "I see. What can I help you with Lord Malovex?"

Malovex did not stop walking. "Captain, your orders from the AuFa were to wait here in the Corvalis system for this transport with the Earth Ambassador and his DAG team, and then to take them to Torsalli, correct?"

Kimmel kept walking as well. "Yes, sir. That was the plan. Until I got a communication from his DAG team saying they were on Braccus."

Malovex stopped cold. "Braccus? Did the orders change?"

Kimmel now stopped and looked at Malovex. "Not on my side, sir. But the DAG team was adamant about meeting them there and canceling the original orders."

Malovex then questioned, "Then why are you still here?"

Kimmel was stern. "I was waiting on my patrol ships to all get back. They were conducting a complete sweep of the area looking for Terrorists. After the Earth attack, the AuFa sent a communication putting us on alert that Taz might be here for the Ambassador. I sent my First officer and a couple of fighters on a T141 transport to Braccus. They are to keep the Ambassador, with BRG help, in a lockdown at the AuFa base on Port Braccus."

Malovex pondered this for a second. "So the orders did not come from the BRG or anyone else? Just a communication from this DAG team?"

Kimmel said, "Yes, sir."

Malovex then continued, "And you told no one on Braccus that you were sending your first officer on a T-141 transport to reach them?"

Kimmel "Not yet, sir. I imagine they won't know until my first officer gets there."

Malovex continued to walk, with Kimmel about a quarter step behind. As they got to the flight deck bridge, Lieutenant Wilcox came up, out of breath from running, and stood at attention in front of both of them, saluting. "Captain. Lord Malovex. I just got a communication. There is a terrorist incident near Port Braccus. They believe it was Taz, sir."

Kimmel was slightly stunned. "We will leave for Braccus as soon as all the patrol ships are in."

Malovex was not as confident. "I am sure the BRG and AuFa are doing all they can do. In the meantime, our best chance of catching Taz is staying right here. If the intended target is still the Earth Ambassador, Taz must think they are heading here to the Corvalis system."

Kimmel turned to Malovex and said, "Or he already found out that the Ambassador and his DAG detail were already on Braccus."

Malovex pondered. "Perhaps...."

Lieutenant Wilcox added, "Captain, the AuFa gave us orders to head to Braccus to assist at best speed."

Malovex thought for a moment before speaking, "What else do you have on this BattleCruiser, Captain?"

Kimmel responded, "Four F-81 Sirator fighters, one more T-141, and 8 P-21 Patrol ships. It is a Battle Cruiser Lord Malovex, not a carrier."

Malovex acknowledged. "Understood. Then we are going to delay those orders, Captain."

Captain Kimmel raised an eyebrow. "Excuse me, sir?"

Malovex gave an order. "Captain, your Battle Cruiser will stay here with me while we wait for Taz to show up. The Ambassador is safe on Braccus. If there is any danger, have your first officer escort him to Torsalli on that transport you sent."

Captain Kimmel was not happy. In his head, he thought, 'taking orders from Malovex?'

He did not like this at all.

BELINEA 3.3

Third Moon of Braccus - Vandabri

Ambassador Bird still seemed annoyed, even though it had been well over an hour after the arguing. Everything had been explained, and he had time to get something to eat. The Ambassador was now going over some reports, sitting behind his desk. Alexis Devanoe walked into the room and handed the Ambassador a file. "The file you wanted, sir."

The Ambassador spoke, but it was undoubtedly disingenuous. "Thank you, Miss Devanoe."

Alexis could tell something was still troubling him. "Still upset, sir?"

The Ambassador responded, "What makes you think that?"

Alexis crossed her arms. "Because when you are miffed about something, or at me, you call me Miss Devanoe instead of Alexis."

Ambassador Bird looked up. He stared at Alexis for a few seconds. "Just because I understand their intentions, doesn't mean I have to like it. These two DAG officers, Willits and Jones. Their unorthodox methods are just an unnecessary burden. These precautions are ridiculous. And then these two pilots are nice boys, but they have no experience. I will be speaking with Director Kimakawa about this."

Alexis decided to offer her two cents. "I cannot speak for Willits and Jones. Their actions are not exactly gaining my trust... "

Ambassador Bird interrupted her quickly. "You think? They are out there playing cards with two hookers!"

Alexis came to their defense, "Well, it is confusing but not the worst cover. Vandabri certainly has a reputation, and an Ambassador here to get laid certainly wouldn't raise a red flag to anyone."

Ambassador Bird countered "Except to any of my constituents or Earth Delegates. And what were you thinking? Walking outside to a bar! What if someone had spotted you?"

Alexis smiled and continued, "I was getting a drink, it's not breaking the law. And, if you let me continue..., I do trust the two cadets. Tunsall is very professional, very smart. Trujillo, despite being a bit arrogant, wouldn't let anything happen to us."

The Ambassador went back to reading but continued to speak. "Your enthusiasm is misguided. He wouldn't let anything happen to *you* because he has a crush on you. I could get kidnapped by a platoon of SS soldiers, and I doubt he would notice."

Alexis was now puzzled. "Crush? Trujillo? On me?"

The Ambassador never looked up. "Don't act surprised. I see the way he looks at you. Following you outside to go bar hopping."

Alexis spoke again "It was one drink Ambassador. And I was trying to figure out what Willits and Jones were doing."

Ambassador Bird replied, "Well, soon it won't matter. Once we get on that Battle Cruiser, we will be in joint BRG control, where I hate to admit it, will probably be more professional than these two."

Commander Jones suddenly knocked on the door. "Ambassador?"

Ambassador Bird and Alexis wondered if Jones had heard what Bird had just said. Jones shouted, "Sir, we just got word there has been an attack on Braccus City."

Ambassador Bird and Alexis looked at each other in disbelief. The two got up and went into the common area, where Willits and Jones had just finished playing cards with the two hookers. Willits spoke first. "Based on these initial reports, it looks like a bombing of a Quill Temple near the Port Braccus Terminal. There was an incident there as well, possibly related to the bombing. Publicly they are not confirming it, but the BRG is saying it was Taz."

The Ambassador's face turned to disbelief "Taz?"

Alexis was shocked. "There was a bombing of a Quill Temple?"

Jones continued, "Many dead, hundreds wounded. No count yet, but they said the Temple was packed. Apparently it's a Quill holiday."

Alexis answered, "It's The Offering Sun."

Trujillo asked, "It's the what?"

Tunsall responded. "The offering of gifts to the Quillisars."

Trujillo could not help himself, "The Quilla-what?"

Alexis continued, "Quillisars. The Red Priests of the Quill. Four times a year, offerings or gifts are made to the Quill Diamond's four corners. Today is the Offering Sun."

Ambassador Bird finally spoke, "If there was extensive damage to this Temple, I want to go see it personally."

Willits interjected, "The scene is too hostile right now, Ambassador. The chance of another attack is still very probable."

The Ambassador was dead set on it, though. "Command Willits. Did you not call for our Battle Cruiser to meet us at Braccus?"

Willits, still looking at the computer screen for more information. "That is correct, Ambassador. If they were still in the Corvalis system, they should already be on their way here."

The Ambassador then stood right next to Willits. "Then it will leave me time to go down to Braccus City and witness this damage first hand."

Willits countered. "Sir, the plan was to hide here, wait til the Battle Cruiser got into a safe orbit around Braccus, then meet on the ship when I felt everything was secure. Never to go down to the city. It's chaos down there. The BRG would likely just put you in a security tent far away from the bombing."

The Ambassador was not having it. "Commander, the purpose of my trip to Belinea is to talk to the Council about terrorism. I am demanding more security for the Ambassadors, the need for the DAG to have an expanded role in combating this aggression. My credibility is enhanced, not hindered if I go down there and report my findings to the Council. Not letting a Council Ambassador assess the damage would make the BRG and AuFa look like they are hiding their incapabilities."

Willits continued to look at the Ambassador. He then looked at Jones, who gave him a slight shoulder shrug before turning back to the Ambassador's stare. It was clear he was not going to budge.

The Ambassador offered one last argument. "I am not going to sit here in hiding while my mere presence can win our message at the bombing site. We are simply letting the BRG assist us in this detail, slightly earlier than planned."

Willits finally acquiesced. Looking at the hookers, he said, "Ladies, it has been delightful, but I am afraid our time is up, and we must say goodbye. Tunsall, Trujillo, prepare the ship for takeoff. We are going to Port Braccus."

BELINEA 3.4

Braccus

The T-141 was in HyperEXtension before slowing down as it approached Braccus. Through the atmosphere, the pilots were hitting controls, pulling the throttle back, and communicating with the Port Braccus Control Tower. "BC54-1, we have you on our system. Proceed with caution to strip 8-1B."

Commander Nickalis Devanoe was riding in a chair directly behind the two pilots. Out of the window, he could see the destruction from the incident on the Port. One bridge had an explosion hole in the middle while a crew was trying to patch it back together. One of the landing strips had been squared off, with almost a hundred AuFa soldiers investigating. In the distance, he could see the smoke from the Temple, which was still smoldering.

Commander Devanoe thought what one of the pilots said out loud. "What the hell happened?"

The T-141 gently touched the ground. It was a massive ship. It had two F-81 Sirator fighter's, wings folded up, in its cargo bay. As the engines began to shut down, the back belly door opened up, and Commander Devanoe walked down it. One of the pilots was next to him. Nick looked at him and said, "Get the two fighters off this ship and prepped, immediately."

The pilot nodded and walked off to find the necessary tow carts to get the Fighters off the ship. Commander Devanoe, once on the ground, turned around and began walking towards the docking bridges. This was the military section of the Port, surrounded with security. A soldier ran up to him and saluted.

"Commander Devanoe. Captain Kimmel informed us of your arrival time. The BRG would like a word with you."

Commander Devanoe had to ask. "Soldier, what happened here?"

"Terrorist attack. Over a hundred dead at the Temple."

Commander Devanoe kept looking around until the soldier escorted him to a ride transport. "Follow me, sir."

With the roll bars' assistance, they both got on the ride transport car, called a TC. The TC was a sort of flying jeep, with four horizontal fan blades for wheels that kept it afloat. The soldier whizzed by the security checkpoint, eventually climbing slightly in altitude. It gave Devanoe an incredible view of the bridge-tunnel with the explosion Taz left in it. The soldier continued to fly, over and around the Port Terminal building, and then toward the Temple's site. In the process of the flight, the smoke seemed to be rising everywhere around the city, as if the whole city was somehow ablaze. He then saw a few rockets go off in the distance, a few mild explosions, and then heard the sound of a firework exploding. Nick Devanoe turned to the soldier and asked, "Is the city under attack?"

The soldier pointed to the Temple and spoke. "The Temple bombing was there, sir. In the hours after the attack, there have been riots, some protesting. Not all the people on Braccus are happy that the Belineans and the Quill are here."

The soldier landed the craft a few blocks from the Temple, with medical crews still working on the wounded. A few press members had gotten by, managing to record the damage with reporters adding their commentary. The soldier, walking towards the security entrance, signaled for Commander Devanoe to follow him. "Right this way, Commander. Captain Vincella would like to see you."

Near the Temple, billowing smoke continued to rise through the dusk of the sunset. Ambassador Bird was still looking around, Alexis right next to him. Cadets Tunsall and Trujillo, armed with rifle blasters, flanked the Ambassador and Alexis. Cheap parlor fireworks, firecrackers, smoke bombs, and broken bottles were thrown, highlighting the streets' chaos a few blocks away. All four of them could hear this, occasionally grimacing when a firework went off. Tunsall and Trujillo kept looking around, trying to see if the minor rioting in the street led to something worse. Many medics were still assisting the wounded, with most of the critical wounded already transported out to local hospitals. There were some dead bodies with sheets over them, yet to be recovered. The Ambassador kneeled and saw the body of a dead boy and mother. They were entirely burned crispy black, still holding hands.

Alexis got up and walked away. She could not take any more of the devastation. She began walking away from the Temple. Instinctively, Trujillo followed her, leaving Tunsall to guard the Ambassador by himself. Alexis Devanoe walked toward the security tent area, noticing a small TC had just landed, and two men jumped out. They walked through the security entrance, both men showing off their credentials. As she got closer, one of the men looked oddly familiar. The man was then staring at her, with the same odd look on his face. It took almost three seconds for the two of them to recognize each other.

The soldier, who could not understand why Commander Devanoe was suddenly jogging toward this lady, shouted, "Commander Devanoe, Captain Vincella needs to see you."

The two suddenly embraced in a long hug. Trujillo strolled behind, keeping his distance but never turning his eyes off Alexis. Trujillo kept a close grip on his rifle, not knowing who this guy was.

Alexis asked, still in an embrace, "What are you doing here?"

Nick let go, putting her small body back on the ground. "What are *you* doing here?"

Alexis was still in shock, "Ambassador Bird. We are on our way to Belinea, and stopped here to survey this attack."

Nick then quickly put it all together. "And you were supposed to meet up with a Battle Cruiser in the Corvalis System, correct?"

Alexis then looked puzzled "How did you know?"

Nick answered, "Because that's my Battle Cruiser. I am Captain Kimmel's first officer."

Trujillo decided to stay about twenty feet back, just staring at the two of them.

Nick asked, "What's with the guy with the rifle?"

Alexis answered, "He is part of my security detail."

Nick then asked, "He is DAG?"

Alexis interjected again. "I think. He is actually a cadet."

Nick looked astonished and now was a little upset. "A cadet? Handling the Ambassador's security? And why didn't you go to the Corvalis system as planned? Who is in charge of your detail?"

Just then, the soldier who flew Commander Devanoe over had walked up. He reiterated, "Commander Devanoe, Captain Vincella needs to see you."

The four walked over to the security tent, Trujillo, about ten feet behind now. When they walked inside the tent, they came upon a circle of six officers who were disagreeing with something. The older gentlemen, Captain Vincella of the BRG was making a point. "Commander, I understand your concern, but this is the safest option…"

Commander Willits interrupted with "Safe? That word is too big for you, Vincella. I am not sure you know what it means."

Captain Vincella said, "Watch it, Commander."

Willits immediately countered. "No, you fucking watch it. Your security team let this guy escape, and the city is in chaos. The AuFa has declared Martial Law, whatever good that is doing, and you want me to leave him in your protection?"

The soldier and Commander Devanoe then joined the circle. The soldier then spoke. "Captain Vincella, this is Commander Devanoe, from AuFa Battle Cruiser 54."

Captain Vincella felt like he finally got a break. "Just in time. Commander Willits, if you do not feel the Military Side of the Port's accommodations are adequate, this is the Commander assigned from the AuFa to handle the security for the rest of your trip. I assure you he has a T-141 that is perfectly fine to keep the Ambassador in while we wait on that Battle Cruiser to get here."

Willits had had enough. "Vincella, he is an Ambassador, not the fucking ship cook. I am not storing him on some cot on a transport ship. I need him on his Ambassador ship, with an entire BRG security detail, inside a Cruiser or a major AuFa ship."

Captain Vincella was now annoyed. "Willits, every one of my BRG officers is assisting with security and keeping the peace. Every available AuFA officer is out looking for Taz. I can barely give you two guards, let alone an entire detail. I keep hearing you guys want to handle security, well here it is. The base is under control, so your Ambassador can park his ass there."

Willits was growing more agitated by the second. " Vincella, people are rioting in the streets! You don't think they can get past the security at the Port Terminal building and onto the base? If this were a Belinean Ambassador, you would have an entire AuFa battalion guarding him."

Nick decided to interject. "Excuse me, I am not sure who you are?"

Willits was still fuming. "I am Commander Nolan Willits, Delegate Ambassador Guard, who the fuck are you?"

This took Nick back for a second. There was no civility in the room now. Alexis, noticing the same thing, tried to ease the tension. "Commander Willits, this is my brother, Nick Devanoe."

Nick looked at her before looking back at Willits and offering his hand, "Commander Nick Devanoe."

They shook hands, with Jones asking from behind Willits, even though he saw the uniform and already knew the answer. "You are AuFa?"

Nick nodded his head. "It's not a costume. You two are in charge of the DAG detail team assigned to the Ambassador?"

Willits almost laughed "If 'detail team' you mean two pilots and us, then yes."

Just then, Trujillo stuck out his hand from outside the circle into it, right in front of Nick. "I am Miguel Trujillo."

Nick Devanoe did not shake it, still slightly confused as to who Trujillo was. Nick then turned to Willits and asked, "And who is guarding the Ambassador right now?"

Willits looked at Trujillo and barked, "You left the Ambassador?"

Trujillo, now withdrawing his unshaken hand, looked at Willits and said, "Tunsall is guarding him, I was following Miss Devanoe."

Willits scolded him and said, "Get your ass back to the Ambassador. She is unimportant."

Nick chirped out a "Hey?"

Willits apologized. "Sorry, no offense Miss Devanoe."

Alexis gave a hand gesture to not worry about it. Nick then said, "No, your right, he should be guarding the Ambassador. She is not important."

Alexis smacked her brother across the chest and said, "Hey…"

Captain Vincella was not interested in pleasantries. "Now that everyone knows each other, can we get to the task at hand. My orders are to get you *SAFELY* on Commander Devanoe's Battle Cruiser and to Torsalli by all means possible."

Nick Devanoe was still very much in the dark. "Captain Vincella, I apologize, but can somebody please tell me exactly what happened? I was on a T-141 to meet up with the Ambassador and flew into all of this."

The BRG officer next to Captain Vincella began to explain while pointing at the map in front of them. "We looked at the security footage. Taz was disguised as a Quillsar Priest and laid, we think, three explosives inside this Temple. The Temple was packed because of the holiday. The devices went off as Taz was escaping through the Port Braccus terminal. A BRG officer identified him, leading him on a chase across one of the tunnel bridges and eventually out to one of the landing strips. Taz was assisted by a crew, and he escaped. As of now, we have 96 people confirmed dead, at least 200 wounded at the Temple. Plus another thirteen dead BRG officers who Taz killed in his escape."

Nick tried to process all that information. He then responded, "Any relation to the attack on Space Port Earth? Obviously Taz must have come directly from Earth to here."

Willits and Jones now perked up as did Alexis. Jones, confused, asked, "What attack on Earth?"

Nick Devanoe, now realizing everyone did not know of the Space Port Earth attack, seemed almost reluctant to say anything. He looked at Captain Vincella for clarity before turning to Willits and Jones and saying, "You don't know about the attack?"

Alexis then asked as well. "What attack?"

Captain Vincella explained. "Taz struck Space Port Earth approximately two days ago. It was a solo attack, designed to hit one of the docking ports with a small ship. He shot down two fighters as he escaped."

There was a hush among the group. Alexis, Willits, and Jones all looked at each other. Willits, after the initial shock wore off, grew frustrated. He looked directly at Captain Vincella and said, "Which slip? Why didn't you tell us?"

Captain Vincella sounded sincere, "I thought you knew. It is also why the BRG wants to inquire about why your ship left three hours before its scheduled departure. "

Willits was still pissed. "Well, good call by us. You are fucking welcome."

Then Nick chimed in. "And why did you not follow your manifest and go directly to the Corvalis System as planned."

Commander Willits was almost glad to answer. "Well, excuse me for not trusting any of you. You guys are fucking incredible. It's like asking me why I put a parachute on the Ambassador when I pushed him outside the door of the aircraft."

Nick then responded, which drew the ire of Captain Vincella, "Except that bringing him here was not exactly a better choice than keeping with the plan and taking him to Corvalis."

Willits quickly added, "I did not have the Ambassador here."

Vincella now asked, "Yeah, where did you have the Ambassador hidden?"

Willits and Jones just looked at each other, knowing they were not going to say anything. Unfortunately, Ambassador Bird just walked into the tent, with Tunsall and Trujillo in tow. Now was the awkward look of what should we say. After a few seconds of silence, Alexis let the cat out of the bag. "We were hiding on Vandabri."

Captain Vincella was flabbergasted. "You hid the Ambassador on Vandabri?"

Nick looked at his sister in a disapproving way and said, "You were on Vandabri?"

Alexis looked at Nick incredulously. "Like I had a say in where we went?"

Willits quickly responded. "Well, clearly, it was safer than being here."

Captain Vincella responded, "Well, no soldier's cot will do for what you guys needed."

Willits was too pissed. "Thanks, Vincella, you are right. Remind me to thank your team of ass-hats guarding us. I feel so much safer."

Vincella went to grab Willits. Willits was ready until Jones, and the other two BRG officers got in the middle. Commander Devanoe finally stepped in, as Vincella and Willits were trying to fight each other. Nick finally shouted "Enough gentlemen….,"

The two were still being pulled apart as Commander Devanoe continued, "Fighting will not get us anywhere. We are all on the same team."

Jones interjected because Willits was too hot and bothered. Jones said, "That may be true, but that does not change the fact that these incidents are related, and likely that Taz is still on the hunt for the Ambassador."

The Ambassador was now confused. "Incidents?"

Willits was happy to answer. "There was an attack on Space Port Earth from Taz, likely directed at you, at the time we should have left. I am certain this incident is tied to it."

The Ambassador was still a little astonished by the new revelation. "There was an attack on Space Port Earth? And it was directed at me?"

Captain Vincella softly said, "We believe so, sir."

Commander Devanoe hoped he was the voice of reason, being both a respected officer in the AuFa but also being human. "Ambassador Bird. I can assure you that Captain Vincella of the BRG has made the necessary arrangements to ensure your safety and will allow you to keep your DAG detail at all times. Is this acceptable to you?"

Willits and Jones looked at Ambassador Bird, both with a look of disapproval on their faces. For the first time, Bird had realized their unorthodox approach, while appearing overly cautious, had likely saved his life. Before, privately, he could not wait to get into a BRG detail. Now he was not so sure. He looked at both of them for a long time, before finally responding to Commander Devanoe, "I would like to hear if Commander Willits has any suggestions."

Willits turned to Devanoe and Vincella. "It is clear Taz has made the Ambassador a priority. I am not sure if he knows he is here or not. I understand that Battle Cruiser is our safest way out."

Nick was about to cool off Willits. "Well, Commander, if you had followed your manifest, you would be in the Corvalis System right about now, on a Battle Cruiser headed to Torsalli. So let's not throw stones in a glasshouse.

Let's work together to get him safely out. The Battle Cruiser should be here soon. It was about an hour behind me."

Captain Vincella responded, "That is not accurate, Commander Devanoe."

Commander Devanoe looked surprised. "Excuse me?"

Captain Vincella continued, "We got a communication from your Captain Kimmel...."

Trujillo looked immediately at Tunsall, who, ever so slightly, shook his head no when glancing at Trujillo.

Vincella continued, "... It seems Lord Malovex has joined the Battle Cruiser. They are going to stay in Corvalis temporarily believing Taz will show up there looking for Ambassador Bird."

Willits and Jones just looked at each other. Commander Devanoe was taken aback by this revelation. "Well, it seems I am wrong. We might be here for a while, Commander Willits. What do you need?"

Willits paused for a moment to reflect on the new information. "Until the Battle Cruiser arrives, we must keep the Ambassador on our C-62T. We need a BRG security detail outside. And we want the Ambassador's ship to be flanked by two F-81's in case we need to make a quick getaway."

Vincella answered, "I can't give you those types of resources, Commander Willits. I do not have two F-81's to spare, nor do I have an additional security detail for you."

Commander Devanoe countered with a hopeful solution. "I have two F-81 fighters on my T-141 transport ship right now. They're not being used to pursue Taz."

Commander Jones looked at Devanoe. "They come with Belinean pilots?"

Devanoe was astounded by the rudeness of the question. "They are highly trained, professional AuFa pilots Commander Jones."

Willits saw the opening. "I am sure they are fantastic, but why don't you give us the F-81's and we will handle the rest."

Vincella practically laughed. "Willits, are you fucking crazy? Who is going to fly those fighters, you?"

Willits stared him down. Pointing at Tunsall and Trujillo, he said, "No, these two will…"

Commander Devanoe was taken aback slightly. Looking at the rifle security guards in a new light now, he said, "You two are qualified to fly an F-81?"

Tunsall and Trujillo both responded simultaneously, "Yes, sir."

Commander Devanoe was caught off guard. But this was a compromise. He knew getting Ambassador Bird on that Battle Cruiser is all that mattered now. "Ok, how about your two pilots share detail with my two pilots. It should not be too long before the Battle Cruiser gets here anyway. Is that acceptable, Commander Willits?"

Willits looked at Jones, then at the Ambassador. Finally, he looked at Devanoe and nodded as he spoke, "I'm fine with that, Commander Devanoe."

Commander Devanoe exhaled. "Good. Captain Vincella, if your BRG officers are needed elsewhere, perhaps it is best if we take over the Ambassador's transport from here, with your permission?"

Vincella nodded.

Devanoe continued. "Then, Ambassador Bird. If you are done surveying the scene, let's escort you back to your ship."

BELINEA 3.5

Earth, Japan

Director Kimakawa sat behind his desk. Vice Director Franklin Meyers was on the opposite side, in front, hunched over. Both looked at a 3-D data screen, assessing the information they had received a few minutes ago. A buzz was heard on his intercom, followed by a voice. "Ms. Anella Devanoe is here."

Kimakawa quietly said, "Send her in."

The doors opened to the cold, dark, spacious office of the Director of the DAG. Annella Devanoe, a woman in her mid 60's, short, with salt and pepper hair, walked in. Without waiting to be addressed, she practically shouted across the room in her Scottish accent. "Thank you for returning my calls Director."

Kimakawa looked up as Meyers turned around to address the lady dressed in a suit. "My apologies Ms. Devanoe."

Annella continued. "I tried three times. I was beginning to think some-one killed you and left your body out on the mountain."

Kimakawa stood up as Ms. Devanoe made her way to the desk. "There was a terrorist attack on Braccus. Initial reports are that it was Taz. He bombed a Temple."

Annella asked, "How many dead?"

Meyers shook his head, "BRG won't confirm, but at least 50, maybe 100."

Annella then asked, "And Ambassador Bird?"

Meyers spoke again. "No update from the DAG detail team, so we cannot locate the Ambassador, but according to his manifest, he should already be in the Corvalis System. There is a significant time difference in the communications."

Annella Devanoe then sat down in the chair and crossed her legs. She let out a sigh. "So Director, you have no update on my daughter. Is that why you did not return my calls?"

Director Kimakawa sat down as well, behind his desk, as Meyers chose to stand. He crossed his hands in his lap and replied, "I told you I would let you know when we knew something. We just found out about this attack on Braccus ten minutes ago. It is classified."

Annella looked at Kimakawa dead in the eyes. "What *can* you tell me about my daughter?"

Kimakawa first looked at Meyers before looking back at Annella. He replied, "Commander Willits and the detail should be in the Corvalis System. If that happened, and it is likely it did, they should be leaving now for Torsalli. Given the circumstances, I requested the BRG that an AuFa Battle Cruiser escort them the rest of the way to Belinea."

Annella patiently asked, "And what did the BRG say?"

Kimakawa raised his eyebrows. "They haven't gotten back to me yet. But the C-62T they traveled in is very fast, and once they get to Torsalli, they will be deep in Council occupation."

Annella paused to digest this information. After a few seconds, she said, "And the Battle Cruiser in the Corvalis System. Which one is it?"

Kimakawa looked puzzled. He looked up at Meyers, who then haphazardly guessed, "I believe Battle Cruiser 54? I will have to check that, Ms. Devanoe."

Annella gave another sigh. "Please do. Battle Cruiser 54 is the ship my son Nickalis is on. He just got assigned there a month ago."

Kimakawa leaned back in his chair, still with his hands crossed in his lap. "The Commander in the AuFa, yes. I did not know where he was assigned."

Annella paused before looking up. "Vice Director Meyers, will you please give me a moment with the Director?"

Meyers looked at Kimakawa, who, ever so slightly, nodded. Meyers then said, "Of course."

Meyers walked out of the room. Annella waited until the door closed before continuing. "These are troubling times, Taichi."

Kimakawa pulled out from the drawer and held up a bottle. "Scotch?"

Annella responded, "As long as it's mine and not the Japanese stuff."

Kimakawa chuckled, "I have both, but I'll pour your Lagavulin."

Kimakawa poured into two empty glasses, pushing one towards Annella. Anella held up her glass, Kimakwa responded with the same gesture, and Annella took a good swig.

Annella waited for the scotch to go down properly before speaking, "Are your feelings about these two DAG Commanders leading the detail team the same?"

Kimakawa looked at her for a second and took another swig of scotch. He then replied, "The situation has me questioning a lot of things, Annella."

Annella nodded. "Because this Guard is not your little play pool Taichi. And you certainly better not be playing games with my family."

Kimakawa then nodded again before delivering a small crooked smile and replying, "I would never play games Annella, I understand what is at stake. What possibly makes you think I do not know that?"

Annella did not smile when responding, "A mutual friend keeps me informed, and sometimes that paints an alternative picture."

The response brought out a small half-smile from Kimakawa, as he knew who the reference was. He finished off his scotch before responding, "Annella, we share a rather large common vision, that your children are fighting for as well. I promise you, any harm inflicted on any of your children is not intended and out of my control."

Annella finished her scotch now as well. She stood up. "As I expected. Please keep me informed when you hear any information."

Kimakawa stood up as well, saying, "Of course."

Annella was almost out of the room when she stopped, turned around, and said, "Oh, Taichi…"

"Yes…"

Annella put her gloves back on "Next time I contact you, don't ignore me, or I will cut your little fucking balls off."

Kimakawa just smiled as she walked out of the room.

BELINEA 3.6

AuFa Base, Port of Braccus

Standing outside the C-62T were Commanders Willits and Jones. They watched as the T141 Transport ship, flanked by two F-81 Sirator fighters, gently landed around the C-62T. Coming out of the back belly was Commander Nick Devanoe. He walked up to Willits and Jones and immediately asked, "Will this do?"

Willits responded, "Yes."

A BRG officer walked up to them and reported. Devanoe introduced him. "This is Lieutenant Bezra with the BRG. He is here to assist. Lieutenant, this is Commanders Willits and Jones of the DAG."

Willits did not shake hands, nor did Jones, just a nod in acknowledgment. Willits then asked, "How long has the Ambassador's C-62T been out here?"

Both Lieutenant Bezra and Nick Devanoe were confused by the question. Bezra responded, "Probably about an hour, correct?"

Willits continued, "Yes, and has the BRG or anybody guarded the vessel during that time?"

Bezra was already caught off guard. "I am not sure, Commander Willits."

Willits coldly responded, "Well, get sure, Lieutenant. Otherwise, people die."

Bezra nodded his head. Willits continued. "Let's get a detail team to do a complete sweep of the ship."

Bezra looked astonished. "A complete sweep will take at least four people, and it won't be quick."

Willits was not in the mood. "Well, unless someone can assure me with complete certainty that nothing was put on this ship in the last hour, it needs a complete sweep. The attack on Space Port Earth was targeted at Ambassador Bird, and Taz will not change that until he is dead."

A soft explosion could be heard in the distance, likely some more rioting in the streets. All four heard it, glancing back at the Port Terminal building before refocusing on each other. Bezra first looked at Commander Devanoe, as if waiting for him to chime in. Bezra responded, "Do you really think that is necessary, Commander?"

Willits just stared at Bezra and said, "If that were a Belinean Ambassador, you would have ten BRG officers out there performing a sweep of the area."

Bezra waited a few seconds before replying. "An amusing anecdote Commander, because we are still trying to process why someone would try to kill an Ambassador of such insignificance. This notion that we just started security detail last week, ignoring the hundred years we have, is arrogant even for you Earthlings."

Willits gave a sarcastic half-smile. "What is arrogant Bezra is the notion that Belinean's can shit rainbows and gold coins. It stinks, and you wipe your ass just like the rest of us."

Nick had decided to end this before it went any further. "Alright, cool it, both of you. Let's stick to the work. Bezra, can you get a detail team out here to do a sweep, yes or no?"

Bezra was still annoyed. After a deep breath, he said, "I will get a team out here as soon as possible, Commander."

Nick continued. "Commander Willits and myself are appreciative of your efforts, correct Commander?"

Nick looked at Willits. Willits, still a little salty, extended an olive branch. "Thank you for your timely response, Lieutenant."

Bezra nodded and walked off. Nick, still looking at Willits, said, "See what happens when we all learn to cooperate?"

Willits began looking around, as was Jones as if to spot something no one else was looking for. Another explosion could be heard in the distance. "No offense Devanoe, but I do not know how you wear that uniform. I do not trust any of them. They are a bunch of racist pricks."

Nick kept looking around as well. "It's sometimes challenging, but not all of them are like that. You do not do us any favors by shitting on all of them."

Willits gave a cocky half-smile. "If you think I started this animosity, then you have not been in the AuFa as long as I thought. I am shocked you have made it to Commander and not cleaning toilets somewhere."

Devanoe stopped looking around and stared directly at Willits. "Just do me a favor, and keep the barking down to a minimum. We will get the Ambassador out of here fast enough. Speaking of, where is the Ambassador?"

Jones then responded, "Inside the base with your sister, watching the security footage of Taz's attack. Tunsall and Trujillo are watching them. Have you seen it yet?"

Nick responded, "The attack footage?"

Willits nodded. Nick continued. "The thing Taz did with the sword and the fireball? Have you ever seen anything like that?"

Willits shook his head while responding, "I've heard some things, but never seen that. You?"

Nick shook his head also and continued, "Never. I've seen Lord Argo and SS officers of the Quill do some crazy shit with those rings they have, like turning into steel swords. But never fire."

Jones then said, "Well, that makes three of us."

Devanoe then asked, "What do you guys know about Ambassador Bird?"

Jones continued, "Not a whole lot. We met him just before we took off."

Devanoe asked again, "Is this guy going to put my sister in danger?"

Willits looked at him for a second before responding. "He's a politician. Eager to change the universe, in love with his own voice, not overly cerebral. Safe to say your sister is the brains behind the operation."

Devanoe half smiled, "Alexis is the smart one in the family, and the most stubborn."

Willits changed the subject by asking him, "Hey, I need a favor."

Nick responded, "Sure, if I can."

Willits then asked, "Look, this Ambassador likes the ladies, in case you didn't notice."

Nick now looked a little annoyed. "Certainly, the stop at Vandabri was not Alexis' idea."

Willits continued. "No, and I certainly can't take him back to Vandabri to get some action. What are the chances I can sneak the two I had from Vandabri back here?"

Nick just looked at him and said, "Really?"

Willits responded, "Well, it's that, or I send your sister out there to go find some action for him. Your choice."

Nick just loosely nodded his head. "I'm sure we can figure something out."

Willits smiled and said, "Thanks."

The Ambassador and Alexis came walking up, Tunsall and Trujillo in tow, both with rifles. The Ambassador was going on and on about the attack. "I have never seen anything like that. This is much worse than the BRG has ever let out. Commander Willits, have you seen the security footage of the attack with Taz?"

Commander Willits responded, "Commander Jones and I have seen it, Ambassador."

The Ambassador continued, "I need to send a full report to the Council."

As the four of them began walking toward the C-62T, Willits held up his hand and interjected, "Ambassador, not so fast."

As if on cue, two BRG officers were walking up to the Ambassador's C-62T transport. Willits continued. "Your ship needs a complete security sweep before anyone gets on it."

The Ambassador looked confused, "Really?"

Commander Devanoe chimed in with "Better to be safe than sorry, Ambassador."

Then Commander Jones added, "I am sure Commander Devanoe has some acceptable accommodations on the T-141 that we can use temporarily to send over your report?"

The Ambassador did not like the sound of that. "Why can't I just go back inside the base?"

Willits answered, "Until Taz is caught, sir, I will feel a lot safer somewhere I can get you out of here in a hurry."

The Ambassador did not look happy but could see the logic. Nick finally added, "Ambassador, this way. We have a situation room and a private quarters area that I think you will find acceptable."

As all seven began walking toward the T-141, Jones went up to Willits and whispered, "What the hell is up with the girls from Vandabri?"

Willits whispered back, "Just play along...."

Nick and Alexis are walking side by side, in front of the Ambassador. Nick said, "How is Mom?"

Alexis smiled. "Annella is as intrusive as ever. The unhappy hen unless she knows where all her eggs are."

Nick laughed, "Better than not caring at all, I suppose."

Alexis responded, "You and Connor get away with much more than I can."

Nick whispered close to her ear, "How is your assignment going?"

Alexis smiled again, slightly rolling her eyes. Looking around to see if anyone other than Nick could hear her, she continued, "You can keep looking with a brighter light, but the light in that head ain't going to get any brighter."

Nick smiled and said, "An Annella classic. And these guys?"

Alexis sighed before whispering, "Not sure yet. The jury is still out. They are either brilliant or clueless. I trust the cadets the most."

Nick turned to look at Trujillo and Tunsall, both still with rifles in their hands, looking everywhere from something unusual to pop out. Alexis continued. "And you? Flight Commander means you are the First Officer of that ship, only behind the Captain. You gotta be the first human to accomplish that."

Nick embarrassingly half-smiled, almost a gush. "Not quite, but close."

Alexis responded, "Captain in no time big brother."

Nick shrugged, with a wince on his face. The Ambassador walked by and loudly demanded, "Commander Devanoe, where is this situation room?"

Nick began walking forward and then to the left, pointing with an open hand, "Right over here, Ambassador. Alexis, you should find everything you need. This is Sargent Insignot. He can assist you with anything you need."

The Ambassador walked in through some doors with Alexis. Devanoe came walking back to Willits and Jones, who were still hanging out at the entrance to the craft's belly. Willits asked, "Devanoe, I thought the T-141 was a big medical ship?"

Nick Devanoe, just like his sister, was happy to talk about things he knew a lot about. While he pointed, he continued. "They mostly are. But to get more flexible, they shaved the medical and living quarters in half in order to store two F-81 Sirator's in here, provided they fold their wings."

Jones asked, "Why?"

Yet it was Tunsall who answered "Logistics. Getting the F-81's on the Battle Cruiser without sacrificing the Patrol Craft makes it almost a mini-carrier."

Nick Devanoe was a little astonished. "That's correct. Teaching you guys logistics at Odgins?"

All four of them were looking at Tunsall, trying to figure out how he knew that. Tunsall shrugged his shoulders as Nick Devanoe continued. "The Ambassador's C-62T is so big that when we meet up with the Battle Cruiser, we will leave this T-141 here. Unless you want to fly the C-62T outside next to us."

Jones immediately scowled, "No, thanks, inside is fine."

Willits then walked off towards the medical area. Everyone watched him go through the sliding glass doors before Trujillo asked Nick, "How much longer until the Battle Cruiser gets here?"

Nick Devanoe replied, "Should be real soon, I am going to check on that right now."

Willits then came out of the sliding glass doors and said, "Jones, can you come here and give me a hand with this?"

Jones began walking to the medical area while Devanoe started walking towards the situation room.

BELINEA 3.7

Corvalis System

Battle Cruiser 54

Malovex was standing alone, looking out the window of the bridge. He glanced over to the side, looking at a visual of the Patrol Ship in orbit around a moon. Captain Kimmel, a mere twenty feet off to the side in the bridge's body, had an officer approach him and whisper, "Sir, it's been almost three hours....."

Captain Kimmel merely shook his head and held up his hand to tell the young officer to be quiet. Captain Kimmel then walked over to Lord Malovex and stood next to him. "Lord Malovex, there has been no change in the situation. How long do you expect us to wait?"

Malovex said nothing for a few seconds before responding, "Anxious to get to Braccus, Captain?"

Captain Kimmel hesitated before speaking. "Those are my AuFa orders, sir."

Malovex went back to looking at the window before saying, "The AuFa would be much more pleased if you caught Taz then transporting an Earth Ambassador to and from."

Captain Kimmel was confused. "My Lord?"

Malovex was always annoyed when he figured things out faster than everyone else. "Taz is after the Earth Ambassador. The attack on Braccus was a smokescreen, a way of getting this Battle Cruiser to respond there, away from the Corvalis system."

Captain Kimmel understood, he just was cautious. "My Lord, you believe Taz expects to find The Ambassador here?"

Malovex continued. " Yes, and your patrol craft out there has very similar dimensions and weight as to the Ambassador's C-62T. When Taz arrives, we can only hope he takes the bait and doesn't see us hiding behind this moon."

The black transport was drifting through space. Inside, Taz is surrounded by a team dressed in black, around a 3-D screen of the Corvalis System. First Officer Verkato addresses him. "We arrived just outside this area, sir, with a full engine shut down. If they picked us up, they likely dismissed us as an asteroid. Our scanners did a full sweep and only picked up this (pointing) small ship orbiting this moon. We can't tell what it is, but it fits the dimensions of a small transport. I would like to send a probe."

Taz nodded and went back to studying the map. First Officer Verkato then went over to another screen and started punching in coordinates. Taz's ship then deployed a small probe. Slowly it moved before an engine thrust shifted it into high velocity towards the moon the Patrol ship was orbiting. Taz then hit a few buttons, and the ship began a jamming sequence.

Inside the Battle Cruiser, a sonar officer sitting in his chair noticed something on his screen. He shouted, "Captain Kimmel, I have something."

Both Malovex and Kimmel walk over to the screen and see something racing towards the Patrol craft. Kimmel spoke as the two got there. "What is it, Lieutenant?"

The Lieutenant looked confused. "Not sure, sir, It's a small craft, I think. But it's using a jamming sequence, which is not letting me get a reading on it."

Malovex responded. "It's Dretelli jamming code. That has to be Taz. It's either a fighter or a probe."

The Lieutenant responded, "Still can't get a reading, but it's moving very fast now."

Malovex looked for a few more seconds, verifying what he saw. "Captain, fire up your engines, we are going out there."

Captain Kimmel disagreed but followed his orders anyway. "Yes, Lord Malovex. Lieutenant Spires, set a course for the Patrol ship, best speed."

"Yes, Captain."

On the screen that Malovex and Kimmel watched, it was clear that the thing heading toward the patrol craft was about thirty seconds away. Malovex asked, "How did they get here, unnoticed?"

The Lieutenant responded, "I don't know, sir. Perhaps from another ship undetected also?"

Taz continued to look at his screen. A crew member looking at his sonar screen yelled "Sir, I have a reading on a ship that appeared from behind the moon. Engines now engaged and rapidly approaching the patrol craft the probe is heading to."

Taz then looked at First Officer Verkato next to him. Taz shook his head 'no' and began walking back to the big screen, before climbing into a Captain's chair. First Officer Verkato barked out, "Get us out of here. Prepare for Hyper-EXtension, best speed to Torsalli. Put the visual of the probe on the screen."

Immediately, on the map screen behind him, Taz turned his head to see the probe approach. The tiny screen to his side showed the view from the actual probe.

On the Battle Cruiser, Kimmel and Malovex intently watched the screen. The Lieutenant then said, "Five seconds, sir."

Kimmel barked, "How far out are we, Lieutenant?"

Lieutenant said, "Fifteen seconds, sir."

As Malovex and Kimmel kept looking at the screen showing the Patrol Craft, they could begin to tell something was wrong. The approaching craft wasn't a craft at all. Kimmel said, "Shit..."

Taz, in his chair, continues watching the probe come up on the Patrol Craft. He had a button next to his Captain's chair on the armrest. He waited until the precise moment and hit it. Immediately the screen went blurry from the explosion.

Malovex and Kimmel were watching from their screen. Kimmel held up a hand to his eyes, to not let the light from the explosion damage them. The probe exploded right next to the Patrol Ship, which was instantly obliterated. Kimmel shouted, "Halt all engines!!"

The Battle Cruiser slowed down immediately. Everyone inside was speechless, taking a few seconds to process what had just happened.

With Taz looking in the background, the ship went directly to Hyper Extension speed after First Officer Verkato yelled, "Make the jump...."

BELINEA 3.8

Port Braccus, AuFa Base

It was nighttime, as Commander Willits was walking to the C-62T. He walked in through the side door and noticed the two BRG officers still working on the scene. Noticing their backs were turned, he went to a spot in the common room and unhitched a panel on the wall. Willits placed a tiny yellow box inside it and closed the panel behind it. He then turned to the two BRG officers, who were still on board doing a full sweep. "Hey guys, can you come here for a second."

The two officers walked over, and Willits opened the panel and showed them the yellow box. "Any idea what this is?"

The first BRG officer asked, "Who are you?"

Willits responded. "Commander Willits, DAG."

The second BRG officer said, "D-A-what?"

Willits continued. "Delegate Ambassador Guard of Earth. I am in charge of this ship."

The first BRG officer said, "So you are the dumbfuck who has us doing a full security sweep on a ship parked inside a base."

Willits smiled. He pointed at the yellow box and said, "Yes, I am. And you two are the dumbfucks who missed this doing the security sweep."

The second BRG officer looked at the yellow box and said, "Does it matter?"

Willits was almost amused "I guess your idea of security sweep is different than ours."

The first BRG officer responded, "I would assume your idea of a sweep involves vacuuming the floors."

The second BRG officer continued. "Who cares if an Earth Ambassador takes a bullet to the head? Just get the next shit for brains to take his place."

Willits was genuinely pissed now. "Well, for starters, nobody dies on my watch. If you guys are such prestigious BRG officers, how come you are in here doing security sweeps instead out there looking for Taz?"

The first BRG officer got into Willits's face and said, "I do not have to take this shit from you, Egglet's. We would be so much better off if we just left you guys to die during your pandemic, you ungrateful fucks."

Willits kept a half-smile and said, "On behalf of all Earthlings, thank you. Now do us all a favor, and go fuck yourself, because your reproducing is killing everyone."

The second BRG officer got out a "Fuck You."

Nick Devanoe came walking on to the ship. He immediately yelled at everyone. "What the hell is going on here?!"

The two BRG officers stood back. Willits kept smiling. After a couple of seconds, Willits spoke. "The BRG officers were finishing their sweep. They found this yellow box for me to look at, once they get done inspecting it. That right, boys?"

Devanoe looked at the two BRG officers. The first BRG officer, after a pause, said, "We were just finishing up the sweep, and needed to look at the box. Just like the Commander said."

Nick Devanoe kept looking at all three of them. Not really convinced any of them were telling the truth. Willits broke the tension. "The boys here told me they call this yellow box an Egglet. I was unfamiliar with the term, so they were explaining it to me."

Devanoe was now pissed. He walked over to both of the BRG officers and said, "I do not care what personal beliefs you have. You will inspect this ship, from head to toe. If there is so much as a bolt out of place, I am going to have Captain Vincella inspect this box after I bury it in your fucking skull. Do I make myself clear?

The first BRG officer said, "Yes, sir."

As Willits and Devanoe began walking out, the second BRG officer said, "Whatever you say, Commander Egglet."

Willits and Devanoe stopped. Both turned around. Willits went right up to him and said, "I hope that was directed at me and not Commander Devanoe. Because all he will do is have you demoted."

The second BRG officer said, "Yeah, what are you going to do about it?"

Willits calmly said, "I am just going to make sure you don't say it ever again."

Devanoe grabbed Willits from the back of the shoulder and yanked him back. "Enough!"

The two now walked out of the Ambassador's C-62T. Both were steaming, Willits in particular. Willits said, "I do not know how you deal with that shit!"

Nick Devanoe said, "The AuFa is not nearly as bad as the BRG. You just have to learn not to take the bait."

As they got outside, they heard a whistle from the guard gate. Both of them looked and saw Commander Jones in tow with two ladies. Willits smiled and said to Nick, "You mind letting these ladies in for me?"

Nick Devanoe, begrudgingly, looked at Willits and said, "You owe me."

Nick then whistled to the security guards, raised his hand, and motioned to let them in. The security guards obliged, and the ladies walked in with Commander Jones. The three walked up to Willits and Devanoe before Jones said, "Nolan, you remember Harmony and Cocoa. Ladies, this is Nick."

Willits said, "Ladies, welcome. Thank you for traveling on short notice."

Harmony said, "Easiest money we made all week. We love working with professionals."

Both of the ladies then began putting their hands all over Nick. Cocoa said, "You did not tell me how attractive he was, we feel bad charging you."

Nick was blushing. "Thank you, ladies, but you are not here for me, same guy as before."

The two ladies looked at Willits with a little curiosity. Jones said, "Ladies, we are all professionals. Nick needs not here about any details of your excursions."

Willits smiled. This was going to be amusing. "Ladies, I apologize for not letting you get your hands all over Nick, he is a looker. But if we can get you over to the ship, we will begin the task at hand."

Nick just looked at Willits in disbelief. "Willits, my sister is over there."

Willits just looked at him, puzzled. Then responded, "I am sure she has seen it all, Nick."

There was a brief staredown before Willits finally said, "Fine. Jones, take them over there (pointing to the C-62T). Ladies, thank you for your patience."

Jones and Willits exchanged a look, and Jones began walking the girls to the Ambassador's C-62T ship. Willits and Devanoe began walking the opposite direction, towards the T-141 that Ambassador Bird and Alexis were on. Willits asked Nick, "Any news on the Battle Cruiser?

Nick Devanoe shook his head and responded, "No. Probably another couple of hours until it gets here. Personally, I think Taz is long gone."

Willits turned to him and said, "Maybe so, but either way, we have to keep moving. Staying any one place too long puts a bulls-eye on us."

As they were walking up the ramp, without looking, Willits said, "You know your sister really has seen everything."

Nick, still walking side by side with Willits, responded, "Willits, one more word about my sister, and it will be your last. I still haven't forgotten you took her to Vandabri."

Willits just smiled. As they got inside, they passed Trujillo and an AuFA sergeant, who were guarding the door for the situation room Ambassador Bird was in. Willits stopped, while Devanoe kept walking right through the door. Willits asked, "Where is Tunsall?"

Trujillo answered. "On standby duty with one of the F-81's."

Willits answered, "Ok, I need to speak with you when I get done with this."

As Willits walked into the situation room, Nick Devanoe had already delivered the bad news about the Battle Cruiser. Nick continued to say,"..... so I would think a few more hours, sir."

The Ambassador, who was still looking at specific footage and assembling a report for the Council, was not happy. "Damn-it. I am tired of being here. Hopefully, this will lead to catching Taz."

Nick nodded his head. "We hope so too, sir. Now, if you will excuse me, if we are going to be here a few more hours, I am going to make sure the base has taken some extra security measures, maybe Captain Vincella can give me an update on the situation at the Temple. Alexis, a moment please."

Nick and Alexis walked out of the room. They stopped and faced each other. She looked up

at him and said, "What is it?"

Nick reached into his pocket and took out a wristband. It looked like a watch. He grabbed Alexis' hand and put the watch around her wrist. She then asked, "What is this?"

Nick responded, "I got this from Vincella. They give them to the Belinean Ambassadors. It looks like a wristwatch."

Alexis half-smiled, "Why are you giving this to me?"

Once he clamped it on, Nick let go of her hand so that she could begin to inspect it on her own. He then grabbed her hand again and showed her a small button on it. "It's a panic button. If you push this button, it will send out a transmission blip, to let me know you need help. The blip will give me your location (Nick held up his hand with his matching wristwatch), as long as I am within a solar system of you."

Alexis almost sounded annoyed. "Are you tracking me now?"

Nick looked at her and said, "No. The Ambassadors certainly don't want to be tracked. That's why it only gets activated if you push the button."

Alexis joked, "Does it go off twice as loud if I go back to Vandabri?"

Nick smiled at the joke. "It handcuffs you and seals your mouth shut if you even go near Vandabri. Seriously, push the button, and I should find you. I'm not exactly a fan of this assignment you are on."

Alexis smiled and said, "Mom put you up to this, didn't she?"

Nick kept smiling before kissing her head. "I wish this were Annella's doing, but nope, this is me being a pain in the ass big brother. Just humor me, alright."

Alexis smiled at the kiss. "Anything you want me to tell Annella if I speak to her?"

Nick smiled and threw his arms up. "Tell her everything is going to plan?"

Alexis smiled again and walked back into the situation room. When the door closed behind her, she noticed Willits trying to open the bottle of wine he brought in. The Ambassador, without even noticing, said out loud,

"Alright, it's been a long day. I am going to go back to my cabin and rest for a little bit."

Willits interjected, "I wish you could, Ambassador, but the two BRG officers might have found something."

Ambassador Bird turned around and said, "Excuse me, Commander?"

Willits went over to the side area and got two wine glasses. He fidgeted with a few things, before finally pouring the wine into the glasses. He then turned around and handed them to Alexis and Bird. Willits continued, "It is probably nothing, but I want to make sure. In the meantime, I snagged one of your bottles of wine while you and Miss Devanoe wait."

Alexis took a sip and said, "This is the Napa Cab? It's delicious. Maybe as good as the Torsalli wine."

The Ambassador sat down, seemingly okay with this inconvenience. Willits then said, "Thank you for your patience, sir. I'm going to go see how much longer those BRG officers will be."

Jones entered the C-62T with Harmony and Cocoa. The BRG officers were finishing up. Jones whispered, "There is a slight change in plan, ladies."

The three of them approached the two BRG officers. Jones said, "Gentlemen. Commander Willits and myself feel like we got off on the wrong foot. We appreciate you guys taking the extra time to do a full security sweep of this ship. To show our gratitude, we have arranged for the Ambassador not to be around for a few hours. Enjoy these ladies."

Harmony and Cocoa walked over to the two BRG security guards and began kissing them. At first, they were unsure of what to do, especially when Cocoa started taking the clothes off one of the guards. Jones continued with a smile. "Relax, gentlemen. This is an Ambassador ship. No cameras in here, as you have inspected."

Jones turned around and shut the door behind him. As he walked out, he waited outside and lit a cigar. A few seconds passed before he noticed Willits walking out of the T-141 and up to him. Willits asked, "You got one of those for me?"

Jones pulled one out and lit it for Willits. After a few puffs, Willits looked at Jones and said, "Ready?"

Jones looked at him and said, "Relax Captain Anxious. Five more minutes."

Willits was impatient. "You are such a softy. Come on. We get in, we get out, it's over with it. We are not here to fucking entertain them."

Jones laughed. "They are Belineans, not dolphins."

Willits said, "They called me an Egglet."

Jones, genuinely surprised, said, "Really? Those little fucknauts."

After another puff on the cigar, Jones asked, "Is this gonna work?"

Willits laughed this time and said, "If it doesn't, we are only heading back to Earth in coffins."

Jones then asked, "How much do you think the Ambassador's assistant knows?"

Willits took another puff, raised an eyebrow, and said, "Alexis?"

Jones nodded. Willits continued, "Don't know. But she knows more than she is letting on."

They continued to take another puff before Jones said, "Alright, let's go."

Willits began shaking his head as they both turned to walk into the C-62T. Willits continued, "First you are busting my balls about rushing them, and now I can't even enjoying my fucking cigar. Damn you can be a moody bitch sometimes."

Jones just rolled his eyes. "Will you just shut the fuck up….."

BELINEA 3.9

On the way to Torsalli

Taz and his crew were around a 3-D map. His crew members had pulled up the spaceport at Torsalli. First Officer Verkato then turned to the four others and began speaking.

"This is a breakdown of the Port. It has defenses here, and here. Of course, that is if there are no AuFa ships on the base, which is unlikely."

Another crew member asked, "Are you sure it's Torsalli?"

Taz nodded in affirmative.

Another crew member suggested an alternative. "We cannot strike that base without risking serious casualties. We need to come in unnoticed."

First Officer Verkato asked, "Stealth?"

The second crew member then asked, "Civilian Transport Ship."

First Officer Verkato nodded in affirmative. "Better. There is a host of Civilian ships coming in and out of Torsalli. It's a popular vacation planet."

Taz nodded and walked back to his Captain's chair.

BELINEA 3.10

Port Braccus, AuFa Base

Willits and Jones walked out the door of the C-62T toward the security checkpoint. Jones was carrying a rather large duffle bag. Willits looked at him, and said, "Go take that bag to Trujillo. I am going to check the security point to see if our guest is here."

There was a base room next to the security checkpoint. It doubled as a situation room and lounge for those on guard duty and other officers needing a break. There were only three officers in the room right now, one of them being Commander Nick Devanoe. He was finishing up dinner while looking at the screen for an update. Reading the update, he nodded to himself and whispered 'excellent.'

Willits walked into the base room, surprised to see Nick. Willits spoke, "Devanoe, I thought you were going to see Captain Vincella?"

Nick Devanoe responded, "I am. But I was starving, I haven't eaten all day. Battle Cruiser is on its way, should be here in a little over an hour. I need to give an update to the Ambassador and let him know."

Willits answered, "Well, not now, Devanoe. He is a little busy with the ladies."

Nick Devanoe just shook his head. "Shit. I am already late for this meeting with Vincella."

Willits smiled, "I will tell him when he gets done, no worries."

Nick Devanoe said, "You sure?"

Willits smiled. "Tell him we are getting out of here in an hour? It will be the best news he's gotten all day."

Nick Devanoe put on his flight jacket and began to walk to the door. "Thanks."

A man approached the security checkpoint, escorted to the common room by the AuFa security guard. The Guard, now standing at the doorway that Devanoe was about to walk out of, said, "Any of you guys request a Service Mechanic?"

Willits lit up. "Yes, I did. I need you to take a look at that C-62T out there, make sure everything is in place with the engines."

The Service Mechanic did not seem happy about this request. Willits then asked, "Devanoe, you want him to look at the T-141 and the Sirator's while he is at it?"

Devanoe was already one foot out the door but glanced back and gave a thumbs-up before shouting, "Sure, if he doesn't mind."

Willits softly asked, "You don't mind, do you? Just trying to be safe."

The Service Mechanic shook his head but sarcastically said to himself, "No, what else could I possibly have to do?"

The Mechanic walked out onto the tarmac and began inspecting the Ambassador's ship.

As soon as Devanoe left, Willits walked over to the C-62T, where he was cut off by Trujillo and Jones, walking out of the T-141. It was very dark out, not a whole lot to see anywhere. Willits looked at Trujillo and said, "Ready?"

Trujillo looked a little agitated, struggling with his clothing. "I am practically swimming in these, but yeah, I am ready."

Willits continued. "Good, I'm counting on you."

The Service Mechanic then returned to Willits, Trujillo, and Jones, having just been over to the C-62T Ambassador's ship, inspecting the outside. The mechanic said, "Listen, I know you got the house lights down for security, but I can't see a damn thing. If you want me to do a proper inspection, I am going to have to tow these aircraft back to the service hangar."

Willits smiled. "Better yet, how about I save you some time. These fine two gentlemen are going to fly them over to you if that is alright?"

The Service Mechanic replied, "Great."

Commander Nick Devanoe was flying over in a transport craft. It was the same TC he had used before, earlier in the day, with the same driver. He flew past the Port Terminal building and right next to the Temple. The scene was far less chaotic now. A small trail of smoke was still billowing from the Temple. All the dead bodies had been removed. A tape surrounded the Temple, not allowing anyone access. There was a make-shift tent off to the side. As the soldier landed the TC, Devanoe jumped out. He noticed a Belinean State Reporter with a cameraman on her. She was giving a report with a bright light on her. "As of now, we have 109 people dead. The BRG has control of the situation, as most citizens are thankful for their presence here to keep the peace. The Quill has issued a statement saying that all members need to take time to meditate, to come to peace with the souls that have entered the Diamond so unexpectedly. The Quill also has given Chairman Hassara and the Council their full confidence, and will recommend giving the BRG and the SS the power to find these terrorists and bring them to justice....."

Devanoe continued walking by until he got to the security tent where two AuFa soldiers were standing guard. Both saluted as Devanoe walked into the tent.

Captain Vincella was talking to a civilian reporter. "You cannot report people are rioting in the street. It will only create further violence and make it more difficult for us to keep the peace."

The reporter responded, "But people are rioting. We are only reporting the truth."

Captain Vincella responded, "When you report the truth, that we were attacked by terrorists, and that the BRG is doing everything to keep the peace and provide justice, then you will get your credentials back. Get him out of here."

The reporter was taken away by two BRG soldiers, leaving Devanoe with Captain Vincella and two senior BRG officers. Around a small table, a 3-D board had been set-up that showed the entire scene of Braccus City. The Temple in smoke, the Terminal Building, Port Braccus, and the AuFa base off to the side. Captain Vincella was back to working the map with the other two officers as Devanoe now walked up to them and said, "Captain Vincella."

Vincella looked up, "Commander Devanoe, sorry for delaying our meeting."

Devanoe quickly responded, "I am the one that is late, Captain."

Vincella went back to looking at his map. "How is it going with guard duty on the Ambassador? And his little bitch Willits?"

Devanoe only gave a tiny smile, "Not too bad. He is a prick, but you get used to him."

Captain Vincella had a different view. "He is fucking asshole, and he was lucky you were here, or else he would've been a dead fucking asshole. I don't think he knows who he was talking to."

Devanoe half raised his eyebrows. "Battle Cruiser is en route, should be here in less than an hour. Anything you want to go over beforehand? Do you want to send one of your security teams with them?"

Captain Vincella was not having any of that. "Fuck him. If he wants to do his own security without BRG help, let him. I don't give a fuck about him or that Earth Ambassador. Besides, what could happen on that Battle Cruiser that one of my teams could prevent anyway?"

Devanoe was now annoyed. This Ambassador just got dumped on them. "So you want us to take him to Torsalli, no BRG detail team, correct."

Captain Vincella now showed a little sympathy. Looking up, he crossed his arms and continued, "Look, Commander, I need every one of my guys. This place is a shit-show. I now have 109 confirmed dead, including children. A couple hundred wounded. It's a security nightmare, and I got Braccus press interfering with everything. Hopefully, I can get the Belinean State Press to diffuse the situation. So if you could take the Earth Ambassador, it would be a huge help."

Devanoe put his hands in his pockets. "No problem. I am gonna grab a hot shower before the Battle Cruiser gets here. So let me get out of your hair."

Devanoe began walking out before Captain Vincella shouted out. "Commander Devanoe, can I ask one more favor?"

Devanoe turned around and said, "Sure."

Captain Vincella then continued. "I am short on supplies. Rifles, ammo, more security scanners, you name it. There is an AuFa supply station near Torsalli…."

Devanoe interjected, "It's on the second moon on the next planet over, Pyliss…."

Captain Vincella continued, "Exactly. I put in an order, but they have no ships to get the supplies to me. You should have some room in that Battle Cruiser after you drop off the Ambassador's ship, correct?"

Devanoe nodded. "Yes, and I was going to leave the F-81's with you, so there will be a lot of room. You need us to stop by the supply station on our way back from Torsalli?"

Vincella was pleading now. "It would be a huge help, Commander."

Devanoe nodded again. "I will check with my Captain, but it shouldn't be a problem."

Captain Vincella responded, "Thank you. See you tomorrow."

BELINEA 3.11

Third moon of Braccus - Vandabri

As the T-141 and F-81 Sirator came to a nice landing, Trujillo turned the engines down to idle and opened the huge cargo doors of the T-141. Trujillo got out of his cockpit and walked down the bay doors onto the landing pad. Tunsall had parked the F-81 behind the T-141 and began turning off the engines. After hitting a bunch of switches, the wings started folding up. Trujillo walked across the pad and was greeted by the Dock Manager Kovo.

Kovo spoke as he walked closer to Trujillo "Gentlemen, I received a message from Mr. Willits, he said you needed my assistance. What can I do for you?"

Trujillo looked at him and gave him a small sack of Belinean Qusar coins. "We need some elbow grease, and no questions asked."

BELINEA 3.12

Port of Braccus - AuFa base

Freshly clean, Nick Devanoe walked through the security checkpoint in a new military suit. He had taken a quick shower and was now returning to the ships. He poked his head into the common room, to find one of his AuFa pilots and the BRG Lieutenant Bezra waiting for him. Devanoe said, "Battle Cruiser here?"

The Aufa Pilot looked at him and said, "Almost, getting into orbit in the next five minutes."

Devanoe responded, "Excellent, let's get out of here."

The three of them walked out of the common room, and over to the C-62T. It was still dark out, but Devanoe noticed only two crafts, the C-62T, and one F-81 Sirator Fighter. Devanoe looked at the AuFa pilot and asked, "Where is the other F-81?"

The pilot responded while continuing to walk over to the C-62T, "I don't know."

Devanoe was slightly confused. He then said, "Alright, get in the F-81 and escort us up. Shoot first and ask questions later if you see something. Otherwise, after we get onboard the Battle Cruiser, return here and report to Captain Vincella of the BRG until we get back from Torsalli, understand?"

The AuFa officer nodded and said, "Yes, sir."

The officer quickly jogged over to the F-81. Devanoe and Lieutenant Bezra walked over to the Ambassador's C-62T and walked through the doors. They were immediately greeted by Commander's Willits and Jones, both drinking some coffee. Devanoe looked at both of them and said, "Commander Willits, Commander Jones, the Battle Cruiser is about to get into orbit, are we ready?"

Willits looked up and said, "As ready as we'll ever be."

Devanoe then asked, "Hey, by the way, what happened to the T-141 and the other F-81?"

Willits responded matter-of-factly, "They are with the service mechanic, remember? I asked you? The C-62T is good to go, but he found a couple of things with the other two."

Devanoe shook his head. "Got it, yeah, I forgot. I just would have preferred having two F-81's for escort up to the Battle Cruiser."

Jones responded, "We can wait?"

Devanoe shook his head, "No, it's fine. Listen, if you don't mind, Lieutenant Bezra is qualified to fly this C-62T, and has experience docking into a Battle Cruiser. So I was going to let him pilot up, alright."

Willits looked at Jones first before returning to look at Devanoe and responding, "Standard Operating Procedure is to turn over the piloting to the BRG, so we assumed he was going to pilot anyway."

Nick sighed. "Good, just making sure we were on the same page. Did not want to upset your two cadets, what're their names again?"

Jones answered, "Knucklehead and Chatty?"

Willits smiled "Trujillo and Tunsall?"

Devanoe half laughed and said, "Yeah. Speaking of, where are they?"

Willits answered, "In the common room in the back guarding Miss Devanoe and the Ambassador. I believe they are all asleep. It's been a long day."

Nick nodded, "Got it. Alright, Bezra, get us out of here."

The four of them walked up to the cockpit area and buckled in. Bezra fired up the engines and began hitting a bunch of switches. Bezra talked into the speakers. "Tower Control, C-62T - E taking off, course set at Battle Cruiser 54, in orbit, copy please."

After a few seconds, a voice came out, "Copy that C-62T- E, proceed with your escort."

Bezra pulled back on the throttle and got the ship airborne, with the F-81 directly flanking him on the side. The two spacecraft slowly headed upward, gaining speed as they gained altitude. Soon they breached the clouds and were ascending past the atmosphere of Braccus.

Bezra hit a couple of switches before talking again. "Battle Cruiser 54, this is C-62T- E. I have a crew of eight including Ambassador Bird and Commander Devanoe. Permission to proceed with docking lock-in?"

"Copy that C-62T - E, identify confirmed, scan for eight passengers is affirmative. Lock-in will commensurate in twenty seconds, proceed with the current course."

The spacecraft began climbing rapidly. As the four looked out the window, they could still see the F-81 flanking them. Soon, what appeared initially as a speck, eventually became the Battle Cruiser, getting closer. The voice came back on. "C-62T - E, begin docking lock-in now."

There was a jolt, and everyone on board the C-62T shook slightly. Jones asked, "What was that?"

Bezra half-smiled. "Just the auto docking function. New to the C-62T, it's easy from here."

Bezra began hitting some switches to enhance the lock-in. The back doors of the Battle Cruiser began to open up as the F-81 returned to the surface. Flying much slower now, Bezra pulled forward on the throttle and eased into the ship through the back doors. He gently landed the craft, as the doors behind him were closing. When the doors finally closed, Lieutenant Bezra turned off all the engines and unbuckled himself from the chair. "And here we are…."

Commander Devanoe led all four of them out of the spacecraft. As the second set of doors was opening, they were greeted by a four-member security team, each with a rifle in their hands, and Captain Kimmel. Commander Devanoe approached, before standing at attention in front of the Captain and saluting. "Captain Kimmel."

The Captain returned the salute and answered, "Commander Devanoe, welcome back."

Nick Devanoe turned sideways and introduced the other four. "Captain, this is Lieutenant Bezra of the BRG. He will be the pilot for this transport and in charge of the detail towards Torsalli."

Bezra saluted out of courtesy and said, "Permission to come aboard, sir?"

Kimmel returned the salute and said, "Permission granted. And you two must be the DAG team that has the entire AuFa looking all over the solar system for."

Devanoe introduced them, although no handshakes or salutes were given. "Captain, this is Commander Willits and Commander Jones of the DAG. Gentlemen, Captain Kimmel of the AuFa Battle Cruiser 54."

Willits then responded, "Captain, we apologize if we have caused any inconvenience. But we are reluctant, and at this point, it seems rightfully so, to trust anyone regarding the Ambassador's travel."

Kimmel took a couple of steps forward. He said calmly, "You changed the manifest, why?"

Willits responded. "Gut instinct. Commander Jones and myself were not satisfied with the number of people who knew what time we were leaving and where we were going. It just seemed best to play it a little close to the vest, per se."

Kimmel tilted his head and said, "Regardless of what it does to the BRG or AuFa?"

Willits gave a crooked smile. "Again, I apologize for whatever measures you initially took that were somehow changed by our actions. I can assure you, it was nothing personal."

Kimmel now stared at them intently. "Commanders, in my thirty-plus years of experience in the AuFa, a mission's success is largely determined on following orders and crystal clear communication. It seemed we had neither, in this case, did we?"

Willits' smile went away. Calmly, he responded. "No, Captain, we did not. But we did end up with an Ambassador who is alive and not dead, so that's a win in my book."

Captain Kimmel was not a fan of Willits' sarcasm. Devanoe tried a half-smile, but could see that was not going anywhere. Kimmel kept staring at Willits, who was going to let that response linger. Kimmel, after a few seconds, went by, finally said, "Well then Commander Willits, Commander Jones, is there anything that your *gut* tells you we should be doing on our way to Torsalli? Set a course to zig-zag the entire way? Perhaps stop at Vandabri and catch a show before taking off?"

Jones half smiled and interjected, "No, Captain, we already did that. Caught a show, had a few drinks, solicited some entertainment, it was a good vacation."

Kimmel, knowing Jones was being a pain-in-the-ass, was further not amused. He calmly replied, "Glad to hear it."

Nick Devanoe interjected, "Captain, the DAG team stopped at Vandabri to hide. Had they gone on to Braccus, it is possible they would've been right in the middle of the Taz Temple Attack."

Kimmel looked at Devanoe in dismay for getting involved. He then turned to Willits and Jones and said, "How fortunate. Or, you could have just stayed with the manifest and gone to the Corvalis system, where we were waiting hours for you."

Willits lifted a finger and, in a smart-ass tone, said, "...and Taz."

Jones kept right up. "Let's not forget that. You were looking for him. Did you find him, by the way?"

Kimmel took a deep breath. "Gentlemen, as amusing as this is for you, it is not for me. I got real soldiers down there that died today. Taz is very real."

Willits then responded, "And you have my sympathy, Captain. But the Ambassador we are assigned to protect is in real danger also. Maybe you don't like how we operate, but that's two shots on his life, both unsuccessful because of us. We don't find this amusing either."

Kimmel sat in silence for a few seconds. There was a huge amount of tension in the air. Willits had stopped smiling, continuing to stare at Captain Kimmel. Kimmel finally responded. "I am assuming we are keeping the C-62T onboard this ship for security purposes?"

Commander Willits nodded, "With your permission, I believe it is the most prudent thing to do."

Captain Kimmel then said, "Well, my security detail team will assist you in moving your stuff. We have set-up the Ambassador's living quarters on deck three, so he can be much more comfortable. I am sure that Commander Devanoe can show you the way."

Willits responded, "With all due respect sir, the living quarters onboard the C-62T are outstanding. It is only an eight hour trip to Torsalli, and the

Ambassador is currently asleep. So we would feel much safer guarding the Ambassador from right here in the bay."

Captain Kimmel was confused. "Guarding the Ambassador Commander?"

Willits reiterated. "Yes, sir. Me and my DAG team. Taz is still out there, Captain, and you won't need to find him. If you got the Ambassador, he will find you."

Captain Kimmel looked a little insulted. "You do not need assistance from my security team then?"

Willits then responded. "Thank you, Captain, but we will be fine right here. My team can handle this. "

There was a long awkward pause as Captain Kimmel looked Commander Willits up. After a few seconds, Captain Kimmel responded, "As you wish, Commander. Let us know if there is anything you need."

Willits and Jones got back on the C-62T and closed the door. As Captain Kimmel was walking away with Commander Devanoe, Kimmel said, "Most unusual set of circumstances."

Commander Devanoe said, "He is a little odd Captain. I do not entirely trust him."

Captain Kimmel responded, "He is an asshole. But he has been right so far. Let's keep the security detail in the hangar, just to be safe."

BELINEA 3.13

Scotland, Earth

Annella Devanoe was sitting in a chair with a small blanket over her body. She was at home, sitting in a cold brick room that was an extension of her estate, looking over the Atlantic Ocean from the cliffs. A small heater was next to her. A tablet was on her lap, while both of her hands were clutching a warm cup of tea. A red Australian Shepherd laid at her feet. Her tablet vibrated, it was receiving a message. Annella put her tea down on the table next to her and picked up the tablet. She hit a couple of buttons and saw that it was a message from Director Kimakawa. She quickly read it.

> *Ms. Devanoe,*
>
> *Ambassador Bird and Miss Devanoe are fine. They are on Battle Cruiser 54 and should arrive at the Space Port on Torsalli approximately one hour from the time of writing this update. Per BRG protocol, crew will then be transported to a Battle Frigate and transported to Hovorn. The trip will take about three days before making the final trip to Belinea under an escort. Will update upon Torsalli arrival.*
>
> *Taichi Kimakawa*

Annella, with one of her hands, grabbed her cup of tea and took a sip. She put it down and then went back to typing a message on her tablet. The recipient was an encrypted title, the message had no subject, but it was short.

"Torsalli, Approx 10:30 SPE TS, Battle Frigate, three days to Hovorn, escorted final trip. They know. Where?"

Annella hit send. The tablet then spoke. "This is a secure, class four recipient; please provide code clearance."

Annella spoke "Annella Devanoe."

The tablet then had a scanner that read her eyes for a couple of seconds, before stopping. Annella put her tablet back on her lap and went back to holding her tea with both hands.

BELINEA 3.14

Battle Cruiser 54

Commander Nick Devanoe and Lieutenant Bezra walked into the cramped bay of the Battle Cruiser. The C-62T was on the edge, right next to the exterior bay doors. Devanoe walked past his own security team, where the guards saluted. Nick asked, "Anything?"

"Just some food, sir."

Devanoe looked at Bezra, and asked, "Check with the Dock Commander, make sure we are ready to go with our flight plan."

Bezra nodded and walked off in the other direction. Devanoe kept walking towards the C-62T. Outside the doors of the C-62T and sitting in a chair was Commander Jones. There was an empty chair next to his, presumably where Willits once was. Two trays of empty food were next to them, and Jones was half asleep. Devanoe walked up to him and said, "We are coming up on Torsalli. Get some sleep?"

Jones stretched his arms and said. "Yes....., thanks for the food."

Devanoe responded, "You are welcome."

Willits came walking out of the C-62T. "All four of them are sound asleep."

Jones replied, "A happy Ambassador for us is one that does not talk. Let Tunsall and Trujillo sleep a little more. They can go on guard duty after Torsalli."

Willits, looking at Devanoe, then said, "I suppose you are the one that provided us with the extra ammo, grenades, bombs, and blaster rifles?"

Nick Devanoe shrugged, "I can take them back...."

Jones opened his hand as if to say stop. "No, thanks. Hopefully, we won't have to use them."

Devanoe responded, "I got some important cargo back there as well. Speaking of, I was going to say goodbye."

Willits looked at him and said, "If you want to wake them all up, go ahead. But that means you answer all the Ambassador's questions as to why are we here, where we are going, why are we changing ships, where is Taz, why is there no fruit for breakfast."

Devanoe gave a half-smile, "Got it. He's that much of a pain-in-the-ass, huh?"

Jones answered, "Actually, not too bad for an Ambassador, but he definitely struggles connecting the dots."

Devanoe thought about it for a second, before drawing a conclusion. "So you guys really do not do much Ambassador security, do you?"

Jones responded, "It is not our first choice."

Willits added, "Is it that obvious?"

Devanoe answered carefully, as if not to offend anyone. "No, but you clearly do not seem to enjoy it. I get the impression that it's beneath you. Yet, here you are. Why?"

Willits walked right up to get face to face with Nick Devanoe. He tilted his head, smiled, and whispered so no one else in the bay could hear him. "Well, isn't that the billion-dollar question?"

Devanoe thought about it long and hard. Then decided not to pursue the matter any further.

Jones then asked, "What's the plan?"

Devanoe noticed Lieutenant Bezra walking up to them. "We are gonna take the Ambassador's C-62T over to the military side of the Space Port at Torsalli. Once we dock, the BRG has provided an officer with further instruction."

On the overhead speaker, the intercom shouted, "Torsalli Space Port, three minutes."

Jones asked, "Anything else?"

Devanoe responded, "I don't think so. Jones, Willits, this is where we say goodbye."

Both gave a quick side salute, but Nick extended his hand to both of them. After shaking Jones' hand, he turned and shook Willits hand and said, "Tell Alexis I said goodbye. Make sure nothing happens to her."

Willits, very sincere and earnest, still shaking his hand, responded, "You have my word."

Bezra, Willits, and Jones walked into the C-62T and went to the cockpit area. After buckling in, Bezra fired up the engines.

Devanoe walked back through the bay and got on an elevator. He went up eight decks, getting off to proceed down a short corridor. He then went to his right, where he went up a ramp that took him directly to the bridge. As he came into the room, Captain Kimmel asked him, "Everything good? Get to say goodbye to your sister?"

Devanoe stopped, looking slightly perplexed. He walked over to the sonar screen area and said, "Wilcox, run a quick thermal body scan on that C-62T."

Wilcox was in his chair, looking at the screen. Devanoe hovered over him from behind. He watched Wilcox hit the screen a few times before he managed a scan get done on the C-62T. It showed basic frames and then thermal images of heat. The engines were big glowing bulbs. The cockpit area had three bodies, looking like they were sitting and flying the craft. Presumably, Bezra, Willits, and Jones. In the back, two bodies were lying down in the common area, while another two bodies were back in the quarters' area, each on a bed. Wilcox then said, "Seven bodies, sir. Looks like these three are in the cockpit, and these four are asleep in the back."

Captain Kimmel had now walked up. "Everything alright?"

Devanoe stood up. "Everything is fine, sir."

The doors of the Battle Cruiser began to open. Bezra flew the C-62T out of the doors and into the tight 'second room.' With the doors closing behind him, he said, "C-62T-E leaving BC 54, proceeding to dock slip 36."

As the back doors slammed tight shut, the second set of doors of the Battle Cruiser opened up, and Lieutenant Bezra flew the ship out of the Battle Cruiser. A voice came in the cockpit that said on the speakers, "Copy that C-62T-E, proceed to slip 36, we have you in sight."

The Space Port on Torsalli looked very similar to the Space Port on Earth. It was just massively bigger and older. It had multiple rings and antennae 'docks' protruding from it. It was so large, the Battle Cruiser looked like a gnat next to it. Bezra circled around and flew directly to slip 36. The Battle

Cruiser practically dropped them off at the site, so this was a quick trip. As Bezra got closer to the dock slip, he hit a few switches, pulled forward on the throttle, and let the C-62T be docked automatically with the slip tractor. An extension was connected to the door, just like it was docked when the ship was on Space Port Earth. The three men unbuckled themselves and walked out.

As soon as they walked out the door, they were greeted by a BRG officer, with a security team behind him. Bezra immediately saluted and said, "Lieutenant Commander, this is Commander Willits and Jones of the DAG."

The Lieutenant Commander nodded his head and spoke, "Welcome to the Torsalli Space Port."

Willits responded. "Thank you, Lieutenant Commander."

Bezra then quickly said, "Gentlemen, this is where I leave you. You are in good hands."

Willits and Jones nodded as Bezra walked off. The Lieutenant Commander continued. "We would like to escort the Ambassador to a more suitable and secure location given his long travel from Braccus."

Willits immediately frowned. "Actually Lieutenant Commander, the Ambassador is perfectly comfortable given his conditions here on the ship. My understanding is this second transport ship should be here soon, so if we could keep your security team outside on guard, we feel it would be the quickest and best solution moving forward."

The Lieutenant Commander looked confused but nevertheless nodded his head in agreement and said to Willits, "As you wish, Commander. Is there anything further my team can provide you with?"

Willits shook his head no and responded, "No, thank you. However, while your team is guarding the ship, Commander Jones and I are going to conduct a quick security sweep of the area, perhaps find something to do before we file a report to our commanders."

Willits provided that last statement with a half-smile and a wink. The Lieutenant Commander seemed a little less rigid now and more understanding of the situation. "No problem Commander, I am sure it was a long flight. My security team will be more than happy to stand guard here."

Willits continued, "And as a matter of discretion, I need to get the Ambassador's traveling assistants off the ship."

The Lieutenant Commander was now really confused. Jones interjected, "Give us a minute, you will understand."

Willits and Jones walked back into the ship, and within a couple of minutes had come out with Cocoa and Harmony. One look at the ladies from the BRG Lieutenant Commander, and he completely understood now what Willits and Jones were referring to. He, too, had to deal with many other potentially embarrassing Ambassador situations. Willits whispered to the BRG Lieutenant Commander "The Ambassador and is still sleeping with one of his assistants. We will be back in one hour."

The BRG Commander nodded and smiled. Willits, Jones, Harmony, and Cocoa now walked back up the tunnel towards the space station. They went through a security area that got them off the military side, and onto the civilian side. They boarded a transport elevator that seemed to 'shoot' them, along with ten other passengers, across the station to the other side of the port. They walked down a few more corridors until they came upon a vast terminal room. They went up to the desk station where a Torsallian asked them, "How can I help you?"

Willits smiled and asked, "I need two tickets for Braccus."

The Torsallian said, "There is a civilian flight that leaves in thirty minutes, and another in four hours."

Willits said, "Thirty minutes is great. When is the next transport down to the Ascarla region of Torsalli?"

She smiled back and said, "There is a transport that leaves in about one hour."

Willits kept up his smile, "Excellent, just enough time for us to get a drink while we wait. I will need two additional tickets for Ascarla, please."

BELINEA 3.15

Battle Cruiser 54

Second Moon of Pyliss

AuFa Supply Station

The Battle Cruiser pulled into an orbit. Captain Kimmel and Commander Devanoe watched from the bridge as a rather large cargo ship flew up from the moon's surface. The ship pulled up next to the Battle Cruiser, flying side by side. A long tunnel bridge extended out from the cargo ship towards the side doors of the Battle Cruiser, connecting the two ships. One of the bridge officers shouted across the bridge, so Commander Devanoe and Captain Kimmel could hear "Docking Tunnel locked into place, sir."

Captain Kimmel then responded, "Proceed with cargo transport Lieutenant."

Commander Devanoe whispered to Captain Kimmel, "Captain Vincella, thanks you, sir."

Captain Kimmel rolled his eyes slightly. "Captain Vincella has a lot more problems then we do."

Inside a stolen Civilian Transport Ship, Taz and his crew navigated the ship towards the Torsalli Space Port. His First Officer Verkato pointed out the window and said, "The Ambassador's ship is on the military side of the port."

The ship then made a turn, so it was going around the massive Space Station. Over the speaker, a voice came out "Civilian Transport Ship 7481, you are in a restricted area, please leave at once."

First Officer Verkato responded, "This is Civilian Transport 7481, we are a little lost, we are looking for Dock Slip 117."

Alexis Devanoe had woken up with a splitting headache. Squinting her eyes, she looked around the cabin. She noticed Ambassador Bird asleep on the other side of the room. Alexis stood and walked to the door, which she could not open. The electronics in the room were not on either, making the room very dark outside of some running lights on the floor. Alexis shouts at the equipment. "Computer on, give me a status, please."

Nothing happens. "Computer on, please. "

Still, nothing happens. Alexis walks over to the Ambassador and begins shaking him. He slowly awakens to the sound of her saying, "Ambassador, wake up."

The Ambassador turns over and suddenly squints his eyes. "Uggh, my head."

Alexis answers, "Mine too. I did not think we drank that much wine."

The Ambassador then sits up. He asks, "What is going on here?"

Alexis responds, "I don't know. Nothing seems to be on."

The Ambassador surveys the situation for a second before he says, "Computer on, please locate Commander Willits."

Again nothing happens. Alexis, sounding nervous now, says, "The door will not open either."

Ambassador Bird stands up. He tries to go over to the door, stumbling a bit. It does not open. He then says, "Computer, override the door to open."

Still nothing. "Computer, lights, please."

Still nothing. The Ambassador goes over to the screens and tries pushing buttons. Alexis goes back over to the door and begins banging on the door really loud. "Help, anyone!!!"

But still, nothing happens. Alexis stops pounding. The Ambassador looks over at her and says, "I think we are trapped. Any ideas?"

Alexis turns around for a second, then briefly thinks. She is now genuinely nervous, as is the Ambassador. It is clear they are somehow prisoners.

She then crosses her arms. In doing so, she notices the wristwatch she is wearing. She looked at it for a few seconds, finally concluding they have reached all avenues to escape their situation. She pushes the panic button on it.

Aboard Battle Cruiser 54, Captain Kimmel, and Commander Deavnoe are watching the cargo transfer. Nick's wrist-watch tracker suddenly blips. He looks at it and immediately holds it out as it is beeping. He raises a considerable eyebrow as Captain Kimmel looks on, in somewhat mild disbelief.

Aboard the Civilian Transport Ship, Taz and his crew continue toward the military side of the Space Port of Torsalli. Over the intercom, a voice says, "Civilian Transport 7481, Dock Slip 117 is on the other side of the Port, please proceed there immediately."

Nobody on board the ship says anything. They are all looking out the window until it finally comes into view. First Officer Verkato points out the Ambassador's C-62T in the distance on a docking slip "There….."

Willits and Jones are in a bar that has a fantastic view of the entire Space Port. They are sitting on bar stools on a railing, finishing their drinks. Over the intercom, a voice says, "Final boarding for Transport Ship 9255, service to Ascarla."

Willits looked at Jones as they stood up. "That's our ship, time to go."

Jones asked, "Any regrets, now is the time?"

Willits, without smiling, said, "No. They get what they deserve."

The two walked over to the boarding dock and had their identifications scanned. They proceeded down the tunnel and onto the transport ship, which had about forty big chairs and a total of thirty passengers. Willits and Jones got a couple of seats next to the window. Jones asked Willits, "Where?"

Willits pointed out the window until Jones saw it. Once he did, he nodded and said, "Got it."

A hostess came over and said, "Drinks, gentlemen?"

Willits said, "Two Woodfords, neat."

The hostess nodded. She walked away. Willits reached into his pocket and pulled out a switch box. Over the intercom, the pilot said, "Welcome aboard everyone. We are now departing Torsalli Space Port and should be landing on Ascarla in about twenty-five minutes."

The hostess came back with the two bourbons. Willits said, "Thank you."

As the ship was backing up, it began to leave the docking slip. Willits could see the C-62T out in the distance, very far away. He looked at Jones and said, "Ready?"

Jones nodded. Willits grabbed the switch box and pushed the button.

The Civilian Transport had an excellent view. All of Taz's crew looked outside the window and saw the Ambassador's C-62T explode from the inside into a million pieces. It immediately turned into a fireball right next to the Space Port. Most of Taz's crew held up their hands to block the flash of light getting in their eyes. All of them look shocked. Taz immediately turns back to the controls, turning the Civilian Transport ship around. He manages to get the ship out of there as fast as possible.

Commander Devanoe is still looking at his wristwatch, which immediately stops blinking. Devanoe now has a look of panic on his face.

Willits and Jones watched the explosion of the C-62T in the distance. Both had an emotionless expression on their face. The ship continued to fly through the atmosphere towards the surface below. After a few seconds, while both are still looked out the window, Willits turned to Jones and said, "Paper, rock, scissors on who tells Kimakawa."

Jones turned to Willits and held out his fist. Willits held out his. They both said, "One, two, three…"

Jones won with rock, while Willits lost with scissors. Willits, matter of factly, said "Two outta three."

BELINEA - EPISODE FOUR
RITUALS

BELINEA 4.1

Serpia 2137 (Twenty Years Prior...)

The massive cargo ship was stationary, except for a few hisses from auxiliary engines to keep it in place. Commander Kimmel was in the main bridge area, jumping from seat to seat. Kimmel ran the scanners, looking for frozen bodies in the debris. He would fly the ship closer to them and extend a large crane arm that connected Quillisar Sallor, in a spacesuit, by a cord. After attaching a clip around the ankle, Sallor would connect the frozen body to the cord and push it to the outside doors of the ship. Once both sets of doors opened, the outer and then the inner, Quillisar Farra would transfer the frozen body to a floating gurney. Farra then pushed the computer-guided gurney towards the end of the bay. As it floated by an empty gurney heading back to Farra, it continued, past dozens of frozen bodies, until it stopped in front of a medical robot. The gurney turned forty-five degrees, and the frozen body would fall to the floor.

Kimmel spoke on his intercom. "My Quillisar, we have been at this for almost four hours. How many more are there?"

Farra responded while walking back to the elevator that would take her to the bridge of the ship. "Keep looking, Kimmel. We need to get all of them."

Quillisar Sallor, from inside his spacesuit, spoke on the intercom. "Quillisar Farra, do we have a total?"

Farra got on the elevator and responded, "One hundred and thirty-six. We need to find two more."

Sallor then questioned. "Quillisar, you know I will do anything you ask me...."

Farra again spoke into the air but picked up by the intercom. "What do you want to ask?"

Sallor said, "You brought Commander Kimmel and myself here to collect these bodies and perform the Quisessa."

Quillisar Farra was still riding the elevator as it took her to the top of the ship. She got off and walked down a corridor, directly into the small bridge of the ship. She was solemn when she spoke. "And the contents in your bag suggest otherwise?"

Quillisar Sallor responded, "So you would like me to come inside and proceed?"

Farra shook her head. "No, we have to get away from here before we can do that."

Farra, still in her red priest cloak, walked up to Kimmel. Kimmel looked completely confused by the conversation Farra and Sallor had over the intercom. He glanced at the screen, which had an alarm bell go off. The computer voice from the panel said, "Warning, incoming ship, hailing frequency open."

Farra responded. "Is it AuFa?"

Kimmel quickly answered. "No, my Quillisar. All the AuFa ships are gone by now."

Over the intercom, he could now hear the hail from the other ship. "AuFa ship, you are in Serpian Territory. Please identify."

Farra said, "What do we do?"

Commander Kimmel said nothing. He looked at his screen again, doing a ship scan. Kimmel whispered, "It's a Serpian Patrol Cruiser. Sallor, get back in the ship, now."

To Farra and Sallor, that meant nothing. They had no understanding of warships. Farra asked, "What does that mean? Can we get out of here?"

Kimmel looked over at the screen again and began turning the main engines on. He responded almost in wit to Farra. "Maybe if I had a crew or even a ship that had any weapons."

Sallor then spoke while looking out at all the floating debris from the ship explosion. "Quillisar, I think I see two more bodies."

The voice over the intercom repeated. "AuFa ship, please identify or prepare to be boarded."

Commander Kimmel went into military mode. He spoke directly to Farra. "They will board the ship, and dispose of those bodies."

Farra asked, "And us?"

Kimmel responded. "Prisoners if we are lucky. Execution if we are not."

Farra was taken back. "Even a Priest?"

Kimmel looked at her dead serious. "They have no religion, they do not care."

Farra looked startled. Kimmel continued, showing Farra the control board. "This button opens the first set of inner doors, this button opens the second set of outer doors. When you hit this button, and pull back on this throttle, that will get us out of here. Do not pull the throttle back until we are all inside, and the doors are closed. Got it?"

Farra asked, "Where are you going?"

Kimmel answered, "To buy us some more time."

Farra nodded in acknowledgment as Kimmel walked out and took the elevator down. He hit a button on his shirt. "Sallor, you have to get back inside, we need to get out of here."

Sallor, now seeing the bodies, estimated they were about sixty meters away. "Kimmel, we got two more bodies out here, we can not just leave them."

Kimmel now got off the elevator and said, "Sallor, that Serpian ship is about three minutes out, and we will be dead if we do not leave before then."

Farra found the button to communicate with the incoming ship. She said, "This is Quillisar Farra, to whom am I speaking?"

As she stood next to the screen, a voice came over. "Quillisar Farra of unidentified AuFa ship. This is Captain Newton of the Serpian Military Defense. The time allowing AuFa and Belinean ships to retreat has passed. You are now in violation of being in Serpian territory."

Kimmel sprinted to the medical robot. He grabbed a floating gurney and pushed it to the other side of the bay, where a partially destroyed F-36 Pirra fighter was. Sprinting to the F-36, he could hear on the intercom Farra's response. "Captain Newton. We are a cargo ship, retrieving dead bodies. We have no weapons and wish you no harm. "

Outside in space, Quillisar Sallor had gone as far as he could go, still tethered to the crane. He could see the two frozen bodies still floating out in space. It was clear to him that Kimmel would not fly the Cargo ship any closer to the two frozen bodies. Sallor looked at the outer doors of the ship, then looked at the bodies again. In the distance, he could see the Serpian Patrol Ship begin to slow down. He paused for a second, then unbuckled his tether. He hit some controls, and his suit gave some short bursts, gliding untethered, towards the bodies.

An alarm went off in the bridge and bay. "Warning. Safety tether is unbuckled."

Kimmel hit his intercom device on his shirt, allowing only Sallor to hear her voice. "Sallor, what are you doing?"

Sallor was focused on the bodies. "We are not leaving without them."

As Kimmel got to the severely damaged F-36, he noticed a torpedo, loosely locked on the crippled wing. He disengaged the torpedo with his tools, which weighed almost 160 pounds, just as the floating gurney arrived underneath the wing. The torpedo 'dropped' onto the floating gurney, and Kimmel strapped it so it would not fall off. He could hear over the intercom "Quillisar Farra, your AuFa ship is in violation of our treaty. Prepare to be boarded."

Out in space, Sallor was now thirty meters from the floating bodies, adjusting the course of his suit with his mini-thrusters. Untethered to the crane, every tiny movement put him in a different direction. As he got closer to the bodies, he could see a man holding hands with a toddler. He was not used to the suit; he was a priest, not a soldier. As he got closer, he hit the wrong booster, which spun his body around. When he had fully turned three hundred sixty degrees, he was face to face with the two bodies and bumped right into them.

On the bridge, Farra was talking into the intercom again. "Captain Newton. There is no need to board. This is not a military exercise. We are performing a religious Quisessa ritual on these souls, so they can be at peace with the energy around them. We ask that you respect our customs, we mean no harm to you. Enough blood has been shed."

After Kimmel hit a switch on the floating torpedo gurney's side, it began blinking yellow as he shoved it towards the big cargo bay doors. He sprinted to the nearby smaller crane and grabbed the heavy cord, proceeding to run back and jump on the F-36. He hooked the cord onto the F-36 and jumped down to a floating tow car. Kimmel dragged the F-36 across the bay floor towards the cargo doors. The floating torpedo gurney was now next to him, bumping into the doors. He yelled into his intercom, "Farra, open the first set of doors, now!"

In space, the two bodies Sallor bumped into were now spinning away, out of his reach. Sallor hit his mini-thruster, but it turned him the wrong way. He could see the Serpian Patrol ship slowing down more as it got closer to the cargo ship. Sallor spun again and regained visual on the two frozen bodies. He hit the mini-thruster again, this time working it correctly to close in on the bodies. Wiggling his fingers as he got to within inches, he was finally able to grab the wrist of the adult body.

Farra could still hear Captain Newton of the Serpian ship through the intercom. "AuFa Cargo vessel, turn off your engines and open your back cargo bay doors, or you will be fired upon."

Farra was scrambling to find the button that Kimmel had just told her about. She then hit the button that opened the inner doors.

As they opened, Kimmel pushed the floating gurney through so that it would bump into the more massive outer doors on the other side. He then hopped back into the floating tow car. Just as the doors were wide enough, he dragged the F-36 through, and yelled, "Farra, hit the button twice, I need the inner doors closed."

Farra, still clearly not feeling comfortable in her surroundings, looked for a second before spotting the button and hitting it twice. The first set of inner cargo bay doors stopped, and then went back to shutting.

Sallor got a clip around the ankle of the adult body, before attaching a cord and connecting it to his suit. He then turned around and began heading back to the ship, both bodies in tow.

Watching the inner doors close behind him, Kimmel jumped out of the floating tow car that dragged the F-36. He jumped up onto the top of the F-36 Pirra and got in the cockpit. The inner doors behind him were now struggling to fully close because the cord he had attached to the F-36 was preventing the doors from sealing shut. If the doors did not completely close, there would be a breach. It was a risk he was going to have to take.

The Serpian Patrol ship was on final approach, slowing down to a crawl as it was about six hundred meters from the AuFa Cargo ship. Kimmel then told Farra, ``Open the outer doors."

Farra hit the button, and the doors opened. However, because of the crane cord breach, the pressure was not stable. Both the F-36 and the floating gurney quickly escaped the holding area and went out to space. Everything not tied down in the giant bay, including the frozen bodies, began traveling to the inner doors.

Captain Newton of the Serpian Patrol Ship was surprised when he saw the damaged F-36 fighter 'float' out of the cargo bay doors. He looked at his crew and said, "The outer doors are open to be boarded, but why is all that debris coming out? Is that a fighter?"

Kimmel was now being flung into space inside the F-36. The tether cord from the crane reeled off a bunch of slack. After twenty meters, the cord ran out of slack and jolted the F-36 back into some stability. Kimmel's head snapped back. For a brief moment, the F-36 was gently bouncing, almost stable. He began looking for the floating gurney with the yellow flashing lights. He finally saw it, heading out to space towards the Serpian Patrol ship. He turned on his guns and fired four shots at the floating gurney. All four shots missed badly but came very close to hitting the Serpian Patrol Ship.

The Serpian Captain Newton, asked, "Did those shots come from that fighter?"

His sonar officer replied, "Yes, sir. The scanners did not pick it up."

Captain Newton was confused. "Lock on and fire back."

A Weapons Officer looking at the screen yelled "Sir, there is no heat to lock on to, it's engines are off. That's why our scanners missed it."

Captain Newton then said, "Religious ritual or not, take out that fighter."

As a couple of engineers were trying to lock in on the F-36, the crane from inside the cargo bay was slowly giving way. Just as the engineers from the Serpian Patrol craft were about to fire, the crane came unbolted from the cargo bay structure. It moved all the way to the inner doors, banging them head-on. The extra twenty meters of slack caused the F-36 to move instantly closer to the Serpian Patrol Craft, before getting 'jolted' back to stability by the crane hitting the inner doors. The shots from the Serpian Patrol Ship missed the Fighter.

Sallor, who was closing in on the cargo ship from sixty meters away, witnessed the whole shootout. Hitting his little booster, he whispered, "Come on, faster."

In the cargo bay, the crane was still trying to pry its way through the small crack between the inner doors. The frozen bodies were piling up behind it, trying to escape as well.

On the Serpian Patrol Ship, the Lieutenant fired again, just missing Kimmel's F-36, still bobbing in space. Kimmel adjusted his eyes and saw the flashing yellow coming off the floating torpedo gurney as it got closer to the Serpian Ship. As he buoyed up, he aimed and fired two shots.

The second shot hit the floating torpedo gurney square. The torpedo exploded, putting a small hole in the front of the Serpian Patrol Ship, changing its direction. The F-36 that Kimmel was in, still tied to the crane cord, got blown back, then wobbled violently from the explosion. As alarms and flashing lights were going off all over the Serpian Patrol Ship, Captain Newton was trying to regain his balance from being thrown from his command post.

The explosion immediately pushed Sallor back another thirty meters. After stabilizing, he redirected towards the cargo ship, the two frozen bodies still in tow. He said, "Quillisar Farra, I am coming."

Kimmel got a couple more shots off at the passing Serpian Patrol Ship, connecting with the rear engine. Kimmel tried to fire again, but nothing happened. He was out of rounds. He whispered, "Oh shit…."

Captain Newton yelled at his crew. "Status?"

A Lieutenant answered. "Engine Two is hit, sir."

Captain Newton yelled back. "Take out that Fighter!"

Another officer answered, "We have to swing back around, sir."

The Serpian ship was doing a full turnaround. Kimmel was running out of options. He looked on the wing and noticed that the F-36 had one more torpedo on it. He turned on the circuit board to aim it, but nothing happened. There was no way to launch it. The wing had been too severely damaged. He tried turning on the engines. The right one was destroyed, but the left one came on, at a fraction of strength, with smoke coming out of it immediately. The computer voice inside the cockpit spoke. "Engine at twenty percent, and failing. Critical failure."

Kimmel saw the Serpian ship had almost come back around. He thought for a quick second, then looked inside the cabin for a relief mouthpiece. He found it in the emergency drawer, and quickly bit into it, relieved he could breathe. He pushed a few buttons, and the voice inside the cockpit said, "Torpedo activated."

Kimmel blew the emergency hatch for the F-36 fighter. He turned the engine to full throttle. The voice in the cockpit said, "Warning, engine levels not stable, critical state."

Kimmel climbed out and grabbed the back cord that was buckled to the F-36, to keep it from going anywhere. He kept trying to unbuckle it, still struggling because the F-36 was trying to get loose of the buckle with one engine trying to escape. The Lieutenant from the Serpian ship said to Captain Newton, "Sir, the engines are turned on, I got a lock on the fighter."

Kimmel finally got the cable cord unbuckled. The F-36 began spinning out of control, mostly away from the cargo ship. Captain Newton yelled, "Fire!"

As the F-36 was spinning violently out of control, the shot whizzed past Kimmel, between the F-36 and the cargo ship. Still clutching the cord as hard as he could, Kimmel looked up and saw Sallor, in his spacesuit, controlling his mini-thrusters towards him. The computer voice inside the F-36 kept repeating, "Danger, Danger, critical engine overload."

The Serpian Ship, Captain Newton, yelled, "Fire again!"

This time, as the spinning F-36 was near his Patrol ship, the shot connected. The explosion from the F-36 did further damage to the front of the Serpian patrol ship. It also set Sallor's course a little sideways. At the last moment, Sallor missed Kimmel. He was too far above him. But Sallor managed to grab the crane cord and clip it. Holding on to the cord, he guided his thrusters back to the cargo ship. As he looked down, he saw Kimmel had grabbed onto the ankle of the frozen adult he was towing. They had made it back to the Cargo ship, where Kimmel yelled, "Farra, close the outside bay doors, now!!!"

The Serpian ship was floating out of control. It had taken on too much damage, and parts of the front were in flames. Kimmel had barely gotten inside the transition area between the inner and outer doors when he noticed the outer doors closing behind him. The room was finally beginning to destabilize from the pressure. The outer doors shut tightly, and Sallor yelled, "Farra, open the inner doors."

The inner doors opened. The crane was butted up next to where the doors were. All the bodies, debris from the cargo bay, and equipment had all piled up next to the doors as well. Kimmel threw out his mouthpiece, and ran to Sallor, talking into his intercom. "Farra, the doors are closed! Get us out of here!"

Farra, hunched over hurt from the explosion, got back up. She looked at the control panel and then asked through the intercom, "Which button?"

Kimmel was collapsed on top of Sallor. Some debris had punctured his leg. He yelled, "The button next to the throttle. Hit the button, pull back on the throttle."

Captain Newton had managed to get down to the firing position of his Patrol Ship. He threw out the officer who was unconscious in the chair. He sat in, lined up the scope, and saw the transport.

Farra found the button, hit it, and pulled back on the throttle. With a massive increase in speed, the cargo ship jolted just as Captain Newton had fired two shots that had missed. In a few seconds, the ship got to a safe speed that allowed it to jump into Hyper-EXtension speed.

BELINEA 4.2

Twenty Years Later...

Avola

Four beams, supported by multiple large rocks, made a diamond shape in the rocky mountain area. Elevated in the middle was the body of Officer Belbin Marrat, who had died three days prior. The funeral arrangement was made on a high plateau in the red rock mountain area near the Avolian base. On one side of the diamond, four Avolian Quill Priests dressed in red had their hoods on and were praying. On the other side of the diamond, eighty-four soldiers stood at attention. The soldiers were in their dress grey uniforms with red trim. In the front were their leaders, Octavious Killian and Kaya Killian. On the other side of the diamond, between the soldiers and priests, were the dead soldier's family members. Ambassador Syren flanked them as well.

The Head Priestess, Quillisar Balerra, walked up to the diamond. She said, "Energy is added, energy is taken, the peace is the energy around us. The energy is in us, and when the light of our energy is extinct, the energy is added to the light around us. We are the energy."

The rest of the audience responded in unison, "The energy is in us."

Quillisat Balerra continued. "Belbin Marrat's energy has not died, it has moved on, redirected back into all of us. The energy never dies."

The rest of the audience responded in unison, "The energy always lives."

The three other priests all got to one corner of the ceremony site. On each corner, each priest revealed from their rings around their neck, in order: fire, instantly lighting a corner; water, rotating like a sprinkler, and a red rock with silver stripes on the third corner.

Quillisar Balerra went to the final corner, at the top of Marrat's head. The corner pointed to the cliff off the mountainous rock. The sun was setting, casting an orange glow on the red rock of the desert mountain landscape.

She took from her hands some orange-brown sand, manipulating it into a small tornado in front of her. The Head Priest continued. "The Quisessa is a time for rejoice. A time to reflect on the energy we are given, the energy that reforms, and the energy that returns, reborn from the fire and stone."

The rest of the audience responded in unison, "The energy is in us."

Quillisar Balerra continued to move the small tornado of orange-brown sand around the diamond and over the body of the deceased. After a few seconds, Octavious Killian walked to the bottom of the diamond, near the feet of Marrat. The Priest who had lit a small fire there took two steps back. Killian pulled out his ring, making the ring turn into a red saber. He kneeled, placing the red saber on the bottom of the diamond beams. He whispered, "The energy must live on."

After a couple of seconds, the saber was on fire. It then lit all of the beams, until there was a diamond shape fire around the dead soldier Marrat. All of the priests took one step back and held both of their hands up towards the sky. Octavious continued to kneel, as the entire body was now engulfed in flames. As the dead body was burning to ashes, Quillisar Balerra said, "The energy is now in all of us."

In unison, the group responded, "The energy never dies."

After about ten seconds, all of the priests took their hands down and walked over to the family members. Octavious extended his saber, and hooked Marrat's ring out of the fire. It had turned entirely silver now. Octavious then walked over to the family, still holding the ring with his saber. He came up to Marrat's daughter, and let her look at the ring. Crying, she politely nodded, and Octavious held the ring up. He shouted so everyone could hear. "The energy never dies…"

As he held the ring up, the red-orange sand from the ground twirled into a very thin tornado, straight up to the ring on Octavious' saber. It instantly disintegrated the ring, turning it into sand as well. The tornado then disappeared.

Starting with Kaya, one by one, the soldiers came up to the family of Belbin Marrat. As Kaya joined him, she and Octavious began walking away from the funeral. Neither was crying; neither was smiling. As they walked away, their cousin was waiting for them away from the funeral. Donovan was not dressed in the best of clothes; he was still dirty. The siblings walked up to their cousin, and Octavious said, "Donovan?"

Donovan had his head bowed, almost unsure how to address his cousin. Octavious grabbed his shoulders. Donovan spoke, virtually on the verge of tears. "I came to pay my respects. I did not think that I belonged in the Quisessa."

Octavious looked down on him; he was significantly shorter. "My cousin, the Quill welcomes all. The energy is in all of us."

Kaya came over and hugged her cousin. Donovan responded with a half hug, almost embarrassed. "I feel awful. I am responsible for his death."

Kaya looked at him, putting her hand on his face. "Donovan, Marrat was a soldier. He knew what he was getting into. Soldiers die, even the best ones."

Kaya took a few steps back. Donovan didn't know what to say. "But this isn't a war."

Kaya responded, "But it is my cousin. And there are only two sides. Ours and theirs."

Donovan, on the verge of crying, shook his head. "Octavious, I never meant for this to happen. We wish the Guild were back in charge, and we know that's what you are fighting for."

Octavious looked solemn. "Yes, and we will keep fighting. Kaya and I cannot thank you enough for the information. Every bit helps."

Donovan looked at his cousins. "Which is why I am here. We have families, too, Octavious. It is dangerous the information we provide."

Kaya looked at Donovan, almost crying herself, and said, "Of course, Donovan, we know. We can have the Quill provide you with whatever you and your family need. Food, clothing...."

Donovan, now with a tear down his face, replied, "Money?"

Kaya looked confused. "Money?"

Donovan, in almost a pleading voice, responded. "We know what the Vait is worth Kaya. The Majavkee have us working twice as hard, twice as long, for only a fraction more money. We just want what is fair. That is why we came to you. We heard you are selling the Vait through other channels."

Ocativous responded, almost dumbfounded. "Yes, in addition to food and shelter, we use it for ammunition and weapons to provide security for you and the miners."

Donovan shook his head. "We have food and shelter. What we want is a better future for our children. We want fair pay for the work we do. If you just take it and use it for weapons, you are no better than the Majakee."

Kaya now looked angry. "Donovan, I have seen your conditions. The Majakee are treating you like slaves. The conditions are awful. They don't care about you or your families. We can only get back to how it was if we can successfully remove them and the Council. They are the enemy."

Donovan looked at his cousins long and hard. "I am not a soldier, but I have fought for a long time. I don't know how much more we can fight."

Octavious said softly, "Until we make this a safe place for our children."

Donovan walked away. Kaya and Octavious just watched Donovan walk away. They then looked at each other before proceeding to step out in the opposite direction. After a few seconds, they heard a voice shout at them. "Octavious...."

Both Kaya and Octavious stopped, turning to recognize Ambassador Syren. They waited for her to join them. As the Ambassador approached, they continued to walk, now all three of them together. The Ambassador said, "My condolences."

Octavious, who was leading the trio, replied. "That's for the family, not me."

Ambassador Syren questioned, "He was one of your soldiers, correct?"

Kaya gloomily replied, "He was one of mine, and soldiers die."

Syren was struggling to keep up; the siblings were walking fast. "The Council representative will be here within the hour. Have you decided where you would like to meet?"

Octavious replied without looking at her. "You still think this is a good idea?"

Syren said, "I do."

Kaya cautioned, "If they send someone insignificant, it will be a sign that we are weak."

Syren had different thoughts. "That's why the meeting is private, and we decide on the location. Although, I think they are sending someone who speaks on behalf of Chairman Hassara. Definitely a Belinean."

Kaya quickly retorted. "How do you know? Did they tell you?"

"No, but they have no reason to lie."

Kaya was angry. Discussing this after a funeral was not the best time. "They have every reason to lie, and we have no reason to trust them."

Syren continued. "Kaya, they don't want a war, they want a resolution."

Kaya turned around to look at Syren. "They want us dead, Syren. All of us. Starting with that one we just burned (pointing first at Marrat's Quisessa fire) and ending with him (now pointing at her brother Octavious)."

Octavious turned around now as well. "Enough!"

He looked at Kaya, squinting his eyes. "Do you think I enjoyed that? Saying goodbye to another brother in our fight for survival?"

Kaya said nothing. Just staring at her brother, she looked just as angry as she was before. Octavious then looked at Ambassador Syren. "Montabella Pointe, ninety minutes from now. Tell them alone, no security detail. And don't give them the location until the very last possible minute. Understood?"

Syren nodded and walked away. Octavious looked back at Kaya and whispered, "What are you trying to do?"

Kaya, in something louder than a whisper, replied, "What are *you* trying to do? You think they will listen to you?"

Octavious "Of course not. But I also know that nothing we do will bring back Marrat, no matter how many AuFa soldiers we kill."

Kaya still was angry. "Brother, we will avenge his death, that I promise. I will not be told his death was for nothing."

Octavious responded, "Kaya, all of these deaths will be for nothing if we don't come up with a solution. I'm sure they're sending nobody important, and I will have you there if it's a trap. But at some point, they will send someone that can offer a possible solution."

Kaya was pleading, "You said so yourself they are never gonna give us what we want."

Octavious replied, "I know they won't. But a compromise (shrugging his shoulders)? How many Quisessa's are we going to have to go to before you realize there is no scenario in which they leave us alone."

Kaya shook her head. "I would rather die than give them anything."

Octavious whispered, holding her face. "And I would rather our legacy lived, even at the cost of our lives."

BELINEA 4.3

Avola

SS-11, Secret Service Transport

The SS ship was slowing down from hyper-Extension speed. It came up to Avola, a dark grey planet with thousands of electrical storms running through its atmosphere as it slowed down. It was strange even to Argo, who had seen over a hundred planets in his lifetime. They came closer to the AuFa Battle Cruiser. It was directly outside what looked like a colossal round frame of yellow and white lights. As they got even closer, it was clear that the Battle Cruiser would not fit through it, but that a relatively small vessel like the ship he was on would. The ship kept slowing down even more, as it glided toward the entrance of the tunnel.

Going through the entrance was a checkpoint. The tunnel looked tight as if the ship would come close to hitting the outside of it. Then gravity kicked in, and the ship gave the illusion of speeding up by passing all the storms around the tunnel. There was a lot of turbulence as the ship got sucked down the tunnel. For a solid two minutes, all Argo could see through his windows was the storms outside. It was also clear only one ship, in either direction, could go through the tunnel at one time. Once the ship cleared the tunnel, Argo was surprised to see the hazy, red-orange glow of the red-rock mountain and desert floor.

The ship was on final approach and was being guided to a secure Majavkee area. It was a small base, carved out of the rock of the red-orange sand. As the ship landed, Lord Argo turned to Lt Walva. "Walla, there will be no need to unpack, we are not going to be here long, understand?

Lt Walva had given up on the name correction game. He simply nodded and continued looking at the screen in front of him. As the ship touched the ground, something popped up on Walva's screen. "Sir, you have four messages here. One from Chairman Hassara, one from Quillisar Prill, one from the local SS Commandant, Captain Leahy, and one here that has no identification or information, sir. It seems to be encrypted.

Argo had stood up. "Walla, why are you looking at my personal correspondence?"

Walva responded, "Sir, you asked me to construct a message to your sister, Defense Director Tempest. The T-Bar Transmitter now that we are here on Avola will work at a faster speed. I simply assumed you would want to know that you had more messages coming through."

Argo put his black cloak on. "Walla, don't assume. Your stupidity can only hurt our position here."

Argo walked over to the screen and practically kicked Walva off it. "Shoe…"

Argo looked at the screen, and a device scanned his eyes. Argo said to the screen, "Hassara, Argo."

Argo then began reading one of the messages. "Dammit. I am surprised he hasn't lit the whole galaxy on fire."

Walva looked puzzled. "And who might that be Lord Argo?"

"Taz. He attacked a Temple on Braccus, over one hundred dead."

Walva looked shell, shocked, "That is awful."

Argo then began typing something into the screen. "There you go. And no, I don't need that. And I already got that. Alright, let's go. Walla, go fetch my V-fleece armor and my bolster pack."

Argo watched Lt Walva scurry off as he came walking down the back of the belly of the sleek, narrow, charcoal grey SS ship. Captain Leahy of the SS was waiting for Argo at the bottom of the ramp, giving him a salute. Argo returned the salute and said, "Captain Leahy."

Leahy then began to walk side by side with Argo. "Lord Argo. I am here to brief you."

Argo and Leahy just kept walking toward the base. It was clear Argo was annoyed by the whole process and couldn't wait to get this done and over with. "Has anything changed since the briefing you sent my sister and me?"

The two were escorted by two more SS soldiers. Captain Leahy replied without looking. "No, sir. There have been no new attacks in the last three days, once they agreed to the meeting."

The two walked through a set of doors into a situation room. The room had a map of the planet on it with several AuFa officers around it. Argo walked into the room, and they all stood at attention. Argo continued towards the table as Captain Leahy spoke. "The Valmay Group still occupies these territories near Lowell Province while Majavkee Security has strong firm holds here, and here. We have fortified these regions with Eighth Battalion here (pointing on the map) and the 26th Battalion here. Each of the four tunnel entrances are still blocked. You saw Battle Cruiser 34 on your way in, with two AuFa Patrol Ships here. Admiral Holland leads the entire force, and he is waiting for your orders aboard the Command Destroyer guarding this tunnel here."

Argo looked satisfied. "Alright, when am I meeting with this Octavious Killian? And where?"

Leahy pointed across the room to a glass window. "Over there is former Ambassador Syren. Off the record, she seems to be the main contact person the Valmay Group uses for communication. She would provide us no information until you got here."

Argo looked annoyed. "Then what are we waiting for? Send her in."

The AuFa Captain interrupted. "Lord Argo, we were waiting for you so we could construct a plan. The Valmay Group would likely not agree to a Majakee security detail as an escort, but perhaps a light platoon of SS soldiers….."

But before the AuFa Captain could finish, Argo, further annoyed, began walking to Ambassador Syren's room. The Ambassador turned around as he entered. "Lord Argo. I was not expecting The Council to send you to negotiate on their behalf."

Argo did not smile. "That makes two of us. However, it is a critical issue, one that the Chairman takes very seriously. I hope you understand I speak directly for him. He wishes this matter be resolved as quickly as possible."

Syren was still a little stunned. "Of Course, My Lord, we wish the same."

"Then, you will please take me to the Valmay Group leader, this Octavious Killian, I believe?"

Syren nodded. "Of course, this way, my Lord."

The two walked back into the Situation room, everyone back to standing at attention. Argo, now standing by the Ambassador, proclaimed, "Ambassador Syren will now lead us to the meeting, which is at …?"

Syren did not immediately answer. She looked hesitant. Captain Leahy was confused. "Where should I tell our security detail we are going?"

Argo waved his hand. "That won't be necessary."

Captain Leahy responded, "Excuse me, my Lord?"

Syren finally responded. "Commander Killian has indicated he wants no security there except for the negotiator."

Leahy interrupted again, looking directly at Syren. "Clearly, the fucking Commander doesn't know who he is negotiating with! We are not sending the head of the SS out there without security."

Argo quietly responded in annoyance. "Actually, we are. Ambassador, you know where the location is, and when?"

Syren nodded in affirmative. Argo continued. "Leahy, you know how to fly one of these transports?"

Leahy nodded and replied, "Yes, My Lord."

Argo responded. "Good. Leahy, you will fly me and the Ambassador to the meeting point with this Valmay leader. Unless anyone in this room is dumb enough to question my orders?"

The room was silent. Argo looked at all of them. "Excellent, Ambassador, shall we…?"

BELINEA 4.4

Avola

Lowell Province, Sector 9 Mining Center

Sterling was walking off a mine train that had just returned from shaft seven. He and the other fifteen miners had taken off their ventilation masks and mining equipment. A supervisor came up to Sterling and said, "Sterling, bosses want to see you."

Sterling looked curious. He looked back at his crew and before walking over to the main building. He climbed the stairs and walked in through the door. His direct Avolian boss, Chief Supervisor Davis, was standing. One Majavkee Supervisor and Majavkee Lord Bialos were sitting behind a table. As Sterling came in and stood next to his boss, Davis spoke. "This is Crew Seven Supervisor, Sterling."

Sterling nodded. The two Majavkee were looking at their tablets. The Majavkee Supervisor then spoke. "Sterling, shaft seven has produced some great results."

Sterling nodded again. Davis stood next to him with his arms behind his back. The Majavkee Supervisor continued. "A good quarter indeed. Out of thirty-eight shafts, you supervised the second-highest total Vait production. Congratulations."

Sterling nodded again and said, "Thank you, my Lords."

Lord Bialos looked up and said, "We feel you deserve a bonus. We are rewarding you an extra thirty Golda's on top of your salary."

Sterling asked, "Is that a monthly bonus, my Lord?"

Lord Bialos answered, "A quarterly bonus, Sterling."

Sterling looked down and did not say anything. A few seconds went by before he responded. "And the bonus for my men?"

Lord Bialos and the Supervisor were taken aback. The Supervisor said, "Excuse me?"

Sterling looked up, right into the eye of Lord Bialos. Davis tapped him on the foot, so as to not say anything, but Sterling continued. "My men, sir. They have been working unpaid extra hours to produce those results."

Lord Bialos responded, "You are saying your men require a monetary bonus to motivate them?"

Sterling said, "I promised them bonuses. They responded by working more daily hours and sometimes on their day off. The older men in my crew say that we processed 50% more Vait from that shaft then what we did the same quarter two years ago."

Lord Bialos looked at his tablet. After a pause, he said, "Almost, it is forty-eight percent. However, we have invested a tremendous amount of capital in new state of the art Doggo drill bits and D-7 diggers. So, we expected at least fifty percent more processing."

The Supervisor continued. "We also lost over two hundred units from this latest terrorist attack by the Valmay Opposition Group. So whatever you promised your crew is your responsibility."

Sterling was momentarily silent. After another long pause, he said, "Is there anything else, sir?"

Lord Bialos added, "I do not sense much gratitude on your part, Sterling."

Sterling said, "Forgive me, my Lord. Perhaps I felt my crew had earned more."

Lord Bialos answered, "Your crew has earned employment, nothing else. We pay them enough. We can take away the bonus if you prefer?"

Sterling paused again and then looked at Davis, who gave him a scowl. Sterling looked at Lord Bialos and said, "Forgive me, my Lord, that was not my intention."

Lord Bialos replied. "Good, you can leave and enjoy the rest of your Quill Offering holiday."

Sterling walked out of the room and down the stairs. When he turned, he saw his crew waiting on him outside the break room. It was clear they were prepared for the bad news.

BELINEA 4.5

Belinea

Defense Minister Hassara's Office

Tempest was finishing watching a briefing at her desk. It was an update on the Braccus situation. A computer voice on her intercom said, "Ambassador Yi is here for you."

Tempest responded, "Send him in."

Ambassador Yi walked in, noticing Tempest behind her desk watching the video and eating a piece of fruit. He walked toward her desk and responded, "Defense Minister, you wanted to see me?"

Tempest answered after putting her fruit down. "Yes, Ambassador, thank you. Please sit…"

The Ambassador sat in the chair in front of her desk. Tempest had extended her hand and continued, "Something to drink?"

Ambassador Yi, the highest-ranking Earth Ambassador, politely shook his head 'no.'

Tempest continued. "Ambassador, I need some information from you. How well do you know Ambassador Bird?"

Ambassador Yi was thrown off by the question. "I'm sure you know as much as I do, Minister."

Tempest folded her hands together. "Pretend I do not. What do you know?"

The Ambassador continued. "Well, he is American. He had been a delegate for quite some time, he is a career politician. He has certainly worked the system to get where he is at. Bird is backed by some very well funded people, including some with deep interest in the building facilities we will be expanding."

Tempest thought for a moment before responding. Do you trust him?"

The Ambassador smiled. "The better the Politician, the less I trust them. So, I essentially trust no one."

Tempest smiled back. "Understood. However, let me ask it another way. I told you that I would handle the negotiation of Ambassador Bird. Is it possible I have underestimated my desired outcome?"

Ambassador Yi looked slightly puzzled. "Is there an update on Ambassador Bird's status?"

Tempest unfolded her hands. "You are aware of the attack on Braccus. It seems Ambassador Bird is alive and well. He is currently en route here to Belinea as scheduled. My question is, are we sure Ambassador Bird will see things our way? Like you, once the Ambassador sees the personal financial gain, you are confident his support will be unquestioned, correct?"

The Ambassador shifted his weight in the seat. "Defense Minister. If you are worried about his stance on taking resources designated to the BRG and using them for an enhanced Earth Delegate Ambassador Guard, that is simply the Ambassador saber-rattling. Failure to acknowledge the terrorist threat to the Delegates undermines his credibility. I can assure you that after this trip, he will very much question the capabilities of the DAG, and his convictions for fighting the terrorists will be as strong as it ever has been."

Tempest smiled again. "My father once told me 'a man has many convictions, the strongest are bought.'"

Ambassador Yi smiled also. "The Chairman is very wise."

Tempest stood up, and Ambassador Yi quickly did so as well. "Ambassador, thank you for your continued support. It is never taken for granted."

Ambassador Yi bowed his head. "If there is anything I can do for you or your father, please do not hesitate to ask."

The Ambassador turned around and began to walk out. He took five steps before turning around again, back at Tempest. "Defense Minister, If I may ask, any word on your brother's negotiation with the Avolians?"

Tempest gave a crooked smile "He should be meeting with them as we speak."

BELINEA 4.6

Avola, Montabella Pointe

Captain Leahy gently landed the transport ship on a small area of flat rock. The Pointe was a park that overlooked a valley of red rock and sand. The Avolians had long before declared the location could not be touched by either developers or miners. As the engines were being shut off, the belly opened. Lord Argo walked out with Ambassador Syren next to him. Behind them was Captain Leahy and Lieutenant Walva, both of whom had stopped at the ship's entrance.

Argo and Syren walked thirty meters to where Octavious and Kaya Killian were waiting. Twenty meters behind the siblings were eight of Kaya and Octavious's soldiers. All of them were armed with rifles. As Argo got closer, it was clear Octavious and Kaya were very surprised to see him. Argo and Ambassador Syren stopped six meters from the siblings. Octavious, after the initial shock wore off, gave a half-smile, and said, "Argo Hassara….I thought they were sending someone important?"

Argo half-smiled right back. "That is what my sister is for Commander Killian. They only send me when they don't care about the body count. (now looking at Kaya) And who is this eye candy? I didn't know you could afford such attractive talent."

Kaya squinted her eyes in anger. The smile on Octavious had disappeared. "Your intelligence team is failing you, Argo. This is my second in command, my sister Kaya."

Argo kept smiling, looking directly at Kaya. "Not my usual preference, but after a bottler of wine, I might change my mind."

Kaya had already had enough. "There is no amount of wine on my end. I'd sooner go home with Ambassador Syren."

Ambassador Syren blushed, mostly in discomfort. Her usual negotiations never went like this. Argo, smiling, said, "I'm pretty sure the Ambassador doesn't have the same hardware I've got."

Kaya, never smiling, replied, "I'm willing to bet."

Argo, continuing to smile, and countered sarcastically. "I like the spunk. When you get done wasting your time with this leader of the Red Ring Rise, I can show you the best hour of your life."

Kaya continued to stare down Argo. She gave a very small hint of a smile, and replied, "An hour or two minutes? Either way, I wouldn't even fuck you with my brother's dick, but I bet you'd like it if I did."

After a few seconds, Argo continued, "Just don't forget the wine, Princess. (Then looking at Octavious) Your sister is a bitch, but she has a bigger cock than you. My intelligence information is just fine, Octavious."

Octavious continued to stare down Argo. "Noone in our group goes by Red Ring Rise anymore. We refer to ourselves as the Valmay Group."

Ambassador Syren interrupted. "Valmay was a village in the Bosa Provence. After an unstable mining accident led by the Majakee Lords, the entire village was lost, killing hundreds. The leaders of the neighboring villages collectively pleaded to the local government to suspend operations and restore the full power of the Mining Guild. The Majavkee Lords all but laughed, vowing to kill all these village leaders who defied them. They labeled them to the press as The Valmay Group of Opposition, ones against the economic gains of mining. They (pointing at the siblings) use it as a battle cry, simply calling themselves the Valmay Group."

Argo glanced at Syren before returning to look at the siblings. "I honestly don't give a fuck what you call yourselves or what they did...."

Kaya interrupted, "You mean the sacrifice of an entire village for monetary gain?"

Argo was now annoyed. "Their sacrifice, their energy, or whatever the shit is you guys recycle, I am not here to talk about accidents and villages. This is not the Council floor."

Octavious interrupted, "The term Valmay Group is a badge of honor. We do not forget the souls that were lost at the hands of the Majavkee Lords' greed."

Argo took a deep breath and said, "Are we really gonna keep talking about death?"

Kaya intruded, "We could talk about killing you...?"

Argo raised an eyebrow. "Princess, where is that gonna get you?"

Octavious responded, "Careful Argo...."

Argo paused, then stared at both of them before continuing. "Make no mistake, my father, the Council, and most people on this planet would love nothing more than to see the both of you hanging from a noose. Some adage about cutting the head off a snake."

Octavious then responded, "What possibly makes you think you'd get out of here alive?"

Argo looked behind the siblings. "What is that...., ten on one, I like my chances. I'm confident I would still have my hands to pour my wine and enough time to find some miserable fucking whore to suck my cock before sunset. But, on the remote chance that one of you kills me, well...., the shit storm that would create. The Council and my father would have every reason to send an armada to extinguish you fuckers from existence."

There was a long pause as everyone stared at each other. Finally, breaking the tension was Ambassador Syren as she said, "I feel that maybe we got off on the wrong foot...."

But Argo cut her off. "Ambassador, you are no longer needed, leave us."

Syren looked at Argo, then at the siblings. She then bowed her head and walked behind Octavious and Kaya, towards the other soldiers behind them in the distance. Argo looked at Kaya. "You too, Princess, time for the men to talk."

Kaya, in a cold dead stare, grabbed the ring on her side and just whispered, "I'm pretty sure I have the biggest cock here, you said so yourself...."

Argo looked amused. "Wow, Octavious, does she hold it for you when you piss too?"

Octavious only replied, "I trust her with everything, Argo. She stays."

Argo let out a sigh. " Very well, what is it that you want?"

Octavious pounced at the chance while never taking his eyes off Argo. "All Majavkee Lords stripped of power and their territories. A return to the

Avolian Mining Guild and a withdrawal of AuFa forces, with an independent peacekeeping force put in its place. Not SS."

Argo just smiled. "Why don't you just ask if we can hang them by their balls from the highest tower in the city, Octavious? I don't think I should have to pay extra every time I kill a whore during services rendered, but unfortunately, the madam is pissed, and father says I should be more gentle. We all can't get what we want."

Octavious half smiled again. "Can't get anything without having to run to Daddy?"

Argo gave a quick snort. "That's fucking humorous. My answer to this problem is to take one of my SS units through your land and cut every one of your fucking heads off. Don't kid yourself, Octavious. It's Daddy's mercy for you little shit's that is keeping me on a leash."

Kaya interjected. "The Majavkee Lords are killing this planet, and nothing short of their complete removal will….."

Argo stopped her. "The Majavkee Lords are not going anywhere. They make too much money for themselves and the Council. No one is sympathetic to their removal. Your negotiation ends there."

Octavious then replied, "Then we will take our chances…"

The siblings turned around and were about to walk away before Argo quickly interjected, "Octavious, don't be an idiot."

The siblings turned around again. Octavious looked at Kaya first before looking back at Argo. Argo continued, "We know you are mining Vait. But the AuFa has every tunnel blocked. The embargo is preventing you from selling any substantial quantity of it. My sister is about to pass an initiative that will triple the efforts to find Taz, your partner in this mess, and a military invasion that will see most of your people die. Is that what you want?"

Octavious responded, "We both know Taz is no longer with us, and that he hasn't been for a while."

Argo took a step forward. "Perception is reality."

Kaya and Octavious looked at each other. There was a pause before Octavious looked back at Argo. "What does the Chairman propose?"

Argo looked at both of them. "Keep your lands. The AuFa, along with my troops in the SS and with the Quill blessing, will keep the peace. In return, we take control of your mining facilities. Your advisors can stay on to assist in the production and verify amounts. The Council will pay you double what we are paying the Majavkee. Publicly, half the money goes to your mining group so that we can save face with the Majakee. Privately, the other half goes to you, personally, with your sister, if you choose, to keep this agreement."

Kaya looked astounded. "You think you can buy us?"

Argo looked astounded as well. "In my experience, everyone can be bought. The deal would make you two some of the richest people in the galaxy."

Kaya countered, "Rich, yes, but never able to look into the eyes of the people that lost families and friends in Valmay."

Argo then asserted. "Who gives a fuck? The Majavkee don't care, they sleep just fine at night. If you feel that bad, give them some of your money or build a memorial statue."

Octavious then questioned, "And what of the Majavkee Lords? They go unpunished for all of their crimes? How can we trust you to keep the peace?"

Argo looked puzzled. "What crimes? Making money? The Majavkee Lords stop shooting at you for starters. They stop going into your territories. All of you make a shitload of money."

Octavious now smiled. "The Majavkee Lords, I assume your engineers as well, will continue to bleed this planet dry until there is no Vait. There is no price for the environmental damage you are inflicting on Avola."

Argo was still baffled. "With that kind of money, you can leave! Buy yourself a vineyard in Torsalli. (Looking at Kaya) Go find yourself a man and make little cocksucker soldiers, or whatever it is that gets you off. You want a *cause* Octavious, how about survival? Because there is no chance you do if you say no."

Kaya took two small steps forward, stared Argo in the eyes, and said, "Remember this Argo, as the moment I decided I will not rest one minute until I stab you right in your fucking heart."

Argo half smiled again. "I'd win, either way. I'd go out with a hard-on if that happened."

Kaya kept her hand on her ring. Argo now put his hand on his. Octavious took three steps ahead, putting a hand on Kaya's shoulder. Now looking at Argo, he said, "Not now Kaya, our day will come. Tell your father we will not be bought. Remove the Majavkee Lords, restore the Guild, or pay the consequences."

Argo just continued to look before shaking his head and mumbling 'Are you fucking serious?"

Kaya and Octavious took two steps back before turning around to walk back to their soldiers. Each of them had their rifles ready as if they could sense the escalation in the talks. As they got about another five steps away, Argo yelled, "Octavious, last chance. Take the deal, or they will hunt down every last one of you."

Both the siblings turned around. Octavious half smiled and was going to say something, but Kaya had beat him to it. "I don't think you or your Father have the balls to do it. But I will be right here waiting, Princess, if you do."

Argo almost laughed as he watched them walk away. Then he muttered to himself, 'Fucking bitch.'

Argo turned around and walked back to the transport ship. He was walking up the ramp when he heard Lieutenant Walva begin speaking. "My Lord, your father, is expecting a complete briefing on your meeting with the Killians. If you could be so kind as to let me know the details, I will be happy to......"

Just then, Argo spun around, grabbed Walva by the head, and slammed him against the side of the ship's entrance. Walva was in a daze, as Argo pinned his head to the side of the ship. Argo grabbed his ring with his right hand and made a dagger. He then released his left hand from Walva's throat, grabbed into his mouth, pulled out his tongue, and in one swoop, cut Walva's tongue off. Argo then threw Walva onto the ship. Walva was bent on all fours, wailing, bleeding profusely from his mouth. Leahy, who had witnessed the whole thing, just followed Argo up the ramp. Argo, only looking forward and not at Leahy, said, "Leahy, find someone to clean him up after you get me back to the base."

BELINEA 4.7

Avola

Lowell Province, Sector 9 Mining Center

Still in their mining suits, Sterling's entire crew were around a long table in the break room. Most were sitting, but a few were standing. One of the members said, "Thirty Golda's, that is it? For the month?"

Sterling replied, "For the quarter. So fifteen on the crew, each of you gets two Golda's."

Another member said, "What about you, Sterling?"

Sterling shook his head. "I promised you guys bonuses. I know you have worked hard."

The first member said, "That's not a bonus, that's bullshit. Besides, you have a family too, Sterling."

Sterling shook his head again and took a sip of his coffee. He quietly said, "We will figure something out."

Just then, Donovan walked into a small break room, where other miners were having their lunch. Through the window, you can see the Avolians operating the big robot rock crushers, drilling through the mountains. Donovan grabbed a beverage and sat down at a table by himself across from Sterling's crew. One of the miners stood up and yelled, "Donovan. What did your cousin say?"

Donovan took a sip of his beverage. "He doesn't know. He is going to get back to us."

The man, confused now, walked over to Donovan and sat down across from him. "Get back to us? What does that mean? Are we getting anything?"

Donovan stared at the man for a few seconds, not responding. The silence was deafening.

The man noticed Donovan wasn't going to say anything, so he continued in a whisper. "Donovan, what good is providing information on the location of the Vait your cousin steals if we get nothing out of it?"

Sterling got up and said, "I do not need to hear any of this. You guys have a good evening."

Sterling began to walk out as Donovan said to the other miner, "He will give us protection. As well as any food or clothing that we need. You would rather side with the Majavkee?"

Sterling stopped in the doorway and listened to what the member of his crew said. "The Majavkee are not the problem, what they are paying us is. Everyone in this room is working twice as much, twice as hard, to get a few crumbs more than what we were making before. We already have food and clothing. Your cousin has to understand that."

Donovan then tried to reason, "Do you really understand? Fighting a war, no one will back him on so we can get things back to how they were. He needs weapons, ships, soldiers. Are you going to fight?"

The man leaned back, insulted. "If Octavious can't even pay us what we were making before, then why fight? He is no better than the Majavkee."

Donovan leaned in and looked at the man. "I just came from a Quisessa for one of his men. They are dying for us. The Priests trust him. Ambassador Syren trusts him. We have to trust him."

The man grew angry, his voice slightly louder than the whisper before. "The Majavkee are Belinean Quill. Of course, our Priests will not side with them. They will side with whoever protects them, whether its Red Ring Rise or anyone else. And we will do the same. If Octavious cannot protect us from the Majavkee Lords, then it is suicide on our part to provide him with any more information on our mining operations."

Donovan responded, "Then you go tell the Priests how you feel, your lack of loyalty and principle."

The man stood up and looked down at Donovan, as if ready to hit him. Sterling yelled, "Enough, let him go. Fighting among ourselves is not going to solve the problem."

His crew member paused and looked at the rest of the miners at the table. Quietly he said, "Principle does not provide me the wealth to get out of this miserable shithole and give my children a better tomorrow."

The man walked out, as Sterling followed. Everyone left in the room was looking at Donovan now. He had never felt more alone. As he slowly got up, he threw his beverage out and walked out of the room. Putting his mining hat back on, a man approached him, dressed in SS gear.

"Donovan, right?"

Donovan nodded. "I am Captain Leahy of the SS, can I see you in private. We have some unauthorized transmissions we want to talk about."

BELINEA 4.8

Belinea, The Capitol
Chairman Hassara's office

Chairman Hassara was sitting down behind his desk. Tempest walked into the room and immediately questioned her father. "You wanted to see me, Father?"

The Chairman did not take his eyes off his screen. "Yes, Tempest. Take a look at this."

The Chairman had next to his desk a 3-D image that popped up. "This is the security footage from the Space Port at Torsalli."

Tempest began watching the footage. A few seconds rolled by, with several ships going in and out of the space port. "What is it that I am looking for?"

Then on the hologram was an explosion of one of the ships on the dock. It was very bright, catching Tempest off-guard. Chairman Hassara continued. "That."

Tempest whispered, 'Shit...' underneath her breath.

The Chairman continued again. "It was the Earth Ambassador Bird's ship. We believe he is dead."

The screen went away, and Tempest looked at her father. "Taz?"

The Chairman answered. "We believe so."

Tempest continued, "I guess my conversation with Ambassador Yi about Bird was not needed."

Chairman Hassara stood up. "No, apparently not. I will need you to do a briefing for the Ambassadors. The Admiral has specific notes on the bombing. Initial reports look like an internal explosion from inside the ship, so no telling how he got a bomb in there in the first place. I sent a message to Malovex. When he gets it, he will go directly there to find out what happened. The BRG will do a full investigation."

Tempest nodded. "The Ambassadors are going to be outraged."

Chairman Hassara added as he walked around his desk. "Likely. I have some other news."

Tempest just looked at him as the Chairman walked entirely around, and got face-to-face with his daughter. "I got a message from your brother about the talks on Avola with the Valmay Group. It looks like military action may be a forgone conclusion."

Tempest then glared at her father. "I knew sending Argo would be a mistake. I am sure he did nothing but piss them off."

The Chairman put his hands on the shoulders of his daughter. "Tempest, your brother is perfectly capable of handling the situation. I sent him for a reason. He has assured me that he has a plan to, as he put it, 'gift wrap' the situation for you."

Tempest then asked, "Should I brief the Ambassadors about Avola as well?"

Chairman Hassara thought for a moment. He dropped his hands. "No, let's trust your brother and give him a little time. He knows what he is doing."

BELINEA 4.9

Avola

Lowell Province, Majavkee Security Headquarters

Lord Argo was not happy, looking at the hologram map of Bosa Province of Avola. It included the AuFa garrisons, Majavkee Security strongholds, and the areas the Valmay group held. He was standing in the room with four Majakee Security Officers, led by Chief Chamberlain, and four AuFa officers, led by Admiral Holland. The AuFa Admiral had just given his idea for an attack. Three SS officers were flanked behind Argo and Lord Evander of the Majavkee.

Argo looked at the Admiral. "Admiral. You guys have had six months to find the Valmay Group base, not where it might be."

The Admiral was convinced. "Lord Argo, with all due respect. We have it pinned down to this particular area, but we need visual confirmation. We are incapable of taking satellite confirmation because of the atmosphere."

Majavkee Lord Evander interjected. "If I may Lord Argo, the Admiral is right. If we head out with a large enough force, the Valmay would be reluctant to engage."

Argo shook his head and said, "Listen, it only took nine of them to take out your garrison, Admiral Holland. And that bitch Kaya would take on one of your Battle Cruisers by herself. So do not talk to me about being reluctant to engage."

Captain Leahy walked into the room from the rear. He could hear the discussion at the table as he wiggled through the other SS soldiers to stand behind Argo. He whispered, "My Lord, a word in private, please."

Argo looked at him and then said, "Gentlemen, come up with a fucking plan that finds this base without us losing a battalion of soldiers."

Argo turned and walked out of the room with Leahy. They went through a pair of doors and began walking down a corridor. "My Lord, I believe I may have a solution."

Argo was not in the mood for bullshit. "Leahy, please tell me it does not involve us flying out there and finding it ourselves?"

They continued walking. "My Lord, we have been doing surveillance on the Valmay Group for quite some time, and are pretty confident the location is in a mountainside of Bosa. But the lack of a visual and the sandstorms, we were reluctant to attack because casualties would be high."

Argo replied, "Tell me something I do not know Leahy. What is your solution?"

Leahy stopped in front of a door. "Well, I am still not sure how we provide your sister with ammunition for the Council, but I believe we have a way for the Valmay to show us where their base is."

Argo tilted his head in curiosity. The two walked into the interrogation room, where Donovan was sitting in a chair, flanked by two SS officers with rifles. Donovan looked up and was petrified at the sight of Lord Argo. Most people were.

Leahy continued. "Lord Argo, may I present Donovan, who has been a naughty boy."

Donovan pleaded, "My Lord, I ...."

But Captain Leahy cut him off. "Silent. Do not speak unless asked."

Argo stared at Donovan for a few seconds, not exactly sure how this would help him. Leahy continued. "Donovan here is a miner in the Lowell Region for Lord Evander of the Majavkee. Apparently, that is his side hustle because his main job is traitor."

Donovan pleaded again. "My Lord, I had no idea...."

But Leahy cut him off again, slapping him with the back of his hand. He yelled, "Silent!"

Argo was mildly amused, but still not connecting the dots. Leahy then continued. "Let's take a listen to some of our audio."

Leahy pushed a button on the screen table off to the side. The audio was Donovan, apparently talking to someone in his mining group. "My cousin, Octavious, he's the leader of the Valmay Group. They still have old soldiers of the Red Ring Rise, and they will overtake the Majavkee Lords. All we have to do is provide him information on the Vait we are mining. He and my cousin Kaya will steal it, and then sell it for fair value."

Argo was now very intrigued. He asked Donovan, "Your cousin is Octavious Killian?"

Donovan was crying now. "My Lord, I never meant to hurt anyone. The Majavkee Lords are working us to death, and they don't pay us fairly."

Argo smiled now as he continued. "But I bet your cousin is giving you plenty for that stolen Vait, at the cost of dead AuFa soldiers, huh?"

Leahy was standing behind Donovan now. Argo was staring Donovan down, who was still in tears. "My Lord, we did not know. Octavious betrayed us. He offered food and protection for our information. He never gave us anything else, I swear."

Argo looked at Leahy, who returned the glance. Argo continued, "Bullshit. Surely he gave you something. A little extra in your pocket so you can go fuck some whores at your leisure?"

Donovan, crying so hard, was barely audible. "I swear my Lord, nothing. He vowed to return things the old way. We were desperate."

Argo looked back at Leahy, who just shrugged his shoulders. Argo then asked, "Your cousin did not tell you about our little peace offer?"

Donovan began to settle down a little bit. He finally got out, "No, my Lord."

Argo then half-smiled. "Settle down Donovan. We are here to help. It appears you are not the only person your cousins betrayed."

Donovan stopped sobbing and took a deep breath before responding, "My Lord...?"

Argo grabbed Donovan's chin, holding it up to look him directly in the eye. "We offered your cousin wealth, to give to you. But apparently, he and his sister have their own agenda, and it doesn't involve you or any of your mining friends. If it is wealth you want Donovan, we can provide you with that. We will give you the same offer we gave him."

Argo smiled, as did Leahy. Donovan just looked confused as ever. Maybe they would not kill him.

BELINEA 4.10

Avola

Lowell Province

Sterling walked into his house. It had been a rough day. His wife Felicia, walked up to him and handed him their child Nix, who was almost two years old. Barely having time to put his equipment down, Felicia began talking. "Hey. So glad you are home. I still have to wrap the presents for the Quill offerings."

Sterling sat down with his Nix, who was smiling at him. He said, "Alright."

Felicia continued. "I went a little bit over with the gifts, but you told me you should be getting your bonus soon. Certainly, nobody deserves it more than Quillisar Balerra and her orphaned children."

Sterling took a deep breath and slightly rolled his eyes. His son grabbed his face and smiled.

Sterling softly said, "Yeah, about that."

Felicia sounded excited as she said, "Did you get it today?"

Sterling took another deep breath. He looked at her and said, "There will be no bonus, Felicia."

Felicia sat down next to him, disheartened. "Why? I thought you said you were up from last year. They promised."

Sterling looked at her and said, "We were. But costs have gone up, so the bonus was smaller. They only gave it to me, so I gave equal portions to the crew."

Felicia put her hands in her face. "Sterling, no. Why?"

Sterling responded, "Because it was the right thing to do."

After a moment, Felicia responded. "The Majavkee have promised you so much, but it's all the same. More work and less pay. When are they going to come through?"

Sterling whispered, not looking at Nix. "I do not know, Felicia. But what choice do we have?"

Felicia got up, still miffed as she walked to the kitchen area. She said, "What am I going to tell Quillisar Balerra?"

Sterling answered, "Keep the offering gifts. Those children need it more."

Felicia just looked at him and said, "And how do we pay our bills, Sterling?"

Sterling held his son tight and said, "I will work some extra shifts on my day off if I have to. I will figure out a way, I have faith. The energy is in all of us."

Felicia whispered with a lump in her throat. "The energy is in all of us."

BELINEA 4.11

Avola, Bosa Province

Octavious and Kaya were sitting in a private strategy room. Octavious had a drink in his hand. He was pacing around a 3-D image that also had a map of their entire Avola area. Kaya was across from him on the other side of the table. After a moment of silence, Kaya finally spoke. "We can move these troops over here to offer cover, but then this mining area becomes very exposed. We would be removing all of their protection."

An officer knocked and quickly walked in. Holding a tablet, he showed it to Octavious. "Communication intercept, sir. Two in fact, but the same message. The Aufa, by direction of Lord Argo, is directing the Majavkee Lords Bialos and Barrett to round up all mined Vait, and transport it to Processing Center Six in the Lowell Province by 9:00 AM. Payment in full, and signed by Lord Argo himself."

Octavious looked at the tablet again, making sure he read it correctly. "Both at the same time? What about the other Lords?"

The Officer replied. "Not sure, sir. These came from our internal sources in the mining centers. We found it odd that it was the same message. That's a lot of Vait to process at one time and remove from the planet."

Kaya kept looking at the map. After yet another pause in which Octavious said nothing, but instead pondered, the other officer walked out of the room. Kaya continued, "You are gonna have to give up something, somewhere, if you want to fortify our forces here."

Octavious kept looking from the other side of the 3-D map. After a small pause, he replied, "They know we are reeling, trying to fortify our position. Yet, Argo is removing all the Vait from two Lords at once, maybe more. Why?"

Kaya looked puzzled as well, but for a different reason. " I do not know, but I am more concerned about the initial report we got. The AuFa sending two attack force squadrons here and here (pointing) can only mean they wish to take back the Garrison at Mining Sector 14 at the very least. If I was going to attack us here, it is exactly what I would do first."

Octavious took a sip of his liquor and sighed. Taking his eyes off the map, he ran his hand through his hair. "I almost think we should have taken the deal, Kaya."

Kaya was angry at such a notion. "Fuck no, Octavious. They would have never held up to their end of the bargain. Besides, we will not be bought."

Octavious shook his head. "It's not bought if we give it back to the people Kaya. Us, the soldiers, Ambassador Syren, we have strong convictions about defending our home at any cost. But there are others, the one's mining, that see it differently. They might want something more."

Kaya countered. "Do not believe that talk Octavious. That is greed."

Octavious replied, "Greed for wanting to be rewarded for honest work? For wanting a better life for your family? We do not have children, Kaya. Just because we do not share those convictions does not make them wrong."

Kaya slammed her fist down. "Damnit Octavious, enough! It does not matter what they offer. There is no way we can trust Argo and the Council, you said so yourself. The removal of the Majavkee Lords is our only way of negotiating peace. We get rid of them, we take back our planet. That's how we win."

Octavious then looked right at her and said, "At what cost Kaya? Maybe the first step is taking that money and empowering the poor. A bidding war for their labor cripples the Majavkee financially. Not everything is won with the sword sister."

Kaya looked at her brother in the eyes. "You are not dealing with wise, rational men Octavious. They are ruthless. They do not care about our families, let alone our planet. I will die fighting tyranny before I concede the democracy they want to take from us."

There was a buzz at the door. The same officer walked in again and gave a sealed message to Kaya. She saluted and walked back out the door. Kaya broke the seal on the note and read it. "It's from Donovan."

Octavious now looked up. "What does it say?"

Kaya began summarizing the note. "There is a huge Vait transfer at midnight, sending all of their Vait to Processing Center Six. The Majavkee Lords Evander and Nickell have been ordered by Argo Hassara to get all mined Vait off the surface immediately, so they can process it's return to Belinea. They will be loading eight transport ships throughout the night so they can leave by 09:00 tomorrow morning. Same as the message you just got. He included a pass code for the transports also."

Octavious began thinking out loud. That's four out of the eight Lords, at least. And the other four may be ordered as well. It does not make sense."

Kaya thought as she answered it without knowing. "Unless you planned a massive attack and were unsure of the retaliation? You would need to make sure the Vait was safe."

Octavious then said, "Of course. They are planning a wide-ranged, encompassing attack."

Another officer buzzed and walked into the room. As she was walking up to Octavious, he continued to talk. "That's why Argo Hassara is here. They were never going to negotiate peacefully. He is here to eliminate the problem: us. "

Octavious read the note the officer handed to him. He then hit a few spots on the screen until a couple of spots began blinking. Kaya was still slightly confused. " I do not understand the connection?"

But Octavious continued. "Privately they secure a major shipment of Vait, and reward the Majavkee Lords for it. It buys them time. Working together though, maybe they tell the Council differently, that the Vait supply chain is compromised because of us, the Valmay Group. If they get the support of the Council, they will bomb this whole area and worry about the consequences later."

Kaya was still confused. "Then why not attack now and just get it over with?"

Octavious replied quickly. "You said so yourself, the fear of us retaliating. They need to get the Vait off the planet before they attack us. (Pointing to the screen) That's why I just got this recon message about the AuFa Attack Group seen repositioning to eventually take back the Garrison at Mining Sector 14 in the Lowell Province. We took that out so the AuFa wouldn't have a base in close proximity to ours. As soon as they get the Vait off, they are going to attack us from there."

Kaya now understood. "So, what do you want to do?"

Octavious took his eyes off the board and looked at her. "We have no choice. We attack, now."

Kaya was astounded. "What? Attack?"

Octavious, pointing at Processing Center Six, said, "The Processing Center."

Kaya looked down at the board, then back at him. "You want to steal the Vait?"

Octavious nodded. Then added, "All of it. That's how we hurt them."

Kaya shook her head. "It's risky. That center is deep in their territory. Stealing eight transports, that is going to take some planning. And power. We will likely need every ship we got. That will also leave our base completely vulnerable to an attack."

Octavious whispered. "They do not expect us to attack, so we have the advantage of surprise. And the Vait is our hostage because they will not bomb anything until it is safely off the planet."

Kaya then looked at the board again. She said, "How much time do we have?"

Octavious half-smiled. Looking at the clock in the corner of the screen, he said. "If Donovan is correct, transports leave in about 18 hours."

Kaya looked up at her brother and said, "Get me, my crew."

BELINEA 4.12

Belinea, the Capitol

Ambassador Yi was reading a message on his tablet in his private quarters, alone.

> *Ambassador Yi,*
>
> *It is with great sorrow and condolences that I must inform you that Ambassador Bird's transport ship has been destroyed, killing all on board. The only details I can provide is there was an explosion at the Space Port at Torsalli, and we believe Taz was involved. I will be giving a briefing to the Ambassadors on the Council Committee for AuFa Affairs at 12:30 hours, where I hope to have more information at that time.*
> *Tempest Hassara*
>
> *Defense Director of the AuFa*

The Ambassador re-read the message to make sure he read it correctly. He quickly began typing.

> *Confirmed report of Ambassador Bird's ship explosion. Confirm death? Mission Status?*
>
> *Yi*

He then ended his message and spoke clearly into the tablet. "Code Clearance Li Jie Yi."

BELINEA 4.13

Avola

AuFa Flannigard Base, Medical Wing

Captain Leahy walked into the Medical Wing and to the front desk. He found an assistant, who stood up as soon as he walked in. "How can I help you, sir?"

Captain Leahy politely stopped and responded. "I am looking for Captain Walker?"

A portly man had turned around from behind the desk and walked straight up to Captain Leahy, directly next to the assistant. "I am Doctor Walker."

"Captain Leahy, SS. You are the head physician here, correct?"

Walker responded politely. "Yes, Captain."

Leahy continued. "And all the wounded from the Garrison at Mining Sector 14, as well as any other wounded AuFa and Majavkee soldiers, they are all kept here, correct?"

Walker again politely responded, "Yes, Captain, we have eight soldiers we are still caring for."

Leahy nodded. "Excellent Captain. Lord Argo has ordered me to evacuate the wounded to Admiral Holland's Command Destroyer. The medical wing there is just as good as here, and they will be prepped for a likely ticket home, I believe."

Walker looked confused. "They patients are perfectly fine here. And the Majavkee Security Soldiers would likely be coming right back here anyway after they are done being treated."

Leahy stared at the Doctor for a moment. "A moment in private, Doctor?"

The assistant walked away, leaving the two alone. Leahy got a little closer. "Doctor, we are about to have a major attack. We are going to need as many hospital resources as we can get. And that starts with moving these wounded ahead of time to the Command Destroyer up there (pointing to the sky) in space. Got it?"

Walker nodded. "I understand now, Captain, my apologies."

Leahy now continued. There will be a Green Medical Transfer Shuttle waiting for you at 08:30 tomorrow, where they will be picking up further supplies at Processing Center Six. Affirmative, Captain."

Captain Walker hesitantly asked, "Green, Captain? Not the usual white?"

Leahy just looked at him and said, "Not the usual transport Doctor."

BELINEA 4.14

Avola, Bosa Province
Valmay Headquarter Base

Inside the hangar bay of the base, two hundred plus soldiers stood, laser-focused on their two commanding officers elevated on a stage. Behind Octavious and Kaya was a detailed map of Processing Center Six, an eight-story square building with four, twenty-meter wide, one hundred meter long, elevated extension bridges. At the end of each bridge were two spokes that went out an additional forty meters at a forty-five-degree angle. On top of the main building were four large landing areas surrounding a fifty-meter high control tower that overlooked the entire facility.

Kaya was still yelling. "The AuFa will use C-112's to transport the Vait to the Command Destroyer above. These are the massive transports that barely fit through the tunnels. We believe there will be eight total, two at each end of the extended bridges. The four landing areas on top of the main building will likely have at least two, perhaps four, AuFa F-81 Sirator fighters, plus four T220 Tolsar Tower Cannon's located on each corner (Kaya pointing at the map). The main assault, led by General Killian, will be responsible for these other four transports, on this side, with Commander Rendon and myself on the other side. Commander Rendon will recover the C-112 Transports and lead them out with the F-81's as cover. Count on an AuFa attack group joining the fray from Flannigard within 8-10 minutes after we arrive, if we are lucky. Questions?"

Commander Rendon asked, "And if the entire Flannigard squadron is already there?"

Octavious, standing on the other side of Kaya, answered. "Each of your crafts, Rotor V-11 Valkyrie's, and the artillery soldiers all have SPB's. Use them, go infrared, and get out as fast as possible."

Kaya then looked around and said, "Anything else?"

There was a silence in the room. Octavious could sense there was opposition, perhaps doubt among the soldiers.

Ocatvious then broke the tension. "And we will all fly away riding dragons that shit rainbows afterwards...."

There was a collective laugh in the room. Even Kaya managed a small smile. Octavious waited for the laughter to die down. "Brothers and sisters, I know what you are thinking. Soldiers are going to die today. The odds are against us. The Processing Center could have a Batallion waiting for us. How do we have enough men to steal all the transports? Are we coming back to a base that is burning in the ashes? All of those things are potentially true."

There was now a hush in the room and everyone had stopped smiling. Octavious continued, "But never have we had a better opportunity, they do not know we are coming. Any transport ship of Vait we steal brings us closer to getting what we want, justice to the Majavkee Lords, and our planet back. "

There was some scuttle in the room now. Men were lightly cheering, some clapping. "We will bleed a thousand deaths to see our children survive, to ignite the candle of freedom. Do not forget the Valmay and all the brothers and sisters that have died before us. This is our day."

As the soldiers adjourned, they chanted, "Valmay!"

Kaya and Octavious walked off stage. They were immediately greeted by Rendon.

Rendon spoke calmly. "With all due respect, sir, are we sure that giving up our base justifies the risk we are taking?"

Octavious paused for a moment before continuing. "Nervous about the risk Rendon?"

Rendon replied quickly, "Nervous that even if we succeed, we may not have a base to return to."

Octavious looked at Kaya first. She had already given her issues with this plan, but Octavious knew this would be the only way. Octavious looked back at Rendon before continuing. " I have moved all of our resources to Bisi, our last fall back point. If Argo somehow finds this place, it will be months before he finds Bisi. Use the caves if need be. Otherwise, get as many ships as you can. The energy will guide you home."

Octavious grabbed the shoulder of Rendon, who, in turn, grabbed his. They both nodded, and Rendon walked away.

Octavious turned to Kaya. They took a long look at each other. Octavious then said just above a whisper, "If I die today, never forget how proud I am of the soldier that you have become."

Kaya looked back at him and put her hand on his shoulder. "We are not going to die today, my brother. Destiny will not let us."

Octavious grabbed her shoulder and repeated, "The energy will guide you home."

The two then hugged, followed by a final look before running to their ships.

BELINEA 4.15

Avola, Lowell Province, Sector 9 Mining Center

The final loading was going into the transport ship. Two armed Majavkee security guards were watching the forklifts transport the Vait onto the back. An AuFa pilot was waiting at the end of the cargo ship. He turned to the AuFa officer next to him and asked, "Is this the last of it?"

The officer looked at him and said, "One more ship. It's running behind."

Rendon and Kaya were in the cockpit, behind two pilots. Along with ten soldiers in the cargo bay, everyone was dressed like a miner. The female pilot said, "Sector Nine, this is cargo vessel 2-1. We have a Vait load to add. On final approach bearing 1-8-0, copy."

A pause was given before a voice came back on. "Cargo vessel 2-1, copy that. You are late. Please send over your verification code and the weight of your Vait Cargo."

Kaya and Rendon looked at each other. Rendon whispered, "Time to see if your cousin's code is gonna work, otherwise, we might have to implement plan B."

Kaya just looked at him, confused. Rendon pulled his mining outfit to the side and touched the ring on his side hip. Kaya just looked at him and said, "Plan B isn't ideal."

Rendon added, "If you got a plan C, I am all ears."

A voice over the intercom was heard again. "Cargo Vessel 2-1, verification confirmed. Please proceed to loading dock Two and directly onto Transport Ship TS-2."

At the command center at Sector 9 Mining Center, a dispatch officer yelled to the commanding AuFa officer, "Lieutenant, I have something."

The Lieutenant walked over and said, "Yes, Sargent."

The Sargent continued. "That cargo vessel just used the code that the SS and Lord Argo warned us of."

The Lieutenant asked, "You let them proceed, correct?"

The Sargent nodded. "Yes, sir."

The Lieutenant quickly replied "Get me Captain Leahy of the SS."

BELINEA 4.16

Lord Argo was looking out the Command Tower window, as Captain Leahy walked up behind him. Leahy said nothing, only acknowledging his presence with a slight nod. Argo looked at him and said, "Are we ready downstairs?"

Leahy nodded. "Yes. We got a verification code from Mining Sector Nine, so they are inbound on a Transport ship. The Medical Transport just landed and is prepared for boarding."

Argo nodded and returned to looking out the window. "Good. Let's see if they took the bait."

Leahy continued. "Do not kill the messenger, my Lord, but Admiral Holland asked if you would like to join him and the Majavkee Lords on the Command Destroyer above to watch, ensuring that you are out of harm's way."

Argo looked at Leahy with a scowl. Argo went back to looking out the window before he said, "Leahy, I would rather die a death by a thousand cuts."

Leahy half-smiled. "The Admiral would also like to reiterate that he is available to prep the alternative plan if this first one should not work out."

Argo gave Leahy another scowl before responding "Now you really are testing my patience. I see none of the AuFa officers have any faith this will work."

Leahy responded, "It's a big carrot, my Lord. Octavious is going to bite."

Argo crossed his arms and continued to look out the window. There was a long pause before Argo asked. "Is Lieutenant Walla recovered?"

Leahy continued to look out the window as well. "Lieutenant Walva, sir?"

Argo quickly replied, "Walva, Walla, you know who I mean."

With the smile gone, Leahy responded, "He will be fine despite the deformity."

Argo looked at Leahy and raised an eyebrow. Leahy continued. "It's better if you see it yourself, my Lord."

Argo returned to looking out the window. A voice from behind the control panel yelled. "Lord Argo, our sensors are picking up incoming craft. Bearing 2-7-0, from the east, sir. I believe it is the Cargo Transport from Sector Nine."

Argo said, "Hail them and confirm."

The Communication officer said, "Confirmed sir. Directing Cargo Transport to Gate 3-06."

Onboard the cargo vessel, Kaya and Rendon kept looking out the window. Kaya said, "Rendon, I see no fighters on the facility, and all the Tower Cannon's have tarps on them."

The Valmay soldier next to them said, "It is still morning, and they had a sandstorm last night. Patrols have not started."

Kaya and Rendon just looked at each other with an expression of 'could we be this lucky?'.

As the disguised Majavkee cargo vessel touched down next to the elevated bridge, Kaya and her team put on their mining masks. They began to unload the Vait off the vessel as some of the Majavkee security soldiers shouted, "Let's go! You are late, move it! Move it!"

They funneled the shipment of Vait on forklifts, down the long elevated bridge towards the massive C-112 Transport Ships. As they got to the fork of the bridge, half went right with Rendon, and the other half went left with Kaya. They drove the forklifts up the ramp through the belly of the ship. Once through the doors, a loading officer instructed them to dump the cargo a few meters down. Kaya and two other soldiers jumped off before they did, going undetected through the rest of the cargo. They made their way to the cockpit, where one pilot turned around and said, "Hey, who the fuck are you?"

Kaya, before slicing her throat with her saber, said, "Doom."

Argo was still in the Command Tower when the communications officer said, "Lord Argo, picking up incoming aircraft, bearing 0-4-5. Low altitude, about five minutes out."

Argo quickly shouted back, "How many aircraft?"

The officer responded, "Hard to say sir, tight formation. At least thirty."

Argo yelled at the communications officer. "Hail the incoming craft, ask for identification. No one on the ground fires until I say so, understand?"

Argo then turned to Leahy and said, "Notify Admiral Holland, send out Attack Wings Three, Four, and Five. Then, go downstairs and let the animal out of the cage."

Captain Leahy nodded and said, "Yes, sir."

Cortes was piloting her Assault Ship with Octavious in the co-pilot seat when she heard the radio transmission. "Incoming aircraft, This is AuFa Command Tower, please identify."

Cortes responded, "This is medical transport M-878. We are being chased by….."

Octavious hit a couple of spots on his screen, sending a jamming frequency to the airwaves.

The communications officer said to Argo, "They are jamming the frequency, sir."

Argo replied, "Keep trying to hail them…"

Over the intercom,, Cortes heard a voice breaking apart. "M-878, please verify. What is chasing you, copy?"

Ten soldiers in the Assault Ship mounted the Rotor V-11 Valkyries, which were an armed four-bladed personal attack rover, similar to a TC. In a Valkyrie, the pilot sat tilted back at the same level as the four horizontal rotor blades that rotated and pivoted to steer the craft. The upper soldier sat behind and higher, responsible for shooting the T-11 Cannon that could spin a full 360 degrees. Two small thin engines sat behind and underneath the shooter, with a rack of four air-to-ground missiles in between. With the Valmay soldiers listening, Cortes said "Two minutes."

Kaya left a Valmay pilot behind to navigate the transport ship. She ran back to the cargo bay, where three of her soldiers had secured the area. Remounting the forklift, she looked at them and said, "On me...let's go."

With the three soldiers hanging on the side, Kaya drove the forklift down the ramp and onto the landing pads. She navigated over to the second extended bridge where another transport was. Speaking into her intercom, she said, "Rendon...."

Rendon touched his screen and said, "Tower Command, Transport Ship Six does not have the space to take on this extra Vait cargo. Attempting to see if Transport Ship Four does."

There was no response. Rendon did not care. He fired up the engines on the Transport for pre-launch. Kaya drove the forklift up the ramp of the next transport, ignoring the two security guards at the bottom. When she got to the top, two more Majavkee Security soldiers were waiting, as one said, "What are you doing, this ship is full!"

Kaya had all three soldiers, still in mining gear, now helping the crate off the forklift. Kaya yelled at the Majavkee security soldiers. "Find room for this crate."

The two security guards walked past the crate and up to Kaya, both with their rifles drawn. "No miner tells us what to do. Who gave you the authority to leave this here?"

A Valmay soldier popped out of the crate with a rifle drawn and said, "I did."

The two security guards turned around, but not in time, as they were both shot dead.

Kaya reached into the crate and grabbed her rifle with the scope. She slung it around her shoulder and said to the soldier next to her, "You, take the cockpit. Don't leave until we take that last transport."

Cortes yelled, "Fifteen seconds!"

Octavious jumped out of his seat and ran toward the back of the Assault Ship. As they were about to land, Cortes fired the cannon on their attack ship at the Tower Cannon covered with a tarp. Octavious and the other soldiers jumped to the ground. He pointed at the Valkyries, telling the attack rovers where to go.

From the Command Tower, Argo could see the explosion from the Tower Cannon below. He looked back at the Communication Officer and yelled, "Open fire all ground forces. Launch Attack groups One, Two, and Six."

Within seconds, over a hundred AuFa fighters and bombers took off, heading toward the processing center. The RAS was a robot attack soldier, five meters high with a 20MM Cannon attached to its side. As the ground bay doors opened up at the processing center, hundreds of Majavkee security soldiers and RAS's began firing on the Valmay. On top of the extended bridge, another tarp was pulled off, revealing a tower cannon that began firing on Octavious. Despite the Valkyries providing cover, some of his soldiers were instantly killed before Octavious could find them cover behind a divider wall.

Meanwhile, Leahy had made it downstairs to the holding cell where they kept Donovan. He removed his handcuffs and said, "It is time. Get your friends and get to Octavious so that you can end this. Remember, the green ship. You have my word. Riches beyond your dreams."

Leahy gave him a key card. Donovan smiled and ran off down the corridor, making a quick left, then right. He unlocked a door using the key card and found a cell holding ten members of his mining group. Donovan said, "Come on, we are getting out of here."

As they continued down the corridor, they opened a door that led them to a hangar bay. From inside, they could see the entire battle going on outside through the open ground bay doors. The miners began grabbing rifles from a storage area off to the side. As Donovan surveyed the scene, he could see Octavious and his soldiers pinned down behind the divider wall on the other side of the landing pads. Donovan yelled, "We need to get to Octavious!"

A miner grabbed him and said, "Going out there will only get us killed!"

Behind the wall, Octavious grabbed his intercom and said, "Fighters, someone take out that damn Tower Cannon on the extended bridge! It's got us pinned down."

Kaya heard Octavious on the intercom and ran down the ramp of the transport to see the Tower Cannon Octavious was talking about. She got on her intercom and said, "Voldo, Manning, anyone, I need a Valkyrie over at transport Four now!"

As Leahy had made his way back upstairs, Argo looked at his communication officer, barking orders. "All Attack Groups concentrate on the ground forces. Do not attack the C-112 transports."

Leahy walked over to Argo and stood next to him. He said, "The animal is out of the cage."

Argo answered calmly, "Is our green medical ship ready?"

Leahy answered, "Should be taking off right when our attack groups get here. How many ships did the Valmay bring?"

Argo answered, "Looks like thirty to forty."

Leahy continued. "And we got forty in each attack group. Twenty-five F-81's and fifteen A-14 Alvator's, One hundred twenty aircraft total."

Argo gave a small grin. "I like our chances."

Down on the landing pads near the transports, the Valkyrie that Manning was piloting got to within a meter off the ground as Kaya jumped on its side. Kaya put one foot firmly on the rail and as her hand clutched the handlebar. She looked at the officer operating the T-11 Cannon on the back of the Valkyrie and pointed to the top of the extended bridge. Kaya yelled, "Get me to that Tower Cannon!"

With her free hand, Kaya grabbed her rifle as the Valkyrie climbed toward the Tower Cannon, all four blades turned and rotating. She took a shot, as did the T-11 Cannon, all connecting and taking out soldiers on the wall. Without slowing down, Kaya jumped off as they reached the top, knocking the last soldier to the ground. As he tried to get up, Kaya turned her ring into a fire saber and quickly stabbed him. The soldier operating the Tower Cannon noticed Kaya, and tried to grab his pistol. But Kaya stabbed him in the leg and threw him out of the chair before he even got a shot off. After slitting the soldier's throat, Kaya climbed into the chair and began shooting at the Majavkee below. After a moment, she looked up into the distance and saw the AuFa attack groups coming. She grabbed her intercom and said, "Octavious, we got over a hundred aircraft coming, fifteen seconds out. SPB's now!"

The SPB's were Smoke Power Bombs that left a cloud of gas smoke thirty meters wide and high when activated. Octavious put on the miner ventilation mask hanging from his hip and his infrared goggles. He yelled at his fellow soldiers and said on the intercom simultaneously, "SPB's now. Cortes, Rendon, escort the C-112 transports out of here."

Cortes replied, "We are not leaving you, sir."

Octavious replied, "EVAC them, then come back for us, that's an order. The C-112's are more important."

Within seconds the entire ground was a haze of gray gas smoke, making visual nearly impossible for the AuFa attack groups flying in. Following Octavious, the rest of the Valmay soldiers immediately put on infrared goggles and ventilation masks. As Kaya got her infrared goggles on, she began picking off Majavkee soldiers one by one on the landing pad below. The AuFa attack group, not being able to see the Valmay on the ground, began attacking the Valmay fighters and Valkyries above. Rendon spoke on his intercom, "Transports, let's go."

At the Command Tower, Argo saw, through the glass, the C-112 transports slowly rise through the smoke. Getting on his intercom, he said, "AuFa attack bombers, switch to infrared and start bombing the ground area. The C-112 transports are away."

A voice from an AuFa pilot came back. "Lord Argo, we can't see anything. And the Majavkee soldiers are still down there fighting."

Argo, annoyed, walked to the elevator with Leahy in tow. He said, "Take out everything. And someone take out that Cannon Tower firing down from the extended bridge!"

As if on cue, an AuFa F-81 flew directly past Cortes' ship and straight to the Tower Cannon Kaya was firing on below. It fired and hit below the cannon, throwing Kaya off of it. Cortes yelled, "Kaya!"

On the ground, the smoke was still everywhere. Still, inside the hangar, Donovan saw a topless transport shuttle, used for ferrying miners and soldiers around the landing pads. He yelled at the miners again. "Now is our chance! Get in the transport shuttle!"

The miners stopped shooting and got on the transport shuttle. Donovan drove them through the smoke and crossfire towards Octavious, as the miners went back to shooting at the Majavkee. Octavious turned ninety degrees to his right and saw the ground transport shuttle coming in fast towards them. One of the soldiers next to Octavious turned his rifle to fire. Octavious, squinting his eyes through the smoke, saw Donovan driving, and pushed the barrel of the rifle down with his hand. He said, "They are with us. "

Donovan drove behind the divider wall and jumped out of the transport shuttle. He ran up to him and said, "Octavious!"

Octavious was astonished. "Donovan, what are you doing here?"

Donovan, breathing very hard. "We escaped, they held us prisoner, for helping you. Quickly, Octavious, you need to shoot down that green ship."

Donovan was pointing to a transport ship on top of the main building that was about to take off. Octavious yelled back at Donovan, "It's a transport. It's probably not military."

Donovan yelled back. "The Majavkee Lords are on it. All of them!!!"

Octavious's face gave a double-take. "How do you know?"

Donovan yelled back. "I just do. There is no time. We can end this whole thing now!"

Octavious just stared at him, as another bomb went off near him. He looked at a couple of soldiers next to him. "Anyone got any rocket launcher rounds left?"

The soldiers next to him shook their heads, as one of them yelled, "I am all out. I got some grenades."

Octavious looked up. His F-81 Fighters were mostly gone, escorting the C-112 Transports out. He knew none of them could turn back. Even if they did, there were now five times as many AuFa F-81's in the sky. He turned to the soldier next to him and said, "Give me the grenades."

Octavious slung the satchel of grenades around his shoulder and ran ten meters to a transport truck. Jumping on top of it, he ran the length of the truck before jumping again to a Valkyrie that was hovering five meters above the ground. Both hands caught the foot railing, and he immediately swung himself up to get next to the pilot, who looked astonished. Pointing, he yelled, "Get me up. I need to get to that green transport ship!"

As the Valkyrie turned all four rotor blades towards the green transport, Kaya got up from all fours. She was bleeding profusely from a contusion on the side of her head, and her shoulder was severely injured. Grabbing her rifle as she stood up, she noticed the cannon was destroyed. She saw fighters still zooming overhead. Looking back down the extended bridge, she could see another Tower Cannon towards the main building. Through the billowing smoke from fifty meters away, she saw Octavious, flying on the side of a Valkyrie towards the main building. Clearly in pain, she jumped down on top of the extended bridge and began running towards the other Tower Cannon.

Octavious still had a firm grip on his handle of the Valkyrie. He yelled again at the pilot. "Any more missiles? "

The Valkyrie pilot shook his head and yelled, "No!"

As the green transport was now airborne, the Valkyrie was almost on top of it. Octavious grabbed a cable hanging from the side attachment and clipped one end to the side handlebar. He took the other end and clipped it to the belt of his uniform on his hip. He yelled at the pilot, "Keep shooting! And stay with the transport!"

Octavious jumped ten meters off the Valkyrie and on top of the green transport. The T-11 cannon from the Valkyrie kept shooting rounds, but they were barely penetrating the armor of the transport. Octavious ran towards the front of the green transport as it picked up speed and altitude. The cord still clipped him to the Valkyrie, but the slack was giving way quickly as the Valkyrie tried to keep up. As he got to the cockpit, he grabbed the handle on the emergency door hatch and opened it. Reaching into the satchel, he activated a grenade and dropped it inside the transport. Almost simultaneously, the cable ran out of slack, jerking Octavious backward off the ship. As he flew through the air, the green transport cockpit exploded, sending the ship straight to the ground. Octavious just missed the Valkyrie's blades he was clipped to, falling past it towards the ground below. When the slack ran out, Octavious jerked again, this time swinging from the cable below the Valkyrie. As he was dangling, he saw the green transport crash and explode a kilometer away. The Valkyrie flew over the transport truck he jumped from, and, from five meters high, he unclipped himself, falling on top of it. Grabbing his intercom, he yelled, "Cortes, get down here now."

On the extended bridge, Kaya was still thirty meters away from the next Tower Cannon. An AuFa soldier on the wall tried to shoot her while she was running on top. But she rolled, popped up with her rifle, and got off three perfect rounds, killing him instantly. The soldier in the Tower Cannon chair was firing on F-81's above and never saw Kaya. From a kneeling position, she re-focused her scope. She exhaled and took three shots. The third one hit him in the face, as he slumped down and rolled off the chair. Kaya, so focused on the shot, never heard the roar of the engines. She turned almost all the way around to see an AuFa F-81, hovering in front of her. The pilot was ready to shoot, as Kaya rolled from her knee. The shot went over her as she kept rolling. Popping up, she sprinted four steps and jumped off the extended bridge, landing on the nose of the F-81.

Kaya crawled less than a meter, grabbed her ring to make a fire saber, and pierced it through the glass bubble cockpit. The F-81 turned violently left, as to try to shake Kaya off. The blade, however, was now through the pilot's torso, giving her something stable to hold onto. As the F-81 was spinning, Kaya pointed her rifle at the engine with her other free hand. She connected on five shots that sent the fighter into critical failure. Kaya dropped her rifle and reached for her cable gun on her hip. She shot it towards the building, where it connected on the roof and snapped into place. As she pulled the fire saber out of the cockpit, she jumped toward the building, using the cable line as a swing. The F-81 continued spiraling towards the ground as Kaya crashed through a glass window and rolled up on two civilians lying on the ground, ducking for cover.

As Argo and Leahy made it downstairs, they entered a hangar and looked at the fight outside. Leahy pulled a device out of his pocket with a button on it and looked at Argo. "My Lord?"

Argo saw the device and said, "Not yet. Wait."

Both men grabbed their rings and turned them into silvery swords. They sprinted into the smoke and immediately engaged in a fight with two Valmay soldiers with red fire sabers. After a moment of fighting, Argo and Leahy pushed them back and killed the Valmay soldiers almost simultaneously. Noticing Octavious' group, they ran towards the divider wall.

Flying above them and seeing the fight below, Cortes said on the intercom, "Octavious, there is no place to land."

Ocatvious grabbed his soldiers. One by one, the seven of them got in a giant circle, all firing out. They took out their rings and turned them into fire sabers. Octavious yelled at Donovan and the miners, "Get in the middle, all of you."

As they did, a wall of fire came out from the sabers of the soldiers. It extended out some twenty meters around them, disintegrating everything in sight. Argo and Leahy were twenty meters away as the wall of fire came towards them. They both immediately kneeled and turned their silvery swords into two-meter wide shields. The fire never penetrated them.

Cortes got her Assault Ship right above them in the middle of the fire circle. First, the miners jumped in, followed by the Valmay soldiers. Octavious was the last one to hop on. He touched his intercom and yelled, "Cortes, go, go, go…"

As the flames disappeared, Argo and Leahy stood back up. Argo and Octavious locked eyes as Cortes flew the ship away. Octavious noticed another transport loading some of his soldiers on the ground a hundred meters away. Octavious spoke into his intercom again. "Cortes, let's provide cover for that transport, we leave no one behind. Anyone seen Kaya?"

After going through the glass, Kaya's bleeding was even worse. She got to her feet and ran towards the stairwell at the end of the room. Reaching the top, she went outside, next to the entrance of the Tower Cannon. The soldier she shot from her sniper rifle was bleeding out on the ground as she climbed into the cannon's chair. Focusing, she saw the Valmay ships in the distance leaving. Kaya noticed two AuFa F-81's flying around them. She wiped the blood from her face and began shooting.

Cortes had her ship hovering, so the soldiers operating the cannons could provide cover for the other soldiers boarding the transports. She said into the intercom, "Octavious, no sign of Kaya, but we gotta get out of here."

Octavious watched the last two soldiers board the transport. He shouted into the intercom. "Cortes, punch it!"

The two ships began to fly away, now flanked by two Valmay F-81's. From a distance of about one hundred meters, Kaya saw the four ships leaving. Still profusely bleeding from the contusion on her eye, she focused on the AuFa F-81's with her other eye. Hearing a bunch of AuFa soldiers coming up the stairs behind her, Kaya aimed carefully. She fired, and missed badly. The AuFa F-81 was right behind Cortes' Assault Ship as Kaya heard someone below her say, "Freeze!"

Adjusting to the wind and smoke, she got off two shots from the Tower Cannon that connected with the AuFa F-81's engine, sending it to the ground as Cortes' ship flew away. Kaya tried to grab her ring, but was pierced right in her leg by a silver sword from an SS officer. She turned, but the SS officer immediately hit her across the head and knocked her out cold.

The four remaining Valmay ships burst into high speed away from the Processing Center.

As Argo and Leahy stood on the landing pads and looked around, they saw the damage done. An AuFa officer walked up to him and said, "Lord Argo, I have the Majavkee Lords. They want to speak to you now."

Argo, looking dismayed. He touched his intercom and said, "Admiral Holland..."

After a couple of seconds, Argo heard on his intercom, "Lord Argo, this is Admiral Holland."

Argo wiped his forehead. "You got a signal on those Vait transport ships?"

After a pause, Holland replied, "Yes, sending you the tracking device data now."

Argo and Leahy looked down at the tablet the AuFa officer just handed him. They could now see the four blinking dots of Rendon's stolen C-112 Transports heading towards the mountains. The other four blinking dots had just left the Processing Center, bearing the same direction.

Argo then replied, "Holland, have Attack Group One, Two, and Six follow those dots and tell them to wait for the signal."

Holland quickly replied, "Which will be?"

Argo looked at Leahy, who pulled out the device with the button on it from his pocket. Argo replied, "One big fucking fire."

Over to the side, two SS officers were dragging Kaya's body across the landing pads, her hands cuffed in front of her. They were flanked by four Majavkee security soldiers. They dropped her body in front of Argo as he asked, "What is this?"

The SS officer replied, "A little present, My Lord."

The other SS soldier tossed Kaya's ring at Argo, who caught it. With a small grin, Argo said, "And who does this belong to?"

Kaya was still lying face down. There was a trail of blood left behind her, as she was now bleeding from her leg as well as her head. One of the Majavkee security soldiers kicked Kaya underneath the ribs and yelled, "Answer the question, bitch."

Argo stepped forward. He kicked the leg out from the Majavkee soldier and simultaneously struck him across the neck. It knocked him to the ground and had him gasping for air while holding his throat with both hands. Argo softly said, "Anyone that touches her, and it will be the last thing you do."

Argo tossed Kaya's ring to Leahy. Argo squatted down and pulled Kaya's chin up. Her entire face was covered in blood, and the wound to her eye looked particularly gruesome. Softly shaking his head, Argo said, "Not the handcuffs I envisioned for us."

As she barely came around, Kaya let out a barely audible "Fuck you...."

Argo gave another half-grin before replying. "Your unwillingness to concede is admirable. Foolish...., but admirable."

Kaya attempted to spit on him, but only a thick blood trail made it out an inch.

Argo gave a tiny chuckle and shook his head. He heard the message from Leahy's intercom. "Captain Leahy, this is Admiral Holland. The first four dots have stopped moving."

Leahy responded, "Copy that, stand by."

Leahy and Argo looked at each other. Argo held up his other hand, and Leahy tossed him the device with the button. Looking back at Kaya, Argo said, "Bitch, you can spit, talk, cry all you want. I do not want you dead. I want you to suffer."

Argo held up her head higher and showed her the device. "See this, you cunt? I want you to take a good look at it and think about your precious little brother."

Kaya tried to squirm, but to no avail, as Argo had a very firm grip on her chin. He continued. "Yes, think long and hard, because this is the last breath he will take."

Argo held the device in front of her and pushed the button.

At the Valmay base, Rendon was on the side of a forklift that was carrying one of the Vait crates down the ramp from the giant C-112 transport. All four of the stolen C-112 transports had just landed to the cheers of all the Valmay soldiers at the base cave. They stopped and lowered the crate. Opening it up, Rendon noticed there was no Vait in them. Instead, the crate was full of C-4 explosives. Rendon said, "What the fuck?"

All four C-112 transports exploded immediately inside the Valmay Base headquarters in the cave. Simultaneously, the other four stolen C-112 transports exploded, right next to the escorting convoy of ships led by Cortes and Octavious.

BELINEA - EPISODE FIVE
LOVARRI

BELINEA 5.1

Burvilla, Serpia - 2137 (Twenty Years Prior...)

Dr. Fiona Faxon landed her personal TC Rover on the corner spot on top of the five-story medical complex. She got out and walked to the glass entranceway to scan her hand. As she glanced up, she noticed several Serpian Military aircraft flying overhead. This looked particularly odd, and her expression revealed it. After she walked through the doors, she got to the bottom of an escalator, noticing many people looking flustered. Fiona put her hand on another security glass door, this one having an additional eye-scanner. She said clearly, "Fiona Faxon."

With the scan completed, the doors slid open. She walked down the hallway and noticed more people looking distraught and not working. A nurse walked by, and Fiona stopped her. "Melinda, what is going on?"

She looked at her and nervously said, "Serpian soldiers were here. They went through the whole facility. I think some of them are still downstairs. It is happening."

The nurse walked off. Fiona resumed walking, albeit more briskly now and occasionally looking over her shoulder. She turned a corner into another secure area, and she put her hand on the scanner next to the door. It analyzed her eye as she said, "Fiona Faxon, 241858."

Another glass door opened, and Fiona walked in. It was clearly a medical room, mostly white, with an area for scientific study, lab work, and computer analysis. As she turned a small corner, she saw a body lying on the ground with blood everywhere. There were four gunshot wounds to the chest, with one fatal shot to the head. Fiona put her hand over her mouth and walked over to the computer screen. She hit a few buttons, and it pulled up some of the security cameras in the building. On the monitor, she could see the Serpian soldiers going through the building, pointing guns at Doctors, and demanding information.

Fiona looked scared as she turned around and went towards the other computer screen. She pulled up a few files and sent copies of them out. She then hurried out of the laboratory and sprinted up the escalator to the landing pad area. The door to her personal TC opened, and she climbed in. "Home."

The TC took off, all four rotor blades angling it to the sky. After gaining altitude, it flew in with the hundreds of other aircraft above. Fiona grabbed her wrist-watch and said, "Contact Tara."

Glancing up, it seemed there were even more Serpian Military aircraft in the sky. The computer voice came on and said, "Tara is unavailable right now."

Fiona talked into her wrist-watch again. "Tara, contact me now, its an emergency."

The personal TC kept going for another five minutes before descending on a small house in a very wooded neighborhood. After gently landing, Fiona quickly darted out and sprinted through the front door. She walked into the common area and noticed a human-like robot watching a small toddler. The robot turned and said in a computer-like voice. "Dr. Faxon, I was not expecting you back so soon."

Fiona grabbed some baby clothes and said, "Neither was I."

She grabbed a few more items, putting them in a small bag. She then picked up the toddler and said, "Come with me."

The robot followed and responded, "Dr. Faxon, can I ask where we are going?"

Fiona ignored the robot and gently whispered to the toddler, "Time to get out of here, my prince."

Fiona, the toddler, and the robot got onto the TC. Once they were strapped in, Fiona, still holding the toddler, said, "Verasantos Base, best speed."

This time, the personal TC climbed to 500 meters off the ground in almost no time. It quickly accelerated to go ten times faster than it was before. The computer voice came on and said, "It will take twenty-two minutes to get to Verasantos Base at the current best speed."

Fiona took a deep breath. The toddler began to cry, and as a result, Fiona tried to rock the toddler to sleep. As she was, she started crying herself, finally allowing the emotions from the medical facility to consume her. The robot then asked, "Dr. Faxon, is there anything I can assist you in? Are you alright?"

Fiona stopped crying, and muttered out feebly, "I am fine, we just need to hurry."

At Verasantos Base, the personal TC descended to a civilian landing area just outside the entrance gates. The base itself was elevated among the trees, with several landing areas fifty meters off the ground. All three got out and headed toward the security gate, Fiona still holding the toddler in her arms. They walked ten meters before they were greeted by Lieutenant Orbo, jogging towards them. He quickly asked, "You should not be here."

Fiona said, "I need to see Tara."

Orbo analyzed the situation and responded, "She is planning. This is turning bleak quickly."

Fiona said, "You have no idea, Orbo. Please, I need to talk to Tara."

Orbo replied, "Fiona, she can not. She saw that you were coming, that is why I am here."

Fiona practically broke down and handed the toddler to Orbo. "Please, you must take him."

Orbo grabbed the toddler, only because he almost suspected she would drop him. He responded in surprise. "Fiona, this base is no place for him."

Fiona, still crying, responded, "The child is no longer safe with me. They are coming."

Orbo was utterly confused and replied, "Then leave the child with his father."

Fiona burst into tears and screamed, "His father is dead!"

Orbo did not know what to say or do. He was still holding the toddler when the robot turned toward him. The robot reached out its arms to Orbo and said, "Lieutenant Orbo, may I?"

Orbo handed the toddler to the robot. He then grabbed Fiona's hand, still not knowing what to say or do. After a few seconds of crying, Fiona looked at Orbo and said, "The child cannot come back with me, do you understand?"

Orbo nodded. Fiona then looked at the robot and said, "Stay with him. Protect him at all costs."

The robot responded, "Yes, Dr. Faxon."

Fiona then proceeded to kiss the toddler on the back of his head. She turned around and walked back to the landing pads. Once inside her personal TC, she quickly took off.

Orbo and the robot, still holding the toddler, walked back inside the base. He turned to look at the robot and said, "Come on, I need a place to hide you."

Fiona, still crying, received a message on her wrist communication device. She said, "Play message."

The message then played "Dr. Faxon. You are needed back at the Medical Laboratory immediately."

BELINEA 5.2

Twenty Years Later...

Space Port at Torsalli

AuFa Military Side

Malovex was flying his ship around the explosion. The area seemed to still be chaotic, with much of the Port security and the AuFa not knowing what to do. Malovex flew his ship into an open slip and was immediately hailed by a voice on his intercom. "Unidentified ship near slip 38, please identify, you are in a restricted area!"

There was panic in the voice as well as in the background. While docking the ship, Malovex quickly replied, "This is Lord Malovex, I need to see the Base Commander at the explosion site, immediately."

Maolvex did not wait for a response. Once the ship was docked, the dock slip sealed around the side door. Malovex got out of his cockpit chair, through the back, and out the docking slip entrance. At the top of the tunnel, he was met by three armed AuFa soldiers rushing at him, with rifles drawn.

Malovex was as perturbed as ever. He just kept walking and said, "Good job, you caught me."

The soldiers put down their rifles and followed Malovex back up the tunnel. He briskly walked another twenty meters to what was left of slip 34. The door to the tunnel was sealed shut. Black marks from the explosions lined the wall. Debris was scattered all over the room as three of the windows had been compromised and were replaced by the emergency windows that rolled down. A few AuFa medics were working on a wounded BRG officer on the ground. He looked up, noticed Maolvex, and said, "Lord Malovex, forgive me for not standing."

Malovex glanced down and muttered, "Nothing to apologize for Medic. That soldier needs attention, keep doing your job."

Malovex then looked at the face of the BRG officer on the ground. "What happened, son?"

Grimacing in pain, he said, "An explosion, sir, not sure. My back was to the gate. We were guarding an Ambassador from Earth."

Malovex surveyed the room again, attempting to figure out who was in charge. A bellowing voice came in from behind him. "You two, I want that entire area sealed off, barricade those windows. No press anywhere on the base. Lord Malovex, no one told me you were here?"

Lord Malovex, "Nobody knows I am here, Commander...?"

The AuFa Commander immediately saluted and declared, "Commander Abbott, Control Tower Officer on Duty, sir."

Lord Malovex began looking around, as he was simultaneously talking. "What happened?"

Commander Abbott responded, "An explosion happened at or near the gate, possibly a malfunction of some kind. We should have the area cleaned and stabilized in no time."

Malovex kept looking around, assessing everything before taking a deep breath. He then looked back down at the BRG officer on the ground. "Son, is your commanding officer here?"

The soldier looked up at Malovex. Still grimacing in pain, he said, "Lieutenant Commander Waterford, sir, was not present when the explosion happened."

Malovex pointed to the officer next to Commander Abbott. "Lieutenant, go find me Lieutenant Commander Waterford of the BRG."

Malovex then stared at Abbott. "Seen the security footage yet, Commander?"

Abbott responded, "No, sir."

Malovex then asked, "Have you shut down transportation on both the military side of the Port and the Civilian side?"

Abbott shook his head and responded, "No, sir."

Malovex finally asked, "Is there a full Medical transport ship waiting to take these soldiers to the surface so the medical facilities up here can be on proper stand-by, in case there is another attack?"

Abbott looked confused. "I was not aware there was an attack, my Lord?"

Malovex just stared at him. They were interrupted by Lieutenant Commander Waterford, who said, "Lord Malovex, my apologies. We were securing a transmission with a frigate coming in to take the Ambassador to Belinea when we heard the explosion."

Malovex then looked at Waterford before he said, "What did the detail consist of?"

Waterford rattled off quickly. "Four soldiers, guarding the gate. Two scanners on the outside of the slip, no movement recorded, but I will pull up the footage. Two dead on the ship, the Ambassador, and possibly his assistant."

Malovex asked, "No DAG officers in his detail?"

Waterford added, "He had two, they are somewhere on the base, I thought they would have returned by now."

Malovex looked down on the ground and added, "Your soldier here said the explosion got him in the back."

Waterford added, "I will send in a forensic team to outline the area, collect samples. But we are likely looking at an explosion inside the ship."

Malovex nodded. "Agreed."

Abbott was confused. "Lieutenant Commander, it is clear the explosion was a malfunction on the gate."

Waterford looked at Abbott first, then back at Malovex before asking, "Who is he?"

Malovex, without missing a beat, said, "Useless."

Abbott was taken aback. Malovex continued talking to Waterford. "Set up a secure perimeter on the entire section of the Port, and shut it down to civilian transports as well. Evac the wounded on a medical cruiser to the surface. And get me the results of the forensic team before they do."

Waterford said, "Yes, my Lord. I will pull up sensor footage as well as base security data."

Malovex also added, "And find me those DAG officers. Meet me in the Control Tower in fifteen minutes. You are in charge now."

Abbott responded, "My Lord, this is an AuFa base. I will have to check with my Commander…"

Malovex interjected, "...You are in charge of nothing you incompetent fool. Clear your men out of this area, and let Commander Waterford do his job."

Malovex walked back up the tunnel. The three AuFa soldiers with rifles that initially greeted Malovex were standing there perplexed. Malovex glanced at them and said, "Unless you use them on each other, put those away before you shoot someone important."

BELINEA 5.3

Ascarla, Torsalli

Willits and Jones got off the transport, making their way through the Port Terminal of Ascarla. It was an eclectic mix of food markets, spices, clothes, and copious amounts of wine. There were thousands of bottles all over. Torsalli had a Mediterranean climate across the entire planet. It was beautiful, with oceans, beaches, and greenery everywhere. Ascarla, in particular, was closer to the hills with a slightly cooler climate, lots of rivers, and near the sea. It was ideal for growing grapes.

They made their way to the other side of the terminal, where many flying transports were for hire. Several advertisements declared: see the hills, go to the wineries, the beaches, and resorts, etc. Willits found one that had a real driver, not an automated one. He was begging for a fare. "Come gentlemen, you want to see the wine country? I take you there. Or the ocean, yes, yes, wherever you like."

Willits asked him, "You take a couple of Qusar coins for payment instead of Belinean IDP currency scan?"

The driver looked at them again and could see they looked like soldiers. He didn't know what to say. Jones broke the tension with "Just trying to enjoy our three-day pass without our Commanders knowing where we are going."

The driver just nodded and said, "Where?"

Willits handed him two Qusar coins and said, "Take us to the Kapoor Estate in Ishannia Valley."

The small doors of the TC opened, and Willits and Jones climbed in. They immediately took off, never getting higher than 30 meters off the ground, but somehow the driver was a master at navigating the airway regulations for air-paths. They seemed to be following other TC's until they made their way out of the city of Ascarla. They climbed to eighty meters and flew over the gorgeous countryside. It was filled with thousands of rows of grape-vines in between the hills, valleys, and streams. Jones turned to Willits and said, "You sure he will see us?"

Willits answered, "I'm not even sure he is here."

Jones replied, "And if he isn't?"

Willits smiled, responding, "Hitchhike back to Earth?"

The flight continued until they were far from the city. As the TC touched down, they came upon a giant 30-meter high fence. The gate had three landing areas outside. Willits and Jones climbed out and went to the front gate. Before they knew it, a full laser body scan was done on them while standing outside. A hologram of an attractive Torsallian lady appeared in front of them and asked, "Gentlemen, how can I help you?"

Willits responded, "Nolan Willits and Avery Jones here to see Vihaan Kapoor."

The hologram responded, "Gentlemen, I am afraid Mr. Kapoor is not here."

Willits responded, "Well, either way, we are here from the Delegate Ambassador Guard on Earth. Mr. Kapoor has some of our property that needs to be updated and inspected."

There was a long pause from the hologram, in which Willits and Jones could tell the image had become frozen. A few more seconds went by. Jones looked at Willits with a curious 'is this going to work' expression. Willits raised his eyebrows, genuinely not knowing what was going to happen. Suddenly the colossal gate doors opened, and the hologram disappeared. However, the hologram voice said, "Please enter."

There was a larger, more luxurious TC waiting on the other side of the gate. There was no driver as the doors opened automatically. Willits and Jones climbed in, taking a seat in the plush caramel-colored velvet chairs. The TC took off just as the doors closed. It's flour rotor blades seemingly making no noise as it flew. It hovered ten meters above the ground, across the Kapoor Estate of grapevines, guest houses, and streams. After five minutes of flying about 120 miles per hour, they came upon the main house, which was similar to a French Chateau. The facility had over fifty bedrooms and a grape processing center next to the caves of the hills. There was an obnoxiously large swimming pool with rocks, caves, and waterfalls as well. The

TC landed on a spot in between the Chateau and the pool. Willits and Jones climbed out, standing back up in the perfect sunny weather of Torsalli.

As they walked up to the Chateau, four men with rifles approached them from the main house, cocked and loaded. Willits and Jones stopped, and each grabbed their pistol, but not taking it out of its holster. Jones looked behind them as if to find a way to escape, but four more security guards were coming up behind them now as well.

Willits and Jones looked at each other, putting their hands up. From the building behind them, a short man of Indian descent rapidly approached them in casual clothing with a glass of wine in his hand. His assistant, the one in the hologram, was walking directly behind him. Vihaan Kapoor, clearly in anger, began shouting at Willits and Jones, still with their hands up. "Thought it was funny when you left me on Vandabri to take a transvestite into one of the parlor rooms, did you?"

Willits and Jones were speechless. Vihaan continued, "Did you really think the richest man on Earth would forget such a cruel joke."

Seeing Vihaan was still pissed, Jones said in desperation, "It was Madam Rouselle's idea."

Vihaan quickly countered, "I have given that bitch so much money over the years she would never do such a thing. It was you two. I didn't realize it until I slid my hand up her skirt!"

Vihaan just stared at them angrily. He was looking up, not taking his eyes off them. Willits and Jones just kept their hands up, not knowing what to say. After about five seconds, Vihaan finally started laughing, "Never make decisions after four bottles of wine, you mother-fuckers...."

Vihaan came in and hugged Willits. Then turning to Jones to hug him also, said, "If one of my staffers left me that way, I would've cut their fucking eyes out."

Willits, smiling, said, "We honestly thought you knew."

Vihaan continued laughing, "I was so drunk I could've fucked a goat."

Jones broke the tension further by saying, "I thought Parkohov was the richest man on Earth."

Vihaan turned his head and said, "That Russian motherfucker don't have the same money I got, fuck him. "

The three began walking back to the pool area. All the security guards had their rifles down now, escorting them on each side. "What are you two doing here?"

Willits replied, "You keep telling us to come back to Torsalli, drink the best wine in the universe, so here we are."

Vihaan Kapoor snapped his fingers at one of the assistants, pointed two fingers up. The assistant hurried off to find two more glasses. Vihaan held his glass up in the sun and said, "Torsalli wine gentlemen, is no joke. My vinter has been making wine in his family for over fifty years. This is a Lovarri grape, blended with Simsi and a touch of Dartolla grapes. Very similar to a French Bordeaux, but Simsi has more Italian Barolo characteristics, and the Dartolla softens the wine like a Petit Verdot. Still a little leather and boots, some cigar, a hint of vanilla and spice, but a very soft tannin oak finish."

The assistant came back with two glasses for Willits and Jones. They held the glasses up, and Vihaan said "Cheers gentlemen, to old friends."

Willits and Jones, before taking a sip, simultaneously said, "To old friends."

Jones replied, "That's excellent, Vi."

Willits said, "You might just make it as a wine producer after all."

Vihaan said, "Belineans are buying it like crazy. Sell a little bit of it back home, but those cheap bastards can't afford it."

Jones smiled and said, "Been back home recently?"

Vihaan's smile quickly went away as they continued walking towards the pool. "Only when I have to. Why would I leave this place?"

Willits and Jones began noticing the beautiful pool with lots of girls everywhere, music playing, a 3-D hologram image of what looked like a soccer match back on Earth. Jones half smiled and said, "I probably wouldn't leave either."

The three stopped next to his outdoor bar area. It was shaded with bar stools and a bartender. Willits turned to Vihaan and said, "Vi, can we talk?"

Vihaan looked at his bartender and said, "Leave us."

After he walked away, Willits continued. "When you talk directly to Director Kimakawa, how do you do it?"

Vihaan was taken slightly aback. "Listen, Nolan. If this is about construction on the base, I told him we are working as fast as possible. I am producing ships faster than the Belineans."

Jones looked curious. "What base?"

But Willits cut him off. "I am not here about the base. Do you have a direct line of communication with him?"

Vihaan still looked confused. "We have a C-bar communication line. Only takes about twenty minutes for a message to go through."

Willits continued, "Directly to him?"

Vihaan was still puzzled. "His office. So either him or Meyers. I doubt his assistant reads the message. Why?"

Willits then said, "Do you still have those DAG patrol drones and the DAG guest house we set up for you a few years back?"

Vihaan "Of course. The Belineans hate it, but it keeps them out of my business."

Willits said, "Good. Finally, what's the fastest ship you got to take us to Belinea?"

Vihaan smiled big. "I got a Belinean D-21 Sirralo, completely pimped out guys. Four staterooms, gold plated common area, wet bar. It can get from here to Belinea in four days."

Jones looked shocked, "Four days? That should be at least six from here."

Vihaan smiled again "It's fast."

Willits then got a little closer. "Vi, I hate to ask, but we are really in a pinch, and I need your help."

Vihaan looked serious as well. "I will never forget that trouble you two got me out of in Locavores, what do you need?"

Willits practically pleaded. "First, We need one of the shitiest transports you got. One that you don't mind parting with."

Vihaan said, "Take your pick. What else?"

Willits then asked, "Can we borrow the Sirralo to take to Belinea?"

Jones countered, "We will bring it back, of course."

Vihaan just smiled again. "Shit, just take one, I got three of them. The other two are for my boys, but one is here with his bitch Torsallian girlfriend, and the other is rock climbing in Willasar."

Willits smiled back "Thanks, Vi, where is this C-Bar Communication?"
Vi raised his glass of wine. "In my office, of course."

BELINEA 5.4

Earth, Northeastern Japan

After getting off the elevator, the woman scanned her hand and entered the facility's restricted area. She was in full military uniform, with several citations and medals hanging from her coat. She got to the office of Director Kimakawa, and a robot asked. "May I help you?"

"Master Sergeant Sabrina Evans for the Director."

The Robot quickly processed, sending a message to Kimakawa. A few seconds went by, and the doors opened, just as the robot responded, "The Director will see you."

Master Sergeant Evans walked directly into the room, stood five feet in front of Kimakawa's desk at attention, and saluted.

Kimakawa put the stuff he was looking at down. "Master Sergeant Evans, how is Odgins?"

Evans gave up on the salute, Kimakawa did not acknowledge it. She eased back into standing at ease, arms crossed behind her, and said, "Good sir. There will be many qualified cadets at your disposal upon graduation."

Kimakawa kept his head down, glancing at the material in front of him. "Excellent. Something I can help you with?"

Evans took two steps forward and placed the computer stick on his desk. She then took two steps back, going right back to soft attention, and said, "This is from Commander Willits, sir."

Kimakawa raised an eyebrow. "Delivering it in person?"

Evans never looked back down, keeping her eyes focused on the wall. "He did not trust any electronic channels, sir."

Kimakawa gave a look of annoyance. "Why didn't you give it to me when we interrogated you on SPE about the cadets?"

Master Sergeant Evans took a small breath before responding "Before he left, Commander Willits gave me specific instructions to give this to you in the event anything unusual happened regarding his assignment. He also said to give it to you in private, with no one else present."

Kimakawa put the stick into his tablet. He asked, "And you don't know what it says?"

Master Sergeant Evans hesitated for a second before she said, "No, sir."

Kimakawa quickly read the note. He then put his tablet down and said, "They have been gone for almost five days. I am getting this now?"

Master Sergeant Evans thought for a second, then said, "I was unsure if the attack on SPE was related, sir. After I heard about the incident on Braccus, I was certain something unusual was going on."

Kimakawa sat back in his chair. He took a deep breath and rubbed his eyes. "Master Sergeant, did you teach Commanders Willits and Jones at Odgins?"

"Yes, sir."

Kimakawa drew a smirk. "How were they as students?"

Evans replied without hesitation. "Two of the worst students I have ever had. Insubordinate. Lack of focus. Below average aviation skills, and as arrogant as I have ever encountered."

Kimakawa looked directly at her. "And yet, the medal on your chest, The Cross of Valor, would suggest something different, no?"

Evans finally looked down, but did not say anything. With a look of immense seriousness, she just continued to stare at Kimakawa. After what seemed like ten seconds, Evans finally said, "You trust the soldiers you fight with, and you don't leave anyone behind."

Kimakawa looked back and only very softly said, "You know what the note says."

Evans said nothing. Before either could speak, they were both interrupted by Vice Director Meyers, who came bursting into the room. "Director, there was another attack. This one was on Torsalli."

Meyers practically sprinted to the desk, before finally stopping. Kimakawa and Evans looked directly at him before he said, "There was an explosion on The Ambassador's ship. He is dead, along with another fatality they believe is Miss Devanoe."

Kimakawa stood up. He was stunned. "Are you sure? They were supposed to be on a Battle Cruiser?"

Meyers responded, "They got off the Battle Cruiser, and were awaiting further transport. The ship blew up on the military side of the Torsalli Space Port."

Evans then said, "And Commanders Willits and Jones?"

Meyers, almost out of breath, said, "Nobody knows. They apparently exited the ship, but nobody can find them. The BRG is looking for them now."

Evans and Kimakawa looked at each other before Kimakawa glanced at the note on his desk from Willits. Kimakawa said, "Well, that makes two of us. Dammit!"

A few seconds of awkward silence went by before a voice came from Kimakawa's desk. The robot from the other room said, "Director, an urgent message from Vihaan Kapoor just came through."

All three looked at each other. Kimakawa whispered to himself, "Vi is on Torsalli."

Kimakawa sat back down and looked at the message. He thought for a few seconds, then decided to read it in front of everyone else. "It's from Willits. Jones and I are safely on Torsalli. We are staying at the DAG guest house on the Kapoor Estate, with the Ambassador, alive and well. We believe Miss Devanoe is not who she seems and is working for someone else (BRG? SS?) as the explosion that killed the two cadets was her doing. We are arranging private transportation to Belinea in the next twenty-four hours. Willits."

All three looked at each other. Evans finally asked, "Who is Miss Devanoe?"

Meyers responded, "She is the Ambassador's personal assistant. She is traveling with him everywhere. She is also Belinean educated, so very familiar with proper Council procedure."

Kimakawa then said, "And the daughter of an old friend….."

Meyers and Evans just looked at Kimakawa as he continued. "Alright, that message goes no further. Meyers, keep inquiring about the explosion. We must appear to be concerned at all levels and genuinely surprised when we find out the Ambassador was on board. Sargent, go back to Odgins, pull up the records for the two cadets that died so we can notify the families."

Sargent Evans looked at Kimakawa and said, "Anything else I can do, Director?"

Kimikawa paused, knowing Evans was asking a different question. He put on his coat and said, "No, I must do this myself."

BELINEA 5.5

Battle Cruiser 54

Second moon of Pyliss

AuFa Supply Station

Commander Devanoe kept looking at his watch-like tracker that he had for Alexis. It had not blinked or beeped in over five minutes. He was over at the Communications area, where an officer was trying to get information. Devanoe aggressively asked, "Can you get me any information or confirmation?"

The Communications Officer, Lieutenant Wilcox, kept trying his best. "I have a contact, sir, but it seems pretty chaotic right now. But I believe there was an attack."

Captain Kimmel had proceeded to walk back over. He asked, "The ammunition cargo is on-board, we are ready to go. Any word yet, Commander?"

Devanoe looked at his Captain and said, "No, sir. With your permission, I would like to request transportation to Torsalli to look into the matter personally, sir. "

Captain Kimmel softly said, "Nick, I know…."

Devanoe cut him off "It's my sister, sir."

Captain Kimmel did not try another word. This was personal. He waited a few seconds before asking, "Let me see the Tracker."

Nick Devanoe handed it to Kimmel. The Captain inspected it for a few seconds. "Who gave this to you?"

Devanoe answered, "Vincella, the BRG Captain on Braccus."

Kimmel walked a few meters to the other side of the communications area where Lieutenant Hauser was. With the device in his hand, he held it up and asked, "Lieutenant Hauser, Can you explain to me how this works?"

Lieutenant Hauser grabbed it and looked at it for a few seconds. "Yes, Captain. The partner device for this tracker must get activated by pushing the button on it. It will begin blinking and beeping immediately."

Kimmel then asked, "And if it stops blinking and beeping suddenly?"

Hauser said, "It's most likely been destroyed."

Kimmel then asked, "No way it just stops on its own?"

Hauser shook her head "It is possible it had a malfunction, but that is extremely rare. Destroying it or out of range are the only ways it stops, sir."

Kimmel then looked puzzled. "Out of range?"

Hauser replied, "Yes, sir. It has a range of any medium-sized solar system."

Kimmel then asked, "So Torsalli?"

Hauser answered, "Is definitely in range for the device, sir. But let me run it through the system and see if I can find out what happened."

Devanoe came walking up to Kimmel and Hauser and said, "Anything?"

Kimmel said, "She's checking. You?"

Devanoe shook his head. "No. Lieutenant Wilcox is trying to get some information about this attack. Captain, I'm telling you, something was strange about the way Commander Willits was acting. And then not saying goodbye to Alexis? The whole thing was very bizarre."

Kimmel raised an eyebrow. Nothing was said for a few minutes. Suddenly, Lieutenant Wilcox leaped out of his seat and came running over to Kimmel and Devanoe. He said, "Captain, there was an explosion on the military side of the Torsalli Space Port. At least two are dead, several critically wounded. The Earth Ambassador Bird is among the fatalities, but they are not listing the other victim. They are looking for two DAG officers for questioning."

Devanoe was crushed. Kimmel patted him on the back and looked at him, but no words came out. Lieutenant Hauser shouted out behind them, "Captain, I found out what happened."

In a furious tone, the Captain looked down at Hauser and said, "Not now Lieutenant, there was an explosion on Torsalli, and it may have killed the Commander's sister."

Devanoe put his hand over his eyes. But Hauser continued. "But Captain, that tracker watch wasn't anywhere near Torsalli."

Both Kimmel and Devanoe perked up. They practically sprinted to the Communication Area, where Kimmel asked, "What did you say?"

Hauser said, "Here, sir. Look at this map."

All three looked at the image. The blinking dot appeared to be right next to Torsalli. Devanoe said, "That's the image that popped up on my side of the tracker watch. It's right next to Torsalli!"

Hauser then apologized. "Sorry, sir. Let me show you the inverted 3-D hologram version of the map."

Hauser hit a couple spots, and the hologram map appeared on the table in front of them. She then pointed at all the landmarks. "We are here, near Pyliss. Here is Torsalli. But the tracker is all the way down here."

Lieutenant Hauser was pointing on the bottom of the hologram map. Looking at it from a 3-Dimensional aspect, the tracker was so far away, it was possible it was the same distance as flying out of the solar system but in a vertical fashion. "As you can see, whatever ship that tracker was on, was heading this direction. With a sudden turn here at the end to go this direction."

Commander Devanoe was confused. "Where the hell does that go."

Captain Kimmel looked at for a second, then realized the route. He hit a couple of spots on the screen to expand the map size. Pointing at the spot, he said, "Molar. That used to be the back way into Belinea."

Devanoe was still confused. "Why go that way, when you can just go through the Torsalli route, which is so much faster."

Kimmel half smirked "The Torsalli route is the safest because it is the most guarded by AuFa ships. But if you were trying to sneak into Belinea, you go through Molar, where there is little AuFa presence. The smugglers use this route frequently but contend with heavy asteroid belts and solar rays."

Devanoe thought for a second. Then said, "Lieutenant Wilcox, did they give any other information on the other fatality? "

Wilcox shook his head briefly. "No, sir. That is why they are looking for the DAG officers to question. They got off the ship, but no one has seen them since."

Devanoe shook his head. "The other fatality was Alexis. But since they needed a pilot, perhaps it was one of those cadets."

Kimmel asked, "Cadets?"

Devanoe replied, "They needed a qualified pilot for the C-62T, so Willits got two cadets, Tunsall and Trujillo."

Kimmel turned white. He grabbed Devanoe by the back of the shoulder. "What did you just say?"

Devanoe turned to Captain Kimmel. He said clearly, "Willits and Jones were not using a regular detail. They picked up these two cadets, I assume from Odgin's, to help with security........"

Devanoe stopped in mid-sentence. He could see the expression on Captain Kimmel's face changing. "About this tall (holding up his hand to six-foot-one inch), sandy brown hair, green eyes. The other one about two inches shorter, dark hair, brown skin?"

Devanoe just looked at his Captain and nodded and then whispered, "Oh shit...."

Kimmel immediately started barking. "Lieutenant Wilcox, you have the Conn. Take this Battle Cruiser back to Braccus, drop off the cargo to Captain Vincella, and await further instruction."

Kimmel taped Devanoe on the shoulder and continued, "We are taking the other T-141 back to Torsalli to find out what happened."

As they began walking to the elevator, Kimmel continued, "And if need be, find a faster ship."

BELINEA 5.6

On the Way to Malor

The T-141 was still traveling at best speed for a planet Tunsall and Trujillo had never been to. The banging, however, coming from the back of the ship, did not stop. Trujillo turned to Tunsall and said, "They are not going to stop banging."

Tunsall then turned to Trujillo and said, "You know what Willits said."

Trujillo deliberated that for a second. He heard another beating on the door. He got out of his chair and said, "Fuck-it."

Tunsall then yelled, "Trujillo!"

Trujillo countered, "Where are they going to go, Tunsall? They shouldn't be incarcerated."

Tunsall stared at him for a second. Then unbuckled his safety belt to climb out of the chair. He set the ship for auto-pilot and walked to the back with Trujillo. When they got to the back door, Trujillo unlocked it and opened it slowly.

Alexis came storming out. First missing with her right arm, the swipe with her left connected across Trujillo's head. She then connected with a kick to the leg when Trujillo kept his hands up in self-defense. When he grabbed his leg, Alexis punched him right in the mouth. She screamed, "What the fuck are you two doing?!!"

Trujillo, incomplete self-defense mode, took another step back, this time with arms back up. Alexis smacked him again on the side, as he could feel the blood coming off his lip. "Alexis, calm down!"

Ambassador Bird walked out the door with a steak knife in his hand. Alexis tried another punch, this time Trujillo grabbed her wrist to stop it. He looked at her, now with a bloody lip, and said, "Will you stop?"

Tunsall looked at Ambassador Bird and said, "We are the only ones on board, so unless you know how to fly this thing, you need us. Let us explain."

Alexis had momentarily stopped. Ambassador Bird cautiously stopped moving forward, but still had the steak knife in his hand. Alexis pushed the hair out from the front of her face, and said, "Explain why you left us locked up back there like prisoners?"

Trujillo refused to let go of Alexis' wrist. Tunsall softly said, "Nobody is a prisoner. It was Commander Willits's idea to keep you safe."

Trujillo let go of Alexis' wrist while keeping his other hand upright as to make sure to protect himself. Ambassador Bird now asked, "Where are Willits and Jones?"

Trujillo answered, "We do not know."

Alexis countered that answer as if Trujillo was lying. "What do you mean you do not know? Where are we?"

Tunsall began to explain. "We are on the T-141 that we used on Braccus. Willits gave you a sedative in your wine, and it knocked you out for over 24 hours."

Bird, very confused, asked, "Where is my Ambassador Transport ship?"

Trujillo calmly said, "Probably on Torsalli now. You never got back on it. We snuck you out of Braccus."

Alexis was a little calmer now. "Why?"

Tunsall answered, "It was Commander Willits's idea that the best way to hide you was for no one to know where you are."

Trujillo added, "So he put four bodies in the back of the Ambassador's C-62T, two AuFa soldiers and the two prostitutes from Vandabri. He told us he would take them to Torsalli and that he would meet up with us on Molar."

Alexis questioned, "Molar?"

Tunsall answered, "Yes, that is where we are heading now."

Bird was practically fuming. "This is outrageous, treating us like this. Does Commander Willits have any idea who he is dealing with? I need to send a message to Director Kimakawa at once."

Trujillo answered, "I am afraid that is just not possible, sir."

Bird, still pissed, said, "Excuse me? I do not take orders from you."

Tunsall calmly said, "Ambassador, Commander Willits ordered us not to allow either of you any communication outside the ship. It is for your safety that no one can know where we are."

Trujillo added, "And even if we didn't, sir, there is nothing powerful enough on this ship to get a message to Earth. It would be a struggle just to connect to Torsalli."

The Ambassador was still livid as he put down the steak knife. "Safety or not, this is unacceptable. Drugging an Ambassador? I will see to it these soldiers are court-martialed. We should be on a Battle Cruiser right now, in the comforts of my Ambassador Transport, heading to Belinea instead of Molta."

Tunsall said, "It's Molar, sir."

Bird yelled, "Whatever. Nothing about this trip has been acceptable since we left Earth!"

Alexis turned and looked at him somewhat calmly and said, "Except that you are alive."

Tunsall and Trujillo were in a bit of disbelief. It seemed that they had gotten through to Alexis, who was beginning to see the rationale. She continued. "The methods and manners are certainly less than desirable, but the results cannot be argued with. Ambassador, Taz, or someone working with him, is trying to kill you. And like it or not, Commander's Willits and Jones have kept you alive."

Ambassador Bird took a breath before letting out, "Is it possible to protect me without all the theatrics?"

Tunsall then explained, "Sir, with all due respect, there is no manual for this. If we had left Earth when we were supposed to, that attack likely would have left us dead. There is an excellent chance the attack on Braccus was a diversion to attack you again, but we were conveniently hiding on Vandabri."

Trujillo added, "Hopefully, nothing happens on Torsalli, but I feel better knowing no one knows where we are."

There was an awkward silence. Bird finally said, "I will think about it. But I want to talk to Willits and Jones."

Tunsall said under his breath, "So do I…."

Bird walked back into the cabin they were in, asking Tunsall if they could turn on the lights and power. Trujillo wiped the blood from his mouth, which was beginning to swell up. Alexis looked at him, then walked over to the medical portion of the T-141. She quickly took out a rag and some antiseptic spray and walked back over to Trujillo. She said, "Let me see."

Trujillo looked away, putting his hand on his mouth again and said, "I am fine."

Alexis replied, "Sit down and let me see it, tough guy."

Trujillo sat in a chair and said, "It's not the first time I have been punched."

Alexis tilted his head back to see the wound better. She whispered, "Or the last…"

Trujillo rolled his eyes as she cleaned up the wound a little bit, then sprayed the antiseptic on it, which made Trujillo grimace for a second.

Trujillo muttered under his breath, "That's a mean right cross you got."

Alexis, not missing a beat, said, "You should see the left uppercut."

Trujillo gave a minuscule smirk. Alexis held the rag on his lip and very softly said, "Sorry I hit you."

Trujillo's smirk disappeared. He softly said back, "No, you're not, but you oughta be."

That made Alexis give a half-smile. Still keeping one hand on the rag, she cleaned the wound again with the other hand. Then put the rag back on it. She whispered back, "This is gonna leave a scar until you get a professional to look at it."

Trujillo responded, "I will live. Besides, I have heard some women like scars."

Alexis pulled the rag off and looked at him. She then said, "Who told you that?"

Trujillo added, "Not all. Just what I have heard."

Alexis put the rag back on and said, "It works for some guys."

Trujillo gave a small smile. Alexis gently tapped Trujillo's face with her other hand and whispered, "You will live pretty boy."

Alexis took Trujillo's free hand, grabbed it, and placed it on the rag. She began to walk away, but Trujillo, now holding the rag on his face, said, "Alexis...."

She stopped and turned. Trujillo said, "Thanks for having our back with the Ambassador."

She paused, looked at him intently, and said, "You don't. But someone is trying to kill him, which means I am in danger of being killed as well. My list of trust is dwindling by the second, starting with Willits and Jones. Which means I don't trust you or Tunsall either."

Trujillo half-smiled, "I trust you."

Alexis said softly, "I know....but you shouldn't."

Alexis turned around and walked away, leaving Trujillo holding the rag on his face. He could then here the Ambassador yelling at Tunsall, "How the hell do you turn this thing back on?"

Kimakawa said softly, "I could have been an intruder?"

Annella was solemn. "I saw your ship land, and a short man walking from it. Unless it was someone from your office trying to kill me, I ventured an educated guess that it was you."

Kimakawa half smiled "What if I came to kill you?"

Annella answered, "You could've done that a very long time ago if that was your true intention."

Kimakawa walked over, standing next to her and said, "Keep your friends close, and your enemies closer."

Annella looked up at him and gave a small snort. "There is tea and scotch on the table."

Kimakawa walked over and poured himself some tea. "Thank you for the tea. It is too early for scotch."

Annella took a sip of her tea, which had a little whiskey in it. "It is never too early for scotch. Especially when you have had the morning I had."

Kimakawa softly said, "Really?"

Annella said, "A setback from the lab regarding pandemic questions. An area we thought we had a cure for is testing negative."

Kimakawa replied, "The progress you have made is not a setback."

Annella responded, "We cannot move forward unless we have figured out all of the potential conditions and outcomes. But that is not why you are here."

Kimakawa sat across from Annella and took a sip of tea. "I have good news and bad news. When was the last time you spoke to your daughter?"

Annella said, "I have not spoken to Alexis since she left, why?"

Kimakawa then questioned, "You would not be lying to me, Annella, would you?"

Annella, in annoyance, responded, "I find lying counterproductive and annoying. If I do not want you to know something, I will just not answer the question."

Kimakawa then said, "Well, some people believe you have. Namely, my two DAG officers who are on her detail."

Annella responded, "The two you do not trust?"

Kimakawa said, "The two that I suspect..."

Annella said, "You would not be here if you did."

Kimakawa thought about that for a moment. He then said. "I received a message from them saying the Ambassador and your daughter are alive and well. That message came immediately after a message from the BRG saying an explosion at the Torsalli Space Port killed them. My DAG officer now believes that your daughter is a spy."

Annella looked serious before responding. "There was another attack?"

Kimakawa said, "They are alive and well, Annella."

Annella suddenly looked angry. "I told you to stop playing games, Taichi."

Kimakawa answered quickly, "I am not playing games."

Annella raised her voice, "But you are allowing my daughter to be exposed to explosions and assassinations while you put your grand scheme in action?"

Kimakawa raised his voice "We have to be on the same page. If you are giving her information without telling me, maybe that is the cause...."

Annella cut him off by raising her voice. "Do not tell me how to talk to my daughter!"

Kimakawa snapped back and said, "And do not tell me what to do with my spies!"

The two paused, letting the dust settle for a moment. After a moment, Kimakawa got up and went over to the table. He saw the bottle of Lagavulin 16-year-old scotch and poured two glasses neat. He returned to the spot he was sitting in, handing over one of the neat pours to Annella, who took it.

He sat down and stared at Annella for a few seconds longer. Both took a sip of the scotch before Kimakawa quietly said, "Why does the DAG team think that Alexis has a hidden agenda?"

Annella responded in an equally calm voice, "I do not know Taichi. Maybe they are just smart. I swear I have not spoken to her."

"Alright."

Annella was confused. "Alright, what?"

Kimakawa softly said, "Process of elimination. You will let me know if she contacts you."

Annella looked at him and responded, "Can you promise me that you can keep her safe?"

Kimakawa stood up. "No, I cannot anymore. But I promise I will try."

Annella then said, "Do you even know if she is safe now?"

Kimakawa then said, "No."

Annella rolled her eyes a little bit and took another sip of scotch. "Taichi, do you even know who your friends and enemies are anymore?"

Kimakawa stared at her, took another gulp of scotch to finish it off, and replied, "I would not be here if I did not."

The two stared at each other for a moment before Kimakawa walked off, leaving Annella to stare at the cliffs and the ocean with her dog.

BELINEA 5.8

Torsalli Space Port

Commander Nick Devanoe piloted the T-141 to a perfect dock on the military side. Nick and Captain Kimmel unbuckled out of their chairs and walked out of the cockpit area. They proceeded out of the ship and down the docking tunnel. When they got to the end, they were met by an AuFa security soldier. He saluted as Captain Kimmel asked, "Which way to your Commanding Dock Officer on Duty?"

The soldier pointed. "Up those escalators, sir, take the tunnel to the bridge."

Devanoe and Kimmel began walking at a quick pace. Kimmel turned to Devanoe and said, "So you never laid eye-balls on The Ambassador, your sister, or the two cadets?"

Devanoe nodded as they made their way up the escalator. Nick answered, "Affirmative, sir. Like I said before, Willits was acting strange about it."

Kimmel then asked, "He was deceptive?"

Devanoe then responded, "More like a 'stop asking so many questions, I got this' kind of way. I could be wrong, but it would not surprise me if Alexis and the rest of them were somewhere else when that ship exploded."

Devanoe and Kimmel made their way across the bridge, before taking a second set of escalators to the Tower Bridge. The scene was far more chaotic there as officers were running around everywhere. In the distance out the window, they could still see the crews working on the spot that the C-62T had exploded. As they walked further up the bridge, Devanoe saw a security monitor replaying the explosion on a loop, repeatedly. Devanoe looked at it once, before tapping Kimmel on the shoulder to join him. They looked at it a few times before Devanoe said, "The explosion was from within."

Kimmel commented, "Which means someone boarded the ship and planted an explosive or it was planted by someone already on the inside."

An officer walked by, and Kimmel asked, "Lieutenant, who is the Commanding Officer here?"

The Lieutenant paused, not knowing what to say. Ever so cautiously, he turned in the direction of a 3-D table that had five officers around it, a mere five meters away from Kimmel and Devanoe. As the officers parted the board, it was clear the man in the black robes with the scars on his face was in charge. Lord Malovex glanced up at Kimmel before he turned back to the board and said, "Captain Kimmel. Should you not be on your Battle Cruiser back to Braccus?"

Kimmel and Devanoe walked up to the board and said, "Lord Malovex, we thought we could assist here. We have some information."

Malovex kept looking down at his board. "Really, Captain, what is it?"

Devanoe interrupted with, "The explosion was from within."

Malovex was annoyed now. Kimmel wanted to smack Devanoe for interrupting. Malovex continued, "Something we have known for quite some time. Any other useless information you would like to offer, or can the BRG continue doing their job?"

Kimmel scowled at Devanoe, as to say with his eyes, 'Keep your mouth shut.'

Devanoe doubled down, though. "Lord Malovex, I spoke with the two DAG officers, Willits and Jones, before they left for the Space Port."

Malovex then stood up and slowly turned around. Looking at Devanoe now, he said, "Who are you?"

Kimmel changed his expression. "Lord Malovex, this is my first officer, Commander Devanoe. A moment please?"

Malovex paused for a few seconds before looking at his BRG officers and then back at Kimmel and Devanoe. He then gestured with his hand for them to approach.

Kimmel and Devanoe walked up to the table next to Malovex. Once the area had cleared a little from the BRG officers, Devanoe continued. "Lord Malovex, when I asked the DAG Commander Willits if I could see the Ambassador and his assistant, he said they were asleep, and he was acting strange. I had previously given the assistant a tracker watch, the ones the BRG use, in an emergency. When we were on board the Battle Cruiser on Pyliss, the tracker watch was activated. It only was active for less than a minute, but we feel it went out of range because of the distance. If the assistant was still with the Ambassador, it is possible they were never on that ship that exploded out there."

Malovex looked at them for a few more seconds. He then said, in almost disbelief, "And, what else?"

Kimmel added, "Given the explosion was internal, it implies it could've been planted by the two DAG Commanders that were assigned security on the Ambassador."

Malovex was slightly annoyed again. "Which is why I would like to talk to the DAG officers. Is this all you have?"

Devanoe didn't say anything, nor did Kimmel. Malovex continued, "You want me to go on a hunch because someone was acting strange and a tracker watch that went off for less than a minute?"

Devanoe added, "We think they were on their way to Molar."

Devanoe realized that the last sentence might have been a mistake. Malovex looked at both of them with disdain. "I do not care if that tracker was headed to the Torsalli sun. Did you get any verbal confirmation? Did you see the Ambassador or his assistant board this other ship? Are you sure the tracker is even working, either now or then? Do you even trust these two DAG officers? Do you have any actual evidence or just speculation?

Devanoe thought for a second and then shook his head and muttered, "No, sir."

Malovex countered, "Let me tell you what I have. I have a confirmed C-62T explosion out there with two fatalities on board, and another six BRG officers wounded. I have two rogue DAG officers that have already changed the manifest on this assignment twice. They left a ship and an Ambassador behind, rather odd considering the ship exploded, and are now on the run somewhere near Ascarla on Torsalli below. I have confirmed Taz was in the area, on board a stolen Civilian Transport ship. And you would like me to go find some phantom ship that's on the way to Molar?"

There was a long five seconds of silence. Kimmel took a step back, grabbed Devanoe's elbow, and said, "Sorry for bothering you, Lord Malovex. We will be going."

Malovex turned back around to look at his board. Devanoe took a step back with Kimmel. Kimmel had turned around now, still with his hand on Devanoe's elbow, trying to direct him down the platform. Devanoe made one final comment. "The assistant is my sister, Lord Malovex. She is tough as nails, and would have never hit the panic button without reason."

Kimmel practically drew blood,, squeezing Devanoe's arm. Malovex stopped what he was doing. Pausing for another five seconds, he slightly turned his head towards Devanoe and Kimmel, but not enough to see them. Malovex asked, "What is your name again?"

Devanoe stood at attention when asked. "First Officer, Commander Nick Devanoe, Battle Cruiser 54, Aultali Chlorifa."

Malovex paused for another few seconds, processing the information and taking a long look at Nick Devanoe. He then turned his eyes towards Captain Kimmel and said, "Kimmel, I heard your Battle Cruiser is doing an ammo restock on behalf of Captain Vincella's request on Braccus."

Kimmel responded. "It is, sir. It should be halfway there by now."

Malovex turned his head and began looking back at the board. He then said, "Take one of the BRG XG-12 Frigates to Molar. When you get there, report to me what you find."

Kimmel then said, "Thank you, sir."

Kimmel and Devanoe walked off, back down and out of the Tower Bridge. Kimmel whispered to Devanoe, "If you ever do that again, I will kill you faster than he does."

BELINEA 5.9

Near Torsalli

First Officer Verkato on Taz's ship was looking at the panels in front of him. He stood up and walked a few feet over to the Captain's chair. Taz looked at some controls off to his left when the officer poked his arm and showed him the message. Taz quickly read it, then looking at Verkato, nodded in approval. First Officer Verkato announced, "New course. We are heading back to Torsalli."

First Officer Verkato climbed back into his chair. The officer next to him whispered, "Why are we going back to Torsalli?"

Taz, without warning, slammed his fist into the control panel next to him. It caused it to short circuit and smoke. Taz then got up and stormed out of the room.

First Officer Verkato whispered back, "The Earth Ambassador was not on the ship. He is still alive."

Torsalli Space Port

Lieutenant Commander Waterford walked up directly to Lord Malovex. He quietly said, "A moment, my Lord."

Malovex, not taking his eyes off the screen, just replied, "What is it?"

Waterford continued, "I got some results back from the lab, I wanted to share with you."

Malovex looked up. Waterford continued. "DNA analysis of the two fatalities on the C-62T. They were two BRG officers assigned to Braccus, who are currently absent without leave."

Malovex looked puzzled. "No, Ambassador? You are sure there were only two bodies on the ship?"

Waterford whispered, "Positive sir. We did a scan when they docked."

Malovex thought for a second before telling Waterford, "Tell no one for now. We keep that under wraps as long as we can."

Waterford acknowledged and walked away "Yes, my Lord."

BELINEA 5.10

Kapoor Estate

Vihaan was still confused as they got out of the transport craft. He then said, "I don't understand you guys. You have been traveling for days. You spend not even one full hour with the ladies, inhale some food, and now you want to hang out up here."

Willits then replied while carrying a rifle with a huge scope. "I know, but technically we're working."

All three of them continued walking from the craft towards the elevated stand in the trees. "Working on what?"

Jones answered, "Working on figuring out who keeps trying to kill us."

Vihaan just laughed, "Can you wait at least 24 hours. Sit by the pool, get a tan. Have a fucking drink, relax."

Willits responded, "You can go back to that shit Vi. Don't stay here just because of us."

Jones added, "Go sit by the pool, find one of those girls to suck your cock while you're drinking a glass of wine."

Vihaan shook his head. "You idiots, I get that shit every day. I would rather be involved in some military, cloak and dagger shit. Maybe we can blow something up."

Willits continued, "Sorry to disappoint you, Vi, but that's not how this goes. More than likely we are gonna sit up here for twenty-four hours, drink some wine, and get some sleep."

The three of them continued up into the tree stand outpost. When they got to the top, it gave them a clear view of the valley below. Willits asked, "Vi, where is the DAG guest house?"

Vi pointed so both Willits and Jones could see. "Right there, at the bottom of the valley."

They both nodded in approval. Jones said, "Got it."

Vihaan then said, "And you want me to leave that cheap-ass transport ship outside with the running lights on as if waiting to take off, but no security around it?"

Willits answered, "That's the bait, Vi."

Willits and Jones sat down. Willits opened a bottle of wine and poured himself a glass. Jones closed his eyes and sat back in his chair.

Vihaan asked,, "Now what? Call some ladies? Tell them to bring some party favors. Get a little groove up in here?"

Willits calmly answered, "Nope. Now we just wait."

Vihaan sat down. After a few seconds, he said, "This military shit is boring as fuck."

BELINEA 5.11

On the way to Molar

Tunsall was alone in the cockpit. He hit a few gauges on his control panel, but for the most part, was sitting silently. Trujillo approached from the back. He tapped Tunsall on the shoulder and said, "It's been a few hours. Why don't you switch out and get some sleep?"

Tunsall turned to him and said, "You sure?"

Trujillo nodded. Tunsall unbuckled himself, got up, and proceeded to the back. He softly said "Thanks."

Trujillo climbed into the chair and buckled himself in. He checked a few panels, made sure he knew where they were going. He then got comfortable, laying back a little in the chair. About ten seconds went by before Alexis approached from the back of the ship. She sat down in the seat Tunsall had just left and asked, "Do you mind?"

Trujillo looked at her curiously and asked, "Coming in peace?"

Alexis gave a half-smile and replied, "I don't mean you any bodily harm…"

A moment of awkward silence passed before she asked, "How much longer to Molar?"

Trujillo hit a button on the control panel and said, "About four more hours."

A few more seconds went by. Her curious brain never stopping, Alexis leaned in closer to Trujillo and asked, "So how do you fly this thing?"

Trujillo shifted ever so slightly up away from her, towards the control panel. He hit a button that lit the board up. He answered. "This is our course heading, directly to Molar. This is the variance light, which will activate if something ends up in our way."

Alexis asked, "Like a hot brunette?"

Trujillo rolled his eyes and answered, "Like an asteroid field or a comet. This route has a shitload of things that can fly into our trajectory. This is our velocity. This is the fuel capacity in the Vait chamber, and the anti-matter reading. This is the ship oxygen supply, Nitrogen tank supply, gravitational settings, running lights, communication channel, cargo bay doors."

Alexis asked, "Where are the guns? I want to shoot something..."

Trujillo then laughed. "No weapons on this transport. Think of it as a huge cargo ship."

Alexis was puzzled. "We are out here by ourselves with no weapons?"

Trujillo continued, "Hopefully, we won't need it, but that's why Willits left us the F-81 we got in the bay. The wings are folded, but in a pinch, we could get it out and protect ourselves."

Alexis continued, "You'd protect me from the 'bad guys,' Trujillo?"

Trujillo rolled his eyes and said,, "Who needs the F-81 when we got your fists?"

Alexis smiled and blinked. She asked,, "You can fly it?"

Trujillo answered, "The F-81? Of course."

Alexis raised an eyebrow. "Well?"

Trujillo reiterated,, "Very well. I am fourth in my class."

Alexis, with a smart ass tone, said,, "Fourth, and still got this assignment. What happened to the first and second in class? BRG already got them?"

Trujillo then motioned with his thumb backward, "Nope. He's back there with the Ambassador."

Alexis looked slightly astonished. "Tunsall is first in his class?"

Trujillo just nodded and softly said, "Second. But he should be first."

Alexis questioned,, "Should be first?"

Trujillo muttered under his breath,, "I might have had something to do with that."

Alexis continued,, "But he is a better pilot than you?"

Trujillo nodded again.

Alexis countered, "You just stated rather overtly that you were an outstanding pilot."

Trujillo added, "I am. But he is the best I have ever seen. I'll take my chances next to him any day."

Alexis asked, "You guys are close?"

Trujillo answered, "You could say that. We've been roommates since day one."

Alexis said in a sarcastic tone, "Found each other at a mixer for military flyboys?"

Trujillo tilted his head and responded, "Trujillo. Tunsall. They assign rooms in alphabetical order."

Alexis then asked, "How did you two get on this assignment?"

Trujillo just looked at her and said, "You ask a lot of questions."

Alexis leaned a little closer and said, "I seek a lot of answers..."

Trujillo, reluctantly, replied, "Willits and Jones came walking into Odgin's. They asked us if we wanted to go on a high-security clearance mission."

Alexis looked a little astonished. "Really? That was it?"

Trujillo slightly shook his head and answered, "We knew they were DAG, so it likely involved security. It wasn't our first choice, but it sounded intriguing."

Alexis asked, "Like me?"

Trujillo answered, "We certainly didn't know you were on the menu when we were recruited. It might have changed our answer."

Alexis smiled and said, "What was your first choice?"

Trujillo responded, "Flying F-81's in the AuFa. But that's likely not gonna happen for me."

Alexis looked confused, "Why not?"

Trujillo said, "Because I am human, and the AuFa is mainly Belinean, especially the officers. You know that. So does your brother. Shit, I am shocked he has made it as far as he has. I would've liked to ask him how he did it."

Alexis responded, "It's been tough, no doubt. But Belinean education helps. It's not too late for you and Tunsall. There are ways."

Trujillo said, "I was talking about me, not Tunsall. He doesn't have the same obstacles."

Alexis asked, "Why not?"

Trujillo answered, "Let's just say Tunsall will have a lot better options after graduation."

Alexis looked puzzled. "Tunsall has a rich father with lots of connections? "

Trujillo paused. He gave a tiny grin before he said, "Something like that. You'd have to ask him."

Alexis also gave a small grin "I didn't peg him for an obnoxious, spoiled rich kid. He seems too quiet, cerebral, and confident. But not in an arrogant way."

Trujillo snorted. "He is arrogant. He barely studies at school and always gets perfect marks. Trust me, he is smarter than everyone else."

Alexis countered with, "Well, if you are the smartest guy in the room and you know it, I would say that is confidence and not arrogance. It's very attractive."

Trujillo now had a slight expression of annoyance. "Really?"

Alexis continued, "Oh yes. And those eyes….I am sure he has girls all over him."

Trujillo, with a hint of jealousy, said, "Never seen him with one."

Alexis was in genuine shock. "Come on. I doubt that? Not popular with the ladies, like you?"

Trujillo tilted his head, "Who said that?"

Alexis quickly countered, "Am I wrong?"

Trujillo just rolled his eyes and softly said, "I've been with a woman if that is what you're asking."

Alexis just smiled and continued, "Oh, I bet you have."

The two just looked at each other for a few seconds, Trujillo was almost embarrassed about where the conversation had gone. Alexis broke the silence by continuing. "Still, hard to get and overly selective makes him even more attractive."

Trujillo, now full-on annoyed, just said in sarcasm, "Need me to set you up?"

Alexis got up but leaned down next to Trujillo's face. Looking directly into his eyes, very quietly and slowly, she said, "Oh no. If I want something, I just take it."

Alexis very gently patted Trujillo on his face, grabbing his chin right next to his slightly swollen lip. She began walking to the back and said, "I'm going to pour myself a glass of wine and read reports. Let me know if we get hit by an asteroid or if you need my protection."

Trujillo gently shook his head. He grabbed his chin where her hand had been and continued flying the ship.

BELINEA 5.12

Torsalli

Taz remained seated at the cockpit chair on the Civilian Transport Ship they had stolen from before. His four-man team stood directly behind him as the ship slowed down considerably coming out of HX speed. After remarking the numbers and changing the identity manifest, they entered Torsalli air space on the other side of the planet. Despite not being able to physically see the ship, it was picked up by the Control Tower with a dispatched audio transmission. "Civilian Transport, We have you as Shuttle 1738. Please verify destination and cargo."

Taz inserted a card into the control panel. A bunch of numbers lit up the screen, including payload data, speed, and destination: Ascarla. As if the computer was rebooting, the screen went through a series of procedures and algorithms to boot up. Then a green light lit up and began blinking: Access Granted. Taz pulled back on the throttle, increasing the velocity of the ship to the surface below.

Torsalli was a beautiful planet of blue oceans and green hills. The atmosphere was very similar to Earth. As long as you came in at the right angle, it was elementary to enter and exit the planet from anywhere. The ship was heading straight towards Ascarla, making its way through the atmosphere to nightfall's dark skies. Taz suddenly turned the ship and headed for the hills and valleys outside Ascarla. Within a few moments, Taz turned on his cockpit screen to night vision so that he could see the landscape on the ground below. Taz flew horizontally for almost a minute, before finding a soft area to land in a desolate area of the valley.

All five men walked out, unloading the back door of the shuttle to expose a Valkyrie Attack Rover. Taz climbed into the pilot's chair, while his men stepped up onto the side step bars and situated themselves to a stable standing position. Each had a firm grip on the side handlebars adjacent to their heads.

Taz turned on the engines, which made a very low buzzing noise. The Valkyrie took off with all five men, heading over the hills towards the Kapoor Estate.

In their covered tree stand area, Willits, Jones, and Vi were all practically asleep. Jones was supposed to be on watch, but only one eye was vaguely open. A beep was heard on their portable surveillance screen. Jones woke up, turning his head to see what had beeped. He uncrossed his arms, and as the screen showed a blinking light that was moving. Jones hit a few spots on the screen. He stood up and said, "Nolan, wake up."

Nolan Willits rolled over and practically jumped to attention, as if this was an old habit between the two. Still focusing his eyes, he came over and looked at the screen. He said, "What is it?"

Jones pointed at the moving, blinking dot. "That. It barely has a heat register, but it moves way too fast not to be man-made."

Willits looked at it for a few more seconds. He said, "The craft isn't giving off heat, the bodies are. Send in the drones."

Jones hit a few more spots on the screen as the armed drones took off from below.

There was a silence on the bridge. Everyone on board Taz's all-black main ship could hear the engines shut down. The First Officer Verkato, looked out the main windows of the bridge into space. He saw the planet of become larger as the ship finally came into an orbit around Torsalli, on the opposite side of the Space Port. The officer on the communication board very quietly said, " Engine shut down complete, Stealth orbit activated."

The ship was drifting in orbit around Torsalli, with no engines on. The communication officer kept looking at the monitor in front of him. After twenty seconds, he said, "Open bombing bay door two."

The small doors underneath the ship slowly began opening. The bombing bay was utterly dark and nothing more than a vertical tube with a long, thin missile-like bomb. A small ray of light from the Torsalli sun exposed the ship and lit up the bomb bay area. As the cargo bay doors finally opened all the way, the audio from the logistics officer said, "Two minutes."

The ship continued a quiet stealth orbit. They were now making their way around the sun to the dark side of the planet. The bridge officer said over the audio "T-Team, Waiting to acquire beacon signal."

On the Space Port, an AuFa reconnaissance officer saw the dot on the screen of Taz's main ship fall into what looked like an orbit. She then checked a few switches, trying to verify a few things. After a few seconds, she knew this was something. She yelled, "Lieutenant Commander Waterford, I have something."

Waterford was at a table with Malovex in the central area of the bridge. He looked up and walked over. Lord Maolvex, who needed a break, followed over just to see what it was. As the two got to the reconnaissance area screen, The officer said, "This ship, sir, came out of orbit very quickly, then just disappeared."

Waterford questioned, "Disappeared?"

The AuFa officer continued, "Yes, sir. But it showed up on no scanners or radar below, so unless it burned up in orbit, it is still out there. Likely in a stealth orbit."

Malovex's eyes got big. "That's Taz!"

Waterford was astonished at such a quick conclusion, which literally could have had several other explanations. He said, "Can you give me visual?"

Malovex had already turned around and was sprinting off the bridge. "Waterford, send me those coordinates. Launch the four security F-81 Sirator's now!"

Malovex stormed off the bridge towards the docking slips.

Taz continued to fly the Valkyrie at an altitude just above the treeline. A couple of warning lights popped up on his tiny screen. He tapped the officer riding next to him on his elbow. The officer looked down, and Taz pointed to the warning lights going off. The officer repositioned himself with one hand still on the sidebar, the other on the trigger of his rifle. The other three men did the same.

The drones came upon them in the next few seconds. They fired a few shots, but Taz, with his zig-zag flying, maneuvered away. The soldiers on the side got a few shots off with their rifles, mostly missing the drones. Taz had continued flying, going up and down, side to side, to evade the drones in the complete dark. Taz tapped one of the soldiers again and made a circle motion with his fingers. The soldier nodded. Taz spun the Valkyrie around in a 180-degree turn, stabilizing the craft, so it was now practically just hovering. The drones flew right up on it and opened their bellies to stop. But by doing so, they were incapable of shooting except up and away. The soldiers all got clean looks and blasted the drones with their rifles.

Taz turned the craft around again and headed deep into the Kapoor Estate.

Willits was mounting his rifle. He said to Jones, "You got a location for their drop zone in the valley."

Jones kept hitting buttons on the small portable screen. "Few more seconds ….coming up now, got it. They flew in from sector 17, and a small ship was detected eight kilometers prior, going off-the screen in the valley."

Willits was now positioned with the rifle in the window. "Send in the Cannon Drone to that location."

Jones hit a few buttons. Through the commotion, Vihaan was waking up. He stood up and said, "What the fuck is going on?"

Jones turned to Willits and said, "Nolan, they are coming this way."

Willits said, "Alright, don't spray the FH gas until I tell you."

Vihaan was now really confused. "The what gas?"

Jones answered, "FH gas. It knocks you out awhile and leaves you with a huge headache, but it doesn't kill you."

Willits added, "We set it up all over the entrances to the DAG house."

Vihaan, still rubbing his eyes, said, "I thought you said you want to kill these fuckers?"

Willits continued while looking through his scope. "I do. But first, I want to know who they work for."

Malovex jumped into his ship. He buckled in quickly. Before even unlocking the moor lines, he fired up his engines and immediately took off. The moor lines ripped out of place. He was flying around the side of the base to catch up to the other F-81's that had already taken off thirty seconds prior. He yelled into his intercom, "Waterford. I need those coordinates!"

Taz and his Valkyrie were now visually identified by both Willits and Jones. Willits looked out the window with his rifle ready. Jones was looking at his binoculars focused on the craft. Jones stated, "Artillery TC, I believe a Valkyrie. One pilot, two soldiers, riding on each side. Velocity is ninety KPH."

Taz identified the DAG guest house building, tapping the elbow again of the soldier standing/riding next to him. Taz then pointed at the guest house. The soldier had a sack around him that he opened up with his free hand. He took out what looked like a small handheld rocket. He flipped a switch on it. On the back of the tiny missile, a small blue light began blinking. As Taz got closer to the DAG house, he slowed down to almost a hover. He made a pass around the actual house until he was five meters above the front door.

Jones, still looking through his binoculars with one hand and his other on a button on the small portable screen, said, "I got a visual. I believe Taz is the pilot."

Vihaan said in shock, not being able to see that far away. "What!?! Taz?"

Willits, refocusing his scope on his rifle, then said, "Come on, take the bait."

The soldier on the Valkyrie then shot the handheld rocket into the plants and grass directly in front of the DAG house. Taz immediately sped away, going right back out the way he came. Jones, with his hand on the button, asked Willits, "Spray the gas?"

Willits immediately answered, "No! Shit, they never got in range."

Jones, still looking at his binoculars, said, "They are flying away."

Willits then tried to pick them up with the scope, but they were moving too fast. He muttered to himself, "What the fuck are they doing?"

Willits then refocused back on to the house. He focused on the small rocket that landed in front of the house but had not exploded. Through his lens, he saw the blue light flashing on it. Willits eyes got huge as he said, "Oh shit, we gotta get out of here."

He stood up and tapped Jones on the shoulder, who just saw the same thing with his binoculars. Jones first grabbed the portable screen, then Vihaan by the shirt. He yelled, "Come on!"

All three sprinted for the stairs and began going down them as Vihaan yelled, "What the fuck is going on?!"

First Officer Verkato, on the bridge of Taz's main ship in space, kept looking out the windows before finally hearing from the logistics officer, "Beacon acquired. Twenty seconds."

The officer on the other side then said, "Sir, we got company. Four fighters coming in fast, bearing 2-7-0 from our position."

First Officer Verkato looked down at the Logistics officer. "Hurry...."

The Logistics officer looked up briefly at him before going back to his screen. "In range in ....ten seconds."

Taz was in full speed retreat back to the Civilian Transport ship they had come from. He first needed to get back over the hill, quickly. Taz piloted the Valkyrie at top speed and a higher altitude now. Time was far more critical than being seen.

Willits and Jones jumped into their own TC craft, which was directly below their hidden tree stand. Vihaan barely made it to the back seat, before Willits took off. They escalated quickly, buckling themselves in as they flew. Willits got just above the treeline and was trying to get out of the valley. Vihaan yelled again, "What the fuck is going on?!"

The Logistics officer said, "Launch."

Immediately, a missile bomb was launched out of the bomb bay doors of Taz's main ship. It had three little wing pop-ups that flared to help it navigate. It continued, accelerating to the surface of Torsalli, specifically, the Kapoor Estate.

The First Officer Verkato said, "Evasive action, get us out of here, Lieutenant. "

The ship began turning, as all engines fired up. It slowly got out of orbit, facing away from the planet. "Increase velocity, get us to cruising speed."

The ship began accelerating even faster now. The logistics officer yelled, "Ten seconds to make the jump to HX speed."

One of the F-81's could see in the distance the ship was trying to get away. He yelled, "Ship identified. He is trying to escape, fire!"

As the ship was about to make the jump, the logistics officer yelled, "Three, two..."

Two of the F-81 pilots launched missiles, one ahead of the other. Just before the jump, the first one caught Taz's ship in the right engine, sending it spinning. The second one, because of the spin, missed. First Officer Verkato yelled, "We've been hit, get back online. Mount your guns!"

Jones said to Willits, "Nolan, step on it!"

Willits clipped a couple of trees, trying to navigate in the complete dark. He had just made it almost to the top of the hill when Vihaan heard something falling from the sky. He turned to look back. The missile sounded like a rocket overhead, and quickly, by virtue of targeting its beacon, landed directly next to the house. The explosion was massive. In a blink of an eye, everything within a hundred meters was annihilated. It left a hole in the ground twenty meters deep. Dust and debris were shooting out everywhere into the pitch-black night. With all its debris, the explosion had reached them on the TC just as it eclipsed the hill. A chunk of debris rock got into one of the four-rotor blades, disabling it by chewing it up. Once the blade stopped working, it sent the rest of the craft into a tailspin to the forest below.

Willits got a little stability just before crashing it into the surface below. As it spun around and flipped a few times, the TC landed upright, with all three of its passengers still buckled in.

First Officer Verkato on Taz's main ship yelled, "Turn us around, fire at will."

The first F-81 came in closer now, trying to lock its missiles on another target. He kept scanning the screen, but the ship was still spinning because of the first missile hit. As soon as it stabilized, the ship turned toward them and began to accelerate, with smoke pouring out of one of its engines. Just as the F-81 pilot got a lock, a side gun from Taz's ship got off a directly connected shot, exploding the F-81. The other F-81 took a couple of shots at Taz's ship but missed.

First Officer Verkato yelled, "Status?"

The Logistics officer yelled, "Heavy damage to engine two. Internal diagnostic says we can make adjustments to get one quarter HX speed in two minutes!"

The reconnaissance officer said, "Two more F-81 fighter's dead ahead."

First Officer Verkato jumped down to the control cockpit. He yelled, "See if we can outmaneuver them until we can get out of here! Spin move."

Taz's ship went into a spiral towards the planet's surface, spinning and swirling at the same time. The next two F-81's now rapidly approached and slowed down to get a good shot off, before realizing the ship kept spinning all the way around now and was climbing right back towards them. As it flew by, the two F-81's got shots off but missed. One of Taz's gunners got a shot off, crippling an F-81 with a shot to one of its engines. The second F-81 had come back around now as well, getting off a shot that hit Taz's ship in the main body.

Willits and Jones unbuckled themselves. Both had cuts all over their bodies. Willits turned around and unbuckled Vihaan, who only had minor damage because he was sitting in the back. Vihaan yelled, "What the fuck was that?!?"

Willits replied, "That was a Mortar Missile from another ship in space. That thing Taz planted was a beacon telling it where to hit."

Jones got out his portable recon screen and opened it. In a few seconds, the entire area of the Kapoor Estate was on display in front of him. He focused on sector 17, the valley near where Taz and his team landed. " I got a visual on the Cannon Drone."

Vihaan just looked back over the hill and could now see the enormous fireball from the missile explosion, one hundred meters into the sky. In disbelief, he said, "Holy shit!"

Willits said, "Vi, time to call your security and tell them to get us."

Vihaan hesitated, still looking at the fireball before he grabbed his wrist and said, "Security, lock into my location, transportation for three."

Willits walked over to the portable screen Jones was operating. Jones said, "Ten seconds until location."

Willits pointed and added "Scan that area there. I bet they landed right in the valley."

The camera on the Cannon Drone showed the valley, but it was pitch black. Willits said, "Flip to night vision and infrared, the engines have to still be hot."

Jones hit a switch, and as soon as he did, it showed an orange spot further in the distance on the camera. Jones pointed and said, "There. Lock into that heat source."

The Cannon Drone flew right to the spot, and with the assistance of the night vision, Willits and Jones could see it was a Civilian Transport. Willits said, "Fucker flew in on a stolen Civilian Transport. He has to have Belinean connections."

Jones replied, "Yeah, but how? And who?"

Willits, wiping blood off his face, said, "I don't know. But at least we now know where the mole is."

Jones replied, "Blow it up?"

Willits answered. "No. Let's see if we can get a visual and a kill when they get back, should be any second."

Above in space, Taz's main ship was still in a dogfight with three F-81's. One of the F-81's had taken a hit and was flying at fifty percent strength. Another shot on Taz's ship from one of F-81's hit the same damaged engine, crippling the engine entirely. However, the F-81 took a direct hit from one of the ship's guns, blowing it into a thousand pieces instantly.

The logistics officer yelled, "Critical failure, engine two. We cannot get to HX speed."

First Officer Verkato, still next to the cockpit chair, yelled back, "We are gonna have to fight our way out of this."

The F-81 came around again, this time connecting on a shot to the first engine, causing Taz's black main ship to go spinning again. As it did, one of the gunners locked into the wounded F-81, getting off four shots, connecting one. As it did, the reconnaissance officer yelled, "Inbound ship, we got another hostile."

First Officer Verkato was looking at his screen, and said, "Where, I don't see it?!?"

The F-81 squared up and began firing right at the cockpit area as the two ships were on course to collide with one another. The Logistics officer yelled, "F-81! Dead ahead!!"

Both the ships shot at each other, all shots hitting. Taz's all-black main ship, despite destroying the final F-81 with a direct shot, was in critical failure as the F-81 managed to get a shot on the first engine.

First Officer Verkato yelled, "Can we get out of here?"

Malovex's ship came flying upward right next to them, directly hitting the belly of the ship.

The logistics officer, after the ship regained some stability, looked at the screen, and yelled, "Critical failure everywhere. Getting analysis now."

First Officer Verkato, still looking at his screen, shouted, "Where the fuck is that other ship?!?"

The reconnaissance officer pointed to the windows and said, "There!"

Outside the windows, Malovex's ship was coming in a slow spiral, until finally leveling off and getting off four perfect shots that all directly hit Taz's main black ship. The ship exploded immediately as Malovex flew by.

Taz was almost back at the landing site of the stolen Civilian Transport onboard the Valkyrie. As they got closer, Taz could see something odd floating twenty meters away from the ship. He immediately stopped and tapped one of his soldiers on the elbow, pointing at the object. The Cannon Drone was three meters long, with one large cannon being held up by four large rotors.

Taz's soldiers, because it was pitch black, were struggling to see the drone, as the night vision had a hard time picking it up because there was barely any heat coming off it.

Willits pointed at his screen. "There, turn the drone towards that, flash the camera on it!"

Immediately a bright flashlight lit up Taz's Valkyrie from the Cannon Drone. Taz responded by going into a dive, as the Cannon Drone took one shot at the Valkyrie, but missed.

Willits asked Jones, "Did it hit?"

Jones answered, "I don't think so, no explosion."

Willits then said, "Keep them from escaping. Take out the Civilian ship."

By the time Taz had stabilized the Valkyrie, he saw the Cannon Drone turn its aim towards the Civilian Transport. Before his soldiers could get off any meaningful shot, the Cannon Drone fired two shots, back to back, three seconds apart, destroying the Civilian Transport engines.

After the second shot, one of Taz's soldiers connected a shot from his rifle with one of the Cannon Drone's rotor blades. A second shot connected with another rotor blade, sending the Cannon Drone plummeting to the surface.

Once the threat of the Cannon Drone was gone, Taz proceeded to fly away on the Valkyrie, further into the valley and away from the Kapoor Estate.

Willits then looked at Vihaan and said, "How long till your security gets here?"

Vihaan looked at his wrist device and said, "Two minutes."

Jones then said, "Not enough time, they will get away."

Willits said, "Fuck!"

The three of them walked back up to the top of the hill, where they looked down at the sheer damage from the Mortar Missile. It had taken everything out in a one hundred meter radius. Things were still on fire, but mostly everything just smoldered in smoke at this point. After about ten seconds of looking, Jones broke the silence and said, "Damn."

Vihaan looked stunned. Even in the dark, the small little flames showed the destruction. He opened his hand and pointed it out. "Look at this shit, you two! You killed every fucking grapevine in this area, the DAG house, and that old transport ship down there! Who the fuck is going to pay for all this?"

Willits just turned to Vihaan and said, "Send the bill to Kimakawa."

BELINEA 5.13

Molar

Tunsall was back in the cockpit opposite Trujillo as they piloted the T-141 into the atmosphere of Molar. There was no Space Port. Molar was a grey planet of mostly blue and black oceans and mountainous rock. The clouds were perpetually dark as it seemed to rain all the time.

As the ship burst through the clouds, it came upon one of the few inhabited areas, Populis Pointe. The Pointe, as people called it, was a small flat area between two mountains rising above the sea. It had become the main port for the planet.

Tunsall pointed with his hand out the window. "There, Populis Pointe."

Alexis and Ambassador Bird were in the back chairs behind Trujillo and Tunsall. Bird immediately asked, "How safe is this planet?"

Alexis countered with, "If you are expecting a large AuFa or Belinean presence, think again. It's a trading stop."

Trujillo then added, "So just like Vandabri."

Tunsall answered, "No. Vandabri is casinos, bars, and brothels. The Pointe is nothing more than a port. Smugglers exchange merchandise and cargo, refuel their ships, buy narcotics. All away from the watchful eye of the AuFa."

Bird asked, "Is this planet not in the Council?"

Alexis answered, "Technically, it's a Torsallian territory littered with all their undesirables and cheap labor. They let local government, what little they have, run the show. So the Pointe has a fair share of drug lords and crime bosses."

Bird just whispered to himself, "Great...."

As they came closer to the Pointe, there was an area off to the side, next to one of the Mountains, that had eight landing spots. Trujillo pointed to one of the landing spots, the last one on the row. He said, "Tunsall, there."

Tunsall slowed the engines down and turned the ship ninety degrees. As if he had landed a ship a thousand times, the T-141 turned and ever so gently touched the ground, coming to a perfect landing.

Trujillo and Tunsall unbuckled out of their chairs. Trujillo looked directly at Alexis and said, "Stay here……., please?"

Alexis gave him a slightly perturbed look. Ambassador Bird then added, "I am going with you."

Tunsall stopped and asked, "Sir?"

Ambassador Bird continued, "I am an Ambassador on the Council, I should be able to provide some clout. Perhaps get a message to the BRG."

Tunsall just looked at him and said, "With all due respect, sir, you being an Ambassador does not improve our situation. It probably makes it worse."

Bird was baffled. Tunsall and Trujillo just walked out the back of the ship. Bird looked at Alexis and said, "These two cadets are telling us what to do?"

Alexis said nothing. Trujillo and Tunsall continued to walk through the rain towards a small building off the side of all the landing pads. They walked through the door and saw a large, robust man behind a counter. Without looking up, he said, "Cargo declaration and manifest."

Trujillo and Tunsall walked up the counter, trying to wipe the rain from their faces. Tunsall looked at the large man and said, "We do not have a manifest."

The large man now looked up. He seemed annoyed. "I need a manifest, or I will just turn you over to The Pointe Port Police."

Trujillo now added, "Let's not do that when we both can benefit from this transaction."

Trujillo held up the bag of Qusar coins. He took four out and placed them on the counter.

The large man just looked at him and said, "That won't even buy you a refuel."

Trujillo took out ten more coins and placed them on the counter. The man said, "What's the cargo?"

Tunsall answered. "No cargo. Just passengers…."

Trujillo continued, "….and no more questions."

The large man held up his hand, which had four fingers. Trujillo put four more Qusar coins down. Trujillo added, "And we need a cleanout and refuel."

The large man said, "That will take a couple of hours, we are behind. How long are you staying?"

Trujillo and Tunsall looked at each other, and Trujillo replied, "Not long."

The large man nodded. Trujillo and Tunsall walked back out in the rain, towards the T-141. Tunsall then said, "Not long?"

Trujillo looked at him and said, "Remember what Willits said. If we don't hear from him or Jones after we get to Molar, leave with the Ambassador straight to Belinea."

The two continued to walk back towards the ship. They got on and were eagerly greeted by Alexis and Bird. Bird said, "And?"

Tunsall answered. "We are good. Refuel, engine cleanout. Re-supply for a few hours and wait on Willits and Jones."

Bird answered, "Wait on Willits and Jones? Why?"

Trujillo looked right at Bird and said, "Because those are the orders, Ambassador."

It was Trujillo's way of saying they were in charge now, and Bird did not like it one bit. The Ambassador turned around and walked back to his make-shift personal quarters. Alexis just looked at Trujillo and sarcastically said, "This is gonna be fun."

BELINEAN 5.14

Torsalli

Kapoor Estate

The security team landed the small transport shuttle at Vihaan Kapoor's personal transport base. What looked like a small hanger housed twelve space crafts. Directly next to where they landed outside, was a D-21 Sirallo. It was a slick, silver-colored spacecraft that looked like royalty was flying on. Someone had already fired up the engines and was walking out of it when Willits, Jones, and Vihaan all got off their transport.

Willits and Jones, still bleeding from the explosion and crash, looked at Vihaan and said, "Vi, we owe you."

Vihaan, still a little pissed about what had happened to parts of his vineyard, replied, "You guys should really get looked at. That's a nasty cut."

Jones just replied, "We are wanted men, Vi. Got to go now."

Vihaan asked, "Wanted for what?"

Willits answered, "Two BRG officers called me an Egglet, and I did not like it."

Jones added, "So we killed them."

Vihaan said "What is an Egglet?"

Willits said, "It's a derogatory word Belineans use for Earthlings. It means they are dumb, impure, and beneath them from a social class."

Jones, looking at Vihaan, added, "A third class citizen, like what you and I used to be on Earth."

Vihaan whispered, "Assholes…"

Willits said, "Yep. So the BRG is looking for us. And you will tell them?"

Vihaan just nodded "I know, I know. You guys were never here."

Willits added, "And when the BRG or AuFa shows up…"

Vihaan just added, "Somebody stole my Sirallo."

They all just gave a small smile. Willits extended his hand, as did Jones. Willits said, "Thank you, Vi."

They shook hands. Then Willits and Jones practically sprinted into the D-21 Sirallo. They got into the cockpit chairs, hit a few spots on the control screen, and soon the ship was taking off into the night.

Willits and Jones gained some altitude, finally reaching the clouds and heading to space. Willits asked, "You know how to fly this thing, correct?"

Not convincingly, Jones answered, "I think so. You think this ship is as fast as Vi said?"

Willits just smiled and said, "We are about to find out."

On the way from Torsalli to Molar, Captain Kimmel and Commander Nick Devanoe were in their frigate's cockpit pilot's chairs. They had been traveling for a few hours. Breaking the silence, Devanoe's wristwatch tracker suddenly started beeping and flashing. Both the men looked at it, with Nick giving a small smile. He took it off and placed it to the control panel. After a few seconds, the control panel gave a readout. Devanoe looked at it. He looked at Captain Kimmel and said, "Molar."

Both turned back to looking out through the windows into space. They were heading the right way.

BELINEA 5.15

Molar

Populis Pointe

Tunsall was sitting in the pilot's chair of the ship. He was reading something on a tablet before proceeding from the cockpit back to the cabin area. Once he got back there, he noticed Trujillo working on an electrical box, with wires hanging out. Bird was sitting across from him, reading from his tablet, and drinking a cup of coffee. Tunsall asked Trujillo, "What's up?"

Trujillo, working diligently with a pair of pliers in his hand, responded, "Trying to get all the power to the rear cabin back on. Must have shorted somewhere. You?"

Tunsall just said, "There is something here about AuFa and Belinean procedure that I was confused about and wanted to see if Alexis understood it."

Trujillo just looked at him and said, "I thought she was up there with you?"

Tunsall looked at him and said, "No, I thought she was back here?"

Bird now looked up at both of them. He yelled at the top of his lungs, "Alexis!"

But all three of them just stared at each other. No response was heard. Trujillo and Tunsall began looking all over the rest of the ship. Bird stood up and repeated his shout. "Alexis!"

They kept looking and yelling for over a minute, But no response came. They all finally met back at the spot they started, confused and frustrated. Trujillo looked at Tunsall and just said, "You think she left the ship?"

Tunsall, putting on a coat, responded, "Would not be the first time. I am going outside to look for her. Stay here with the Ambassador."

Trujillo quickly responded, "I will go."

Tunsall turned to him and softly, but in an aggravated tone, said, "Stay here…"

Tunsall walked off the ship and into the rain. Trujillo stood there looking at Bird. They continued to look at each other. Trujillo briskly walked to the cockpit area to the control panel on the side. He flipped a few switches and ran a scan of the Pointe. The heat registers and population concluded about a thousand people scattered about. There was no chance he could pinpoint Alexis with that. He then tried to pull up some security footage, but it was murky because of all the rain. He walked back to the cabin area where Bird was still standing, looking out the window. Bird said to him, "You think something happened to her?"

Trujillo just responded, "No. I think she was just stupid and decided to go for a walk or something."

Bird instantly replied, "In the rain?"

Trujillo then said, "Maybe some serious cabin fever, or …...shit!"

Bird replied, "What?"

Trujillo put on his jacket. "Ambassador, wait here. Do not let anyone in."

Trujillo ran outside, back over to the small building with the large man. Trujillo walked up to the counter and said to the large man, "I need to send a communication."

The large man again never looked up. He just replied, "To where?"

Trujillo was hesitant to reveal too much. "Somewhere far. Braccus, perhaps Earth."

The large man shook his head and said, "Just like I told your friend, you need a C-Bar transmission for that. Only one of those on the Pointe. It's up at Rhett's, further up the mountain. And it will cost you."

Trujillo stormed out.

Further up the path, Tunsall was still walking in the rain. He was going through the covered portion of the town, which was nothing more than a series of large tin roofs and solar sails over the paths to help with the rain. The town was littered with all sorts of interesting types of scoundrels of different races. Tunsall was jogging until he got to the entrance of Rhett's. It was a trading post of sorts, with lots of exciting merchandise inside. He walked up to the lady at the counter and said, "I need to send a communication."

The lady pointed to a hallway off to the side. Tunsall walked down it. As he got to the end, he turned and entered a small, darkroom. There was a robot behind the counter. Tunsall saw Alexis typing on a tablet off to the side. Tunsall looked at her and said, "Stop!"

Alexis stopped typing and looked at Tunsall. "What are you doing?"

Tunsall looked at her and said, "What are *you* doing? We told you about no communication!"

Alexis went back to typing and said, "It's not what you think, Tunsall."

Tunsall reached for his side-arm, pointed his pistol at Alexis. He firmly replied, "I said, stop."

Alexis just glanced at him and said, "What are you going to do, shoot me?"

Tunsall fired a shot right next to Alexis, intentionally just missing her. She turned to him and said, "Are you crazy?"

The robot added, "Please stand by while we assess the damage you have caused."

Tunsall kept the pistol pointed right at her. "I am warning you, Alexis. Willits said to look out for this very thing."

Alexis tilted her head and said, "Did he? Exactly what did he say?"

Tunsall replied, "He said not to let either of you send any communications, especially you. He does not trust you, and after this, rightfully so."

Alexis replied, "Really! Did it ever occur to you that it might be Willits and Jones we should not be trusting?"

Just then, Trujillo caught up and turned into the room. He saw Tunsall had drawn his pistol. Trujillo practically yelled, "What the hell is going on?"

Tunsall quickly responded, "I caught her sending a message, just like Willits said she would."

Trujillo turned to her and said, "Is this true?"

Alexis responded, "It's not what you think, Trujillo."

Tunsall asked, "How do people keep finding out our location?"

Alexis answered, "I don't know!"

Tunsall quickly responded, "But you think it's Willits and Jones?"

Alexis answered, "I used to….."

It left Tunsall and Trujillo looking at each other. They were confused by the response. Alexis went back to typing a few more lines. Trujillo yelled at her, "Alexis!"

She then finished typing in a few seconds. She looked over at the robot and said, "Send it."

Tunsall, still pointing the pistol at Alexis, said, "No!"

Alexis took three steps towards Tunsall and held out her hand. She gently pushed the pistol down, causing Tunsall to point it towards the floor. She reached into her pocket, pulled out two Qusar coins, and put them on the counter. She said, "One for the message, one for the trouble."

Alexis turned back to look at Tunsall and Trujillo and said, "I know, now, that it is not Willits and Jones. That's what the message says."

Tunsall then asked, "Then who are you sending it to?"

Alexis said, "I can't tell you that. You are going to have to trust me."

Trujillo responded, "You told me not to trust you."

Alexis looked at both of them. "And you shouldn't. But right now, I do trust both of you. And I am asking you to do the same for me, even though you have no reason to do so."

Tunsall and Trujillo glanced at each other, then looked back at Alexis. After about a six-second pause, Tunsall, with a bit of apprehension, said, "Alright."

A few more seconds went by before Alexis asked, "Where is the Ambassador?"

Trujillo said, "I left him on the ship."

Tunsall and Alexis said in unison, "Shit!"

They ran out of Rhett's back onto the covered path. Eventually, they ran back through the pouring rain to the air landing pads. When they got to the ship, they opened the door, which they noticed had been blasted. All three rushed in, and Alexis yelled out, "Ambassador!"

Tunsall saw the Ambassador's steak knife planted into the wall. Underneath it was a note.

If you want your cargo back alive, you will need five times more than what you had in the bag. You have one hour.

Tunsall ripped the note and handed it to Trujillo. Trujillo read it, and gave it to Alexis. Alexis said, "Damn it. Now, what do we do?"

BELINEA - EPISODE 6
CATACO

BELINEA 6.1

Burvilla, Serpia 2137 (Twenty years prior...)

Dr. Fiona Faxon was operating on the table, one victim after another. She was screaming at nurses around her. "Clamp."

"Suction, I can't see the wound."

"Hold still. He's been frozen, start the de-ice procedure."

Patient after patient kept rolling in. The battle was intense, and the number of wounded was staggering. They triaged by the severity of injury, but now, almost sixteen hours in, there finally seemed to be a slowdown. She put arms back together, iced patients down so that a later procedure could grow a re-attached leg, and reduced the swelling of brain injuries. Two patients were 'deep freezed' on the battlefield and then brought in. It funneled them through a de-icing procedure, which took hours but allowed operation on the brain while minimizing spinal damage. Blood was all over her. She would change, then change again, then change again, and again. It never stopped. It seemed there was no point.

Soldiers were screaming. Grown men brought to tears at the sight of limbs being amputated. Several nurses vomited on multiple occasions, never entirely processing how much blood was on the floor. The room had four operating tables, and never in those sixteen hours was one not in use, either by Dr. Faxon, her counterpart Dr. Higgins, or the two robot doctors who handled the 'minor' surgeries. There were two nurses with each doctor. Dr. Faxon pulled out another piece of shrapnel from one of the soldiers' shoulder and chest area. She then cleaned and sealed the wound and asked the lead nurse across from her, "Can you please finish up?"

The lead nurse nodded. Fiona walked away from the patient and out the door. She ripped her gloves and mask off, and proceeded down the hall to the Doctor's lounge area. She poured herself a glass of water and sat down, taking a small sip as she leaned back. After a very long sigh, she took her scrubs hat off and sprinkled the water over her face. With both hands, she rubbed her eyes and the blood off her cheekbone. Keeping her hands on her face, she took another deep breath and succumbed to her exhaustion.

As she continued to sit alone, a man in full military uniform entered the room. Fiona did not remove her hands from her face. She no longer cared. The man stood next to her with a warm white towel in his hand. Fiona looked up to see the towel extended toward her. She grabbed it and placed it across her face. It felt clean. The rest of her didn't. She muttered, "Thank you."

The man spoke softly. "Dr. Faxon, it is I who should be thanking you."

Keeping the towel on her face, she said, "Why is that?"

The military man continued. "My people tell me you saved at least eleven soldiers. No Gen's, all Serpians, not one death. Impressive."

Still, with the towel on her face, Fiona muttered, "No medal needed."

The military man gave a small smirk. "Some would say the loss of life, while tragic, is the price of victory."

Fiona, still with both hands on the towel, gently pulled it down to her chin. She looked up at the man and said, "But that's not what you say, Commander.....?"

The man walked a few steps away and then turned around. "Captain Merriam. No, I would not. The moral and ethical debate regarding the Gens becomes muted in a time like this. When so much Serpian blood has been spilled, how could one justify they carry the same importance?"

Fiona looked up at him and responded, "Serpian, Tiloian, Generated blood. It's all the same, Captain. No one is more important. All of them die without it."

Captain Merriam gave another small smirk and said, "A philosophical difference Dr. Faxon. Nevertheless, thank you. I am here because of another matter. I assume you are aware of the incident in your laboratory?"

Fiona took a small breath before answering. "If incident is a reference to the murder of my colleague by your soldiers, then yes."

Captain Merriam looked down at her and said, "That, I am afraid, is beyond philosophical difference, Dr. Faxon. Given the circumstances we are currently in, you understand our concern regarding your stance on the situation?"

With a confused expression, Fiona said, "My stance?"

Captain Merriam continued. "The Doctor had a stance that directly counteracted our mission moving forward. Simply put, he was a threat to our survival."

Fiona looked at the Captain for a second, knowing these may be the last words she said. "Like me, he was a scientist first, and a doctor second. The work we did benefited science, no particular race in general."

Captain Merriam crossed his arms. "All his work, Doctor?"

Fiona stood up and got face to face with Captain Merriam. "Our religious beliefs never impede with our work. Which is for the greater good of science, first, and the survival of our species second. How many of your soldiers must I save before you believe me, Captain?"

The Captain uncrossed his arms but continued to look at Fiona in the eyes. " A fact that I cannot deny. I do question, were your actions driven by fear, or your loyalty to the cause?"

Fiona turned around and took a few steps. After a few seconds, she turned around again, half-smiled, and said, "My oath as a Doctor prevents me from having a political agenda, Captain. If you see that differently, then I suppose you are here to deliver me the same fate."

The Captain took a long stare at Fiona. He then turned around and poured himself some water, taking a sip. He turned around again and looked directly at the Doctor. "Surely I would do no such thing, especially to a hero who saved so many Serpian soldiers today, Doctor. I feel you misunderstand my motives. We only wish to extract all your material on all the projects you have been working on. Together, with our research and Doctors, we can build solutions that benefit all of us."

Fiona gave a small frown. "I assume I have no choice in the matter?"

The Captain smiled and responded, "You should assume saying no will only disappoint me."

There was an awkward silence. After ten seconds, Fiona said, "Captain, I still have patients that need follow-up procedures, so if there is nothing else?"

The Captain gave another warm smile. "Of course, Doctor. Forgive me. I will be on my way."

The Captain walked out of the room. Fiona sat back down, now noticing the small red light blinking on her wristwatch. She tapped it and read the short message. She leaned her head back and closed her eyes, trying to process the devastating news. She began to sob.

Overcome with grief, her eyes flooded with tears for a minutre. As she began to breathe normally, she walked over to her locker and opened it. She ripped her shirt off, wearing only a necklace holding a ring with a glowing grey stone. Fiona put on a clean sweater and slammed her locker shut. Storming out of the room, she briskly walked down the hall and took two flights of stairs up towards the aircraft landing pads. As Fiona climbed into her personal TC, she hit some buttons and fired up the engines. The computer on the screen asked, "Destination, please?"

Fiona looked at her wristwatch and then began typing in coordinates onto the computer. The Computer acknowledged, "Coordinates accepted. Expected flight time: Twenty-six minutes."

The TC took off, all four rotor blades directing it up to the sky. It was morning, the sun not quite peering over the treeline yet. But the sheer number of explosions, fires, and overall devastation had left the entire sky in a cloudy haze with little visibility. Fiona continued to cry, wiping the tears away with her arm. No more rockets or missiles were flying overhead. The fighting had stopped, the battle had been won, if there was such a thing. As the TC flew above the trees, she could look outside her window and see its shadow in the branches. But as she got closer to the front, there were fewer trees and more areas of flattened devastation from where the bombs went off.

She continued for another twenty minutes. Through the haze, she finally reached an area that was still smoldering with spot fires. The hole in the surface was massive. Over ten kilometers wide, it looked as if a giant meteor had fallen from the sky and hit the surface. The hole was easily forty meters deep. A few soldiers had red flares and shined them in the direction of her TC. Fiona saw them and hit a few spots on her control panel. She descended towards the surface and landed directly next to the soldiers. The door opened, and one of the soldiers yelled, "This is a restricted area. You cannot go in there!"

Fiona showed her ID bracelet and yelled back, "I am Doctor Fiona Faxon. I was ordered up here to help evac soldiers and prep them for surgery."

The soldier looked at the ID bracelet and then took his tablet out and presented it to Fiona. She put her palm on it, and it scanned her handprint. A light turned green and verified who she said she was. The soldier looked at her again and said, "Sorry, Doctor. We did not get those orders. We have not pulled out anyone alive in several hours, so I am afraid there is very little that can be saved."

Fiona yelled back through the noise, "I understand. I assume you have teams up there searching through the rubble?"

The soldier nodded in acknowledgment and yelled, "Gens."

Fiona continued, "Then I will get up there and see if I can offer any assistance."

The soldier yelled back, "Proceed with caution, Doctor. We still have flare-ups and all the fires are not out. Hostiles are gone, and the area is secure, but it is still a hot zone."

Fiona nodded and closed the door. The TC took off again, this time heading in closer to the gigantic hole in the ground. Never getting more than fifteen feet off the ground, she flew another eight kilometers to the backside of the hole. As it was landing, the four-rotor blades put the TC in a light hover and gently touched the ground. The computer said, "Arrived at destination."

The door opened, and Fiona got out, carrying a small bag over her shoulder. She stood for a few seconds, as the smoke was overwhelming. Still wiping the tears from her face, she looked around, not knowing where to start. After coughing a few times, she took a deep breath, closed her eyes, and put her hand over her chest. After a few seconds, the glow from her ring underneath her shirt got brighter. The light from it protruded through her shirt, and she could suddenly feel where to go.

Fiona began to walk, one small step at a time. There was no direction to go, no path to follow. Slowly, step by step, she walked and cried. The smoke was everywhere. In the distance, she could still see Gen soldiers walking through the rubble, searching for any sign of life. The ground was black and made up mostly of charred metal and debris. No one could have survived this. Anyone that was here died, likely in a ball of fire that burned them to a crisp. For some, it was instant. For most, it was a long ride down, in flames, until they crashed to the surface.

Fiona continued to walk. She would pause to readjust herself. She grabbed her ring inside her shirt again. She continued, stumbling through the black debris. In tears, she finally stopped. The ring was glowing as bright as she had ever seen it. Fiona got on her knees and searched everywhere. She ran her hand through the debris and noticed much of it was still hot. Reaching into her bag, she pulled out a pair of gloves and put them on.

She continued to search, as she ran her hands through the hot debris. Nothing. She turned ninety degrees and repeated. Nothing. She turned another ninety degrees and did the same. Nothing. She took her gloves off and looked into the sky with her eyes closed. Fiona put both of her hands on the ring inside her chest. She took a deep breath, tears coming down her cheek from her shut eyes. The ring glowed again. She turned forty-five degrees to her left and extended her hands out. She began digging.

Through the hot black debris, her hands were feeling it. She kept digging, the debris going back over her spot like digging in wet sand at the beach. Further she went, until finally, she saw a glow. Elbow deep now, Fiona grabbed something that was not debris and pulled it out. In her hand was a ring with a glowing blueish stone, similar to the grey stone she wore around her chest. On both knees, she stared at it, eyes still watery from the smoke.

After staring at it for a solid five seconds, she began to sob while on all fours.

BELINEA 6.2

Twenty Years Later...

Avola

Bosa-Lowell Province Border

When all four of the C-112 Vait Transports exploded in mid-air, the shock-waves extended to the ships flanking them in formation. Some of them closest in proximity lost all control and crashed to the barren red rock surface. Others were seemingly blown off-course and needed some very experienced flying by the pilots to stabilize.

It took Cortes almost ten seconds to regain balance and not crash the Assault Ship. Octavious, riding in the back, yelled into his intercom. "Cortes, what the fuck happened?"

Cortes flew right through a billowing black cloud from the C-112 out in front, now pummeling to the ground. After looking at her control screen, she shouted back, "I don't know, they fucking exploded in mid-air. All four of them, I think."

Octavious could see the damaging debris falling to the ground. The low altitude they were flying at allowed the red rock surface to be scorched from the burning aircraft. Octavious tried to recollect his thoughts. He was honestly speechless about what he had just witnessed. The Transports blowing up. The attack on the Processing Center. The heavy casualties they took on. He whispered to himself, "They knew we were coming."

And yet, if they got the Majavkee Lords and the Vait, it would be worth it. But thinking now, they did not get the Vait, did they? Where was Kaya? Was killing the Majavkee Lords a lie also? Octavious ran to the other side of the vessel. He grabbed Donovan, who looked shell shocked over everything that just happened. He grabbed him by the front of the shirt and yelled, "Who told you the Majavkee Lords were on that transport?"

Donovan was still half out of it. "What?"

Octavious repeated the question. "How did you know the Majavkee Lords were on that ship that I blew out of the sky?"

Donovan, still confused, said, "The SS officer did, Lord Argo's Captain."

Octavious, now incredulous, asked, "Leahy?"

Donovan answered, "Yes, he is the one that freed me, and us (pointing around to all the miners they rescued as well)."

Octavious now was starting to put it together. "Freed you? That's how you escaped?"

Donovan answered again. "Yes! He offered us the same deal he offered you! The same price for the Vait as the Council was paying the Majavkee Lords. We go back to the old Mining Guild ways, except that we would now keep half!"

Octavious looked at him in disbelief. "And you would work for us? All we had to do was kill the Majavkee Lords for them?"

Donovan smiled. "Yes, Octavious, yes!! And now we have that!"

Octavious gently closed his eyes and whispered, "What have we done?"

Cortes broke up the conversation with an announcement over the intercom. "Octavious, we got problems."

Octavious, still with his eyes closed, spoke on the intercom. "What is it, Cortes?"

Cortes responded. "I am going to turn the ship, sir. Look at the base."

When Cortes made the course adjustment, everyone, including Octavious, looked out the Assault Ship's open side. In the distance, they could see the mountain rock that identified where their base was camouflaged. But now there was smoke billowing from it, clearly on fire. Octavious spoke, "Contact the base, Cortes. What is going on?"

Cortes did not sound hopeful. "I have been trying for almost a minute, no response. I can see the AuFa F-81's from the Processing Center on my screen. They could have caught us by now, sir, but they are staying three minutes behind. I also see two attack squadrons converging on us at the base. There is nowhere to go, sir."

Octavious let go of Donovan's shirt, turning to think. He whispered to himself, "This was all a trap. Fuck!!"

Octavious looked at the other soldiers on the vessel, as well as the miners. They were all looking at him, a look of defeat on their faces. They had gotten pummeled at the Processing Facility. The small victory of stealing the Vait was actually a coordinated attack disguised as an escape. Completely outnumbered and crippled, they were now minutes away from being slaughtered by multiple attack squadrons.

Octavious took a deep breath. Wondering what happened to his sister would have to wait. He regained his composure. He yelled, "Man the guns!"

Octavious sprinted through the soldiers up to the front of the ship, going up a small stairwell before getting into the cockpit. He yelled at Cortes. "Where are we?"

The co-pilot next to her hit a few spots on the screen, and then on the center console, a map showed up. Octavious studied it for a second and then said, "Cortes, can we get to the Cataco Mining Shaft, over here (pointing), on the edge of the Bosa Province?"

"Maybe....."

"Alright, bank there. We can escape there, maybe through the tunnels, to the Fall-back point."

Cortes was confused. "And leave the ships?"

Octavious replied, "We will not last two seconds against those Attack Squadrons. And we can not hide in the base. Tell the remaining ships to follow us."

Cortes banked forty-five degrees, and the other twelve ships remaining did the same.

The Leader of Attack Squadron Four spoke over the intercom. "Command Tower, confirm course change in Valmay Attack Group."

Attack Squadrons Two and One, was chasing the Valmay vessels from the Processing Center. They patiently kept a three-minute distance behind them, allowing the other Attack Groups to converge together. It would essentially be a turkey shoot. Admiral Holland replied from his Command Destroyer,

"Copy that Attack Squadron Four. Readjusting variance to intercept with the other Attack Squadrons now."

The Leader from Attack Squadron Four said, "Copy that, and word on what my signal is?"

Admiral Holland replied, "Attack Squadron Four, Lord Argo said it would be a huge ball of fire."

The Leader of the Attack Group kept looking. After a few seconds, in the distance, she could see the smoke billowing from the mountains. "Copy that Command Center, I have visual. Valmay Base is on fire."

Octavious asked, "Cortes, how long until we get to the Cataco Shaft?"

She replied, "Six minutes!"

Octavious got on the intercom again. "When we get to Cataco, any grenades, missiles, rockets, get them on my ship. We need immediate evac into the mines."

Octavious sprinted back down to the bay and began shaking down the soldiers for anything they had left. One soldier managed to find some torpedoes in the ammunition rack. Octavious spoke into his intercom. "Cortes, time?"

Cortes responded, "Four minutes. And one of these attack squadrons is going to intercept us at about the same time."

Octavious replied, "Porter, the F-81's, how much fuel?"

Lieutenant Porter responded after looking at the gauge. "For what?"

Octavious responded, "To get to Bisi?"

Porter was confused. "We have enough, why?"

Octavious nodded, "Do it, best speed!"

Porter yelled, "We are not leaving you behind, sir!"

Octavious responded, "That's an order, Porter. You can not protect us, and the Fighters are too valuable to lose. Go."

Porter, after a split second of contemplation, replied, "Copy that sir. Octavious, good luck."

The four F-81's broke away from the other pack of aircraft. After a few adjustments, they climbed high, for about twenty seconds at top speed. When they got to a safe altitude, Porter looked to see if he had anyone following him. "Valmay Sirator's, light it up."

The four F-81's flew off in a blink, now going ten times faster than they were previously going.

Cortes yelled, "Two minutes!!!"

Octavious went to Donovan and the miners. "We are coming up on the Cataco Shafts, are any of you familiar with them?"

Two of the older miners, Virgil and Lucas, came forward, in front of Donovan. Virgil said, "We mined them a long time ago, sir. It's been dormant for some time, unstable."

Octavious replied, "That's the least of my concerns. When I was a child, there were tunnels, from the mining, that connected to the Bosa Forterra Mountain Shaft, correct?"

The two miners looked at each other before confirming. Lucas said, "Yes, I believe so. Old Tunnel Eleven went out that way, and I believe it connected with those shafts. But there is no more Vait in those mines, Octavious."

Octavious looked at them and said, "I am not looking for Vait. I am looking for a lifeboat."

As the ships were getting closer to the mountain's side, Octavious could now see the opening of the shaft. It looked dusty, almost swallowed whole by the desert storms. One would really have to know what they were looking for to find it. The voice on the intercom was Cortes, causing everyone to look up in the sky. "Octavious, attack squadron, 9:00 to the west, about 40 degrees up."

Octavious looked that way and could see the enormous attack squadron coming. It had over thirty-five fighters and fifteen attack bombers. An engagement with them would not last long. Add in the additional two attack squadrons, and it would become suicidal. Octavious said into his intercom. "Cortes, step on it. Park this thing right next to the entrance."

Cortes said, "Copy that, thirty seconds."

Octavious then turned to his soldiers. "I want one side of this ship blasting the doors open of the shaft. I want the other side to provide cover for all the soldiers getting here. This is gonna be our only chance."

Admiral Holland was listening to the Attack Squadron Leader on the intercom. "Command Tower, I have visual. I count eight ships. They are slowing down to land."

Admiral Holland turned to the Majavkee Lords, who were a distracted bunch. They could not get over what they had witnessed at the Processing Center, and they were getting individual reports about how much of their security they had lost in the battle. Admiral Holland said, "What is out there? Where are they going?"

All of the Majavkee Lords turned and looked at the map, temporarily forgetting their other conversations. After a long pause, Majavkee Lord Bialos said, "That is near Cataco."

Admiral Holland replied in question, "Cataco?"

Lord Bialos answered, "Yes, the Cataco Shaft. It's in Bosa."

Lord Evander added, "It's abandoned, for years now. That area is probably near one of the shaft openings, but we would have to ask our experienced miners, they would know."

Holland looked up and responded, "Attack Leader Two, shoot everything on site. Even if they land, no prisoners."

"Copy that."

Cortes reversed the thrusters and spun the assault ship around. The wing brushed against the desert floor as the ship came to a violent stop in front of the boarded shaft doors. The rest of the ships began landing next to them as the side cannons from the assault ship blasted open the shaft doors. The cannons on the other side of the ship started shooting at the AuFa fighters in the sky. Octavious responded over the intercom, "Everyone out, leave your ships, get to the entrance of the shaft!!!"

Shots from the AuFa fighters connected with two of the landing Valmay ships. As both exploded, soldiers began running out of the other Valmay ships, through dust and smoke, towards the shaft entrance. At Octavious's assault ship, the soldiers dropped off bombs, torpedoes, and grenades before they proceeded into the cave. Octavious yelled, "Hurry!"

Another explosion rocked the ground as an attack bomber connected with another one of the Valmay vessels. Once all the Valmay soldiers were inside, Cortes tapped Octavious' shoulder. With bombs cascading down everywhere, Cortes and her co-pilot got off the ship and ran to the entrance. Octavious remained behind, surveying the bounty of explosives left for him. Putting one bomb on a timer on top of the pile, he ran out of the ship.

As Octavious was running, another explosion went off, causing him to stumble to the ground. He tried to get up, not noticing the burning chunk of shrapnel in his leg. He looked at the doors, which were twenty meters away. Cortes had turned around after the explosion and saw Octavious on the ground. She had stopped, waiting for Octavious to get up. When he did not, she ran back towards him. She helped him up and got his arm around her shoulders. The timer was at ten seconds, and yet another explosion went off behind them. AuFa soldiers were landing, a mere fifty meters away, as Cortes and Octavious skipped and stumbled towards the entrance. The timer was down to three when they got to the doors of the shaft. A soldier grabbed Octavious's arm and yanked both of them in.

The bombs went off, a series of explosions that went through the ships. The AuFa ground forces were instantly killed as the Attack Squadrons pulled back. Soon, a fireball reached one hundred meters into the sky. Watching from video screens in the command center, the Majavkee Lords and Admiral Holland took a small step back.

Inside the cave, Cortes was lying on top of Octavious. Dust was everywhere from the explosion, as the shaft was shaking from the explosions. Cortes turned Octavious slightly over, looking at the wound. She immediately took out her ring, made it into a small fire saber, and dug the shrapnel out of Octavious' leg. Octavious was moaning in pain. She then yelled, "Who has a Pulsator?!"

One of the soldiers ran up with a small first aid kit and immediately pulled out the skin healing device. Within seconds, Cortes had patched up the skin on the open wound. As Octavious got to his feet, he looked back out the entrance door to the mine. It was still a wall of smoke. Octavious said, "That should buy us a few minutes."

Lucas, the older miner, came up to Octavious and said, "I found tunnel Eleven Octavious. And a car."

Octavious recovered but with a small limp, began walking with the miner to the tunnel. He responded, "Open up all the tunnels. They need to guess where we are going."

The miners and soldiers broke apart and began taking down the boards blocking the tunnels. Dust was still settling, but better than it was a minute ago. Lucas and Virgil were scurrying through the Base Tower at the shaft openings. They came out with two packs that they attached to the side of the cars. As the car lit up, Virgil said, "Not much juice left on these Electro-packs, but enough to get us where we are going."

Everyone climbed aboard the cars, which were flat and on tracks. They rolled away from the shaft base, down tunnel eleven, all sixty of them, towards the Forterra Mine Shaft.

BELINEA 6.3

Avola

Lowell Province

Inside the Temple, Sterling and Felicia were giving gifts to the orphans. The children were smiling and appreciative of the toys. Quillisar Balerra, a rather old lady, walked up to them and said, "Sterling, Felicia. Thank you for the offerings. Where is Nix?"

Felicia answered, "With my mother. He does not need to see us give toys to others."

Balerra smiled and said, "Patience my child, he will learn. How are both of you?"

Sterling smiled, Felicia did not. "Sterling is working way too many hours."

Balerra said, "He is providing for his family, Felicia. I am sure there is a financial reward for his dedication."

The smile from Sterling's face disappeared. He said, "Well,..."

Felicia said, "No, there is not Quillisar. The Majavkee have him working more for less money."

Sterling interrupted, "That is not true, Quillisar."

But Felicia cut him off again. "It is. There are no bonuses. The conditions are getting worse and something needs to be done."

Balerra nodded her head. "Walk with me, my children."

They followed Balerra outside, so they were now in the children's playground. Balerra continued. "I hear this from all in my congregation. The energy is not bright, everyone is hurting. Their faith is being tested. Do you remember what happened at Valmay?"

They both nodded their heads as Felicia said, "Such a tragedy."

Balerra continued, "Indeed. There is an Opposition group that has retaliated those actions. Have you heard of them?"

Sterling just looked at the old lady, while Felicia looked puzzled. "You mean the terrorists? The ones that call themselves the Valmay Opposition Group?"

Balerra stopped walking and looked at both of them. "And why do you call them terrorists?"

Felicia said, "The videos that were shown, they were more responsible for what happened than the Majavkee. I have even heard they have old members of the Red Ring Rise."

Balerra looked directly into Felicia's eyes and said, "Do not believe everything you see unless it is with your own two eyes."

Felicia continued. "But Quillisar, the Majavkee Lords preach faith in the Quill. It may be a different form, but they are at least spiritual. Violence and greed is the only faith the terrorists practice."

Balerra said, "That is what the Majavkee want you to believe. Where has the faith you have given them got you? Who has more faith? The person who quietly meditates on their own daily or the person who boasts about the Quill and all it's good, but never actually goes to Temple?"

Felicia and Sterling said nothing. Balerra let them think about that for a moment before she continued. "You may not approve of their methods, nor do I. Violence only leads to more violence. But never say that Octavious Killian is a man with no morals or principles. I promise you, his heart, his faith in the Quill, is just as strong as mine."

The two continued to look at Balerra when someone shouted across the playground. "Quillisar, there has been an attack at the Processing Center. Hundreds are feared dead.

All three looked at each other. Sterling looked at Felicia and said, "Get Nix and go home. I need to get to work."

BELINEA 6.4

Capital City, Belinea

AuFa Headquarters, Military Services Building

The Council Security Group Board Room

All eighteen Ambassador's of the Council's Security Group were in the boardroom. Also in the room were Chairman Hassara, Admiral Magloan of the AuFa, and three of his officers. Everyone was seated around a huge circular conference table with a 3-D hologram image of Avola's attack in the center. Defense Minister Tempest Hassara was standing while giving the presentation.

She continued speaking. "As you can see, after the initial attack, there is an additional attack here on this medical transport by their leader Octavious Killian. Thirty-four people died, including wounded soldiers, civilians, and children...."

The hologram's image showed Octavious Killian taking down a clearly marked white medical ship instead of a green transport ship. The footage had Octavious dropping the grenade satchel into the medical transport cockpit and then images of children killed because of the explosion it caused. It was damning evidence of a terrorist group causing collateral damage at the highest level. Tempest continued to speak. "The Valmay Group continued their destruction by taking out these massive C-112 Cargo ships, eight in all, each full of Vait. We estimate a twelve percent loss of our entire Vait supply with this attack."

Ambassador Yi asked a question. "Defense Minister, may I ask, why were the Vait transport ships all pulling out at once?"

Tempest quickly answered, "My brother, Argo Hassara, was sent to Avola to negotiate on our behalf. He quickly determined the situation was much graver than previously reported. It was his decision, along with the Majavkee

Lords, to extract as much Vait from the planet as quickly as possible before another major attack could take place. Unfortunately, they were too late."

Ambassador Campova of Braccus leaned back in her chair and spoke next. "Ambassador Yebba, this is nothing short of an act of war."

Many of the Ambassadors were nodding their heads. Ambassador Yebba of Avola looked at the map, then around the rest of the room. He stood up, and Tempest moved to the side, pausing the image on the hologram right as the medical transport was burning on the ground. Yebba spoke. "I have received a joint statement from the Majavkee Lords, demanding retribution. Ambassador's, my planet needs your help. This is not a civil war. This is an injustice, by a small group of terrorists over the peaceful, hard-working, greater majority of Avolian citizens. I, like them, are outraged. The financial implications of losing such a large amount of Vait, as well as transport ships and weapons, further adds to the weight this Council must now bear. Innocent Avolians died. Soldiers, both Belinean and Avolian, died trying to protect those innocents. This vicious, unprovoked attack came at a time when we were negotiating a compromise. We are past peaceful solutions. We need leadership from this Council that protects all of us moving forward."

Yebba sat down. Chairman Hassara immediately spoke after. "In conjunction with the terrorist attacks by Taz on Earth, Braccus and Torsalli, the latest killing Earth Ambassador Bird, the Valmay Group is a much stronger organization than we previously thought. In front of you is Admiral Magloan's analysis, describing in detail the challenges we are facing. Issue one is Avola's numerous logistical problems. A full battalion will be needed to eliminate the threat entirely and not disrupt Vait production. Issue two will be what other terrorist organizations they are working with? Taz could just be the tip of the iceberg. Hunting down a potential larger network of terrorists will require an additional battalion and a twenty percent increase into both the AuFa and BRG budget."

There was a hush in the room. The Ambassadors had their heads down, not knowing what to say. Ambassador Campova spoke again. "The attack on my planet alone, where over a hundred innocent people died, is enough to consider drastic measures. Combined? The message needs to be clear. No price is too high for our safety and security."

Another long pause at the table. Tempest had walked back over to the middle of the table, where she was ready to ask for a vote before a voice at the end of the table spoke.

"Where are we going to get the money?"

Tempest looked down at Ambassador Garvalin. Garvalin leaned in a little more so that Tempest could see her. She said, "Excuse me, Ambassador Garvalin. What did you say?"

Ambassador Garvalin put her arms on the table, leaned in, and now slightly louder, said, "Nothing about this will be cheap. I assume the Council will be responsible for taking the funds out of something else or, even worse, raising taxes. Is that part of our recommendation as well?"

Chairman Hassara interrupted, "We have a few options regarding that. Before proposing this to the full Council, being in unison here with our decision was more important."

Ambassador Yebba of Avola quickly followed, "And we agree with you, Chairman, the sooner the better."

Ambassador Garvalin leaned back in her chair. She crossed her hands in front of her and continued. "Defense Minister, the incident on Nuhalla eighteen months ago...."

Tempest was led into the question, and she answered without adequately thinking. "Another tragedy Ambassador. Yet the AuFa, in a joint task force with the BRG, found the small terrorist groups and eliminated them."

Ambassador Garvalin nodded her head in agreement. "Yes, they did. Quickly and efficiently."

Tempest was slightly annoyed. "It was a difficult operation, executed flawlessly. Yet, these crimes presented before us today are a mere fraction to those. We are simply asking you to do our jobs."

Ambassador Garvalin, still with her arms crossed, waited a few seconds before replying, "Except, that is not what you are asking, Defense Minister."

Tempest gave a scowling look. "Excuse me?"

Everyone was looking at Ambassador Garvalin. Uncrossing her arms, she said clearly, "Defense Minister, surely the mission on Nuhalla was not flawless? The AuFa and BRG must have had some limitations to their capabilities. Perhaps the terrorists even exposed a potential weakness?"

Chairman Hassara tried to interrupt. He took a small breath and got a syllable out before Tempest took the bait and interrupted with "Ambassador, the AuFa and BRG are the finest military and security in the galaxy, respectively. No weakness was exposed, and there are certainly no limitations to their capabilities."

The Ambassador staring at Tempest, plainly asked, "Is it possible there is something out there the Ambassadors have not seen that you have, that can defeat the AuFa and BRG?"

Tempest stared at Ambassador Garvalin and responded, "Nothing."

Garvalin replied, "Then why the extra money?"

Tempest was going to say something, but only took a deep breath and could not immediately get an answer out. She got out a couple of words of "I mean to say…."

Ambassador Garvalin interrupted her and continued. "No one is saying this is not a tragedy. You asked to do your job. Your job is providing safety and security for our citizens. If every time there is an uprising somewhere, and you come in here asking for more money to do your job, then effectively, you are not doing it."

Tempest was speechless. Chairman Hassara knew it was too late, so he tried damage control. Even though Garvalin was still looking at Tempest, he replied to her, "Ambassador, do you own a house?"

Ambassador Garvalin continued to stare at Tempest. She finally stopped, gave a smile, and, looking at the Chairman, answered, "I have two. One back home, plus my small residence here on Belinea."

The Chairman smiled as well. He now crossed his hands and continued, " Until I spoke to Quillisar Prill, I had no idea about owning a home. Sure, I have one, but I am never there. See, I give a huge donation to Quillsar Prill, out of my own account, every few months. My dedication to my faith. The Quillisar will come to me from time to time and ask me 'Chairman, it's a shame what they found in the children's Temple school, termites in the walls.' Naturally, I give the Quillsar more money. He then comes to me and says, 'Chairman, did you hear about the pillars in the main temple, rotting.' Again, I give the Quillisar more money. He comes up to me again, asking, 'did you hear about…'. But I cut him off. I say, 'Why don't you just give me a list of the problems ahead of time, and I will write you a check beforehand each year. The Quillisar says to me, 'As if I know the problems before they arise, I am not the God of Prognostication."

Everyone in the room chuckled for a bit, including Ambassador Garvalin. The Chairman continued, "The problems in your house Ambassador happen when they happen. There is often no foretelling before they do. When we know where the terrorists are, when we know where the problems exist, then eliminating them is very possible. However, sometimes it requires more resources to find them."

Ambassador Garvalin gave a small smile. "Chairman Hassara, the ability of the BRG and AuFa to execute their jobs is not in question. No one has more respect for the work they do than I. However, finding these terrorists in the first place? Is that the best use of their resources?"

There was another pause. The Chairman looked as if he was going to say something, but Garvalin interrupted again. "Ambassador Bird gave a speech before he left about the need for local securities to take on a greater burden of responsibility. Since Ambassador Bird is no longer with us, I would like to hear what Ambassador Yi has to say about this?"

Ambassador Yi was in the middle of the room, directly across from Tempest. He looked back at Ambassador Garvalin. "I think Ambassador Bird was merely trying to spark ideas about how to best solve the Terrorist problem."

Ambassador Garvalin continued, "By proposing to increase your own Delegate Ambassador Security instead of using those funds to go directly towards the BRG and AuFa?"

Ambassador Yi looked like he was caught off guard. "I think there were a number of possibilities Ambassador Bird was willing to discuss, and those possibilities were to be covered privately before the next Council meeting."

Ambassador Garvalin looked at the tablet in front of her, hitting a few spots before continuing. "Ambassador Yi, I have a copy of that speech. Ambassador Bird said, ' we share the same vision as the Belieneans, we must let these terrorists know...we will shine the light of justice upon them, ...working together on that mission, we shall also not forget our primary vision of a better Earth. We cannot tolerate becoming prisoners to a plan that will lead us into an economic abyss, simply to remove an evil we all must extinguish together.' What does that sound like to you, Ambassador?"

Yi smiled, looking at everyone in the room. Staring at Tempest, he said, "I think The Ambassador wanted us to work together to fight these terrorists."

Ambassador Garvalin obviously disagreed. "Perhaps. It sounds like to me that Ambassador Bird's constituents believe your local security can do a better job of protecting themselves at a fraction of the costs."

Tempest interjected. "I am sure all of us would like to know what the Ambassador meant by his comments, but he is not here, is he?"

Garvalin leaned back in her chair again. Taking a deep breath, she said, "Tragically, no, he is not."

Tempest looked focused again. Staring at Garvalin, she said, "But we do have the enemy in our crosshairs Ambassador. Citizens of this Council have died at their hands. Justice needs to be served. Do you have the courage to remove them, or do you want to argue about how it should be done?"

There was an awkward silence in the room. The tension level had gotten high. Everyone in the room was staring at Garvalin. Garvalin finally said, "I think we should be given time to discuss all of our options before presenting a recommendation to the entire Council."

The Chairman stood up. Everyone else followed when he did. The Chairman said in a serious tone, "Take whatever time you need, Ambassador. But in about an hour, I will release the footage of the Avolian attack to the rest of the Council. At some point, I am sure it will leak to the press, which, when I am asked by the press what we are doing, I will refer to this group's planning of a counter-attack. At that point, all of you will have to talk to your constituents as to why you have waited."

The Chairman proceeded to walk out of the room, leaving the rest of the Ambassadors, Tempest, and Admiral Magloan, to just stare at each other.

BELINEA 6.5

Avola

Captain Leahy walked up to the door. He did not knock, nor did he open the door. Instead, he just patiently waited. Some noises could be heard on the inside, but Leahy stood at a very casual attention. A minute went by, and finally, the door opened. A naked girl walked out, with a huge bruise across her face. Her hands were bleeding, and she was clearly in tears. She ran past Leahy, leaving the door open behind her. Leahy was confused but could hear things still in the room. With the door being open, he took a few steps inside. Softly, he said, "Lord Argo...?"

He took a few more steps in. He could now hear clearly, yet still not see, Argo with another girl. The girl was yelling, "Give it to me, give it to me, give it to me, yes, yes, right in my face...."

Leahy could now hear Argo yelling, "Take all of it, you dirty little whore....."

Taking a few more steps in allowed Leahy to see everything. Argo had his back towards the door, naked and standing. The girl, also naked, was on her knees in front of him. There was a little more noise, as Leahy decided to turn around and walk back out the front door.

As he got there, he waited for about twenty seconds, leaving the door open. As he waited, Lieutenant Walva walked up. Pointing at the open door, he said to Leahy, "Is he in there?"

Leahy half-smiled, still not used to the voice. Walva's voice had changed to an uptight English Butler. Leahy answered, "He is busy."

Walva just looked at him and said, "He is late..."

Leahy tilted his head and said, "You wanna lose your head this time?"

Walva kept looking at him, annoyed. A few seconds went by. Walva tried not to say anything, but finally continued in frustration, "They are waiting."

Leahy kept looking at him and said, "Then let them wait...."

A few seconds went by. The girl carried her clothes in her hand and passed in between Leahy and Walva. She said, "Excuse me…."

Leahy smiled and said, "And now we enter…"

Leahy and Walva walked in the door for a few steps and stopped. Leahy announced his presence loudly. "Lord Argo?"

Argo yelled back, "Come in, Leahy."

They turned the corner, and Argo was sitting down, already halfway putting his clothes back on. Argo then said, "I am almost ready. Those fuckers can wait. Walla! You are alive!"

Lieutenant Walva then said, "Nice to see you too, Lord Argo."

Argo squinted his eyes and asked, "What the fuck is wrong with your voice?"

Walva explained. "It seems there were complications with the surgery."

Argo immediately said, "They made you likable?"

Leahy smiled, Walva did not. Walva continued. "These Avolian doctors are not as good as the Belineans. So, my vocal cords were accidentally cut in an attempt to attach a clone-based tongue. They managed to insert an artificial vocal box in me, temporarily, until I can get back to Belinea."

Argo said, "Any surgery they can do to make you less annoying or did they already try that?"

Walva gave a half-smile and said, "Same annoyance, different voice."

Argo finished putting on his boots and said, "To be honest, though, the voice isn't half bad. It suits you."

Argo stood up and put his black cloak on. He walked up to Walva and said, "Glad it turned out alright, let me see."

Walva said, "Excuse me, my Lord?"

Argo tried to look into Walva's mouth, and repeated, "Let me see."

Walva, slightly confused, stuck out his tongue. It was blue, circulation was struggling, and you could see where they tried to re-attach it to the root of his old tongue. Walva said, "Ahhhh…."

Argo gently slapped him on the shoulder and said, "You will be as good as new once we get back home. But you should keep the voice, perhaps as a little reminder?"

Walva asked, "And when are we going home, my Lord?"

Argo's smile turned to a frown. As they walked out, he said, "Not soon enough."

On a long rectangular table, all of the Majavkee Lords sat, as well as AuFa Admiral Holland and Commander Bullmo, head of Majavkee security. Majavkee Lord Bialos spoke. "Eight Transports, six cannons, the damage to the facility will be costly. It will take some time to recover properly."

Majavkee Lord Evander added, "But the root of the problem may be gone."

Majavkee Lord Bialos answered, "At what cost? Not to mention all the soldiers."

Majavkee Lord Evander answered, "Peace is not cheap. At least the transports were empty, so we did not lose any Vait."

A few seconds went by before Majavkee Lord Bialos said, "Him making us wait is insulting."

Argo had just walked into the room and said, "So is your hospitality, but who is keeping score?"

The room went silent. Majavkee Lord Bialos, embarrassed by his statement, immediately countered with "Lord Argo, forgive me, no one informed us of your delay."

Argo sat down at the head of the table and said, "I was unaware of my tardiness. I was doing more important things."

Admiral Holland then said, "Lord Argo, I have a status report if you wish."

Argo leaned back in his chair and folded his hands together. He said with a smug smile. "Can we confirm Octavious Killian's death?"

Admiral Holland continued, "I am afraid we cannot at this time. There is a small group of Valmay fighters yet to be captured. They have fled inside the Cataco mines, where we have them surrounded. We are not sure if Octavious is with them."

Argo shook his head. "I want him alive, Admiral. Make that very clear to your troops. I want to bring him and Kaya back to Belinea and hang them in front of the entire Council."

Admiral Holland nodded in acknowledgment. Majavkee Lord Bialos then added, "We have a current casualty report as well, Lord Argo."

Argo then replied, "And that report is not nearly as important as finding Killian."

Bullmo, the Head of Majavkee Security, then stood up. His voice full of anger, he said, "I lost almost three hundred of my men out there today, for you. I suggest you make it important."

Argo then stared at him. Shrugging his shoulders, he said, "Who are you?"

He answered. "Bullmo, Head of Majavkee Security."

Argo, pointing at the Majavkee Lords, continued, "You did not do it for me. You did it for them. Also, if they were any good at fighting, maybe you would not have lost so many soldiers."

Bullmo stared at him, turning a deep color of red. Looking at the Majavkee Lords at the table, he continued, "I serve them, and (looking back at Argo, pointing), we followed your orders. Show some remorse for the soldiers that died at your hands today."

Argo sat up in his chair and replied, "Head of Majavkee Security is a useless title at this table. You might want to check your tone."

Bullmo replied, "I am not convinced we needed your help in this matter."

Argo was now annoyed. He stood up and said, "Leave this meeting now before you say more things you will regret."

Bullmo took a few steps towards him, going around the table, grabbing the handle of his handgun. As he kept walking towards Argo, he began pointing at him with his other hand. His voice was rising as he got closer. "How dare you address anyone in this room that way. Show your proper respect for the blood that was spilled...."

In one quick motion, Argo grabbed the ring on his side and tilted his head ever so slightly. Holding the handle on his ring with both hands in front of his face, the ring transformed slowly into an extending silver blade. Bullmo said, "You would not dare...."

Argo pointed the sword towards Bullmo as he approached, extending it ten feet in an instant. It pierced Bullmo through his eyeball, straight out the back of his head. He wobbled for a second as Argo then retracted the blade back to its ring form. Blood from the wound came out, splattering onto one of the Majavkee Lords sitting at the table. Bullmo fell to the ground, blood pouring all over the floor. Argo, still holding the handle on his ring, said, "Anyone else want to talk about casualties?"

Argo waited for a few seconds. All the Majavkee Lords were in shock. Most kept their heads down. No one said anything. Argo said, "Good."

Argo put the ring back on his hip and took a deep breath. He sat down and said, "I lost AuFa soldiers out there today as well. We will properly mourn their death back on Belinea. But let me make this very clear to everyone at this table. This is your fucking problem. And every time you need us to resolve your problems, we question leaving you in charge."

Majavkee Lord Evander then quietly said, "Lord Argo, I speak for all the Lords here when I say we thank you and the AuFa for the assistance you have provided...."

Argo cut him off. "Save it, Lord Evander. If there was no Vait here, we could care less about any of you. Mine as much as you can, by whatever means necessary. We will continue to purchase all of it at the fair price you have always received. But I promise, the Council will be just as happy letting someone else go out there and mine that Vait if you can not handle these fucking distractions on your own."

Argo stood up and looked at Admiral Holland. "Admiral, get a message to that small group in the mines. Tell them I have Kaya Killian, and she dies unless Octavious peacefully surrenders. If he is still alive, that will snuff him out."

Argo walked out of the room. He navigated around the dead body and its blood on the floor. As he did, he said, "Lord Bialos, you are going to need a new head of security. May I suggest one that does not talk as much."

BELINEA 6.6

Avola

The Cataco Mines

Huddled in the middle of a long narrow cave were all sixty survivors. The older miners were discussing different options. Some of the soldiers were still tending to wounds, trying to clean themselves up. Others were on security at both sides of the cave, waiting for an attack from the surface. Octavious sat alone, contemplating his next move. He looked tired. He got up and walked over to a spot where Cortes and Donovan were fixing the control board on the cable car. As he came up, Donovan was attempting to reconnect wires underneath it. Donovan asked, "What about that?"

Cortes, who was on the top of the car with the control board in front of her, said, "Negative."

Donovan kept trying to re-wire. Octavious asked Cortes, "Any luck?"

Cortes shook her head no. Cortes then asked, "Have the miners come up with a plan?"

Octavious replied, "Six hours, and all they can tell me is we are stuck. A blocked twenty-meter section of tunnel going to Forterra. Even if we made it, by this time, they have likely set up forces on the other side. It is only a matter of time for the Majavkee to figure this out."

Donovan from below asked, "What about now?"

Cortes just repeated "Negative."

After a few seconds, Octavious slightly shook his head and very quietly said, "We should have just taken the deal."

Cortes responded, "Do you think you could have trusted Argo Hassara? Or the Council for that matter?"

Octavious sighed. He then replied, "Maybe not. But at least we could have survived. This will only end with all of our deaths. And I knew that going in."

Cortes quickly replied, "So did we. So did your sister, if she is dead. We are not giving up."

The Control panel suddenly lit up. From below, Donovan, said, "What about now?"

Cortes sat back up, looking at the entire control board. Lights kept flashing, but quickly the board was coming back to life. Octavious, already standing, looked over at it now. Cortes yelled, "It's back on."

Donovan crawled out from under the board and stood on the other side of Cortes. He hit a couple of buttons, and a map showed up on the screen. Pointing at the screen, he said, "Alright, here we are."

The two older miners, Lucas and Virgil, heard the commotion and came walking over. The digital map allowed them to decipher what they had been verbally discussing. Pointing at the map, Lucas said, "Octavious, we went down tunnel eleven, so our only out is through here, the Forterra Shaft, without going back the way we came."

Octavious then said, "Can you enlarge the map?"

Donovan did, and it began showing maps of all the tunnels and shafts in the area. Octavious noticed something. "What is this over here? That's back to Lowell Province, no?"

Virgil said, "We used to call it the Cataco Cut. It goes back and down, deeper into the mountain towards Lowell. The entrance used to be here (pointing), but they had an accident over ten years ago, collapsing the entire area. So there is no way into it now."

Lucas said, " Except for the CCP."

Virgil responded, "That is a myth."

Lucas countered with, "No, it is not."

Octavious interjected and asked, "What is the CCP?"

Virgil said, "CCP was the code for Cataco Cut Pass. A few miners were rumored-"

Lucas cut him off and said, "It wasn't a rumor, I went down it a few tines. We used that code so the Guild wouldn't find out."

Octavious asked, "Find out what?"

Virgil continued. "They were acting without permission from the Mining Guild, and subsequently selling Vait to non sanctioned buyers. Smuggler's mainly. Trying to earn a little extra money."

Lucas followed up. "And we did, for a few times. But the smugglers ended up paying us less and less, threatening us every time. That was no accident. Some of the older miners destroyed that entrance so the Guild would never find the evidence."

Octavious shook his head. "Alright, so where exactly is the CCP?"

Lucas replied while pointing at the map. "It's right here. It's sealed shut from this side, but it's a four-kilometer pass that connects to this abandoned shaft over here, which then connects to Sector Nine shaft at Lowell, probably the seven tunnel."

Octavious then replied, "That is where most of you worked, correct?"

All the miners in the area nodded. Lucas said, "Sector Nine, yes sir."

Octavious, looking at the older miners and pointing to the map, said, "And if you were to find a way to open this Cataco Cut here, it will connect to the CCP? Do any of the older miners know about this CCP?"

Virgil replied, "Who are you calling old?"

Octavious grinned. Virgil continued. "Sure. It's been years, but some of them know where it was sealed shut."

Octavious looked at Donovan, who was still standing next to Cortes. "Can you quietly get a rescue message out to them?"

Donovan just looked at him. "Octavious, the mine entrance was destroyed on our side. Even if we dug through that, it is sealed from the other side. The message to them would have to get through, risk not getting caught and know where it is. I did not."

Octavious gave him a stern look, remembering what happened. "There is a lot you do not know."

The two just stared at each other. Octavious spoke. "The miners that work in that area, sector nine, tunnel seven. Just send this message, CCP-SOS. Alright? They either understand it or, just like the Majavkee, they will not."

Donovan, begrudgingly, began typing onto the control board. Octavious turned to the two older miners and said, "Take the rest of miners with you to that Cataco Cut entrance, figure out a way to get through."

Virgil and Lucas nodded and walked off. They started yelling at some of the other miners to "Roundup, get ready."

Cortes and Donovan turned to Octavious and said, "We got a message coming in Octavious. It's from the Majavkee."

Ocatvious said, "Open channel message?"

Cortes nodded in affirmative. Donovan said, "They have Kaya. They demand our immediate surrender, or they will kill her."

Octavious looked at the board. "She is alive? How do we know?"

Cortes pulled up the picture. She said, "She looks like they beat her."

Octavious was tearful and joyful. He took a huge sigh as if the weight of the planet was off his shoulders. Kaya was alive, barely. His sudden joy was overcome with anger. "They only want me. I can trade my life for her."

Cortes grabbed Octavious's arm. "No. There is no trusting them. They will just kill you both. Besides, it is not what Kaya would want."

Ocatvious looked down at Cortes and said, "But it is what I want."

Cortes replied, "And she would want you to fight. She would never forgive you."

The two stared at each other for a few seconds. Octavious gently shook his head and said, "It's not her decision."

There was another pause. Cortes finally said, "Let's get out of here first. Then we go get her."

Octavious said, "We may not have the time."

Cortes added, "Argo will keep her alive until he gets you. She is the bait, and you are the prize."

The two continued to stare at each other as they watched a group of miners start walking down the cave towards the Cataco Cut.

BELINEA 6.7

Avola

Argo was walking down a hallway. Lieutenant Walva was next to him with a tablet in his hand. Captain Leahy of the SS was directly behind them. Walva, in his new British Butler voice, said, "I have a message for you. It came through on your SS-T account."

Argo held out his hand, and Walva handed him the tablet. Argo was reading while he was walking. He was lip-syncing until he finally let out an "Excellent, another target eliminated. Walla, forward that message to my Father, same channel, and security code."

Walva, giving up on the name change, just took the tablet back and said, "Yes, my Lord."

They walked down another hallway to a locked door. Argo put his hand on the palm reader to the right, and the door open. Kaya was sitting in a chair, head down, with her wrists cuffed to the arm-rests. The room was dark, with no windows and only one small overhead light. Captain Leahy walked in behind Argo. An Avolian Doctor was looking at Kaya and stood up when Argo got closer. Argo asked, "How is she?"

The Doctor tilted her head. She replied, "She needs surgery, Lord Argo. The leg wound has left a substantial gash, and she has lost a lot of blood. Her left eye has major external injuries, while her skull sustained an internal fracture behind the eye socket. I won't know until I perform a complete scan."

Argo asked, "So she is in pain?"

The Doctor nodded. "Yes. Or her body is in shock, and she is numb."

Argo asked, "Will she live?"

The Doctor nodded again. "With surgery, yes. Without it, she could die."

Argo took a breath. After a few seconds, he said, "Well, shit. That changes things."

He took a few steps towards Kaya. He grabbed her by the chin and turned her head up. "Looks like you have been in pain long enough. The Doctor here says we need to fix your leg and head, give you a little blood, or else I lose my prized hostage."

Argo turned to the Doctor and said, "Bare minimum Doc, leg, head, blood. Do not touch the lacerations or the eye."

The Doctor replied, "She might lose it."

Argo answered, "She has another one."

Turning back to Kaya and keeping her chin up with her hand, Argo said, "Right, Princess?"

Leahy even smiled at that one. The Doctor looked revolted. As she did, Kaya managed to mutter out of her mouth, "Argo….you are still here?"

Argo tilted his head and said, "Excuse me?"

Kaya took a breath and, with Argo still grabbing her chin and smiling the best she could, said slowly, "I thought you were looking for your little cock that your sister stole?"

Argo half-smiled. He squatted down to get eye level with Kaya. Still holding her chin, he said, "Spunky to the end."

Kaya painfully said, "It's not her fault her's is bigger."

With the half-smile still on his face, Argo kept her chin up so she could hear every word. Softly, he said, "If your brother is still alive, he is going to trade his life for yours. I then will cut his head off and feed him to the rats. But, I do not think he is. Which means after the doc fixes you, I am going to let every one of my SS officers come in here and rape you. Either way, bitch, know that you are going to suffer for the rest of your miserable fucking life."

Argo grabbed his ring and made the silver into a dagger. He pierced it right through the back of Kaya's hand. Blood came out, and Kaya grimaced in pain. Gritting her teeth closed, she let out, "Fuck You!!!"

Argo took the dagger out, stood up, and put the ring back on his hip. As he was walking out, he said to the Doctor, "You can fix that too, but not the eye."

BELINEA 6.8

Chairman Hassara's Office

Capital City, Belinea

Tempest was still fuming. The Chairman poured himself a drink. Her arms were crossed as she looked out the window. She said, "I cannot believe that fucking bitch. The audacity to go after me like that!"

The Chairman then sat down behind his desk. After a sip of his drink, he looked at Tempest and said, "You fell right into her trap Tempest."

Tempest turned around and said, "You knew what she was going to say?"

The Chairman smiled and replied. "No, I did not. But you must prepare for every possible scenario. Charm and disarm."

Tempest took a deep breath. Walking over to the bar table, she began pouring herself a drink and said, "I don't need a lecture, father."

The Chairman tilted his head and said, "I am not giving you one. Just reminding you, we all have a role to play."

Tempest took a sip of her drink and then let out, "I had everyone in that room until that cunt opened her mouth. I want to scratch her fucking eyes out."

The Chairman leaned back in his chair. "Relax. You will do no such thing. She did not hurt you or even embarrass you. She surprised you. Any retaliation will look foolish and petty."

Tempest stared at her father. "And what if she convinces the others to vote no?"

The Chairman merely shook his head gently side to side, and said, "She will not."

Tempest replied, "How do you know?"

The Chairman took another sip of his drink. "Because this is politics. Walk softly and carry a big stick, my child. And never forget, I have the biggest stick."

Tempest walked over to the front of her father's desk and sat down. She said, "I told you I was in no mood for a lecture."

The Chairman continued, "They can bark all they want, but no one is going to defy me in that room publicly. Your brother gave you more than enough material to paint the picture you want. Feed that to the press and the public will demand justice. Everyone will want to blame someone for the innocent lives lost. Combined with the political agenda of the rest of the Ambassadors and no one will care about the cost. It is justice, which has no price. Her own people will turn on her for even suggesting anything otherwise."

Tempest just quietly said, "Fuck her."

The Chairman sat up. He continued, "Tempest, keep your friends close, and your enemies closer. There will be a time to deal with her properly, be patient."

Tempest leaned back and said, "If that were Argo or Malovex in there, she would have never said that. And if she did, they would have cut her head off."

The Chairman gave a small chuckle. "Probably. But that's why I sent you instead of them. They only know how to lead through fear. Your presentation was magnificent. But you have to know every angle, know what every Ambassador wants, and what they fear. That's why, one day, it will be you in this chair and not them."

Tempest took another sip of her drink. "Do they know that?"

The Chairman smiled again. "Do you think they care?"

Tempest was genuinely curious. "I have no idea?"

The Chairman took another sip of his drink, letting the liquor roll around the large ice cube in his glass. He then took a breath and said, " Malovex has little patience for diplomacy, and Argo has none. That is why I sent him to Avola. Do you think I sent him there to negotiate?"

Tempest had an even more curious look on her face. She shook her head in confusion. "The Vait is too important. We had to strengthen our position and secure the trade channels. That is why you sent him."

The Chairman continued. "Yes, the Vait flow is essential to our overall plan. But I sent him because the Majavkee are weak. They fear us, and Argo exemplifies that. The Valmay are not scared of us, and thus would be much harder to deal with."

Tempest said, "But you offered the Valmay Group a deal?"

The Chairman got up and walked over to the bar table again to pour himself another drink. " A deal we would have never honored even on the slim chance they took it. Argo was sent there to gain public support and eliminate the Valmay. And so far, he has done just that."

Tempest made a small joke. "Maybe you *should* think about putting him in your chair."

The Chairman replied while he sat back down. "You are missing the point, Tempest. He is not a politician. He is a warrior and a killer. Him and Malovex both. They do not want all the regulations, cordial formalities, and bureaucracy of sitting in this chair. They want to be the fear that this chair puts into the people."

Tempest just took another sip of her drink. "Argo gets all the easy jobs."

The Chairman chuckled and said, "And all the ones most people can not stomach. By the way, did you read the message I forwarded to you?"

Tempest answered, "Yes."

A robot voice came over on the intercom. It said, "Urgent message Chairman Hassara in your C-Bar T-box."

The Chairman hit the spot on the tablet on his desk. He then said, "Well, his ears must have been burning."

Tempest asked, "Argo, again?"

The Chairman shook his head no. He replied, "Malovex. It seems our Ambassador Bird might be alive after all."

Tempest sat up and said, "What?"

The Chairman half-smiled and said, "It seems he may not have been on the Ambassador Transport ship like we thought. Which means someone out there is being clever as to not let us know where he is. Perhaps one of these messages is not true."

Tempest asked, "I thought Argo had a very reliable spy?"

The Chairman answered, "According to him. Malovex disagrees."

Tempest asked, "Should we tell Ambassador Yi about Bird?"

The Chairman leaned back. "Maybe it is time we found out what Yi does and doesn't know."

BELINEA 6.9

Capital City, Belinea

In a very high-end wine shop, Ambassador Yi walked through the aisles looking at the bottles. Two DAG officers were casually following him. As he turned to go down another aisle, he walked straight into Ambassador Garvalin. Yi said to her, "Ambassador, I did not know you procured your wine here?"

Ambassador Garvalin looked at him and said, "Yes, so unusual running into you."

Ambassador Yi looked at his guards and said, "Leave us."

Garvalin looked at her guards, and they did the same. Once alone on the aisle, Garvalin said to Yi, "Did we have to go through all the cloak and dagger just to have a conversation?"

Yi looked at her and said, "The rebuttal with Tempest? I do not think you are getting invited to the Defense Minister's birthday party. Expect the SS to watch your every move."

Garvalin smiled and said, "I am only doing what we discussed."

Yi smiled back before answering. "It is working. You rattled her cage. It will keep her preoccupied long enough to not worry about Bird until he gets here."

Garvalin said, "So the rumors of your fellow Earth Ambassador being dead are not true? He is still alive?"

Yi nodded and replied, "According to my sources. They are unsure of his whereabouts, and the bullseye is still on his back. But as of now, alive."

Garvalin took another look around to make sure no one was listening. "What happens if someone finds the bullseye, and he doesn't make it here to the Council meeting?"

Yi looked at her and said, "We win either way. The only difference would be me giving the speech instead of him. His assassination, while not planned on our end, nevertheless gives me the proper ammunition to give the same speech he would have."

Garvalin asked, "Alright, what is the next step?"

Yi gave a couple of glances to make sure no one was listening either. "Publically, you must say nothing. Once the Chairman finally gets the press involved, issue a statement, we are diligently working on a solution. Play coy. Say the Chairman and the Defense Minister are more than welcome to join us during these negotiations."

Garvalin then asked, "When they come down there, demanding things again, and my constituents demand justice, then what?"

Yi answered, "By that time, we should have Bird back alive."

Garvalin asked, "And if we do not?"

Yi smiled, took a deep breath, and just said, "Then I will give the speech a little earlier than I wanted to."

Garvalin smiled, nodded, and said, "Alright, I will walk out the other side of the store in ten minutes if you go out the front now."

Yi smiled, turned around, and began walking away. As he did, he said, "There is a '48 Lovarri blend from Kapoor Estate on Torsalli on the next aisle over. A friend of mine produces it. Expensive, but great for a special occasion."

Garvalin said as he walked away, "I hope we have one."

BELINEA 6.10

Avola

Cataco Mines

Octavious had watched for over an hour. The miners, through a series of small explosions, rock cutting devices, and ventilators, had broken through the blocked entrance of the Cataco Cut. Dust was everywhere, and light was almost non-existent. The crew was off the shaft trains and now on foot, a rocky and unstable path that was slow to navigate. Once they had gotten through the entrance, however, the Cut was spacious. It was six meters high and ten meters wide, deep underneath the mountains.

They finally got to the other side, when Lucas turned to Octavious and said, "That's it. The Cut stops here."

Octavious was sipping on a cup of water. Dust was all over his face. He looked at Lucas, a little short on breath, and said, "What now?"

Lucas, while pointing at a section of the cave, said, "The CCP is up there somewhere, but we would be cutting blind. It's not on any of the maps, so without proper tools and lighting, it could take us days, maybe weeks."

Octavious looked down before looking up to take another sip of water. Octavious said softly, "I'm open to ideas."

Nobody said anything. Finally, Donovan replied, "I sent the message Octavious, through the internal miner channels. I got no response."

Virgil responded. "And nor would you. If I got that message, I would think it was a trap from the Majavkee, testing us on our loyalty. "

Octavious looked at Cortes and realized he was probably right. He looked at Virgil and Lucas and said, "Alright, start trying to find the entrance. We wait here as long as it takes."

Lucas said, "We are gonna need some more light. And what are we gonna do about food and water, Octavious?"

Octavious shook his head gently and said, "I will figure something out."

Belinea 6.11

Torsalli

Kapoor Estate

The BRG officer was still interrogating Vihaan Kapoor when Lord Malovex's ship landed. Malovex, in all black as always, headed straight for them. As Malovex walked up, he could hear Vihaan say, "How the hell should I know?"

As the BRG officer turned slightly, he noticed Malovex standing next to him. He immediately turned ninety degrees and stood at attention. As he was saluting, he got out, "Lord Malovex."

Malovex stood there, eyeing Vihaan Kapoor up and down. He finally said, "Vihaan Kapoor, I was told there is a big black crater in your backyard and that you were robbed?"

Vihaan let out a small smile before he said, "Sansigar Malovex, so glad you are here. I was robbed. I am trying to file a report right now."

Malovex squinted his eyes and tilted his head ever so slightly. He softly said, "It's been quite some time since someone other than my Uncle called me by my first name."

Vihaan just stared back and said, "It's been quite some time since someone had the balls to rob me, but who is counting?"

The two gave each other a courteous smirk, neither sincere. Malovex took a deep breath and said, "Well, we already killed the guys responsible for the crater…"

Vihaan quickly said, "Thank you, where can I leave a tip?"

Malovex continued, "But what was stolen?"

The BRG officer interrupted and said, "Mr. Kapoor claims two D-21 Sirallo's were stolen from his property."

Malovex replied quickly, "You have *two* D-21 Sirallo's? One is not enough?"

Vihaan looked directly at Malovex and said, "I got three, but again, who is counting?"

Malovex looked at Vihaan and said, "Why two Vihaan? If you are one person, I see stealing one. But if you got a team, why steal two? Why not just take all three of them?

Vihaan wiped the smile off his face and just said, "What am I, Sherlock Fucking Holmes?"

The two just stared at each other. The BRG officer said, " As I was trying to explain to Mr. Kapoor. The Earth DAG maintains his property, so his report will need to be filed with them. We are here strictly in the capacity to offer assistance and find the culprits."

Malovex then said, "Pity. You know, Vihaan, I can arrange for the BRG to provide you security. Might be a little more expensive, but we could probably stop the theft of your personal transports for starters."

Vihaan just smiled and said, "For now, I will take my chances with my fellow Earth business partners. Perhaps you can leave a card and a quote if I change my mind."

The BRG officer interrupted again. " We were about to ask Mr. Kapoor for his security footage to help us catch those responsible."

Vihaan just chuckled. "Good luck with that."

Malovex slightly tilted his head in confusion and replied, "Kapoor, when did you become so uncooperative?"

Vihaan said, "Let me summarize the security footage for you, Malovex. There was my vineyard, and the next millisecond it was gone all black. So I have nothing on the Sirallo's."

Malovex quickly added, "I am pretty sure the BRG can stop that from happening as well."

Vihaan said, "Losing my vineyards?"

Malovexx shook his head, looked at the BRG officer, and said, "Bombs falling from the sky. Leave us."

The BRG officer walked away. Malovex turned to Vihaan and said, "You have a contract to build Belinean ships as well, Vihaan. We are all concerned. Why not tell me what happened?"

Vihaan, politely said, "You think I got answers? A bomb fell from fucking sky. What's next, my lucky numbers?"

Malovex only replied, "I am sure aristocrats everywhere are sobbing at a particular vintage being lost. I was referring to the two DAG officers that showed up on your doorstep."

Vihaan replied, "I don't know what you are talking about."

Malovex crossed his arms and said, "Oh, I think you do because that bomb was not the only thing that fell from the sky, and you got a missing Sirallo."

Vihaan held up two fingers and said, "Two."

Malovex said, "Glad you can count. Which brings me to my next question. Were the Sirallo's stolen at the same time?"

Vihaan answered back, "I woke up from a wine hangover, got an afternoon blowjob, and then discovered they were gone. I have no idea."

Malovex replied, "Here is the situation, Vi. I wish I cared about that crater out there and all the precious wine you lost, but honestly, I don't."

Vihaan interjected with a sarcastic "Refreshing…"

Malovex answered, "What I do care about is the ground team that navigated that bomb on your house. So, if your two DAG officer's left in two separate Sirallo's, well, that seems very generous and a bit over-indulgent even for you. But if they only left in one, then I am interested in who stole the second one. Otherwise, the team I am really looking for could still be here."

Vihaan thought for a second, before replying, "Do I look like a generous, over-indulgent prick?"

Malovex answered, "Is this a trick question?"

Vihaan crossed his arms and said, "In an effort to maintain a good relationship with your father and yourself, hypothetically, if I allowed two friends, who asked if they could borrow one of my transport crafts, they certainly would not have enough balls to ask for two."

Malovex tilted his head the other way. "See how easy that was, Vihaan?"

Vihaan replied, "Maybe, but I don't see you or your father paying for that big black fucking crater out there, do I."

Malovex turned and began walking away. He shouted, "Relax, Vihaan. We will just get you another contract to build some fucking thing."

BELINEA 6.12

Capital City, Belinea

Ambassador Yi was nervous. He had gotten the private message as soon as he left the wine shop to see Chairman Hassara and Tempest Hassara at once. He was now outside, leaving his palm print and eye scan for proper identification. He got through the two security guards and entered the office doors, where the robot assistant said, "The Chairman will see you…"

Ambassador Yi walked in and noticed Tempest Hassara and Admiral Magloan joined chairman Hassara. The Chairman spoke first, "Ambassador Yi, please come in and sit down."

Ambassador Yi acknowledged everyone before sitting in the chair in front of Chairman Hassara's desk. This was already a curious meeting. The Chairman had a drink in his hand and usually only had one when the day's work was over. This then was an unexpected meeting. The Chairman asked, "A drink Ambassador?"

Yi smiled kindly and said, "A little too early for that Chairman. I usually drink wine."

Tempest walked over to the bar area and poured two glasses of wine. She turned around, walked over to Yi, and presented him a glass before returning to her seat. "Torsalli Simi."

Yi smiled again and crossed his legs in his chair. "Well, that changes things. Too good to pass up, thank you. Cheers."

Yi raised his glass, as did everyone in the room. It seemed even Admiral Magloan had a hi-ball glass, neat, of whatever the chairman was drinking. The Chairman took a sip and then asked, "Ambassador, we have several conflicting reports that I wanted your perspective on. What do you know about Ambassador Bird getting here?"

Yi took a sip of his wine. He was prepared for this. He answered, "Chairman, as I told the Defense Minister, I know less than you."

Admiral Magloan interjected. "You have an individual security staff, the Delegate Ambassador Guard, correct?

Yi glanced at the Admiral before refocusing on the Chairman. "Yes, the DAG for short. I have a detail team assigned to me by the Guard's top officer, Director Kimakawa. He, and his deputy, Vice Director Meyers, handle all the assignments and the details for each mission."

Tempest then asked, "And you trust them?"

Yi glanced at Tempest a little longer before returning his eyesight to the Chairman. He realized quickly as if there was any doubt, who was actually running the meeting. Yi continued with a smile. "I have a team of eight, and they have kept me alive this long."

The Chairman smiled and then said, "The reports coming from Torsalli regarding Ambassador Bird are not definitive. There was an explosion of his Transport craft, but we cannot get confirmation that he was on it."

Tempest added, "It is possible his DAG team pulled him off of the ship. We were curious as to what you have heard from your end, perhaps from the Director or your DAG team?"

Yi was very good at playing dumb. "Like you, I have only heard the transport had blown up. My channels assumed he was onboard."

The Chairman reshifted in his chair and continued. "Tempest asked if you trust them because candidly, everyone in this room has little confidence the DAG is capable of doing their job."

Tempest continued, "I do not often speak for my cousin, but I assure you, Lord Malovex, shares the same views. We have no doubt the BRG, through his guidance, is far better equipped and trained to execute security for all the Ambassador's, including yourself."

Yi took a sip of wine and answered, "I appreciate your concern. It is difficult for me to comment when I am unaware of all the facts present. I know the DAG does not have a spotless track record, nor does the BRG for that matter. My commitment is to stop the terrorists by all means necessary, recognizing that should be our common focus."

Tempest continued, "Were you aware of what Ambassador Garvalin was going to say today?"

Yi was slightly nervous. "No. Her position surprised all of us."

Tempest added, "It blind-sided us, and we do not like to be caught off guard like that."

The Chairman took a sip from his glass and said, "Yet, you know the Ambassador fairly well, no?"

Yi could see where this was going. He shifted gears. Even if he was wrong, better to cover his ass now than never be trusted again. Yi said, "I sought her counsel. I spoke to her about the need to reconcile, move forward, and collectively come up with an answer to bring the terrorists to justice."

Tempest replied, "You have seen her since the meeting?"

Yi continued, "I met her privately in the city. Forgive me, but I did not think any of you reaching out to her would change her position. I felt I could reasonably persuade her differently."

The Chairman asked, "And did you?"

Yi shook his head slightly and said, "I do not believe so. She said she would give it more thought, but my assessment is the position will change when the pressure is too much."

The Chairman asked, "So, communicating with her in private will not help?"

Yi shifted in his chair as well. "In my opinion, Mr. Chairman, it is not necessary. And the inability to change her mind when confronted would make you or Tempest look weak. I have shown her what is at stake, let the plot run its course."

The Chairman and Tempest looked at each other. After a few seconds, The Chairman said, "I concur, Ambassador. Your solidarity in this matter is not overlooked by the people in this room. You are a true ally."

Tempest stood up and, looking at Yi, said, "Thank you for your timely response. I am sure you have other business to attend."

Yi stood up as well, putting his glass of wine down. "Defense Minister, I am at your service."

Yi bowed his head and walked out of the room. He proceeded down two different hallways, his DAG team directly behind him. Yi whispered over his shoulder, "Lieutenant Orlando."

The Lieutenant came up a couple of strides, so that he and Ambassador Yi could be walking side by side. "When Director Kimakawa sends a message to you, and you respond, is it over a private channel?"

The Lieutenant nodded and said, "Yes, Ambassador. It's the same C-Bar Channel you use."

They turned a corner and went through a door outside. The Ambassador said softly, "Alright, no more communication at all. If you receive a message, do not respond, understand?"

The Lieutenant then claimed, "I will be disobeying orders, Ambassador."

Yi stopped and looked directly at his Lieutenant. Very quietly, he said, "From this moment on, you only take orders from me, I will deal with Kimakawa."

Yi turned and walked away. Under his breath, he said, "We are being watched."

BELINEA 6.13

Molar

Populis Pointe

Alexis, Tunsall, and Trujillo continued looking through the T-141 to what other assets they had. Trujillo opened a cabinet and found two rifles, being stored vertically. A box of ammunition was on top of the storage. Trujillo, holding a rifle, said, "Yes…..."

Tunsall nodded his head. Alexis turned to him and said, "Great, how does that help us?"

Trujillo answered, "This will provide us cover."

Alexis continued, "From whom? We don't even know who we are dealing with?"

Tunsall replied, "I am willing to bet it is one of the crime Lords. It's probably not the first abduction/ransom transaction they have done."

Trujillo, smiling, countered sarcastically, "Maybe we can inquire with the locals and see who has the best reputation in times like this? One with Ambassador kidnapping specialization?"

Alexis quickly answered, "They did leave us a note…."

Trujillo continued, "Yes, but do we even know if Bird was on board?"

Tunsall, turning directly to Alexis, added quickly, "Maybe he took a walk and tried to communicate with somebody, like you."

Alexis rolled her eyes slightly, took a small breath, and said, "But the door was blasted?"

Trujillo added after a little silence, "They could have blasted it, just to leave the note. Don't you think he might have left? Or that it is even likely?"

Alexis looked at Trujillo and said, "Shit. You should not have left him."

Trujillo looked right back at her and said, "Nor should have you."

The two just stared at each other for a few more seconds, before Tunsall broke the tension with "Trujillo, I am going to need a hand getting the Sirator out."

Alexis looked at Tunsall and said, "You think these guys are going to fight you in space?"

Tunsall sarcastically responded. "Yeah, I am sure they have a Battle Cruiser."

Alexis continued. "It's probably a crew of four to six guys and small weapons. Instead of the Sirator, perhaps try a pistol?"

Tunsall looked at her and said, "You have no idea what I can do in that thing. Besides, I hope I am wrong, but I bet they got a lot more than six guys."

Alexis replied, "Great. You two got a plan?"

Tunsall looked at Trujillo. Trujillo cut in and said, "We do, if he is thinking what I am thinking. "

Alexis asked, "Which is….?"

Tunsall, still looking at Trujillo, said, "You with the rifle out there…"

Trujillo continued, "You in the Sirator for cover…."

Tunsall nodded his head towards Alexis and said, "She negotiates…"

Trujillo finished with "Yep."

Alexis was confused as to how fast they thought and talked. "Wait, what…?"

Tunsall added, "If only she knew how to fly, then we would really have something."

Trujillo grabbed Tunsall by the shoulder. He looked at him before looking back at Alexis and said, "How much do you remember about what I showed you in the cockpit?"

Alexis, still confused, said, "What?"

Tunsall looked at Trujillo and asked, "You cannot be serious?"

Trujillo quickly replied, "It's not a fucking Sirator. It's a transport ship. It's like flying a personal TC."

Alexis said, "Will one of you tell me what you are talking about?"

Trujillo said, "Let's get the Sirator out, then we teach."

Alexis replied, "Teach what?"

Trujillo gave her a small smile and said, "Teach you how to fly."

Alexis answered, "Are you fucking crazy? That would take hours. That can't even be an option."

Tunsall, on his way walking out, just said, "You got thirty minutes."

BELINEA 6.14

Earth

Northeast Japan

Director Kimakawa was standing in his office next to a shelf. On it was several books, a few medals of admiration, models of spaceships, pictures with each of the Earth Ambassadors, and a Samurai sword that hung horizontally by two handles. A buzzer went off, and Vice Director Meyers entered the room. He said, "You wanted to see me, Director?"

Kimakawa turned around, still standing, and said, "How long will it take to get a DAG team to Marist?"

Meyers was confused. "There is an eight-member DAG team with Ambassador Santos. She is en route to Belinea and should stop at Marist in about five to six hours."

Kimakawa said, "Get a message to that DAG team that we need them to hold on Marist for a day. They have another Ambassador joining them."

Meyers asked, "May I ask who, Director?"

Kimakawa strolled a few steps to the side of his desk. He continued, "I received a message from Alexis through her mother, Annella Devanoe."

Meyers asked, "Why didn't Alexis just send it to you?"

Kimakawa answered, "The Ambassador still doesn't know she works for me. They are together, and it would be suspicious to claim to have access to me. I am sure she suggested her mother as an option. It was very clever on her part."

Meyers asked, "What was the message."

Kimakawa said, "It appears Willits and Jones have gone rogue, perhaps negotiating with someone else. They left her and the Ambassador alone in the guest house at Vihaan Kapoor's estate, which made Alexis suspicious, so they fled. It turns out her suspicions were true."

Meyers looked confused. "In what way?"

Kimakawa answered in a dull tone. "Thirty minutes after she left, the entire Guest House blew up. She believes Willits and Jones detonated a bomb or sold the coordinates to someone else."

Meyers asked, "Have you heard from Willits and Jones?"

Kimakawa shook his head slightly. "No. Nor Vihaan. And I do not expect to. It's possible they still believe the Ambassador and she died in the explosion. Luckily Alexis caught on and got the Ambassador to Ascarla. She then booked a private Civilian transport for the two of them, which should be in Marist in a couple of days..."

Meyers then asked, "I will send a message to the DAG team. They will not like it, but this kind of emergency, they will understand."

Meyers was about to walk out when Kimakawa said, "And Franklin...."

Meyers turned and said, "Yes, Director?"

Kimakawa, still standing next to his desk, said, "I know Willits and Jones have had differences with you. You have been very vocal about not trusting either one of them for some time. I appreciate you refraining the urge to tell me 'I told you so.'"

Meyers looked at him and said, "I am just trying to do what is best for the DAG, sir."

Kimakawa kept his head up, and solemnly replied, "And so am I."

Meyers walked out of the room. A few seconds went by, once Kimakawa knew the place was clear. He walked over to the cabinet with the sword again, touching a spot on the Sun Tzu book, and the cabinet opened. Inside, still holding a glass of scotch, Annella Devanoe walked out. Kimakawa walked back to the chair behind his desk, where he already had a scotch out next to his tablet. Annella walked over to the chair across from the desk and sat down.

After adjusting herself in the chair and taking a sip of scotch, she said, "You are sure?"

Kimakawa replied, "Yes, he is the only answer."

Annella replied "Meyers may not, but I never resist the urge to tell you 'I told you so.'"

Kimakawa just gave her a scolding look. He quietly said, "You never knew either."

Annella quickly answered, "I always knew who it wasn't. Which is more than I can say for you."

Kimakawa took another sip, before leaning back in his chair and crossing his arms. "You don't have to be so smug about it, Annella. It wasn't a contest."

Annella replied, "Maybe not. But any time you admit I was right and you were wrong should be declared a holiday."

Kimakawa rolled his eyes and took a small breath. Annella continued, "Why are we waiting?"

Kimakawa answered, "I may have the evidence. But I don't have the motive, or the puppeteer pulling strings. Until I get that, we keep playing along."

Annella finished her scotch and put the empty glass on Kimakawa's desk. She stood up and said, " The motives rarely change Taichi. Vengeance, financial, or fear, that's it. Your puppeteer? The culprits along the way may surprise you, but we both know where the trail ends."

Annella walked out of the room. Kimakawa just continued to lean back in his chair, pondering, while finishing his scotch. He pulled out a cigar from his humidor, cut it, and took a couple of puffs before reassuming his position. He continued thinking long and hard about what he had to do.

BELINEA 6.15

Avola

Cataco Mines

Octavious was talking with Cortes about their options for Kaya. Both were sitting with very minimal light to expose their faces. All of the light was being used for the miners to continue to dig holes in the rock, looking for a 'dead-spot' to cut through to this mythical 'Cataco Cut Pass.' Cortes then said, "What about a quick strike deployment team?"

Octavious then said, "Even if we knew where she was, we would have to break in and get her. We would likely lose the whole team in a rescue."

There was another pause between the two. Cortes asked, "Can we infiltrate the security?"

Octavious replied, "Possibly, but how do we navigate an escape without knowing where we are escaping from?"

Suddenly, the older miner Lucas yelled, "Everybody quiet!!!"

Octavious and Cortes turned to look up. The other older miner Virgil repeated: "Everybody quiet now!!!"

The room became silent. Lucas began feeling on the rock with both his hands. He moved a few meters until he found a spot just above his head. He moved his hands around it, eventually putting his ear to listen. Quickly walking away, he yelled, "Back up, back up!"

The cave began to shake mildly. A hollow drilling sound could now be heard, and it was getting louder. The room started shaking even more, as if a small earthquake was happening. Dust began flying everywhere. Cortes and Octavious both looked at the ceiling of the cave, waiting for it to collapse. Ten more seconds went by, and the drilling got louder. The spot Lucas was listening to began to shake violently. A large spinning drill bit, over one meter wide, pierced through the rock. Once all the way through, it continued another three meters before finally stopping.

Everyone in the room was still silent. Octavious walked over to Lucas and said, "The Majavkee?"

Lucas said, "Or the rescue team. Hard to say."

Octavious paused for a second. He walked over to the mining teams supply area and pulled out a spray paint can. He walked back over to the drill bit and began spraying paint on it. He said to himself, "Either way, we can not stay here."

Octavious sprayed out "VALMAY" on the drill bit. He then grabbed Lucas' rock hammer and beat the drill bit with it three times. The drill bit ever so slowly, began spinning the opposite way it had come out. It went back out the hole and away, no longer in visual sight. The cave still shook but not nearly as much. A soldier on the other side of the cave yelled, "Ocavious, we got a problem!"

Octavious turned, then quickly walked to the other side of the cave. The soldier was backing up a little as a hefty amount of smoke was coming in. Octavious came up next to him and said, "I think the AuFa found us."

The smoke kept getting thicker and began to come inside the cave. The soldier turned to Octavious and said, "Smoke bombs?"

Octavious nodded and said, "Fire throwers and smoke bombs, then seal the exits. It is what I would do."

He turned to the other miners and said, "Quickly, seal this hole as best you can."

Donovan said, "But how do we breathe? That's our only way out!"

Octavious replied, "Not anymore."

Octavious sprinted to the hole left by the drill bit and shined a light up through it. It looked to be roughly twenty meters high, where he could still see the drill bit spinning out. Octavious then looked at Lucas and said, "What is the protocol for this?"

Lucas said, "They know they broke through. If I were up there, I would send a Zip-cell down to get us."

Octavious nodded, acknowledging what he suspected. He looked over to the side and could see the smoke getting worse. Donovan was helping them and yelled, "Octavious, the smoke is coming through the rock. We can not stop it."

Octavious yelled back, "Keep trying…."

The tunnel stopped shaking for a minute, before mildly shaking again. They could hear something coming down the shaft. A few seconds went by. Finally, a Zip-cell carriage emerged from the hole. It was a tube-shaped cage, with a pointed steel top attached to a cable. When Octavious opened the cage door, someone inside had painted 'RRR.' He smiled. He looked at Lucas and two other miners and said, "Get in, two at a time. Hurry."

The two miners got into the cage, and Octavious hit the cage three times with the rock hammer. The Zip-cell quickly went up the shaft. Thirty seconds went by, and the Zip-cell had returned, empty.

Belinea 6.16

Earth, Northeast Japan

Meyers had walked out of his meeting with Kimakawa down a long hallway. He went to his office and opened the door with his palm print. Once inside, he spoke to the computer and said, "Computer, lock office, no visitors."

The Computer voice said, "Acknowledged."

Inside the office, Meyers walked over to the bookshelf. He pulled a specific book out, and on the other side of the room, a hanging art piece swung open. As he walked over, he pulled out a black box from behind the art. After pushing a button on the side, a tablet came out of the box, and Meyers furiously began to type. After a minute, Meyers stopped, the tablet blinked green and slid back into the box. The computer voice said, "Message sent."

Meyers put the black box back into the wall and shut the art piece in front of it. He walked over to his desk and reached for his tablet. He said to the tablet computer, "Get me a C-Bar transmission to the terminal at Marist."

BELINEA 6.17

Avola

Cataco Cut Pass

Two by two, the remaining soldiers and miners were being jettisoned out of the shaft through the Zip-cell. The cave was getting hot. It was clear flames were outside the hole they had patched outside the shaft. The smoke in the cave filtered to the point of almost zero visibility. Octavious and Cortes were left with another soldier, Donovan, and two older miners, Lucas and Virgil. All six were huddled on the ground waiting for the Zip-cell to return. When it finally did, it nearly crashed next to Cortes.

She opened the gate to let Lucas and Virgil get on, but both went to the side, attempting to let Cortes get on. She yelled at them, "Go. We will be right behind you."

Virgil said, "We will go last. There is no time to argue."

Octavious looked at the old men and said, "We do not leave people behind, go."

But the older men just shook their heads. Donovan then jumped in, followed by Cortes pushing the other soldier into the Zip-cell cage. She slammed the door behind them while Octavious banged on the cage three times. The Zip-cell shot up and out of sight through the hole. As it went away, Octavious grabbed Lucas and said, "Listen to me, you got us this far, we would have never made it without you. You are getting on that next car."

The older men looked at each other and just shook their heads. Lucas said, "We leave last."

Octavious yelled. "This is not a debate; this is an order!"

Lucas said, "We do not take orders from you. You lead them, not us."

Virgil added, "We were born in these caves. We knew one day we would die in them."

The Zip-cell cage landed next to them. Lucas grabbed the door and opened it for Cortes. She climbed in. Octavious climbed in and yelled, "I am sending the cage right back for you!"

Lucas said, "Nobody is going to follow us, but they will follow you!"

Virgil hit the cage three times and, as the Zip-cell was leaving, said, "Give our children hope!"

As Octavious and Cortes were zipping through the shaft hole, they both looked down and could see the smoke through the grate. As they kept going, they eventually saw the flames below engulf the cave. As they got to the top, Cortes and Octavious quickly got out. There was a room of about twenty people. When Octavious emerged, one miner yanked him out while another miner threw him mining clothes. Sterling said, "Change clothes, now."

Octavious yelled back, "There are two more down there!"

Octavious and Cortes were now out of the Zip-cell as the gate closed, and it zoomed back down. Both of them, in front of everyone, changed into mining clothes. Once they changed out, they looked back down the hole. A few filter ventilators were managing most of the smoke from pouring into the cave they were in. Sterling looked at Octavious and said, "You sure, there were two more?"

Octavious yelled, "Yes, two more!"

They waited. And waited. Ten seconds turned into thirty seconds quickly, but there was nothing. Sterling yelled to the miner operating the Zip-cell. "Pull it up."

Octavious yelled, "Did they bang on the cage?"

Sterling looked at him and said, "They are gone."

After twenty seconds, the Zip-cell came up. It was entirely black, burned in a couple of spots.

There were no signs of the old miners. It was clear they died in the flames. Octavious looked distraught. Cortes was still on an oxygen ventilator when Octavious screamed, "Fuck!"

Sterling grabbed Octavious's shirt and said, "Quiet! We still have to get you out of here."

They began heading down a tunnel. They slowly made their way up a two hundred meter path of rocky terrain, narrow passages, and low ceilings.

At the end was a train car, grabbing ten miners at a time. As they sat down, Octavious looked at Sterling and asked, "What is your name?"

The train car began to move. He replied, "My name is Sterling. I am the crew supervisor."

Octavious answered, "Octavious Killian."

Sterling replied, "I know who you are. We all know who you and your sister are."

Octavious nodded and said calmly, "Thank you for rescuing us."

Sterling continued, looking down at the old guy at the end of the train. "Do not thank me. Thank that old guy down there, Butler. When we got that SOS-CCP message, I had no idea what it meant, and I have been mining for twelve years. Butler was the only one who knew."

Octavious nodded and said, "Will do. How do you suppose we get out of here?"

Sterling said, "Walk out of the mines as miners like everyone else. They have not checked security badges for over a year. Where the Guild prevented child labor of any kind, the Majvakee are fine with it. A lot of miners began bringing in their children to help make ends meet, so the Majavkee turned a blind eye. If more was getting mined, they could care less about how it was done. They only care about money."

They continued on the train and now could breathe easier as they got closer to the surface. The small train they were on stopped. All the miners, including Octavious, Cortes, and the rest of the soldiers, crossed an area to a much bigger train car that carried over one hundred miners. Some of the miners were dumping the Vait into large containers off to the side before getting on the open-air train. Finally, the train began moving, and it accelerated to top speed in about a minute. It was a ten-minute ride back up to the surface. When the train met the station, all the miners got off. They lined up to walk through the scanner in a straight line.

Sterling looked at Octavious and said, "It's fine. They are only scanning you for Vait."

There were three scanners, each with a single file line of miners moving through them. Octavious walked through the vertical door frame scanner. Sterling followed Octavious, and when they got out, they continued towards the villages. Octavious got next to Sterling and asked, "Where are we going?"

Sterling glanced at him before answering, "You are coming with me. Every one of your soldiers is going home individually with one of my miners."

Octavious raised an eyebrow. "You trust all of them?"

Sterling looked puzzled at the remark. "You trust all of your soldiers?"

Octavious said proudly, "With my life."

Sterling answered, "So do I. Keep walking, we need to get you somewhere safe."

They walked down a few more blocks and finally entered an apartment complex made from the red rock and hills of Avola. Sterling walked into his place, and Octavious followed. They were greeted by Sterling's wife and his toddler. Sterling said, "Octavious, this is my wife Felicia and my son, Nix."

Octavious said, "Hello. Sterling, I need to get out of here with my soldiers. I am sure they are still looking for us."

Felicia was not happy to see him. She looked at Sterling and interrupted with, "Why is he here?"

Sterling said, "There is no time to answer that Felicia. He will be gone soon."

Felicia, looking at Octavious, said, "Do you know what they have done? What he has done?"

Sterling nodded his head. "Felicia, everyone knows about the attack on the Processing Center. They are trying to escape."

Felicia grabbed her tablet and said, "Have you seen this?"

Sterling grabbed the tablet and began looking at it. It was the press release of the attack on the Processing Center. Octavious looked over Sterling's shoulder. The doctored video showed Octavious attacking a white medical transport as the narrator continued.

"The unsolicited terrorist attack has killed over a hundred, including thirty-seven people on this clearly identified medical transport. Of the thirty-seven people on board, ten were injured children trying to escape the attack. The Majavkee Lords are working closely with

the AuFa to bring the Valmay Opposition Group and their leader, Octavious Killian, to justice."

Octavious looked at Sterling first, before looking back at Felicia. Felicia asked, "How could you kill children?"

Octavious replied. "That's not what happened. The transport was not identified that way. The footage is doctored. We attacked a ship we believe had all the Majavkee Lords onboard."

Felicia just looked at him and said, "Do you think that makes your mistake, justifiable?"

Octavious bowed his head and paused before speaking. "I guess it does not."

Felicia said, "All I know is those children are dead. Who killed them is irrelevant. We do not care about your rebellion. We only care about the collateral damage it causes. A man of faith would understand."

Felecia walked out of the room, still holding the newborn, who was now crying. Sterling just looked at Octavious and said, "She does not mean that."

Octavious wiped his hands on his face and responded, "Yes, she does. I am going to leave."

Sterling said, "Not now. You need safe passage out of here. We have contacted someone. They are coming, be patient."

BELINEA 6.18

Molar

Populis Pointe

The rain began to fall harder. The back bay door to the T-141 was open, with small running lights accenting the ramp. Alexis was at the top of the ramp with a pistol in her hand. She looked down the ramp outside, raindrops splattering everywhere. Alexis re-positioned her earpiece and softly said, "Any movement?"

The voice on her earpiece was Trujillo, who said, "Negative."

Alexis readjusted the light armor she had put on. She replied, "They are late, which means they are likely canvassing the area."

Trujillo answered, "I am looking everywhere, I don't see shit. Wait…., Yep, I got them. Looks like eight, maybe nine guys. Ambassador is in the middle, and he is handcuffed. Walking your way, thirty meters from the ship."

Alexis said, "They didn't teach you counting at the Academy? Is it eight or nine?"

Trujillo replied in an agitated tone, "Eight, plus the Ambassador."

Alexis said, "Copy, that."

Each of the eight men guarding Ambassador Bird had a helmet, a rifle, and wore black trench coats. Three of them wore a night-vision visor while the others suffered through the rain. The Ambassador continued to walk in the middle while the guards kept looking everywhere for movement. Trujillo talked into Alexis' earpiece again and said, "Fifteen meters."

Alexis only said, "Trujillo, don't miss."

Trujillo replied, "Don't worry, it's not counting."

Alexis began walking down the ramp and got to the bottom. The group was ten meters from the ship when Alexis yelled out, "That is close enough."

The group stopped. The man in front took off his helmet and said, "Who are you?"

Alexis answered, "The negotiator. Who are you?"

The man in front just laughed. He continued, "My name is Hendrix. I am the law on this island."

Alexis yelled, "Boss, you alright?"

Ambassador Bird yelled, "Alexis, what are you doing?"

Hendrix looked back at Ambassador Bird while he talked, only to turn his head around towards Alexis. He continued, "Alexis, such a pretty name. Where are your friends Alexis?"

Alexis yelled back, "Just me, Hendrix."

Hendrix smiled again and said, "Come on now, Alexis, the Dock Master said you went into the city with two male friends. He never lies, at least not to me."

Alexis answered, "Maybe you should rethink that relationship. Are you just going to talk, or are we here to barter? You have something of mine. I am willing to pay."

Hendrix laughed again. "Feisty little bitch, I like that. I already told you what I needed. Five times more than what you had in that bag I stole. I see that and your two friends, you get your boss back."

Alexis answered, "I have an equal amount in Belinean credit. It is waiting in the office of your Dock Master via e-currency."

Hendrix said, "That will not work, cupcake. Credit is not popular around here, it leaves a trail. I want the coins. No coins, no return of the Boss man."

Alexis replied, "Well, I guess we got a problem then, don't we?"

Hendrix smiled again and continued, "I am sure a girl of your beauty can negotiate something else. Take this transport ship you have. I might be willing to trade that for the boss man."

Trujillo said into the earpiece. "I got two more guys coming up behind the ship. They are directly behind you, twenty meters. Shift your stance if you copy."

Alexis was standing, with all her weight on her right leg. She shifted all the weight to her left leg to copy Trujillo. The two men strolled slowly with rifles out. They had gotten to fifteen meters now. Alexis said, "I need the ship to get out of here, so that won't work either."

Trujillo was elevated deep in the rocks, twenty meters high, and some thirty meters away with the rifle. He spoke again through his piece. "Tunsall, it's time."

Tunsall spoke into his piece and said, "Copy that."

Hendrix was no longer amused. He simply asked, "What is to stop me from taking the ship from you?"

Alexis just smiled and said, "You think you can?"

As the two guys had crept up to ten meters behind her, Trujillo set his mark and shot. The first shot hit the soldier square in the neck, practically decapitating him on the spot. The other soldier behind Alexis was temporarily stunned. He stopped moving and turned to see where the shot had come from. Looking at the area Trujillo had shot from, Trujillo shot two more rounds directly into the second soldier's faceguard, killing him instantly.

All seven other guys guarding Bird now held their rifles up, not knowing where the shots were coming from. Hendrix grabbed his pistol, and with his other hand, grabbed Bird by the shoulder. He pointed the pistol right at Bird's head and said, "Not cool bitch. Quit shooting or your boss' brains are going to be all over this landing pad."

Alexis walked the ten meters up to Hendrix with her pistol out. She got right up to him, pistol now six inches from him, and said, "Or we can try Option number two, which is you say hello to my friend with the rifle…"

Hendrix was pissed. He pointed his pistol right at Alexis' head and said, "One rifle will not stop me from opening your head up bitch."

Alexis stood still and simply said, "….no, but my other friend might."

Tunsall had come flying in with the F-81 Sirator, engines blazing. He managed to dust up five meters above the ground, and was now hovering directly behind the eight guys. Every single one of them turned when they heard the engines, including Hendrix. In that brief second, Alexis, with her pistol hand, smacked Hendrix's pistol out that he had pointed at her. Trujillo immediately said, "Duck."

Hendrix turned back around after Alexis punched his pistol away. In one swoop, Alexis kicked out the leg of Ambassador Bird, causing both of them to fall to the ground. Hendrix looked at Bird and Alexis, now face down. It was the last thing he saw, as Trujillo put a bullet right in his face. After he saw Bird and Alexis go down, Tunsall started firing away. He killed four instantly, as the other three escaped out the sides. He turned the F-81 a bit to reposition as Trujillo said into his piece, "Alexis go!"

Alexis yelled into Bird's ear and said, "Get up, we gotta run."

Alexis and Bird got up and ran back to the ship and up the ramp. A couple of shots were fired at them, but they missed. Alexis hit the lock on the ramp, and it slowly began to retract. Bird yelled, "What the hell is going on?!"

Alexis climbed into the pilot's cockpit. She tried to remember the procedure, and after hitting a couple of buttons, the engines to the T-141 roared to life. Outside, Trujillo was following one of the guards with his scope. He took a couple of shots, but missed. Tunsall took off high and returned back down, trying to narrow in on a guard running away. Alexis hit a few more buttons, and she pulled back on the stick. Slowly, the T-141 began to take off. One wing was dragging on the ground. Suddenly a man off the landing pad emerged with a handheld rocket launcher. He aimed it at the T-141, which was slowly flying away. The missile fired, and it directly hit the engine below the small wing, exploding it on impact. Alexis lost all control of the T-141, as the body, from five meters high, crashed right back down to the surface. Trujillo yelled, "Alexis!"

Tunsall flew around and now saw where the rocket launcher had come from. He fired his guns on the target, and eventually, after thirty rounds, eliminated the guard. Trujillo saw the other guard running down the pad, and clipped him with a couple of rounds in the leg. Tunsall talked on the radio. "Trujillo, I got one guard running away down the side of the hill, copy visual."

Trujillo was now navigating the rocks back down. He said, "No copy on visual. As long as he keeps running, let him go. I need your backup here."

Tunsall replied, "Copy that."

Trujillo kept climbing down the rocks until, eventually, he got down to the landing surface. He then sprinted over to the crashed T-141. He said into his earpiece, "Alexis, you alright, copy please?"

Nothing. Trujillo kept sprinting, all the way across the landing pad, almost one hundred meters to where the T-141 crashed. The side of the T-141, near the wing, was in flames. The main hull was not. An emergency door had been opened. As Trujillo came running up, Alexis was helping the Ambassador walk out. He had injured his ankle from the crash. Trujillo ran up to them and offered assistance. Both of them were now assisting the Ambassador walk away. Bird kept repeating, "I am fine."

As they got about fifteen meters from the ship, they found a small waiting area off to the side, where they sat the Ambassador down in a chair. Tunsall had landed the F-81 Sirator near them and was already climbing out. Trujillo asked Alexis, "You alright?"

She nodded and replied, "You?"

He nodded. Trujillo then looked at the Ambassador and said, "Are you alright?"

The Ambassador looked at him and nodded. Trujillo followed with, "Good, never leave the fucking ship without us again."

The Ambassador replied, "How do you know I left the ship?"

Trujillo turned away without answering. Tunsall by now had jogged up to them and immediately asked, "Everybody good?"

Alexis answered, "I think the Ambassador sprained his ankle on the crash. Otherwise, we are alright."

The three of them just looked at each other for a few seconds before Alexis said aloud, "Shit, did that just happen? Flawless execution, gentlemen."

Trujillo answered, "Except for your flying…"

Alexis replied, "Really? That guy had one of those rocket things…."

Tunsall reluctantly answered, "A handheld surface to air missile?"

Alexis answered, "Yes, one of those things. And, I managed to fly the T-141 away, so he did not get a clean shot."

Trujillo responded, "You actually call that flying?"

Alexis answered, "What would you call it?"

Trujillo answered, "If I dropped a brick from a building, I guess it's technically flying."

Alexis quickly came back, "Never a lesson in my life, at least I got it off the ground. And what about my move on the Hendrix asshole? Knocked his pistol out, got the Ambassador to the ground? Nothing on that, huh?"

Trujillo answered, "Who dropped that guy like a sack of potatoes? Oh wait, you couldn't see because you were lying on the ground."

Alexis replied, "You *told* me to hit the floor! And, are you sure it wasn't Tunsall that got him because he practically laid out the whole bunch in one swoop."

Trujillo was almost pissed. He instantly replied, "I had a rifle, he is in a Sirator fighter, how did any of them even escape?"

Now Tunsall interjected. "Really? I flew in at twenty percent fighter speed, reversed full throttle, and did a three-sixty degree spin five meters off the ground. After stabilizing, I knocked out half of their crew without a single shot hitting the Ambassador or Alexis. You really think you could have done better?"

Trujillo answered instantly, "Absolutely."

Tunsall replied, "Are you insane?"

Trujillo said, "I knocked out three with a rifle. If I had the Sirator, we'd be halfway to Belinea by now."

Ambassador Bird finally had enough. He yelled, "Will all of you shut the hell up! How are we going to get to Belinea, not that the transport crashed?"

Tunsall, Trujillo, and Alexis looked at each other for a few seconds. None of them had anything to say. Trujillo just muttered to himself, "Shit..."

Alexis then pointed to the sky and said, "Look...."

A light was growing bigger. It was clear after a few seconds that it was a ship coming into land. It was coming right where they were, and as it slowed down, gave the impression it was going to land right next to them, which it did. Trujillo and Tunsall tried to identify the markings, which they realized were AuFa. Trujillo drew his rifle, and Alexis drew her pistol as the frigate landed. Once the engines shut down, the front door of the landing ramp lowered. A few seconds went by, and a man emerged walking down the ramp onto the surface. The ship was twenty meters away, but the man approached quickly, at a brisk walking pace. Trujillo still had his rifle pointed, when Tunsall grabbed the front of it and gently pushed it down. Trujillo said, "Is that...?"

Tunsall softly said, "Alexis, drop your weapon."

Reluctantly she did. As the man got closer, he began to slow down his walking pace. He looked at all three of them, specifically at Tunsall, and said loudly, "Sal... "

Captian Kimmel began walking closer now until he was five meters from Alexis, Trujillo, and Tunsall. Tunsall looked right at him and said, "Hello, Dad..."

BELINEA - EPISODE 7

THE MOLE

BELINEA 7.1

Scotland (Two months prior...)

Annella Devanoe was looking at her daughter. Alexis had grabbed her last bag and was about to walk out the door. Annella said, "Are you sure you have everything?"

Alexis turned around and said, "Yes."

Director Kimakawa walked up behind Annella and stood next to her. Alexis looked at him and said, "Any decision?"

Annella asked, "Decision on what?"

Kimakawa looked at Alexis with a scowl and said, "No. I will be talking with them shortly. I placed initial information and schedule execution in the dossier file BirdFlight on your tablet. There is one more thing."

Alexis straightened up and answered, "Yes, Director?"

Kimakawa continued. "I cannot explain everything. But many factors drove my decision to choose you for this assignment, the biggest one being trust. I need to know that you will not reveal yourself to anyone. Trust no one. You must not give any indication that you are anything more than a bright, helpful assistant. Understand?"

Alexis nodded and said, "Yes, sir."

Annella took a few steps forward and hugged her daughter. She said, "Safe travels."

Alexis returned the hug and whispered, "Bye."

Alexis walked out of the room and outside to a personal TC, which promptly brisked her away. Annella and Kimakawa walked down the path towards her porch area. Annella's dog walked beside her. Annella said, "I presume you are going to tell me about this assignment? I don't like you putting her in a situation where she cannot protect herself."

Kimakawa responded, "I am telling you now, with Yi. Annella, Alexis, is perfectly capable of taking care of herself. She knows the risks."

As they entered the covered patio, Ambassador Yi was already seated, enjoying a hot tea. He stood up as Kimakawa and Annella walked into the room. Yi said, "Alexis get off, alright?"

Annella nodded and poured herself some tea. "Taichi, is now going to explain why he has summoned us."

Yi and Kimakawa looked at each other. Everyone was sitting now, as Kimakawa began. "We have a potential problem. The Belineans have been made aware of our DAG team looking for a Vait supplier."

Yi interrupted, "How?"

Kimakawa answered, "That is what we do not know."

Yi continued, "I can tell you our Council security group has heard nothing. Nether Tempest nor the Chairman have inquired."

Kimakawa answered, "It could be they believe you do not know, and the DAG is doing this alone. It could be they are trying to discover how much you do know. Perhaps find out how much they should trust you, or use as leverage later."

Yi thought for a second before he said, "Possible. The other Ambassadors and I have heard rumblings that the Majavkee on Avola have problems with the Vait flow and production. The local rebels, the Valmay Group, have been wreaking havoc. The belief is they are selling Vait on the Black Market, refusing to sell any of it to the Council or Belineans."

Annella looked at Kimakawa and said, "The Valmay. That is who your DAG team is trying to contact, correct?"

Kimakawa nodded. He continued. "Yes. We can continue to buy it from the smuggler's who purchased it from the Valmay, but the amounts are minimal. Our goal was to set up a purchase agreement directly with the Valmay for much more, but we have yet to make contact."

Yi countered, "Then how did the Belineans find out? Is it possible your team accidentally made contact with the Majavkee instead of the Valmay? At least that would explain how the Belineans know."

Kimakawa continued. "It is possible. There is another theory, though. Perhaps the DAG group went rogue. Bribed and are now working as spies for the BRG. Either way, I believe the leak came from them."

Annella countered, "A mistake or the Majavkee simply finding out and relaying it to the Belineans is more plausible. Working for the BRG is a crazy theory, even for you, Taichi."

Kimakawa continued, "Is it? My source tells me a mole in our group channels information to the SS and BRG. The belief is the mole is in my inner DAG circle at headquarters. But I trust the four in the circle and both of you. Therefore I must consider other options. The DAG team would make sense."

Annella asked, "Who is leading the DAG team?"

Kimakawa hesitated, then said, "You know I can not tell you that."

Annella responded, "If we are going to flush out the mole, we need to start by trusting each other on everything."

Kimakawa hesitated again before replying, "The DAG team is led by Commanders Nolan Willits and Avery Jones."

Annella smiled and leaned back in her chair. "Willits and Jones? I know those two. I highly doubt they are conspiring with the Belineans. And if it were someone on their team, they would know. If there is a mole, Taichi, it is internally in your office. Or one of us."

Kimakawa smiled, and while looking at Yi, continued, "Nevertheless, I have come up with a plan to sniff the mole out. Ambassador Garvalin is still on our side about expanding personal security, intelligence, and small military among the planets, correct?"

Yi nodded and answered, "Privately, Garvalin and I are aligned. Defense Director Hassara has let me know that at some point, there will be an initiative to ask the Council to increase the BRG and AuFa budget by ten percent. Perhaps that is the reason for leaking the rumblings, using Avolian turmoil as the excuse. Garvalin and I are merely waiting our time to drop the counter-proposal for an expanded guard."

Kimakawa said, "What if we give them Ambassador Bird, instead?"

Annella questioned, "What do you mean?"

Kimakawa, now looking at Yi, continued. "You said Bird has wanted to talk about reducing our budget to the AuFa and BRG and allocating the money to our own defense. So let him. In fact, encourage it. Let him start the rhetoric, make big speeches, write memos, make it his public platform. Let's see what the BRG does in response."

All three looked at each other, pondering what Kimakawa just said. After ten seconds, Yi said, "Hassara and the rest of the family would likely be pissed, but I could spin it where I still had their trust. I could say let me talk to the new junior Ambassador, smooth things over. It might work. But what about the mole? You said sniff out?"

Kimakawa answered, "I am going to pull Willits and Jones off assignment and tell them I need the best two officers to lead Bird's security detail, mainly because of all his new rhetoric. If they are the mole, and I think they are, the BRG will be ecstatic to have a spy that close to the guy giving public speeches questioning their effectiveness. The BRG would certainly want to talk to Bird, at the very least, monitor him. They would likely go through Willits and Jones to do it. Alexis will observe the whole situation and report any unusual activity when it does."

Yi countered with, "You will take the whole team off assignment?"

Kimakawa quickly answered, "Just the two of them. I found an apparent loophole. I will let Meyers pick a couple of his pilots to join the detail team."

Annella asked, "Meyers knows your plan?"

Kimikawa answered, "Not entirely. The inner four in my circle know the DAG team is inquiring about Vait, but nothing about Willits and Jones seeking out the Valmay group. Meyers will suspect something when I pull them off assignment. My disdain for their insubordination, which doubles as the truth, and the lack of progress with the Vait inquisition will be reason enough."

Yi asked, "What if Alexis finds something that proves Willits and Jones are the moles. How will she contact you? What do we do?"

Kimakawa smiled. "She can always contact me through Annella. We have another DAG team waiting for them on Belinea. Arresting the two DAG officers who are spying for the BRG in front of the Council on Belinea? This is how we save face with Hassara, the family, the BRG, and the SS. We are secretly buying Vait? You are spying on us. We are even."

Yi asked, "What if you are wrong about Willits and Jones?"

Kimakawa answered, "If they get Bird to Belinea without incident, and Alexis doesn't witness anything unusual, then the mole is likely in my inner-circle. I will deal with that accordingly."

Annella took a sip of tea before responding, "I am alright with this plan, as long as neither of you interferes with Alexis. I do not believe it is Willits and Jones, so I am sure Bird will get to Belinea just fine. But any communication has to go through me. Otherwise, it sets off a red flag, and her life is in danger, understand?"

Yi and Kimakawa, reluctantly, nodded in approval. Annella continued, "However, Taichi, I think this is a big waste of time. If there is a mole, it is right under your nose."

BELINEA 7.2

The Frigate - Leaving Molar

Nick Devanoe was in the cockpit chair of the Frigate. The Frigate was a small patrol cruiser, usually with a crew of fourteen. This particular one, a loan from Lord Malovex, had a two-person crew of Captain Kimmel and Commander Devanoe. They now had an additional four passengers. Cadet Miguel Trujillo was in the chair next to Nick, as Nick gave him a brief rundown on how to fly the Frigate. Nick continued, "Your fuel gauge is here, bearing and course is here, speed and trajectory are here, got it?

Trujillo nodded, "Yeah, easy. I got it. This thing moves faster than I thought."

Devanoe nodded and said, "These new ones are faster than the Battle Cruisers. I am going to the back to talk with Alexis as long as you feel good."

Trujillo turned to him and said, "How do you know I won't turn this thing around and head back to Molar? I still think we should have waited on Commander's Willits and Jones."

Devanoe answered, "There is no guarantee they even made it off Torsalli. They have the entire AuFa and BRG looking for them."

Trujillo responded, "Willits told us if we didn't hear from him to get the Ambassador to Belinea by any means possible."

Devanoe countered with, "And that is what you are doing, onboard an AuFa Frigate no less."

Trujillo said, "But we didn't wait, and those were my orders."

Devanoe replied, "Given the circumstances, you are following orders. You guys did well."

Trujillo looked back at his control panel and said, "Willits also said not to trust anyone."

432

Nick gave a small smile and said, "That is wise. I don't know who you trust at this point. If I wasn't Alexis' brother, I am not even sure how much you should trust the AuFa."

Trujillo added "Or the BRG?"

Nick looked at him again for a second before responding. "Look, I have worked with a lot of solid AuFa officers, including Captain Kimmel back there, who don't look at me differently for being human."

Trujillo asked, "Are you saying I have a chance in the AuFa?"

Nick asked, "I thought you and Tunsall wanted to join the DAG?"

Trujillo responded, "We got recruited for this assignment. We would rather be flying Sirator's on a Carrier."

Nick smiled again and said, "So would I. Despite what you have heard, it's getting better. You will find out, the AuFa is changing, becoming more diverse. The BRG and the SS? That's completely different. Lords Malovex and Argo have their own agenda; it doesn't include anyone that is not full Quill Belinean."

Trujillo went back to looking at his control panel. "Good to know."

Nick continued to walk out to the back, past the empty Captain's conn chair. As he left, he said, "We'll talk later."

Tunsall and Alexis had got done wrapping and fixing Bird's ankle. Tunsall said, "Stay off it for an hour or two, the blood-mix infusion will help the swelling, and you should be fine."

Alexis looked at Tunsall and said, "Thanks."

Tunsall nodded and walked up to the map board and communication center, where Captain Kimmel was surveying the screen. Nick Devanoe arrived from the other direction at the same time Tunsall did. Nick spoke first, "Trujillo has the conn. He will alert us if anything unusual pops up."

Kimmel looked up at Tunsall and said, "Become good pilots, have we?"

Tunsall said nothing. Kimmel looked back at the screen and said, "This course will get us to Hovron in under two days. After that, we will look at options."

Nick replied, "Get the Ambassador on a Battle Cruiser to Belinea?"

Kimmel looked up again. "No. We will find a way to get me back to Torsalli. No communications. You take this Frigate, on my orders, all the way to Belinea. After everything that has happened, this will be the only way to get Ambassador Bird there safely. Nobody needs to know he is alive and onboard except us."

Nick nodded in agreement and simply said, "Yes, sir."

Captain Kimmel then asked, "Commander Devanoe, will you give us a moment?"

Nick nodded and continued to walk to the back where Alexis and Bird were having a discussion. Kimmel looked at Tunsall and calmly said, "How did you get on this assignment?"

Tunsall calmly responded, "Two DAG officers asked, so we volunteered. We thought it would be good experience for our careers."

Kimmel responded, "You should have told me. These morons clearly cannot go from A to B without getting shot at."

Tunsall quickly replied, "They are not incompetent, sir. They are good soldiers."

Kimmel gave Tunsall a stern look and said, "They are glorified security guards, and this is too big for them."

Tunsall shook his head and said softly, "That is not true. I have learned a lot. Willits and Jones are smart tacticians...."

Kimmel now raised his voice slightly, "Willits and Jones almost got you killed. Without us, you and Trujillo would be waiting for them on Molar with your thumbs up your ass."

Tunsall quickly replied, "I still think we should have waited for them ...."

Kimmel was now annoyed and said, "Son, do you really think they made it out of Torsalli alive? Even if they did, you think they would still try to find you two?"

Tunsall looked up and took a breath. Calmly he said, "I do. Just because they are not AuFa does not mean they lack principles. They are loyal and smart enough to get out of Torsalli."

Kimmel softly said, "You think those two could flee the entire BRG and AuFa?"

Tunsall cut him off and said, "Yes. I think you should give them some credit."

There was a long pause between the two of them. Kimmel finally said, "There was another attack on the Torsalli Space Port. It was an explosion of the Ambassador's C-62T. It killed two people on board, which, given it was none of you four, means they were likely BRG or AuFa. You better get used to the fact that you will never see Willits or Jones alive again because the BRG and AuFa are not looking, they are hunting them."

Tunsall said nothing.

Behind them, Nick had joined his sister Alexis and Ambassador Bird. Nick asked Bird, "You feeling better?"

Bird nodded and just said, "I am fine."

Alexis asked, "This Captain Kimmel you serve under….he is Tunsall's father?"

Nick just nodded and softly said, "Yeah…"

Alexis replied, "You trust him?"

Nick looked oddly at his sister. "He is my commanding officer and a highly respected Captain in the AuFa with almost thirty years experience."

Bird acknowledged, "This is the safest I have felt on this entire trip. I am not losing any sleep with him in charge instead of Willits and Jones. It is a wonder we are not dead."

Alexis looked at her brother and said, "Do you know where they are?"

Nick shook his head and responded, "No. They were last seen boarding a transport to Ascarla on the surface. The Ambassador's C-62T blew up just after, in the Torsalli Space Port. Everyone thinks the Ambassador is dead. (Now looking at Alexis) You too."

Bird asked, "Wait, *another* attack? How did you find us?"

Alexis held up her wristwatch tracker. Nick replied, "I gave Alexis a wristwatch tracker on Braccus. I have the match. She hit the panic button, which activates it."

Bird responded, "Thank you, Commander. I feel that if you and Alexis were in charge of my security detail instead of Willits and Jones, we would be on Belinea by now."

Nick gave a smile. Alexis squinted though, still thinking about this. She then said, "Willits and Jones are not the problem, Ambassador. They split us up because they thought there would be another attack, and they were right."

Nick countered, "Or they caused it. The explosion was internal, and the ship was docked."

Alexis thought for a second. Then, looking at Ambassador Bird, she said, "They wanted everyone to think you were dead. At the risk of them being fugitives and being on their own. Why?"

The three of them looked at each other for a few seconds, not saying anything. Finally, Nick said, "Captain Kimmel told me when we get to Hovron, I am to take you to Belinea myself on this Frigate, no communication to anyone. He will find a way back to Torsalli."

Bird said, "I was unable to get a message to Kimakawa when I was on Molar, but I'll be damned if I will not send him one when we get to Hovron. This entire experience has been unacceptable from the start...."

Alexis had her head down and kept thinking as Bird kept talking to Nick. After a few seconds, she popped her head up and said to the Ambassador, "You will do no such thing."

Bird was taken aback. He politely answered, "Excuse me?" May I remind you who you work for, Miss Devanoe?"

Alexis kept thinking and then answered, "I work for you, sir, but that's not the point. The Captain is right, no communication to anyone."

Bird, still a little miffed at the insubordination, said, "Why?"

Alexis replied, "Willits and Jones have been one step ahead of everyone this entire time. We keep getting attacked at where we *should* be, not where they lead us. Tunsall!"

Tunsall turned around from talking with Captain Kimmel. He said, "Yes?"

Alexis asked, "The DAG team did a full security sweep on the Ambassador's C-62T before we left Earth, correct?"

Tunsall nodded and added, "Yeah. Willits made us do a quick sweep on Vandabri. And the BRG team did a full sweep on Braccus. They found nothing."

Alexis turned to Nick and Bird and whispered more to herself, "We were not being tracked. But they knew where we were supposed to be. It's not Willits and Jones….."

Nick was confused, as was Bird. Nick said, "What's not Willits and Jones?"

Alexis kept whispering to herself. "Torsalli was not random, that was their out….they knew it was internal…."

Alexis then turned to Captain Kimmel and yelled across the room. "Captain Kimmel, thank you for understanding. You are correct. No communication is the best policy. Any further assistance you can provide for us is greatly appreciated."

Alexis then grabbed Nick's elbow and said, "Come with me…."

Nick followed her down the back hall to the private quarters' area, Whispering, Nick said, "What the hell is going on…."

Alexis looked around to make sure they were alone and said, "Big brother, I need a favor out of you when we get to Hovron."

Nick looked confused, "What?"

Alexis said, "Get a secure message to mother."

Nick frowned. He said, "I would rather piss a pair of scissors. Why can't you?"

Alexis answered, "They might be tracking my communication channels. You can send it via a secure AuFa channel, and it won't raise a single red flag."

Nick was confused. He said, "Red flag with who? Who would be tracking your communication?"

Alexis continued, "Whoever is trying to kill the Ambassador."

BELINEA 7.3

Lowell Province

Avola

Sterling had left, leaving Octavious waiting for over an hour, alone in his living quarters. Felicia, Sterling's wife, walked into the room, this time without the toddler Nix. Octavious stood up, out of politeness. He said, "Forgive me, I will be gone soon."

Felicia said nothing as she stood there looking at him. After a long pause, Octavious said, "I would have already left had Sterling not been so adamant about me staying."

Felicia asked, "Where is he?"

Octavious replied, "I do not know. He said he would be right back."

Felicia took a deep breath. After a few seconds, she said, "You know, Sterling tries to defend the Majavkee. They made him a supervisor, but all I see is him working more hours for almost the same pay."

Ocatvious took a step forward and softly said, "I am aware. I hear that from all the miners."

There was another pause as if Felicia was pondering what to say. She took another breath and said, "We sometimes argue because my field stone is blue, my passion is the Quill. Sterling's is orange, although he doesn't use his stone the way that you do."

Octavious quietly responded, "Few of us exist anymore. If the Council found out we were teaching our children *our* Quill, and not the Belinean Quill, they would come for our heads."

Felicia looked at him for a second and very softly whispered, "Red Ring Rise...."

Octavious, reluctant to ever admit such a title, nodded and whispered, "Yes...."

Felicia took another breath and said, "And the Majavkee? They believe you twist the Quill. That you use your power for weapons."

Octavious asked politely, "You believe they have faith?"

Felicia replied, "I do not know. They appear to be loyal servants of the Quill."

Octavious replied, "A facade. I doubt any of them have set foot in a Temple. But they certainly preach like they do. It allows the Belineans to choose sides."

Felicia replied, "There are different variations, but we all believe the same Quill principles. Why would the Belineans and the Council not back you?"

Octavious answered, "Greed. We would fight them, while they see the Majavkee as allies in their pursuit to mine as much Vait as possible, regardless of what it does to our planet. "

Felicia was emotional. "I see children dying. Innocent people slain. They say in the name of the Quill, but who wins? The Majavkee seem to get richer, and we are no better off. We are trying to make a better place for our children, for Nix…."

Octavious interjected, "So am I…."

Felicia said, "But how does killing Belineans and Majavkee do that? The more of them you kill, the more of us they kill. It never ends. And there are more of them, and less of us. If they only care about the Vait, why not give it to them so we can live in peace."

Octavious replied, "It is not that simple…."

Felicia replied, "Why not? What makes it complicated?"

Octavious did not know what to say. Felicia began to cry. He stood in silence for ten seconds, trying to articulate his next words. "If the Council and the Belineans stopped their aggressive mining and restored the Guild, I would no longer fight. If they left us free to practice my religion with my family, I would not fight. But they will not stop, nor will I."

Felicia, in tears, interjected, "You threaten the children in our homes…."

Octavious, tilting his head, said, "It's my home too!"

Felicia looked at him for a second, wiping a tear from her face. Octavious continued, "And they do not play by our rules, they have no moral compass or faith. I am fighting for my home. I am fighting so your children will still have a home, long after we are gone."

Felicia looked at him, tears still rolling down her face. A few seconds passed. She took a small breath and said, "Then win."

Octavious's eyes got a little bigger. The door opened, and Sterling walked in. He said, "Ready?"

Octavious nodded and put a hood on over his head. He walked over to Felicia and grabbed her shoulder. He looked at her and waited until she was looking back at him. He whispered, "I will, or I will die trying."

Octavious then walked out, with Sterling right behind him. Sterling caught up and got to the lead. Sterling asked Octavious, "You alright?"

Octavious replied, "I am fine. Where are we going?"

Sterling half smiled and "Time to pray…."

Octavious asked, "You do not have to help me."

Sterling said, "I am aware."

Octavious stopped. Looking at Sterling, he asked, "Then why do you?"

Sterling replied, "I do not know. I am not sure if I believe in you or not. But Balerra does, and I believe in her, and my faith."

Sterling pivoted to walk, and Octavious followed. They turned at another block and continued four more blocks, closer to the center of town. Octavious said, "I thought we were trying for a low cover?"

Sterling responded, "We are, just right under their noses."

They passed a couple of Majavkee Security Officers in the street. They then turned one more corner, and in front of them was a Quill Temple. Octavious looked at Sterling and said, "You are joking, right?"

The two walked into the Temple. They saw the diamond shape figure on the wall, and both bowed their heads. They began walking down the middle aisle. Approaching from the back was a Quillsar, that met them at the front of the aisle, underneath the Diamond-shaped emblem on the wall. Octavious gave a small bow as he said, " My Quillisar…"

Balerra was a very old lady, her red Quillisar Priest cloak looked ragged and used. Octavious bowed, as Balerra had no time for pleasantries. She said, "Come with me, my child, your face is far too recognizable."

Octavious followed Balerra behind the wall of the Temple. As she was walking, she continued talking, "We evacuated most of your soldiers, but you will be a bit trickier."

Octavious replied, "My soldiers are already out?"

Balerra had turned a corner and came up to a small dressing room, where she began rummaging through a closet. She replied, "Yes, with the help of an old friend. They are easier to hide because the Majavkee are not looking for them; they are looking for you."

Octavious was still slightly confused. Quillisar Balerra shoved a Red Priest Cloak into his chest. She said, "This is from Quillisar Yovollo. He was killed in the bombings. It might be tight, but it should work well enough."

Octavious looked at Balerra and said, "You want me to be a Quillisar Priest?"

Balerra looked at Octavious and replied, "Really, Octavious? We need to get you out of here."

Octavious looked at her and said, "I have done many terrible things, Balerra, but pretending to be a Quillisar feels like a sin."

Balerra looked at him and said, "The goal is for you not to talk, but on the off chance you do, The Blue Code 17?"

Octavious looked up, trying to recite it. "Out of the mouths of our children, the sacrifices and offerings yet to be disposed, the energy has prepared the body for existence, one that has taken no pleasure, one that has committed no sin, but only a voice that cries, the energy is now folded into all of us."

Balerra added "Although, in these troubling times, I prefer 'So also the tongue is a small muscle, capable of the strongest things, how great a forest can be set ablaze, by the slightest of fires.'"

Octavious nodded and said, "The Orange Code 11, one of my favorites."

Balerra grabbed his cheek and said, "Octavious, I have known you your entire life. You know as much as any Quillisar does. Let the energy come for me and take me away if this is a sin. Now, put the damn red cloak on."

Octavious put the red cloak on and covered most of his head with the hood. Octavious looked up, before looking down again, and said to Balerra, "Following you."

Quillisar Balerra began to walk out the back of the Temple, Octavious following in his red cloak, Sterling a few steps behind. They walked down to the playground area. Even though it was just nightfall, some of the older children were still playing. They found the entrance where a woman was standing. A voice came out, "Alright, children time to go."

Octavious recognized the voice, but continued to keep his head down. He whispered, "Syren?"

Former Ambassador Syren was ushering the children out of the playground. As she was waving her arms, she quietly whispered to Octavious, "Do not say another word."

Syren said much louder now, still waving her arms, "Come along children, right this way."

Syren, Sterling, another adult caregiver, Balerra, and Octavious began walking with ten children towards the landing pads that were two blocks away. Once they got there, it was a rock area, flat, made up of six pads. Three aircraft were parked. A beat-up transport, with Quill markings on the side, had a door open. It was clearly the Quill shuttle. Two armed Majavkee Security and two AuFa soldiers were guarding the landing pad facility. The AuFa guards were sitting down, having a drink, while the Majavkee soldiers guarded the entrance.

As they came through, Syren began guiding the children through the entrance, towards the beat-up transport shuttle. The Majavkee soldiers said, "Hold on, where are you all going?"

Syren replied to the Majavkee soldiers, "I am Ambassador Syren, let us through. We are taking the children to the Bosa Temple for the night."

One of the Majavkee soldiers said, "We will need identification for everyone."

Quillisar Balerra walked up next to Syren and said, "These are children, and I am their Quillisar. The children have nowhere to stay tonight. "

The other Majavkee soldier said, "I do not give a shit who you are. We need to see everyone's identification."

Syren looked over at the two AuFa soldiers, who had now got up and started walking over. Syren politely yelled at them, "Excuse me…"

The two AuFa soldiers came up next to them, and one of them said, "Can we help you?"

Before Syren could say a word, Balerra walked up to the AuFa soldier and said, "Would you like to explain to your Quillisar back home about how you roughed up some children and Quillisar's on Avola? Perhaps if I told Quillisar Prill of your actions, he could speak to your Commanding Officer about your bravery."

The one AuFa soldier just said, "Quillisar, what is the problem?"

Balerra looked at the Majavkee soldiers and said, "Them."

The AuFa soldiers turned and looked at the Majavkee soldiers as well. One of the Majavkee soldiers said, "We need to see their identification, we have orders."

The other AuFa soldier said, "Are you kidding? Them?"

The other Majavkee soldier pointed at Sterling and said, "What about him?"

The other AuFa soldier looked at Sterling and asked, "Who are you?"

Sterling whipped out his identification and said, "Sterling Oppenmeadow. I am a Miner, Crew Supervisor in Lowell Province. My Quillisar asked for help."

Nobody looked at his identification, though. The AuFa soldier just looked at the Majavkee Security and said, "This is why they hate you guys. The Valmay burned up in those caves. There will be no survivors. But you two want to harass a couple Quillisar's, some children, and a miner because they pose a threat?"

The other AuFa soldier had already opened the gate and started allowing them through. He said to Balerra, "My apologies Quillisar, please come through."

As everyone was now walking through, Balerra looked up at the AuFa soldier that was letting them pass, and said, "When was the last time you went to Temple?"

The AuFa soldier gave a small smile and replied, "Over a week ago, Quillisar. At the Sun Offering."

Everyone had passed through and was now boarding the shuttle. The engines had turned on, and a little dust had popped up. Balerra looked at the

AuFa soldier and said, "Then make sure you come to Temple this week. You can come to mine. It's a couple of blocks away. And bring these two (looking at the Majavkee soldiers), they could use the guidance."

The AuFa soldier just smiled and said, "Yes, Quillisar."

As Balerra was walking to the shuttle and being assisted on to it by Sterling, she could hear the AuFa soldier behind her talking to the Majavkee soldiers. "Seriously, what is wrong with you two? Octavious Killian is dead, and you want to mess with the clergy and children too?"

As the transport shuttle took off, Balerra and the other caregivers said to the children, "Settle down children, you will only get a reward if you behave."

Syren sat down next to Octavious, while the transport was already flying away. Syren said, "I did not expect to see you alive. We heard about the attack on the Processing Center and the base being destroyed. We were shocked. Do you know about Kaya?"

Octavious said, "She is alive, correct?"

Syren said, "From what we know, yes. Lord Argo wants to trade her life for yours, but he believes you are dead."

Octavious said, "Oh, I will give him that trade if he wants it. Where are we going?"

Syren just looked at him and said, "Home."

The transport shuttle took a small banking turn and headed across the desert rock.

BELINEA 7.4

Avola

AuFa Base Six

Lord Argo walked into the control room. Around a large screen, table were several AuFa officers, including Captain Leahy of the SS. Lord Bialos and Lord Evander of the Majavkee were behind an old miner, who was at the center of the table pointing. Argo walked up to the screen table and said, "Status?"

Everyone turned and looked at Argo. Leahy, pointing at the screen, was the first to say something. "My Lord, the Valmay Group was chased here, to the Cataco Mines in the Bosa Province. The AuFa made their way down each of these shafts, leaving a company behind at every entrance, here, here, and here. Based on some newly mined debris, we believe the Group went down this abandoned tunnel, number eleven. They were likely trying to hide and ride it out. But we sent in a smoke team, pouring flamethrowers down the tunnel. It has yet to clear of the smoke and fire, but without protective gear, which they did not have, there is no way they survived."

Argo looked at the screen and replied, "When the flames subside, get a team in there and verify the bodies, whatever is left of them."

Lord Bialos replied, "My Lord, is it safe now to get the Vait shipments to the AuFa ships?"

Argo answered, "Yes. It will take some smaller transports since we blew up the big ones. But that is the price you pay for peace. Send out a final call, process it here. I want all the Vait on the Battle Cruiser that will return with me to Belinea tomorrow."

Lord Evander spoke, "The price we agreed upon, my Lord?"

Argo just tilted his head. "Lord Evander, the price we have always paid. Be thankful I am not taking the Vait for free after all the shit you guys have created for us, miserable pricks."

Lord Evander was taken back and said, "My Lord, I meant no disrespect."

Argo turned around to walk out, "No, it's just your native tongue."

Argo kept talking as he was walking out, and said, "I do not care if it is char-broiled. I'm not leaving this shithole until someone brings me the body of Octavious Killian."

BELINEA 7.5

Hovron

The Frigate was on a landing pad at the AuFa base on Hovron. It was a small base, with about fifty AuFa vessels scattered around. Alexis was standing in the doorway on top of the ramp, which led inside the ship. She was looking around to make sure no one was watching. Nick finally came walking up the ramp. Nick said as he walked up to Alexis, "Message sent, although it doesn't make any sense."

Alexis answered, "I know, but it will to her."

Nick shrugged his shoulders, and said, "Alright, what now?"

Alexis answered, "Kimmel got back from the Control Tower a couple of minutes ago. I believe he is inside gathering a couple more things and saying goodbye to Tunsall."

Tunsall and Kimmel were standing inside the quarters of the ship. Kimmel took a breath and said, "The plan after graduation still involves you becoming an officer in the AuFa…."

Tunsall snapped back and said, "That was always your plan…not necessarily mine."

Kimmel responded, "So now you want to be a pilot in this incompetent security group, chauffeuring Ambassadors to and from? Did Trujillo put you up to this? He is the reason for you not graduating first in your class, and now this."

Tunsall rolled his eyes a little bit and responded, "Trujillo did not put me up to this, and he is not the reason I am not graduating first in my class. We still want to fly Sirator's. We are just looking at all our options."

Kimmel looked at Tunsall and said, "And you can fly Sirators, in the AuFa, I can arrange that."

Tunsall asked "And Trujillo?"

Kimmel just tilted his head and said nothing. After a few seconds, Tunsall said, "I never asked for your help. Regardless of what happens, we prefer to do it on our own."

Kimmel took a deep breath and said, "Understand there is no future for this DAG security force. Joining it would be a huge mistake."

Tunsall responded, "And it would be my mistake, not yours."

Kimmel took another deep breath and said, "After graduation, there are things we need to discuss at home, alright?"

Tunsall nodded and said, "Sure…."

Kimmel hugged Tunsall and said, "Despite my misgivings, I am proud of how you have handled this assignment Salvador, with honor."

They embraced for a couple of seconds before Tunsall finally said, "Thank you, father."

As they let go of each other, Kimmel said, "Trust Devanoe, he will get you there safely. No communication with anyone until you get to Belinea, understand?"

Tunsall nodded and said, "Yes, sir."

Kimmel walked out with Tunsall behind him. When they got to the ramp that led down to the ground, Trujillo, Alexis, Nick, and Ambassador Bird were all there. Kimmel looked directly at Bird and said, "I am using my best judgment and not turning you over to the BRG, as I should. I hope we have an understanding that you, in turn, will not try to communicate with anyone until you get to Belinea."

Bird looked at him for a few seconds. "I trust my assistant, and it is what she recommends as well. I am grateful for your assistance, and will let your commanding officers know what you have done."

Kimmel gave a crooked smile, "Thank you, Ambassador, but it's better my commanding officers know nothing about this."

Bird nodded, understanding. Kimmel looked directly at Tunsall and Trujillo and said, "Commander Devanoe is in charge until you get to Belinea."

Tunsall and Trujillo both nodded. Kimmel looked at Nick and said, "Your manifest says this is a cargo frigate for Admiral Flynn, bound to Belinea. Once you get there, leave them (nodding at the Ambassador) with the local BRG. Check-in with the Admiral, explain to him what happened. Tell him my orders are for you to take the Frigate back to Torsalli unless he has another mission for you. Understand?"

Nick gave a quick salute and said, "Copy that, sir."

Kimmel returned the salute and walked down the ramp. He said, "Safe travels."

Kimmel got almost to the bottom before Nick said, "Captain…"

Kimmel stopped and turned around. Nick continued, "Thank you, sir, this won't happen again. Moving forward, I will not let my personal feelings affect my judgment to perform the duties of being your first officer."

Kimmel just chuckled and said, "I hope they do…."

Nick paused and tilted his head, a little shocked by the answer. Kimmel waited a couple of seconds before he replied, "If I did not think you had the acumen to handle the job, you would not have it."

Kimmel turned around and started walking away. Never looking back, after a few steps, he said, "You are a good soldier, Devanoe."

Kimmel walked out of the site, leaving Nick to ponder what Kimmel had said. He briefly smiled before hitting the lever to lift the ramp door. It locked into place, as Nick and Trujillo walked to the bridge area. They slid into the cockpit chairs, Trujillo on the left, Nick on the right. Trujillo touched some spots on the screen while Trujillo fired up the engines and said into his intercom, "Tower, this is Frigate 1182. I have a flight plan for Belinea, request permission to take off."

There was a pause, and the Tower said, "Permission granted."

The Frigate roared to life and gently began to ascend into the sky. After a few minutes, they were in space. They hit the switches, and the ship was jumping into HyperExtension speed. After a few more minutes of gaining proper momentum, Trujillo said to Nick, "I got first shift. You and Tunsall take a break."

Nick replied, "You sure?"

Trujillo nodded, and Nick unbuckled himself. Nick got up and walked back off the bridge towards the back. He noticed Tunsall lying down on a sofa next to Bird's quarters. Alexis was looking at the Communications screen, then walked up to Nick. "How long before Mom gets her present?"

Nick answered, "The AuFa has a C-Bar communication. So from here, maybe forty-five minutes?"

Alexis said, "Alright. We should be fine in the meantime."

Nick replied, "I spent most of the flight piloting the Frigate to Hovron. I am going to try and get a few hour's sleep. Alright?"

Alexis nodded, and Nick went further back into the quarters to go lay down. Alexis went up front to see Trujillo. When she got there, he was already very comfortable in the chair. He glanced behind, almost sensing her presence. She said, "Hey…"

Trujillo nodded and returned to looking at the screen. He replied, "Hey…"

Alexis got right next to him, right behind his ear, and whispered, "You took out those two assholes on Molar…."

Trujillo nodded and said, "And the Hendrix asshole…."

Alexis smiled and continued, "And the Hendrix asshole…although I could have handled him on my own."

Trujillo slightly grinned and still looking at the screen in front of him, continued. "I am sure you could have."

Alexis said, "You didn't miss….

Trujillo continued. "No, I did not…"

Alexis kissed him slowly on the cheek and said softly, "Thank you."

She pulled away, but Trujillo grabbed her wrist and pulled her down to sit on his lap. They looked at each other for a few seconds before Trujillo said, "You're welcome."

Trujillo leaned in and kissed her. Alexis put her hand on the side of his face and kissed him back. After a few seconds, she pushed away and stood up. As she left the cockpit area, she said, "I will thank you properly later…."

Trujillo asked, "What was that…."

Alexis, still walking away, said, "Warmup."

Trujillo smiled and returned to flying the Frigate.

BELINEA 7.6

Avola

Bisi Provence

Octavious was looking at his tablet, making calculations, and occasionally looking out the window. A colossal desert dust storm was raging below them. Syren was only looking at her tablet. Octavious asked, "The children….a prop to get me out?"

Syren never looked up. "Yes and no. They are orphans. Quillisar Balerra and Sovinna jointly watch them from each of their Temples."

Octavious looked at the window. After a few seconds, he said, "It was risky…."

Syren looked up. Staring at Octavious, she said, "I am not a military officer, Octavious. I do not plan attacks and escapes. It was the best I could come up with."

Octavious quietly whispered, "I cannot handle any more innocents dying because of me, Syren."

She looked at him and said, "You told me that was the price we paid."

He shook his head softly as Syren touched him on his thigh.

The Transport flew for another minute, before slowing down and dropping altitude. The ship went through the dust storm and eventually made it to the side of a mountain. Octavious gave a small grin. He knew where they were. Where red rock, stone, and natural mountain were, two small doors broke apart from each other, wholly camouflaged at the base of the mountain. The opened doors revealed a small tunnel that the transport flew through. Through the tunnel and further inside the mountain, it revealed an enormous cavern of multiple ships. Fighters, transports, crates of ammunition, and Vait were everywhere. There were at least sixty people on the ground scurried about.

As the transport landed on one of the pads, a group of about twenty Valmay soldiers were waiting. Octavious and Syren came down the ramp and were immediately greeted by Cortes and Porter, who saluted Octavious. Cortes said, "Welcome to Bisi Base, sir."

Octavious saluted and said, "Our supply warehouse and former base from long ago is our new home? Outstanding work crew. When did you get here?"

Cortes replied, "I came in on a transport with five others about thirty minutes ago. Porter has a better understanding of what is going on."

Octavious looked at Porter, waiting for a status. The Fighter pilot replied, "All four of the C-112 transports, led by Rendon, exploded at Bosa. Prentein and Kuriss, on the base floor, survived the attack, as well as about seventy personnel. Gathering what they could, they back-tracked through the tunnels to the exit on the other side of the mountain, torching the rest of the base as they left. They waited until nightfall and made their escape here, making sure the AuFa did not follow them."

Octavious gave a small grin, proud of his team. "Good. What kind of supplies do we have, what is left?"

Porter took another deep breath "The four Sirator's we flew back in, plus the two that were being worked on here. We have three C-11 Transports, six AT-32's, about a dozen Valkyries, fifty full ammunition crates, surface to air missiles, almost a thousand T4 Bombs, and eighteen full crates of Vait. We still have almost a hundred soldiers and another forty personnel. They keep coming in, those that escaped."

Octavious replied, "Alright. Any information on Kaya?"

Porter looked at Cortes, before looking back at Octavious and said, "Nothing, sir."

Octavious said nothing. He started looking around before he muttered, "We are in a better position than I thought. Any status on AuFa and Majavkee movement? Have we been able to get out any patrols?"

Porter said, "Their main concentration has been snuffing us out of the Bosa Base, and your detour into the Cataco mines. Otherwise, they seem to be defense mode."

Sterling walked up to the three of them. He said, "I am sorry to interrupt, but the transport is going to take me back. I just wanted to say good-bye."

Octavious turned around and looked at Sterling. "I owe you my life. Please stay awhile. I would like to know more about your miners."

Sterling said, "Wish I could, but I just got an all-hands callback."

Octavious asked, "What does that mean?"

Sterling said, "It means they bring back all the miners to load the transports for processing. They do it when they are ready to make a large Vait transaction. Like when a large AuFa transport is here for purchase."

Octavious thought for a second. Then quietly, he said, "They are pulling out all the Vait to take back to Belinea."

Porter asked, "Are they leaking it to set up another trap?"

Octavious replied, "No, I saw on my tablet, the media, everyone assumes no one survived the caves. If we are no threat, it's a perfect time to get the Vait out."

There was a pause until Octavious asked, "Sterling, if they lost all the C-112's to transport the Vait, what would they use to get in on the ships above?"

Sterling thought about it for a second and said, "The bulk of the loading will have to be at the mining centers on smaller transports, before taking it to the Processing Centers, likely Six and Two. It will take more time, but it can be done."

Octavious replied, "If we could steal the Vait, that would be a bigger bargaining chip, then me in getting Kaya back."

Porter asked, "You want to plan an attack?"

Octavious paused for a second, before looking at Sterling. Putting his hand on his shoulder, he said, "No, a revolt....."

Cortes asked curiously, "A revolt, sir?"

Octavious paused again as he was formulating the plan in his head. He continued, "We have two huge advantages that we didn't have last time."

Porter asked, "What is that?"

Octavious said, "This time, we will be laying the trap."

Cortes asked, "And what's the second?"

Octavious smiled and said, "They think I am dead."

BELINEA 7.7

Molar

Populis Pointe

Willits and Jones landed the D-21 Sirallo on a pad that was next to the crashed T-141. The T-141 was still smoking, with one of its engines charred black and in shambles. Jones turned to Willits and said, "What the hell happened?"

The two came down the ramp, each with a hand on their side piece. They began inspecting the T-141 to try to determine what caused the explosion. Jones was looking at the still-smoking engine when he said, "This engine got hit by artillery…."

Willits added, "But it was close to the ground, so it was either trying to land or take off."

Jones then said, "I am going to check inside…"

A man had appeared from behind them and said, "You will not find anyone…."

Willits and Jones immediately turned around with pistols drawn. Not recognizing the person, they kept their pistols up. The gentlemen mildly raised his hands and said, "I am the Dock Master. You know the people that were on this ship?"

Willits responded, "Yeah, where are they?"

The Dock Master walked up slowly and said, "Long gone. I sure would like to find them, though. I got to figure out how to get this burning hunk of shit off this pad. Who is going to pay for it?"

Jones replied, "What happened?"

The Dock Master replied, "A shootout, right here on my landing pad. I would have expected that from Hendrix, but not from your crew."

Jones asked, "Who is Hendrix?"

The Dock Master continued, "Look, there ain't a lot of law around here, Mister. Whatever kind we do have, Hendrix is one of the bosses. Or was."

Jones asked, "Was?"

The Dock Master took his hands down as Willits and Jones dropped their weapons. "Got killed. Asked your group for a little toll for passing through, they shot'em all up. I had nine dead bodies out here after one of them got in one of those AuFa Fighters…"

Willits and Jones turned to each other before Willits said, "They did what?"

The Dock Master continued, "Well, Hendrix was holding the older fellow as collateral. Maybe they took it the wrong way. But there was no need for all that shit. It took me hours to get someone up here to clean up all the bodies."

Willits and Jones continued to look puzzled. Jones then asked, "And you don't know where they went? Is there a commercial port you can fly out of?"

The Dock Master just laughed and said, "Shit, you obviously ain't ever been here. No commercial flights, you would have to hire one of the smuggler's to get you out, not that you guys have that problem in that Sirallo you are on. Your crew left in one of those AuFa Frigates."

Willits, completely perplexed, asked, "An AuFa Frigate? With a full crew?"

The Dock Master shook his head. "Couldn't say. They were in and out of here right after this T-141 got shot down. Not often we see any AuFa craft here."

Jones and Willits just looked at each other. After a few seconds, Willits reached into his pocket and took out some coins. He walked over to the Dock Master, handed him the coins, and said, "My name is Willits. This is Jones. I am sure we will be back this way. This is for the trouble with the bodies. Can you also resupply the Sirallo."

The Dock Master counted the coins, which was more than enough. He tipped his cap and said, "What about this T-141?"

Willits said, "Buy an engine for it and fix it. It won't be cheap, but after that, you can paint it and sell it to one of these smugglers for a lot more. I promise the AuFa is not going to come looking for it."

Willits and Jones began walking back to the Sirallo. Standing outside, Jones reached into his pocket and pulled out his cigar-case. He opened it and took out two, one for each of them. Jones lit both as Willits and he took a few puffs. Jones said, "Any ideas?"

Willits paused for a second, taking another puff, before he said, "Where do I start. An AuFa frigate? Half of me thinks they are dead. The other half thinks it was BRG related, and they were forced to go to Belinea without us."

Jones replied, "It could not have been Taz. We left Torsalli before he did, *if* he did. No way he made it here in that time."

Willits continued, "I would like to think the kids were forced to leave without us, but who the hell knows."

Jones took another puff. "What do you want to do?"

Willits shrugged. Jones answered his own question. "We can't go back to Torsalli. I'm sure the BRG is still looking for us. At some point, they will figure out its two BRG officers on that transport and not the Ambassador."

Willits held up his cigar and immediately said, "I got a plan for that."

Jones continued, "Good, because otherwise, that will probably involve putting us up against a wall to be shot. We could go back to Earth?"

Willits chuckled again. "I am not convinced our boss doesn't think we are some sort of spies or traitors. Until we convince him otherwise, that crazy Samurai might decapitate us."

Jones continued, "What about Alexis? You still think she is working with Kimakawa?"

Willits took a puff and looked at Jones. After a pause, he said, "I think so, but I have no clue what she is telling him. I know Kimakawa is close to her mother, Annella."

Jones spun around quickly, "You mentioned that before, have we met her?"

Willits nodded and replied, "That time in London a few years back, remember?"

Jones nodded his head, took another puff, and said, "In the pub with the Belineans. We ended up back in Scotland and killed that bottle of Oban. She had that fucking dog, what was it?"

Willits smiled. "It was an Australian Shepherd."

Jones snapped his fingers and said, "That's right. It spent the entire night trying to hump my leg. That's Alexis' mother, huh?"

Willits just said, "Yep."

Jones continued, "Seems like a pretty smart lady. I am sure she has figured out that whoever is trying to kill Bird is getting fed from inside his office."

Willits asked, "How would Annella know?"

Jones countered, "Alexis, you idiot, not Annella."

Willits rolled his eyes and said, "Fuck off."

Jones replied, "Bite me."

A few more puffs, and they could see the Dock Master working on the Sirallo. Jones asked, "So where do you want to go?"

Willits shook his head and said, "I want to go on vacation to Vandabri with Vi, but I have too much principle."

Jones replied, "For the DAG? Or Kimakawa? May I remind you he has served us up on a platter to get killed."

Willits half smiled and said, "Neither. For Trujillo and Tunsall."

Jones took a puff and groaned. He said, "Oh no...."

Willits looked at him and said, "What?"

Jones said, "Why did you have to bring those two into this discussion?"

Willits answered, "Because we gave them a job, and they executed it. Shit, they took out some Molar Crime Boss and eight of his henchmen. It's impressive. If they were a part of our crew, and I am not sure at this point they are not, would we leave them behind?"

Jones took a puff and then quietly said, "I hate you sometimes..."

Willits, talking through his cigar, said, "Principle.....we leave no man behind."

Jones asked, "Belinea?"

Willits half-smiled and nodded in affirmative.

Jones shook his head. They both turned around and started walking back to the Sirallo. He said, "You know they still got BRG officers on Belinea?"

Willits said, "Belinean officers on Belinea? Since when?"

Jones replied, "They are either going to arrest us or more likely, shoot us on site."

Willits answered, "I told you, I got a plan for that."

Jones asked with skepticism, "Really?"

Willits answered, "Just blame it on the people trying to kill us."

BELINEA 7.8

Avola

Lowell Mining Center Six

Donovan and twenty other miners walked into the facility. With them were Cortes and four other Valmay soldiers, dressed like miners. They walked through a Vait detector device that allowed field stones and rings. The Majavkee Security was not searching for weapons or even paying attention. They were more focused on workers leaving the facility and the transports on the pad. Nevertheless, Donovan, Cortes, and the rest walked through security, past the loading areas, and straight down into the shafts.

They got to the staging area, where there was a supervisor. Sterling was in charge and nodded when they came in. He then yelled at them and said, "There are two large drop pallets of Vait at the entrance of tunnel four. Grab them, take one to pad seven, and one to pad eight."

They marched down to Tunnel Four and noticed the Four large drop pallets, two with Vait, two that were empty. Cortes and another Valmay soldier got into one empty crate, while two more Valmay soldiers got into the other empty crate. Donovan and the other miners put a lid on the crate, and semi-sealed it shut. They jumped on the forklifts and loaded the crates on, driving them out of the tunnel and over to the Landing Pads. Donovan drove the forklift straight up the mall transport and dropped it off. He drove the forklift back down the ramp.

A few minutes went by, and the two AuFa pilots entered the transports, walking up the ramp and into the cockpits. After buckling in, one of them radioed in "Processing Center Two, this is Transport 8152, requesting take off from Mining Center Six. Cargo in hand."

A few seconds went by before on the radio, a call was heard. "Transport 8152, copy that, expected ETA twenty-two minutes."

The two cargo ships slowly took off. As they did, Cortes and the other Valmay soldier unlocked the top of the crate and climbed out. When they slowly and quietly walked up to the Transport's cockpit area, they got right behind the pilots. Cortes and the Valmay Soldier turned their ring's into daggers and placed them in front of the throats of the pilots from behind.

Cortes asked, "What are your orders?"

A suddenly very nervous pilot responded, "Take the Vait Cargo to Processing Center Two."

Cortes said, "Not anymore. If you want to live, change your course to 2-7-0 for four minutes."

The pilot and co-pilot changed course without resistance.

BELINEA 7.9

On the way to Belinea

Nick Devanoe had slept eight hours. He felt refreshed. He walked out of his quarters and to the common area. Tunsall was sitting in a chair guarding the hallway that led to the Ambassador's quarters. He was reading on his tablet. Nick went over and poured himself some coffee. He said, "I don't think anything can happen to the Ambassador on this ship, so you can ease up on the guard duty."

Tunsall put his tablet down and said, "Willits gave us a direct order to never not have eyeballs on him. He got away from us for five minutes on Molar and look what happened."

Nick sat down opposite Tunsall and said, "Your loyalty is commendable, but my officer insight points out there was a lot more threat on Molar than this ship. I don't think Bird has the ingenuity to do anything stupid at this point."

Tunsall gave a small smile and replied, "I know. I have been asleep for most of the time. I woke up about an hour ago and started reading some things I downloaded when we were on Hovron."

Nick took a sip of his coffee. "Like what?"

Tunsall looked back at his tablet and said, "A situation on Avola. Terrorists calling themselves the Valmay Opposition Group are killing hundreds of locals and disrupting Vait production. The Press releases claim Taz is working with them, coordinating the Braccus and Earth bombings together."

Nick put his feet up on the corner chair. He replied, "Interesting. I do remember reading a security clearance memo on the Valmay on Avola. I guess it has gotten much worse, but I don't recall anyone tying them to Taz."

Tunsall put the tablet down and said, "You cannot believe everything in the press releases. They have their own initiative that does not necessarily align with everyone else."

Nick asked, "I'm not supposed to believe Taz attacked Space Port Earth?"

Tunsall responded, "There was an attack on Space Port Earth, an explosion happened, lives were lost. Those are facts. Who did it and why, at this point, is speculation until I see evidence that I trust and is undoctored."

Nick took another sip of coffee. He paused for a second, before he said, "That is not exactly a popular Belinean opinion."

Tunsall responded, "I am not Belinean."

Nick looked confused. "Your father is the Captain of a Belinean Battle Cruiser...."

Tunsall replied, "And he is not Belinean either...."

Nick was now perplexed. "But, then, how...."

Tunsall replied, "He is from Verona."

Nick turned his head sideways and said, "That is practically the same thing."

Tunsall, trying to find out how much Nick knew about Belinean culture, said, "Is it?"

Nick answered, "Sister planet, same solar system as Belinea. Allies for centuries, a good number of Veronians in the AuFa, representation on the Council is exactly aligned with the Belineans. You both practice the Quill, it's essentially the same."

Tunsall, questioning that fact, asked, "Is there a good number of Veronians in the AuFa?"

Nick answered, "A lot more than Earthlings."

Tunsall half-smiled and said, "That is true, but not as many as you think. It is probably why you did not know your Commanding Officer was a Veronian. They do not exactly go around parading it. And the Quill is different."

Nick was now actually curious. He asked, "Really? What is the difference?"

Tunsall sat up as he tried to explain. "The Quill started on Verona, with the Four Founders Points…"

Nick interjected, "I knew that, but it was carried over centuries ago to Belinea, where it is practiced equally, no?"

Tunsall answered, "Veronian Quill understands the energy from the planets is different on each planet and thus will produce different results with their field stones. The spirituality of believing that we are all energy, is the same. Belinean Quill believes the pure Quill comes from their planet alone. It ties the Water Field blue stone into passionate Quillisars and dedicated warriors. It does not recognize Fire Field stone warriors, mainly because Belinea has no rock or desert landscape to draw that energy from like it does on Verona."

Nick asked in an almost joking manner, "So your father is an orange stone warrior capable of making flaming swords?"

Tunsall replied, "No. The Belinean Quill quickly made it an offense for the orange field stones to have weapons. My Dad is an orange stone, but that practice has long been removed. There are no more fire swords. Well, until I saw that security footage of Taz."

Nick now sat up. "Yeah, what the hell was that?"

Tunsall replied, " I do not know. It was undoctored security footage and sure looked like a fire circle to me."

Nick paused for a second. He then asked, "Your father taught you a lot. His Quill passion is obviously strong."

Tunsall shook his head and said, "Captain Kimmel is practically a non-believer, I think he only wears his stone to keep in good grace with the AuFa. I do not have a stone, so I am a non-believer like you. What I learned was mostly from my mother when I was young."

Trujillo had now come walking up from the front cockpit area. He interrupted with, "What are the chances one of you can relieve me? I've been up there for over eight hours."

Nick then asked, "Wait, Tunsall and Kimmel? Why the different last names?"

Tunsall got up and looked at Trujillo. "I got you, as long as you got guard duty?"

Tunsall took one step toward the cockpit/bridge area. Trujillo navigated around as if waiting to get into the chair Tunsall was in. "As long as it is sleeping guard duty."

Nick stood up and said, "Wait, I got the conn. Get some rest, both of you. I can pilot the ship, and I promise the Ambassador isn't going anywhere."

Trujillo asked, "You sure?"

Nick nodded and then grabbed his coffee, taking a couple of steps towards the cockpit/bridge. Tunsall gathered his tablet and began to walk down the corridor to the personal quarters. Nick quickly turned around and said, "Tunsall…."

Tunsall and Trujillo turned around at the same time. Nick asked, "Why the two names?"

Trujillo and Tunsall looked at each other. After a two-second pause and a deep breath, Tunsall said, "Tunsall is my mother's maiden name."

Nick tilted his head in confusion. After another pause, Tunsall continued, "It's a long story, some other time."

The two walked out, while Nick turned around and walked up to the cockpit chair. Nick slid into the chair and broke out his tablet, starting to read it. As Trujillo and Tunsall were walking back to the quarters, Trujillo whispered to Tunsall, "I don't like the fact we left Willits and Jones looking for us on Molar."

Tunsall softly said to Trujillo, "Neither do I, but that is if they are still alive."

Trujillo said, "Alexis seems to think they are."

Tunsall replied, "And you trust Alexis now?"

Trujillo paused and took a deep breath. He looked around for a second and then said, "Yeah, I think I do."

Tunsall looked at him for a second, then said, "Alright. Just remember, pretty boy, you do not gain trust through your cock, okay?"

Trujillo replied, "Fuck you…"

Tunsall answered quickly, "Since when have I ever let my cock do my talking?"

Trujillo fired back, still in a whisper voice, "Never, that's the problem. It's like you're not human."

Tunsall quickly retorted, "I am not. Any other quick facts you want to verify?"

Trujillo sarcastically smiled and said, "I am going to sleep. Go fuck yourself."

Tunsall replied, "I am going back to the common area to keep my eye on Bird."

Trujillo answered, "Why? He is not going anywhere? Even Nick said so. He ordered us to sleep."

Tunsall replied, " I can just as easily sleep up there as back here. Better to be safe than sorry."

Trujillo, watching Tunsall walk back to the common room, just said, "Alright…."

Trujillo entered his room quarters and closed the door. The room was tiny, consisting mainly of a cot-like bed for one, steel drawers off to the side, and a small stool with a fold-out desktop. He turned the low light on and noticed someone in his bed. Alexis turned over wearing nothing but a thong and a button-down shirt that wasn't buttoned anywhere. Trujillo was confused and immediately said, "Sorry, wrong room."

Alexis held a hand up to her eye to block the lowlight and said, "No, right room."

He stared at her for a second while she slightly got up, putting her weight on her elbow. He looked down at her whole, soft, white body, before saying, "What are you doing in here?"

She replied quietly, "Waiting…."

Trujillo took his shoes off and sat down next to her in the bed. Very softly, he asked, "For…?"

Alexis took her hand that she was using to block the light and grabbed the side of Trujillo's head. She pulled it towards her face. Before kissing him, she whispered, "You…"

The two had a long, passionate kiss. Trujillo took his hand and gently slid it inside of her shirt, caressing her breast. Alexis sat further up and began taking Trujillo's shirt off. As he was kissing her, he said, "Aren't you worried about your brother?"

Alexis just kept kissing him back and said, "No, but where is he?"

Trujillo got his shirt off, and then was rolled over by Alexis, who was now on top without her shirt on as well. She began unbuttoning Trujillo's pants. Trujillo responded, "He is upfront flying the ship…."

Alexis got the pants and underwear off. She whispered, "Good, that will keep him busy while I thank you properly."

Alexis proceeded to go down on Trujillo. Trujillo leaned back and began to softly moan as he had his cock inside Alexis' mouth. Taking almost no time at all, Trujillo's cock became hard. After a minute, Alexis stopped and got up on top of Trujillo. She quietly asked, "What are the chances you can do this quietly?"

Trujillo, putting his arms around the small of her back, replied, "I've done it quietly before…"

Alexis raised her ass and grabbed Trujillo's cock. She slowly guided it into her, then relaxing as she fell back on top of him while still riding his cock. She began kissing his neck and then his ear before softly replying, "Yeah, but you've never had me before…."

BELINEA 7.10

Avola

Medical Facility 4

Kaya was waking up. She was lying on a table, naked except for bandages, with a white sheet over her body up to the neck. She kept blinking her eye, finally realizing there was a patch on the other one. She whispered, but could barely get out "Where is….."

The Doctor was next to her, finishing up wrapping a bandage. She said, "Be quiet. You are coming out of surgery. It will take you a few minutes to get adjusted."

The Doctor then checked her eye for twenty seconds before putting the bandage and patch back over it. After looking at her shoulder, she used a device to look at the fracture in her skull when she said, "You lost a lot of blood, and your shoulder was shattered. I surgically repaired the shoulder, polsared the skull fracture, and pumped you back up to a normal blood amount."

Kaya blinked her non-bandaged eye. She muttered out, "The eye…."

The Doctor looked at her and said, "Be quiet. Do not say a word. I treated the eye, but it needs further surgery that I could not give because we do not have the time. I need to get you out of here before he returns."

Kaya's eye got a little bigger. She turned her head as the Doctor went over to the table and grabbed a syringe. Walking back around, she inserted the needle into her bicep. The Doctor continued, "This will essentially numb your body. Any motion will be very difficult, so do not try. But you will be able to hear and blink your eye. In order for me to get you out, you have to be dead. Understand? Blink twice if you do."

With a lot more difficulty than she thought it would be, Kaya blinked her good eye twice. The Doctor then put the sheet over her head. Kaya could see hospital lights through the sheets. The Medical Center still seemed to be in some slight chaos after the battle. The Doctor was coming up to two glass doors. Two AuFa Security guards, their backs to the doors, were directly on the other side. The Doctor looked through the glass and saw a nurse. She nodded at the male nurse, who gave a small nod back. The male nurse proceeded down the hall and made a turn right next to the guards. Holding on to Kaya's gurney, the Doctor waited.

The male nurse turned into a room, and, within five seconds, had gotten into an altercation with a patient. The male nurse yelled, "He has a knife, Security!!"

Trays and equipment were being overturned. The male nurse and patient, who was a miner injured in the Processing Center attack, continued to struggle with each other. The male nurse had grabbed his patient's wrist, holding back the scalpel in his hand. A female nurse walked by and tried to intervene, but she got pushed back into the hall. Looking at the security guards, she yelled, "Will you help us!!"

The two AuFa Guards walked fifteen feet to the doorway of the room. Once they saw the struggle, they went in and helped the male nurse subdue the patient. The Doctor pushed Kaya's gurney fifteen feet to the glass doors. She put her hand on the scanner, and it opened. The Doctor pulled the gurney through and was down the hall in under ten seconds. She could overhear the commotion from the room, where the male nurse said, "I don't know what set him off, I had given him a shot for the pain, and he freaked out."

The elevator doors were closing just as the guards returned to the security post of the glass doors. The Doctor took the elevator to the second floor, pushing the gurney down a very long corridor. A sign on the side said "Morgue Processing" with an arrow. She continued down the hall towards the outdoor bay. Upon arriving to the immediate right, personnel were working with a Quillisar. The Doctor counted over twenty dead bodies. To the left was another small corridor that led to a loading dock. The greeting AuFa officer, a female Lieutenant, looked at the Doctor. The Lieutenant said, "Soldier or Miner?"

The Doctor said, "Miner."

The Female AuFa Lieutenant pointed to the left and said, "Down that corridor, leave the body at the end."

The Doctor nodded and pushed Kaya's gurney down the small corridor, which stopped after about twenty meters. There were already five other bodies, in bags, piled up on the side. The Doctor released the lever on the gurney, which dropped to almost ground level. The Doctor reached into her pocket and pulled out a canvas bag and some medical tape. She cut a piece off and taped the canvas bag to the sheet. She lowered her head and whispered into Kaya's ear, "Stay still, close your eye. Someone will be here soon."

The Doctor got up and began walking back. She almost got to the doors when the female Lieutenant asked, "You are not taking the gurney back up?"

The Doctor looked puzzled. Not knowing what to say, she hesitated and spoke in fragments. "I was....well, it....honestly, I have never been down here before. They needed help upstairs. This was my patient I lost, so I volunteered to take it down."

The female Lieutenant said, "Wow, a damn Doctor bringing a dead one down here, never seen that before. Yeah, you gotta take that gurney back up, otherwise, we get in trouble for keeping them down here."

The Doctor looked back and around as she said, "Alright,..... I guess, ... I just never...."

The female Lieutenant then said, "Never flipped over a dead body? Let me give you a hand."

The female Lieutenant began walking down the corridor, the Doctor followed quickly behind. The Doctor kept looking around to see if anyone else was watching, but the other AuFa officers were all concentrated on their side of the bay. They got to the gurney with Kaya's body, and the female Lieutenant asked, "Why isn't he in a body bag?"

The Doctor replied, "She...I don't know. I think they were running low on them upstairs."

The female Lieutenant kneeled to grab Kaya. She said, "This whole thing is a cluster fuck. I am sure they didn't want to waste a bag on a miner, even a female one."

The Doctor grabbed Kaya's shoulder, while the female Lieutenant grabbed Kaya's ankles. The Lieutenant said, "One, two, three..."

They lifted the body and tossed it next to the other dead bodies. The bag dislodged from the sheet and fell to the ground. The female Lieutenant reached over to pick it up. She said, "That one was still warm. She must have just bit it."

The Doctor held out her hand to get the bag back. She responded, "Just lost her in surgery."

The female Lieutenant asked, "What's in the bag?"

The Doctor grabbed the canvas bag from her hand and said, "Her Field stone and some personal artifacts she had on her."

The female Lieutenant asked, "Anything good?"

The Doctor tapped the bag back to the top of the sheet. She said, "Show some class."

The female Lieutenant turned around, grabbing the gurney, and said, "Damn, stop being so sensitive. It's just a fucking miner."

The female Lieutenant pulled the gurney as the Doctor trailed behind. When they got to the glass doors, the Doctor took over pulling the gurney, and said, "Thanks for your help."

The female Lieutenant waved and said, "No problem."

The Doctor went through the doors with the gurney. The female Lieutenant waited about twenty seconds, then began to walk back down the corridor slowly. She looked around to see if anyone was paying attention, which none of the other AuFa soldiers were. She was about two meters from Kaya's body when a light from a shuttle blinded her eyesight. Coming in for a landing was a small transport shuttle. The female Lieutenant looked directly at the bag and thought for a second about going for it. Behind her, she heard an AuFa soldier yell, "Lieutenant, we got a problem over here."

She stopped and looked over. Then looked back at the shuttle that had now landed. She looked at the bag one last time.

The female Lieutenant turned around and yelled, "Hold on?!"

Two workers got off the shuttle, dragging a gurney, and said, "You in charge?"

The female Lieutenant heard a soldier from across the corridor say, "They got two bodies, down by the processing center that never got picked up."

The female Lieutenant yelled back, "Why is that our problem?!"

She then turned around and looked at the workers from the shuttle. Pointing at the now six bodies on the ground, she said, "Yeah, I am in charge. Those six bodies are yours."

One of the workers said, "Is there something I need to sign?"

The female Lieutenant simply said, "No, they are just miners."

She turned around and started walking back to the other side of the corridor. She yelled, "Unless they are AuFa soldiers, we are not going out there to get those two!"

The workers shook their heads at the Lieutenants' remarks. They grabbed Kaya and put her on a gurney. They pulled the gurney back to the shuttle. Once inside, they lifted Kaya's body onto a sofa. One of the workers asked, "Is that her?"

The other worker opened the sheet to reveal Kaya's head. He nodded. He grabbed the bag that was taped to the sheet and opened it. Inside was Kaya's field stone and ring. There was also a syringe. He took it out and immediately injected it into Kaya's bicep. He whispered, "My name is Hamilton, I am a field medic in Lowell Province and a friend of the Doc. What I am giving you will help reduce the effects of the numbing agent. You should start gaining your motion back in a few moments."

Hamilton and the other worker went back to get the other bodies. One by one, they loaded them onto the gurney, took them back to the shuttle, gently dropping them in the cargo area. When they came back with the last body, they saw Kaya standing. Holding a sheet around her waist and a flaming sword with her other hand, she had nothing else on except the patch around her eye. Breasts exposed, she looked at the workers, and calmly said,"We need to get the fuck out of here."

BELINEA 7.11

Avola

AuFa Base Six

Argo and Lieutenant Walva were walking down a corridor. Argo said nothing, and for once, Walva said nothing. They turned and went down another aisle. Argo finally spoke. "Leahy said it was urgent, not you, correct?"

Lieutenant Walva only reiterated, "Affirmative, my Lord."

Argo replied, "And you have not seen the information?"

Lieutenant Walva answered, "No. Captain Leahy said only you."

Argo continued until he got to the control room. He entered, and around the screen table were four AuFa officers, two SS officers, and Captain Leahy. Argo immediately said, "This better be good, Leahy."

Leahy turned to the side. Everyone around the table stood at attention. Leahy spoke, "This came five minutes ago for you."

Everyone looked down at the screen, which changed over from a map of Avola to a transmission. Octavious Killian appeared on the screen. He was standing in front of four Transport Carriers, parked on a patch of rocky terrain. "Lord Argo, greetings. I got your message, you do not look good. Are you eating alright? Avolian cuisine does not agree with everyone. Let me get to the point, these four ships behind me represent four missing transports that have not reached Processing Plant Number Two yet...."

Cortes and the Valmay soldiers, dressed in AuFa uniforms, are sending down crates off the transports. As they enter the caves, they are opened. Inside are several rifles, air-to-surface missiles, bombs, and grenades. Donovan and his crew disperse the weapons, then load Vait back into the crate, where it is sent out again to be transferred back to the Transports. Argo is watching the entire two minutes on his screen, as it is narrated by Octavious.

"..... I am sure by now, those clowns you call officers (an AuFa officer is handing him a note), are handing you a note confirming what I just said. What they have not figured out yet, is that I am picking off shipments right and left. Where do you ask? Well, remember, these are the same officers that let me escape, so you will have to find out on your own. Unlike you and those Majavkee pricks, I have left the miners a little something. Call it a reward for loyal behavior. So, while I am touched that you offered Kaya's life for mine, I have a counter. You can have all your Vait back, in exchange for my sister. Here are my coordinates. You got thirty minutes from the time of this transmission. And come alone, Argo. I do not have time or patience today to deal with one ounce of your bullshit."

The transmission ended. Walva took two steps back, anticipating what would happen. Argo looked at the AuFa officer next to him. He calmly said, "Is this transmission real?"

The AuFa officer looked speechless. In a very jittery tone, he said, "My Lord, all the caves were surrounded, there was no possible way in or out, we were sure Killian was dead, no one could have survived that."

Argo yelled, "Well, he looks alive to me, you incompetent fuckers!!"

Argo went back to looking at the screen, which had turned back to a map of Avola. After a few seconds, he said, "How much Vait have they stolen? Is it possible he is bluffing?"

Leahy replied, "They only have four small transports, but we can't confirm how many runs he has made. Because of the lack of large ones, the small transports keep running back and forth. It's possible he has twelve, maybe sixteen full crates."

Argo yelled at the other AuFa officer. "Why are there no fighter escorts with the transports?"

The AuFa officer replied, "Admiral Holland has the bulk of our forces sifting through the exploded Valmay Base and at the Cataco caves, trying to root out the last of the Valmay soldiers."

Argo replied, "Great fucking job, they are out. Did you catch any of them? Because while you have been holding your dicks waiting, they have been stealing transports."

Nobody said anything. Argo turned to Lieutenant Walva and said, "Walla, contact Medical Facility Four. I want Kaya Killian here, now. I do not care if she is still in surgery or not."

Walva turned around and went to the other side of the room, immediately hitting a few spots on the screen and contacting the facility. The group could overhear him saying, "Yes, Lord Argo needs the transfer....."

Leahy looked at the map again before speaking to confirm what he had. He said, "Lord Argo, these coordinates, he must have been mistaken.....It's our Garrison in the Lowell Province, Sector 14 Mining Center."

Argo then replied, "What?"

Leahy responded, "I have checked it twice, sir."

Argo asked, "Is it possible he took over the base?"

The AuFa officer hit a few buttons on the screen to get a visual of the base with the security cameras. The AuFa officer said out loud to the screen, "Garrison Fourteen, this is Base Six, do you copy?"

The other AuFa officer hit a couple more spots on the screen. There were three functioning cameras on the base. The rest were now non-operational. One showed an empty hanger, the other an empty corridor, and the final one showed the same four small transports, on the rocky terrain path of the landing pads. If you looked closely at the ships, ventilation smoke came out of them, which meant their engines were on. The AuFa officer repeated, "Garrison Fourteen. This is base Six, do you copy?"

Still, nothing. The officers started looking at each other. Argo asked, "What about the other cameras?"

The AuFa officer replied, "Disabled my Lord."

Argo asked, "And any overhead shot from above? Perhaps Holland's camera from the Battle Cruiser?"

The AuFa officer simply replied, "No visual reading because of the atmosphere, my Lord."

Argo asked in an angry tone, "How did they retake the Garrison?"

The AuFa officer replied quickly, "My Lord, all the Fighters on the base were reassigned to Cataco. Most of the defense turrets were still not operational after the last attack. There were probably twenty to thirty personnel on the base. It would not have taken much."

Argo asked, "How did we not know about this attack?"

The AuFa officer only speculated. "It's possible, my Lord, the fact that we cannot communicate with them now, that the Valmay knocked out their Communication tower."

Argo thought for a second. He kept looking at the screen before finally looking back up at the AuFa officers. He finally said, "Tell Admiral Holland to pull out all fighters and personnel from the Cataco's and the Valmay base. I want two fighter escorts per every transport, to and from the facility, and to and from the ships in space. Got it?"

The AuFa officer asked, "My Lord, that will require every fighter we have. There may not even be enough without pulling some from the Mining Areas and Processing Centers."

Argo answered, "Reinforce Processing Centers Two and Six, but leave the Mining Centers. The Majavkee security didn't help when they were there, so what does it matter if we pull out? Most of the Vait is already on the ships or the Battle Cruiser above. No excuses, Lieutenant, make it happen."

The AuFa officers nodded in agreement. Argo looked at Leahy and continued, "Alright, we handle Octavious my way. Gather your SS team and meet me at my personal transport in ten minutes. Walla!"

Leahy nodded, and Lieutenant Walva turned around from the station he was on. Walva responded, "Yes, my Lord?"

Argo replied quickly as he and Leahy were walking out. "I changed my mind. Have Kaya Killian waiting. We are going to pick her up on my transport."

Walva looked scared like he just saw a ghost. He turned to Argo and said, "My Lord, Kaya Killian, is gone. The Medical Wing cannot find her. Or her Doctor."

Argo stopped. He looked at Walva, and for a second, he thought about taking it out on him. Instead, he looked up and said, "I hate every person on this miserable fucking planet."

Argo took a deep breath. Walva took a step back, knowing from experience not to be in the way of Argo's anger. After a few seconds, Argo looked at Leahy and said, "Alright, time to go to plan B."

Leahy raised an eye-brow. He said, "Yes, my Lord."

Argo quietly said, "I need you to go to Temple…."

Argo turned to the AuFa officers, still looking at the screen. "And you fucks, get me, Admiral Holland, now!"

BELINEA 7.12

Quillisar Balerra's Temple

The Lowell Province

Kaya walked into the Temple, now with a makeshift robe on. She was pulling a gurney with a dead miner, while Hamilton was pulling another. They came in through the back door, where Quillisar Balerra greeted them. Kaya had her head down and a towel over her head. As she came up to Balerra, the old lady immediately whispered, "Get inside, now…."

Kaya pulled the gurney inside, followed by Hamilton. Once inside, Balerra ushered them through a few doors until they were behind the Temple's altar. Balerra looked at Hamilton and said, "You have done good, my child. Give us a moment, please."

Hamilton walked out of the room. Kaya looked at Balerra and only asked, "Octavious?"

Balerra poured a glass of wine, and answered, "He is alive."

Kaya then asked, "You know for sure?"

Balerra turned around and looked at Kaya. Before taking a sip, she said, "Have I ever lied to you, my child?"

Kaya quickly responded, "When I was twelve, you told me I would never be as good as the other male soldiers."

Balerra looked at her and gave a small chuckle to herself. "I said you would never be as strong or as quick, but I never said you would not be as good."

Kaya tilted her head slightly. She looked tired, and it was clear she was not one hundred percent yet. Balerra looked at the patch over her eye and the area around it. She continued. "Octavious managed to slip through the Cataco mines, back out the Lowell side."

Kaya asked, "How?"

Balerra answered, "Some of the older miners, members of this Temple, found a shaft that connected. They smuggled him here, and I contacted Syren, who took him to Bisi."

Kaya asked, "Bisi?"

Balerra now realized Kaya did not know the whole story. "Lord Argo apparently left bombs inside the transports. They exploded at your base, destroying it. Your troops have rallied back to Bisi."

Kaya thought for a second. She whispered, "Rendon…."

Balerra replied, "Excuse me?"

Kaya paused for a second and put her hands on her forehead. She then said, "How many died?"

Balerra replied, "I do not know for sure. They have been covering it all day on the state media. If you believe them, you lost several hundred soldiers, and the last of your rebellion was destroyed in the Cataco mines."

Kaya went over to the table with the wine and poured herself another glass. She took a few huge gulps before putting it down. She then answered, "I need to get to Bisi, now."

Balerra replied, "Kaya, you know there is no communication inside or out in Bisi. I have left a message for Syren. When she gets it, she will come here for you. She can take you to Bisi."

Kaya reiterated, "I need to go now."

Balerra half laughed. "By yourself? You would not last two seconds without coming into contact with Majavkee Security.."

Kaya stared at her and said, "I would kill anyone who tried to stop me."

Kaya took another sip of wine. Balerra tilted her head before walking up to Kaya. She stopped in front of her. Balerra was a short woman, and she put her palm on Kaya's cheek. "My dear, how many do you think that is?"

Kaya looked down at her. Kaya had an expression of hatred, solace, and pain, all boiled together. Balerra turned and went to the wine table. She poured herself some more and continued. "Two years ago, when the Mining Guild was removed, and you and Octavious began rebelling in earnest, what did I say to you?"

Kaya was slightly annoyed, gesturing like a person who wanted to get out of there. She replied, "You told us peaceful protest is the answer to our salvation. Violence only leads to more violence."

Balerra took a sip of wine and turned to hear Kaya's answer. She replied after, "I was beginning to question if you listened to anyone?"

Kaya tilted her head and slightly raised an eyebrow. Balerra continued. "Octavious is one of the smartest men I have ever met, but his heart is conflicted. Like you, he is deeply passionate about his beliefs. The principles, as he references, of living free from religious persecution, being at peace with the energy of the planet, and practicing fair wages for fair labor. Unlike you, he also understands that not everyone shares his convictions on these principles. While they want them, they desire peace more. In their minds, violence does not lead to prosperity. "

Kaya was confused, not understanding Balerra's rationalization. "What are you saying?"

Balerra continued. "You were captured. You became a prisoner. The violence suddenly had a real consequence."

Kaya replied firmly, "I have always been prepared to die fighting for what I believe in."

Balerra gave the tiniest of grins and continued, "There is no question to your unwavering commitment. But your potential death left him questioning his motives. Had he gone too far? Is there a compromise where you do not get everything you want, but the miners, these people you are fighting for, get something and can live in peace?"

Kaya thought for a moment. After a long pause, she looked down at Balerra and said, "My Quillisar, I am simply willing to die for what I believe in. To compromise is to become a prisoner in their society."

Balerra countered with, "And Octavious agrees. Yet, he is willing to give himself up, so that you can live, in any capacity."

Kaya was confused. "What do you mean?"

Balerra answered, "When you were captured, Argo offered an exchange. You for Octavious."

Kaya answered, "He would never do that. It's against his principles."

Balerra gave another small half-smile, and said, "Kaya, you are his principle."

Kaya was angry. She put the wine down. She said, "I cannot just stay here. I have to find them. I have to do something."

Balerra answered, "Kaya, you must stay here and wait for Syren. It is not safe for you out there."

Kaya looked at her and said, "I am leaving. You can either help me or not."

Balerra thought for a second. After a five-second pause, she said, "What can I do for you, my child?"

Kaya began taking off her makeshift robe and replied, "You can start by giving me something proper to wear."

Balerra replied, "I have just the thing."

BELINEA 7.13

Avola

Lowell Province

Sector 14 Mining Center

Two F-81 Sirator Fighters, along with two bombers and Argo's personal transport shuttle, were flying to the Mining Garrison about two hundred meters off the ground. Argo was sitting behind his two pilots. He hit a couple of buttons on his screen, and Walva, who was back at AuFa Base Six, appeared. Argo said, "Any new information? Anything on the camera feeds."

Walva answered, "Nothing, my Lord. However, Majavkee Lord Bialos got back to me. They estimate that Octavious has about twelve full crates of Vait."

Argo answered, "More than I thought, but worth the sacrifice if he is dead for good."

The ships were coming up on the Garrison. The towers were still there, but still heavily damaged from the attack they had weeks ago. Only one turret was operational, but as they flew closer, it seemed to be abandoned. The SS officer flying with Argo repeatedly tried to make contact with the garrison, but to no avail. They did a flyby of the facility and saw four transports, still parked in the same spot. The ventilation was still coming off them, so the engines were on. After Argo did another pass, he said over the intercom, "Order Number One…"

The two bombers, escorted by the two Sirators, made another pass. Each unloaded a payload of four bombs from a higher altitude than when they did the flyby. The bombs were huge, and within minutes, the entire Garrison had been destroyed. A ball of fire and smoke extended one hundred and fifty meters high. One of the AuFa pilots confirmed the destruction and said over his radio, "Target confirmation. Garrison is destroyed."

The ships turned around and began heading back to Base Six.

Lieutenant Walva was watching the bombings from the screen in the control room of AuFa Base Six. The three functional cameras all went to black after the bombs were dropped. About thirty seconds after, a transmission popped on the screen. One of the AuFa officers could be heard saying, "Yes, are you sure?"

Walva had a curious look on his face. The AuFa officer then said to him, "I have someone claiming to be Octavious Killian."

Walva replied, "Put it through....., who is this?"

The voice over the transmission said, "This is Octavious Killian, who is this?"

Walva replied, "This is Lieutenant Walva of the AuFa."

Octavious spoke again. "Where is Argo?"

Walva replied, "He is not here."

Octavious replied, "Well, at least he got that part of the message correct. Patch me through."

Walva answered, "Excuse me?"

Octavious replied, "I know he just got done blowing up Garrison Fourteen, so please patch me through wherever he is because he missed the target."

Walva looked worried now. He hit a couple of buttons, and spoke: "Lord Argo, I have Octavious Killian on the speaker."

Argo replied, "We just blew up the Garrison, how is that possible?"

Octavious was now patched through and answered, "You did, Argo. I am sending over the video transmissions from the other cameras we disabled so you could get a better look at your work."

There was a long awkward pause until a video transmission popped on the control screen at Base Six. Walva hit the view buttons, so the feed patched indirectly to Argo's personal transport. As the video showed the other cameras, it became apparent that not only did Octavious take over the base, he left all of the AuFa soldiers handcuffed and sitting on the ground as prisoners. Twenty four in all that died as soon as the bombs from AuFa's squadron exploded. Octavious had it on a loop with different angles of the base, and began narrating as Argo was watching. "Let me commend the accuracy of the bombings. That is some exceptional work out of your crew. I wish I had an entire air-wing capable of this kind of destruction, but who needs one when you are willing to do the work for me."

Argo grew enraged with every different angle showing the soldiers getting blown up from the bombings. He finally replied, "Octavious, you are a dead man."

Octavious replied, "You may get your wish soon enough. In the meantime, Argo, you did not play by the rules. I said to come alone with Kaya, and you brought bombers and fighters instead. In more ways than one, you only have yourself to blame."

Argo angrily answered, "You and me, right now, Octavious, just tell me where."

Octavious said, "I tried that, but you reneged, so that deal is no longer on the table. But thank you for pulling out the AuFa soldiers. Despite a few more Majavkee security I had to deal with, it has allowed me to take over Mining Center Six in Lowell Province."

Argo angrily replied, "I am coming for you, and the Vait, Octavious. Don't go anywhere!"

Octavious replied, "As long as you bring Kaya, you have something to barter. I should warn you though. You might want to contact whoever is in charge of that Battle Cruiser up in space, first."

Argo gritted through his teeth, and he was pointing at his pilots to turn the ships around. "I don't have time for your fucking games Octavious."

Octavious replied, "No games Argo. However, right about now, your engineers are going through those crates, (Above on the Battle Cruiser, the engineers are inspecting the Vait crates.) and realizing there is just a layer of Vait on top. It is only about twenty percent of a full crate. The rest is rocks. The other eighty percent of the Vait never left this Mining Center. And since I am now in charge here, I have considerably more Vait than you realize."

Argo, hitting a switch so that only Walva would hear him, yelled into the speaker box. "Walla, confirm with Holland how much Vait he has?"

Octavious continued, "Your assistant is going to get back to you with that confirmation. You have twenty minutes to get here. And this time, if you do not come alone, you can add mining center, Majavkee Security, *and* Vait to the list of things I am going to blow up."

The line went silent. Argo yelled, "Walla!!!"

Lieutenant Walva answered back. "My Lord, Admiral Holland, has confirmed. The crates were not full. He is counting now, but it seems likely they are about 70-80% short."

Argo paused and put his hand on his forehead. He shook his head and whispered to himself, "Fucking shit….."

Argo thought for a second. There was an awkward silence. The pilot in front of him said, "Lord Argo, we are about fifteen minutes from Mining Station Six."

Argo said nothing. He kept thinking, trying to figure a way out. The pilot asked him, "My Lord, do you want me to tell the AuFa Wing to stand down?"

Argo said nothing. He kept looking out the window. Five, then ten, then fifteen seconds went by, Argo not saying anything. He whispered to himself, "Wait, he thinks I still have her…"

Argo sat up. He flipped a switch and spoke, "Walla. Tell Leahy to bring the cargo to Mining Station Six."

Walva responded, "The cargo, my Lord?"

Argo answered, "He will know what I mean. And get me Admiral Holland, stat."

Argo, now looking at his pilots. "You guys, tell that AuFa wing to drop back six minutes behind us, but no more. No fucking way we are going in there with our fly undone."

The Pilot turned around and asked, "My Lord, If he ties the bombs to the Vait, it will create an explosion that will destroy everything in the Mining Center."

Argo just half-smiled, and replied "Good, because I do not care anymore. If it costs me my life, so be it, but Octavious Killian is not leaving that Center alive."

BELINEA 7.14

Avola

Lowell Province

The Quillisar Priestess walked down the streets dressed from head to toe in her bright red cloak. Turning a few blocks, she would make her way to the Mining Center. It was dusk as she noticed more people walking. Joined by others, there seemed to be a mob growing as the Quillisar Priestess, her head completely covered, whispered to a civilian, "What is going on?"

The civilian responded, "Quillisar, the miners. They are revolting. They say Octavious Killian is alive and leading them."

The Quillisar Priestess continued to walk that way. With each block they walked, the mob got bigger. By the time they had walked eight blocks to the Mining Center entrance, they had grown to a crowd of almost three thousand people. Twenty armed Majavkee Security blocked the entrance to the Mining Facility. The crowd began getting rowdy, threatening to overrun the security guards, who now looked worried.

The Quillisar Priestess made her way to the front, wiggling through the civilians. She noticed some of the miners on the other side of the fence inside the facility. They had mining equipment such as hammers and chisels, while the others were throwing rocks at security. They were positioned some forty meters away from the fence, but the danger was imminent. When the Majavkee security fired a gas-like substance into the civilian crowd, it only made the crowd angrier. Three of the civilians tried to climb over the fence. One of the Majavkee security soldiers fired four shots directly above the civilians climbing the fence. Fifty miners rushed the Majavkee Security from behind. Once one got a hold of a rifle, the miner turned and used it on a Majavkee Security guard. Within seconds, chaos had broken out. The civilian crowd began tearing the fence down. Within a couple of minutes, over thirty civilians were wounded or killed. The rest had breached the fence, overtook the security, and ran into the facility.

First in line was the Red Priestess, as she made her way forward. The crowd was chanting "Val-May, Val-May, Val-May, Val-May."

Inside the Mining Facility, Octavious has taken over the Control Room. He was waiting, looking at all the security camera monitors to gauge what was going on. Cortes, standing next to him, said, "They are over-running the facility, sir. Word has gotten out."

Octavious nodded. "The revolt part is working. Now we just need Argo to play along."

Cortes asked, "You trust him to bring Kaya and not bomb the whole facility? No offense, sir, but he only cares if you are dead."

Octavious kept looking at the screens. He replied, "There is certainly a chance. He showed his intentions at the Garrison. But the amount of Vait we have, and the number of civilians will give him pause. It is a simple exchange."

Cortes asked, "When will we know?"

Octavious replied, "He has ten minutes. He will probably show up alone. If he does not, he will bomb and burn this place to the ground. One other thing Cortes…."

Cortes looked at him and replied, "If you see any AuFa ships show up after we are talking, or I give you a signal, get all the civilians out of the facility. Have the miners and soldiers escape through the caves if you have to."

Cortes asked, "Signal for what, sir?"

Octavious turned and looked at her. Quietly, he said, "The signal that Argo does not have Kaya. And that means he was never going to give her up for anything. And I will end it, one way or another with Argo, right there."

BELINEA 7.15

Avola

Lowell Province

Mining Center Six

The miners and civilians were now shooting, along with throwing rocks, at Majavkee Security. The Red Priestess saw a Majavkee Security guard shooting into a defenseless crowd. She pulled out her ring, and a fire sword came out. Running up to the guard with flames flashing around her, the guard had difficulty shooting her. She dodged a couple of rounds as she flipped up, behind the security guard, and sliced his head off in one motion.

Two more security guards ran up, but the Red Priestess took them on simultaneously. They tried first to shoot, but the Red Priestess first blinded them fire, then cut their hands off. After stabbing one in the neck and cutting the leg off another, she took her free hand and removed her hood. Kaya took her flaming sword and stabbed the security guard with the missing leg through his eyeball.

With smoke now everywhere, Octavious was waiting with five of his Valmay soldiers on the landing pads near the caves. Behind the soldiers were four transports, engines running. A shuttle from the sky appeared, gently touching down in front of them. The engines never stop running as Argo emerged from the lowering ramp. He walked down and stopped ten meters away from Octavious. Octavious yelled, "Argo, I was worried. My soldiers thought you would just bomb this place like a coward. Welcome to the party."

Argo looked up at the smoking buildings and civilians throwing rocks on the other side. "Love what you have done to the place Octavious, they call this the revolution look, no?"

Octavious yelled, "Where is Kaya?"

Argo yelled back, "We will deal with that in a second. Where is the Vait? The Majavkee Lords say you have forty full crates."

Octavious shook his head and yelled, "Their counting is as good as their shooting. I have over sixty, but you will not see one crate of that until I see Kaya."

Argo kept staring at Octavious. After a pause, he said, "A lot of people underestimated you, Octavious. Not me, but the Majavkee and the AuFa. It is a shame we are on opposite sides of this conflict."

Octavious replied, "Argo, I got four transports behind me, each carrying four full crates of Vait. There are four more transports outside the base. They each have four full crates and a Majavkee pilot waiting with a gun to his head. That is thirty-two full crates of Vait in exchange for Kaya."

Argo smiled and said, "I thought you said you had over sixty crates?"

Octavious was not smiling. "I do, the rest I am keeping. Had you kept the original deal, you would have got all of it. Now, where is she?"

Argo turned around and looked at the horizon. Coming up was another transport, with AuFa markings. The ship gently touched down right next to Argo's transport. This time the engines shut off. As the ramp came down, it was Captain Leahy and another SS officer. Behind him was Quillisar Sovinna and ten Avolian children, the same ones that helped him escape the Temple. As they all got off, they were followed by eight more SS soldiers. Octavious closed his eyes briefly, and took a deep breath. He knew this would end badly.

Argo yelled, "I am tired of you dictating the rules, Octavious, so here is my counter-proposal. I take off with the Vait, and you can have these precious little children you seem to care about."

Octavious yelled back, "This was not part of the deal, Argo. Children? You spineless piece of shit."

Octavious grabbed his earpiece. Argo yelled back, "It's my deal now after you killed the AuFa soldiers at the Garrison. Right now, one of your soldiers is telling you they picked up two air wings, heading this way, probably eight minutes out. They are gonna blow this whole place up, unless I stop them."

Cortes yelled in Octavious earpiece, "Sir, you got two air wings headed this way, each has ten fighters and eight bombers, with military transports as well. They got AuFa soldiers, sir."

Octavious yelled, "What are they going to do, Argo? Blow up the base with you in it?"

Argo yelled back, "That is exactly what they are going to do because they do not even know I am here. They will not stop unless I call them off, which I am not inclined to do because as long as you die, I have won."

Octavious was pissed. He yelled, "Kaya and the children, and you get all the Vait, Argo. That is the last offer."

Argo smiled and said, "Well, then I guess we are going to die because I cannot give you what I do not have."

Octavious yelled as loud as he could, "Where the fuck is she!?!"

Argo yelled back, "She is dead, Octavious. The surgery never saved her. I was bluffing the whole time. It was the only way I could get to you."

Octavious looked stunned. What had happened? He had played this entirely wrong. Argo continued, "But for good measure, once she was dead, we carved her heart out and pinned it against the wall in the control room as a reminder. I, too, was shocked she had one."

Kaya was running through the facility, killing Majavkee security along the way. A mob of miners were behind her, some with rifles. When they got to the Control Room, they noticed it had twelve Majavkee soldiers outside, trying to get in. Turning around, the soldiers fired on them, and Kaya took her mob down the corridor for cover.

Ocatvious turned around and looked at his soldiers. He grabbed his earpiece and said, "Cortes, get far away, into the caves. They are going to bomb the whole thing, and I cannot stop them."

Cortes said, "We are not leaving you!"

Octavious said, "I will buy you as much time as possible. This is between Argo and me now."

Octavious looked at his soldiers again and said, "Are you ready? This goes no further."

The soldiers all nodded. Each of them grabbed their rings, and all in unison extended their red flaming sabers. The eight SS soldiers behind Argo, plus Leahy and the soldier next to him, all grabbed their rings and extended their silvery swords. Argo said, "What are you doing, Octavious?"

Octavious looked at Argo and said, "It ends here, Argo…"

Argo smiled. "What about the children?"

Octavious, not smiling at all, only said, "That's on your conscious, they could fly away now. As long as you are dead, that is all that matters to me."

Argo smiled and nodded. He looked back at the children, saw their pilot, and looking directly at Quillisar Sovinna, said, "Get them out of here!"

As Argo turned back around, he grabbed his ring and extended it into his silvery sword. Just as he was about to engage, Leahy and the SS soldier next to him ran past him and engaged in a fight with Octavious. The Valmay soldiers followed suit and engaged with Argo and the rest of the SS.

Cortes yelled at the Valmay officer next to her, "We gotta get out of here. They are going to bomb the whole facility."

The officer yelled back, "We can't! Majavkee security is right outside the door."

Cortes pulled up the security screen and saw the Majavkee security outside. She pointed and said, "Someone is fighting them from the corridor."

Kaya told two of the miners who had rifles, "Put down a base of fire, empty your round, and then retreat down the corridor. Do not come back until the fire is gone. The rest of you take cover down the corridor now. Ready?"

The two miners nodded. They jumped out from their position and began firing at the Majavkee security. Kaya jumped out after them but quickly jumped over them towards the security. One of the miners got shot in the head and died instantly. The other one kept firing.

Kaya was fifteen feet in front of them now but still twenty feet from the Majavkee. She kneeled on one knee and held her blade up vertically in front of her. She made it the shape of a diamond, still with flames on it. The diamond got more prominent, even as rounds from the rifles whizzed by her. She took a deep breath, closed her eyes, and the blade turned into a giant diamond fireball. As she exhaled, the fire went down the corridor right at the Majavkee security. In an instant, most of them caught on fire as the flames extended to the whole area right up to the door of the Control panel. Kaya took another deep breath, and a second diamond-shaped fireball came out of her sword again, engulfing the security in flames.

Down on the landing pad, the SS and the Valmay soldiers were in an epic battle. The shuttle with the children had taken off, but Argo's personal transport was left behind. Octavious swung his saber, clashing with both Captain Leahy and the soldier who was next to him. Argo was battling with one of the Valmay soldiers, who was holding his own with him.

Leahy managed to strike Octavious in the shoulder, briefly bringing him to his knees. The other soldier attempted a hard swing, but Octavious blocked it. Wasting no time, he struck the soldier in the chest. The move, however exposed him to Leahy, who extended his silvery sword to eight feet and struck at the same spot on Octavious' shoulder.

Argo continued to fight back and forth with the Valmay soldier, finally getting him in a bad spot. He took a good swing and ripped both of his legs off. Standing over him, he extended his sword straight through his mouth.

Octavious swung again and ripped Leahy's sword right out of his shoulder, causing blood to go everywhere. Octavious was fighting one-handed now. He kept trading blows until he finally saw an opening. Leahy swung and missed. Octavious rolled over onto his bad shoulder and landed on his knees. In pain, he swung and chopped both of Leahy's legs off, just below the knees.

Octavious got up and walked over to Argo. The two began trading blows with their weapons. Octavious tried a fire blast, which Argo stopped by turning his sword into a shield. Argo tried to extend his sword ten feet to pierce Octavious, but he brushed it to the side with his flaming sword. The two resumed trading blow after blow. Octavious, with his wounded shoulder, was still struggling.

As the flames dispersed, Kaya walked up the door. Cortes and the other Valmay officer shoved it open with their shoulders. When the door opened, Cortes yelled, "Kaya!"

Kaya asked, "Where is Octavious?"

Cortes, still stunned to see Kaya, pointed through the glass, and said, "He is down below, with Argo. We gotta get out of here. They are going to bomb the whole facility."

Kaya looked down and could see Argo and Octavious trading blows. She yelled at Cortes and said, "Come with me!"

Argo swung and gave Octavious' face a brand new scar, cutting it across his eye and down his cheek. Octavious swung, but missed badly. Argo went for a crushing blow, cutting Octavious' arm instead. Octavious tried the same move again, rolling on his bad shoulder, but his arm affected his balance, and as he swung, he only got one of Argo's legs, cutting it straight through the ankle. As Argo was falling, he struck his blade right through Octavious's bad shoulder, sending him to the ground.

Argo released his extension and got up on one knee from his good leg. With his other leg missing a foot and bleeding out, he pierced Octavious in the forearm just as he was rolling over, causing him to drop his fire saber. Octavious rolled around on the ground, struggling to find his saber. One of the SS soldiers found it and threw it ten meters away. Argo, with the assistance of the SS soldier, got up and limped over to Octavious. He grabbed the back of Octavious' head.

Kaya and Cortes came out of the tunnel and onto the landing pads. From sixty meters away, both had their fire blades ready. But Kaya stopped, so Cortes did as well. Kaya and Argo locked eyes. A shot was fired near him, causing Argo and the soldier to readjust. As they did, they looked up and noticed the revolting miners, a few thousand of them. They were on top of the facility looking down and on the landing pad, some thirty meters away, ready to rush them.

Argo smiled, blood on his face. Argo had pierced his sword into Octavious' shoulder, twisting it. It caused such excruciating pain, that Octavuious could not move and was helpless. Argo looked up at the crowd and saw there was no way to get out of this. With three thousand miners ready to rush him, he yelled at the top of his lungs, "This is your leader? This is your God? This worthless mortal?"

The crowd was restless. One by one they began to chant, "Val-may, Val-may, Val-may..."

Hesitant to rush Argo, he leaned down and spoke into Octavious' ear. "I am going to kill each and every one of them, Octavious."

With blood running down his forearm from where Argo pierced it, Octavious raised his hand as high as it would go. Still on his knees, he tried to ball his hand up into a fist. The crowd sensed he was going to speak and stopped chanting. Octavious closed his eyes, took a deep breath, and yelled, "Red Ring Rise!"

Every one of the miners pulled the diamonds or rings out that were hanging from their neck. The stones all began to glow, some blue, some red, some green, some yellow. They looked at each other in awe. Argo was utterly perplexed as well, for he had never seen anything like it as well. Kaya and Cortes, still standing on the pad, had their stones glowing a bright red. The miners began yelling, "Red Ring Rise, Red Ring Rise, Red Ring Rise....."

Despite the chanting, the sound of aircraft engines deafened the skies. Some twenty F-81 Sirator fighters came in from everywhere, starting their runs. They fired on the miners everywhere, as hundreds were killed instantly.

Octavious opened up his hand from the clenched fist position. He held his head up, and somehow, his fire saber ring moved through the air, some ten meters, right into his hand. Octavious swiftly pierced Argo right where his ankle had been cut off. It caused Argo to lose balance and let go of Octavious' head. The SS officer next to Argo took his saber and pierced it through Octavious' back.

Kaya and Cortes ran toward them. Argo was helped back-up by one of the SS soldiers. He saw the other four SS soldiers firing at Kaya and Cortes, who were forced to take cover. Argo picked up Octavioius' head from his now motionless body. Kaya peaked out with her one good eye and saw Argo turn his sword into a large dagger. In one swing, he cut through Octavious' neck, just as he was shot in the shoulder and lost his balance.

Kaya ran towards them. One of the SS officers shot her in the shoulder, causing her to spin towards the ground. Argo dropped Octavious' almost severed head as two SS Officers helped back to his personal transport. Helped by the remaining SS officers, Leahy, still bleeding and screaming profusely from his injury, sat next to Argo. As a robot medic looked at his ankle, Argo yelled, "Get us out of here and bomb this fucking facility."

Watching Argo's transport fly away, Kaya got back on all fours, blood pouring out of her shoulder now. She jogged over to Octavious' almost decapitated body, and grabbed it. With blood everywhere, she saw his head almost completely severed and began to cry. She looked up at the billowing smoke, as her blood-soaked arms wrapped around his chest.

One of the SS officers got in the Vait transport, and followed Argo's ship. He said on his intercom, "Give us a few seconds before you start your bombing run. We have a full load of Vait."

Cortes ran over to Kaya and said, "We gotta get out of here."

They both grabbed Octavious and dragged him to the one transport that was left. Kaya and Cortes got Octavious' body up the ramp, where Cortes dropped him and sprinted to the cockpit.

The AuFa pilot said, "Lord Argo and the Vait transports are clear! Start your run!"

The bombers all lined up. Once Argo's transport was a kilometer away, the bombers turned toward the facility. One of the bomber pilots said, "Bay doors open, bombs away."

Cortes hit the throttle and got the transport turned around, three meters off the ground. Talking to herself, she said, "Come on, come on, fucking move!"

The transport went directly underneath a crossing bridge, gaining speed as it went past it. Cortes could see the explosion of the bombs coming up behind her. They were compounded by the remaining Vait as they soon engulfed her ship. Cortes lost control of the transport as it crashed to the surface.

BELINEA - EPISODE 8

TAZ

BELINEA 8.1

Capital City, Belinea (Six Weeks Prior...)
Chairman Hassara's office

The four chairs in front of Chairman Hassara's desk were facing each other, forming a perfect X with a small diamond-shaped table in the middle. Chairman Hassara and Tempest sat across from each other. Malovex stood by the bar table, pouring himself a drink. Malovex said, "You told him the time for the meeting?"

Tempest had her elbow on the arm of the chair, using it to hold her head up. She replied in annoyance, "Of Course…."

Malovex closed the top to the liquor bottle and responded, "Any chance he has forgotten how to tell time?"

Tempest answered, "That would imply he used to…"

Malovex walked back to the chairs with a triple pour, neat, in his glass. He quickly continued, "Any chance a sniper took him out on the way over here?"

Tempest replied, still in annoyance, "Only if wishing made it so…"

The Chairman interrupted, "Punctuality is not your cousin's strength."

Malovex now sat in the chair in between the Chairman and Tempest. "Even monkeys can tell time, and yet you never think to just give him a time that's 30 minutes earlier?"

Tempest replied, "It might need to be an hour…."

Malovex quickly continued, "Doing the same thing over and over and expecting different results is the definition of insanity. I no longer blame him, I blame us."

The Chairman interrupted again with, "We could just start the meeting without him."

Tempest half-smiled and said, "Argo has important information and a proposal."

Malovex added, "Perhaps it is a cooking recipe?"

The Chairman added, "We all have things we could be doing right now, Sansigar."

Malovex took a sip of his scotch and rolled his eyes. The Chairman quickly added, "Perhaps I should get him an officer, and assistant, that strictly kept him on-time…."

Malovex added, "…or a monkey."

Argo came walking through the doors with a tablet in his hand. He quickly asked, "What is the monkey for?"

Malovex quickly replied, "You."

Argo went over to the bar and poured himself a drink, asking aloud, "I need a monkey?"

Tempest inserted, "You need a lot of things…."

The Chairman said, "You are late, and we have been waiting…"

Argo put the bottle down and asked, "I do not see how a monkey would have solved that."

Tempest added, "Perhaps a wristwatch?"

Malovex gently nodded and quickly added, "A monkey with a wristwatch…"

Argo was walking back to the chairs with the neat drink in his hand. He asked, "You can teach a monkey to tell time?"

Malovex quickly responded, "And somehow you cannot…"

Tempest added, "The whores, they work by the hour. Perhaps I could get them to teach you."

Argo sat down, with the drink and the tablet, and said, "My whores work all day sis…."

The Chairman raised his voice and said, "Enough. Let's get started. Argo, you have some vital information for us?"

Argo replied, "Remember about a month ago I told you one of my spies said the Earth Security Group, the DAG, was poking their heads around Avola and inquiring about purchasing Vait?"

The Chairman responded, "And I told you not to do anything about it. We do not have direct evidence, but we do have an excellent relationship with one of the Earth Ambassadors."

Argo replied, "Which one?"

Tempest replied, "Ambassador Yi."

Argo continued, "Alright, not that one, but another Earth Ambassador is running his mouth about independence, and do we need the BRG. Here, look…."

Argo put the tablet on the table in the middle of all of them. He hit a button, and a 3-D hologram of Ambassador Bird popped up, giving a speech.

"Yes, we share the same vision as the Belieneans, we must let these terrorists know….that there is no place for them to hide. We must work together on that mission, but we shall also not forget our primary vision of a better Earth. We cannot tolerate becoming prisoners to a plan that will lead us into an economic abyss. We cannot allow the Council to place us in financial shackles of dependency. Earth must, AND WILL, do what is best for EARTH. Earth will choose our own direction. And most important, Earth will fight for the right to protect its own citizens…(applause)."

Malovex quickly responded, "He's got balls…"

Chairman Hassara quickly asked, "Who is this, weasel?"

Tempest answered, "That is the new Earth Ambassador Bird."

The Chairman continued, "A new Ambassador saying that? Is he an idiot? Another pandemic might change his tune."

Argo continued to speak. "He has been making a bunch of these speeches. Combined with my spy telling me they are trying to get Vait, and I think these people from Earth are going to try and start their own military."

Tempest concluded, "Your vital information for this meeting is speeches that have you concerned Earth is trying to create its own army? That is a stretch, Argo."

Malovex added, "Yes, and if they were, why have I not heard anything from my spy?"

Argo replied, "Because my spy is far more connected than your spy."

Malovex sat up and said, "Tell me your spy, and I will tell you mine."

Argo replied, "Sansigar, you know I am not going to do that."

Malovex smiled and said, "Do not be embarrassed by the fact your spy is sucking some officer's cock. That is your kind of crowd, Argo."

Argo smiled back, "Not going to admit you might be wrong on this?"

Malovex answered, "I never said you were, just that I have heard nothing from my spy."

Argo replied, "And it's not true until you do?"

Malovex answered, "It makes it reliable."

Argo answered, "Why is your spy more trustworthy than mine?"

Malovex answered, "For starters, mine can tell time...."

The Chairman interjected again, "Stop. Let's work on the problem. If they are building some independent military, which I do not think they are, what do we do?"

Tempest replied instantly, "We absolutely send them a message letting them know we will not tolerate such an act."

Malovex answered, "Certainly, nothing drastic?"

The Chairman pondered for a second. "No, through back channels. We have too much invested in Earth, with our shipbuilding facilities and cheap labor to jeopardize the production in that way."

Malovex added, "I am not even sure letting them know *we know* is the best thing."

The Chairman responded, "Agreed. Perhaps do nothing until we have factual verification?"

Argo interjected, "Illuminating. However, I do not propose problems without providing solutions."

Tempest gave a quick sarcastic interjection "If only you had the same dedication with all your faults...."

Argo took a breath and said, " What if we just killed Ambassador Bird?"

There was an awkward silence in the room. After about six seconds, Tempest finally responded, "Are you serious?"

Argo responded, "Yes."

The Chairman responded, "I appreciate the fear you put in people, my son, no father could be prouder. But that kind of behavior leads to riots and civil wars when the people turn on you for being a masochistic prick."

Argo responded, " You know I would slit his throat in front of a hundred cameras and not care about the ramifications, but I was referring to someone else. What if Bird was assassinated through a controlled terrorist attack?"

Tempest said, "You mean Taz?"

Argo nodded in affirmative. "We have kept him under wraps for weeks. I can arrange a situation where my Earth spy gives information to Taz regarding Ambassador Bird's travel schedule. Taz finds the perfect time to assassinate Ambassador Bird. That's the spin we use as evidence that we need to increase the budgets of the BRG and AuFa."

Malovex asked, "What if any of the older Ambassador's see it as 'someone spoke, and someone got executed'?"

Argo answered quickly, "Is that a bad thing?"

There was another silence in the room. After a few seconds, The Chairman looked at Malovex and asked, "What do you think?"

Malovex leaned back in his chair and waited a few seconds before speaking. Finally, after taking a sip of his drink, he said, "As much as I would like to disagree with my cousin, I do not. If this is done right, we could pin this on the DAG watch, avoiding any BRG criticism. How does Taz communicate with this spy of your's?"

Argo wiggled his finger while sipping on his drink and said, "Good one, cousin. You almost got me to bite."

Malovex replied, "I was referring to the fact that Taz is a man of very few words."

Argo half smiled and said, "Let's just say Taz gets the information from either me or Verkato, his first officer."

Malovex continued, "As long as the information is reliable. You do not need this blowing back up in Taz's face. This would also mean we call their bluff. Privately, we let the DAG know, even if the Ambassadors do not know, this is what happens if they even think about building a military."

Tempest asked, "You can get a message to them, discreetly?"

Malovex smiled. "Apparently, Argo can get a message through his trusted spy."

Argo, wiggling his finger again, sarcastically replied, "My cock sucker knows how to get straight to the top."

The Chairman asked, "Their DAG Director, what is his name, Kamaka?"

Malovex answered, "Kimakawa. We do not go through the spies, but I can arrange a face-to-face meeting disguised as something else entirely."

The Chairman turned to Tempest and said, "Tempest....?"

Tempest replied, "It's ambitious, and I do not know if it is enough *spin* to get the increased budget for the AuFa and BRG, but it certainly helps if it is done correctly."

The Chairman stood up. "Alright, Argo, make it happen. Tell Malovex when to deliver the message. Malovex, confirm with your source what they are doing."

Everyone stood up and began walking out when the Chairman said one final thing. "Oh, and Argo. I am getting you an officer to help with your punctuality."

Argo replied, "Is that necessary?"

Tempest replied, "Not if you could tell time."

BELINEA 8.2

Northeast Japan (Six Weeks Later...)

Vice Director Franklin Meyers walked into Kimakawa's office. Annella Devanoe sat in front of Kimakawa's desk while the Director sat behind it. As Meyers walked up, he asked, "You wanted to see me, Director?"

Kimakawa opened his hand and said, "Please sit down, Meyers."

Meyers sat in the chair opposite Annella. Kimakawa then got up and walked over to the bar. He politely asked, "Would you care for a drink?"

Meyers said, "I am good, sir."

Kimakawa poured himself some scotch. He then walked back over, around the chairs, and got right behind Meyers. In Kimakawa's left hand was his scotch. With his right hand, he pulled out the small pistol hidden behind his waist. He pointed it right behind the back of Meyers' head and gently tapped it. Kimakawa said, "You know what this is?"

Meyers felt his head go slightly forward. He moved his arms slightly up and said, "Director?"

Annella Devanoe got up and sat back down in Kimakawa's chair behind the desk. She reached into a drawer and pulled out a pistol, pointing it at Meyers. Kimakawa, still holding his gun as well, said, "Over twelve years ago, when this Guard group was in its infancy stages, we knew the only way it would have merit is if it had its own intelligence agency. Under the camouflage of being a Delegate Guard, we worked tirelessly training operatives, like yourself, to gain access and knowledge of all the planets we were suddenly working with. Trusting one person's viewpoint is never a good idea when deliberating between ally or foe."

Kimakawa took a sip of his scotch and put it down on the front of his desk. Keeping his pistol in one hand, he used his other to pull up a chair next to Meyers. He continued. "One of my first operatives was Miss Devanoe's daughter, Alexis. What better way to gain knowledge on your new ally then be educated by them. We sent her off at ten years old, to a school on Belinea. She learned everything about their history and culture."

Annella thought back to that precocious ten-year-old girl, in school attire, learning next to Belinean children. As Kimakawa had his flashback of reading to Alexis when she was young, he continued. "Alexis barely knew her father, so in many ways, I have accepted that role for her. I trust her more than anyone in this universe, perhaps even more than her mother. So when I got this note from her, it was not as shocking as it would have been months ago. She had become the operative I always knew she could be."

Annella held her tablet up with the hand that wasn't holding the pistol. She said, "Would you like me to read it?"

Meyers was nervous. He said, "Director, I really do not know what this is about?"

Annella began reading the note, not caring what Meyer's answer was. "This came over on my son Nickalis' account, making sure it was not read by anyone here. It says, 'Alexis said she will be home for Christmas this year, she is bringing Willa and Jonna to meet the family. Hopefully, K can come too, once he figures out who in his office would keep him from going.'"

Meyers was painfully nervous and was beginning to sweat. "Miss Devanoe, I do not understand what that message means. Should I?"

Annella threw the tablet down and said, "How dare you put my daughter at risk so that you could seek some personal gain?"

Meyers repeated, "I have no idea what you are talking about."

Kimakawa calmly said, "Alexis is referring to who in my office has been spying on the DAG. I wanted you to know she already figured it out but did not want to risk it in a communication."

Meyers looked at both of them, practically pleading while he said, "Certainly not me. That note could apply to anyone."

Kimakawa said, "I have known for over forty-eight hours that it was you, Meyers. Tell me who you work for, and you may just walk out of here."

Meyers looked at both of them. "Willits and Jones sent the message through your son, and it was not her message at all."

Kimakawa got up and walked over to the library shelves of books. He continued. "I had surveillance on you. We monitored your office and found the C-bar transmission hidden in the wall. It is very advanced. It seems to work without a locator. The engineers will undoubtedly be looking at it closer once they can take it apart. Now, tell me who you work for?"

Meyers began to sweat. He said in a panic, "I never sent any classified documents."

Annella grew angry. Raising her voice, she said, "What documents did you send and to whom?"

Meyers grew jittery. He was gripping his armrests tightly. He continued, "I was never told where or who would get the information, I swear!!!"

Annella replied, "Lying to me will not get you out of here alive. We monitored the last two transmissions. You were given the location of Ambassador Bird and letting someone know he is not dead, but alive. Why?"

Meyers yelled back. "I know nothing about the Ambassador, I swear."

Kimakawa broke his silence. He put down the pistol and grabbed the sword from the shelf. Turning around, he said, "This is a Samurai sword from the Edo period that has remained in my family for many generations. The Samurai were a proud and loyal group of dedicated warriors that I have often tried to model this guard on. Do you know what they did to traitors?"

Meyers yelled back, "Willits and Jones knew where the Ambassador was. I just verified for them. They performed the crime. The Belineans, along with Willits and Jones, tried to kill Ambassador Bird. Not me!!!"

Kimakawa continued, "They were given a choice of punishment. The Samurai would allow the guilty soldiers to commit *seppuku*, a form of suicide in which the warrior stabs himself."

Meyers spoke again, this time more calmly. "Please, Taichi, you do not understand...."

Kimakawa walked closer and pulled the blade out of its case. He got face-to-face with Meyers and calmly continued. "Otherwise, there would be a public decapitation at Kozukappara, next to the Emmeiji Temple, so all could see what happens to the disloyal. You swore an oath, Franklin. So, one last time, who are you working for?"

Meyers began to cry. He said, "Please, Taichi, I never knew they were going to kill Bird."

Kimakawa answered, "Yes, you did, and you gave them the information to do it."

Kimakawa then took one giant swing with the sword and cut Meyer's hand off. Blood went everywhere, splattering all over the desk and onto Annella. Meyers was waving his arm with no hand, blood spewing out of it. He tried to move, but Kimakawa turned the sword onto his throat and held it there.

Kimakawa returned to talking. "We were the only ones that knew Willits and Jones got Ambassador Bird off his transport at Torsalli. We were the only ones who knew they were keeping Bird at Vi Kapoor's guest house. And then it got bombed. Who did you tell?"

Meyers was screaming in pain. "It was Willits and Jones…."

Kimakawa continued, "No, it was you! Because Willits and Jones never had Bird at the guest house. They never even had him near Torsalli. They smuggled him out of Braccus undetected, where he has been with the cadets the whole time!"

Meyers grew white. Kimakawa saw the betrayal in his eyes. Annella then read another piece off her tablet. "This was from Alexis over two days ago from Molar. 'The Crowe and I are with cadets. W/J whereabouts unknown, but they smuggled us out of Braccus separately and have kept us alive. Beginning to think we are barking up the wrong tree."

Kimakawa continued, "You were always going to blame it on Willits and Jones. The execution would have worked perfectly had they used the pilots you picked, and they left Earth at the right time. But Willits changed the departure time and used the cadets as pilots instead. They would have ambushed Bird in Corvalis when you gave them the manifest, but Willits changed their course direction to Braccus instead. And they would be as dead as the ten billion people that lost their lives in the pandemic if they were in that guest house on Torsalli……."

Meyers cried. He held his severed arm with his other hand, blood still coming out of his wrist. With snot coming out of his nose and mouth, he muttered, "Taichi, I never knew…."

Kimakawa screamed with the blade now directly in Meyer's face. "WHO THE FUCK DID YOU TELL!"

Meyers, in a barely audible voice. "A man approached me. I think he was Belinean."

Kimakawa replied, "How long ago?"

Meyers answered, "Six, seven months ago. He offered me money, lots. Get me out and far away from here with just a little bit of information. It was small, useless stuff like how big DAG was, how we were training operatives, and looking to expand. I lied mostly."

Kimakawa asked, "Did he ask you about the DAG looking for Vait?"

Meyers, still in a lot of pain, nodded. He continued, "Yes. I told him we were looking for Vait to build security ships. I was done, he said one more job before getting me out. He needed the travel information for Ambassador Bird. He threatened me. Said he would turn me in."

Kimakawa asked, "Turn you in to whom?"

Meyers, still whaling in pain, said, "Another spy on the inside. I thought he might be working for Willits and Jones, looking for Vait. Then the assassination attempt happened with Bird on Space Port Earth. I realized I had given the information. I refused to help, but they insisted Bird was dead either way. They would get me out and give me the money only if I helped."

Kimakawa replied, "And you trusted them?"

Meyers grew hysterical. He continued, "It was better than trusting Bird! You heard his speeches! The Belineans saved us! They are our ally in fighting terrorists, not the enemy."

Kimakawa continued as Meyers was fading from so much blood loss. "How did it work?"

Meyers answered, "They gave me the C-Bar. Somehow it can send a message to a ship, not a designated C-Bar portal on a planet. It has an encryption key, so I never knew who I was sending or receiving information."

Kimakawa said, "Did you ever think it was Taz you were sending the information to?"

Meyers shook his head and said, "I never spoke to Taz, I swear!"

Kimakawa replied, "Yet he always knew where Ambassador Bird would be."

Kimakawa swung the blade back, preparing to strike. Meyers said, "Please, Taichi, I never meant to kill anyone!"

Annella finally interrupted and said, "But what you would have gladly killed my daughter. May God have mercy on your soul."

With those final words, Kimakawa struck his sword across Meyer's neck and instantly decapitated him. His head went rolling off and onto the floor. Meyer's body was still in the chair, slightly reclined. Kimakawa put his sword down on the desk. He went over, picked up Meyer's head, and took a picture with his wrist device.

Annella, still wiping blood off her face, softly asked, "What are you doing that for?"

Kimakawa calmly replied, "Letting Alexis know mission accomplished."

Annella answered, "Alexis is not who you need to worry about it. What are you going to say to Willits and Jones?"

Kimakawa just stared at Annella, pondering that question.

BELINEA 8.3

Belinea, Capital City

Ambassador Landing Facility, Ambassador Compound

Willits and Jones walked out of the Belinean D-21 Sirralo, escorting a young girl in robes. Two armed BRG officers greeted them. One was walking slightly ahead of the other and said, "You have no manifest, you are in violation of Belinean travel code. Please identify."

Willits smiled and said, "There is no manifest."

Jones grabbed the young lady's arm and said, "Right this way, my Lady."

Jones rushed her through the two security guards who now looked perplexed. Willits continued, "This is from Captain Kimmel of the AuFa. We were told to check her into the Hotel Lavender and await instruction from an Ambassador Vollach of Braccus."

The first officer said, "No manifest? Captain Kimmel didn't use the BRG?"

Willits continued, "The lady is a personal *friend* of the Ambassador, but one that cannot travel with him publicly if you catch my meaning. So Vollach had Kimmel take care of travel for the lady."

The second officer tapped his wristwatch and spoke clearly into it. "Tower, can you please confirm a Captain Kimmel in the AuFa, possibly somewhere near Braccus."

The BRG officer looked at Willits and said, "And who do you work for?"

Willits just flicked his head up and said, "Private security for Ambassador Vollach. I do not wear a uniform like you guys."

The BRG officer said, "And you do not travel like us either. That's a D-21 Sirralo, correct."

Willits said, "Perks of the job."

The message came across from the wristwatch. "Captain Kimmel's whereabouts are unknown at this time. His ship's current assignment is transportation from Torsalli to Braccus, and await further orders."

The second officer spoke into the wristwatch and said, "Alright, thanks."

The first officer said, "I need you to sign in for the Sirralo."

Willits looked around and grimaced a bit. He continued, "Look, the more I keep this on the hush-hush, the better. The Lady has some friends that she is getting for us. What time do you guys get off?"

The second officer said "In about two hours."

Willits responded, "Alright, once we get the Lady checked in, meet us back here. We will take the Sirralo for a little joy ride party with the other ladies."

The first officer said "Are you serious?"

Willits said "The very least I could do for you guys looking the other way for a few hours. Just make sure no one else boards it, alright?

The second officer replied "Not a problem. Do you know where you are going?"

Willits smiled and said "Not my first time to the Hotel Lavender gentlemen."

The first officer then asked "Hey. This is my last week here, the BRG is transferring me to an assignment on Braccus. Is Vandabri everything that I hear it is?"

Willits nodded as he walked off and said "Absolutely. Best time in the galaxy. Go find a place run by Madam Rouselle. Tell her Vi Kapoor sent you."

The officer looked confused "Vi Kapoor?"

Willits smiled and said "Trust me."

Willits sprinted to catch up to Jones and the girl. Willits came up from behind and Jones said, "Everything good?"

Willits said "Yep..."

The girl spoke very quietly. "So, what now?"

Jones said "We are going to work. You are gonna have the easiest assignment of your life."

The girl said "What's that?"

Willits replied "To sit around all day at one of the finest hotels in Capitol City. Go layout by the pool, have a refreshment, go to the spa, get a meal, all while still getting paid just to be quiet."

The girl replied "You guys can hire me anytime."

BELINEA 8.4

Avola

Lowell Province, Mining Center Six

Three miners were putting out the flames around the crashed transport. Two others were prying open the cargo bay door with rudely elementary equipment. When they finally got it up, they ran inside and began taking the bodies out. They handed Kaya's body to two other miners, before coming out with Octavious' body, followed by Cortes, who surprisingly seemed slightly coherent. One of the miners said "That's all of them."

They loaded all three bodies onto gurneys and then directed them onto a transport. Cortes shook her head ever so slightly. The Doctor that had previously worked on Kaya was on this medical transport and began scanning Octavious. She immediately said "He is gone, there is nothing I can do."

She then went over to Kaya, still in her red priest clothes. The Doctor scanned her everywhere. She whispered to herself "I put you back together only so you could tear yourself up again."

She scanned her for a few seconds and said to the pilot "If we do not get her back to Bisi now, I am going to lose her."

The pilot nodded and said "Let's go."

The transport took off. The Mining Center was in complete chaos. Most of it was on fire, billowing smoke. Almost a thousand miners had been killed, the rest had gone into hiding in the caves or dispersed back into the city. The AuFa had left after the initial attack, but would be back soon to retake the base after the fires calmed down.

As they flew off towards Bisi, the Doctor asked "How long til Bisi?"

The Pilot yelled back "Thirty minutes!"

The Doctor began patching up Kaya's shoulder, first by removing the round that was in it. She whispered again to herself "Come on, Kaya, hang in there."

BELINEA 8.5

Belinea , Capital City
AuFa Base One

The AuFa Frigate landed on pad Eleven. An entire AuFa platoon came out on the base, six guards on each side. They were holding their rifles, not pointing and aiming, but at a loose position. Nick Devanoe walked down the ramp off the ship and was immediately greeted by an AuFa officer. The Lieutenant saluted at Nick and said, "Commander Devanoe, I am Lieutenant Nichols. Admiral Flynn would like to see you at once."

Nick then spoke. "Yes Lieutenant. This is your platoon?"

Lieutenant Nichols confirmed "Yes, Commander."

Nick continued "Post them here Lieutenant. Do not let anyone on or off of this ship, including BRG. Do you understand?"

Lieutenant Nichols nodded his head and said "Yes, sir."

Nick then asked "Which one of your men can direct me to Admiral Flynn's office?"

Onboard the frigate, Tunsall and Trujillo got into full-body gear. Alexis was in a standard business suit with her tablet in a small carrying case. She spoke to the cadets "Listen, we stay together until we find a DAG unit. Not BRG. Understand?"

The cadets both nodded. Trujillo, readjusting his armor, said, "Although, technically, we only take orders from Willits or Jones."

Alexis checked the clip inside her handgun before wedging it into the small of her back, hidden by her coat. "I never thought I would say this, but I wish those two were here right now."

Tunsall replied "So do I."

After a pause, Trujillo asked, "Alexis. Do you think they are alive?"

Alexis took a deep breath and shrugged her shoulders. She answered "I would be more surprised if they were."

Ambassador Bird came walking into the room and said "Are we preparing for battle? I thought we were safe now that we are on Belinea?"

Alexis answered "Just taking some extra precautions. Did you get ahold of Ambassador Yi or any local DAG?"

Bird said "Yi, yes. He is sending his DAG team here and leaving the Capitol Building now. He was under the impression I perished in Torsalli."

Alexis answered "That is probably a common belief around here. Which is why from now on, you trust the three people in this room until Yi gets you a proper security detail."

Tunsall turned around and said, "Proper security detail? What are we?"

Alexis answered quickly. "Tired. And unless you want to keep up with exhausting twenty four hour shifts, we need some help. This isn't Molar. We can't just shoot everyone."

Trujillo responded "I'd like to forget Molar..."

Bird chimed in with "No one is forgetting Molar..."

Tunsall quickly added "Or Braccus..."

Trujillo, looked at Alexis with a devilish look, and added, "Or the trip to Hovron..."

Alexis tilted her head at Trujillo and said to everyone, "Everyone tighten up. A little less talk and a lot more ears up."

Bird asked "What are we waiting on?"

Alexis answered "My brother to get back."

Tunsall asked "He is coming back?"

Alexis just gave him a dirty look and continued looking out the window before replying "He should not bother with Christmas if he doesn't."

BELINEA 8.6

Avola

Bisi Province

Kaya was beginning to come around. The Doctor was checking her eyes. One still had a bandage over it, but the other was flickering open. She spoke quietly. "Kaya, can you hear me?"

Kaya, slowly turning her head, responded "Yes, where am I?"

The Doctor answered, "Bisi Base. You had several skull fractures from your crash, and getting shot in the shoulder required a lot of regeneration to the bone and tissue. But you should be alright. Look at me over here."

Kaya looked around with her one good eye. Kaya asked, "What about Cortes?"

Still looking at Kaya's eye, she answered. "Better than you, just one small skull fracture."

Kaya asked "My brother's body?"

The Doctor took a breath and quietly whispered. "We have it, I am so sorry for your loss."

Kaya paused, and whispered "I am sorry for everyone's loss."

After a moment, The Doctor continued. "Kaya, there is something you should know. I wasn't able to operate properly on the eye the first time. As a result it got infected. The multiple fractures and structural damage behind the eye socket forced us to remove valuable tissue that cannot be regenerated. Frankly, I am not sure if the scar around the eye can be repaired, it is not my field. I do not think you will ever see out of that eye again."

Kaya took a moment to process the information. She slightly nodded and said "Doc, you saved my life, I am not upset with you. Thank you."

The Doctor said "I have to go check on some other patients."

She got up and walked toward Ambassador Syren. She grabbed her hand on the way out and said, "Kaya will be fine."

Syren walked over to Kaya and looked her over. Kaya said "You know the Doc? Because I do not know her name."

Syren half smiled and said "The Doctor is Melana Bell, and she is my partner."

Kaya looked confused. She said, "I never knew…."

Syren spoke softly "She works at the Avolian hospital, but does work with the AuFa units as well. Her relationship to me would present a problem at work, so we keep it pretty close to the vest. She did recognize you, though, and she was responsible for getting you out of there. She will be our surgeon now because she will never be able to return."

Kaya looked stunned. "I am sorry, Syren."

Syren responded "These are all going to be tough decisions moving forward. Everything has changed after today. The AuFa killed several hundred innocent Avolian Miners. I am sure the Belineans will attempt to cover it up, but this is not going away. The Miners are united in a way they were not before."

There was a long pause before Kaya managed to get out, "You know about Octavious?"

Syren nodded and whispered "Yes, I have notified Quillisar Balerra. When you are well enough, there will be a ceremony."

Kaya responded "The second day Syren, Quill tradition. Even if I cannot walk, wheel me out there, understand?"

Syren nodded and then said "Kaya, Octavious might be dead, but you are still in danger. They know you are alive, they will come for you. We still need to keep you hidden. Perhaps even get you off the planet."

Kaya shook her head gently. "I am not going anywhere. This planet will blow up before I leave it."

Syren shook her head and said "How many lives have to be lost for you to understand we need to find a peaceful solution?"

Kaya looked to the side, away from Syren. After a couple of seconds, she looked back at Syren and said "Everyone is allowed to follow their own path, I will not stop them. But I have nothing now. I no longer have my brother, my family is my remaining soldiers. My path involves saving this planet and killing Argo Hassara. And I will do nothing else until that happens."

BELINEA 8.7

Belinea, Capital City
Ambassador Landing Facility, Ambassador Compound

The Ambassador Landing Facility had over three hundred spots for Ambassadors to park their private transports. Some of the junior Ambassadors were forced to park at a second facility nearby. The ramp came down on the D-21 as it had parked three spots away from the other D-21. Four guards came out, flanking a red Quillisar Priest that had his hood over his head. The guards were all carrying rifles, with one of them carrying a long skinny bag harnessed around his shoulder. They marched over to a luxurious personal TC, where two BRG officers were waiting for them. The Lead BRG asked "Credentials?"

The Lead Guard of the four held out his wristwatch so the BRG officer could scan it. He read the results out loud. "Commander Mastera of the SS, where can we take your Quillisar?"

Commander Mastera replied "We will take this TC and be on our way."

The BRG officer said "We cannot allow that sir. We were told to take you wherever you would like to go."

Mastersa only replied "This is a delicate matter for Quillisar Prill. Confidentiality and discretion is a must. Tell your Commander we took the TC and if there are any questions to take it up with Defense Minister Hassara herself, understand?"

The second BRG officer said, "Yes, sir."

He signaled for the pilot to get out of the TC. As he did, the other SS officers got onboard with the Quillisar. The BRG officer said to Mastera "A Quillisar in a Sirralo? We are in the wrong line of work. Second one today no less."

Mastersa said "What did you say?"

Worried that he might have offended Mastera, the BRG officer replied "Just a fact. We had another D-21 Sirralo land about two hours ago. Not with a Quillisar though."

Mastersa paused, and then said, "Are they still there?"

The second BRG officer answered "No, the ship is empty."

Mastersa said "When they return, detain them and wait for me to question them, understand?"

They both nodded in affirmative and said "Yes, sir."

Mastera climbed into the TC, and the door closed. With all five people inside, it took off, clearing the trees. It was a cloudy day with a small misty rain in the air. As they got near the Ambassador's Quarters, the TC found a landing spot next to one of the condo's. The pilot turned the engines off, and everyone got out. Masters and the Quillisar, opened the long skinny bag. They took the parts inside and assembled them into a long, handheld rocket launcher. They made their way through the path and found a spot in the trees to get into. The Quillisar took his red hood off, allowing him to see through the lens of the rocket launcher. Taz lined the scope up so the other guards could see the specific condo of Ambassador Bird.

BELINEA 8.8

Belinea, Capital City
AuFa Base One

Admiral Flynn was pouring himself a drink as Nick Devanoe stood at attention in front of his desk. The Admiral almost gave a half-smile, when he noticed Nick still standing that way. He said "At ease, Commander. Something to drink?"

Devanoe crossed his hands in front of his body and said "No, thank you, sir."

Flynn did not bother sitting down. Taking a sip of his drink, he said "Before this BRG officer gets here, you mind telling me what is going on? I do not often get random transports with unidentified cargo."

Nick looked directly at him. "Captain Kimmel and I were on Braccus sir. Our orders were to transport an Earth Ambassador, Bird, from Braccus to Torsalli and drop him off to BRG control from there. After the attack on Braccus, compounded with the explosion on Torsalli, we investigated the matter a little further."

Admiral Flynn asked "Why are you and Captain Kimmel investigating the bombing of a transport and murder of an Earth Ambassador? That is BRG jurisdiction"

Nick paused for a second, trying to figure out how much he wanted to reveal. "The bombing took place on the AuFa base at Torsalli Space Port."

Admiral Flynn paused for a second. He replied, "Are you aware Lord Malovex is on Torsalli?"

Nick answered "We saw him sir. He gave us the frigate to use as transport."

Flynn looked puzzled. "Malovex gave you the frigate you flew here? Really?"

Nick replied, careful to reveal too much. "Bird's assistant is my sister, sir. Captain Kimmel cut me some slack. The Ambassador and her were alive and well on Molar, where we found them. Through a series of events, two Earth Delegate Ambassador Guard members kept them alive."

Admiral Flynn responded, "If the Earth Ambassador is alive, why is the BRG searching for these two Earth Guards?"

Nick paused and said "They believe they caused the explosion on Torsalli. Which they might have, I do not know. But they did not kill the Ambassador."

Admiral Flynn took another sip. "So Kimmel told you to get this Ambassador and his assistant, your sister, here personally without turning them over to the BRG?"

Nick paused a second before making the eventual accusation. He said "Yes, sir."

Flynn half smiled and took a sip of his drink. Well, Kimmel and I share similar views of the BRG. Sounds like you do too. Alright, and you do not know where these two Earth DAG officers are?"

Nick quickly answered "No sir. It is possible they are still alive, but I doubt it."

Flynn nodded. He took another sip of his drink and said, "Alright. Off the record Commander, I spoke with Captain Kimmel about you. He reviewed the files of ten other candidates when searching for his new XO. I recommended someone else, but he was adamant about you. I promise, his loyalty does not come easy, but he clearly saw something in you. I advise not taking advantage of that in the future."

Nick answered firmly "Yes, sir."

Flynn continued "Let me deal with the BRG officer when he gets in here. I will have Lieutenant Nichols and his AuFa platoon escort the Earth Ambassador to the Ambassador Compound at Capitol City. What orders did Kimmel give you?"

Nick said "I am to take the frigate back to Braccus, unless you had other orders for me."

Flynn chuckled and said "The asshole has a sense of humor, dumping this flaming pile of shit right in my lap. And you can tell him I said that. Take the frigate back to Braccus, Commander."

Nick half smiled and said, "Yes, sir."

Lieutenant Orlando came walking up with five other DAG members to the frigate. He looked at the AuFa soldiers guarding the frigate and asked "Who is in charge here?"

Lieutenant Nichols turned around and answered "I am."

Lieutenant Orlando walked directly up to him and said "Thank you for your assistance, Lieutenant, you and your platoon are relieved."

Nichols practically laughed and said, "Lieutenant…?"

"Orlando, Earth Delegate Ambassador Guard. It is my understanding Ambassador Bird and his assistant are onboard this frigate. We will take over their security from here."

Nichols half smiled and said "That would matter only if I took orders from you Lieutenant. However, my AuFa Commander's orders were to let no one on or off this frigate."

Orlando never cracked even the smallest of grins. "By Council decree 21-A.2. - All Ambassadors will have their private security for travel around Belinea and Capitol City. This includes but is not limited to: Transportation crafts, Ambassador Complex, Private Quarters, and Social Engagements. Once inside the Council Assembly, security is extended back to the Belinean Rosash Guraan, or BRG."

Nichols stopped smiling. "Congratulations Lieutenant, on finally conquering reading, but I do not give a shit about you or any BRG decree. You are on an AuFa base, which is my jurisdiction. And my Commander gave me an order. If you would like to discuss it with him, he is up there talking to Admiral Flynn right now."

Orlando continued to stare. He got face to face with Nichols. "I am going aboard this frigate to check on the safety of my Ambassador."

Orlando started walking toward the ramp. Nichols stated very loudly, "Lieutenant, do not force us to shoot you."

At once, the entire platoon raised their rifles at Lieutenant Orlando. Orlando stopped and turned back to look at Nichols. Simply and confidently, he said "Do what you have to, Lieutenant. But if you shoot me, it will be the last thing you do."

As he said this, the five other DAG soldiers raised their rifles and pointed them at Nichols. Orlando turned back around and continued to walk up the ramp of the frigate. Nichols softly said "Let him go, but no one else."

Orlando got to the top of the ramp and made a left into the quarters. He was met by Alexis, Tunsall, and Trujillo, who were all standing in front of Ambassador Bird. Tunsall and Trujillo were holding rifles, but did not point them at Orlando. Orlando then declared "Ambassador Bird, I am Lieutenant Orlando, DAG. I am the head of Ambassador Yi's detail team. He sent me here to escort you back to the Ambassador Compound. Are you alright?"

Ambassador Bird responded "I am Lieutenant. This is my assistant Alexis Bird. Where is Ambassador Yi?"

Orlando looked at Alexis before looking back at Bird and saying "Now that we have verified you are alive, he told us to meet him at your personal condo with two of my soldiers to perform a security sweep. He does not trust anyone right now, sir."

Bird replied "Understand Lieutenant. We are ready."

Orlando looked at Tunsall and Trujillo. After sizing them up, he asked, "Who are you two?"

Alexis answered for them. "This is Tunsall and Trujillo."

Orlando looked perplexed. "DAG uniforms, but no insignia. What is going on?"

Tunsall answered "We were recruited to fly the Ambassador for this mission, sir."

Orlando was now really perplexed. "Recruited?"

Trujillo answered "We are cadets at Odgins, sir."

Orlando was astonished. "Cadets? Who the hell is the Commanding Officer on this detail?"

Tunsall answered "Commanders Nolan Willits and Avery Jones, sir."

Orlando raised an eyebrow. "Willits and Jones?"

Trujillo also answered, "Yes, sir."

Orlando shook his head. "Willits and Jones were on security duty? And they recruited the two of you to fly on this mission?"

In unison, Trujillo and Tunsall answered "Yes, sir."

Orlando asked "What about Mollanari, or what's her name, Rix?"

Trujillo and Tunsall just looked at each other before Trujillo responded "We do not know those people, sir?"

Underneath his breath, Orlando whispered "Security Detail? They must have really done something to piss off Kimakawa."

Bird asked loudly "What was that Lieutenant?"

Orlando half grinned and replied "Nothing, sir. If you will follow me."

Orlando turned around and the four of them followed him back towards the ramp. Alexis asked "Lieutenant, speaking of Director Kimakawa, it is urgent I get a message to him, letting him know of our arrival. I assume you have a C-Bar Transmitter in your DAG office that I can use."

Orlando, still walking, but not looking at Alexis, replied "I do Miss, but Ambassador Yi gave me specific directions not to let anyone communicate in or out."

Alexis stopped on the ramp down and grabbed Orlando's arm. "Is Kimakawa your boss?"

Orlando nodded and said "Yes."

Alexis said "Then you will take me to your office to deliver this message. Whatever punishment Yi gives you, will be marginal to Kimakawa's."

Orlando paused for a second before finally saying "What the fuck is going on?"

Alexis smiled and said "Chaos...smartest person wins...."

Alexis continued to walk down the ramp, now in front of Orlando. As they got to the bottom, Nichols had his rifle up and said "I was alright with you checking on your Ambassador. You see, he is fine. But I cannot permit you to leave with him."

Orlando walked directly up to Nichols again and confidently said. "We are leaving, and the invitation to shoot us is still there."

Nichols replied "I am serious this time, Lieutenant."

Orlando kept walking and said "So I am. Just remember, we shoot back."

Nichols pointed his rifle right at Orlando and yelled "Halt!"

Alexis went right up to Lieutenant Nichols and said "What are you doing? Just check with Commander Devanoe."

Nichols replied, "I have my orders."

Alexis stated, "This is no time to start an incident. We are on the same side."

Orlando turned around and said "Exactly Lieutenant. Remember, we are on the same side."

Nichols stared at Orlando, continuing to point his rifle right at him. He did not say anything for ten seconds, never taking his rifle down. Orlando asked, "Are you gonna shoot, or are you just going to point it at me all day?"

A few more seconds went by, until finally, from behind, Commander Nick Devanoe yelled "What the hell is going on?"

Nichols, not moving, yelled back as Nick was walking up "My orders were to not allow anyone on or off the frigate, sir."

Nick Devanoe walked up to the two and looked at Orlando and said "Who are you?"

Orlando replied "Lieutenant Orlando, DAG. I am here to get Ambassador Bird."

Nick responded "Alright, relax. The Lieutenant was only following my orders and this is an AuFa base you are on. We are all on the same side."

Orlando looked Nick up and down and said, "Are we?"

Nick looked at Orlando and said "Excuse me, Lieutenant?"

Alexis got in between both of them and said, "Lieutenant, relax. This is my brother, Commander Nick Devanoe."

Orlando said "AuFa?"

Nick noted with his expression that this was odd behavior. He nodded, and simply said "Yes."

The two said nothing for a few seconds Orlando afterward said, "We all got a role to play. DAG team, let's go."

The DAG team began escorting Bird out. Tunsall and Trujillo were curious about the exchange. All through school, all they wanted to be were pilots in the AuFa. And yet, in this exchange, both, far more surprising to Tunsall, their loyalty seemed to be for Lieutenant Orlando and his fellow DAG soldiers. Alexis looked at Nick and said "I will talk to you later."

Nick smiled and said "No you won't, I am leaving."

Alexis walked back to him, a look of confusion on her face. "I thought…"

Nick continued, "Once I get this frigate refueled and restocked, I gotta take it back to Torsalli."

Alexis shook her head and said, "I don't know what to say….."

She gave her brother a big hug, and Nick said, "Gotta get back to my day job. Make sure Tunsall and Trujillo stay close to you, alright."

Alexis, still hugging him, said "I will. Thank you."

She let go and stood there for a few seconds. Tunsall and Trujillo stared at Nick. Tunsall said, "Thanks for everything."

Nick, nodding at Alexis, said to Tunsall and Trujillo, "Make sure you watch her."

Trujillo half-smiled and said, "I think she can take care of herself."

Nick gave a small grin and said "She thinks she can. You guys know better."

Alexis gave a small frown and turned around. Sprinting up to Lieutenant Orlando, she asked, "Lieutenant, where is this DAG office?"

BELINEA 8.9

Avola

AuFa Base Six

The Robot Doctor had attached a titanium foot and ankle back to Argo's leg. He sat on the table, wiggling it around to see what kind of flexibility he had with it. Argo put a sock over it while the Robot Doctor asked, "Lord Argo, we are not done with the procedure. We still need to attach regenerated flesh and skin to the skeleton frame."

Argo however, had enough. "Nope, we are done. This will get me back to Belinea where a real surgeon will operate on it."

He strapped on a boot and hopped off the table. Lieutenant Walva was waiting for him outside the medical wing, where he addressed him walking by. "Lord Argo, are you feeling better?"

Argo looked at him and said, "I am missing a foot, Walla, what do you think?"

Walva responded with, "They were able to attach an artificial foot to your body, no?"

Argo kept walking, Walva followed. Argo continued, "Is there another explanation for my walking?"

Walva continued, "Speaking of my Lord, the Majavkee Lords would like a final word with you before you go."

Argo kept walking, with a small limp now. They turned a corridor as he said, "Unless it's a thank you, let's try not to arrange that."

Walva continued, "Yes, my Lord, I understand your hesitation. But there are some issues they would like to bring up."

Argo answered, "Like their incompetence?"

Walva answered, "Like the body count, sir. There are over nine hundred and fifty dead miners out there."

Argo kept walking with the small limp. He continued, "I like to call it dead protesters..., and will I at least get a thank you?"

Walva quickly said, "Not likely my Lord."

Argo kept walking while talking, "Nope. We do their dirty work for them, and instead of an ounce of gratitude, I am going to get a one minute lecture on the chaos I have created them."

Walva inserted "There is the loss of the entire Mining Facility, my Lord."

Argo continued "Do they not have others? See how many miners revolt now after what we did. Shit, you could guard them."

Walva replied "Flattering as always, my Lord, but I think there is a point that may have been missed..."

Argo snapped back, "You want to lose your tongue again?"

Argo stopped, and Walva froze. Neither said anything for a second before Argo said, "Which way to my transport? I cannot get out of here fast enough."

Walva responded, "You are going the right way, sir, it's just that..."

Argo cut him off and said, "You packed all my shit, my armor, everything?"

Walva answered "Of course, my Lord, it's just that..."

Argo interjected again, "And Leahy is doing alright?"

Walva answered, "Captain Leahy is still in surgery but the Doctors say he will make a full recovery."

Argo turned a corner and said, "Good, make sure we get a transport to Belinea when he is well enough to travel."

Walva answered, "Of Course my Lord, it's just that..."

They turned one more corner and twenty meters in front of them was Argo's transport. There were eight Majvakee Lords waiting next to the ramp. Argo stopped and looked at Walva and said, "You just forgot to tell me the Majavkee Lords are waiting next to my transport?"

Walva continued "The thing is sir, with all due respect, I was unable to finish a sentence, so the opportunity did not present itself in our conversation..."

Argo grabbed Walva's chin and said, "Walla, do me a favor and pretend I cut your fucking tongue out again for the rest of the trip back, understand?"

Walva nodded while Argo was still gripping his chin. He attempted to say 'Yes, my Lord.' But the grip caused it to sound like "Hes, ny ord."

Argo let go and walked over to the ramp. Lord Bialos was the first to talk. "Lord Argo, we have a situation."

Argo answered, "If you are responding to the attack on Mining Center Six, let me say…"

Lord Bialos continued, "There are over nine hundred dead miners out there. How are we going to keep them from revolting?"

Argo took a breath, then said, "The first thing you can do,…is develop,…I mean make them understand,….tolerance can be a surprising.….you know what? Fuck it! "

All the Majavkee Lords were taken aback. "Bialos, and the rest of you dickless shits, grow a pair. Yes, this should have never happened. If you guys had half a brain, you would have figured out a way to keep the Valmay, the Mining Guild, and the miners happy. So you are gonna have to go with plan B and rule by fear. The Council will spin this as a full military revolt, forcing us to leave multiple Battalions of AuFa soldiers behind. Trust me, the miners are so scared, they will not revolt again."

Lord Evander continued, "And the Valmay?"

Argo practically laughed, "You are welcome? No Octavioius Killian, no Valmay."

Lord Bialos said "It is not that simple my Lord…."

Argo replied, "But it is. Mine the Vait, protect the Vait, sell the Vait. You want to keep the miners from revolting? Every now and then, try giving them some money, you greedy fucks."

Argo turned to walk out, and now next to the ramp was Quillisar Balerra. She was standing there with her hands folded in front of her robes. Argo looked at her and said "And who are you, Quillisar …"

Balerra took her hood off and said "Balerra…I heard you were leaving without saying goodbye."

Argo smiled and said, "Quillisar, I did not even know we were friends. Now, if you will excuse me…"

Balerra continued without moving, "An SS officer leaving a Quillisar who has a direct message for your boss? Where is your faith, my child?"

Argo smiled. He continued. "My apologies, Quillisar. I was in a hurry to meet up with a ship that is going home."

Balerra continued, "Certainly they will not leave without you Lord Argo. Did you see what happened out there, at the Mining Facility?"

Argo replied, "A lot of unnecessary dead miners?"

Balerra corrected him, "A lot of unnecessary dead members of the Quill, my child."

Argo replied, "Do not protest and there is a good chance you will not get shot."

Balerra countered, "Not exactly a positive declaration for change. Physically, the body can take a lot. But the spirit, the soul of the energy, cannot exist without purpose to live. That is what my members were seeking. But that is not what I was referencing."

Argo answered, "Hopefully you are going to tell me before the next Offering?"

Balerra answered, "I have been around for quite some time my son. There are very few Quillisar's older than me…"

Argo, in a sarcastic tone, replied, "A fact that surprises no one…"

Balerra continued, "A long time ago, a Quillisar Priestess went off on a Spaventa. Do you know what that is?"

Argo responded, "Probably not a weekend on Vandabri…"

Balerra continued. "Spaventa is an enlightenment. It is a walk for one hundred days into the rocks, caves, and mountains of Avola. You can drink water, but you cannot eat. You only take in every bit of energy the planet and its surroundings give you. Only the highest, most dedicated of Quillisars can achieve this pinnacle. When they do, they come home and engage their newfound energy, glowing in their field stone, among the rest of the Quill. But, only one Quillisar, in all my years, has been able to light up all the field stones in a mass, regardless of color."

Argo asked, "You, Quillisar?"

Balerra shook her head. She said, "No. But your Quillisar will know who I am referring to. I thought I would never see it again, until it happened yesterday in front of you."

Argo was now silent. He just stared at her. He replied, "What would you have me do with this information?"

Balerra responded, quietly but confidently, "You tell Prill what you saw and that it was no Quillisar that caused it. You watch his reaction."

Argo paused for a few seconds with an odd look on his face. Balerra took a step forward and whispered. "Containment is an illusion if you cannot see what you actually possess."

Argo stared at Balerra for a few more seconds. Finally, understanding the full reference, he asked, "Anything else, Quillisar?"

Balerra stepped to the side, and Argo proceeded to take a step onto the ramp. As he was taking his next step, Balerra said, "Lord Argo, one more thing."

Argo stopped and slightly shook his head. He turned around, and Balerra continued. "Hating these people is your problem. Having the power to kill them without consequence has now become mine."

Argo looked at her and, while nodding to the Majavkee Lords, said, "You can start with that collection of imbeciles right there."

Balerra responded, "You tell yourself that if you want. Just do not tell that to someone who lost a loved one yesterday."

Balerra turned around and walked away. Argo shook his head again and walked up the ramp.

BELINEA 8.10

Belinea, Capital City

Ambassador Compound

The two TC's landed as the six DAG soldiers led by Lieutenant Orlando all got out. Tunsall, Trujillo, and Ambassador Bird, followed. The entire group of nine walked down the path next to the rows of Ambassador condos. All were naturally camouflaged by the very tall pine trees. The misty rain gave a fog-like condition everywhere, making it a little easier for security and ideal for privacy. Lieutenant Orlando led the group, and said, "Ambassador this way."

Bird looked over at Tunsall and Trujillo, each with armor on, each with rifles. He asked, "Where did Alexis go?"

Trujillo answered, "She is at the DAG office. She said she had to send a message."

Jones was looking out the window while Willits was eating a piece of fruit. Jones said, "Hold on, I see something."

Willits asked sarcastically "Adult entertainment? Or something else?"

Jones answered, "Definitely something else."

Willits got up and stood next to Jones. Jones squinted his eyes trying to see better. "That looks like two DAG soldiers escorting someone in front of Bird's condo, but that is not Bird."

Willits added, "That person is too short."

Jones asked "Who the hell is that?"

Ambassador Yi was walking with two DAG soldiers from Lieutenant Orlando's team. He had a hood on as he tried to camouflage himself a bit so no one would recognize him. He stopped in front of Ambassador Bird's condo and tried to open the door. He was talking to himself as he whispered, "The master code is here somewhere…."

Taz was in the treeline. All he could see was the back of the Ambassador and the two guards looking around for anything unusual. Taz adjusted his scope a bit, relaxed his muscles, and squeezed the trigger.

Trujillo saw the flash of light come from the trees. In a second, there was another flash from the explosion hitting Bird's condo. It was immediately followed by a deafening boom. Everyone on the detail stopped. The DAG soldiers rushed to Bird and got him on the ground. Trujillo, Tunsall, and Orlando started running towards the explosion. Trujillo was first in line running along the path.

The explosion from the rocket shattered the window in front of Willits and Jones. They were lying on the floor, with broken glass all over them and Ambassador Yi's condo. Willits looked at Jones and said, "You alright?"

Jones reached for his side pistol and said, "Yeah, what the fuck was that?"

Willits reached for his side pistol and said, "That was a handheld rocket launcher. Ready…"

Jones nodded, and both started blindly shooting through the window frame across the foggy treeline some twenty meters towards where the rocket came from.

Trujillo, still running with Tunsall and Orlando, who were about five meters behind him on the path, saw a few people in the treeline firing at a condo. He stopped about ten meters from Bird's condo, which was now in flames. In front of the doors were the remains of the three dead bodies, including Yi, all charbroiled and still on fire. Trujillo could hear rounds coming from the condo that was fifteen meters down from Bird's. Pistols from the condo followed by rifles from the treeline. Trujillo took out his rifle and began firing at the treeline from where the rocket came from. Tunsall and Orlando stopped right behind him and started doing the same.

Some of Taz's soldiers now began to fire upon Trujillo, Tunsall, and Orlando. Trujillo could see through the trees that whoever shot that handheld rocket launcher was reloading. He looked closer and could barely make out it was Taz. Trujillo, not knowing who was in the condo, decided Taz was an enemy of everyone. He yelled at the top of his lungs, "He's reloading!! Get out of that condo!!!"

Willits and Jones looked at each other confused. Willits said, "Was that Trujillo?"

Trujillo yelled again, "Now!!!!"

Willits and Jones took one last look before Willits went through the door, and Jones went out the window. Jones took a round in the shoulder and rolled down the path. Willits took three steps on to the path and jumped into a creek in front of the condo. Trujillo, Tunsall, and Orlando kept firing, laying down recovery fire. Taz launched the rocket a second later, and it exploded Yi's condo.

The firing stopped for a second, as the dust and flames settled from Yi's condo, which was now on fire. Willits was laying in the creek, but managed to roll over and get behind a tree. He yelled across the flames still coming from Bird's condo. "Trujillo?"

Trujillo looked over at Tunsall before he yelled, "Willits?"

Willits yelled, "Bird safe?!"

Trujillo yelled back, "Yeah. I got Tunsall and Lieutenant Orlando."

A few more shots fired around them, but again, visibility was poor because of the fog. After ten seconds, Willits yelled, "Jones?"

Jones had crawled over and gotten behind a pine tree. Sitting with his back against the tree, he had blood coming from his shoulder wound. Clearly in pain, he yelled, "I will live."

Willits yelled again, "Trujillo, ready?"

Trujillo said, "For?"

Willits said not quite as loud, but just loud enough for Trujillo, Tunsall, and Orlando to hear him. "Our turn…."

Willits stood up and came out, firing his side pistol. Trujillo, Tunsall, and Orlando did the same as they got up with their rifles. They crossed over the flames of Bird's condo and saw Willits, who was in a full sprint up the path. Willits passed Jones, who was struggling to get up from his wound. Willits weaved in and out of the walkway path. Through the trees, up and down, he finally got to a clearing where he could see forty meters ahead of him. Taz and his soldiers were running the other direction. Willits stopped and shot at them, barely missing. One of Taz's soldiers stopped, turned around, and began shooting at Willits, causing him to jump behind a tree. When he got up, he looked over at the door of one of the condo's and saw an explosive device in front of it beeping.

The firing stopped as Trujillo, Tunsall, and Orlando came running up. Trujillo looked over at the door and saw the same thing. He asked, "What is that?"

Willits responded, "Probably their exit strategy."

Jones looked at Tunsall and said, "Grab it."

Tunsall said, "Are you kidding?"

Jones replied, "No. Throw it into the trees."

Very reluctantly, Tunsall grabbed the bomb and chucked it into the trees. Willits then said, "Come on."

They continued to run up the path, which split into two, a right and left fork. Willits said, "Orlando, Tunsall, go with Jones that way. Trujillo, come with me.

Tunsall, taking off down the left fork, was in front of Orlando, followed by Jones, who was struggling along with his damaged shoulder. When they got to a hill, Tunsall and Orlando could see forty meters to the bottom.

Matching the surroundings, a thirty-meter high, five-meter wide tower, all in green camouflage, stood at the bottom. The tower was in the middle of a clearing that had twenty pads. BRG soldiers ran to the eight attack Valkyries still on the ground while the other twelve were already airborne flying above the treeline towards the blazing condos. Next to the Tower were four small buildings that provided housing for BRG soldiers. Tunsall could see two of Taz's soldiers talking to a BRG officer. One of them pointed at Tunsall and Orlando. The officer yelled, "Up there!"

At that moment, twenty armed BRG officers whipped their rifles around and began shooting to the top of the hill. Tunsall, Orlando, and now Jones, who had just come up from the rear, all took cover behind the trees. Orlando yelled, "Why are they shooting at us?"

Two armed Valkyries circled back around, hovering above them. They began shooting down on the three of them. Orlando yelled, "Shit, any ideas?"

Tunsall yelled, "Drop your weapons."

Jones yelled, "Are you fucking crazy?"

Tunsall yelled, "No way we shoot ourselves out. Drop them, put your hands up.

After a couple of seconds, they could hear more soldiers coming up the hill. Reluctantly, Orlando threw his rifle onto the path after Tunsall did it. Jones immediately followed by throwing out his pistol. All three soldiers got up and put their hands on their heads. Tunsall kept repeating, "Do not shoot, we are unarmed. Do not shoot, we are unarmed."

One of the BRG soldiers, with his rifle pointed right at them, yelled, "Get your hands up!"

Orlando yelled back, "They are up, asshole! The culprits are getting away!!!"

One of the BRG officers punched Orlando right in the stomach, causing him to fall over. He said, "Shut up!"

Tunsall yelled, "That is a DAG officer. We were guarding an Ambassador when the rockets exploded."

Another BRG officer, who was now pointing his rifle right at Tunsall, said, "Sure you were."

Two of Taz's soldiers that went left on the fork had just taken off in a medical TC. A mere three meters above the ground with all four rotor blades pointing upwards, the medic asked the soldier, "Alright Commander, where are you hurt?"

Taz's soldier, disguised as an SS officer, said, "Here…"

He took a dagger out and stabbed the medic in the chest. The pilot turned around, but it was too late as the other soldier had sliced his throat. He dragged him out of the pilot's chair and climbed in himself.

Trujillo and Willits continued another kilometer down the right fork of the path winding through the trees. They could occasionally see two soldiers and Taz, still running, sometimes shooting back. The track had circled back to the BRG base, on the other side of the landing pads opposite where Tunsall, Orlando, and Jones were being held. Taz and his two soldiers waited. The medical TC his other soldiers had taken over was descending upon them. One of the soldiers was on a knee, scoping the area behind them. As Trujillo got forty meters away, he lined up his rifle and took a quick shot that went straight through his head. The other soldier whipped around and fired at Trujillo. He was met with more rounds from Willits side pistol. As the medical TC next to them landed, Taz and his soldier jumped in. Taz grabbed a tablet from his backpack.

On the other side of the BRG base, Orlando, Jones, and Tunsall had been escorted down the hill. Approaching the base, they still had their hands on top of their head. They stopped next to a refueling truck parked at the edge of the forest. Ten armed BRG officers were still yelling at them to "Shut up, get down, make a move, and I will kill you,...."

Tunsall, Jones, and Orlando kept yelling at them. "We are DAG, you are letting them get away, check with your other officers."

Finally, Tunsall, who was looking off to the side, noticed a bomb sitting next to the refueling truck. Tunsall yelled, "Hey assholes, that's a bomb over there!"

The BRG officer that was guarding him pointed a rifle in his face. Never attempting to look for the bomb, he yelled back, "Shut the fuck up before I make you shut up."

The other BRG officer was holding his earpiece more closely now and said, "You got Ambassador Bird safe? Copy that, please."

Another few seconds went by before he spoke again "Yi is dead, as are two DAG soldiers. The rest of his detail went into pursuit down the path. Copy that. Can you give me the name of the head of his detail?"

Orlando was standing but with his hands on top of his head. He looked at the BRG officer with the earpiece having this conversation and said, "It's Orlando asshole."

The BRG officer listened to his earpiece and then dropped his rifle. He then looked at the rest of his soldiers and said, "These are not our guys..."

Another BRG officer asked, "Then who were those SS soldiers?"

Orlando had enough. He said, "The enemy, you dumbass!"

Another BRG officer said, "Cool it. We need to work together.."

Meanwhile, Jones had gotten up and started to walk towards the parked Valkyrie. Tunsall looked at the guy guarding him and said, "You still got a bomb over here, shitheads...."

The BRG soldier guarding Tunsall walked right up to him and said, "I do not care who you are. Nobody talks like that to..."

But Tunsall cut him off and head-butted him right in the nose. He then punched him in the gut, took the rifle out of his hands, and with the back end, struck him across the head, causing him to fall. Four BRG soldiers immediately pointed their rifles at Tunsall. Because of Tunsall's ruckus, Jones had jogged to the Valkyrie, practically unnoticed. As he climbed into the Valkyrie, Jones yelled, "Tunsall...."

It caused all the BRG soldiers to look over at Jones, but still keeping their rifles on Tunsall. Jones climbed into the pilot seat of the Valkyrie. Tunsall, still holding the rifle he had taken out of the BRG soldier's hands, looked at another soldier. He tossed it in the air toward him, and said, "Fuck it."

Tunsall immediately took four quick steps toward the back of the Valkyrie. One of the BRG officers shot a round into the air, trying to stop him by scaring him. Tunsall pulled the hook attached to the cable on the back of the Valkyrie. He took three steps back to where the bomb was and hooked it onto the cable. The BRG soldier that shot the round into the air yelled, "Stop!"

Tunsall raised his hand and waved at Jones. He yelled, "Go!"

Jones saw Tunsall wave through the rearview mirror and pulled down on the throttle. Another BRG soldier yelled, "What are you doing?"

Jones had the Valkyrie one meter off the ground, dragging the bomb behind him from a two-meter cord.

On the other side of the base, Taz kept the door open on the medical TC as the soldier next to him picked up his rocket launcher. He aimed it back at the surface, where Willits was shooting his pistol. Taz was hitting buttons on his display while the soldier fired the rocket launcher. As the rocket soared towards Willits, he jumped to take cover. The explosion sent him flying in the air towards the trees.

Jones never got the Valkyrie more than two meters off the ground. As he accelerated across the pads, away from the BRG soldiers, he flipped the Valkyrie in reverse and spun. He hit the lever on the hook dragging the bomb, which uncoupled and rolled into the forest.

Inside the medical TC, Taz hit one last button on his tablet, and all the bombs went off at once. The two in the forest next to the Ambassadors condos and the third one that Jones just sent rolling into the woods. The bombs caused a massive explosion, a fireball forty meters high. As the Medical TC began to climb higher, Trujillo got on one knee and aimed his rifle. He kept firing on the rotor blades of the TC until he finally connected on one. He switched aim and hit another blade, causing the Medical Rotor Rover to spin and spiral towards the ground. The pilot managed to pull up at the last second and crash land it.

The Medical TC was slightly on fire, smoke pouring out of it. Jones had gotten out of his Valkyrie and started walking to the crash site thirty meters away. Tunsall grabbed the rifle he tossed on the ground and started running toward the crash site as well. Several BRG officers followed, still in awe over the explosions. From the other side of the crash site, Trujillo began walking towards it, thirty meters away, rifle drawn. After a moment, the door to the Medical TC opened up, and Taz walked out. Bleeding through his red suit, he took out his ring and made it into a diamond. Trujillo, Jones, and Tunsall all stopped at once. The eyes on all three of them got huge. They turned around and yelled, "BACK UP!"

Taz let the diamond fire blade go over his neck. He got on both knees. A couple of BRG soldiers did not back up. They broke out their rifles and tried to shoot Taz. Taz took a deep breath, and the firewall came out, going in every direction, forty meters around him. Jones had taken shelter behind his Valkyrie. Tunsall had gotten behind the Tower. Trujillo had made it back to the forest and got behind a tree. The fire extended for fifteen seconds before it stopped. The four BRG officers caught in the wake burned to a crisp. The ten that had listened to Jones, Tunsall, and Trujillo had managed to take cover, the worst only getting minor burns. Taz stood up and looked around.

A ship appeared from the sky. It was breaking through the fog. Taz, delighted to see it, was convinced this was his way out. The ship came down and landed ten meters from Taz's crashed Medical TC. Smoke, from the crashed TC to Taz's fireball, seemed to be everywhere. Combined with the fog, the entire area was a smokey blur. As the dust settled, Malovex walked down the opening ramp from the ship.

In his all-black robes, Malovex continued towards Taz. Malovex grabbed his ring and suddenly stopped. He had an instant flashback to Serpia, twenty years prior. It was a clear vision, as if he was looking into a cockpit, he could see the controls. He could see the helmet, a reflection in the glass, and hands moving frantically, shooting. Malovex continued to keep his eyes close, not moving. In the vision, he could see the troubling flight through the cockpit glass, everything moving in a flash of light. Ground artillery fire and explosions went off right next to the craft, but it barrel rolled out of it. And for a quick second, he could see the eyes in the reflection. Just as quickly, the eyes blinked, and the vision disappeared.

Malovex opened his eyes, and Taz was still in front of him. Only a few seconds had passed. He extended his ring to a silvery sword and continued towards Taz. Taz raised both his arms. His fire blade was a dagger, and he did not bother extending it to a saber. As Malovex kept getting closer, the speed of his steps increased. Taz caught off guard by the whole thing, took a step back. Taz extended his dagger into a fire sword just as Malovex was running toward him. It caused Taz to go reeling back with a swing, as Malovex struck him with an overhead blow. Taz defended it with his blade, as the two connected. One with a fire blade, the other with a thin silvery sword.

They continued their fight, blow for blow, Back and forth they went. At one point, Malovex got Taz on the ground. As he was ready to strike, he put his blade up and made a stream of fire. It set Malovex's hair ablaze as he narrowly missed it. When he went to swing, Taz rolled over and got another stream of fire off, this time blocked by Malovex, making a two-foot wide shield with his sword. Taz got to his feet, and the striking continued. Back and forth they went. Taz finally got Malovex on the floor. When he went for the striking blow, Malovex made a semi-circle ring with his sword around his body. Taz's flaming saber connected with it, but it did not penetrate his semi-circle shield. Malovex kicked out Taz's foot, causing him to stumble, which allowed Malovex to jump back to his feet.

The two continued to exchange blows. First, Malovex had a long narrow strike with his extending sword. It did not connect, as it just missed Taz's head. Then Taz tried a fire burst that burned Malovex's hands. They took a few seconds catching their breath, Malovex flip-flopping his sword between his burnt hands, Taz pacing around him with his fire saber. They went back at it, blow after blow. This continued for another thirty seconds until Malovex watched Taz lunge. Malovex stepped sideways and rolled over on his shoulder. When he came out, he was sideways with Taz, slightly behind him. He swung and slashed him across both calves.

Taz fell to the floor. Malovex took a step forward after the swing, and then another one. Taz rolled over, unable to get up. Malovex took a step to the side and turned around. He was now facing Taz, standing in front of him almost two meters away. Malovex went for the striking blow, but Taz, closing his eyes, held up his fire saber, and it let out a stream of fire one meter wide. Malovex had taken a step before his crushing blow and had managed in one clean motion to flip over Taz. When Malovex had landed, he was behind Taz, sword drawn. Taz was finishing his fire stream. When he opened his eyes, he couldn't see Malovex until it was too late. Malovex had positioned his sword in between Taz's helmet and chest armor. From behind Taz's head, he kept extending his silvery sword until it pierced through his neck, just above the chest. Taz began to wiggle during his dying moments.

After a few seconds, Malovex retracted his silver sword. With Taz rolling and wailing, he took a massive swing at his head, causing his helmet/mask to come off. His eyes and nose had blood coming out of them while his mangled black hair almost hid the 'T' branded on his forehead and nose. Malovex took his sword, and with one devastating blow, pierced it right through Taz's face, straight through his skull, taking the life from him.

BELINEA 8.11

Avola

Bisi Base

Kaya got up out of bed. She put her full black uniform on, including the ring on the side. The patch over her eye was still there. The surgery to fix it was unsuccessful. She walked down to another room and saw Cortes in her bed, mostly recovered. Kaya looked at her and said, "Get dressed."

Cortes did, and together they walked out of the temporary medical center. A transport ship was on the other side of Bisi Base with two of Kaya's soldiers outside the ramp. As Kaya and Cortes approached, one asked, "Are you alright?"

Kaya gave just a very somber nod. Kaya stared at him for a full five seconds before whispering, "Come…"

A few more soldiers joined in, all curious to see her. Eventually, they followed Kaya and Cortes to the transport. Together, all eight of them got on board, found seats, and buckled in. Cortes fired up the engines. Kaya sat next to her in the co-pilot chair. Cortes looked at Kaya. Without having to ask, she was asking where to go. Kaya replied, "Balerra's Temple…"

Cortes nodded, hit a couple of levers, and the ship took off. Kaya hit one button and said on the radio, "This is Kaya, open up the gate."

The doors slightly opened, enough for the transport to slip through and out the mountain. Cortes, still focused on where they were going, asked Kaya without looking, "You worried about them finding you?"

Kaya shook her head. She responded, "They will not be looking for a small transport. They also think we are all dead."

The ship gained altitude and began the thirty-minute journey back to Mining Center Six. Kaya looked out the window. She thought about her brother, the battles, and disagreements. She thought about how he fought, where they had come from, and how far they had come. She looked at the mountains, the rock, the desert. A tear ran down her face. Still looking at the window, she said, "I love it, all of it…"

Cortes responded, "What?"

Kaya looked at her and said, "Home…"

Cortes nodded and looked back at where they were flying. No words were spoken for the rest of the flight. There was nothing to say. Cortes was coming on a final approach for a landing pad a few blocks from the Temple. Kaya unbuckled herself and walked back to the other six soldiers. One by one, she grabbed their shoulders, and looked them in the eye. Each stood up when she got to them, taking their arm and hand and placing it on her shoulder. Each would nod, a symbol of respect that went way beyond a salute. They had fought together. They watched fellow soldiers die together. The transport landed just as Kaya got to the last soldier. She put a hood on to disguise herself, as did Cortes. The other six soldiers did not use any disguise. All eight of them walked out the ramp together.

There was no AuFa or Majavkee security presence. There was some rioting, but for the most part, there was a peaceful sadness to the town. The AuFa and Majavkee would wait a few days before re-taking the Center, letting tensions subside. It was dark, and visibility was reduced. Kaya walked up the steps of the Temple. There was a service for one of the Miners going on, and the family was in front. Crying could be heard all through the Temple. Another dead miner's body was waiting. A Quillisar was giving the ceremony. Kaya saw people as she walked through. Even with the hood, many people recognized her. They came up to her and showed respect. They grabbed her arm, and in return, she looked them in the eye. Without any words, she somehow expressed, *'I know, I feel your pain, we are all in this together….'*

Kaya walked down the center aisle. A wife was crying out loud, trying to be comforted by her eight-year-old son. Her dead spouse was in front of the Temple, the Quillisar giving a pre-ritual. Kaya walked up behind and bowed her head. The crying woman went up to her dead spouse, only to be turned away by the Quillisar and another family member. After thirty seconds, they managed to turn her around, backing her away from the dead body.

The woman, while being helped back, then locked eyes with Kaya. She ran to Kaya and began hitting her. She was screaming, "WHY! WHY! WHY…"

Cortes tried to step in between them, but Kaya brushed her off with her arm. Kaya grabbed the crying woman with both hands on her shoulders, looking her in the eye. After a few seconds, both of them got to their knees. The crying woman stopped hitting Kaya, and within a few seconds, allowed Kaya to embrace her. The woman cried and cried, loudly. It caused Kaya to cry as well. She cried for another thirty seconds, all the while Kaya held her tightly. The crying woman let go, slightly pushing Kaya away. Looking at her directly in the eyes, she said, "His name was Lewis….Lewis…."

Kaya nodded, still looking at her directly in the eyes. She took a huge breath, still crying herself, and said, "I will not forget…."

They touched foreheads. Kaya now grabbed the side of the crying woman's head with both of her hands. After another thirty seconds, a family member pulled her away, as both her and Kaya stood up. Kaya nodded again at her as if to say 'I understand.'

Kaya walked to the side and saw the next dead body that was up and locked eyes with a woman who was crying also. Kaya stared for a few seconds before walking out the side door of the Temple. Cortes and the other six soldiers followed her. When she got outside, the landing areas and playgrounds were filled with people. Dead bodies, hundreds of them with families standing over them, were everywhere.

Kaya stood there for a few seconds, trying to understand and accept the enormity of the situation. She surveyed the landscape again and again, eventually closing her one good eye because of an inability to process all the collateral damage. She took some steps down, and walked to an aisle that weaved between the bodies. She saw a familiar face, a family member. She looked at her, not fully processing why she was here. She was crying. As she embraced Kaya, Kaya looked down and saw the dead body of her cousin Donovan. Kaya closed her eyes and held her cousin's spouse closely. Tears began streaming down her face. This continued for another thirty seconds before Kaya let go and looked at her cousin's spouse in the eyes. They touched foreheads. Kaya grabbed the back of her head and placed it in her bosom. She looked up and around, now fully processing all the death and loss.

After a few seconds, she let go of her cousin's spouse and moved on. Row after row, aisle after aisle. Bodies, all dead from the massacre. Loved ones were crying, passionately wailing in frustration and loss. Kaya swallowed hard, trying to get the courage to make it through. She walked another thirty meters, through a few more aisles of tens of dead miners.

Sterling walked up to her and said, "You do not know who I am. My name is Sterling."

Cortes stepped in and said, "Sterling rescued us in the caves."

Kaya nodded and said, "I am Kaya."

Sterling said, "I helped your brother escape. He stayed with me while the AuFa were looking for him. I am so sorry. You have my deepest condolences."

Kaya swallowed again, another tear going down her face. She said, "Thank you. Did you lose someone also?"

Sterling tilted his head. There were a few seconds of silence as he tried to process a correct answer. Finally, he said, "We all lost someone. Friends, family, co-workers. Everyone here is greiving."

Kaya grabbed his shoulder and nodded. Sterling waited a few seconds before he continued. "But no more. We all want to fight. We will train if you will teach us, in all your ways. We will be silent no more."

This caught Kaya off guard. A few seconds went by before she finally just nodded, not knowing what to say. She let go of Sterling's shoulder and continued to walk. Another twenty meters and she got to Quillisar Balerra. The older lady was preparing a dead miner's body for the service inside. She was kneeled over. After a few seconds, she got up, and embraced the family. She nodded her head at them, turned, and saw Kaya. They stared at each other for ten solid seconds, neither knowing what to say to the other. Finally, Kaya walked over, got down on one knee, and bowed to her. Cortes and the other six soldiers immediately did the same. Balerra took a couple of steps towards them. When she got to Kaya, she placed her frail hand on top of Kaya's head. A tear ran down her cheek.

Balerra quietly said, "Rise my child…"

Kaya stood up. She looked down at Balerra, and after a moment, embraced her. While hugging her, Kaya whispered in her ear, "I am going to kill every single one of them…."

They stopped embracing. After a moment, Balerra said, "It will not bring Octavious back, Kaya. It will not bring any of them back."

A few seconds went by, another tear going down Kaya's face. She said, "But these deaths cannot go unavenged. Otherwise, they died for nothing."

Balerra asked, "Does it ever stop my child? How many deaths will it take?"

Kaya answered, "Until they leave our home...."

The two looked at each other for a few seconds. There was a concession by Balerra. She knew Kaya would never be Octavious, and vice-versa, Kaya would never stop. Kaya turned to walk away. As she got a few steps, Balerra said loud enough for Kaya to hear, "From this moment on, I beg you to think about the children as well as our planet, our home, before you do anything."

Kaya stopped. No longer with any tears, but still watery eyes, she turned to look at Quillisar Balerra. She softly said, "My Quillisar, it is all I think about...."

Kaya, Cortes, and the other six soldiers walked away, back towards the Temple.

BELINEA 8.12

Belinea, Capital City

Ambassador Compound, BRG Patrol Post

Alexis made her way down the path until she finally saw the BRG Post. A BRG soldier attempted to stop her, but she showed enough credentials to get by. She continued down the path to an area where Tunsall, Trujillo, and Orlando were standing. Orlando was being treated for some scratches. Trujillo was bleeding from a cut on his head, but was otherwise fine. Alexis jogged right up to him and hugged him. "Are you alright?"

Trujillo hugged her back and replied, "I'm fine."

Alexis let go and looked at him. She then asked, "You hurt? Did you get shot? What happened?"

Trujillo answered, "Taz and his crew blew up Ambassador Bird's condo. We chased them down here, and there was a fight. Lord Malovex killed Taz."

Alexis quickly responded, "But you are not hurt. Did you break anything?"

Trujillo, now slightly annoyed, said, "I am fine."

Alexis was grabbing Trujillo's shoulder and looking at the cut on his head before Tunsall interjected with, "I am fine, thanks for asking."

Trujillo gave a half-smile, as Alexis turned around and walked three steps over to Tunsall. She grabbed his shoulder, then put her hand on his cheek and said, "Tunsall, you alright?"

Tunsall gave a smirk and said, "Just another day at the Academy..."

Alexis looked at him for a few seconds before turning around to address all of them. Looking directly at Orlando, she said, "Yi is dead. He was at the front door with two of your DAG soldiers when the explosion happened."

Orlando quietly said, "We know. We are still being detained here, which is why I am not back there. Bird is safe?"

Alexis was looking at their detainment with curiosity. She then nodded about Bird. "He is currently in the BRG safe house, but the rest of your detail refuses to leave him."

Orlando nodded and whispered in admiration, "Good…"

Alexis asked, "Why are you being detained?"

Trujillo responded, "BRG will not let us go until everything checks out. I don't think they are worried about us anymore, but Willits and Jones don't seem to be going anywhere."

Alexis, completely dumbfounded, responded, "They are here?! Alive?!"

Trujillo nodded further down toward the Tower, in two chairs were Jones and Willits. They were unarmed, but being guarded by ten BRG soldiers. A medic was still working on Jones' shoulder, trying to patch it up. Willits arm was in a sling, and there was a bulky bandage wrapped around his thigh, which was extended straight out. Alexis immediately left the three of them and began walking down the path. Trujillo asked, "Where are you going?"

Alexis made it further down and then was stopped by a rather tall BRG soldier. As Alexis tried to get past him, he said, "No one goes through Miss."

Alexis looked up at him and said, "I need to see those two DAG officers, please."

The soldier looked at her and said, "No one sees these two except that medic."

Alexis asked, "Are they prisoners?"

The soldier turned to the side, looking at another soldier, before replying, "Not exactly."

Alexis then stared at him straight in the eyes. Showing her credentials, she said, "My name is Alexis Devanoe. I am the Executive Assistant for Ambassador Bird, who just had yet another attempt on his life. Those two men are responsible for his detail, and I am going to question them. If you try to stop me, I am sure Ambassador Bird will let the Council know how unco-operative the BRG was in letting him communicate with his own security."

The soldier tilted his head and then took a step to the side to allow Alexis to pass. Alexis walked down to Willits and Jones. The medic was taking something out of Jones' shoulder. Alexis asked, "You two, alright?"

Jones responded, "What does it look like?"

Alexis walked over to Willits and looked at his shoulder before looking down at his leg. She asked, "What happened?"

Willits responded, "Taz shot a rocket near me, I dove. Dislocated shoulder and a piece of shrapnel in my leg."

Alexis asked, "Why hasn't anyone worked on you yet?"

Willits grinned. "Apparently, candy-ass over there has a worse wound that needs to be taken care of first."

Jones gritted his teeth and said to Willits, "When I am able to use this shoulder again, the first thing I am going to do is punch you right in the mouth."

The medic responded, "I am working as fast as I can. Please hold still."

Alexis looked around at the BRG soldiers, and said, "Looks like you are being detained."

Willits responded, "I don't think the BRG has forgotten about that incident on Torsalli."

Alexis said, "My brother told me on Molar. Something blew up?"

Jones answered, "The Ambassador's C-62T. And some BRG cargo inside."

Alexis, now remembering everything, responded by slamming her fist down on Willits injured thigh. He gritted his teeth and let out an "Owww…"

Alexis said, "That was for leaving the Ambassador and me with two cadets to get us here."

Jones answered, "It was better than getting shot at. How did they do? Is Bird safe?"

Alexis looked at Jones and responded, "Bird is safe, but it did not go without incident…"

Willits, still grimacing in pain, said, "Did they screw up?"

Alexis grinned and said, "Actually, no. The incident was mainly caused by Bird. Those guys are alright. I like them."

Jones gave a small grin as well, and said, "So do we."

A few seconds went by before Willits asked, "You gonna tell us what Kimakawa said, or are we gonna keep this charade up?"

Alexis looked at both of them for a few seconds. After a long pause, she asked, "When did you find out?"

Willits answered, "No child of Annella Devanoe is just an assistant to an Ambassador."

The medic was done with Jones. He got up and was about to walk over to Willits, when Alexis said, "Give us a minute please…"

The medic turned around and walked away. Alexis asked, "When did you find out Kimakawa had doubts about you?"

Jones was moving his shoulder in a circle, trying to regain his range of motion. He smirked when he answered, "About two seconds after we walked out of his office with this assignment."

Willits continued, "We knew it was bullshit from the get-go. Putting us on security detail? We knew we were being watched and that he no longer trusted us."

Jones added, "We just didn't know why."

Alexis asked, " The incident on SPE? And Braccus?"

Willits looked at Jones before he responded, "We knew they had to be related. Not trusting us, and then the attempts on the Ambassador? It's exactly what we predicted in the note."

Alexis looked puzzled. "The note?"

Jones answered, "We left a note with our old Sergeant at Odgins to give to Kimakawa."

Willits continued, "It said 'if something is happening on this trip to Belinea, I promise you it is not us. The cause for the trust you no longer have in us is from someone else."

Alexis was speechless. She had no idea Willits and Jones knew all along. She then said, "So you kept changing the manifest and where we were going…."

Jones continued, "Where ever we were supposed to be, that is where an incident was. We didn't know if it was you or someone in Kimikawa's office."

Willits added, "Once the explosion happened at Vi's guest house on Torsalli, we knew for sure."

Alexis looked puzzled. "There was another incident on Torsalli?"

Jones smiled. "That's when we knew it wasn't you because you knew nothing about that. It had to be someone in Kimakawa's office. We hoped Kimakawa was smart enough to figure it out."

Alexis paused for a second. It was clear Willits and Jones had finally come clean with her. It was time to return the favor. She held up her wrist-watch device, which held up an image. "Well, he figured it out."

Willits saw the image of Kimakawa holding the decapitated head of Meyers. Willits added, "Could not have happened to a nicer guy."

Alexis then showed the image to Jones, who added, "I've never seen him look better."

Willits then said, "Well, glad we are back on the good side, even though I am not sure why we were ever doubted in the first place."

Jones added, "That won't do us much good getting out of this predicament."

Alexis asked, "What's your plan?"

Willits said, "I had one, but I am not sure if Lord Malovex's incident out on the pad is going to help or hurt us."

Jones added, "Unless you got any other suggestions?"

Alexis thought for ten long seconds. She walked over to Willits's wrist transmitter and held her wrist-watch device next to it. She hit a couple of buttons. The image of Meyers was transferred over. Alexis said, "Talk with Lord Malovex, barter."

Jones asked, "Barter?"

Alexis said, "Kimakawa said Meyers was a spy, so ask yourself who he was feeding the information to? It certainly wasn't just Taz."

Willits and Jones looked at each other for a moment, before realizing this might work.

Lord Malovex was in a room with his three of his Lieutenant's and one Commander. The Commander continued, "My Lord, I do not know all the details of Torsalli. But I have looked at the surveillance and heard from other officers. Had those two DAG officers not got that bomb away from the fuel truck, several soldiers would have killed. Not to mention the bomb left in the Ambassador Compound...."

An excited Lieutenant added, "Or how many people they saved when they told everyone to back up before Taz launched that fireball."

Malovex added, "They clearly saw the security footage on Braccus. Some of you have not seen that yet."

The Commander continued, "My Lord, it is your decision, but I have no reason to keep them until you order me otherwise."

Another BRG Lieutenant came in and said, "My Lord, the two DAG officers request to speak with you."

Malovex turned, with a puzzled look on his face. He said, "Send them in."

Willits and Jones walked in. They were not handcuffed, but it was clear they were unarmed and not allowed to leave. They stood in the room, and then asked, "Lord Malovex, can we speak to you alone?"

Malovex was now really confused. After a moment, he looked at his Commander and nodded. The rest of the BRG officers began to leave. The excited Lieutenant added, "My Lord, would you like one of us to stay for security?"

Malovex looked at the Lieutenant with a combination of disgruntlement and annoyance. The Commander, very perturbed, grabbed the excited Lieutenant by the back of the collar and walked him out of the room. As he did, he gritted his teeth and quietly said, "He just killed Taz by himself. Do you think he can handle two unarmed humans?"

Malovex turned and looked at Willits and Jones. He said, "I wish to thank you. My officers tell me that without you two, many BRG would have lost their lives today."

Willits responded, "Thank you for killing Taz. We have been trying to do that for some time now."

Malovex answered, "I am aware. I was on SpacePort Earth, Braccus, and Torsalli after each one of his attacks. It seemed I was always one step behind him, and you two as well. Which brings us to our little problem. The death of two BRG officers onboard the Ambassador's C-62T that blew up at the Torsalli Space Port."

Jones responded and said, "We are aware, sir. We believe it was Taz."

Malovex asked, "Taz blew up the Ambassador's C-62T? From an internal bomb on the ship? Detonated from outside, where the two of you were conveniently fleeing the explosion to Vihaan Kapoor's Estate below?"

Jones and Willits said nothing. After a pause, Malovex noted, "There is very little that I do not know. Including a missing D-21 Sirallo from Mr. Kapoor's estate."

Willits decided to call the bluff. "We might know a little more than you think, Lord Malovex."

Malovex crossed his arms and asked, "Really? Like what?"

Willits held up his wrist-transmitter. It showed the image of Kimakawa holding up Meyer's decapitated head. "Shame about our Vice Director, Franklin Meyers…"

Jones continued, "Slipped on a banana peel and fell right on Kimakawa's Samurai Sword. Tough break…."

Willits added, "Clumsy fellow…"

Malovex replied, "What does this have to do with me?"

Jones answered, "It seems Meyers had a lot of friends…"

Willits added, "A lot of friends in your office, based on his transmissions…"

Jones continued, "To the point, we couldn't take a piss without someone trying to blow us up."

Willits finally added, "So yeah, we did what we had to do, to get the trail off of us. Sorry, it was your two officers, it was nothing personal, except for that Egglet comment."

Jones turned to Willits and said, "Yeah, that was personal…"

Willits quickly added, "…and certainly unnecessary."

Malovex stared at them for a few seconds. He quietly asked, "What are you proposing?"

Jones answered, "The truth does no one any good."

Willits continued right after. "You pin their death on Taz. We pin this Meyers situation on Taz as well."

Malovex asked, "And if I say no?"

Jones answered, "Well, likely you just shoot both of us, and we are out of your way, justice served."

Willits continued, "But the Ambassador's assistant is telling Kimakawa all this as we speak. In turn, she or he will tell Bird, who then addresses the entire Council as to why the BRG feels the need to spy on us."

Jones continued, "Our dainty, little, mall-cop security."

Willits added, "Only if we were to perish, or something happened to us."

There was a long pause. Malovex took a deep breath and said, "I think we have all had enough killing for one day. I will deal with my officers. Besides, Taz was actually near the Space Port at Torsalli when that bomb went off. I wasn't entirely sure it wasn't him that detonated that bomb. Now I know the truth, so thank you."

Willits and Jones looked at each other, not knowing that last part. After a second, they looked back at Malovex, who returned the look and only said, "Gentlemen, you are free to go."

BELINEA 8.13

Belinea, Capital City

Ambassador Compound, BRG Safe House

Ambassador Bird was in the room, still looking at his tablet. He was looking at the security footage from his condo unit, and the moment that Yi was murdered. It was beginning to sink in that someone died, a mentor, from someone trying to kill him. He was shaken up. The six DAG soldiers that stayed to guard him had not left his sight. They were in the room with him, along with four other BRG officers outside. Bird honestly did not know where he was, but despite it being safe, he felt anything but.

The door opened, and Ambassador Garvalin entered. She talked with the head BRG agent before sitting down next to Bird. She said softly, "I am so sorry, Ambassador Bird. You have my condolences. Are you alright?"

Bird seemed scared. All of the other instances on his life he was not present for. This one happened forty meters from him. It should be him that was killed, not Yi. He looked at Garvalin before looking back at his tablet. A few seconds passed before he said, "Yi was a good man."

Garvalin put her hand on Bird's knee and said, "Yes, he was…"

A few more seconds passed before Bird opened up a little bit. He said, "I never looked at the situation from a security standpoint…."

Garvalin tilted her head, slightly shaking it in the confusion of the statement. Bird continued, "Yi and myself had discussed it, a lot lately, about the financial impact this would cause our economy. The resources we could save by putting it back into our development, not theirs. "

Bird stopped for a second. He looked at the tablet again, watched the moment Yi had blown up. After a few seconds, he continued. "But these guards in front of me, they are sworn to protect me at all costs. At their own mortality. The ones here in front of me have not left my side since the bombing."

Garvalin looked at Bird and said, "They found Taz. Lord Malovex killed him."

Bird nodded and continued, "I heard. I am just … I don't know what I am. These men...Even the men whose competency I questioned...they still swore to protect me. I did not know what that really meant until now."

After a pause, Garvalin said, "These are elite soldiers. We should give them every resource we can, so they can do their job."

Bird looked at her when she said this. After a moment, he reached into his pocket and pulled out a note. Bird handed it to Garvalin. She asked, "What is this?"

Bird responded, "Lord Malovex gave me a note before I left Earth. It was a sealed message from Ambassador Yi. He did not trust any other communication methods. I think you should read it."

Garvalin was confused. She opened the note and read it to herself.

Ambassador Bird,

I hope this note finds you in good spirits. We are in difficult times. Your presence, and speech, to the Council is crucial for the success of what we are trying to build. It is possible you may have a difficult journey to Belinea. Trust the people closest to you for guidance, but no one else. When you get to Belinea, I will explain everything. If, for some reason, something has happened to me, chaos has developed. Trust your judgment and seek out Ambassador Garvalin. She is aligned with our position.
It will be the most important speech you ever give, our survival depends on it.

Yi

Garvalin folded the note and looked at Bird. After a moment, She looked at the DAG guards and the BRG guards. She said, "Will all of you give me a moment alone with the Ambassador, please?"

The BRG officers walked out of the room and outside. Now that Taz was dead, they felt no real danger. The other six DAG soldiers slowly walked out except one, the de facto leader with Orlando not present. He looked at her, and she at him. Garvalin said, "You remember me from the wine shop?"

The DAG member nodded his head. Garvalin continued, "That matter I discussed with Ambassador Yi is what I am discussing now. I promise we will avenge his death together."

The DAG officer hesitated for a second, before nodding and walking out. Garvalin then looked at Bird and said, "I was unaware he gave this to you."

Bird shrugged his shoulders. He said, "I had a speech prepared, I even sent it to him to review. But he said he would discuss it with me when I got here."

Garvalin stood up and paced for a moment. She said, "Ambassador, I have a copy of the speech Yi wanted you to give. I think the time to deliver it could not be more appropriate."

Bird asked, "You have it with you?"

Garvalin reached into her pocket and pulled out a small stick. She gave it to Bird, who put it into his tablet. The speech was uploaded, and Bird began reading it. After thirty seconds, he looked at Garvalin and said, "You want me to say this?"

Garvalin said, "Yes, and so did Yi. There will never be a more right time."

Bird took a deep breath and said, "I am not sure I can do it."

Garvalin replied, "I understand. It will take a lot of courage. But the power of the message will be so much greater from you than me."

Bird thought for a moment. He then said, "What about Santos? She is more senior than me."

Garvalin replied, "They did not drop bombs on her."

Bird thought long and hard. A solid twenty seconds passed. He then looked at Garvalin and said, "Something needs to be done, not for you or me. But for the legacy of Ambassador Yi."

Garvalin nodded and said, "Let's go to the Council meeting."

BELINEA 8.14

Belinea, Capital City

The House of the Council

The room to house all two hundred and eighty-four Ambassadors of the Council was enormous.

It looked like a giant theater, each Ambassador given a swiveling chair that exited with a tunnel out the back. Each chair had an arrangement of gadgets that were all within arm's length reach. The room was horseshoe-shaped. Ambassadors with lower credentials and junior in rank were closer to the circular floor at the bottom. The more prestigious or senior the Ambassador was, the higher the chair was in the room. Thus, the entire top row of thirty Ambassadors was the most influential in the Council. Eye-level with them was a grand stage at the open end of the horseshoe. It faced the Ambassadors, with a large screen behind it, and a splendid magnificent chair for Chairman Hassara. Just below his right was Defense Minister Tempest Hassara, head of the AuFa. Below and to the left of the Chairman was Lord Malovex, the head of the BRG.

Malovex did not attend many Council sessions, but given the nature of what happened and the topics, his presence was needed.

Directly across the grand stage, all the way on the other side of the room was the Quill Box. It was in the middle (and slightly higher) on the top row of Ambassador chairs. It had a large chair that Quillisar Prill sat in, with an empty seat next to him for Lord Argo, head of the SS, or Secret Service of the Quill. Currently on the screen behind the grand stage was a 3-dimensional hologram of the Quill Diamond. All the Ambassadors were there in attendance. Ambassador Bird was at the bottom, directly next to the circle. In the tunnel behind him was Alexis, followed by Willits, Jones, Orlando, Trujillo, and Tunsall. Ambassador Garvalin was in the second row from the top. Because of the bombings, there was a more significant presence of BRG soldiers, double than usual.

Chairman Hassara stood up, which caused everyone else to do the same. The grand stage moved, slightly out about ten meters, and then down another fifteen meters. The Chairman spoke, the audio system amplifying his voice. "Greetings to all. Before we begin, we lost a member of our family yesterday. Ambassador Yi, from planet Earth. He was killed by a horrific act of terrorism. I would like Quillisar Prill to say a few words."

Quillisar Prill took a step up in his box. The entire area that held his seat moved five meters forward, and down another three. Four spotlights turned on and directly casted light upon him from above. He spoke, "We are the Energy. When energy is added, energy is taken, peace is the energy around us. The energy that was in Ambassador Yi is now in all of us. The light and power of that energy cannot be extinguished. It merely grows stronger in all of us. The energy is eternal, and the memory of Ambassador Yi's energy will never be forgotten. We are the energy."

The rest of the audience responded in unison, "The energy is in us."

The area Quillisar Prill was on retracted back to its original spot. Everyone sat back down in their seat. The Chairman then said, "A word from Ambassador Santos, now the senior Ambassador from the planet Earth."

Ambassador Santos, A Spanish woman whose seat was only two rows above Bird's, now had the spotlights shine on her. Nervously, she said, "Thank you, Chairman Hassara. Ambassador Yi was a great man. Kind, endearing, compassionate. He represented everything good of what humans can be. He had no family. His life was this Council, and he considered many of you in this room his extended family. Let us hope this tragedy will serve as a platform to develop the necessary solutions to stop these unnecessary deaths. Defense Minister Hassara has been gracious enough to host a service this evening in his honor at the Grand Belinean Estate Ballroom. I hope to see all of you there so we can properly celebrate the life and legacy of a truly great man. Thank you."

The Chairman acknowledged the quickness and continued. "Thank you, Ambassador Santos, for your kind words. Let us begin the session. I yield the podium to Defense Minister Tempest Hassara, to update the situation."

Tempest stood, and now all the spotlights were on her. She said, "Thank you, Mr. Chairman. Ambassador Santos, Ambassador Bird, my deepest condolences."

The screen behind Tempest began showing the events she was describing. "Let us begin with the Valmay Group, the Terrorist Cell based on Avola. They have grown stronger, targeting local Avolian miners and the Majavkee Lords. The Majavkee process the Vait and distribute it to the Council. Their success is critical for our development and security. Almost three weeks ago, this Valmay attacked an AuFa Garrison. As you can see, this particular attack killed twenty soldiers, as the group also seized four cargo units of Vait. Then, less than a week ago, they attacked a mining facility in Lowell Province. Their leader, Octavious Killian, is seen here attacking a Medical Transport with Avolian children onboard. Eight children died because of the attack, including fifty-eight AuFa and Majavkee soldiers. The attack on the Processing Center two days ago was the worst yet. The Valmay killed hundreds of innocent Avolians with an arsenal of bombs, missiles, and guns. Almost a hundred Majavkee security soldiers were killed, and thirty cargo units of Vait were stolen. I now recognize Ambassador Yebba of Avola. Ambassador, can you please elaborate for us?"

Ambassador Yebba, his chair located on the highest row, stood up. Three spotlights suddenly shined on him. "Thank you, Defense Minister. My fellow Ambassadors, I am pleading for your help. My planet is being ripped apart at the seams. The fear these terrorists are putting into the innocent Avolian people is real. The Majavkee Lords have processed an abundant amount of Vait, more than any previous regime. We should praise them for their efforts. But their security needs our help. These terrorists are not only killing innocent citizens of this Council; they are threatening the Vait production this Council is so dependent on. We need your help. We need the help of the AuFa. This Council, and our planet, simply cannot stand another day of uncertainty and tragedy. "

Tempest Hassara continued. "Thank you, Ambassador Yebba. We have seen how far the tentacles can reach with this Valmay Group in the last three weeks. Taz, a lead officer in the Valmay and trained by them, has made several attacks starting with Space Port Earth. The brutal attack on Braccus followed that. As you can see, this left over a hundred innocent citizens of Braccus dead. Killed going to Temple for the Sun Offerings. Twenty more AuFa soldiers and local security were killed in the pursuit to catch Taz and his accomplices. Another attack orchestrated by Taz took place on Torsalli. The final act of terrorism, right here in your Ambassador Compound, the brutal murder of our friend and colleague, Ambassador Yi."

The screen showed the security footage of the Yi attack, as a somber silence fell onto the room. Tempest let the images sink in. After a long ten second pause, she now wanted to see if Garvalin would speak in objection as she did in the private meeting. Tempest continued. "These are vicious acts of hate. We will not allow our citizens to live in this fear. They deserve better and demand better. We, as a Council, are obligated to provide them with the security to prosper and grow. I now yield to Ambassador Garvalin. I understand you had some concerns regarding the funding of this proposal. Would you care to elaborate at this time?"

Tempest had Gravalin right where she wanted. The pressure, in front of this whole Council, would be too much to overcome. Garvalin took a couple of seconds to get up. When the spotlight shined on her, she took a deep breath and said, "Thank You, Defense Minister. First, I would like to offer my deepest condolences to the hundreds of Avolians and Braccusans that have lost their lives to terrorism. I would like to yield the rest of my time to Ambassador Bird from Earth."

This wholly caught Tempest off guard. Malovex and Chairman Hassara readjusted themselves in their chairs. Tempest let out, "Excuse me, Ambassador?"

Garvalin continued. "Defense Minister. During the last three weeks, at least two of these attacks were directed at Ambassador Bird. I believe he has gained first-hand knowledge of the situation, and I can offer us greater insight."

Tempest hesitated until she finally said, "The floor is yielded to Ambassador Bird."

Bird stood up, but no spotlights were on him. He cleared his throat, a bit nervous. He said, "Thank you, Ambassador Garvalin, and Ambas- I mean ...."

The audio took a second to catch up before it was amplified. The spotlight finally got on him, one at first, then two more after a few seconds. Bird was not used to them, and immediately held up his hand. Clearing his throat again, he said, "Sorry, thank you, Defense Minister Hassara."

The Chairman, Tempest, Malovex, and honestly, everyone else had no idea what was going on. Almost no one ever yielded their time, especially to someone on the Ambassador rows' bottom ring. Bird began reading from his tablet.

"The effects of terrorism simply cannot be put into words. The scars they leave are emotional and physical. Ones that can last an eternity. This is not the time to point blame. We must be focused on the problem...."

Bird stopped. A few seconds of silence went by. He looked up and around at all the other Ambassadors. Alexis took a few steps up and got right behind him. A few more seconds went by before Bird turned and gave the tablet to Alexis. From atop, Tempest spoke. "Ambassador Bird, is there something wrong?"

Bird looked up again, this time at the grand stage at Tempest. A few more seconds of silence went by before Bird finally responded. "Yes, Defense Minister, something is very wrong...."

Tempest looked over at Malovex to get an idea of what was going on. Malovex only looked back in bewilderment. Bird continued.

"None of us were born Ambassadors. We were born children. Some of you were born citizens of this great Council. And some of you, like me, were born without knowing its existence. All of us have been blessed with different educations, different upbringings, even different religions. But all of us seek a place where no one's voice would go unheard and is united in the common belief that every person mattered. On Earth, we say that is what makes us human. Until the day this Council rescued us from oblivion, I was unsure if that fundamental principle could be a reality. But when all of us went from citizens to Ambassadors, we not only shared that principle, we swore an oath to defend it at all costs."

Bird turned as his voice gained confidence. He began to look around at all his fellow Ambassador's. He continued. "Most of you have never been to my planet, but this I can assure you, when you back a human into a corner, we do not cower and hide. We come out swinging, scratching, and crawling. Earth was saved and rebuilt, brick by brick. A Phoenix rising from the ashes into the magnificent planet we are today. So now, while we all stand here in the face of this new terror, we see the damage they have done. We see the children at the Temple in Braccus, the life burned from their bodies. We see these dedicated soldiers, sworn to an oath to ensure us a blanket of preservation, and sacrificing themselves fulfilling that obligation. We see an Ambassador, killed in the sanctuary we call our home!"

Bird was getting louder. The Ambassadors were fidgeting, yelling in support. Bird continued. "These Avolians, innocent citizens of our galaxy. We owe them the opportunity of freedom. Now is not the time to look away and ignore, or shamelessly shudder to a bully fighting with fear. These innocents are not nameless or faceless. They have a heart and a soul. They are my brothers, my sisters, our family! These innocents are not blind, and they are not mutes. They have looked through the lens of distress and the cries of despair for far too long. It is our duty to provide them the eyes of righteousness, and the voices of a thousand angels singing the verse of courage...."

The room was a frenzy. Ambassadors began standing up, clapping, and cheering. They soon all joined in. Bird continued, "Defense Minister, I have seen the budget proposal, I have seen what you ask of this Council. You ask me, us (raising his arms), to stand behind you. How dare you ask so little, when you have given us so much? My message to you is the message this Council should inscribe on the tombstone of Ambassador Yi. My friend, my colleague, your death will not be in vain. Your death will be the symbol for justice, a symbol that will burn in our memory for eternity and become the beacon of solidarity to our cause. Defense Minister, you ask me, is there something wrong? Yes, there is! And the answer is YOU ARE NOT ALONE! We do not stand behind you. We stand with you, together. You will get all the money and troops you need. Each of us will raise our own security, our own guard to protect all the citizens of our planets and the Ambassadors that serve them. Your troops, our troops, our pledge is simple. WE WILL LIVE IN FEAR NO MORE! JUSTICE WILL BE SERVED!"

Bird slammed his fist down on his podium in front of him. An eruption like no other filled the room. Every Ambassador was on their feet, clapping, whistling, shouting. Tempest was dumbfounded. She sat there, not believing her eyes or ears. The Chairman knew they had no chance. Bird had given the speech of a lifetime. He stood up, looking down at Ambassador Bird, and began his own applause from the grand stage. Malovex, who rarely smiled, even had a small grin on his face, to go along with a slight shaking of his head. He, too, stood up with the Chairman applauding. It took Tempest a few more seconds to process it. She saw Malovex get up and glanced back to see that her father had done the same. Finally, she stood up to the thunder and began clapping.

Down below, Ambassador Bird folded his hands above his head and gently shook them. He then slowly began turning around, an effort to acknowledge all the applause. Garvalin was clapping as well, a small tear running down her face from the memory of Yi and what it had created. In the tunnel behind Bird, Alexis was smiling and clapping simultaneously. She whistled. Willits unfolded his arms. He looked over at Jones, who gave him a fist bump, Jones whispered, "Time to drink…"

Willits replied, "You damn right…"

The two walked out, leaving everyone else behind.

BELINEA 8.15

Earth, North East Japan

Annella Devanoe and Director Kimakawa watched the speech from their monitor. After the last thunderous applause, with Bird holding his hands above his head, Kimakawa looked over at Annella and said, "Well, that was not awful."

Annella countered with, "Nothing is going to make up for the loss of Yi. We have no one to replace him, but they have enough money to find their next Meyers traitor spy quickly."

There was a long silence after Kimakawa paused the monitor with Bird, still clutching his hands together above his head. Kimakawa then spoke. "Maybe….Perhaps Bird can be that trusted soldier for us."

Annella took a sip of her scotch before she replied, "One that has the pulse of the Hissara's, that had built up clout with his fellow Ambassador's, yet was still aligned with our mission? Is Bird even trustworthy enough to be brought into our circle? Or is he a clawless puppet that follows the Hassara's like Santos. This will set us back two years."

Kimakawa took a sip of his scotch and said, "We goto the Delegate ranks and begin our search on the next elected Ambassador, grooming him from there."

Annella shook her head. "We do not have that kind of time, Taichi. Provided they don't kill you when they return, you send Willits and Jones back out and find a supplier for what we need. You get Vihaan Kapoor to start doubling his production. The next Ambassador should be one that helps you with the Delegates on how we pay for this, now that Bird has put that burden on us. If Bird can be half of what Yi was with the Council, that will be a bonus. Otherwise, we move forward without that asset at our disposal."

Kimakawa looked down and paused to think about what Annella said. After a few seconds, he looked up, nodded, and said, "Today, we start phase two."

BELINEA 8.16

Belinea, Capital City

Grand Belinean Estate Ballroom

People were packed around Ambassador Bird. He had become an overnight sensation with his energized speech. Standing next to him was Alexis, introducing all the other Ambassadors and political figures. The mood was somber because of the celebration of the life of Ambassador Yi. But Bird continued to soak in the opportunity to meet as many people as possible. Lieutenant Orlando stood behind him to provide security, even though the BRG had soldiers everywhere. Ambassador Garvalin walked up to Bird and shook his hand. She said, "Great speech…"

Bird shook his head slightly and said, "I do not know what came over me. One minute, I was reading Yi's speech. The next, I went with my gut, right off the cuff."

Garvalin leaned in and whispered into Bird's ear, "It is more than we could have ever hoped for."

At the same moment, Defense Minister Tempest Hassara and Chairman Hassara walked into the room together. They shook a couple of hands before stepping up to Ambassador Bird. Garvalin introduced them. She said, "Chairman Hassara, Defense Minister, may I have the pleasure of introducing to you, Ambassador Bird."

Chairman Hassara extended his hand. Bird enthusiastically shook it. Hassara said, "Ambassador Bird. I would like to offer my condolences on Ambassador Yi. His loss is particularly hard for Tempest and me. We both considered him a trusted colleague and loyal friend."

Ambassador Bird nodded and answered. "Thank you, Mr. Chairman. I could not agree more. We lost a great man. Defense Minister…"

Bird extended his hand to Tempest. Tempest shook it and replied, "Ambassador Bird. My condolences…"

The Chairman continued. "How is it that we have never met?"

Bird smiled and said, "Perhaps you cannot see all the way down to my seat Mr. Chairman?"

Nobody laughed. A couple of seconds went by before the Chairman let out a laugh. He then said, "Old age gets the best of all of us, I am afraid."

There was a pause while everyone briefly chuckled. Then Tempest continued, "That was a compelling and moving speech today, Ambassador. I was not aware of Earth's dedication to the cause until today."

Bird continued, "There is a long history of terrorism on our planet. We have spent centuries fighting it. Unification is the key to fighting the fear they spread."

Tempest asked, "I agree. I noticed in your speech, the call for your own military…"

Bird interjected with "Security, Defense Minister. I would never call it military."

Tempest continued, "Alright, what kind of security force are you talking about?"

Bird continued in confidence, "I consider Lord Malovex and his BRG force to be the finest in the galaxy. It is clear we all can learn much from them. My Delegate Ambassador Guard would simply expand to keeping the peace on Earth, and helping us fight the terrorists."

Tempest replied, "So, while Lord Malovex killed Taz at the Ambassador Compound, you understand the threat is still there?"

Bird countered, "Absolutely. And without the heroics of my DAG team, Taz would have killed me. Without both, I would not be here. I see no reason why we can not work together to accomplish a common goal."

The Chairman interjected, "I could not agree more, Ambassador."

A BRG officer came up and whispered something into the Chairman's ear. The Chairman then said, "If you will excuse Tempest and me, something needs our attention."

Ambassador Bird bowed his head and said, "Of Course Chairman, Defense Minister, it was a pleasure."

The Chairman and Tempest walked through a door and then down a corridor. When they got to the end, they walked through a doorway into a very plush room. Malovex was standing near the bar area, pouring himself a drink. The Chairman immediately said, "Not one word since you killed Taz. I paged you three times, and you came and went during the Council meeting without talking to me."

Malovex replied, "I am very busy keeping your kingdom intact. You are welcome."

Tempest replied, "You could at least help me with all these Ambassador's out there."

Malovex poured a glass of wine for Tempest, and before handing it to her, said, "Argo will give up sex before you get me out there. All you get is wine."

The Chairman sat down in a chair and said, "What happened yesterday when you killed your cousin's little pet?"

Malovex answered, "I have been following him for three weeks. He was becoming sloppy and less controllable. The distraction attack on Braccus was unnecessary. By the time he got to the Ambassador's Compound, he had done his damage. I met him alone in front of my BRG soldiers. What else was I supposed to do? Let him go?"

Tempest sat down next to her father and said, "Argo is going to be pissed."

Malovex answered, "No, he will not. He can just put another one of his SS goons in a mask and have them blow shit up."

The Chairman said, "I found the attack on Baccus excessive as well, even though it did strengthen our position with the Council."

Malovex continued, "A position we already achieved with Avola. Which, speaking of, fear has a new face."

The Chairman answered, "Who?"

Malovex, still standing, grabbed his tablet, which was in front of him on a table. He hit three buttons on it and a picture projected on the wall. It was a red Quillisar killing a Majavkee soldier back on Avola. Malovex continued, "That is Kaya Killian, and I suppose her new uniform. One that will certainly suit our needs."

Tempest asked, "Where did you get that?"

Malovex answered. "Argo sent it to all of us, check your box. Security footage of the Mining Center uprising. He said he lost a foot."

The Chairman replied, "A foot?"

Malovex replied, "Apparently it was an intense battle between the SS and the Valmay. Knowing him, he will be more pissed about losing his spy on Earth."

The Chairman asked, "How do you know?"

Malovex took another sip from his drink. He responded with, "I put two and two together after talking with these DAG officers. We still have mine, that is all that matters."

Tempest spoke, "Good, because the speech this Ambassador Bird gave has me worried they are building an army."

Malovex countered, "An Army? Try a glorified security force. Besides, you got what you wanted out of that speech."

Tempest questioned, "Did I?"

The Chairman interjected, "Perhaps at a cost, but Malovex is right. They cover the increase in spending, with no answer on how they will fund their own situation."

Malovex continued. "We can easily exploit their lack of experience in security and military, and still get the biggest fleet this galaxy has ever seen."

Tempest seemed less convinced. She only whispered, "Perhaps...When does Argo get back?"

The Chairman answered, "Tomorrow. We have a meeting with Quillisar Prill about something that happened within the Quill on Avola while Argo was there. Argo sent the video to Prill, and he is concerned. (Looking at Malovex) Would you like to join us?"

Malovex was distraught for the moment. The same vision came back to him. The cockpit, the control panels, the chaos outside the craft, the barrel roll. He then saw the eyes again. They blinked. And when they did, The Chairman raised his voice, "Sansigar, are you alright?"

Malovex snapped out of it. Bewildered, he said, "Excuse me?"

The Chairman asked again. "Would you like to join myself, Argo, and Quillisar Prill looking at this video from Avola tomorrow?"

Malovex slammed his drink. Leaving the glass on the table, he stood up. "I would rather light myself on fire."

As Malovex was walking towards the door, Tempest asked, "Seriously, you are not gonna help us with the Ambassadors out there?"

Malovex walked out of the room, and yelled, "Same answer…"

Alexis kept trying to break away from Bird when she saw Orlando talking with Trujillo, Tunsall, Willits, and Jones. But they were a good forty meters away, on the other side of the room.

Willits, handing Orlando a stick for his tablet, said, "Orders from Kimakawa. He wants you to round up whatever eight-man team you need, your new detail will be Bird."

Lieutenant Orlando said, "Yes, sir. No longer in charge, Commander?"

Jones interjected and said, "No more security detail. Back to the daytime job."

Orlando looked at both of them and said, "I heard a rumor…"

Willits quickly answered, "Keep it that way."

Orlando smiled and, nodding at Trujillo and Tunsall, said, "Taking them with you?"

Tunsall answered quickly, "We were not invited."

Jones said, "Who said that?"

Willits added, "We just figured you were going back to school, try to join the AuFa."

Trujillo added, "Is that even an option, to come with you guys?"

Willits and Jones just looked at each other for a few seconds. Jones said, "They did perform pretty well getting the Ambassador here. We heard about Molar."

Willits said, "And we certainly will never have more clout with Kimakawa about picking our own team than we do now."

Jones continued, "It won't be flying fighters, you two…."

Willits added, "But it will be a lot of sticky situations and undercover work. What do you say? Lieutenants of the Delegate Ambassador Guard?"

Trujillo and Tunsall just looked at each other for a few seconds. Trujillo then said, "You know how I feel. But I understand what you have to do. I go where you go."

Tunsall thought for awhile. Willits and Jones were surprised by Trujillo's answer. They had noticed it first hand, but these two acknowledging out loud that they made decisions together really demonstrated their trust for each other. Tunsall continued to think. After another moment, he looked at Willits and said, "Where is loyalty and trust in the job description?"

Willits cracked a tiny grin and said, "Number one on the list."

Jones followed with, "We don't leave any man behind."

Tunsall thought a few more seconds, before he said, "My father will not be happy. But if Trujillo and I are assigned to you two as our Commanding officers, we would like to join."

Trujillo and Tunsall saluted. Willits and Jones casually saluted back. Willits said, "Welcome, gentlemen. Let's get out of here and get to work."

Willits gave a quick nod to Orlando, who saluted back. As the four of them began to walk away, Trujillo asked, "Start work now?"

Jones replied, "First, we gotta return the D-21 Sirralo to Vihaan Kapoor. Two of them actually."

Tunsall said, "A D-21 Sirralo, really? And who is Vihaan Kapoor?"

Willits stopped, causing the other three to stop. "A friend on Torsalli. However, perhaps we can get Vi to meet us on Vandabri?"

Jones, speaking very seriously as to confuse Tunsall and Trujillo, said, "Probably need to stay away from Torsalli for a while anyway. Do you think Vihaan could be persuaded to meet us on Vanadbri?"

Willits crossed his arms. In a solemn tone also, he answered, "I don't know, very serious man. He has a lot going on. It might be tough."

Alexis came walking up. She then said, "Gentlemen, enjoying yourselves?"

Willits said, "We were just leaving."

Alexis said, "Leaving, without saying goodbye?"

Jones replied, "Our apologies Miss Devanoe, how rude of us."

Alexis asked them, "Headed home?"

Willits answered, "Not exactly…"

Alexis looked confused. She then said, "I figured Trujillo and Tunsall needed to get back to graduate, no?"

Jones replied, "I guess this mission was their graduation. They are joining the DAG."

Alexis was a little stunned. "Really?"

They both nodded. After a pause, Alexis asked, "Commander Willits, may I have a moment with Trujillo?"

Willits, a little puzzled about the question, replied, "Yes…."

Alexis grabbed Trujillo's hand and whispered, "This way…."

They walked around a corner. Willits looked at Jones and Tunsall and said, "What is that all about?"

Jones and Tunsall just shook their heads. When Trujillo and Alexis got around the corner, she looked at him angrily and said, "Gonna leave without saying goodbye?"

Trujillo countered, "I didn't know we were leaving until a minute ago."

After a pause, Alexis asked, "You're joining DAG? What about flying fighters for the AuFa?"

Trujillo paused for a second and said, "Joining a family was more important."

Alexis said, "Agreed."

She kissed him. After ten seconds, he said, "I gotta go. How do I contact you?"

Alexis just said, "Don't worry. I will find *you*."

Alexis walked back down the corridor and back out to the main room. Passing Tunsall, Willits, and Jones, she said, "Tunsall, watch him for me. Willits and Jones, good luck, thanks for everything. I owe you one."

Willits and Jones nodded, as Alexis never stopped and walked right back into the crowd. Tunsall looked at Willits and Jones, who provided the same confused expression. A few seconds went by, and Trujillo joined them again. Willits asked Trujillo, "Something you want to talk with us about?"

Trujillo left them behind and continued to walk towards the exit. He said, "Nope."

Trujillo made it about ten meters, but none of the three followed him. He stopped and turned around at all three, and said, "Are you coming?"

They all looked at each other, smiled, and then proceeded to walk toward him, out the door.

BELINEA 8.17

Avola

Bisi Base

Kaya was alone looking into a mirror. Quillisar Balerra walked into the room. Kaya turned around and said, "My Quillisar…"

The old lady, dress in bright red robes, walked up to Kaya, and said, "Is there anything you would like me to say?"

Kaya shook her head. "I am not sure what to say, how can I ask you to say anything?"

Balerra grabbed Kaya's hands. "You are not alone, my child."

Kaya looked up, over Balerra's head, and whispered, "Octavious was the one who always did these. I just listened."

Balerra looked up at her and said, "Anyone can talk. Listening is the virtue, now more than ever."

Kaya had a small tear run down her face. "I'm afraid, and that never happens to me."

Balerra smiled. She said, "Did you see what happened before Octavious died?"

Kaya did not understand. She looked down at Balerra with confusion, not answering the question. Balerra continued. "The energy moved on, in a way I have only seen once. His energy was so bright, that he has put the power of that energy into others."

Kaya shook her head. She said, "I do not understand my Quillisar."

Balerra said, "Do you understand why some of you with orange Quill field stones have the ability to manipulate the fire, to turn them into sabers, and some of you are just workers?"

Kaya said, "I thought it was our dedicated faith, beginning at an early stage for training."

Balerra said, "Yes, it is your training. But the faith, the faith rewards you for believing."

Kaya gently shook her head again. "My Quillisar, I still do not...."

Balerra now quoted, "If you believe in the Energy of the Diamond without seeing the Power it imposes, your faith will be rewarded in ways that cannot be explained...."

Kaya said, "The Quill, Orange Code Four?"

Balerra nodded and said, "Yes, my child. I believe you are about to see something extraordinary."

Cortes walked into the room. "Kaya, it's time."

Kaya, still confused, began walking away. She looked at Cortes and said, "Just the soldiers, right Cortes?"

Cortes said, "A few more people have joined. Some through the caves."

Kaya started walking to the door and said, "As long as it is only a couple..."

As Kaya walked out of the room, she took a few steps into the base's interior. The giant cave now had all the aircraft pushed to the sides. In the middle of the room were the four wooden beams that made a diamond shape, holding the dead body of Octavious Killian. The rest of the room was packed, over two thousand people, all kneeling in prayer. Kaya did not turn around, as she still gazed at all the people. She said, "Cortes?"

Cortes was right behind her. She said, "Kaya, these people have been showing up all night. Most of them walked. It took them twenty hours. We could not say no."

Kaya paused for a second. Kaya continued, "What if this is a trap? What if the Majavkee followed them here, or worse, they are among the crowd?"

Cortes said, "I do not think so. The Majavkee have laid low, probably reassessing the situation. Most of these people came through the tunnels. It would be nearly impossible to track them. They lost people too, Kaya."

Kaya kept looking. She put her hood on, as to try and go undetected into the crowd. After about twenty steps, though, people began to recognize her. As she strolled down the aisle, people stood up and bowed to her. Some touched her arm. The emotion was real. People felt something being next to her, touching her. Step by step, she made her way to the middle of the diamond. It took her five solid minutes, but she finally got next to it. Everyone went back to kneeling. There was silence now in the cave. Quillisar Ballera and Cortes were next to her. Kaya, taking her hood off and glancing at Balerra, finally spook.

"There is nothing I can say that will bring your loved ones back. We all lost someone two days ago, so did I. I have lost many friends, over many days, it does not seem to end. I feel your pain, and I feel your loss. My friends, my Avolians, go home. Be with *your* loved ones now, in this time of reflection and sorrow."

Sterling got up from several rows back. "We came to pay our respects, Miss Killian. Octavious was a great man."

A few people talked out loud, agreeing with the sentiment. Kaya said, "He was, I know that. And I thank you for the concern. But the threat moving forward is real, and we all must individually decide how we are to handle it."

Another person stood up and said, "We are with you, Kaya!"

Another person stood up and yelled, "You paid your respects to us, to our families! We are only doing the same."

Kaya shook her head. "I promise it is because I care about each of your families that I ask you to return home. The Majavkee and the AuFa are still out there. They want me and my soldiers, not you."

A woman got up and said, "Do you think that anyone in this room would let the Majavkee take you away? Or Octavious' body?"

Kaya said nothing. A few more got up. An older man said, "Now is not the time to garner peaceful solutions. We pay our respects, yes. Then we plan our retaliation. We seek justice to avenge all that they have done. We are ready to fight Kaya, with you!"

Everyone in the room stood up. A few more claps and yelling could be heard. Kaya looked at all of them before signaling for them to keep it down. "Fifteen years ago, we began to train harder, dedicated ourselves to our Quill, even though the Belineans did not allow it. When the Majavkee had the massacre at Valmay, we changed our name to that. Yet, here we stand today. In more despair, with more loved ones lost than ever before. Countless times Octavious tried to tell me this. I would not listen. And this is what you ask?

You still want to fight? Because if we keep fighting, it will not stop until all of us are dead. And I am prepared for that, but only if you are too."

There was an awkward silence in the room. After a few seconds, one of the older women yelled, "Red Ring Rise!"

Another few men began saying it as well. "Red Ring Rise, Red Ring Rise...."

After about ten seconds, everyone in the cave began chanting "Red Ring Rise, Red Ring Rise, Red Ring Rise!"

Balerra then closed her eyes. Kaya continued to look around, sensing an energy in the air. Balerra raised her arms towards the sky. Instinctively, Kaya took out her ring and held it with two hands in front of her. The flame extended from it, but not in a saber-like fashion. She stared at it for a few seconds before closing her one good eye. A ray of fire shot from it and ignited Octavious' diamond. Balerra yelled, "Energy is added, energy is taken, the peace is the energy around us. The energy is in us, and when the light of our energy is extinct, the energy is added to the light around us. We are the energy."

Everyone was still chanting, "Red Ring Rise!"

Kaya still had a flame as she softly said, "The energy is in all of us...."

As she spoke, the flame turned into her fire saber. She pointed it up towards the top of the cave but was still looking at the wooden diamond. Suddenly water came out from all around Octavious's body, and began to extinguish the flames around it. Balerra continued, "The energy never dies, the energy is reborn again."

Kaya repeated, "The energy is in all of us...."

A forceful wind blew through the cave, almost knocking a few people down. The crowd was still chanting "Red Ring Rise, Red Ring Rise...."

Balerra yelled at the top of her lungs, "The energy is here in all of us, let the energy show us the light....."

A mini sand storm tornado formed over Octavious body. It rose circular towards the top of the cave. Many of the people went back to their knees, witnessing something they had never seen before. Kaya closed her eyes and said, "The energy is in all of us..."

Her fire saber grew larger, rather quickly. In one deep breath, she lowered it, pointing it at the diamond. A massive burst of fire came out of it. The fire engulfed the entire room. Anyone not kneeling was now. It was the most exquisite fireball anyone had seen come out of a saber, and it swept through the entire room in six seconds.

The chants had then stopped. Kaya opened her one good eye, petrified, expecting to see hundreds of people on fire. In astonishment, her brother's diamond, and entire body, were gone. No ashes, no more wooden pillars, nothing. Everyone else thought the fire burned them, but looking at their bodies, they realized they were fine. Balerra had waited all this time to open her eyes. When she did, she looked at Kaya. Kaya was looking at her stone, which was glowing bright reddish-orange. Everyone there began taking out their Quill field stones, most of them hanging from their neck. They were all glowing. Blue and green ones, as bright as they could. But the orange ones were glowing the most luminous. Cortes was staring at her field stone, glowing a brilliant orangeish-red, before looking at Kaya in disbelief. Kaya turned to look at Balerra. Balerra took one long look at her and said, "The energy is in all of us...."

BELINEA 8.18

Belinea

Outside Capital City

Lord Malovex Residence

Malovex got out of his personal transport, alone. He walked over to the front gate of his residence and had the scanner read his palm. As the gate door opened, he walked through the garden. When he got to the primary residence, he sidestepped and walked around back. In the backyard was a tranquil looking Asian-style garden, with pebble paths and small wooden bridges over Koi ponds. The giant redwood trees of Belinea were all around his residence, keeping him very secluded. He walked across a small bridge and got to a small shrine temple area. There was a pagoda over it, with wisteria growing all throughout. The shrine was a small tombstone with a diamond on it. A small Vossai tree grew in front of the tombstone, with a little spot to put a stone. Malovex took his ring out and removed the blue stone that was in it. He got on his knees, placing the stone in the base of the Vossai tree. He closed his eyes, and immediately he could see the image again.

Inside the cockpit. The control panel. The chaos of bombs and missiles going off outside the cockpit glass. The barrel roll. The eyes.

Malovex opened his eyes again. He then thought back. The flashback that was as clear as the present day to him.

Twenty years before...

Malovex was walking through his residency towards the front door. The injuries from the battle were still present on his body, causing a small limp.

He had a drink in his hand as he opened the front door. Dr. Fiona Faxon stood in the rain, a hood over her head. She looked up as the two stared at each other for a few seconds. Fiona reached into her pocket and pulled out the ring and stone she had retrieved. She held it in her hand for Malovex to see.

Malovex looked at it for a few seconds. Softly he said, "It belongs on Serpia, with you."

She began to cry. She said, "They will deface it, if they do not destroy it, once they find out."

Malovex continued to just stare at her hand. He accepted the stone. Sometime later, he would place the stone in the base of the tiny Vossai tree. Flash forward to the present, Malovex just stared at the tree. After a few seconds, it started to rain. The pagoda blocked most of it, as he never stopped staring at the stone.

Twenty years before

Commander Kimmel, Quillisar Farra, and Quillisar Sallor were all standing around the table. The toddler on the table was no longer frozen, but he lay there, motionless. They had a couple of tubes in his arms. The operating spotlight was above his head. Sallor was looking at the toddler's chest. Kimmel said, "I do not understand why they are taking so long to defrost?"

Sallor said, "This was not operating Freeze. These were combat freeze. They are not meant for the cold of space, so when you combine the two, it is not just a frozen brain and spinal lock. It turns into an entire frozen body lock that cannot be defrosted with Callopa drugs and heat lamps. The entire body has to defrost on its own, and I am not even sure it will work."

Quillisar Farra asked, "What do you mean you do not know if it will work?"

Sallor simply answered, "I have only read about it. I have never seen it done. I am not a surgeon, my Quillisar. My education translates to a Doctor Assistant, a practitioner, a combat nurse essentially."

Farra responded, "Try your best, my child…."

Sallor tried a few more things, trying to get a response. After a moment, Kimmel asked, "Why the toddler first?"

Sallor answered, "Because he has the least body mass, he will defreeze faster."

Sallor did a few more things until he then saw a finger move. His head snapped back, and he said, "Hold on, we may have something."

The three of them hovered over the toddler, waiting with anticipation. About ten seconds went by before Sallor whispered under his breath, "Come on….."

Sallor grabbed the toddler's hand. A few seconds later, two fingers moved. Sallor whispered, "Yes,.... you can do it…."

A few more seconds went by. All three were looking at the toddler's face now. After another ten seconds, the face began moving, and suddenly, as if waking from a deep sleep, the toddler's eyes opened.

End Season One

PROLOGUE (BONUS SCENE AFTER CREDITS):

Vihaan Kapoor is in his office. He read the message from his C-Bar Transmitter on to his tablet. He smiled big and wide and said, "Willits and Jones have both of my Sirralo's!"

He kept reading, and after another few seconds, he said, "Fuck yeah!!"

He stood up and yelled out, "Ladies, pack up your shit, bring the wine! We are going to Vandabri!!!"